THE DRUID TEMPTRESS . . .

The Roman lines! he mused. Home at last! And Melangell was willing to come with him. Chuckling to himself, he tried to imagine how her face would light up when she actually saw the Great Pyramids, the temples of Rome, a camel, a crocodile . . .

Glancing over his shoulder, he saw her happily splashing in the distant pool; surfacing and diving like some sleek dolphin. And then suddenly she was out of the water, effortlessly sliding onto the rocks, sitting with her bare back toward him. As she tossed her wheaten hair, the drops of water flew in a glittery cascade around her head and his hands fell still as he watched her. Of all the marvels he'd seen, he mused, in all the Roman world, few could match the stark beauty of these barbarian women's soft, white skin . . . so pure, so clear, like the soft white breast of a swan . . .

With slim arms she reached upward, spreading and untangling her drying hair, a movement so sensual he felt himself stirring beneath the short Celtic breeches he wore. Closing his eyes and turning his head, he groaned softly to himself. Mother Hera! I shouldn't have done that . . . shouldn't have looked . . . for that when we get back to Rome

D1052416

The SILVER LAND

Nancy Harding

POCKET BOOKS

New York   London   Toronto   Sydney   Tokyo

Grateful acknowledgment is made to the following for permission to reprint previously published material:

Routledge & Kegan Paul PLC: excerpts from *A Celtic Miscellany* by Kenneth Hurlstone Jackson. Copyright © 1951, 1971 by Kenneth Hurlstone Jackson. Reprinted by permission of Routledge & Kegan Paul PLC.

An *Original* Publication of POCKET BOOKS

POCKET BOOKS, a division of Simon & Schuster Inc.
1230 Avenue of the Americas, New York, NY 10020

Copyright © 1989 by Nancy Harding
Cover art copyright © 1989 Joseph Csatari

ISBN: 0-671-63409-7

First Pocket Books printing February 1989

10 9 8 7 6 5 4 3 2 1

POCKET and colophon are trademarks of Simon & Schuster Inc.

Printed in the U.S.A.

*Dedicated to the latter-day Celts
of the Lost Cause,
Who tried again and failed,
But not for lack of valor.*

Tout est perdu fors l'honneur.

With a special thanks to the good people
of Pennant, Powys, Wales,
whose lovely legend of "Melangell's Lambs"
served as direct inspiration for the heroine
of this book.

Tell me, men of learning, what is longing made from?
What cloth was put in it, that does not wear out with use?

—Welsh

Contents

Contents

BOOK *I*
Wayward Song

*The sun rises when the morning comes,
the mist rises from the meadows,
the dew rises from the clover;
but oh, when will my heart arise?*

—*Welsh*

Part 1

BELOVED OF LOUCETIUS

*T*HEY WERE THE PEOPLE-OF-NO-TRIBE. GENERATIONS EARLIER they fled their southern homeland, the land of the Silures, seeking only peace, and freedom, and an end to the menace of Rome. But always the Romans followed, like some great creeping plague; northward into the land of the Ordovices, where brave Caratacus tried to stand off the armies of the Emperor Claudius; through the sprawling Brigantian confederation, stretching from sea to sea; across the rolling lowlands of the Selgovae, gateway to Caledonia. With the northern Damnonii people these Silurian refugees stopped, built a waterside hamlet on log pilings sunk into the shallows of a narrow loch, and tried to eke out a living. Her potters made milk-glazed vessels from the coarse local clays, the men hunted for food and furs, and splendid gray, buff and cream freshwater pearls that washed ashore below their village were gathered for trade. Their chosen chief tried to cement an alliance with area tribes, who showed little interest in the mere handful of warriors the alien People-of-No-Tribe could produce. Tolerated for their trade goods, the small band of wanderers was otherwise ignored, left to hunt and fish and bargain for food as best they could, far, far from their native lands, the resting places of their ancestors, and the power of Rome.

This was home, here where the great red stag belled his call over dark, forested hills and the lowering silver moon turned the lake mists into twisting wraiths and spirits. Home to a terrified young girl who huddled by the central hearth of her family's small round thatch hut, her slim fingers toying with a misshapen gray pearl that hung from a bit of yarn around her neck. With each clang of weapons from beyond the security of the wall, each shriek from the wounded, she huddled her knees tighter under the coarse brown shift she wore. Wet autumn leaves nearly obstructed the smokehole in the roof, but the girl did not dare venture out to clear it. To do so would be to risk a lance in her back or a stone to her skull. She tried to keep the fire low, waving away the tendrils of smoke that curled downward from the blackened ceiling, and wondered desperately where her mother and uncle were. When the attack on her village began three days ago, they, like everyone else in the small hamlet, knew their duties. Seizing their weapons, they had gone to defend the palisaded fortifications with a stern final command to the bewildered girl: Melangell, pack our things and remain in the hut until we return.

She had been thankful for that order, for it relieved her mind of the burden of decisions as the terrifying days stretched out. She packed most of her family's few belongings in a large carved cedar trunk her uncle had made and then she waited, as day turned to night and night to day. Once she took a long iron pot-hook and pried a hole in the thick reeds that formed the side of the hut; all she could see was the reed wall of the adjoining hut, and an occasional cloaked figure hurrying by. Sighing, she had returned to the fire, trying not to panic when a sudden rending scream sounded just beyond the walls. And still she waited, lying sleepless in the hollow night, her familiar straw pallet scant comfort as she listened to the thuds of lance and dart hitting the packed earth outside, looking up in awe when sling-stones landed on the roof, rattling dryly and sending down small showers of dust and debris. She knew this was no Roman raid, though why a neighboring tribe had chosen to attack them she could not guess. Their pearls, perhaps, or their food? One thing she did know was the small size of their defending forces; maybe twenty-five men and women. They could not hold out forever. . . .

With the first gray light of a new dawn her fragmented sleep was shattered by the sudden sharp tearing of a bronze spearpoint, longer than her two hands, that forced its way through the thatch wall opposite her, next to the barred wicker door. She sat up, realizing that the chaotic noises of the past few days had ceased. The whine of slings and thuds of lances had stopped. For one breath-span all was still, and then the final horror began. In the sounding screams and pounding feet and harsh, insistent clanging of fierce hand-to-hand combat, Melangell knew the truth.

The simple stockade walls had been breached; their defenses had failed.

Panic closed tight around the girl's throat. Stumbling to her feet, her tattered cloak clenched helplessly in one hand, she looked around the tiny round room for a place to hide . . . anyplace . . . surely there must be . . .

Loud shouts and angry male voices came from beyond the door. Desperately the girl shoved the massive cedar chest across the room, climbing over it and attempting to hide in the curve behind, where it abutted the wall. She pulled the old cloak over her head and peered through a crack at the end of the trunk where it fitted loosely against the thatch.

The protruding spearpoint twisted, jerked, and disappeared, showering dried reed and grass to the floor inside.

What is there to fear? she sobbed, flinching at the fierce poundings that battered the bolted door. Only that the sky may fall upon me, the earth open up and swallow me. There is nothing beyond that to fear.

The door was sturdier than the flimsy walls around it, for beneath the savage onslaught it was not the door that gave way, but the adjoining thatch, which crashed inward. From the sagging ceiling came a choking cloud of dried reeds and a gust of fresh air that sent hearthsmoke swirling through the hut.

Three tall warriors pushed into the room, spears and swords in hand, and stopped to peer through the smoke. Desperately the girl suppressed a cough and watched them through watering eyes. The men came forward slowly, wary of an ambush. Their broad swords poked at straw sleeping pallets and overturned low wooden crouching-stools. A shorter, fair-haired one stooped near the doorway to scrape in the dirt floor at something that caught his eye, while the second fair-haired one, taller and with a heavy, drooping mustache, pulled her uncle's best cloak from its hook on the wall, eyed it appreciatively, and tossed it over his shoulder. Her family's meager rations held no interest for these well-fed fighters, and clay jars and baskets of food were quickly dumped to the floor in their search for booty. She saw the tallest one, fair-skinned and black-haired, pull her grandfather's revered cloak from a shelf where it was stored, eye it scornfully, and toss it to the ground in disgust, but not before ripping the simple gold pin from its corner. He looked aside when his companion spoke, arched his dark brows arrogantly, and gave a short laugh. The girl's rage at this desecration was quickly overcome by sick fear when the dark one spied the storage chest she was hiding behind and strode toward it. As his hands reached for the lid, he saw her huddled figure, and a slow smile crossed his lips. The girl suddenly knew, with some sharp animal instinct, that she was discovered, and turned her face upward. The look in his eyes, his pale sand-colored wolf's eyes, as they bore into hers, she would carry with her to the end of her days.

She tried to bolt away from him, but he gave a low laugh and seized her shoulder. As effortlessly as if she were a doll, he flung her to the earthen floor. Clenching her eyes shut, she awaited the slice of the sword, the stab of the lance point. Instead the pearl was ripped from her throat, strong hands tore at her shift, a heavy body fell atop hers, and a blinding pain shot through her. Involuntarily she screamed and her eyes flew open; it was the dark-haired wolf atop her, her face almost smothered by his neck. Futilely she struggled, beat on him with her fists, but it only excited him more and he bit her savagely on the neck. Sobbing her hurt into the swirling smoke, she lay still, and waiting, praying for a painless death. This was the fate of women in war, she knew, and it did no good to fight it. Mother! her heart cried silently; Mother!

The wolf soon finished and his two companions took their turns, and the strange, sweaty smell of their bodies brought her near to vomiting. When it seemed they were through, the girl rolled onto her side, groaning in pain, and tried to rise. She could see by their dusty bare feet that they stood nearby, watching her. When one laughed at her attempts, an odd anger welled up and she forced herself to stand, to face them, and to die on her feet, a free woman, not groveling in the dirt like a cur.

A foot came out, gave her a shove, and she toppled

sideways onto the floor. Undaunted, she tried to rise again, and again the foot pushed her down. By her third attempt the men were laughing heartily, and her pain was increasing so that each try was more drunken than the last. But her rage, too, increased, and when the third shove brought her within reach of the iron pot-hook by the hearth, she seized it triumphantly and with her last bit of strength leapt to her feet, swinging it wildly at them. It seemed to catch them momentarily off guard, but soon a sword flashed and a bone-jarring clang sent the hook flying from her hands. Melangell remained standing, facing the long-haired blond giant, and awaited her death. With a grin the man whirled his sword in slow circles overhead, then abruptly sent it slicing toward her neck.

A voice broke the stillness and the sword was lowered. The wolf strode over to the girl, threw her grandfather's discarded cloak at her, grabbed her arm, and pushed her toward the fallen wall. As the stupor of her death-watch dissipated like the smoke in the room, the reality of her situation became clear: she had been spared, she was alive, and she was now the captive of the light-eyed wolf.

And she was only fourteen years old.

The old cloak wrapped tightly around her thin shoulders to ward off the autumn chill, Melangell was shoved forward to join the small band of captives herded like cattle by the compound gate. Behind her the straw huts were set alight and an occasional pathetic scream broke the still morning. A young black-robed druid crouched outside the smoke-shrouded gate, his brown hair damp with sweat, and counted the meager booty, the cattle passing by, a few scarcely valuable trinkets spread on a blanket at his feet. Druids were the only ones who could count the higher numbers, and their memories were well trained by twenty years of druidical learning; it was their task to keep a reckoning for the chiefs.

An easy enough task, Melangell thought bitterly as she eyed her people's poor possessions lying naked in the morning light. Bronze chains and armbands, rings and hair ornaments of shiny black jet, the chief's massive iron cloak-pin, and only a spattering of gold amidst the dross.

Their real wealth, their only wealth, their pearls, were missing; they probably lay blackened and crumbling in the fires that raged behind her.

Her hand went absently to her neck, seeking the now-vanished pearl she had worn, and she lifted her gaze to the druid's flushed face. The heat is making him uncomfortable, she thought maliciously, a small satisfaction that eased her hurt. With that instinct druids so often seemed to possess, the man suddenly looked up, his gray eyes catching hers. Uncomfortable, Melangell looked down at her dirty feet, the ill-guided pleasure gone from her heart.

The wise man's gaze had been pitying.

The warriors returned, trotting to outrun the spreading flames, and gave their captives bundles of loot to carry. Under watchful guard they were herded through the gate of the wooden palisade and over the small log causeway that crossed the boggy ground, their weary feet stumbling on the rough planks. A brief glance over her shoulder was the last the girl saw of her home. It was blazing brightly with the rest of the village, no more than a huge straw bonfire.

"What is to become of me?" Melangell sobbed, stumbling weakly beneath the heavy sack she carried over one shoulder. "Only fourteen of us are here in this group—seven girls, five young boys, and two infants. I know my family must be dead, like everyone else. Dead . . ." She swallowed the gathering tears as the group made its way down a narrow path through small vegetable patches, patches she had helped tend in happier days. With a silent prayer she commended the souls of her kinfolk to a better future than their past had been.

Am I to be given to his wife, or his mother? she wondered. Am I to work in a farmyard or a household? I hope I am not to be his slave. . . . She shuddered at the memory and tried to push it from her mind. The pain of her wounds increased and she wondered when they would stop to rest. The bite on her neck was throbbing, her back was scraped, her shoulder had been wrenched and, like many of the other girls she noticed around her, blood trickled down her leg. From the cramped way they walked, she knew their fates had been the same as hers. A panic rose within her when they left the stubble of the harvested wheat fields, the lands of her people, but she fought it down. It would do no good. Things could never go back to the happy life she had once known. Prodded at spearpoint, they entered the gloomy forests by a twisting, rutted cart track.

They did not stop all day, and she wondered if her captors were in a hurry. By evening the weary captives were supporting one another in an effort to stay alive. A few girls sobbed aloud; hungry infants wailed unceasingly; and the boys marched resolutely forward, eyes dull with shock or livid with hatred and revenge. When the cartmaker's young son fell to the ground on a badly swollen ankle, he refused to rise. After watching in brief silence the children's efforts to rouse him, a guard stepped up and in one swift stroke sliced the boy's chest in half. He met his fate without a sound. The lesson was not lost on the captives and they struggled more desperately to stay afoot until a halt was called for the night in a clearing by a stream where heavy blue twilight hung in the humid air.

"What do you suppose will happen to us?" Whispered a soft-spoken girl with large hazel eyes, daughter of one of the wealthier men in the village, as she nervously fingered her bowl of gruel and fat pork. "I hear they sell slaves to the Scotti across the Western Sea, who are the most savage people there are."

"I think," an older boy replied, "that if they wanted slaves to sell, they would have kept more of us. Only fourteen from a village of forty-three . . ." He shook his head sadly.

"Yes," another agreed, "they must intend to keep us for themselves. At least they are the same people as we are, and we can understand their speech."

Melangell held a corner of her cloak to her throbbing neck and poked at a chunk of fat in her cup. "Does anyone know where their village is? How many days we must walk like this? These rations are less than the little I used to eat."

As one the group turned toward the member with the most education, the rich man's daughter. She had no idea. "A girl is seldom taught such things," she said quietly.

"I do know they were awfully familiar with the land around our village," the older boy mused. "They must have been scouting us out for some time."

"Our people are tradesmen and farmers, not warriors,"

the pot-maker's nephew interjected defensively. "Why should they notice enemies lurking in the woods?"

"Well, maybe if they had been trained for such things, we wouldn't be here now like this and—" the older boy began.

"And who knows what will happen to us?" sobbed a young girl.

"I know," snapped Melangell, "that we should stop this talk. It will only weaken us." She wiped angrily at the dried blood on her leg.

"Yes," agreed another, "right now we must only think of how to survive."

A looming shadow dropped across them and they looked up in alarm. It was one of the guards, tall and stern and forbidding.

"Sleep now," he ordered, kicking dirt over their tiny campfire. In silent obedience the captives rolled into their cloaks and lay close for comfort, and Melangell was not the only one who cried herself to sleep that night.

It seemed to Melangell that sleep had just embraced her when a foot jabbing her side woke her again. "Get up," a guard commanded. She sat up, pulling her grandfather's cloak around her torn clothes. Without a parting word to her companions she followed the guard from the camp, past hastily penned cattle still dozing in the dawn, by tethered chariot horses and stolen carts loaded with her village's plundered winter rations.

A group of elite warriors lounged around a campfire ahead, swapping tales and laughing loudly while they awaited the morning meal, and the air was heavy with the smell of roasting meat. When she and her guard approached, Melangell saw one man stand up, and she recognized his dark hair at once. He motioned them toward the waiting vehicles, and, one hand clenched in her hair, the guard forced her aside to an especially splendid chariot, its wicker sides set with ornamental bronze plaques. The lean dark-haired wolf left the group and walked toward them, and a nervous fear began to churn in her stomach.

He must have spied the guard's hand in her hair, for his first word was a sharp question.

"Trouble?" he asked.

"Some," the guard replied.

The wolf grabbed her chin in one powerful hand and jerked her face up, and she winced when the sudden movement violently pulled the hair still held by her guard.

"If you are trouble for me, girl," he threatened, his pale eyes narrowing, "I will give you to him as punishment." He motioned with his head toward the man behind her, and a faint smile creased the corners of his eyes. She heard the guard snort a laugh. He released her hair and retreated a few paces.

Freeing her chin, the wolf looked down at her. He had bathed since the raid, for his skin gleamed like ivory and his dark hair hung thick and shaggy behind his neck.

"By midday we will reach our fortress," he began. "You are to be a slave for my crippled mother. You are to help care for her, wait on her, help her walk; whatever she requires. Do you understand?"

Silently the girl nodded. He seized her chin again and his hand tightened around it uncomfortably.

"But if you are any trouble to her . . . any trouble at all . . ." He gave her head a little shake for emphasis. "I will give you to your guard there. He can be very . . . rough with women." He rolled the words out slowly for emphasis. "Do you understand?"

She managed a small nod of her head as he held it fast. She shuddered at the thought of someone this man would consider "rough with women."

"What is your name?" he suddenly asked, releasing her.

"Melangell."

"A strange name." His fierce wolf's eyes seemed to bore into her for a moment. Then he gazed slowly down her body and up again, over her tangled wheaten hair, pausing when he spied the scabbed and oozing bite mark on her neck.

"I will have some ointment sent," he said simply. "And clean clothes. You will ride with me in my chariot today. I will leave you here to wash yourself. But remember my warning, girl," he cautioned, turned, and strode back to his companions. To her surprise, the blond guard followed him. Alone, she sat on the rear deck of the chariot. She must, at any price, behave, she reflected. To belong to an elderly woman was infinitely better than belonging to the wolf . . . or his guard.

The size and grandeur of the fortifications around her captor's village awed Melangell when they approached across the harvested fields. The town itself was many times the size of her own small village; it sat secure atop a cleared dun, surrounded by massive timberwork, earthen, and stone walls that seemed to reach to the sky. Horses and chariots, carts and bellowing cattle, clumped and clattered through high earth outerworks, over a heavy log threshold and into the town. She could see silent guards standing atop the defenses, watching them enter. There was no ceremony, no grand welcoming; everyone unwounded and able to, simply alighted and went his own way, leaving servants and slaves to attend to the animals and baggage. Soon wails and cries dotted the compound as families learned that their husbands, sons, and fathers would not be returning from this foray.

The first sight of her new home was also impressive. Melangell followed the wolf as he left his chariot and the milling throng enshrouded in dust and noise inside the front gates. They walked past tiny shops and craftsmen's homes; down narrow, twisting streets where small striped pigs and noisy geese roamed freely; around smithies and stables, past racks of drying barley and wheat, clay pits for food storage and piles of neatly stacked firewood; by the large round homes of powerful warriors, many with clattering trophy heads hung boastfully outside the doors. They came to a green clearing at the fringes of the settlement, and a sturdy round timberwork house set apart from the rest.

Pushing open the door into a dimly lit interior, the wolf descended a few small steps to the excavated floor, Melangell close behind.

"Mother," he called out, evidently having trouble seeing in the gloom. A rustle to the left made them both turn.

"Here, son," a quiet voice said. "The fire is too low—" she began.

"Where is that lazy Seonaid?" he demanded angrily,

striding across the hut. "How long has she been gone, leaving you like this?"

"Since morning. But no matter. You are home safe and that is all that concerns me now." Even through the gloom the girl could hear the love in the old woman's voice, and she saw a small figure near the wall struggle to rise. With surprising tenderness the wolf stopped, leaned down, and helped the woman to sit.

"I have brought you something, Mother," he announced. "A slave, to tend to your needs." Reaching back, he grabbed the girl's arm and jerked her forward. As her eyes adjusted to the darkness, Melangell could see a surprisingly youthful-looking woman, a woman who did not seem old enough to be the wolf's mother, and a woman who had clearly been a striking beauty in her prime. Now, however, her face bore a large palm-size puckered scar on one cheek, and in her struggle to sit it was evident that one leg was tiny and withered.

The woman peered at the girl, her gray eyes intense and her faded golden hair showing ashen silver streaks in the guttering firelight.

"She looks healthy and strong enough," the woman finally said. "How old are you, girl?"

"Fourteen."

"Your clothes are very fine. Have you ever worked hard in your life? I won't have a lazy good-for-nothing cluttering up my home and eating all the food. Well—have you?"

"Yes . . . ma'am . . . these are not my clothes, ma'am. Your son gave them to me. I . . . I am of free but humble birth and am used to hard work . . . ma'am." She tried to make a good impression, to act as a slave should; to gain the old lady's approval. The woman finally leaned back against the wall.

"Yes . . . I suppose you'll do. We must get you some more suitable clothes, though. Go now and build up the fire while my son and I talk. Go!"

Melangell nodded obediently, turning and searching the room for firewood and tools. An evening meal was being prepared when the door burst open and a young woman with wildly flying red hair rushed in.

"Maia," she gasped, with a quick glance in Melangell's direction as she hurried past, "are you all right? I saw the smoke and thought . . ." She stopped abruptly when the wolf suddenly stood and confronted her, his hands clenched angrily at his sides.

"You thought what? That she might be burning up in here? Or maybe starving while you were out gossiping with your friends, or buying yourself more pretty trinkets, or daydreaming down by the stream?"

He seemed ready to strike her, and Melangell watched the unfolding scene with interest.

"Nechtan!" the redhead gasped in shocked injury, "I only left for a little while. I knew she was all right, and that someone would look in on her. See! She is fine! No harm was done!" She put her hands on her hips and leaned forward toward him, pouting prettily. Is this his wife? Melangell wondered. This red-haired . . . Seonaid? Was that her name? She could see his eyes change as he searched the young woman's face for something; then his gaze ran down over her ample body. His mouth suddenly broke into that odd lopsided grin, and with the same short laugh she'd heard before, he grabbed the redhead around the waist, jerking her toward him. She pretended to protest until a fierce kiss silenced her. Shrieking with glee, she was hoisted over his shoulder and the two happily left the house. As the door scraped noisily behind them, his mother spoke.

"That Seonaid! He can never stay mad at her for long. She has more than enough body, but not enough of anything else, which is fine with most men, I suppose."

Melangell looked at the old woman. She still sat upright on the earthen ledge which jutted from the wall, and which seemed to have been made especially for her needs.

"Ma'am," the girl ventured, "supper is almost ready. I will do my best for you, but you will have to teach me what to do because I don't know how to . . . how to . . ."

"Care for a cripple? Of course, child. You seem intelligent as well as sturdy. We may as well talk. We will be very close companions for quite a while. Bring the food over here when it is done. We'll chat while we eat."

"Should I save some for . . . ah . . ."

"Nechtan? Well, you may save it. He might be hungry

later, but I am guessing he and Seonaid will find food elsewhere . . . when they find time from devouring each other. Of course, she cooks about as well as a goat, so perhaps you'd better set aside some for him."

"And for her?"

"Her? By the names of my ancestors, no! She can feed that well-rounded body of hers at her own hearth."

So the girl knew that Seonaid was not his wife. He must not be married at all. And his name was Nechtan. Melangell settled back on the ledge, spreading the food between them, while the old woman began to talk.

"Now, to satisfy your curiosity about my afflictions, my leg and hip were crushed many years ago in a riding accident. My horse slipped on a wet stone, fell atop me, and in the process forced my cheek into the hot embers of a campfire. I could not rise until the horse had been removed." Her voice grew distant at the memory, and Melangell shuddered at the thought of such an ordeal.

"I had been quite a beauty until then. Proud, impetuous. Afflictions teach one patience and humility soon enough. No man wanted me then, and who can blame them? A scarred and crippled shell of a woman, and unable to bear children. I never married."

Melangell lowered her bread and honey in mid-bite.

"But then Nechtan . . . your son . . . I mean . . ."

"My son?" She laughed lightly. "He is my foster child, the natural child of some near relatives. His parents were killed by invaders when he was a baby, but a loyal servant saved him. As his only living relative, I raised him as my own. And you, girl. Melangell? That is an odd name. Are you foreign?"

"No, ma'am. My village is . . . was . . . to the northwest, on a lake. It is said our people long ago came from the south, the land of the Silures. Mine is an old family name. I don't know much about it."

"And your neck? My son got to you, did he?"

The girl's hand flew up to the wound on her neck and she lowered her head in confused embarrassment.

"Yes, ma'am," she muttered.

"Your first time, too, no doubt. Yes, well, men are like that. I'll never understand why, though. Why violence appeals to them so much more than peace. Well, you're mine now and he is not to touch you. I'll have a word with him tomorrow"—she lowered her cup of ale—"or whenever he returns. We'd best get some sleep now. The welcoming feast is tomorrow afternoon, so we must be well-rested. The food was very good, Melangell. You have different ways of fixing things. Good, but different. Now, if you will help me onto the pot, we can retire. Fix your bed on the floor here beside me in case I need you during the night."

In the brief time the weary girl lay awake on her straw pallet before drifting to sleep, she pondered the day's happenings. The old woman . . . Maia . . . was kind, and she seemed glad to have someone to talk to. She was lucky to belong to her, she supposed, and wondered briefly at the fate of the thirteen others from her village. And Nechtan . . . she still knew little about him. Today she had noticed an odd spiral tattoo on his upper right arm, stretching along the muscle nearly from shoulder to elbow—what did that signify? And he had no mustache, as most Celtic warriors did. Yet he wore a heavy gold Celtic torque around his neck, with two boars' heads at the front, glaring at each other in eternal enmity. The boar, fiercest creature in the forest . . .

Well, she mused as the firelight danced along the walls, she was glad, from the leer on his face when he walked out with Seonaid, that she no longer belonged to him.

The feasting began at midday and lasted well into the night. As Maia's personal attendant, Melangell was allowed to enter the Great Hall with Nechtan's small retinue. He led the way, splendidly attired in a saffron shirt Maia had embroidered; a red-brown-and-yellow-checked cloak; new ankle-length red wool breeches; and he had ornamented himself with plundered gold bands around his wrists and arms and several heavy gold rings on his fingers. He walked proudly, his heavy sword at his side, and followed by his four spearmen, all finely dressed as well. Behind them the girl aided and supported his mother, who seemed in pain as she hobbled one slow step at a time. Maia's hair had been dressed with gold bands, and the only other jewelry she wore was a large enameled gold pendant on a heavy chain; the design of a wheel, symbol of Loucetius, god of thunder. In an attempt to impress the gathering with a touch of the exotic, Melangell was made to wear the captured finery Nechtan had given her, and murmurs broke out around them when they passed. Although his band was small—most warriors could afford to keep ten or more men—they made a fine and impressive spectacle, and no small measure of respect was shown to Nechtan and his crippled mother as they entered the hall.

And what a splendid hall it was! Of round stockade construction, it was large enough to hold several normal houses. A huge fire roared on the central hearth and the smell of roasting meat hung heavy in the air, mingled with the pungent tang of wine. The king and his nobles and warlords sat on several fine bearskins opposite the door, where the king could watch his guests arrive. At his side the young druid sat cross-legged and silent, his black robe unrelieved by any show of jewelry or color. Nechtan and his men turned to the right on entering the room, while a slave escorted his mother and Melangell to the near left side of the hall, where the women were seated on folded cloaks and cushions. A low stool was provided for Maia's comfort, and Melangell stood behind her, thankful that she was near enough to listen to the men's loud swaggering and boasting, jokes and laughter, instead of the dull chatter and gossip of the women around her. Occasionally the men would fall silent, listening to a song in praise of one of the warriors who had perished in the last raid, or a bardic recital of long-ago heroics; then their ribaldry would resume, growing louder as evening approached and the wine flowed more freely.

The king speared a chunk of the choicest boar meat with his dagger and slowly chewed on it while he listened to a loud argument between two warriors. A fair-haired shield-bearer was questioning the claims of a redheaded spearman across the circle of seated men, whose boasts of loot in the recent raid did seem ridiculous to Melangell, in light of what she knew of her village's poor state. Goaded beyond endurance by his tormentor, the redhead leapt to his feet and drew his knife. The blond did likewise, letting his cloak fall to the dirt floor behind him. They glared hotly at each other, exchanging vile curses, and the girl could see that there had been bad blood between them for some time. A few of the older warriors laughed drunkenly, but the king clearly had

had enough of the two young hotheads. He silently held up one hand in a cautionary gesture, and the two warriors hesitated. Then Nechtan stood, smiling slightly, the firelight gleaming off the gold at his arms and neck, and spoke to the king and the assembled warriors.

"There is one here, Annos," he said, nodding to the seated king, "who could settle these boastful claims. A slave I captured from that village, an intelligent girl, who sits yonder with my mother."

Melangell's legs turned to butter beneath her when she heard his words, and she sensed Maia stiffen uncomfortably. The women's chatter died away as they became aware of what was being said around the central fire. Melangell felt a hot redness creep up her neck when several of the women peered curiously at her. If he summoned her, she knew she must go, but she felt she would rather face a thousand deaths than enter that circle of drunken warriors and rich nobles gathered around the hearth. Visibly quaking, she saw the king nod once and heard Nechtan call out her name. She stumbled blindly through the seated women, across the packed earthen floor, and halted at the outer ring of shield-bearers who stood guard at the fringes of the festivities. Impossibly tall men loomed around her, as if she stood in a forest of huge trees, and for one blind moment she wanted to run; then the circle parted, a spearman took her arm, and she was guided into the group, halting near the roaring fire. Terrified, she picked out Nechtan's face, thankful for once for his presence. When he motioned to her, she circled the hearth till she reached him. Seizing her shoulder, he turned her to face the group.

"This is Melangell, of noble birth," he lied. A few heads nodded approval. "Tell these men what riches your village once held."

Her terrified mind went blank at the prospect, and when she opened her mouth to speak, no words would come. Desperately she tried to think, to no avail. She felt his hand clench tighter on her shoulder, his fingers digging into the bone. Loud laughs broke out around them.

"Eh, Nechtan, which end of her did you rape, anyway?" an older man called out.

"Or did she make a fool of you on that score too?" another shouted.

"Speak!" he hissed furiously into her ear. Her shame only added to her muteness, like wave upon wave of engulfing water. Their argument now forgotten, the two hotheaded warriors roared along with the rest.

"Forgotten how, Nechtan," one taunted, "or has Seonaid worn you out that much?"

"Look how she blushes!" cried the other. "Like a red currant-berry! I do believe she is still a virgin, Nechtan, and not a bad-looking one at that! Shall I remedy that for you?" The blond warrior strode forward drunkenly and reached for the girl with a grin. Melangell was so insensate with fear and confusion that when Nechtan, in disgust, almost bodily threw her at the warrior, she landed in a heap at his feet.

"Take her," he snapped, "she's yours."

The laughter grew to a roar through which the girl dimly heard Maia's voice, protesting loudly; but soon even her voice was lost in the midst of the deafening, drunken crowd of men. The warrior bent, slid his hands around the girl's slim waist, and effortlessly hoisted her over his shoulder.

"No!" she screamed, finding her voice when he began to walk away with her. Squirming and kicking, she tried to escape, but he clamped her legs tightly in one arm and resumed walking unsteadily through the sea of laughing faces.

"No!" she screamed again, pushing away from his back with her hands, trying to slip free of his grasp. "No . . . *No!*" Her terror mounted until a loud crash exploded around them and the girl, hanging upside down behind the man's back, heard a sudden silence fall on the crowd. Her captor froze in mid-stride, his muscles growing tense beneath her. At the sound of a second crash, a few women gasped, springing to their feet, and the warrior hastily dumped the girl to the floor and retreated.

"Loucetius!" someone whispered. Melangell felt them move away from her as another crash of thunder split the air. Pulling herself into a huddle, she buried her face in her knees and cried brokenly at the nightmare the day had become. The silence around her became near-absolute—no whispering, no thunder; only her own soft sobbing and the crackling of the fire drifted through the hall.

Then Maia called to her and broke the tension.

"Melangell," she said softly, "come, child, and help me home."

The girl crawled to her knees and stumbled toward her mistress. Guests muttered uneasily throughout the hall and the druid leaned forward, watching the slave girl intently. Wiping away her tears and brushing the dirt from her clothes, Melangell helped the old woman rise, and together they made their way across the room as the crowds parted before them. As they passed into the chill night air, frightened whispers followed.

"Loucetius!"

"Loucetius . . ."

The thunder god.

Nechtan did not return for two days, and when he did, the girl soon wished it had been two hundred instead.

A sharp kick to her back jolted her from a sound sleep and she instinctively thrashed around in reaction to it. A hand quickly clamped around her mouth while another took her arm and lifted her to her feet. She knew at once who it was, and she knew at once that he was drunk. She also knew that his obvious intent was to not awaken his sleeping mother. He dragged her across the floor and up the steps to the door with such force and fury that she could scarcely get her feet to the ground to match his angry strides. A blast of cold night air hit them when they stepped outside, a chill late-autumn breeze coming in off the nearby river, heavy with dampness. The stars glittered wildly overhead as he jerked her forward.

Violently he heaved her along, behind the house, past the woodpile and covered storage bins, almost to the outer wall of the fort itself, where he stopped and threw her full force against a farm wagon. Its heavy side slammed hard into her and she fell in pain and breathlessness, trying to cling to the spokes of the wagon wheel for support.

"Make a mockery of me, will you, in front of everyone?" he spat out in a rage, his fists clenched.

Feebly Melangell tried to pull herself upright, protesting.

"No, Nechtan, no . . . I tried to . . ."

"Shut up!" he hissed, and his fist came up hard into her stomach. Groaning, she sank back to the rutted earth, the wagon sailing dizzily above her.

"Please . . ." she gasped, "no . . ."

He kicked her in the side, and when she rolled over, his foot landed in her back. Pain shot through her and she clawed at the ground, trying to avoid his blows, cowering like a helpless animal. Grabbing her by the back of the neck, he lifted her upright and pressed his knife to her throat.

"I ought to kill you now and be done with you," he whispered violently into her ear as he held her against his chest. She hung limply in his grasp, her stomach churning from fear and the reek of old wine that surrounded him. She had seen animals die from a slit throat, and it was not a pretty sight, but almost anything was better than this.

". . . but for my mother, who values you so highly, I . . ." She heard his words drift brokenly across her mind.

"Bah!" he exclaimed, and she felt him move to replace his dagger. Before she could relax, his fist smashed into her face, and in the hot tide of blood that erupted, she fainted.

He dropped her to the ground and left. In her unconscious stupor the battered girl crawled under the wagon, where she was found the next morning, still unconscious, bloodied, and shivering in the cold.

She awoke to the sounds of a furious argument between Maia and Nechtan, and a skilled hand gently bathing her battered face. A woolen blanket covered her, and she could smell the sharp odor of medicinal herbs in the air. Opening her swollen eyes, she saw a young man bent over a large bronze bowl. Shortly he wrung out a cloth, turned toward her, and continued bathing her face. She recognized him as the druid who had so unsettled her outside her village. His face had a soft, cultured look to it, his gray eyes shining with an odd, compassionate light, and only his wavy brown hair, cut shorter than a warrior's, seemed unruly and untamed, tumbling forward across his forehead. He smiled slightly when he saw her attempting to look at him, but he sternly motioned her to silence when she tried to move her injured lips to speak.

"There is nothing you need to say," he responded quietly. His voice was low, controlled, soothing to her battered spirits. "I will tell you what you need to know, and then you must rest. You have been very gravely injured. I have cleaned you and applied poultices to your back and abdomen. There is a plaster on your lip and cheek, to aid in healing where the skin was split, so you must not try to speak. I have medicines for you to take, but for the next few days you are to remain here; you are not to get up or be moved.

"Nechtan will pay for my slave to come and care for both you and his mother; what he has done is a grave offense. Beating another person's slave is a violation of the law. His mother is a freeborn woman with her own property, so neither she nor her possessions belong to him. If she chooses, she can have a Lawgiver summoned to settle the issue; and if he persists in his behavior, one must be brought in."

He turned aside to the bowl, then back to Melangell, gently dabbing the medicine on her cuts and bruises.

"You are to have only broths and liquids for a few days. I will instruct my slave as to your care. He is a learned man, with some limited knowledge of healing. Now," he concluded, setting aside the cloth, "drink this and sleep."

His mouth curved into a half-smile as he took a little gold whisk and briskly stirred the contents of a small bronze cup to a froth. Melangell groaned in pain when he lifted her head and held the cup to her mouth. It felt odd, she noted; the first metal cup she had ever in her life drunk from. The foamy liquid tasted bitter but it had a faint sweet aftertaste, and she savored it for a moment while her head was laid back on the pallet, the spilled medicine wiped from her chin.

"Rest now," he seemed to command, and his fingers ran as lightly as a butterfly's wings across her forehead. In a moment the pain eased, the fear vanished, and she sank into a deep, contented sleep.

She awoke to the dimness of twilight coming through the partly open door. She could see Nechtan on the ledge across the room, wrapped in his woolen cloak and sleeping off his drunkenness. An involuntary moan escaped her lips when

24

she tried to turn her head, and in a breath-span the sound of scraping and shuffling told her that Maia was being escorted across the floor to see her. Forcing her head to move, she turned and saw Maia, looking older and grayer than she had ever seen her, leaning heavily on the shoulder of . . . a Roman!

Melangell's breath caught in shock, and as she struggled to rise, Maia's alarmed voice cut through the silence.

"Melangell—no! Be still! No!"

She needed no more commands. Quickly she fell back to the straw pallet, pains tearing at her stomach. Maia shuffled nearer, a stool was pulled out for her, and she wearily settled down on it. Then Melangell felt a man's hand lift her head, a cup came to her lips, and an almost tasteless liquid trickled down her throat. She knew it must be the Roman.

A Roman!

Her bruised eyes drew open and she glared at him in hatred.

"A Roman . . ." she muttered bitterly. He nodded gravely in reply. He was dressed in a slave's plain cowled tunic and short breeches, and his face looked ordinary, in a rugged sort of way, as if his features had been chiseled out of sturdy oak. His dark curly hair was ludicrously long, like a sheep's wool at shearing time, and his grim eyes were the darkest Melangell had ever seen.

"Anarios, at your service," he said in a clipped tone.

"He is a physician," Maia interjected. "The druid sent him."

"But," the girl whispered, "a Roman? I want no Roman tending me. I—"

"Young lady," he interrupted, "although I am a Roman, at the present time I have more in common with you than with my fellow countrymen, for we are both war captives and slaves. Like you, I do my job and try to please my master; like you, I try to stay alive. Nothing more." He rose and walked to the fire, and she stared at Maia in silence.

"We have all suffered at the hands of the Romans," the old woman said simply. "He is here to serve you now. He is a physician, not a soldier. You must set aside your hatred for a time, rest, and recover your strength."

"He . . . is a Roman," Melangell stated again flatly, unable to say any more; unwilling to tell the old woman that it was the Romans who'd killed most of her family before she was born; all except her mother, heavy with new life, and her uncle, who'd wrapped his sister in their father's cloak and saved her, escaping into the bogs, where they were hunted like animals until their pursuers had given up.

But he had been right. Like him, she intended to survive. The unspoken bond between all slaves had passed between them as well. Like him, she intended to escape.

Obediently she drank the warm broth when he returned with it, and Maia sighed in satisfaction. But the girl could tell, just by looking at his dark eyes, that the Roman knew he had struck a chord within her.

"You will not touch her again." Maia's voice was low and firm. "She was given to me. It is common knowledge. You can no more damage her than you could damage my wagon or cow or dwelling. Is that understood?"

Melangell lay still in the darkness and listened to the hushed conversation as Maia berated Nechtan.

"By all laws, you are my son, Nechtan, but that does not mean that you can abuse those same laws when it suits you. The Chief Druid, the Lawgiver, will bless us with his presence at Samhain, and there are those who say I should present my grievance to him regarding what you have done. What have you to say?"

The girl wished she could see how Nechtan looked at this moment. Was he still haughty, or contrite? His voice, when he spoke, carried only a slightly softer edge to its usual deep pride. For him, it must resemble shame and sorrow, or as close as he could come to it.

"I am sorry I damaged your property, Mother. I was drunk and I was angry. I know I gave her to you as a gift, outright, and as such I have no more claim on her. But as for her, I would do it again, and she is lucky to still be alive. I have no regrets as far as—"

"Be quiet," Maia snapped. "Do you surely want me to go before the Lawgiver? You will be found completely in the wrong if I do, Nechtan. Because she shamed you unwittingly is no cause to do what you did. She is the best worker, the best attendant, I have ever had. I would have great difficulty replacing her. Besides, I like the child. She is intelligent, thoughtful, dutiful—"

"I'll hear no more of this," Nechtan interrupted. "Any slave is dutiful if beaten enough times. They say that Roman's back is—"

"Think of the precedent you seek to set, son." The old woman's voice rose. "Just because she humiliated you—"

"Yes!" he nearly shouted. "She did, and for that she paid, and lightly, too, in my opinion!" He rose angrily to his feet.

"And if a neighbor's cart splattered mud on you, or his cow dropped dung on your foot and humiliated you, could you justify destroying his cart or—"

"This is different!" He paced away from her. "I wouldn't consider—"

"Yes, it is different," she said dryly. "And I wonder why. Do you feel ashamed for what you and your men did to her, or do you have feelings for her that you deny to yourself? Perhaps that is why she annoys you so. Just remember this, son: by the sacred names of all the gods who dwell around us, she is watched over by Loucetius. And he is the god of this household, as well. You've said yourself you don't know why you spared her life and brought her to me. It was the will of Loucetius—"

He snorted in derision.

"Listen to me, Nechtan!" she continued. "How else can you explain it? You saw what happened at the feast. Loucetius protects this girl. If you harm her again, you will surely bring disaster down upon this household. Would you go so far as to offend a god?"

"I don't believe in your superstitions, Mother. The world is what it is, and no god will intervene to change it. What god decreed my fate?" he retorted.

"Hush!" Maia whispered in fear.

"What god denied me my inheritance at the hands of a bunch of filthy barbarians? What god decided I should build myself up from nothing? I did it, Mother. All that we have, I did, and not some woodland spirit."

"You condemn us all, son. It is your bad blood that speaks out. It is not your mother's blood, my sister, the blood of our people. No—it is your father's blood. Your foolish black-haired father's blood; the blood of the Picts—"

27

"You will not use that Roman name, Mother!" he growled, whirling on her. "Yes, I am Cruithni, and proud I am of it, too. My blood is noble blood. More noble than that of the chieftains and petty rich men who live here. I am grateful for what you have done for me and I have tried to be a good son, but now I think it is time I lived on my own. Tomorrow I will go to live with my men in their quarters until other arrangements can be made. I will help you whenever you need me; but you have chosen her over me and I cannot live with that. This is your house and your holding, so I will leave. Now, good night, Mother."

The girl heard Nechtan carry his mother to her resting place on the ledge, and they quietly settled in for the night. Nechtan poked the fire a few times and laid several more logs on the hearth, half-buried in ash to last till morning. Then, his cloak wrapped around his shoulders, he brooded, staring at the low flames while the boars' heads at his throat gleamed and sparkled across the room at the girl. Weary, Melangell fell asleep while Nechtan remained musing by the hearth.

When she awoke the next morning, he was gone.

"Well, that druid certainly knows his business!"

The Roman's compliment came amidst winces and jumps from Melangell as he peeled and flaked and scraped the dried plaster off her lip and cheek.

"It is healing nicely; a small scar you will probably carry for life, but not bad, considering how extensive the injury was."

The girl could not reply, for he had pulled the skin beside her mouth taut in his fingers while he picked off the last of the hardened cake.

"But of course," he continued, "it will matter little as to whether a man will want you with a scar or without, because you will only marry whomever and whenever they decide, anyway." He peered over his shoulder as he spoke, to be sure Maia was beyond hearing. "The choice is not ours to make, is it?" he concluded, lowering his hands.

"I hadn't thought about it." Being a fellow slave, and an intelligent person as well, the Roman was the only person she could talk openly with. "I hope I am never married to anyone."

"Oh, ho!" he laughed. "You'll probably get your wish. Maia will keep you for herself for as long as she's around, and by the time she's gone, you'll be too old."

He motioned the girl to lie down, pulled the blanket aside, and began removing the poultice from her abdomen. He shook his head when he saw the large blue bruise beneath it.

"Savage brute, isn't he?" he muttered.

"He was angry . . . and drunk. I shamed him in front of everyone. A warrior must not be shamed."

"How you people stick together! Even after all he's done to you. Destroyed your village, murdered your family, raped you too, I'll wager, eh?"

Melangell averted her eyes.

"Yes, I thought so," he continued. "Beats you to a pulp, and you still try to defend him. But I, on the other hand"—he gestured dramatically with one hand—"am the hated Roman, the dreaded enemy. Don't you people have any discipline? I would never do this to a woman."

"You're not a soldier. All soldiers are the same. Your soldiers killed my family and destroyed my home too."

"War makes animals of all men," he stated simply, and a grave look settled on his dark face. "They give me so little to work with here!" He sighed in frustration. "Your abdomen does not look good to me. I think I'll get the druid with all his magics to look at you again. You need more treatment. Turn over now, and let me see your back."

He helped her roll over and as he tended her back she asked him questions.

"Anarios—that's not a Roman name, is it?"

"No. I was born in southern Gaul. Do you know where that is?"

She shook her head.

"Far, far to the south of here. Across mountains and fields and great waters. My parents were Roman, and I was educated in Rome."

"Rome! What was it like?"

"Ha! A great, great city. Greater than you, in your most fantastic dreams, could imagine. But no matter. Two years as a physician with the army in Britain, and our outpost was overrun. They realized my value, I suppose, so I was spared death and was sold into slavery, which is almost the same thing."

"Then you are not so old? You Romans are so dark, it is hard to tell your ages."

"Oh," he laughed, "I am all of thirty years old. But no more," he continued seriously. "I'll discuss my past no more. Discussing your former life would make you sad too, and so I don't question you. And believe me, I have plenty of questions about you; caring for a beaten girl is quite a new thing for me, and very different from treating the hideous battle wounds of soldiers. But people like us, Melangell, we can have no past and no future. Only the present, the here and now; that is what we live for. For that only do we struggle and survive. Remember that, Melangell. Now, let's turn you back over so I can give you more broth and medicine, and then I'll go and visit that druid again."

Brennos, the druid, agreed with Anarios, and after some painful poking and probing the two withdrew and carried on a solemn and brief conversation, which only increased the girl's fears. Without a word to her, the young druid left and Anarios returned to her side.

"He will prepare medicine for you. It is also his opinion that if you are not better in a few more days, you should go on a pilgrimage to a sacred spring somewhere and make offerings to your goddess of healing . . . What's her name?"

"Arnemetia."

"Yes. He sees that as a last resort, but I'm not sure I agree with him."

"A pilgrimage! How do I do that? I can barely walk, I cannot sit up alone, I must be helped to the pot . . . It is a very long trip! How can I possibly—"

"Well, I am to accompany you, and your gracious mistress will provide us with a cart for you to ride in. She's very worried about you, you know; she must value you highly. And no doubt we'll have some guards along, too, to keep an eye on us."

"No doubt."

"Well"—he stood up—"I will go and fetch his medicines

and we'll see if they help any. Maybe between his potions, my skills, and the old lady's prayers, you won't have to make that trip at all."

But the medicines and broths and bed rest did little good. At times her stomach ached unbearably and Anarios had to fix teas to give her rest. Her food—broths, stewed fruits, and watery gruels—did not digest properly. She lost weight, her eyes became gray and sunken, and everyone realized the pilgrimage was necessary.

A small, sturdy two-wheeled farm cart was provided by an increasingly worried Maia, loaded with provisions and a pallet for the girl to lie on, and two of Nechtan's spearmen were detailed as guards, one to drive the wagon and the other to ride alongside. When all was ready, Anarios helped Maia to sit at the girl's bedside for a moment.

"It is twelve days before Samhain, the coming of the New Year," she said. "Perhaps if the weather holds, you can return in time for the ceremonies." She looked down at the bony face of the girl and inwardly cursed her irresponsible son. Patting Melangell's hand, she slipped her enamel pendant of Loucetius beneath the girl's limp fingers.

"For you . . ." Maia whispered, "to watch over you on your journey. He is your protector as well."

"Oh, no!" the girl started to protest. "I shouldn't have this. It is yours."

"Nonsense!" She smiled. "I want you to have it. It might bring you good fortune on your journey. I want you to get well, dear, and return as soon as possible. Melwas and Niall have been instructed to watch over you carefully, and they will obey my instructions, I am sure."

She turned aside briefly when Nechtan's shadow fell across the doorway.

"It is time to go," she said gently, fearing she would never see the girl alive again. "Nechtan!" she called. "Come here!"

Silently he strode across the floor, and Anarios rose quickly, moving away from the young warrior's hostile glare.

"I will carry Melangell to the cart," the Roman offered.

"You will escort me, Roman," the old woman stated. "Nechtan, you must make some sort of peace with

Melangell before she departs on her journey. To do otherwise would be bad luck for her. You, son, carry her to the cart."

"I will not," he protested. Melangell closed her eyes in weariness at yet another fight between mother and son. She could see that her trip was starting out badly, and it would probably end that way too—with Anarios and the two guards returning the necklace to Maia, leaving her poor battered body buried beneath the frozen turf somewhere. She had hurt for so long, been ill for so long, she almost didn't care. If only life would be done with, and quickly.

She felt strong hands slide beneath her and powerful arms lift her into the air. She opened her eyes, expecting to see the familiar face of Anarios beside hers, but instead she saw Nechtan, his yellow wolf's eyes looking down at her face with a brief moment of tenderness. Then his face clouded over again, his lips tightened, and his haughty expression returned. Clutching Maia's necklace, she felt herself being carried across the room, up the steps, and out to the waiting cart. He held her effortlessly, never once jarring her injured stomach, and she wondered idly if dying was like that—being borne quietly and gently away, away. . . . He laid her on a straw pallet in the cart and pulled a fur covering to her chin. For another brief instant his gentle look returned and he wiped her tears aside. Speaking quickly and quietly, so no one else would hear, he leaned toward her ear.

"Melangell, I'm sorry—for everything."

His emphasis on the last word puzzled her. Straightening up, he withdrew when Anarios climbed into the cart beside her. As they lurched into motion, Maia waved farewell, but Nechtan stood sullenly at her side, staring blankly ahead, not looking as the cart rolled through the gateway, down the incline, and along the rutted path across the fields.

Melangell watched the fortress recede from sight in the early-morning haze. She had not noticed, nor had anyone else, the brief nod Nechtan gave his man Melwas, on horseback, while the cart slowly lumbered away.

The first night was spent in a little forest clearing. Both Melangell and Anarios were thankful for the presence of the two guards, who soon had a nice fire burning and a small haunch of beef roasting for supper. Anarios tried to make conversation with the men but his attempts were met with brief statements and hostile glares, so he abandoned the effort.

"Not very talkative, are they?" he commented as he sat beside Melangell's pallet.

"Unlike you Romans," she replied irritably. "Rome must be a very noisy place."

"Ha! That it is!" He laughed cheerily. "We are not at all like you taciturn northern races. You only talk when you're drunk, which seems to be quite often."

"And you only *stop* when you're drunk," she retorted. He seemed to enjoy the comment, but the girl was in no mood for their usual banter.

"I don't know which is worse," he observed casually, "the degree to which he irritates you or the degree to which you irritate him."

"I don't know what you're talking about," the girl muttered, turning her face away and into the edge of her blanket.

"Oh, I think you do—and I also think the cake is about evenly divided between the two of you. A physician must be observant, you know."

"You're insane. The brightness of the moon has touched your mind."

"Perhaps," he said, stretching his legs and pulling the medicine bag onto his lap. "But I think not. . . . Let me give you something to help you sleep. I can see from our friends over there that it must be time to retire." He poked around in the leather bag until he pulled out a wooden vial and dropped two round pills into his hand.

"Here," he said. "The druid had me make these in case we could not boil teas. The herbs are powdered and mixed with fat. These are very strong and you should be asleep in short order."

He held her up to swallow the pills and watched her drift to sleep. If only my old army comrades could see me now! he chuckled. A slave and a nursemaid to a young pagan girl.

He settled back to study the two spearmen. Melwas, the shorter of the two, had already rolled into his cloak and was sleeping soundly, while Niall, his long hair nearly as yellow as the golden torque he wore, sat watch by the campfire. The tall warrior seemed to studiously avoid looking at the two slaves, but Anarios got the clear feeling that the man's keen blue eyes never missed a move they made. He couldn't put a finger on it, but there was something about the two guards that he didn't like. Well, the druid said they should be at the spring in about six days, so maybe it would all work out. He dismissed the thought of trying to escape. Those spears looked too wicked, and one of the men was always on the alert. No, he'd just have to wait and see what happened. The gods sometimes decreed their will in very odd ways.

The trip soon became a nightmare for the injured girl. On the second day the road through the woods became impossibly rutted. The cart lurched and bounced wildly down into holes and up over tree roots, till Melangell clenched her teeth to keep from crying out. Anarios walked behind, carrying his precious bundle of medicines and trying to steady the jarring of the wagon. Unable to endure the girl's suffering any longer, he called a halt. Melwas rode back to see what the trouble was.

"This road is killing her," Anarios snapped. "Look at her . . . she won't even make it to the spring at this rate."

"It is the only road," the warrior replied. "It is much traveled and badly worn."

"Why don't you people fix it? Make it a *decent* roadway?"

"Fix it?" Melwas seemed amused at the idea and leaned forward over his pony's neck for emphasis. "And who will fix it, Roman? Many tribes use it. Which tribe fixes it? It belongs to no one. It is the road, that's all. Now we go!"

"Wait! Can't you carry her on your horse? She can't take much more of this."

"I do not carry slave girls on my horse," he replied haughtily, and turned to ride away. In frustration, Anarios slung his pack over his back and picked up the girl. Trying to avoid the holes and roots, he followed the cart as it lurched into motion again.

On the third day the ground turned soft and boggy, and Anarios guessed they might be nearing the spring. The road, too, became softer, and eventually the cart sank to the flooring in thick mire and could not be moved. Pulling themselves in mud to their thighs, the three men dragged the horses free and unloaded the cart, passing bundles and food from one to the other until drier ground was reached. Lastly

Melangell was lifted out by Melwas, handed to Anarios, and on to Niall, who laid her on a knoll of high ground.

Together the men gathered timber and saplings and tried to hoist the wagon from the mud, without success. Anarios suggested a sling to lift it upward, using the horses as muscle-power, but the spearmen were skeptical that it would work. When darkness gathered, bringing to a close the short winter's day, Niall called a halt to their efforts.

"We sleep now," he declared, "and tomorrow we walk."

"Walk?" protested Anarios. "How many more days' travel is it?"

"Two."

"I am worn out now. I cannot carry her for two more days."

"I will help carry her," Niall said. "Melwas will stay here with the horses and try to free the wagon while we are gone. Now we sleep."

It seemed pointless to argue with him. Anarios moved Melangell closer to the fire and, exhausted, lay down to sleep beside her.

They walked until nearly dusk the next day. The ground remained spongy and wet and they often had to skirt deep pools and dangerous bogs. At least the warrior seemed to know exactly where he was going, Anarios was relieved to note. The smoother trip seemed to revive Melangell, and she even managed to eat a little, which cheered Anarios' flagging spirits. He did not like to see his patients fade away and die. Maybe there was something to this sacred spring after all. Although he never thought he'd hear himself thinking it, he would be glad to see that stinking little village again, once this trip was over. How he missed the wide, straight, firm Roman roads he was used to, instead of these infernal footpaths and goat tracks.

At nightfall Niall found a hill to camp on, propped the girl by a scrubby hawthorn tree, and unslung the pack from his back. Anarios dropped his medicine sack to the ground, stretching to unlimber his stiffened muscles. He hadn't thought thirty was so old, but he was having difficulty keeping up with this strapping young warrior of . . . Twenty? Twenty-two? He belonged in a nice civilized city, not out here hiking through a marshland like an overloaded jackass. He poked through their rations while Niall lit a small campfire, and soon they were eating hot barley gruel and cheese. Niall sat by the fire, watching Anarios help the girl. Leaning forward, he extended a horn flask toward them.

"Here," he offered. "It is good wine—Roman wine. It might help to revive her."

Anarios took it in surprise. "Roman wine? Where did you get Roman wine?"

Niall leered good-naturedly at him.

"From the Romans. Where else?"

"Yes . . . well . . . I'll not ask *how* you got it. I don't think I want to know. It might help her, at that, more than the stale beer we are used to drinking." Unplugging it, he held the polished rim to Melangell's lips and let a little wine trickle into her mouth. She looked up at him in surprise.

"Wine?" she muttered, her sunken eyes puzzled.

"Yes," he laughed. "Roman wine, according to Niall. See what I've been missing all these years!"

"You have some too, Roman," Niall interjected.

"Yes? Oh, why, thanks!" Anarios took a deep swallow and closed his eyes happily.

"Ahh, yes! Roman wine." He sighed, and gave some more to the girl, then took another deep drink himself before returning the horn to Niall.

"May Bacchus bless you for that, Niall, it was just what . . ." He stopped when he felt the girl slump unconscious in his arms. Understanding quickly hit him and he looked at the smiling warrior, fear and hatred in his eyes.

"Why, you . . ." he began, attempting to rise before unconsciousness hit him and he, too, fell to his face across the little rise of land.

Niall gave a low laugh, poured the rest of the wine onto the ground, and finished eating his meal.

"The wolves will finish them off before long, if they haven't already," Niall muttered as he and Melwas loaded their provisions on the horses. "They are hungry from the long, dry autumn."

"And if not, they will drown in a bog before the day is over." Melwas grinned, mounting his horse.

Leaving the cart abandoned in the mire, the two rode off down the mud trail as the sun crept above the horizon.

Anarios woke groggily, the bitter taste of leaves and soil in his mouth. He spat noisily and heard Melangell softly call his name behind him.

"Anarios? Anarios . . ." She choked back a sob. "I thought you were dead."

He rose quickly to his hands and knees, looking around the knoll as a rage rose within him.

"The dirty bastard," he gasped. "He took everything . . . everything—food, medicine—everything."

He stood unsteadily and looked out at the bog, trying to quell the unaccustomed feeling of panic he felt rising within him. The perfect nightmare, he thought briefly, the civilized man, abandoned in the wilderness.

"Anarios," the girl called again. "Help me up!"

He turned and saw her sitting upright against the small tree, a surprising bit of color showing on her pale face. How ironic that she should now begin to improve; now, when their life expectancy was only days, at most.

"We are free, Anarios! Don't you see!" she said, excitement sparkling in her eyes. "They left us here to die, but if we find our way out, then we are free!"

"But how?" he argued. "We have no water, not even a knife. *Nothing.*" His mouth fell open in astonishment when he saw her pull a long slim dagger from one red leather boot and hold it triumphantly before her.

"Maia was worried about my safety." She grinned, her eyes bright.

"Why, bless that old lady to the heavens and back again!" he shouted, sweeping her into his arms in a joyous hug. She laughed delightedly.

"Free!" she sang out. "Free!"

Abruptly he stopped and lowered her to her feet, looking grimly into her face.

"Do you know the wilderness, Melangell? I am a foreigner and know little of how to survive here. My meat has always come from a butcher and my bread from the baker's oven."

"I know some, yes. This is my country. If it will be enough or not, we will just have to see. But you can be sure I will try.

Perhaps with my knowledge and your strength, we can succeed!"

Things were looking infinitely brighter and he impulsively squeezed the girl again. "Then let's get started!" he announced, laughing.

"'Walk when you have to and eat when you can,' my uncle always told me," Melangell explained, splitting some tough creepers to make ropes.

"Sound advice." Anarios nodded as he watched her deft fingers extract the tough fibers. "A Roman general could have coined the saying, since the army mostly marches here and there and seldom eats a decent meal."

She handed him a cluster of the stripped cords. "Tie these together as if your life depended on it, because it might one day," she instructed. "With these, and our sharpened sticks, we should be able to escape these bogs in a day or two. Then it will be much easier to travel, and food will be more plentiful."

"Yes," he agreed as he worked, "I've noticed very little wildlife out here."

"So if, as we walk, we spy something edible, we stop and eat it. Then we walk some more," she added. "Now," she said, rising unsteadily to her feet, "we tie these around our waists, and around our walking sticks, so both we and they may be retrieved from the mire."

He looked up at her admiringly. "Your color is back and your strength returns," he remarked.

"A taste of freedom is the best medicine there is, eh, physician?"

"I would not have lasted a day out here without your resourcefulness," he said.

"As I doubt I would last a day on the streets of Rome, without yours. We are the children of different cultures and different gods, that is all. There is no great mystery to that. As there are different birds and different stones, so are there different peoples."

He laughed again, tying the cord around his waist. "Obviously those two did not take you into account when they abandoned us here."

"No, nor did Nechtan," she answered bitterly, her face

hardening. "Revenge moves me almost as much as does freedom. One day I will pay him for this debt I owe him."

"I hope you and I both will live to see that day," Anarios replied. "Masters always underestimate the abilities of their slaves, don't they? Well, let us begin!"

He helped her down the slippery grass of the knoll and she prodded the ground ahead, picking out a secure footing for their path. Following behind, Anarios held a steadying hand on her shoulder as they crept forward across the great bog.

Midday they caught a sluggish, sleeping turtle that had not yet hibernated and ate it raw. Melangell's stomach, unused to solid food, rebelled at the meat and soon she vomited it up while Anarios watched in dismay. She would not last long, he knew, if she was unable to keep down even the scant rations they could find. When she finished she walked with a stoop, as though her stomach pained her again.

"Melangell," he protested, watching her, "we must stop so you can rest. If you can eat but little, at least you can get enough rest. You have been in bed for half a month; you are not used to such exertions."

"But we must go on," she muttered, "get out of this swamp. There are evil spirits and demons . . . swamps are dangerous."

"No!" He stopped her. "Take my hand and I'll lead the way until we find a suitable place, and then we'll stop for the night. Maybe with your advice I can start a fire. I'll try to find something you can eat, and perhaps some clean water for drinking. Come now . . ." he said, taking her hand and passing to the front. He probed the muck with his walking stick, advancing toward a distant hillock where, he hoped, they could camp.

Night was gathering rapidly when they reached it, and as he helped the girl up the slope he thought it to be about as much of a blessing as one could expect in a place like that; it was dry, and a little thicket of bushes gave them some shelter from the abrupt chill of the evening breeze. After a laughably long time he managed to get a fire going in some dry leaves and seed-down, and he put water in the turtle shell they had saved, to warm near the fire.

"There." Melangell pointed to some reeds rattling dryly

in the wind. "Dig up the roots and boil them. And young shoots, if there are any."

The Roman took his walking stick and probed in the damp soil, and soon he had dug a handful of small nut-size tubers. Brushing off the dirt, he dropped them in the hot water. It seemed to take forever before they were tender, and he ate his share at once, then mashed hers with the knife point. She scooped them into her fingers and wolfed them down, and Anarios was glad to see that she didn't throw them up.

"Anything else?" he asked, looking around the hilltop.

"There might be little fish in the shallow pools, but that's all I can think of. Maybe a rat in the tall grass. It's too late in the year for eggs . . ." She seemed wearied by the talk.

"Why don't I just put more wood on the fire and we get some sleep?" he suggested. The girl nodded, wrapped her cloak tighter against the wind, and lay down. In minutes she was asleep, but Anarios sat up well into the night, deep in thought.

The next day's trek brought them to firmer ground and the sight of trees in the distance, and their spirits rose when they saw them. He was supporting her now with one arm while he tapped their way along with the other, and he wondered how much longer it would be before he'd have to carry her again. She tried valiantly, he had to give her that—much more so than any Roman society lady could ever manage— but she was just not up to the ordeal. Could he make it alone, he wondered, if she should die? When a mule foals! he snorted. Aside from her knowledge, she was one of the natives. What chance would he, a Roman, stand alone if he met up with townspeople or warriors? Butchered on the spot, or enslaved again and sold to a master far worse than the druid had been, or, worse yet, sacrificed to one of their infernal gods. He shuddered at the thought of the tales he'd heard. Still, on his own he could make better time; head south, maybe find a Roman patrol. His mind turned eagerly at the thought, but then he looked down at the strained face of the girl. No—he couldn't abandon her and run off on his own, not while she was still alive. Maybe get her to a farm somewhere, or a village, and then leave. Yes, that was it . . . get her to safety and then head back to the Roman lines.

To his dismay, wetness on his cheeks interrupted his thoughts and he looked up to see snowflakes beginning to fall. Snow! The worst thing that could happen! Everything would be covered and they would not be able to see where they were going through the pools and mires.

"Melangell!" he said urgently, trying to rouse her. "We must find shelter. Maybe in that copse of trees over yonder." He motioned with the stick. "Come . . . let's hurry!"

Snow was swirling thickly and beginning to collect on the freezing ground when they reached the scrubby trees, and he knew there was little chance of starting a fire. Melangell slumped sideways when he sat her on the icy ground.

"Branches . . ." she muttered. "Make a shelter."

Hastily he cut branches and tried to prop them along a central pole suspended between two saplings. It was better than nothing and it seemed to keep the snow out. He covered the shelter crosswise with evergreen boughs and put more inside, on the cold ground.

"Crawl in there, Melangell," he said, trying to cover the ends with more branches. His hands were growing stiff with the cold and he abandoned his efforts and crawled into the shelter beside the huddled girl.

"We'll be warmer if we curl up together under both cloaks," he suggested. She was shivering violently and he wrapped his arms around her, trying to keep her warm.

"Anarios," she muttered quietly, "think of me when you reach freedom. I don't think I will make it."

"Nonsense!" he replied, pulling the cloaks up around her face. "This storm will be over by morning and then we'll reach solid ground by midday!" He tried to sound reassuring—more reassuring than he felt. "Now let's lie down and you can sleep." They reclined on the boughs and he pulled her closer, trying to warm her with his body. What he wouldn't give for a fire right now, he mused as he felt her shivering next to him. She snuggled her head against his chest, sighed softly, and was soon asleep; but sleep would not come to Anarios as he listened to the storm swirl around them.

* * *

It seemed as if she had slept for days when Melangell awoke to the smell of broiling meat.

Meat!

She sat up stiffly. Bright sunlight and blue sky shone through the end of the shelter, and a small fire burned just beyond the opening, protected from a brisk north breeze. Both their cloaks still covered her, but Anarios was gone. On hands and knees she crawled from the shelter. Anarios sat to one side of the fire, cloakless and huddled close for warmth, turning a green branch with two roasting chunks of meat on it. He rose quickly when he saw her.

"Here, I've cleared a spot for you to sit, over by this tree," he said, helping her to her feet. The long rest seemed to have done her good; she looked stronger, and he marveled at the resiliency of these northern races.

"But the meat—where did you get it?" she puzzled.

"I thought it was time for me to be a little resourceful too if we are ever to get out of here alive, so when morning came I went scouting around. There must have been a road near here at one time, because down the far slope, I saw a wagon wheel jutting up from the snow, and on closer inspection, animal tracks all around it. Big swamp rats. It was easy enough to spear two, they were so fat and stupid. There are enough to last us quite a while. Then I found some of those rushes you'd pointed out, and dug more tubers. And after quite a lot of effort, I managed to get a fire going too! So at least we have food and heat now, and we are going to stay here for a while to let you recover."

"Did you . . . say a wagon wheel?" she asked slowly.

"Yes. An overturned cart, buried beneath the snow. The rats are living under it, but all you can see now is the wheel. Maybe we could find the track it came on and . . ."

He stopped when he saw she was lost in thought, and her hand slowly rose to the pendant around her neck.

"Loucetius . . ." she whispered, half-afraid. "The wheel is his symbol. Maia said he was my guardian and would watch out for me, and he has."

She looked up at him, her eyes wide with an unearthly fear, and despite himself Anarios felt a chill prickle the back of his neck. He was a Roman! It was absurd! He did not believe in these pagan gods, and yet . . .

He returned to the spit and turned it, then pushed the turtle shell full of tubers and melted snow closer to the fire. He could not get the girl's awestruck face out of his mind, and those big green eyes . . . Funny, he'd never looked at her close enough before to notice what color her eyes were. A striking sea green, like a shallow Mediterranean inlet.

After nightfall, Anarios sat outside the shelter entrance, stared absently into the dancing flames, and ran a hand through his tangled hair. "Damnation!" he cursed himself. "Why did I let something like this happen to me? The first rule of the physician—never let yourself become involved with your patients—and I have violated it!"

His fingers ran over his chin, across the new beard growing there. A beard! he snorted. How must I look? Dirty, unshaven—a Roman never wears a beard. If only I could get cleaned up, shave, decent clothes . . . No, it wouldn't matter to her. She is just a child . . . or is she? Rural girls mature faster than city girls. She has the body of a Roman girl three or four years older. She's a puzzle . . . yet, sometimes, I swear, when she looks at me with those sea-green eyes, she looks at me in a different way . . . or do I imagine it? She was raped . . . does she even know what love is like?

He tossed more wood onto the fire and stood.

"I am her physician but oh, dear Venus, I am also a man, and it has been so long, so very, very long . . ."

Turning, he entered the shelter and lay down beside Melangell. He studied her peaceful face before drifting off to sleep, and found himself dreaming endless dreams of being home once more, under warm and sunny skies, and strolling arm in arm with a fair-haired girl in white beside the turquoise Mediterranean waters.

"I know it's better than starvation," Anarios observed, eating his meal the following day, "but I think I will very quickly come to hate rat meat."

"And I!" Melangell laughed. "If only there were some plants growing here that I could use for seasoning. Some herbs, wild mustard seed, onion tops . . ."

"My mouth waters just to think of it," he replied. "We Romans love onions, and a paste made from crushed mustard seed and vinegar. Very good with cold meat."

"It sounds tasty enough. Maybe someday I can try it. We salt our meat and slowly dry it in aromatic wood smoke. Properly done, it will last for years, and is very good too."

"I suppose all the different peoples have their favorite dishes," he observed, drinking some water. "You dry your meat, to last the winter. We spice ours, to cover the taste when it goes bad in the heat."

"I hadn't thought of it that way," she said. "The world must be so full of marvels I haven't even considered. Tell me some of them." Melangell put her bark plate aside and reclined on her cloak expectantly. Anarios gazed up at the bare treetops in thought.

"Well," he began, "in a very hot country called Egypt there are huge mountains made of stones and put together by men."

"Really?"

"Yes. I have seen them. They say they contain vast treasures, but I don't know. And the people there, when they talk, sound like birds chirping."

"That must be funny!" she laughed.

"But they are also a very old people, and their country is full of wisdom. It belongs to Rome now."

"Tell me more."

Her appetite for knowledge seemed insatiable, and he wondered how she could live in a place like this, backward and ignorant as it was. He glanced at her earnest green eyes and for a moment envisioned the two of them touring the Empire together, and her constant awe at the wonders he could show her.

"Well," he continued, setting his plate beside hers, "in Egypt they have giant lizards, bigger than a grown man."

"I don't believe you!"

"It's true. In fact, they even eat people on occasion. Some of the natives hunt them, but some think they are sacred and will not harm them, even if they eat their children."

She stared at him, unblinking, and pondered this strange bit of news.

"And what are called 'river horses,' only they look more like huge pigs . . ." He threw his arms wide to show the size. "They live beneath the water and will capsize a boat to kill the people aboard."

"They sound very terrible," she agreed. "And what else?"

"No more for now." He shook his head. "We cannot sit and talk all day with so much work to be done. I must catch more rats for supper and dig more tubers, and you should sit here by the fire and rest."

He stood, pulled his short patched slave cloak around his shoulders, and picked up his walking stick.

"Rest and stay warm," he instructed, and walked off into the scrub.

"Do you think," Anarios asked later while they ate their evening meal, "that you could shave my face for me?"

"What! I?" she responded in surprise. "Why?"

"I have no mirror, and with this sharp knife I hate to think of the damage I'd do to myself. This beard . . . I want it off. Romans don't wear beards. It's barbaric. Do you think you could?"

"Well . . . I don't know." She hesitated. "I have never shaved anyone before."

"I could instruct you. At least you could see what you were doing, unlike me. Haven't you ever shaved anyone before? An elderly relative, perhaps?"

"I had none. Only my mother and an uncle." She looked at him briefly. "The Romans killed the rest of my family before I was born."

"I am truly sorry," he said quietly. "I just thought that I . . ."

"You look less like a Roman with a beard, if that helps you decide. You are still too dark, but the beard helps to hide your true identity."

"Yes." He nodded. "I suppose that's true. Still, I am not used to it. I have never in my life had one, and I—"

"All right!" she sighed, rising to her knees and crawling over to him in mock exasperation. "Let me see it. Our men have mustaches but seldom wear beards either, so I am not familiar with them. I can promise you, though, that my attempts will probably be as bad as yours!"

She seized his chin in one small hand and turned his face from side to side.

"It is odd," she observed. "Different from the hair on one's head. I don't know . . ." She seemed dubious. "Why don't you leave it until later, when you can . . ."

She looked up and found him staring into her eyes. The words faded from her lips and she seemed unable to pull away from his gaze, as surely as if chains bound them together.

"I . . ." she began, and stopped. Strange thoughts were pouring into her mind and she did not want to look away. His hand reached up to touch her cheek, and then he jerked it away. Awkwardly eyeing the ground, they sat down and finished eating in silence.

It was not his imagination. He sighed, looking up at the brilliant stars in the brittle night sky. That look in her eyes . . . that longing. She was no child, inexperienced though she might be. He'd heard tales of the passionate nature of these barbarian women. Were they true? And yet, he reflected, despite her rape, she is still a virgin. She wants something, but she doesn't know what it is. If the day ever comes, I must be as gentle with her as with the most high-born Roman maiden. Nothing rough to remind her of Nechtan. I must draw on all my memories of the sweetest of warm Roman nights, with the gentlest of girls in my arms, and . . .

He lowered his head to his folded arms and stifled a sob. I must stop thinking like this. I must . . . and yet, it has been so long! Nearly three years, with only the occasional foul-smelling slave girl behind a shed somewhere to satisfy my needs when my needs grew too urgent. Filthy and stupid, the only ones who would consent to lie with a hated Roman.

He sobbed aloud. Oh, gods! It has been so long.

"She's *what?*" Maia exploded, and tried to rise unaided on her good leg. Alarmed, the hired girl and Nechtan rushed forward.

"Dead, ma'am. In the bogs. She and the Roman," Niall said flatly.

Rage swept across her face. She picked up her walking stick and struck him angrily on the side of the head. He took an involuntary step backward and his hand flew to his scalp as blood began to ooze from the wound. A mixture of anger and bewilderment crossed his face and he looked in desperation to Nechtan for help.

"You imbecile! How my son ever selected such fools as you two to serve him, I'll never know." She swung again, but Niall dodged the blow and the old lady nearly toppled forward from her ledge before Nechtan caught her.

"Get your hands off me, you fool!" she shouted at him. "Dead! How could such a thing happen? You know the path, Niall. Everyone does. How could they die? Tell me!" she demanded, fire in her eyes.

"The weather was bad, lady," he began hesitantly, glancing at Nechtan again. "Much rain. The waters were high and the path was difficult to find. The Roman carried the girl, and they stepped into a pool and sank from sight before we could rescue them. Conditions were so bad we also had to leave the cart behind, mired in the mud."

At this Maia exploded anew.

"My cart too! Two good slaves, and my cart! Did you bring anything back with you besides your own precious hides?"

"The horses, ma'am."

"The horses? Well, that's very fine! You—Nechtan—you know you must pay me for the girl, and the cart."

"I know, Mother. I will."

"And the value of the Roman to the druid, which will be a considerable sum."

"Yes, Mother."

"And while you're at it, why don't you get two decent warriors instead of these two buffoons? Send them to the Romans as a gift; then they will be sure to lose against us."

She waved them away angrily. Niall stiffened visibly at her insult, but Nechtan motioned him to the door.

"I will pay you extra for your efforts," he whispered to Niall. Behind them Maia slumped against the wall and held her head in her hands.

"Oh, poor Melangell," she moaned in genuine anguish. "What a horrible death, a horrible waste. Those fools . . . those fools . . . poor, poor Melangell."

"Lady, you should calm down. It is bad for your health."

The druid's level gray eyes peered over the rim of his bronze wine cup, seeming to search Maia's face for something, something only he could see. She ignored his remark and leaned forward toward him.

"Brennos, do you have any word of flooding in the bogs around the sacred spring of Arnemetia?" she asked him. He lowered his cup and thought a moment.

"Not that I have heard. A carpenter with an afflicted liver just returned from there two days ago. He had no unusual reports, except to say that he is now much improved, praise be to Arnemetia."

"Yes . . . praise be . . . but no flooding? The roads were clear, the pathway across the bog unhampered?"

"So he said. The road, as usual, was nearly impassable, but he had no difficulties whatsoever with the path across the bog . . ." His words died as he picked up the import of her questions.

"Yes"—he nodded—"that is curious. Are you sure Nechtan's two men know the way? That they didn't stray from the path themselves?"

Maia sat up with a snort of disgust.

"Those two? They have been many times. What fighting man doesn't know the way to the healing spring as well as he knows his own face?"

"Yes, that's true," Brennos agreed. "But what could have happened to them . . . and why?"

"I gave the girl my pendant of Loucetius, for protection. It was gold. Perhaps robbery was the reason . . ."

"Did they carry any other valuables?" the druid asked.

"No," the old woman stated. "Only food—provisions. Your medicines. The wooden carving you made for the girl to leave as an offering."

"That would be worthless to anyone else. The invocations made over it were for her affliction only. I suppose they could have traded the medicines for a few trinkets at a farmstead along the way." He fell silent for a moment before looking at Maia again.

"Perhaps I should send someone to investigate . . . go to the bog and see what can be found. Maybe there will be some trace of them."

"That's what I hoped you would suggest." The old woman smiled. "Whom could we send?"

"I have just the man," Brennos said. "Calum. They say he

can track a mouse across water. If they are out there, dead or alive, Calum will find them."

"Yes," Maia agreed. "He sounds like what we need. This will be our secret for now, of course?"

"Of course." He nodded. "For now," he added ominously.

"Samhain comes in two days," Melangell suddenly announced across the flickering campfire as she gazed at the nearly full moon on the horizon.

"What?" Anarios looked up. "I have heard of that and often wondered what it is."

"A sacred festival marking the start of the New Year, and the worst night of the year. The spirits of the dead walk abroad, seeking to be appeased. Druids are about and will protect your household in exchange for a gift. The veil between the world of the living and the world of the dead is for that night pulled aside."

She gazed out at the moon again and Anarios felt a chill go down his spine. Curse these damned superstitious people, he thought angrily. Even the most intelligent of them are the most superstitious lot in the world . . . worse, even, than Egyptians.

"And how do you know that?" he asked casually.

"The full moon," she stated, nodding toward the sky. He turned to look at the brilliant orange moon rising over the bogs, turning pools and puddles to molten bronze. Again he shivered as a breeze sprang up, and he pulled his old patched cloak closer and huddled toward the fire for warmth. When he glanced up, Melangell was staring at him.

"We must get ready," she informed him.

"For what?" he replied irritably.

"We have no druid here. We must put out offerings to try to appease the spirits. Otherwise they will haunt us for the coming year."

"And you really believe this?" he snorted. "You're as bad as the old women in Rome who read chicken entrails. As a doctor, I believe in science, that's all. As one with the army, I might pray to Mithras. But as—"

"You are no longer with the army," she stated coolly, leveling her green eyes at him. "Mithras cannot help you

49

here. You are in the domain of my people and my gods, and you'd better take it seriously or disaster will befall us."

He stared back at her for a moment, but her gaze was too intense for him and he looked down absently at the leather strips tied around his feet.

"All right", he said. "I still don't believe it, but for your sake I will help you do whatever needs to be done."

Glancing up, he saw her smile slightly at him.

"Thank you," she whispered in a voice so tiny he could barely hear it.

Samhain fell cold and windy. Remaining patches of snow flickered eerily in the bright moonlight, and the dancing black shadows of bare winter trees took on a life of their own. Patiently the Roman helped the girl gather food and set it on bark plates around the edge of the campfire—a few tubers, some nuts and acorns, a handful of seeds. He found himself worrying more about the approaching fury of winter than about any wandering spirits; they would have to leave, and soon. Go to her people, or try to reach the Roman lines to the south. They could not survive the winter in this open, windswept bog, as poorly equipped as they were.

A lone wolf howled in the distance, raising the hair on the back of Anarios' neck, and he looked to see where the girl was. She huddled miserably in her cloak at the entrance to their shelter, staring too intently into the blazing fire.

"Melangell?" he said quietly. "Are you all right?" She looked up at him and he saw a hint of terror in her eyes, a look he'd seen often enough on the faces of young soldiers who faced death for the first time. Sympathy moved him. He placed two more logs on the fire before sitting beside her.

"Here," he said, wrapping an arm around her shoulder, "why don't we talk? I'll tell you more about the foreign lands I've seen—"

Another howl cut him off and he peered into the darkness nervously.

"Do you feel it too?" she whispered, sensing his body grow tense beside hers.

"Feel what?" He tried to laugh. "Ah . . . oh, no, I—"

"Shh!" she hissed. "I think they . . . are coming . . ."

The words died on her lips and he felt her begin to shiver violently.

"Hush!" he tried to reassure her, clenching her tighter in his arm, but he did not feel too reassured himself.

Suddenly she turned and buried her face in his cloak, and her voice came muffled and broken, a note of panic beginning to sound in it.

"I know . . . they're coming . . . I can feel it . . . Vintios, wind god, brings the dead. They come . . ."

He slid the knife closer with one hand while trying to reassure her with the other. Again he peered out into the surrounding gloom. I am imagining things, he told himself. Her fear has infected me. Any soldier knows how infectious fear is—like some plague of the East. There is nothing—"

A sudden blast of wind roared across the knoll and Melangell clung desperately to his cloak with both hands. "They come . . ." he heard her sob. "Vintios, spare us. They come . . ."

He tried to remain calm, to sit upright by the shelter, to put the lie to her foolish dreads. But the wind blew harder and harder. Small branches sailed through the air in front of him.

"Don't look!" she screamed in his arm. "Don't look!" Her hand reached up blindly, groping at his face, and tried to pull it down toward hers. Resolutely he remained sitting. Still the wind howled, and a fine, gritty sand blasted his face and scrabbled at the fire. It flared, danced, flickered, and died before his watering eyes. He could stand it no longer. Wrapping his free arm around the girl, he buried his face in her hair and tried to find huddled refuge with her against the gale. He could hear her sobbing below him.

It is only the cold, he told himself. This shivering of mine . . . it is only the wind, the cold. I shiver because of the cold.

As abruptly as it began, the wind stopped and an eerie stillness settled on the hillock. Low clouds scudded across the moon and the trees sat silent, as if in shock. He felt Melangell stir in his arms and slowly he looked up, around the clearing. A few embers still glowed in the campfire, he noted thankfully. Branches and leaves littered the ground and the drying rat skins seemed to have blown away.

Melangell peered out below his chin, her face pale and drawn in the white moonlight. "See? It's over!" he said softly, brushing the straggling hair from her eyes. She still looked wildly into the darkness as if she could hear something he couldn't, and when he moved to rise and tend the dying fire, she clung to his arm and held him down.

"No!" she whispered. "Something comes!"

She sat as still as a frightened rabbit, listening, watching. Resigned, he settled beside her, wondering when this long, strange night would be over, when the barest sound of a twig snapping in the stillness sent him sitting upright in watchful tension. One hand closed around the knife handle at his side, and he shifted the girl to be free of her should action be called for. She didn't seem to notice; all her attention was focused on whatever was out there.

There! To his right. Did he see it? A glimpse of white in the moonlight . . . a shade from the dead . . . a bit of mist from the bog . . .

No. It moved again, clearer now, and closer. What was it? he wondered, his panic rising. Could he fight it? The impulse to run coursed wildly through his veins. Run! Run from this unearthly peril, this unholy night.

Melangell's hand fell softly onto his arm, and he sensed her relaxing beside him. Baffled, he glanced down at her. Her face shone with a strange kind of radiance, a peacefulness, an awe. Following her gaze, he saw the white shadow move into the far edges of the clearing, and out of the darkness . . . a pure white deer, a doe, delicately sniffing the food offerings the girl had insisted on placing around them. The bark plates filled with tubers and nuts and seeds.

Like a leaden weight dropped into the sea, his stomach sank within him. The plates of food still sat around the clearing, despite the driving winds which had blown nearly everything else away.

He closed his eyes sickly. Gods above! he thought. Gods above, I am beginning to believe this.

Opening his eyes, he saw the deer slowly crunching the nuts in her soft pink mouth. Then she moved on to the tubers, snuffled them delicately, and ate them. Lifting her head, she gazed at the two huddled humans with pale, unearthly eyes and walked over to the seeds. Seeming to find them unsatisfactory, she spilled them onto the cold ground and walked on, staying to the edge of the shadows, around the circle of their camp, until she approached to within a few paces of the two. They saw that she was heading for the turtle shell filled with fresh, clean water. She sniffed it for a moment, then slowly drank it dry. Raising her head again and showing no fear, she stood silently and studied them, as if with a certain intelligence known only to her kind; then, appearing satisfied with what she saw, the young hind turned and walked away, disappearing into the hushed trees and waiting shadows as if she had been only a dream.

The two sat in stunned silence for a time, and then Melangell exhaled in a rush as if she had not breathed through the whole event.

"A messenger from the gods," she whispered. "They send messengers in the shape of animals, many animals—but a white deer, a pure white deer on such a night as this . . ." She shook her head, finding that words failed her.

"What do you people know?" Anarios muttered, half to himself. He wanted to deny it, debunk it in fashionable civilized skepticism, yet he couldn't . . . he couldn't deny what he had just seen, felt, experienced. The ghostly white deer on the heels of the unearthly wind, on the night when the veil between the two worlds is pulled aside.

A wolf howl shattered the spell and Melangell jerked back into reality.

"We must follow the deer," she stated.

"Follow—" he began. She cut him off.

"Yes . . . now . . . the deer knows the way, and we will follow it, while the moon is bright and the tracks are fresh. We will get out of this bog tonight. The deer was sent to guide us."

"Guide us?"

"The wolf you heard—another sign. We are being tracked. Hurry! We must go."

It took only a moment to gather their few belongings, and he had learned better than to argue with her on matters such as this. She seemed to have a set of eyes, an understanding, that he did not possess.

The trail was easy to follow, tiny hoofprints leading starkly out across the patches of snow, down the slope, heading to the south—the direction of the Roman lines.

Leaving the hillock, they passed the old upturned wagon, the wheel now blown aside and lying submerged and barely visible in the dark peat-water.

"See!" Melangell said, pointing to the wheel. "Loucetius has abandoned this place. It is time for us to go."

He squeezed her hand and nodded an answer. Yes, he agreed. And, gods above, he believed.

Hand in hand, they followed the doe's trail across the moonlit patches of snow. Behind them, the snow slowly melted, leaving no trace of their passing.

The rising sun welcomed them onto dry land. Walking into the shelter of the forest and away from the flat, open bogs, Anarios and Melangell continued their trek until the sun had climbed high into the sky. The deer's trail had long since been lost; vanished as they approached firmer land where the small hoofprints could not penetrate. They walked until they stumbled on an open thicket of blackberries, where they ate their fill, wrapped themselves in their cloaks, and fell into an exhausted sleep on the fragrant forest floor.

They awoke to moonlight filtering through the treetops and flooding their weary faces. Refreshed, they gathered more berries into the turtle shell and resumed their journey, keeping to the south as much as possible.

The level forest floor gave way to rocky, rolling hills, and then increasingly difficult slopes and gullies. In the distance they could hear a rushing stream, and soon the mellow, damp smell of rich soil and water spray told them they were near it. Struggling over the last rill, they saw below them a tossing mountain stream glittering in the night, jumbling and falling over huge boulders in its path.

"Fish!" Melangell said eagerly. "There will be fish down there! Something besides rats to eat!" She glanced up at Anarios, who stared silently down the steep hillside.

"Let's go," he muttered. They drank slow and long when they reached the water, and Melangell reclined on a sloping rock while Anarios scouted the dark valley. When he returned there was a look of concern on his shadowed face.

"There is a hut upstream. It looks abandoned, but we can't be sure. Come," he said, extending his hand to her, "we'd better check this out. It might not be a good idea to stay here after all."

Her heart fell at his words. She had so looked forward to fresh fish to eat, clean water to drink, a refreshing swim after the sun had risen and warmed the water . . . and a good, long, restful sleep.

Carefully they stepped along the boulders at the river's edge. She soon spied the hut, crudely built of interwoven saplings on a sturdy circular foundation of river rocks. It looked abandoned to her too. One side had slipped down and leaned toward the water, a thatch roof sagging precariously atop it. The moss-covered stones beneath it looked more permanent, and much older, as if a succession of rickety shacks had been built on them, perhaps for generations. The hillside rose steep and brushy directly beside it, and it seemed to be in a safe, sheltered position.

They advanced slowly, the knife ready in Anarios' hand, looking for signs of life around the hut. Cautiously he pushed the sagging door, and an accumulation of dust, dead leaves, and mouse dung fell in front of their faces. In the patches of moonlight that littered the interior they could see no signs of recent habitation. A cold, black hearth-pit was scratched in the center of the dirt floor. A few overturned clay cups and bowls littered one corner, beside a moldering straw pallet. But Melangell's sharp eyes spied something infinitely more interesting: hanging from the wall above the pallet, several gut-strings with bone fish hooks still attached. Fish! she thought hungrily, and stepped into the room, Anarios warily following her.

"Let's sleep," she said quickly, "so that we may awaken with the dawn, catch some fish, maybe go for a swim."

He nodded in weary agreement.

"Five is enough," the Roman decided, pulling another flopping fish ashore. "We will eat our fill tonight, and let the rest dry near the fire. We can take the extra with us on our journey." He looked at Melangell, who was cleaning the fish on the broad flat rock behind him. "It shouldn't be more than a few days' walk to the Roman lines."

She glanced up at him, a frustrated frown on her face.

"Here," he said, reaching for the knife. "The sun is warming things nicely. I'll do that—you go for a swim."

She seemed grateful as she handed him the knife. "Many thanks!" she said, smiling. "Aside from the fact that I have half a sack of bog mud all over me, I really do hate cleaning fish."

"Ah! We Mediterranean races are used to it, well enough." He laughed, and watched her skip from boulder to boulder, seeking the deep, quiet pool they had found downstream.

The Roman lines! he mused. Home at last! And the girl was willing to come with him, to see some of the wonders he'd told her about. He'd get out of the army, go into private practice, have ample time for travel. She was so curious, so eager to learn about everything; traveling with her would be a never-ending delight. Chuckling to himself, he tried to imagine how her face would light up when she actually saw the Great Pyramids, the temples of Rome, a camel, a crocodile . . .

Glancing over his shoulder, he saw her splashing happily in the distant pool, surfacing and diving like some sleek dolphin. And then suddenly she was out of the water, effortlessly sliding onto the rocks like a seal, and sitting with her bare white back toward him. As she tossed her wheaten hair, the drops of water flew in a glittery cascade around her head, and his hands fell still as he watched her. Of all the marvels he'd seen, he mused, in all the Roman world, few could match the stark beauty of these barbarian women's soft white skin . . . so pure, so clear, like the soft white breast of a swan.

With slim arms she reached upward, spreading and untangling her drying hair, a movement so effortlessly sensual he felt himself stirring beneath the short Celtic breeches he wore. Closing his eyes and turning his head, he groaned softly to himself. Mother Hera! I shouldn't have done that . . . shouldn't have looked. Time enough for that when we get back to Roman lines. Besides, she's just a child.

I must remember that. Time enough for that when we're safe.

They sat in silence as night fell into the valley around them, Melangell huddled into her old cloak, the physician watching the firelight sparkle and dance in the roiling waters beside them.

"I think we should extinguish the fire for the night, lest whoever tracks us should see it," the girl blurted.

Anarios glanced at her. The events of Samhain had seemed real enough at the time; he did not for a moment doubt that they had occurred; but in the clearer reality of this little valley he was no longer so sure he believed her superstitions as he once had. She seemed to read his mind, for she leveled her gaze at him and spoke quietly.

"I know we are followed. By whom, I do not know, though I can guess it is from our former homes, seeking to return us to our former masters. The deer did not lie; the wolf does not lie." She stated the last simply and clearly, as if there was no room for argument. The Roman knew her well enough by now; he did not argue. Rising to his feet, he collected some firewood. "I will light a small fire in the hut," he agreed, "just enough for warmth. Help me. Then we will extinguish this one."

A chilly rain was falling by the time they settled into the hut. Occasional stray drops sizzled loudly when they found their way to the fire, but the hut was tolerably dry.

"We leave tomorrow," Anarios said, glancing sideways at Melangell.

"You say it should only be a few days' walk before we reach your people?" she said, almost in a whisper, and he suddenly realized a truth he had long overlooked in his romantic daydreams: she was afraid of this future he had planned for them. He gazed at her silent profile a moment, her lips slightly full, her nose small and straight, the effect as delicate as a fine Greek statue, and tried to think of what to say to her. She must come with him! She must! They were so near to home, to freedom, after so long.

His home, he knew; not hers.

Reading his thoughts again, she looked at him and admitted the truth aloud.

"Anarios, I am afraid."

"I know," he replied. "I can tell."

"Even when I was captured by Nechtan it was still my people, my land. But this . . . this . . ." She shook her head, searching for words to express her dismay. "I cannot speak the language, I do not know the customs, the clothing, the foods, the religion. I know nothing. I will be laughed at, ridiculed. I will have no friends, no family. Can a fish live in a tree with the birds, Anarios? Can a calf swim with the seals? I . . . What am I?"

His heart moved at her overwhelming anguish, and he saw tears slide down her cheeks. Fighting them, she clenched her eyes shut and threw her head back. Slowly she spoke again.

"You Romans, you do not understand us. You travel the world, adopt new ways, learn new things. What I am is this land, this land around us. Its spirit gave me birth; its life nourishes me. I know each tree, each rock, each bird and animal. My soul and theirs are bound together, Anarios." She opened her damp eyes and looked at him sadly. "When I climb a mountain, I know its history. I know the field where my grandfather died fighting an invading army. I know the waterfall where my parents conceived me. In a grove the oak spirits Dervonnai whisper to me; at the stream the water spirits Niskai sing me to sleep. Vitucadrus, he of brilliant energy, illumines us our souls. All these things, Anarios, they are *me,*" she said almost fiercely, clenching her small fist to her chest and staring at him, and then her eyes brimmed over again.

"What shall I be without them, Anarios? What shall I be?"

She buried her face in her hands, doubled over, and began to cry softly. He sat in stunned silence, unable to think, unable to respond, as all his plans crumbled around him. I, who have traveled the world, still miss my home. It is only natural that this girl, who has been nowhere, should fear missing hers. He turned toward the fire and ran his hands through his hair, bewildered, and gazed at the low flames. She must come with him! She must!

Her sobs broke through his stupor and he moved to her side, taking her gently into his arms.

"Hush, little one," he whispered, stroking her hair and pressing her to him protectively. "I think I have a solution. Come with me to the Roman lines, just for a while. It will at least foil our pursuer, and then you will be safe. Safe from slavery. Then give my life a fair chance . . ."

He could feel her sobs subsiding as she listened to him. She was a sensible girl; she would see the wisdom in his words. He took her small, wet face in his hands and turned it up to him. This time it was his heart that turned in anguish as he looked at her and spoke.

". . . and then, if you don't like my life, my ways, I will have you taken back to your people."

There! He had said it! Her face took on a stunned expression at his words.

"You . . . you would do that for me?" she whispered, disbelieving. His eyes roamed her face tenderly and he wiped the tears from her cheeks.

"Yes," he said, nodding, "I would." Their eyes met again in that same awkward gaze, but this time neither of them looked away. Slowly he leaned down and kissed her mouth, and to his surprise he found her lips responding. He kissed her again, gently opening her mouth with his, and she seemed as willing to learn about this as she had everything else.

Oh, gods above! he thought in happy desperation, and a fire began to grow wildly within him. Control! he reminded himself. Control! Don't frighten her.

He kissed her lips, her neck, her face, her closed eyes, as his hand slid down along the soft curve of her hip, found the bottom of her shift, and slowly crept upward, his fingers hot against her bare skin.

She rolled her head backward, her eyes still closed, and when his fingers found her breast an involuntary shudder racked her body. He was desperate for her now; to feel her, all of her, nakedness against nakedness.

"Melangell," he whispered hoarsely, reaching for the bottom of her shift, "take this off."

She roused and studied him, a dreamy look in her eyes.

"So this is what it is like, then? Making love . . . this is what it is like?"

"Yes, my love," he replied, kissing her again, "and better

yet to come." Quickly he pulled his old tunic off and she gazed at his chest, the skin as dark as that of his face. He reached for her gown and she pulled it up over her head, tossed it aside, and knelt, naked, before him.

"Oh, gods!" he said, closing his eyes, his breath coming in short, quick gasps. How white she was, how pure and perfect and white.

"Anarios?" she questioned, afraid that something was wrong. He looked at her, rose to his knees, quickly untied his breeches, and kicked them away. Reaching for her, he held her full against his body, soaking in the feel, the warmth of her. Her hands crept slowly around his back and lingered on the whip scars she felt there. The smell, the warmth, the strength of him felt so good, so comforting to her. She shivered as his hands ran down her back and slowly caressed her buttocks. Then he was kissing her again, his mouth more insistent, exploring her neck, going lower and lower until she gasped aloud when his searching lips found her breast and lingered there. A raging torrent filled her head when his fingers lightly stroked her breasts, and then his mouth returned. He was fairly sobbing in his eagerness, and she thought the roaring in her head would drive her deaf; and then he was embracing her feverishly again, bearing her down onto their cloaks. She thought then that she would explode, and when she felt his body move between her legs, felt him carefully enter her, felt him begin to move against her, she shattered into a thousand fragments, as a tree explodes when struck by lightning. He clenched her tight in his arms and she heard him sobbing aloud. Then he was still, his arms holding her close, his cheek resting in her hair. He did not want the moment ever to end.

She could see nothing through the dark mists that surrounded her. Stumbling blindly, she tripped over rocks and tree roots and tried to brush aside heavy, dripping leaves that blocked the way and tangled in her hair. Her desperation grew; some light! An oil lamp! A burning brand! Anything.

"Anarios!" she called wildly, but still she could see nothing. "Help me, Anarios!"

And then she felt his presence nearby; felt him but could not locate him in the dark, swirling mists. Stumbling, she fell to her knees, her arms flailing out against the blackness.

"Anarios . . ." she cried again, but her voice seemed to shrink and fade into uselessness. At last she found him . . . his leg . . . his hand. She pulled herself upright in relief, until a flash of lightning illuminated his face, the face of . . . not Anarios . . . a strange man . . . a cunning-looking man, standing silently with a spear, gazing triumphantly at her, and with a captive at his feet—Anarios, bound hand and foot and looking at her in hopelessness.

No! she cried out silently. No! and tried to run from the man, but he held her fast. In desperation she sank to her knees in the smothering night.

No!

Another flash of lightning hit and his grip fell away from her hand. Before she could think or retreat, she was enveloped in a cloud of flame. A gentle flame that did not burn or hurt her.

The man disappeared; Anarios disappeared; only she remained, burning brightly in the succoring mists.

No! Anarios! No!

A hand caressed her forehead and someone shook her shoulder.

"No!" she heard herself screaming aloud. "No!"

"It is all right, Melangell," Anarios soothed. "It was only a dream. I am here. It is all right."

She opened her eyes and looked at him in terror. He lay back on the cloak and held her close in comfort.

"I am here," he repeated, stroking her hair, trying to ease her fear. She began to cry into his neck.

"We must go," she sobbed. "The man . . . he comes . . . we must go . . ."

"Yes," he agreed, "we will go soon. Have no fear."

"Loucetius has warned me . . . we must go . . . we must go! You are in great danger! We must!"

"We will," he whispered. "Soon. We will go."

Calum had great difficulty finding their trail once they left the knoll in the bog. The footprints at the campfire seemed to follow those of a deer into the woods, and then they all vanished into puddles of melted snow. Cursing, he headed south across the great swamp by the only trail he knew. They, too, seemed to be heading south, probably the Roman trying to get back to the encampments; but if they took the same trail that he now followed, he couldn't see it. As carefully as he looked, he could find no sign of their passing. He knew they were too inexperienced to be able to leave absolutely no trail at all. Muttering again, he decided he'd get to dry ground south of the bog, then skirt the edges, looking for some trace of them. It was the only thing he could do. There'd be hell to pay when he got back with them, that was a certainty. A Lawgiver summoned, an inquiry . . . find out what possessed Niall and Melwas to abandon them like that. Yes. He nodded to himself as he loped silently across the bog. Hell to pay. If he could catch them, that is. Losing their trail like this could cost him several extra days. Unless something held them up, they would easily make it to the Roman lines before he could capture them.

He did not like to fail on a mission. Hoisting his spear over one shoulder, he pulled his blowing cloak close and broke into a trot, hurrying his way across the great empty marsh.

Anarios held Melangell as the morning sun spilled into the hut, drying the dampness of the previous night's rain. The fire had gone out, but he didn't mind. They were warm enough, the two of them, without it.

Melangell raised herself on one elbow and gazed down at his face in concern, her long hair spilling onto his bare chest.

"Are you sure you can't recall it?" she asked him. "I know it was a terrible nightmare. Then you were holding me, and I went back to sleep. What was it about?"

"I don't remember either," he lied. "It couldn't be so important, if neither of us can remember it, can it?" He smiled at her, playing with her hair in his fingertips, and she gave her head a slight shake.

"It bothers me. I can't get it from my mind . . ."

He slid his hand to her face and caressed it gently.

"We have other things on our minds now, dearest," he whispered, and pulled her mouth down to his. She collapsed on his chest, her arms crept around him, and their tender lovemaking began once more.

"Here," he said, laughing and picking her up in his arms. He climbed the last boulders and stood, naked, with her naked in his arms, by the deep, still pool where they bathed. The afternoon sun warmed them nicely and Melangell kicked her legs, threw back her head, and peals of laughter rang from her throat. How beautiful she looks, Anarios thought, all naked in the sunlight, her hair flying in golden waves around her. Fiercely he began kissing her soft neck, and then, filled with mischief, he tossed her into the water. She rose, sputtering and laughing, and floated lazily on her back, gliding away from the shore. With a grin he dove in after her, closing the gap between them as she playfully tried to escape.

"That's them," Calum observed aloud, shifting his position behind a boulder atop the surrounding hills.

"Just like two children they are, playing and frolicking around." He watched them with more than casual interest. The girl, now . . . quite a tasty-looking morsel she was. Nechtan always did have good taste in women. But the Roman, well, that was a different matter. He did not for one moment like the idea of a damned Roman smacking bellies with one of their women. Fool girl! Has she no pride at all? Slut, he thought bitterly. Nechtan and the others will hear of this; he'd see to it.

Silently he continued to watch them. He had plenty of time. The best plan would be to surprise them at night, in the dark, while they slept. Only his fear of Nechtan kept him from considering having a go at the girl himself. But that damn Roman . . . He shook his head in disgust.

I have plenty of time, he thought, narrowing his grim brown eyes. I'll wait.

"Leave the fire out," Melangell suggested to Anarios as they entered the hut for the night. "It is not so cold and, besides, we'll be leaving in the morning."

He nodded agreement. "It will save me having to mess with the damned thing, anyway," he said, slipping an arm around her waist. "Just think," he mused, squeezing her to him, "this time several days hence we will be safe, with a nice sturdy building to sleep in, good food just waiting for us, and a whole new world for you to experience." He laughed, shaking his head. "I never thought I'd see the day when I called army food 'good food.' Well, tomorrow our future begins!"

Calum waited till the night was half over before he began his descent into the valley, pulling his cloak tighter against a brisk wind gusting in from the west. Looking up, he saw on the horizon a low cloud bank reflecting in the waning moonlight. Best hurry this along, he thought to himself. It looks like a storm is coming and soon the moonlight will be gone altogether. Carefully he watched each foothold so as not to dislodge any loose rocks that might alert them. He'd go for the Roman first, before he had a chance to wake up fully and put up a fight, as he had no doubt the Roman would do. What man wouldn't? He sighed. Life is a dirty business; he just wanted to get this over with and get back home, back in his own warm bed, with his woman beside him. He could understand any man's wish for freedom, even a Roman's, but he had a job to do and he would do it.

His bare feet hit the soft ground of the valley and, his spear at the ready, he crept as quietly as a rustling breeze through the waving streamside grasses, toward the distant hut, nearly hidden in the dark shadows of the hillside.

Melangell tossed restlessly, haunted by the dream she could not remember. Anarios, soundly sleeping beside her, did not believe such things, she knew, but she could not deny it—it was in her blood. She gazed up at the sagging thatch roof, waiting for sleep to come, when a barely perceptible scraping sound caught her ear and an instant and instinctive terror flared within her. The door! Someone was opening the door! She leapt to her feet with a scream and Anarios' eyes flew open just as a spearpoint was leveled at his chest.

"Get up!" a stern voice commanded him. Melangell backed away to the wall, her eyes staring in horror at the man's face . . . that face . . . the cunning-looking man in her dream . . . the same man, with Anarios bound and helpless at his feet.

"No!" she sobbed as Anarios slowly stood, knowing full well he could do nothing against the wicked spearpoint, poised and ready to strike. He looked in hatred at the man. Then for one instant his gaze met Melangell's, and she saw in his dark eyes the end of all dreams, the end of all hope, all life, everything.

"No!" she sobbed again, quietly, defeated. The man pulled a rope from his heavy leather belt and tossed it sideways toward her. It landed near the cold hearth.

"You!" he ordered. "Tie him up! Now!"

She stared at them mutely, unable to move. She? Tie him up? Return him to slavery with her own two hands? Never! How could she possibly, possibly . . .

Stopping in mid-thought, she began to scream hysterically.

"No! I will not! How can you do this, you spawn of every demon that ever lived! I will never do it! Never!"

Sobbing, she collapsed in a huddle on the cold dirt floor, her fists futilely beating the packed earth.

Damn women! Calum thought angrily. He could have guessed something like this would happen. He prodded Anarios' chest impatiently with the spearpoint, moving him around toward the rope and the huddled girl.

"Get up!" he ordered again. "Get up and tie him, or he dies. Now! I shall take you back to Nechtan, but as for this Roman devil, I care little one way or another. Now, get up!" he shouted.

Her sobbing eased and he saw her begin to move. Then, before he could react, she threw a handful of fine dry hearth ash directly into his eyes. Stumbling, his eyes a burning agony, Calum swung out with the spear, but he was too late. He heard the door scrape, and they were gone.

"Water!" he moaned, clawing at his face and trying to find the doorway.

Run! Run! Like a raging torrent it filled her head, her mind, her heart, her soul. In sheer blind terror they ran, fleeing for their lives, their freedom. Every drop of blood in her body seemed to scream it. Run! Down the slope and across the boulders they flew, crashing into the stream and fighting the torrent as it pulled at them, supporting each other until the far bank was reached and, gasping and cold, they crawled out of the water. Stumbling in the mud, they disappeared into a thicket of brush at the base of the jutting hillside.

Calum lowered his face into the water once more and shook his head violently. The last of the ash seemed to have washed from his eyes, but they still smarted and watered painfully. Damn that girl, he thought angrily. He should have been expecting some trick like that. She was a Celtic woman, and they were fighters, not quitters. Cursing his own stupidity, he peered around for some sign of the two and saw the bushes across the stream shake and waver as they passed through them. Picking up his spear and wiping his burning eyes, he splashed off into the stream after them.

The higher they climbed the cliff face, the stiffer the wind became, until, nearing the summit, they beheld a breathtaking sight: a huge wall of clouds, flashing yellow and orange beneath it, bearing down on them from the west. Like the drowning villages of a shoreline, the stars vanished one by one beneath the approaching storm. In the dying light they could see the man a short distance below them.

"Go!" Melangell gasped to Anarios, clenching his hand in hers. He looked at her, his face tight with fear.

"No! I will stay and we will defeat him, or die together trying."

She smiled and ran a quaking hand across his sweaty forehead.

"You begin to sound like one of my people now, hotheaded and impetuous and a romantic at heart. You are the practical Roman, remember? I can hold him off—sidetrack him for a while . . ."

She paused painfully and looked away.

"Maybe even escape him. It's me he wants. Go! Go back to your people. You must regain your freedom. Now, here . . . go!"

She pressed the golden medallion of Loucetius into his hands, and he understood the wisdom of her words.

"Go quickly now!" she said in alarm, looking down the

hillside. Anarios lifted a large stone and heaved it at the pursuing man.

"We have ignored a warning from Loucetius," she said softly. "We are doomed; we cannot escape this destiny we have chosen for ourselves. Go, my love! Go to your freedom . . . go."

He clenched her desperately, as if to impress on his memory the feel of her in his arms,

"I will come back for you. Back to this valley. Wait for me . . ."

She nodded. He threw another stone down the hillside, and another, then held her face in his hands and quickly kissed her. Without a parting word he clutched his blowing cape, scrambled up the last few paces of hillside, climbed over the edge, and was gone.

Her hair blowing wildly in the approaching gale, Melangell lifted her face to the black clouds above.

"Loucetius, protect me," she whispered. "I have made the greatest sacrifice in the world for you. I can give no other. I have torn out my heart, and now it blows away on your winds. I can do no greater than this."

He did not like his position one bit . . . coming up from below them like this. And he did not like the ominous feel to the air as the monster storm approached. A boulder rattled past him and he ducked to the side, and when he looked up again he saw the Roman vanish over the top of the cliff. Let him go! he mused in satisfaction. He could still get the girl, his primary goal.

Cursing, he dodged another rock, and another. She was trying to delay him, he knew; give her lover time to escape. He couldn't say much for the Roman, but the girl was certainly brave enough.

A veritable shower of rocks suddenly rained down on him and he wrapped his cloak tighter against the rising winds, clung resolutely to the hillside, and waited them out.

When the barrage ceased, he looked up, only to see the girl skitter away to his left, along a jutting lip of rock. She'd chosen wisely, he noted; below the lip was nothing but a crumbled field of loose shale, impossible to cross. He'd have to climb up and over the same route she took; a slow process. Scouting ahead before he resumed the climb, he guessed her destination: a huge boulder poking out into midair from the side of the hill, with a large dead tree leaning out over the gorge. Damn! he cursed again. Why couldn't Nechtan have picked a stupid wench instead of this one? What could he do on a spur of rock like that? Risk having her go over the edge, lost forever . . . or risk himself going off instead. She had almost all the advantage over him, like a squirrel and a cat in a tree. Doggedly he climbed onward.

She stood at the top of a gentle slope that rose about ten paces from the rocky ledge to the projecting boulder that was her destination, and methodically aimed rocks, one by one, down at him. He tried to shield his face with one arm as he crept forward, her determination matched only by his. The larger rocks she seemed to have trouble aiming and they missed him, bouncing crazily at his feet and rattling off down the crumbling slope below; but the smaller ones throbbed and stung painfully and his anger was beginning to rise. An icy rain pelted him as the first low roll of thunder echoed down into the gorge and back again, and the tracker looked up tensely. When a god such as Loucetius was manifesting his powers, one should not be caught in the middle of it. The sky above was nearly obstructed by the looming mass of clouds, and lightning danced jaggedly from one side to the other.

Only a little farther . . . he had to get her now! One mad rush, through the stones, and he'd have her. The storm was upon them . . . he could delay no longer.

With a deafening crash, lightning struck a large pine tree on the opposite cliff and it toppled silently down the hillside. Then the rain picked up, driving in great waves, and Calum huddled down in fear. When it slacked off he looked up and to his amazement saw the girl still standing, looking down at him, her hair and clothes hanging dripping on her slim body.

She does not wish to hurt me, he realized, only to pin me down. As long as I do nothing, she does nothing. If I am to rush her, now is the time.

Tensing his muscles to sprint the last few paces, he suddenly fell to the side, against the cliff face, when a bolt shattered the dead tree to their left. Looking up in a daze, he saw the girl slumped sideways but still standing, and as he rose to his feet, she stood erect, raised her arms heavenward, and turned her face to the sky.

"Loucetius!" he heard her scream through the thunder and wind and driving rain. He could barely see, but still he advanced, his long hair wet in his eyes, the spear clenched in his hand. Another crash of thunder split the air and he fell to his knees—from the shock, from fear, from awe at what he saw before him. Bright blue flames danced at the girl's outstretched fingertips, ran down her arms, and flickered like a halo across her head. Cold-looking flames; unearthly flames.

No! he shouted angrily. I will not give her up! He tried unsteadily to rise from his knees. Pulling back the spear, he let it fly . . . and then he collapsed facedown on the wet rock.

She felt it slide easily into her upturned arm, felt the jarring snap when the bone was split in two, felt the pain like fire consume her body as her arm fell lifeless to her side. Then she was grasping the spear shaft in her good hand, groping blindly and in mute agony. Her knees buckled and she crumpled to the stone above her pursuer, the driving rain washing away the pouring blood, the black sky above luring her into the black nothingness within. . . .

Anarios ran blindly, desperately, clutching her medallion to his wet chest. He glanced over his shoulder in horror as the bolts of lightning sliced and flashed over the valley behind him, and for one wild moment he resolved to go back, to help her; but her words returned to him vividly and a violent crash split the heavens around him. In sick hesitation he stood in the blasting wind and sobbed aloud, unsure of what to do, where to go. Then the driving rain hit in hard, incessant waves, pounding him fiercely, pushing him onward before it . . . away, away, to the south, toward home.

Part 2

NECHTAN'S STORY

DESPITE THE CHILL WIND, NECHTAN SWEATED PROFUSELY while he worked his newest field, clearing out the rocks in preparation for tilling. It was the custom to turn under the year's first snowfall, and from the looks of the sky it would not be far off. He should have known better than to contract with Annos for such a rocky new piece of land so late in the season.

Placing a large boulder on the sledge behind his horses, he straightened up wearily and cast an eye on the darkening skies, then gazed across the plot of land. It was fertile, loose; he figured on a nice crop of wheat, maybe oats, growing there next summer. It depended on the dampness and length of the spring which of the two he planted. Wheat was more tender but also more valuable; oats were hardier and always had a ready market. Exhaling heavily, he resumed his work. He hoped the next summer would not be as dry as the last one had been; the drought and lack of food was the cause of their raid on the foreigners' settlement where he had captured the girl.

The girl . . .

He heaved a large rock angrily onto the sledge and cursed the luck that had ever made him decide to spare her and bring her home. Well, he thought in grim satisfaction, prying another stone out of the soil, if his two men had done their jobs right, he'd no longer have to worry about her.

Across the field Niall leaned wearily on his spade and hailed Nechtan. Turning, the young man saw his mother slowly hobbling up the weedy slope, her cane in one hand and the other supported by the hired girl. He felt a mixture of anger and concern for the old lady; she had no business being out here, climbing hills and evidently intending to struggle over rocky fields as well. Sighing in resignation, he eyed the thickening clouds, wiped his brow, and tossed his shovel on the sledge. Picking up his cloak, he walked across the soft earth to greet her.

"Mother, what in the name of Ialonus brings you out here so late in the day and with snowfall approaching?" he said sternly, gazing down at her.

"Son, we have had so little chance to talk since you left," she began, stopping as if waiting for him to reply.

He rolled his eyes heavenward at her statement.

"Mother," he began, trying to be gentle despite his irritation, "I have contracted to work this new field. As you can see, I am trying to clear it of stones so I can plow under the first snowfall, which might be tomorrow morning, from the looks of the sky. The druids say it will result in a much better crop next year—"

"I know about farming," Maia snapped. "I am not a child, even though you sometimes treat me like one."

"If I do, Mother, it is only because I am concerned about you."

"Concerned, is it?" she said, her gray eyes narrowing. "My health has been poor from worrying ever since poor Melangell . . . disappeared. It is of great concern to Brennos. If I am such a worry to you, then why did you—" She stopped abruptly, her face locked in an awkward gaze with his until she quickly looked away.

Nechtan straightened and studied her in suspicion.

"Why did I what?" he said slowly. "What have I done that would harm you?"

"Nothing," Maia replied, seeming to look out over the field. "Yes, I see you do have a lot to do. Perhaps I was foolish to come out here to talk."

She looked up at him again. His thick, dark hair framed his face in shadows, making his features nearly indistinguishable in the brief winter's twilight.

"It's just that with both you and the girl gone, I have no one to really talk with. This fool here," she said, giving the hired girl a cuff on the ear, "barely knows the language. How can I talk with her?"

Nechtan sighed impatiently. He was losing the daylight; he had to get back to work, and soon.

"Yes, Mother. I know. But the girl is gone, and I will not move back in."

"Then surely you can spare a little time from your fields and your weapons practices and your Seonaid to visit me! I must talk to you, Nechtan! Can you come to dinner one day?"

"Yes . . . one day . . ."

"Tomorrow?"

"No. I will still be too busy with this field. The next day. For the evening meal; I promise," he said, turning to go.

"Alone?" Maia asked. "Come alone . . . no Seonaid. I don't have that much food . . . and then we can talk, just the two of us."

He nodded and walked away in silence. Maia watched him go, an ache in her heart.

He is in such trouble, and he doesn't even know it. Me . . . I would never bring the Law down on my own son. But it is out of my hands now. All I can do is try to warn him.

Maia's low oak eating table was scrubbed with wood ash and rushes until it shone like polished stone in the firelight, and then a coating of beeswax was rubbed on to add more luster. The old woman had driven the hired girl tirelessly; she wanted everything to be perfect for this meal with her son. Her small golden table service, brought from far-off Greece by her roving grandfather, was laid out on the gleaming table. A precious blue Roman glass vase which Nechtan had brought her from one of his raids sat in the center of the table, holding a few sprigs of holly and hemlock greens. Greens in the house in winter meant luck; she hoped it was so, for she certainly needed luck now, and so did Nechtan.

My son, my son, she thought, shaking her head as she gave a final check to the arrangement in the vase, *why have you done this terrible thing? Why you, among all the village; why you?*

She started at the sound of his hand on the door, and as he entered, the serving girl scurried forward to take his cloak.

"Well!" he said, smiling, eyeing the resplendent table, "this is very impressive, Mother! Very nice. I haven't seen these golden dishes since I was a little boy and one of the Chief Druids came to feast with us."

Maia beamed with pleasure at his compliments.

"I wanted things to be very special," she explained as he took one foot and slid out a low stool, squatting opposite her at the table.

"Oh, they are!" he said, still smiling but inwardly puzzled at what this "special occasion" might be. Despite the questions, his stomach turned in hunger when he smelled the foods she had prepared for him.

"Girl!" Maia commanded. "Serve everything to us at once, and then you may go."

The girl nodded obediently and turned to the pots by the hearth. Maia snorted a laugh.

"That girl is so thick-headed she does anything I say without one word of question. If I said, 'Girl, walk across the ceiling,' she would break her foolish neck trying to do it."

Nechtan laughed and watched the girl serve some of his favorite foods: hot ham, barley with butter and honey, dried berries stewed in a spicy wine, fresh bread fried in fat, little butter cakes . . .

"It's been a long time since I've eaten so well!" he exclaimed, spearing a chunk of ham on his knife point.

"No doubt," Maia said dryly, scooping a mouthful of stewed berries from her bowl. "Here, son, pour the wine for us. It's the last of my Roman wine."

His eyebrows rose appreciatively as he poured, and he sipped it slowly in delight.

"Nothing better!" he proclaimed. "The only good thing about the Romans is their wine."

"Yes," Maia agreed. "But now tell me . . . how is it with you? Did you finish your field?"

He nodded between eager mouthfuls. How he eats! Maia thought. Like a hungry little boy.

"And did you plow under yesterday's snowfall? It was not a significant amount, but I suppose it was enough to please the druids."

"Yes, Mother," he said, wiping his mouth with the back of one hand and rising to fetch more food from the fire.

"One edge, several paces wide, was uncleared and still too rocky, and I did not want to risk breaking the plow, so I left it. But the rest we got turned under. Maybe I will leave that strip barren next spring; it probably wouldn't produce very well, and it would just be a waste of my time and seed."

She nodded. "That sounds like a wise decision," she said. I will talk of idle matters until he finishes his meal, she thought to herself—let him enjoy it before such unpleasant things are discussed.

"Mother," he interrupted her thoughts, his pale gold eyes staring at her from the hearthside, "you didn't go to such trouble just to talk about my field. Why did you invite me here like this?" He returned to the table, his wooden trencher piled high with food.

"I have missed you, son. You have been in my home for twenty-one years, and now suddenly you are gone, and I miss you. Can't I extend the hospitality of my hearth to you without being suspected of things?"

"I'm sorry," he said, and resumed eating in silence, but she could tell by the look on his face that he didn't entirely believe her answer. He was a hard one to fool, she knew; those pale eyes of his seemed to see into everyone.

"The Lawgiver will honor us with his presence this year."

His eyes momentarily flickered up to hers, and then he resumed eating.

"Will you and Seonaid be marrying soon?" she asked, trying to delay.

He shook his head and swallowed a mouthful of crumbling butter cake.

"No. I've never thought of marrying her. You know what kind of a wife she would make."

"But no other man will attempt to win her while she seems to be yours, and she too is getting older. Before long she will be too old."

He shrugged. "If she doesn't like it, she can tell me. She has said nothing so far. I have no claim on her, nor she on me. We enjoy each other—that's all."

"But you are a respected and feared member of this town,

one of Annos' warriors. No other man would dare try to claim her if he thought for one moment that—"

"Mother," he said, placing his hands on his upturned knees and looking at her, "what Seonaid and I do is our business, not yours. We are adults—"

"I was only concerned about the girl, that's all."

He looked at her skeptically. "It would be the first time, wouldn't it?" he said slowly.

Maia lowered her eyes to the golden dishes.

"Yes . . . I suppose. But I grow old, Nechtan. We all do. I would love grandchildren. A happy home. Laughter, smiles . . . all the things any of us want. Seonaid is the only girl who ever really interested you, and yet you say you have no idea of marrying her."

He poured himself another fortifying cup of wine and listened blankly to her tale of woe. Are all mothers formed from the same mold? he wondered. How they all seem to go on so—marriage . . . babies. He snorted cynically. Mothers begin the domestication of men that wives finish.

"Nechtan!" Maia's sharp voice interrupted him. "You daydream. You did not hear my question! Is there any other girl who interests you?"

He shook his head.

"Seonaid is fun, that's all," he muttered. "She leaves me alone. She doesn't nag. To be blunt, she is a bit stupid. She gives me what I want, when I want it. Why should I want a nagging wife? Squalling babies? I have what I need with her, and beyond that I am free."

"You talk like a child," Maia snapped with unaccustomed irritation. "You want no son to raise in your footsteps? No son to bring pride to your heart? Beautiful daughters to love you in your old age, dote on you and spoil you?"

"Sons to be murdered by the Romans," he retorted. "Daughters to be carried off into slavery. I want none of that. Maybe I will be the last of my line, but it is the way of the world, Mother. The way you knew is dying; the world is changing. The Romans come, and none can stop them. We, as a people, are doomed. When we are at peace, I will take my pleasures where I can find them. When we are at war, I will fight them to my last breath. Old age? I will not live to see old age. I will die on a battlefield somewhere, run through by a Roman spear. But I will die a free man, Mother, a free man."

He stopped abruptly, his anger subsiding when he saw his mother's scarred face contort with grief at his words. She lowered her face to her bony hands.

"I hope I shall not live to see that day!" she sobbed. "My son, my beautiful son, all that I have in this world, lying dead in the mud . . ."

"Mother," he said quietly, reaching for her hands and lowering them from her face, "don't cry. I could be wrong. Perhaps the Romans will halt their progress. We may defeat them one day. When they are no longer a threat to us, then I will marry. I promise. You know me." He grinned. "I will soon give you a houseful of grandchildren! Now, don't cry. Don't cry." Gently he wiped her tears away, and she looked at him with a pain that seemed all out of proportion to the events of the evening.

"Mother?" he said softly. "Something else troubles you, and I think it must be the reason you had me come to talk. What is it?"

She stared at him in silence for what seemed like an eternity; at his dark, shaggy hair, his pale eyes and aquiline nose, his sensitive mouth drawn back into a slight frown. Oh, gods above, she thought as desperation raged in her heart, don't let anything ever happen to him! Gods above, don't!

"Mother?" Her odd behavior was beginning to worry him. "Are you ill? What is wrong?" Leaning over the table, he clenched her hands tightly in his.

"I don't know how to begin," she muttered quietly, looking down. "Something . . . there is something wrong. But I . . . we don't know yet what it is."

He straightened up, puzzled.

"Wrong? Mother, I do not understand such riddles. What is wrong?"

"Your man Niall—he lied. There was no flooding in the bog." She glanced up at him, and to her horror she saw his face go white with shock. He knew! He was in on it! Her heart shattered within her. My son! My son!

He did not reply, only sat woodenly, waiting for her to go on.

"Brennos sent Calum to look for traces of . . . of the girl and the Roman . . . to find out what really happened. Do you know Calum?"

He nodded silently, numbly, and his stomach felt sick. Calum . . . the best tracker in all the northern Damnonii lands.

"He is not back yet. We do not know what he will find. Only Brennos and I know this, son. At first I was angry, angry at losing the girl. I wanted to find out what those two fools of yours had been up to. But as time passed, I thought it over . . . and I became afraid." She looked up into his distant eyes, and he lowered them to their clenched hands.

"Why, son?" she whispered. "In the name of all the gods, why?"

He slowly shook his head as she watched him.

"The girl . . ." he began. His voice dropped away, unable to go on.

"Why, Nechtan?" Maia protested. "To violate the law so . . . and not only my slave, but the druid's as well? A *druid's* slave? What crime so enormous could one small girl commit against you to make you do such a thing?"

He looked up at her, his eyes two pools of fear.

"The curse, Mother . . . the curse," he said quietly. A silence as thick as honey descended on the room as they stared into each other's frightened eyes. Maia drew her hands back and sat upright.

"You mean . . . she is the one?" she mumbled incredulously. "And you . . . you thought to escape it by doing this?"

He nodded silently.

"When did you realize this about her?"

"When . . . when we raided her village. There was something about her that struck me. She . . ." He swallowed hard. "She tried to die on her feet, despite what my men and I did to her."

"I don't want to hear that," Maia interjected.

"Time and again she tried to rise. She got a pot-hook and tried to fight. And when Niall was about to cut her down, she stood erect and . . . and looked him in the eye! Mother! I . . ." He shook his head, bewildered, and went on.

"But I knew it for a certainty at the banquet. Drunk as I was, I felt such a rage when that stumbling fool tried to carry her off for himself that I was . . . was glad when Loucetius saved her. I had been shamed enough already; I could not have taken her back myself, after I had thrown her to him. But then . . . it scared me, Mother! And it angered me. My fears angered me, and she angered me. A warrior must not be frightened by a mere girl. I had to . . . to do what I did . . ."

"And what was it you did?"

"I told my men that she must die. Not the Roman, unless it was necessary. But she must. And then I . . . I almost changed my mind. It was hard, but I went through with it. I could do nothing else, Mother! Do you see?"

She nodded slightly.

"I think so. But what did they do with them? Do you know that she is dead?"

He shook his head slowly.

"I don't know. They didn't say, and I didn't ask. Don't be so hard on them, Mother. They are good men; they were only following my orders. It is I who am the fool, not they."

He buried his face in his hands.

"It is too late now," he mumbled. "I have gone through with it. It is too late."

"And you, son, did you love her?" Maia asked softly.

She could barely detect the slight nod of his head in reply.

Nechtan sighed and rolled over onto his back.

"It is no use, Seonaid. I . . . I cannot," he muttered absently.

The redhead propped herself up on one elbow and gazed down at his worried face.

"It's all right, love," she cooed, tracing his lips with one forefinger. "What happened at your mother's tonight? It seems to have upset you." Her steady blue eyes looked into his and he slowly turned his face aside.

"Just talk, that's all. The usual. It angers me—you know how mothers are."

She laid her head on his chest and listened to the reassuring beat of his heart beneath her ear as she ran her fingers down his neck.

"Yes," she agreed. "All mothers are the same. Mine too . . . get married . . . have babies. You know," she began, propping herself up again, "I want to be rich! I want to have beautiful things. Gowns and cloaks and jewelry. A fine house. Slaves. Herds of cattle. How can I, if I have a bunch of babies underfoot? No"—she shook her head emphatically and lay back down beside him—"I will wait for what I want."

He nodded silent agreement and sat up.

"Go and fetch the ale," he said, giving her a pinch on her rump. "All of it. I feel like getting drunk tonight."

She laughed and stood and he watched her well-rounded bottom appreciatively as she walked across the hut to get the drink. She is such an armful! he mused, and yet tonight he felt nothing stir within him, for the first time in his life. Nothing.

"Here!" he snapped when she returned, grabbing the clay jug from her startled grasp. Before she could speak, he raised it to his lips and poured the ale in great gulps down his throat. She stood and watched him, the two unused cups in her hand. He finished, belched loudly, and set the jug down. Reaching for her wrist, he jerked her to the mat beside him. Seizing one ample breast in his hand, he pulled her to him and began to violently kiss her mouth, her neck, her body, growing more insistent and angry, his kisses turning to bites, until she struggled in his arms and tried to pull away.

"Nechtan! Stop it! It hurts! Stop!" she protested, but he persisted as if he didn't hear her.

"Stop!" she screamed, louder, but still he continued. Frustrated, she slapped him fiercely across the face and he jerked his head back, looking at her in muddled surprise. Squirming from his grasp, she stood and pulled a cloak around herself, anger flashing in her eyes.

"Seonaid, I—" he began.

"Get out!" she snapped.

He rose unsteadily to his feet and attempted to reach for her.

"I said I . . ." he muttered as she backed away from him.

"Get out of my house!" she repeated. "Just who do you think I am, anyway? Some serving wench or war captive you can rape?"

She picked up the nearly empty jug of ale and sent it flying toward his head. He ducked and it shattered against the far wall.

"Get out!" she screamed. "Out! Get out!"

He stared at her in drunken silence, picked up his clothes, stumbled his way to the door, and left.

If she had not been so mad, she would have laughed at the fact that he was still naked when he went.

Niall and Melwas sat in silence on a log near the girl's house. Exchanging knowing glances, they grinned when they heard Seonaid's loud protests. That Nechtan was something, all right, they commented . . . he really knew how to drive the ladies wild. But they knew something was wrong when the girl's screams rose to anger, they heard a clay vessel shatter, the front door opened, and their master, drunk and naked, stumbled into view. Exchanging another glance, they rose and approached him cautiously.

By the gods! Niall thought in astonishment. He must have drunk the whole pitcher dry in one gulp. He extracted Nechtan's cloak from the bundle he clenched to himself and draped it around his master's shoulders. Melwas, surveying the situation, turned and walked back to Seonaid's door and gave it a sharp knock with his hand.

The door opened a crack and the girl's face peered out.

"Yes?" she snapped. "What is it?"

"His sword," Melwas replied. He heard her walking around inside; then the door opened a scant crack and she threw the sword out angrily. Melwas caught a brief glimpse of her bare thigh before she pushed the door shut in his face.

"Get that drunk away from here!" she shouted through the door at him. Melwas picked up the sword, turned, and rejoined the other two, visions of lusty nights with Seonaid dancing in his head.

"What wouldn't I give to trade places with this one for just one night!" he chuckled, pulling one of Nechtan's arms over his shoulder.

"And I!" Niall agreed, prying the bundle of clothes from Nechtan and taking his master's other arm.

"Well, we heard the lady," he continued. "Let's get this poor fellow home."

"Lower that damn fire!"

Melwas turned from the piled furs where he sat polishing his sword blade with wood ash and looked in surprise at Nechtan.

"Awake so soon?" he questioned mildly.

Nechtan groaned and rolled onto his side.

"Fix the fire, I said! The light is killing me."

Melwas rose and pulled a rack of drying meat between Nechtan and the hearth pit. "We need some light in here. We are trying to get a little work done."

"Here," Eber said, rising from a squatting-stool by the fire and picking up a wooden cup. "Try this. A special tea from Brennos. I use it all the time."

Nechtan rose shakily on one elbow and reached for the cup. He swallowed the contents in two quick gulps and flopped back onto his folded fur pallet.

"Gods above! What's in it?" He grimaced. "Cow dung?"

The other men laughed.

"Oh, some herbs . . . I don't know," Eber said with a grin. "It helps, though. You'll be up and around by evening."

"Evening?" Nechtan groaned. "You mean I've slept all day? What did that witch put in her ale, anyway?" He lay silent on the pallet, gazing up at the low thatch ceiling as his spearmen exchanged puzzled glances.

"Someone get me some food . . . something decent to eat, and . . ." He sat up and looked around the room. "Where's Niall?"

"Out. I think he went to get a haunch of beef at the butcher's . . ." Melwas began.

". . . And see what he can get from the butcher's little dark-haired daughter!" Osla roared, winking slyly at Melwas.

"Well, knowing Niall, he won't—"

"Go get him," Nechtan snapped irritably as Melwas rose to cut him a slab of pork. "I want to see him and you, Melwas, at once. You other two, go," he said, waving them off impatiently. "Go to the wine shop or find yourselves a woman or something. Just leave us for a while." Worn out by the effort, he held his aching head in his hands.

"We'll go down and fetch Niall and send him back," Eber said, crossing the cramped room.

"And maybe take over where he leaves off, eh, Eber?" Osla grinned as they exited the door, laughing.

Nechtan sat still, enjoying the silence for the brief time it took Niall to return. He seemed annoyed and, unpinning his cloak, he tossed it to his sleeping pallet.

"Yes?" he said stiffly as Nechtan looked up at him.

"Sorry to interrupt you," Nechtan began, "but I think you will find this matter of more importance than the butcher's daughter."

"I hope so, because it was finally beginning to look like I—"

Nechtan held up a hand to silence him.

"What do you two know of Calum?" Nechtan said simply, but something in his voice made the warriors shift uncomfortably.

"The best tracker around," Melwas began. "They say he never misses; that he once tracked a murderer for two months, for the gods' sake, but eventually he found him."

"He can track through the rain, the snow, day or night. He can see clues the best of us would miss. They say he even has a special sense for it . . . knows just where to go and what to look for," Niall added. "Why?"

"And does anyone know where he has been for the past few days? Has anyone seen him around here anywhere?" Nechtan continued.

They shook their heads, baffled by what he was hinting at.

"Well, I know," Nechtan snapped, slamming his fist to the bearskin pallet in a rage. "He is tracking the girl and the Roman!" he shouted. Niall and Melwas reeled at his words.

"He's *what*? You mean . . . How do you know? What does . . ." they both spluttered in fear.

"Never mind how I know." Nechtan waved his hand distractedly at them. He ran his fingers through his tangled hair as he tried to think. Then he stared at them, his eyes narrowing ominously.

"Just what did you do with them, anyway?" he asked.

Niall and Melwas looked at each other and shifted uncomfortably.

"Well?" Nechtan repeated. "What did you do with them?"

"We . . . ah . . . left them . . ." Niall began. "That is, I did. The cart got mired in the mud on the road so Melwas stayed behind with it and the two horses. I walked the Roman and the girl out into the bog, got them good and lost, gave them some drugged wine, and while they were unconscious, I left, and I took everything with me."

"Everything?"

Niall nodded. "They had nothing. No knife, no food or water, no medicines. I took it all."

"But you didn't kill them? The wine—was it poisoned?"

"No, just drugged. But the girl was half-dead already, from the hard journey. She wouldn't have lasted long, not in the shape she was in."

"And the Roman?"

Melwas snorted in derision. "I doubt he'd know enough to eat a berry off a bush out there . . . if he was lucky enough to find one. No, he wouldn't have lasted long either," he said.

"And do you think Calum will be able to find where you left them?" Nechtan asked Niall, who nodded a reply.

"Oh, no doubt. But I don't think there will be much for him to find . . . wolves, you know."

"Yes," Melwas agreed. "Wolves were howling all around us every night. They would finish them off, if they didn't sink into a bog first, trying to get out."

"Then you think we have nothing to worry about?" Nechtan asked suspiciously.

"Nothing," Niall muttered, "except for the fact that we said they sank in a bog before we could rescue them. If Calum finds traces of them, it could be hard to explain."

Nechtan speared the slab of meat with his knife point and took an angry bite.

"Well," he said sourly, "I guess all we can do is hope Calum doesn't find them, or any signs of them."

* * *

A loud banging jolted the men from their sleep. Instinctively they grabbed their weapons, and Osla rose and approached the barred door.

"Who's there?" he called out.

"Angus. Of the king's guard. I have a message from Annos."

A blast of cold air rushed across the central hearth and flared the low fire when the guard entered the hut; stern, red-haired, and one of the tallest men in the town.

"I am here to summon Nechtan and his two men Niall and Melwas before the king," he announced formally, looking at Nechtan.

"Now?" the princeling asked in disbelief. "It is halfway through the night!"

Angus nodded. "Yes. Now. I am to wait for you. Hurry!"

A bright fire blazed in the great central hall when the four men entered through the heavy wooden door, ornately carved and painted with elaborate interlace patterns. In the gloom surrounding the fire Nechtan could see Annos, slumped back on his piled bearskins, the gray at his temples shining out like two cat's eyes in the darkness; still a strong and vigorous man, despite his age. Beside him Brennos, wearing his black druid's robe, sat cross-legged on an otterskin mat, his hands calmly folded in his lap. On the king's other side Nechtan recognized the leathery old face of the Lawgiver, Artogenos, like Annos, sitting stiffly on a skin of his namesake, Artos, the bear. The man's little gray eyes were stern and unblinking, and Nechtan felt his stomach knot up tensely. This . . . all this . . . could mean only one thing.

Calum had returned.

As they respectfully approached the hearth, he noticed for the first time the tiny stooped figure of his mother, sitting on a low stool across the fire from him, the serving girl behind her. Maia looked so small and insignificant, alone in the empty vastness of the Great Hall, that his heart went out to her. He longed to go over to her, to embrace her fiercely for the love he felt for her.

But Angus led the three men to the opposite side of the

fire and they stood at stiff attention, weaponless and waiting, all eyes on Annos to begin the proceedings.

The king rose slowly, and when he spoke his voice was icy cold.

"Good people, and distinguished guest," he said with a nod of recognition to Artogenos, whose gaze barely flickered in reply, "I have summoned you here on a very grave matter—to hear the tale of a witness who comes before us." Annos' voice was loud and clear, as if he were addressing a gathering many times larger than the handful he had assembled.

"And then, when all the testimonies are in, our visitor, one of the most revered Lawgivers of our time, will render the verdict."

He paused for a few moments, waiting, and then abruptly he sat. "Let us begin," he said, with a nod to the guard posted by the door. The man turned, opened the door, and the erect figure of Calum strode into the circle of firelight, a dark green cloak billowing splendidly behind him as he walked. Only a few years older than Nechtan, the tracker was not exceptionally tall, but his body was tightly muscled, in the manner of a cat. His long brown hair, like his clothes, was dirty, but he had taken pains to comb it back from his face before entering the room, securing it at the nape of his neck with a length of braid. *He is a fine-looking man,* Nechtan thought admiringly. *Proud. Skilled.* He sensed Niall and Melwas shifting nervously beside him.

"Calum," Annos began when the man stepped toward him and bowed slightly, "is it true that you were hired by the druid Brennos to go to the sacred spring of Arnemetia, to search for traces of the two missing slaves—Anarios, a Roman, who belonged to Brennos; and Melangell, a serving girl who was given to Maia?"

"Yes," Calum replied evenly. "I was."

"And did you find traces of them? Any at all?"

"I did, sir."

"What were they?"

"Many, sir. I found a knoll in an out-of-the-way area of the marshland, littered with footprints, a cold campfire, wood shavings, split vines—"

"A campfire?"

"Aye. Where they had camped."

"And the other? What of that?"

"Where they made walking sticks and ropes. To escape the bogs, sir. They were abandoned there, and they were alive."

A stir passed over the assembled group, and Niall closed his eyes sickly.

"And how do you know they were abandoned there? It is a serious charge to bring, without proof," the king began.

"Niall's footprints, wandering around the bogs with them; Niall's footprints on the knoll, and going off again. A campfire such as a warrior makes, not the clumsy, amateurish ones I found later . . ."

He paused while another shock rippled the room.

". . . a campfire made by Niall, who led them there and abandoned them, no doubt thinking they would die. With the walking sticks and ropes they left the knoll and attempted to escape the bogs. I continued to follow them."

"Go on," Annos said. "What else did you find?"

"They camped on several other knolls. Made crude campfires, ate from pieces of bark—they ate a turtle, tubers, seeds, and rats. Once they camped for several days on a hillock, even built a little shelter. They left offerings for the dead at Samhain, and the girl regained her strength while they were there, for when they left, her track was a normal one. They went off after a deer, and I lost them for a time."

Nechtan found it hard to believe that this capable-looking man could lose even a single footprint of their trail, and he realized how stupid his whole idea had been. To think that he had believed he could pull it off successfully! He had failed, and now she was alive. He jumped at the thought. Alive! Or . . . was she? Calum had not brought her back . . . had he? Was she here? He tried to peer around the shadowed hall, looking for the small figure, the long wheaten hair . . .

". . . and then I found it again, to the south of the bog," Calum's voice went on. "Heading toward the Roman lines."

Nechtan's head whirled around in disbelief and everyone in the room leaned forward attentively. Calum seemed to grow uncomfortable, and Annos fixed his gaze on him kindly.

"We realize the hour is late and you are tired from your

journey, but you must finish your tale. Continue," he urged the tracker.

Annos sat back in the furs, his fingertips perched together at his chin, and waited.

"I found them, sir, in a valley. Two days from the Roman lines. They . . . ah . . . they . . ." He cut his eyes around nervously to Nechtan, whose face frowned incomprehension at his gaze.

"Continue!" Annos ordered again.

Calum took a deep breath before he spoke.

"Lovers, sir. They were lovers," he said, his voice dying away.

Rage clouded Nechtan's features and he started forward toward the man. "Lies!" he shouted. "It is lies!" Angus and Niall seized his arms and held him back. Maia looked over in alarm and her face filled with sorrow for her son. "Not a Roman!" he shouted. "No! She wouldn't—"

"Silence, or I will have you silenced!" Annos thundered ominously. "You will have your chance to speak. Let this man finish. Continue," he said with a nod at Calum.

"I can understand your feelings, Nechtan," Calum said quietly, "for I, too, felt anger when I saw them . . . together."

"You saw them?" Annos asked in surprise.

"Yes . . . ah . . . naked, cavorting on the rocks, swimming in the stream, making love . . ."

Nechtan groaned and rolled his head back. Lovers! The Roman lines! She must be gone now, as surely as if she were dead. Gone.

"And where are they now?" Annos questioned.

"I crept in by night, while they slept, to capture them, but the girl tricked me and they escaped. They crossed the stream and scaled the opposite hillside, very steep and rocky. Near the top the Roman went on, while the girl stayed behind to delay me and make good his escape."

"The girl?" Brennos exclaimed. Calum nodded.

"Yes. I could not catch them both, and the Roman was gone, so I went after the girl. She threw rocks down at me, but not trying to hurt me—only delay me. Then she scampered over the cliff face, luring me after her. A terrible storm was rising—it was difficult to see, hard to keep good footing in the wind. Lightning was hitting the trees . . ."

He paused and looked aside when Maia gasped loudly.

". . . but she still continued. It did not seem to bother her, until a bolt landed beside us just as I was about to rush her, knocking us both against the hillside."

Stopping again, he looked slowly around the room. Everyone listened to his tale in rapt attention. He took a deep breath and resumed.

"Then she retreated to a rocky point jutting out over the valley. She . . . she . . . ah . . ." He seemed to have difficulty in getting the next words out. "She raised her arms heavenward and called out the name of Loucetius, and . . ."

He saw Artogenos lean forward eagerly.

"And a cold blue fire sprouted from her fingers, ran down her arms, and across the top of her head."

He closed his eyes as if he could scarcely believe it himself, and listened to the loud gasps of astonishment around him.

"And then," he continued, "I am ashamed of what I did next. Fear and anger overwhelmed me. I did not want her to escape me as the Roman had done. I . . . I threw my spear at her . . . and then I collapsed on the rock near her feet."

"And did it strike her?" Annos asked.

"I believe so, for there were traces of blood on it the next morning when . . . when I awoke and found it lying on the rock beside me."

Nechtan felt his knees grow weak. Dead. So she was dead, after all.

"And the girl?" Annos continued. "What of the girl?"

Calum gulped.

"Gone, sir. I searched the valley, the hills, the surrounding flats; nothing. No trace of her at all. She is gone, sir, vanished, as if she had been only a dream."

Melwas and Niall stood together before the king and druids. Melwas was instructed to go first, and his testimony was short.

"We went to the springs, sir," he began. "The journey was hard on the girl, and the Roman carried her much of the time. When the cart bogged down in the mud, we removed the girl and the baggage. Then the two slaves and Niall continued the journey on foot, while I waited with the horses."

"Had you been given any orders regarding the girl?" Annos asked him.

Melwas swallowed hard and nodded.

"Well, what were those orders?" the king prodded.

"I cannot say, sir," Melwas stated, and Annos exhaled in mild frustration.

"Who gave you the orders?" he snapped. Melwas stared silently ahead and did not answer. Annos studied him for a moment, then turned to Niall.

"You—what is your story?" he ordered. Niall straightened up and began to speak.

"The same as Melwas', sir," he said. "When the two slaves and I left Melwas and the horses, we journeyed for two days on foot across the bogs. Then I lost them."

"You lie!" Calum snapped from the side.

"It is you who are mistaken," Niall said, turning to face Calum. "Yes, I abandoned them. I am a warrior, not a murderer. I could not kill them outright for no reason, so I abandoned them to their fate. But that knoll you found could not have been the one where we camped. You are mistaken there, Calum. For you say you found wood shavings and split vines on the hill. I took everything with me. They had no knife to use to sharpen sticks or make ropes. I took everything . . . everything. They no doubt died on some other knoll, and you followed someone else's trail."

"No!" Calum protested. "I know who I saw; who I threw my spear at. I—"

"Annos!" Maia called out sharply. The king looked in her direction and waved Calum and Niall to silence.

"Speak," he said.

"Let this suffice for my testimony," she began quietly, "for I have only this one thing to say. I was very fond of the girl, and I worried for her safety. When she left, I gave her two things—my gold medallion of Loucetius, and a small dagger, which I hid in her boot."

She looked levelly at Niall's pale face.

"Did you take that knife too, Niall? For if not, then that is the one they used."

Dumbly the warrior shook his head. Annos turned back to him as Calum smiled in vindication.

"And who gave you these orders regarding the girl?" the king asked, but Niall, like Melwas, refused to answer. Annos waited, and when it became clear that they would not incriminate their master, he dismissed them.

"The final witness," he announced. "Nechtan, come forward."

Grimly Nechtan stepped out and halted in front of the seated king.

"Sir," he began, "let me first say that my men seek to protect me. I am grateful for their loyalty. It was I who gave them the orders, and my word was that the girl should die. That was all."

He fell silent and waited for Annos' next words. The king studied him thoughtfully and then leaned forward.

"And why did you give such an order?" Annos snapped. "You had already beaten her—your mother's slave. Wasn't that trouble enough for you? Why did you seek her death too?"

"It is a private matter, sir," Nechtan said quietly, and Annos' fist came down on his pallet in a rage.

"It is no longer a 'private matter,' boy! You will answer me now or I'll have your head on a pole by sunup. Now, speak!" he thundered at Nechtan, fire in his eyes. Maia gasped aloud.

"Because of the curse," Nechtan muttered.

"What?" Annós snarled. "Speak clearly!"

"The curse," Nechtan repeated. "A curse on my family, for as far back as anyone can remember. The druids know of it," he said. Artogenos stared at him a moment until understanding came and he spoke in surprise.

"Then you, boy, are of the royal house of the Cruìthni?" Nechtan nodded.

"And the curse," the old man went on, "is that the royal heirs shall meet their fates at the hands of a woman. And she—this serving girl—is that woman?"

Again Nechtan nodded.

"Are you sure?" Artogenos asked.

"Yes," Nechtan muttered. "She is the one."

"Fate? What fate?" Annos snapped as everyone in the room listened curiously to the unfolding tale.

"Various fates," Artogenos continued, turning to the king. "All unpleasant. Betrayal, slow poisoning, impaling, burning alive . . ."

Nechtan tried not to listen. He knew the stories well enough. Various fates . . . *His* fate.

"All painful, all tragic. Pain of the heart as well as pain of the body," the old druid went on, casting a knowing glance at the silent young man before them. "They say an offense against their gods began it, untold generations ago. The fairest maid was to have been sacrificed to end a plague, but the king kept her for himself. His love was so great, he dared to defy the gods. Many of his people needlessly died as a result, and the gods, in a rage, produced the curse: it would be the misfortune of each of this king's male heirs to feel an overwhelming love for a woman—a woman who would, in the end, bring about his death or destruction."

He looked at Nechtan sadly.

"They can know no happy love," he concluded.

The king stared at the princeling.

"And you sought to circumvent your fate by having her killed?"

Nechtan nodded, fearing to look at the king. Maia lowered her eyes and gazed at the packed earthen floor.

Poor devil, Calum thought, pity moving him. And now he doesn't know if she is dead or alive, where she is, or anything more about her.

"Do you have anything else to say?" the king asked. Nechtan wordlessly shook his head.

"Then let the Lawgiver render his verdict. Melwas . . . Niall . . ." he called. The two warriors came and stood tensely at each side of their master, the entire room waiting in strained silence while the old man pondered their fates. Time stretched out like reaching vines as Artogenos sat in pensive silence. Finally he looked up and his gaze fell on the three, not unkindly.

"Previous cases," he began slowly, "where one man has killed or forfeited the valued slave of another, have been settled in one of two ways. For a highly valued slave and a man of lesser importance, the penalty would be death."

A quiver ran around the room.

"For a valued slave and a man of greater importance, the man himself would be sold into slavery and the purchase price would be returned to the slave's owner as compensation."

He paused, collecting his thoughts, while the group waited. What would it be? Death? Slavery? Death for Melwas and Niall, and slavery for Nechtan?

"But this is no ordinary case. Even a highly valued slave is no equal to a prince of royal blood. There can be no comparison. And besides," he said, looking Nechtan in the eye, "I feel this matter is out of my hands. It involves issues beyond the knowing of mortals such as ourselves . . . a girl so obviously blessed of Loucetius, and a girl who is the fulfillment of an age-old curse, at that—a curse lowered upon princes by angry gods. I cannot—I will not—interfere in matters such as this. You, Nechtan, will suffer enough at the hands of your people's gods . . . and yet, some sentence must be decreed. And so, I declare your punishment: for you and your two men, banishment from this village and this territory, for a period of two years, one for each slave you have lost. Brennos will oversee your holdings for you during that time, for the benefit of your mother and the repayment of his own lost slave. You may take your other two men with you or not—that is for you to decide. You may also take with you only what you need to survive and can carry on your own backs. No horses. You will depart on the morning after the coming one."

He stood swiftly.

"So, my judgment is banishment for two years; and beyond that, I leave you to your own fates. May the gods be kind."

A hushed crowd gathered outside the low entrance to the Great Hall to see the three outcasts off. A large war chariot stood waiting to carry them away, the grooms trying to calm the nervously prancing horses. A murmur suddenly rose to one side and spread around the circle when the three men, escorted by Angus and their families, came into view. They walked proudly, despite their shame, and each carried a large leather pack slung over one shoulder. Approaching the waiting chariot, they deposited their gear on the deck and turned to bid their families farewell.

Maia stood trembling between the sturdy presence of Osla and Eber.

"Good-bye, lady," Niall and Melwas told her with a curt nod before turning aside to their own kinfolk. Nechtan took her small, withered hands in his and gazed silently into her face before looking up at the two flanking warriors.

"Take good care of her," he ordered them. "I will be back in two years."

They nodded solemnly. Looking down at her again, Nechtan wrapped his arms around her frail body and lifted her off the ground in a great embrace, burying his face in the familiar gray-streaked hair that had comforted him all his life.

"Good-bye, Mother . . . good-bye . . ." he choked. She patted his back lightly.

"Come back to me, son. I will wait. Come back," she whispered. He placed her on the ground and nodded.

"Good-bye," he said again, swallowing his tears as he kissed her cheek. Then he turned and mounted the chariot with his two men.

Brennos stepped out from the throng and stood with one hand resting on the wicker chariot side.

"Fellow tribesmen," he announced loudly, "by authority of the Lawgiver, the Great Druid Artogenos, I now pronounce the princeling Nechtan ap Oenghus and his two spearmen Niall and Melwas outcasts from this tribe for a period of two years. They are hereby banished from these lands and territories; they are not to be sought out or spoken to; they are as dead men, until the sentence is completed."

He stepped away from the chariot and the people walked from the clearing. The word had been given. The three were now dead men.

"It is done," he said, with a nod to Angus.

Reins in hand, Angus slapped to the horses and they broke into an eager gallop. Nechtan stood, one hand on the wicker side, and stared at his mother's tearstained face until the chariot drew through the gate, turned, and she was gone from sight.

Their territories were large, and they rode slowly until nightfall, Angus never speaking a word to them. At last he slowed the weary horses and pulled them to a stop.

"This is our northernmost limit," he said, pointing to a rocky ridge beyond which a hill fell away into thick forest.

"You are not to crest this ridge again for two years. There are no villages around here; no people. Now, go, and may the gods be with you."

He turned, took the reins, and waited for them to leave. Quickly the outcasts stepped down, took their packs, and walked toward the rocky crest, not turning to look when the chariot clattered away behind them and was soon lost to their ears. Reaching the crest, they paused, and Nechtan took a deep gulp of the cold night air.

"Well, let us begin," he said, and started the descent down the slope. Melwas silently followed, but Niall stopped, leaned over, and picked up a small rock from the ridge . . . his homeland, land of the Damnonii. Tucking it into his traveling pouch, he trotted down the hillside behind them.

They awoke well past sunrise, stiff and cramped from sleeping on the cold, damp forest floor.

"Gods above!" Melwas yawned, pulling his woolen cloak tighter as he sat up. "It is cold out here! We'd better find some food, and then get some sort of shelter built."

Nechtan nodded, staring up at the patches of pale blue sky through the overhanging trees.

"We will need a good roof over our heads before the snows come," he said. "Dry a lot of meat before the lean times, as we have no grain to tide us over."

Niall sat up eagerly.

"We could raid a village. Steal a cow," he said.

"Ha!" Melwas laughed. "Steal a woman, you mean."

Nechtan looked at him sternly.

"Quiet, you two," he snapped. "We do no raiding, no stealing, no raping. We do nothing to anger neighboring villages we might come across. Here, we have no safety in numbers. Our survival for two years depends on our own skill, and the goodwill of any people hereabouts. Do you understand?"

He eyed Niall threateningly, and the blond warrior nodded.

"Yes," he agreed, "you are right. But what if we run out of food, especially this first winter when we are so unprepared?"

"We don't," Nechtan stated. "We hunt, we fish, we do what we must. We lie low, like a cunning fox. If we raid, we will no doubt die; if we go to a village peacefully to ask for food, we might end up as slaves ourselves. We stay here, quietly, and we survive for two years. That is all we *can* do."

He rose to his feet and pinned his cloak around his shoulders.

"Now, get up! We have too much to do to lie around all day like lazy women." He opened his pack and pulled out several leather water bags. "One of us hunts, one looks for water, and one begins cutting down saplings to make a shelter."

By the third day the circular wall of their hut was erected, a roofing framework was lashed in place, and the men began to lay a roof. Scouting the adjacent hillside, they were unable to find enough rushes to cover it in thatch and finally settled for an awkward-looking mixture of grass and sods cut from the meadows.

"I know this will leak like a woman's veil with the first good rain," grumbled Nechtan, kneeling atop the rickety framework and trying to hammer the sods down firmly with the butt of his sword. Niall hauled several more sods up by vine rope.

"I think it's pretty good, myself. Especially since none of us have ever built a house before," he said.

"And it's better than the rain we'd get with no roof at all," Melwas added, looking up from the wicker door lashed with deer hide that he was making.

"It will go easier if you overlap them," a voice spoke up. The three men looked around in surprise, and Nechtan seized his sword hilt as he turned toward the sound. A wizened old man slowly approached them, a smile on his wrinkled face, his blue eyes twinkling merrily.

"I said, it will go easier if you overlap them . . . the sods," he repeated, indicating what he meant by overlapping his outstretched hands.

"Like the scales on a fish," the old man laughed. "A fish is watertight, is it not? Fix a support around the top of your wall, and place a row of sods along it. Overlap the next row above that, and so on, to the peak of your roof." He stopped by the house wall and looked up at the two men. Nechtan stared at Niall, a look of surprised understanding on his face. Then he began to pull up the sods he had so laboriously hammered into place.

"I think he's right!" he exclaimed as Niall turned to help him.

Melwas motioned the old man to sit by the fire.

"You are welcome to what little we have," he told him while he resumed his work. The old man sat on an upturned log end and extended his hands to the warming fire.

"Many thanks," he replied, "but I will not take your food."

"Do you live nearby?" Melwas asked. "We were told this area was uninhabited."

"So it is." The old man nodded. "For the most part, except for an occasional wanderer like myself. A satisfactory place, I suppose—neither the best nor the worst. And where do you hail from, that uses no sods on the roofs of houses?"

Melwas smiled and glanced over at the man.

"The adjacent lands of the Damnonii. We are outcasts— for two years."

The old man raised his eyebrows in surprise.

"Outcasts, are you? And for two years? Your offense must not have been too grave for that . . ." He leaned forward, seeming to expect an answer.

"A matter involving some slaves. And you? Where do you hail from?"

The old man wagged his head from side to side.

"Ah—here and there," he said. "I wander about, you see. I am a druid, but one of that rare sort who have forsaken the power and politics of kings for the true wisdom of the gods."

Melwas nodded and looked at the man in open admiration. "Semnotheoi," he said. "A holy man."

The old man laughed. "Is that what they call us now?" he

said. "At other times it is 'madmen.' Anyone who forsakes power must be mad, you see."

Melwas shook his head vigorously. "That is not true," he protested. "Many admire you. Perhaps it is only those with power themselves who call you 'mad'—or those who envy them their power."

"A wise answer." The druid nodded. "Have you ever considered joining us, I wonder?"

Melwas stood, laughing, and heaved his newly completed door upright.

"No, old father, I am a fighting man. I could never become one of you—I haven't the patience for it."

Carrying the door to the house, he propped it against the wall and turned to the old man.

"You are welcome to stay the night with us in our new home. A druid under our roof will bring us luck, no doubt. We haven't much, but we will gladly share it with you."

"Why, yes, I would like that. I am far from my own shelter, and the nights are very cold to my old bones."

"And what brings you here, old father?" Nechtan called down to him.

The old man shrugged his shoulders casually.

"This and that," he said, his eyes twinkling again. "Some and then some. I seek my medicines, my herbs and potions, with which I tend to sick and injured animals. It is the task the gods have chosen for me. That is all . . ." Turning, he extended his hands again toward the campfire as the three young warriors completed their chores in amused silence.

Icy gales howled around the makeshift hut at the base of the winter-brown hillside, driving snow into the few cracks that had not been chinked with river mud and chopped straw. A tanned deerhide tied down over the wicker door crackled and bellowed inward as the wind heaved against it. Snow, already knee-deep, drifted higher against the north wall of the house. Inside, Nechtan, Melwas, and Niall sat huddled around the hearth-pit, bundled under furs and wool cloaks and trying to stay warm.

"Gods above!" Nechtan shivered. "I hope this will not be a long winter. With this weather, we cannot even go out to hunt."

Niall nodded miserably, pulling his cloak over his head. "I used to think winters at home were bad, but what wouldn't I give to be there now, cozy and warm!"

"Aye! A Great Hall with a roaring blaze, a fat boar dripping into the fire, good wine to warm the belly . . ." Melwas mused, pulling his rough fur mittens off and extending his hands to the hearth.

"I only hope we have enough food to last the winter," Nechtan said, huddling closer to the fire. Melwas suddenly sat erect, his head cocked to one side.

"What is it?" Nechtan asked.

"A noise . . . shhh!" the warrior answered, still listening. He stood and walked to the door.

Abruptly they, too, heard it—a soft, whining sound and a scratching at the wicker door. Pulling the door inward, Melwas peered out into the swirling dimness of snow. Suddenly he saw, peeping out from a drift, the small red face of a fox.

"What is it?" Nechtan asked again, approaching the door. "Hurry and close it. The cold is—"

Before he could finish his words, a larger form appeared and the fox slipped through the doorway, bounding into the room and vigorously shaking the snow from its thick fur. Behind him the old druid stumbled into view, a large bundle tied to his back and a shrouded figure limp in his arms.

"Here . . ." he gasped in near-exhaustion. Niall took the sagging form as Nechtan and Melwas pulled the old man inside and, kicking away the snow that had fallen in, pushed the door shut against the howling blizzard.

"Old father!" Nechtan gasped against the cold. "What in the name of all the gods are you doing out in this storm? And what is the meaning of this?" he said, waving his arm from the fox to the still-shrouded figure now lying by the fire.

"Here!" Niall said, handing the old man a handmade wooden cup. "Some hot tea, to warm you."

The druid took the cup in his stiffened hands and quickly drank it down.

"Many thanks," he mumbled through icy lips. "If you had . . . built your home a few paces yonder . . . I fear I would not have reached you."

101

Nechtan handed the old man a fur wrap. He pulled it around his shoulders before walking to the recumbent form by the fire.

"Some broth, if you please," he directed, pulling the woolen cloak aside from the pale, lifeless-looking face of a young man. He knelt beside him and began to rub his deathly cold hands and arms.

"Some help, eh?" He looked up at Nechtan, who fell to his knees on the other side of the youth and began to assist the druid. He didn't see why, though; the boy looked dead already, or near it. His hand felt as cold as the snow outside the door.

"To the fire . . ." the druid said calmly, removing the cloak from the young man and pulling him to the edge of the hearth. Taking a cup from Niall, he poured a scant trickle of hot broth into the boy's slack mouth, only to see most of it run back out.

"Come on!" he muttered to the lifeless face, and began vigorously rubbing and smacking the boy's cheeks and chin and forehead.

"Help me!" he commanded, without looking up, and the three warriors began rubbing and pummeling the youth's arms and legs as the druid did.

"Come, boy . . . come . . ." he muttered again, and again he poured a little broth into the boy's mouth. To the old man's evident relief, the broth did not run back out. The fox, lying near the fire licking its wet paws, looked up in bright-eyed interest when the young man coughed once . . . twice . . . and his cold-swollen eyelids crept open. Satisfied, the old man sat back on his heels and studied the boy. The youth looked blankly around the room, as if his eyes could not yet focus nor his brain adjust to what had happened to him.

"In my pack—some wine," the druid said to no one and anyone. Melwas dragged the heavy pack to the fireside and awkwardly untied the ice-stiffened laces on it.

"Here," he said, handing a goatskin wine bag to the druid, a type such as the Romans often used. The old man cradled the boy's head in one arm and trickled the wine down his throat. The boy drank it eagerly.

"Now, then," the druid said, seeming satisfied with the

situation at hand as he pulled the fur from his shoulders and tucked it around the boy, "I will answer your questions."

He gazed around the fire at the three young men, his eyes once more twinkling in merriment where moments before they had been clouded and gray. The fox stood up and trotted happily to crawl into the old man's lap, where it immediately curled up, its bright eyes peering out from behind the bush of its tail.

"You should not have come out in a storm like this!" Nechtan scolded him.

"Ah! But it was not 'a storm like this' when I set out upon my journey," he paused and gazed up at the ceiling in thought, "four days ago. And as you can see, it was a trip that needed taking, my friends," waving his hand toward the boy.

"Yes," Nechtan continued. "Who is this boy? Where does he come from?"

"Who he is, I do not know, nor where he comes from, nor why he was out without even a cloak. I only know that I came upon him after the storm had begun, curled up to die beneath an alder. I have carried him since yesterday, knowing I was closer to your hearth than to my own."

Nechtan stood and looked from the old man to the pale boy and back again.

"And now what is to be done, old father?" he asked. "We have little enough to eat here, and nothing for a convalescing youth."

"Never fear!" The old man smiled and began rummaging in his pack.

"The reason I set out on my journey was to bring you some things. See? The wine yonder . . . some barley . . . a small pot of honey . . . a few medicines . . . and . . ." He held up a lumpy pouch.

"This I knew would be the most valued gift of all." He grinned mischievously, holding it out to Nechtan. Niall and Melwas watched with interest as their master opened the bag, and he broke into a loud laugh when he looked inside it.

"Soap!" he roared, tossing the pouch to Niall. "And just when we thought our choice was to be as dirty as a German mercenary or as oily as a Roman scraping himself to remove his dirt. Many thanks, old father! Many thanks!"

"And there is one other thing." The old druid pulled out a small, soft deerskin pouch, meticulously embroidered with a series of bright scarlet spirals. Nechtan took it and studied the craftsmanship, felt the buttery softness of the hide.

"This is very fine; very fine indeed," he observed. "Rare skills did this. Where does it come from, old father?"

"A friend made it, while recovering from a misfortune." He waved his hand when Nechtan tried to return it to him. "No . . . it is yours. When I saw it, I knew at once that you must have it. It is only fitting for a leader of men such as yourself."

Nechtan laughed at the remark. "A leader? Me? My friend, look around you. I am an outcast! Whom do I lead? My two men?"

"Three," the druid said, pointing to the pale young man by the hearthside. "The gathering of your warriors has already begun."

Shouts and laughter broke the stillness of a hazy summer afternoon in the clearing at the edge of the great forest, interrupted by an occasional dull thud as another arrow found its mark in the straw-and-deerhide target. Soft breezes from the nearby river lifted the heat from the forest floor and stirred the trees into gentle motion.

Another thud came, and a louder cheer indicated the arrow had centered the target exactly.

"Well done! Well done indeed!" Nechtan applauded, lounging back against the hillside, a cup of ale in his hand.

"You, Mael, are you truthful in stating you have never used the bow before?" he questioned a tall thin young man with red hair who started forward to retrieve his arrows.

"In truth, sir, I never had use for one before," Mael answered, turning toward Nechtan, a bow clenched in his hand. "I was a miller's son, who had never fought nor hunted till now."

Nechtan nodded admiringly. "Well," he said, "you certainly have a skill for it. The old druid would no doubt say it is your destiny."

Mael laughed good-naturedly along with the rest of the group perched around the clearing, now numbering six men: Niall and Melwas; Cathal, the Parisi archer the old druid had saved from the blizzard; Mael, the miller's son; and Eber and Osla, who had joined them in the spring.

"You two," Nechtan said, motioning to Osla and Eber, "I want you to practice too. All my men will be expert with all weapons, not just a few. We will practice fighting with spears, javelins, darts, swords, and daggars. The Romans practice unceasingly, I'm told, and so must we if we hope to ever defeat them."

He set his cup aside and beckoned to Cathal and Niall. "We must talk," he said, and instructed the others to continue with the archery practice as he walked away.

"I have heard from the druid," he said quietly when the two joined him. "The Romans are on the move again, and heading north. There was much activity in their camps all spring, new men brought in, shiploads of supplies . . ."

He paused in thought.

"I think perhaps we should go on a little hunting trip to the south and see for ourselves what is happening with the Romans. Just the three of us, to travel faster. The rest will remain here to tend our crops and finish enlarging the hut . . . and in case any others come to join our army."

"As well they might," Cathal agreed. The boy had grown and matured much in the past six months, and already he looked like a man, not a mere youth of seventeen. His long brown hair was braided in a single plait down the center of his back, but he'd chosen not to wear the usual warrior's mustache. His shoulders were broad, his large hands showing the promise of much growth yet to come. Despite his youth, his skill with weapons was so great that Nechtan had chosen him to be one of his personal guards. "I hear from traders that there is much dissatisfaction among the young warriors of many tribes," Cathal went on. "The kings sit for too long; the old men are afraid. No one will act against the Romans—until it is too late."

Nechtan nodded. "Well, then that is all the better for us, isn't it?" he said, clapping his hand on the young man's powerful shoulder. "And we *will* be ready for the Romans."

A glint of cold hatred shone from his pale golden eyes, and Cathal thought with a shudder that he was glad he was not a Roman on the receiving end of Nechtan's sword.

* * *

They journeyed on foot for four days, over rocky hillsides and soggy fens, through deep forests and across flower-decked meadows, always avoiding the well-traveled paths and the busy settlements. They did not want to risk a confrontation with the local people, and they could not afford a long delay, even for pleasant reasons; and Nechtan and Niall pushed the idea of finding a willing woman from their minds, however long it may have been since they'd had one. The Romans were up to something, and they had to try to discover what it was.

When they reached the gentler slopes and grasslands that marked the beginning of the no-man's-land between native and Roman-held territories, they dropped weary and thirsty beside a rushing stream that cascaded from a distant valley and between the bases of two low hills.

"Gods above, we must do this more often!" Nechtan gasped, raising his face from the fresh, cool water. "It certainly keeps you fit!"

"Better than sitting around our compound all day, doing women's work," Niall agreed, splashing the water over his dusty blond hair to cool his hot aching head.

Nechtan looked to Cathal. "Well, boy, your Parisi people came this way when they fled the Romans to the south. What is the best route to circle them and get a closer look?"

The boy threw his arm out to the east. "The valley yonder rises into small mountains, which dip down like a finger jutting onto the plains. They are heavily wooded and afford excellent cover. I would hunt there many a time, and I could watch the Romans moving about on the flats below. What a place for an ambush." He grinned wickedly, and Nechtan laughed.

"Indeed," he said, standing. "Then let us begin."

They loped upstream, toward the deepening valley. At the mouth of the valley they halted to eat, and Cathal was ordered to remain there and wait for them to return.

"But I know the way!" he protested vehemently. "I can show you!"

"Exactly," Nechtan agreed. "We two are experienced warriors and, looking out for each other's safety, we will be able to get close to the Roman lines to observe. We know what to look for—you don't. We need someone to stand guard at the mouth of this valley, and that must be you, Cathal, because you do know the way. If danger comes, you can more quickly and easily find us and warn us."

He looked at Cathal, who nodded glumly.

"Good," Nechtan concluded. "Remain here, unless there is great danger. We will return by sundown tomorrow. Find some good game for supper, for we'll be hungry by then."

Nechtan and Niall belted their patterned cloaks around their waists and, thus concealed, walked away, the soft patterns of the cloth melding into the dappled forest light.

Cathal dejectedly wandered into the valley and climbed up to the scrub along the lower slopes of the hillside. He had nothing to do now but wait and watch till tomorrow, when he would go hunting for a fat red squirrel or a succulent young boar newly born that spring. His stomach turning at the thought, he settled himself comfortably behind a large bush, keeping one sharp eye on the valley entrance while composing a lyric in his mind to the fair-haired daughter of a trader he had met not long ago on his wanderings.

Nechtan and Niall crept along the slope of the hillsides, going higher into the small mountain range and through dark hemlock forests along its crest. At dusk they paused for a short nap, each taking turns while the other watched. A sliver of moon rose as they resumed the journey. When the sun crept above the hills to the east, the land began a slope downward to the point of the jutting finger, and the men stopped, gazing in awe at the sight below them.

The Roman legions were already active in the gray morning light, and the faint sound of horses neighing and voices calling drifted to their ears. A huge stone-and-timber fortress sat directly beside a wide road that ran nearly as straight as a lance into the mists of the far horizon. A large building occupied the center of the compound, surrounded by several smaller ones, the outer edges rimmed with long, narrow buildings—barracks for the men, Nechtan guessed. Outside the palisade, row upon row of large leather tents of newly arrived soldiers stretched across the cleared ground, surrounded by a makeshift wall of earth and branches. Grooms walked several splendid-looking horses in a nearby field. Small groups of men were practicing maneuvers, their moves as precise as a school of shoaling fish, their armor glinting like scales in the morning light. Rows of supply wagons sat along the road, some empty and some yet to be unloaded.

So this is the might of the Romans, Nechtan thought bitterly, watching the camp activity. If only I had a thousand men, we could sweep down and butcher them in their beds. But I see no signs of campaign. They have more men, and many supplies, but I see no evidence of the army itself moving. The Romans take everything with them. There would be wagons and pack mules loaded with goods; equipment of the engineers; their awesome war machines; chariots for their leaders. No, I do not think—

He felt the sharp point of a sword suddenly press against his back, and a heavily accented voice spoke.

"Stand slowly," it said, and anger rose in Nechtan like a flame at the note of mockery he detected there.

The sun crept high before Cathal woke with a jolt, confused at first in his sleep-numbed brain until his mind cleared and he realized where he was. He stretched stiffly and stood, deciding that he might as well go and hunt; nothing was going to happen here at the valley's mouth. Hoisting his bow over his back, he ascended the rocky valley, looking for some sign of game.

He came to a small meadow tucked between boulders, where hazel nuts and berries grew, and he found signs of a squirrel's feasting there, but not the animal itself. He should have looked in the evening, when boars were out and feeding, he cursed himself. Skirting the meadow, he continued to search. When he climbed atop one of the surrounding rocks, a gleam of triumph came to his eyes; a fat young badger was scratching in the dirt, diverted by its search for grubs or mice. Not much of a meal, Cathal mused, but better than nothing, and the animal's fine pelt would make a splendid traveling pouch. As slowly as he could, Cathal reached for the bow on his back, but the movement alerted the animal and in an eye blink it was off, darting back and forth among the boulders, seeking its burrow or some other safety. With a low whoop of delight the boy sprang from the rock and raced off after the frightened animal, the excitement of the chase flaring through him. This, he swore, was one badger that would not get away.

He leapt lightly over the rocks and once thought he had lost the badger, but it cowered breathlessly by a fallen log and, when discovered, skittered off again, deeper into the valley. *It will run out of space,* Cathal thought triumphantly as he pursued it. *I will corner it, and it will be mine!*

The badger was close now . . . very close. His hand went to his daggar hilt when he saw it scamper desperately up a final grass track between two huge boulders, up and up, caught between the rocks, until it emerged above him. Before Cathal could stop, he ran into the boulders, caught himself with one hand, and watched the badger run into the folds of a long black cloak and cower, gasping, at the feet of a . . . a druidess, swathed in a black robe, a black hood pulled over her head and low across her face, leaving it almost hidden in shadow except for a grimly stern mouth.

Cathal looked up at the shadowed face, back to the trembling young animal, and his hand fell away from his knife. The cloak rustled softly around the exhausted badger as the druidess moved, and she spoke in a cold, hard voice.

"Go," she said simply, and Cathal backed away.

"I . . . I'm sorry . . . I didn't know . . ." he stammered, with a mouth that didn't seem to want to work properly.

"Boy," she commanded again, "go at once. Your master needs you."

She bent, picked up the trembling animal, and cradled it in her arms.

"Go! At once!" she repeated, and turned to walk away. Rousing, Cathal felt her words sink into his frightened brain. "Your master needs you."

Taking a shortcut across the stream and up the far hill, the boy raced to the ridge and down over the encumbering rocks along the mountain crest.

The Roman soldier laughed as he backed Nechtan and Niall at sword point against a large mossy tree trunk.

"Ha! Now, what will I do with you two barbarians?" He sneered. "Spying on us, eh? Should I kill you here or send you to Rome to fight in the Colosseum? You don't look like you'd make good slaves . . . but good fighters, yes . . . put on a good show. Yes"—he nodded—"I could get a nice bit of gold for you two barbarians." He eyed them up and down. They were a good head taller than he was, and in superb fighting condition. He jabbed Niall in the stomach with his sword point.

"Make you fight each other, eh? See what that would look like."

His greedy eyes fell on their gold torques and armbands, and he threatened to press the sword point full into Niall's abdomen.

"Let's have your gold, then, before I march you down into camp." He held out his left hand impatiently, but neither Celt moved.

"Come on, then, let's have it or I'll butcher you here and take it. Don't you want to live to see Rome? Better than any of these hog wallows you've got around here, eh?"

He paused for a moment, then whirled at the sound of footsteps behind him. In that instant Niall seized his wrist and wrenched the sword from it as Nechtan sprang forward, his daggar drawn.

Niall clamped the struggling Roman firmly against his chest, one hand tight across the man's mouth to silence him. Nechtan pressed his blade to the soldier's neck and glanced over his shoulder. Cathal approached, a look of alarm on his dusty face.

"You disobey me, boy, but, by Medocius, I am glad to see you!" Nechtan said quietly before turning back to the subdued captive.

"Our language—you speak?" Nechtan asked him. The man gave a brief nod in reply, the Celtic knife still at his throat.

"You stay quiet? Answer questions?"

Again the man nodded, terror evident in his dark eyes. Nechtan glanced at Niall, who removed his hand from the man's mouth but still held him firmly in one arm.

"Your orders—what are they?" he asked, pressing harder on the man's throat for emphasis. The soldier tried to draw his head away, pushing it back into Niall's broad chest, and spoke in a slow, garbled voice.

"I . . . we . . . stay here till spring, then . . ."

"Then what?" Nechtan said fiercely.

"New governor . . . they say . . . he advances next year." His voice began to plead, quaking in fear.

"Please . . . I am only a legionary . . . infantryman. I know little . . . please . . ."

Nechtan and Niall eyed each other, communicating without words. Nechtan, chewing on his lower lip, replaced the knife in his leather belt. The soldier slumped in relief.

"Your physician," Nechtan suddenly asked. "Is he Anarios?"

The soldier shook his head, a puzzled look on his face. "Anarios . . ." he mused aloud. "No, he is with the Syrian archers. Not here."

"He is alive?"

"Yes. He returned from three years as a slave and . . ." His voice died away as he began to understand the warrior's question.

"And a girl . . . did he have a Damnonii girl with him?"

"A girl?" the soldier repeated. "No . . . I don't know. I never heard that he did. He is alone now—a physician."

"Where are these Syrian archers?" Nechtan demanded. "Where is Anarios?"

"To . . . to the east . . . near the coast . . . several days' march by road. A small garrison." His voice dropped away and he watched the dark-haired Celt turn from him. With a slight nod to the blond warrior, the man walked away, lost in thought.

Cathal watched in horror as Niall drew his knife, held the struggling young Roman firmly in one arm, and despite the man's pleas for mercy, quickly slit his throat from ear to ear. The soldier fell to earth, thrashing wildly, and attempted to rise, but Niall kicked him to the ground and calmly watched as his struggles grew weaker. Finally the soldier lay still, his gleaming body armor streaked with blood, his dead fingers still clutching the forest floor.

Nechtan turned as silence descended, and eyed the sprawling body.

"Take his head," he ordered Niall, who swiftly bent, seized the soldier's dark, matted hair in one hand, and pulled the head up to cut it free. Cathal turned away, sick at the sight. He was an archer, and he often hunted, but he had little experience in actual battle and nothing as cold-blooded

111

as this. His empty stomach turned in nausea and he walked away, sitting on the far side of a tree, away from the grisly scene behind him.

Nechtan looked around at the trees as Niall lifted the dripping head.

"Wedge it in the fork of that tree, so that his companions will find it," he directed his spearman.

Without a word, Niall obeyed.

"Now, cut off his genitals." Nechtan continued, but Niall drew to an abrupt halt.

"What?" he said in disbelief. "I will not touch the filthy organs of a Roman dog, no doubt full of disease and cursed from all of our women he has raped. I will not."

Niall stood solidly, wiped his knife blade on the Roman's tunic, and returned it to his belt, his mind obviously made up. Nechtan stared at him, walked over, and kicked the body onto its back. Jerking up the man's tunic, he drew his knife and in one swift stroke cut the Roman's genitals free. Striding across the forest floor, he stuffed them savagely into the dead soldier's mouth, and when he turned to Niall, the cold hatred in his eyes made Niall's blood turn to ice.

"That will be my mark, the fate of every Roman dog I capture. Let them learn my sign, and let them tremble when they see it."

He turned, wiped his blade and replaced it, and silently walked away. Niall quickly followed. The girl haunts him still, he thought grimly. The girl haunts him still.

Cathal leapt to his feet when the two men passed him. Nechtan's mood seemed sour, and like Niall, he stayed out of his chief's way, doing nothing to antagonize him and speaking only to answer his questions. Swiftly they traversed the rocky mountain crests, dropped back to the lower slopes, and came to the hills surrounding the small valley, where Nechtan halted.

"Boy," he called to Cathal, "the quickest way to our supper, if you please."

Cathal approached him fearfully, receiving a sympathetic glance from Niall as he passed.

"I . . . I have none," he began. Nechtan whirled on him angrily, his hand ready to strike and fire in his eyes. Niall stepped forward to intervene.

"Nechtan, the boy saved our lives," he cautioned, his hand raised toward Nechtan's upturned fist.

Nechtan lowered his arm and looked at Cathal darkly.

"Yes—true," he muttered. "But you'd better explain yourself, Cathal, for if anyone had come this way, and you gone from your post . . ."

"I went after game, like you said," the young man began. "I found a young badger and chased it to the end of the valley, where it escaped by hiding beneath the cloak of . . . of a druidess, robed in black and standing on a rock."

Nechtan's eyes narrowed as he looked at Cathal.

"Is this the truth, boy?" he said sternly. "You know the three rules for living as a good warrior: truth in the heart, strength in the arm, and honesty in speech."

Cathal drew himself up to full height, now as tall as Nechtan, and anger sparked from his eyes.

"I do not tell lies," he answered hotly, glaring at his chief. Nechtan nodded.

"All right. Finish your tale," he said, and the boy relaxed.

"This druidess sheltered the animal, and she told me, 'go.' I began to apologize, and again she said 'go,' but then she said, 'your master needs you.' She picked up the badger and silently left, and I ran by every shortcut I knew to come to your aid."

"What did this . . . this woman look like?" Nechtan asked.

"Her head and much of her face were covered by the hood of her robe. I could not see. Her voice was cold . . . stern . . . like a voice from beyond the grave."

Nechtan and Niall looked at each other nervously.

"This rock . . . take us to it at once!" Nechtan said, and followed the boy's steep descent directly down into the valley.

"There." The youth pointed to a large boulder, split by a grassy cleft. "Atop that rock."

Nechtan eyed the rock, and then looked carefully around them. No one else was to be seen. He started forward alone and climbed to the top of the huge boulder.

That's odd, he thought, reaching the top and looking at the sandy soil covering the rear where the rock sprang from the hillside. The soil looks undisturbed . . . no footprints of human or animal.

Pausing, he drew out his daggar and held it high over his head. Facing the hillside, he spoke in a loud voice.

"Good mother, I thank you for my life . . . and from this day forward we will not disturb your creatures or the peace of your valley. But be warned, good mother; we have this day killed a Roman. Be on your guard, for his companions will no doubt come to avenge his death. I leave as my thank offering this knife of mine, with which I repaid a small debt owed the filthy enemies of our people. Take it, good mother, with my thanks . . ."

He laid the knife on the bare rock, backed off the boulder, and in reverent silence the three men left the valley to begin the long trek home.

From behind the scrub brush high along the valley wall, a pair of shadowed eyes peered down at him as he spoke, a head nodded in approval, and a slight smile tugged at the corners of a silent mouth.

"They will not listen," Osla said grimly, scooping hot barley into his rough wooden bowl. Eber nodded agreement.

"That is why we left," he said. "All the traders, the shopkeepers, the craftsmen, they fear a war. Even under the Roman yoke they can still make a profit. That is all they care about."

Niall nodded cynically at their words. "Yes," he said. "I thought we were proud warriors, but living out here, I come to see how soft and lazy we truly had become. How can we fight the Romans if all the townsmen are meek and the warriors so idle?"

Nechtan rose and cut a chunk of meat from a roasting boar sizzling over the hearth. "I still say they must be warned. If only one king, one village, will listen, that might prod the rest to action. We must try. Beyond that, all we can do is get ourselves ready to fight."

"All seven of us?" Mael snorted.

"More will come, once the word gets out to others like ourselves who wish to fight, not sit idly by and wait for the yoke of the Romans to fall upon our necks. In a year's time we will have a large army, fit and well-trained. If the Romans win, it will be a hard victory they claim." Nechtan looked around the shadowed circle of faces. They all nodded approval.

"Then we set out—now, while the weather is still good. Cathal, to the south. Osla and Eber, to the northwest. Niall and Melwas to the northeast. Warn the villages and farms. Try to rouse them. But return here by fall. Alone, or with other warriors. We begin our practice, even if the snows surround us; we practice in the new hall we have built, if we must. By next summer we will be a fighting army!"

"And I?" Mael said, raising his hand. "No doubt I am to remain behind?"

Nechtan nodded and Mael shrugged good-naturedly.

"I would just as soon stay, actually," he admitted. "Being a miller's son, I have few real fighting skills and little gift of eloquence. I would do you little good on your travels."

"Good." Nechtan nodded. "Then you remain here, tend to the crops, keep the house in repair."

"And what of you?" Melwas asked.

"I return to our village."

A loud chorus of protests greeted his words and he held up a hand to silence them. Only Melwas grinned at him, the plan evidently meeting with his approval.

"Yes, it has been less than a year of our banishment," Nechtan concurred, "but I will sneak in by night. If their defenses are as lax as you say, it will not be a difficult task. No one need see me but the king, with whom I will speak in secret, and my mother, whom I wish to visit."

"And Seonaid?" Eber prodded, slapping his knee merrily. Everyone laughed; they all had heard of the near-legendary Seonaid. Nechtan shook his head and smiled.

"No time, I'm afraid," he said.

"Then bring her back for us," Osla jested, and the group roared its approval of the idea.

"Another time, perhaps," Nechtan continued over the noise. "So it is settled. We leave tomorrow, and may the gods of this land bless our journeys."

Part 3

ESUS, OAK KNOWER

GREAT WAVES OF PAIN CRASHED AGAINST MELANGELL'S CONsciousness, tossed her like a stormy sea, and subsided into tranquil pools of nothingness. Feverishly she groped for her upper arm . . . stop the unending pain . . . if she could only clench it tightly enough in her hand she could squeeze the pain away, like a great festering sore.

It seemed as if time, sun-crossings and moonspans, had abandoned her to this never-ending sea of agony. On and on it went, tossing and burning, till she wearied of the struggle and allowed herself to slowly sink down, down, into the black water, gulping great mouthfuls of this sea, warm and bitter, till it overwhelmed her and she sank into peaceful oblivion, death, nothingness.

Something pulled gently at her hair and she brushed it away.

"No, Mother," she muttered, "I will get up later. I am so tired. Let me sleep."

Again the tug came, at first tentative, then more insistent. Slowly she opened her heavy eyelids just as a soft black doe's nose whiffled gently against her forehead. Startled, she attempted to rise, but a great clash of pain caused her to cry out and fall back, her head reeling. The deer, startled, backed away a few steps and at the sound of clapping hands the animal turned and bounded away.

Exhausted and waiting for the pain to subside, Melangell lay limp, her eyes tightly closed.

"Here, little apple," a kindly voice said, and a hand slowly lifted her head. "This will help the pain."

Opening her eyes a crack in startled curiosity, she saw the friendly face of an old man, his blue eyes looking at her in concern, like two calm, tranquil pools in which she could lose herself if she tried.

"Did you move your arm?" he asked quietly. She tried to shake her head no.

"Ah! Good! I tried to bandage it in place, but with no assistance and at my age, it was a bit difficult. The bone is severely shattered—it must not be moved. Do you understand?" He peered into her face and she half-nodded.

"Wh-who are you?" she began. He smiled and shook his head sternly.

"Rest, little apple. I am merely an old man who found you, that is all. Now rest."

His potion seemed to be taking effect, for she felt her mind slowly slipping away . . . away . . . .

"The deer seems to like you," the old man said, sitting beside her and putting a bowl of hot gruel on the floor. Melangell smiled as she stroked the young deer's soft forehead with her good hand.

"Shoo now!" he said, waving his arm at the doe, who rose to her feet and reluctantly walked away from the girl.

"She will eat this gruel for herself if you're not careful." He chuckled, propping the girl up and feeding her from the bowl.

"She is your pet?" Melangell asked softly.

"Oh, I healed her once, and she decided she liked my food better than her own. I have many such friends. Now, eat. You are badly underfed. Where have you come from, child?"

She told him her story as she ate. He nodded.

"So that explains your friend there, who wounded you."

"You saw him?"

The old man nodded. "Oh, yes. When I took you away, I left him on the rock, and returned his spear to him. He was unhurt and not needing my attentions. You, however, were quite a different matter." He smiled at her again, and she imagined, as he looked down at her, that the wispy gray hair framing his head was like the soft down of a nestling bird.

"You were seriously wounded; had lost much blood. It will take many days before you can be up and around."

"And then where will I go?" she wondered aloud, looking away.

He stood and shrugged his bony shoulders. "Go rejoin your Roman friend." His eyes creased in merriment at the surprised look on the girl's face.

"Yes, I saw you. From the time you first entered my valley. Even your tracking friend could not find my cave here on the cliff face when he searched for you. No one can find it, unless I allow them to. I see everything that goes on here. I saw your bravery and sacrifice to save your Roman, and I saw Loucetius in his turn save you. You have a power, child, a rare power, and I did not choose to let you die there on that rock. So, yes, go and rejoin your Roman among his people, for that is where he is now. He arrived there yesterday . . ." He paused when he saw tears of pained relief trickle down the girl's pallid cheeks.

"You really love him so much, then?" he asked gently, and Melangell, nodding, choked back a sob.

"Then it is settled, isn't it?" he said, patting her hand. "To your Roman you shall go."

"Easy now, little apple!" the old man cautioned Melangell as, one arm around her back, he helped her to stand. The cave whirled dizzily when she got to her feet, and she slumped into his chest.

"I . . . I'm sorry," she gasped. "It hurts too much. I am too weak."

"Here!" he said softly, pulling an overturned wooden bucket closer with one foot. "Sit. Get your breath back. You must have lost more blood than I realized. Sit! Your wound is a bad one," he explained, clenching her hand reassuringly. "The ancients thought that to break that particular bone would result in death, so difficult was it to heal. I don't agree, but you must get stronger, for I have a short journey to make." He pulled a small wicker table closer and sat down cross-legged on the dirt floor. "I will leave you with food, and you are not to leave the cave. You'll have all the instructions you need to fix foods and medicines for yourself. I think you'll be all right for a few days. Here . . . some wine . . . it is good for you." He pushed a small metal cup across the table to her; the same type, smooth bronze with an elaborately engraved rim, that Brennos used. Picking it up, she sipped some wine and then studied the cup thoughtfully.

"Are you a druid?" she asked. "You don't seem like the druids I have known."

He smiled merrily at her. "Yes, I am a type of druid, I suppose. Not your usual type, though. I prefer to live in seclusion, learning the true wisdom of the gods in natural poverty, rather than the rich wisdom of men that most druids prefer. Ah"—he shrugged—"what good will riches or earthly wisdom do me?"

"Then you are what they call a 'holy man'?" she said in awe. He nodded.

"Semnotheoi, some call us. 'Those who reverence the gods.'"

"And you have chosen me to save," she mused, gazing at the druid's cup again.

"No, little apple," he said gravely, "Loucetius chose you to be saved. I am only an instrument of the gods . . . of Loucetius and his consort Nemetona of the Groves, of great Bran, Arnemetia, and Dagda the Good, Aramo the Gentle, the all-knowing Ollovidius, and all the rest. They seldom act directly on this dark earth; they use intermediaries, vessels into which they pour their wine. Me, another; an eagle or a lightning bolt; a sacred bull or a fog at sea. All are tools of the gods."

"And your journey? Is this for the gods; are you a vessel again?"

"Partly. I have had a vision that I am needed. But partly because of you, dear child. There is a special fern, and even though the season is late, I hope to find enough of it to help restore your blood and regain your strength."

"And for me you do these things?" she said, gazing at his twinkling eyes.

"Of course!" he said happily. "Are you of less importance to me than my friends the deer, the raven, the fox? Would I do less for you than for them? All life is precious, little apple, especially one chosen by a god."

Taking another sip of the wine, she fell silent, and he watched her solemn face. Such inner beauty she had, such peace and radiance! Yes, surely she is the beloved of Loucetius. What a pity she will be wasted on a lot of pagan Romans who only destroy, destroy, and never create. Still, if that is her wish . . .

He stood abruptly. "I will get you some food. Surely you are hungry?"

Rousing, she looked up at him. "Yes . . . a little. Something gentle on my stomach. It is still queasy. No rich meats."

He laughed and she looked at him, puzzled. What had she said that was funny?

"We eat no meat here," he explained. "What would my friends think? That I cure them with one hand and kill them with the other? And what would that make me? A clouded vessel expecting to receive the pure wine of the gods? No, here we do not seek life by feasting on death."

"I . . . I am sorry," Melangell stammered. "I never thought . . . never realized . . ."

"Oh, that's all right!" he laughed. "My friends' feelings are not easily hurt. One bowl of oats and they will readily forgive you! There is time . . . you will learn. Now, eat, and recover your health!"

"I'm sure you'll be all right while I'm gone," the old man said. "Why, in just these few days you have recovered to a remarkable degree!"

Melangell slowly nodded. To be honest, she did not want him to leave. She had already grown fond of him, like the father or grandfather she had never known, and she would be very lonesome when he was gone.

As if reading her thoughts, he spoke again. "I will be back before you have a chance to miss me, Melangell! We all must learn to live alone with ourselves. Let this be your time. Make the most of it! Think! Create! Any unpleasant thing can be an enriching experience if only you use it right. Our souls need such trials to overcome. Very few people know that."

He paused when an idea occurred to him and he walked over to the small cedarwood chest in which he kept his few possessions. Rummaging through it, he pulled out a packet and handed it to the girl. She opened it and unfolded a small square of buttery soft deerhide. She looked at the druid, uncomprehending.

"It is deerskin. But I thought you . . ." she began.

His face grew pained. "It belonged to a friend of mine. A very fine stag of pale sand color, most unusual. He died in a fall from the cliff, and I left him to nourish the wolves in the winter; but before I did, I took the softest part of his skin and prepared it myself. I promised him that with it I would make something of very great beauty . . . a promise, as you see, that I have not yet kept. He was a grand friend. I am sure that he would be honored to have you make something instead. Will you?"

She looked at his wrinkled old face, at the obvious grief she saw there for the dead deer, and nodded.

"Yes, I would be honored."

Sadly Melangell watched the old druid descend the concealed path down the hillside. He was soon lost to view behind the thick brush and trees. Turning, she made her way back along the narrow passage and into the small cave that was now her home. She surveyed the room; everything seemed well taken care of and conveniently close at hand. Firewood was piled along one wall, on the far side of her bed. The straw pallet had been moved closer to the fire for warmth. At one end of the bed were extra woolen blankets; at the other end sat a wooden barrel of fresh water. Sacks of grains and packets of medicines lined the rickety wooden stand he had made long ago, when his hermit life first began. On the low table, next to a few wooden cups and bowls he had ornamented with carved woodland scenes, sat "her project"—several bone needles, a small knife, fine red thread she had pulled from an old shawl the druid had given her, and in the center a makeshift stand of wicker on which he had stretched the deerskin, to hold it taut while she did her one-handed embroidery.

I will rest first, she thought to herself, and then I will begin my sewing. I think I'll make a leather pouch, embroidered with a series of spiral designs.

By the third day Melangell had fallen into a convenient routine of caring for herself and her home; meals, tidying up, a few moments of attention to the druid's pets, and always a cup of willow tea nearby for the pain from her aching arm. Gradually the embroidery on the deerskin took shape, the spirals neatly and meticulously sewn by firelight in the evenings before she retired for the night. And always, early the next morning, the stirrings of the tame animals in the cave roused her by sunup, to begin another long, busy day.

On the fifth day of the old druid's absence a raucous calling from the raven who roosted near the cave entrance roused Melangell from her evening meal and she went to look outside. The dirt ledge beyond the door had been scraped and scratched and she saw a trail of drying blood running under a nearby rowan bush. Inching her way toward it, she pushed the dense branches aside and saw, panting heavily, a young wounded badger with an ugly gash running down one flank. It raised its sleek head weakly to look at her, and fell back again. "Poor baby," she muttered, running her fingers down its heaving side.

"Come . . ." she said, slipping her good hand under its body and sliding it out from beneath the bush. The animal was heavy, though; too heavy for her to lift with one hand. Returning to the cave, she fetched a folded blanket onto which she slid the injured animal. She dragged it into the cave and near the fire; close enough for warmth but not near enough to frighten it. With a cleansing herbal wash she bathed the raw wound, and after applying a poultice of crushed leaves she bandaged the animal. Her arm now hurting from the exertion, she made herself a fresh cup of the painkilling willow tea and sat by the badger, watching it. It seemed to have calmed, and when it raised its curious black nose and looked around, she set a shallow bowl of fresh water before it. The badger lapped it eagerly, its dark eyes shining in the firelight. Scraping off some soft cheese, she offered it to the animal, and after sniffing the pieces, it began to eat.

"What brought you here, little one?" she wondered aloud. "Did you know a kindly man lives here—or was it me you sought?" Melangell finished her meal while keeping an eye on her patient, and when it fell into a weary sleep she resumed her evening embroidery.

She tended to the badger with her good hand for four more days. In the evenings, her day's embroidery done, she would lift it into her lap and rub her fingers through its gray fur, singing it softly to sleep while she watched the dancing firelight. And when, on the night of the ninth day since his departure, the old druid returned, he smiled and nodded at the sight of Melangell sleeping beneath her blanket, one arm curled around a small bandaged badger at her side.

"How was your trip?" she asked, wincing as the old man unwound the bandages from her upper arm. Blood from the wound had seeped and dried, and it pulled painfully when the bandages came off.

"Very successful!" he said, never taking his bright blue eyes from her arm. "I found my fern roots, and more besides. A fungus I have long sought; some seed-heads I can scatter in the valley come spring."

He paused and picked the last of the bandage loose, and Melangell's head began to reel from the sensitivity of the wounded arm.

"No . . . don't move it," he commanded. "The bone needs much more time to heal—many days."

Studying the girl's arm, he sat back on his heels and dropped the crusty bandage to the floor.

"I think I'll pound some comfrey roots to pack it in," he said, nodding absently to himself. He looked up at her and smiled. "Look if you must, but not if you are squeamish. It is not pretty."

Slowly Melangell looked down. A large jagged scab ran from under her upper arm, at an angle toward her shoulder, and back down again, almost to her elbow. The skin around it was vivid blue and purple from the shattered bone beneath.

"Dear Arnemetia!" she said in a shaky voice, looking away. "No wonder it hurts so. It looks hideous."

"Oh, no," he said, patting her hand, "it looks just as it should look. It was a very bad wound. Now let me crush the roots and apply them around your arm. Not only do they heal, they also dry and harden into a cast to hold the bones in place. Don't move even one finger of that arm while you wait. Let me tell you about my trip."

He fetched a sack of large brown roots, kept moist and plump in damp sand, and began mashing them on a flat stone.

"I saw many beautiful sights on my journey," he began. "Sunny hillsides still cloaked in late-autumn flowers . . . yellow and white and pink. A great misty waterfall surrounded by leaves the color of flame. A little grove of aspen trees, carpeted in emerald moss and bespangled with yellow leaves."

He paused as he recalled it.

"Aye," he said, resuming his work, "that was a sight worth a king's treasure. Gold, and emerald, and the silver-white trunks of the trees. A place where the hushed mystery of the gods reaches out and touches you; truly a sacred grove blessed by Nemetona, unlike the blood-soaked sanctuaries of my fellow druids."

He snorted a laugh and continued his tale.

"And my calling, little apple, was a true one, for I was needed. Three fine young men, newly banished for some small crime, were trying to build a shelter against the coming winter; a job they had never before attempted."

He grinned at the memory as, with skilled fingers, he began to pat the sticky mass of crushed roots onto Melangell's arm.

"Slowly . . . a little at a time, and let it dry before the next layer is applied, until we build up a solid amount," he explained.

She nodded and tried not to jerk in pain, despite his cautious efforts not to hurt her.

"The tea of ferns is steeping," he said, glancing at her pale face in concern. "You shall have some soon, and more tea for the pain."

"Yes," she whispered. "Go on with your story."

"Nice boys they were, but inexperienced. I gave them some advice, and spent a night in their new home. They were of your people, I believe. Damnonii?"

She nodded in surprise, and wondered if she might know them.

"Their names?" she asked. The old man only shrugged.

"We exchanged no names. They called me 'old father.' "

"That's not surprising," she suddenly realized, "for I do not know your name either!"

He looked at her again, his fingers a sticky mess, and a big smile crinkled his eyes.

"That is so! I hadn't realized. Names are so unimportant, are they not? It is Esus."

"Esus," she repeated softly while he patted another layer of root on her arm. "And these men—what of them? What was their crime? What did they look like?"

"Oh, a matter involving some slaves. They did not say. All warriors, I'll wager. Two fair ones, and the third with hair as black as a raven's wing."

He sensed a wave of tenseness sweep over her, even through his messy hands, and he looked at her curiously.

"You know them, then?" he asked, wiping his hands on a scrap of wool. "I could bring them here sometime, for I will be going back to take them some things they may need. The winter will be long and harsh for three inexperienced exiles. Would you like for me to—"

"No!" she gasped abruptly. "I do not . . . no . . ." Her face turned suddenly grim, and a disturbing glint of hatred shone through the fear in her eyes.

"All right, then." He patted her knee reassuringly. "Let me fetch your tea while the cast dries." Stiffly he rose to his feet and walked to the fire, nodding pensively in understanding.

That look on her face . . . that reaction—he must be the one she told me about. How odd, the ways of the All-Knowing.

"The young one sickens." Melangell fretted as Esus fixed their morning gruel. The little animal lay quietly on its side, its breathing rapid and shallow. The old druid turned from the fire and knelt beside the girl, helping her unwind the bandage from the badger's flank. Thick yellow matter clung to the cloth and oozed from the wound, and the druid shook his head absently.

"As I feared," he said. "Whatever animal seized this little one was a meat-eater, and their teeth and claws are always dirty. The dead flesh, you know. Poisons have taken hold; we must clean it at once, and then pray.

"This," he said, prying the lid from a small clay jar, "is a special soil we druids know about, and every good healer keeps some in supply. It comes from a secret glade near a spring, and is thrice-blessed by Arnemetia, Ialonus, and Coventina, for it contains a mysterious ingredient which stops the festering poisons of a wound. Packed against the injury and tied in place, it will cleanse it in a matter of days."

He extracted a fingerful of thick gray mud from the jar and pressed it to the gash down the badger's side. The animal flinched in pain at his touch, and Esus' eyes shone in sympathy.

"Its pain is great, poor thing," he said quietly. Covering the wound with the mud, he wrapped a clean cloth around it.

"Now let it rest while we eat," Esus suggested. He rose to leave, but Melangell lingered by the young animal. "I'll give it some tea," she said. "After it has had some sleep."

The night crept by, but Melangell stayed awake and sat near the fire, the suffering animal in her lap. Esus had long since fallen asleep, the hearthfire burned low, and outside the cave a cold wind whistled noisily. Pulling her cloak tighter around her neck, she gazed down at the badger and found her thoughts wandering to Nechtan, to the news Esus had brought her of his fate.

He must think I am dead, she mused, her fingers stroking the sleek black-striped head of the sleeping animal. Dead, by his own command, and for what? Injury to his pride. For that I was to die. . . .

The badger stirred, stretching one clawed foot stiffly and spreading its toes.

Poor thing, she thought. Such pain, such suffering. If only I could relieve it, help you somehow. . . . She looked at the creature, seeing and yet not seeing, her mind drifting back to Nechtan.

. . . And I could find him now, extract some revenge from him for what he did to me. Esus helps him to survive, and yet I, if I wanted, could seek his death.

The badger whimpered, a tiny, drawn-out sigh that spoke

eloquently of its sufferings. But this time pity moved Melangell, and she turned her attentions to the animal. Her hand slid over the bandage, but the animal did not stir . . . and yet she seemed to feel an ache, a queasiness, in the pit of her stomach when she did so. Could it be? she wondered. Is such a thing possible?

Another fevered sigh stirred the badger, and again her heart moved. Again her hands caressed the small body; again she felt the pain—its pain.

What is my hatred? she suddenly realized. Nursing my hurt like some wounded hero, when I could let it go if only I tried. And all the while this creature, this innocent, suffers real pain. I must turn my thoughts to this animal the gods have sent to me, and help it, and turn this hatred from my heart. Without doing that, I cannot be a clear vessel for the gods . . . and that is what I truly desire.

Without knowing what she did, or why, acting only on instinct and intuition, she focused on her concern and empathy. Let love heal you, she thought; little one, let some small measure of my health and strength infuse you, restore you, while your own fragile self is on the mend. I give it willingly to you . . . do not suffer so . . . take what you need of me.

Wearied, she drifted to sleep, still propped near the fire, as the first light of dawn glimmered over the purple hillsides beyond the cave. When Esus roused, he saw the girl slumped sideways in sleep, a look of tranquillity on her face, her good hand resting on her badger . . . the badger who now looked around bright-eyed and eager, hungry for some food.

I know not what she has done, he mused as the next evening fell, but the creature is hale and hearty. My potion should not have worked for days. What gifts does this girl possess? What rare talent for this child of Loucetius? I must teach her what I can, while there is time. She must learn, grow, expand, to the limits of her capabilities—which could very well exceed my own.

He glanced aside at the girl, one arm in a bandage, the other extended to feed her pet, and he shook his head again in disbelief.

"In pain herself, and yet she aches so for the pain of a little animal. Such a one as this is a rarity. How blessed am I that she comes in my lifetime! It will not be easy for her, nor for me." He sighed wearily. "Already she has passed through the White Martyrdom, the abandoning of family, friends, home. Now, I think, she approaches the Green Martyrdom —living in seclusion in the wilds of nature. I pray for her sake that she does not enter the Red Martyrdom—a bloody death to achieve her goal. And yet, if that is what Loucetius requires of her, who am I to question it? The rewards will so greatly exceed any suffering on her part."

"Well, little apple, today we remove your cast, so we may see how you fare for a few days without it. If all goes well, I must then go on another journey."

Esus looked at Melangell as she stirred a pot of barley by the fire, and she smiled in eager anticipation.

"Now! Can we do it now, while the gruel cooks? It takes so long, and I am so anxious to have this removed."

Laughing, he nodded and rose to his feet. "Sit on the bucket, and let me fetch a knife and some warm water. Then we'll see what there is to be seen."

Not waiting for him, she sat and began pulling the knots loose on the cloths that held her arm bandaged in place. By the time he returned to her side, most of the cloth hung loosely from her shoulder.

"Well, are we so eager for breakfast?" He chuckled, watching her feverish efforts.

"Oh, you have no idea the torment this has caused me," she said.

"I think I can well imagine! Now then, let's see what we have . . ." He pulled the last of the bandage free and dropped it to the floor. With the knife he broke loose the hard, dried roots that formed her cast. They came apart in large chunks and soon he was brushing the last bits of crumbs from her upper arm. She looked down at it apprehensively. The ugly red scab was now a clean pink scar, and the blue-and-purple bruises over the shattered bone had vanished. The arm looked healed, and almost as good as new.

Melangell looked at him and they smiled at each other.

"You did it! Esus, you healed me!"

"*We* did it," he corrected. "You were a good patient, as well."

She laughed and stretched the arm out tentatively.

"Be careful with it the first month or so," he cautioned. "The bone is not yet strong, and the muscles are weakened and will need rebuilding. Too much sudden stress could split the newly healed fractures again."

"Whatever you say!" she laughed, flexing her fingers and bending the arm. "This is the most wonderful feeling in the world!"

"Let's eat, then, and discuss my upcoming trip," he said, gathering his things from the floor.

"I see why you want to return to visit the three men, but why now, Esus?" she worried aloud over barley, wild honey, and fresh cheese. "The winter is upon us, the trip is long, and . . ."

"And I am so old?" His blue eyes crinkled merrily at her. "Not so old as all that. Living in the wilderness ages you faster, that's all. I promised them I would return, with some things which they might need. They can get to no civilized place to acquire the little comforts we all take for granted, and I have been lately trading my services with some nearby farmers for a few things. See?" he said, pointing to the wicker stand. "Fresh honey, more grains, newly made soap . . ."

"And when will you be leaving?" she asked slowly.

"In two more days. Time enough to see how your arm is doing. Gather a bit more firewood for you, make other preparations . . ."

She nodded and fell into quiet thought.

"The dark-haired one," she said suddenly, looking down awkwardly at the rough table. Esus paused in mid-bite, waiting for her to continue.

"Will you give him something from me, and not let him know where it comes from? I . . . I am afraid for him to know I am here, or even still alive."

She glanced up at him almost shyly, and his wise old eyes could read volumes behind the look on her face. He swallowed the cheese and nodded.

"Of course . . . yes," he said.

She rose without a word and walked to her sleeping pallet, looked among her few belongings, and returned.

"Here," she said, placing the embroidered deerskin pouch by his elbow. "The stag . . . he was your friend. You don't mind, do you?" she asked apprehensively. He gazed at the delicate design in silence, the stitches as tiny and perfect as seeds. Picking up the bag, he looked at her in surprise.

"No, I don't mind. But you . . . this means a great deal to you. Are you sure you want me to give it to this man?"

She nodded solemnly and turned away. "Yes," she said over her shoulder as she walked to the cave entrance. "I have . . . an old tally to settle with him, and I wish to do it this way—with forgiveness."

He nodded in sudden understanding. The girl knows, he realized. She knows. She wishes to become a clear vessel for the gods, and before that all else must fall. Even her hatred, he mused, his fingers closing around the soft pouch. Even that.

When he returned many days later, Esus knew by the look on her face and the quiet manner in which she conducted herself that the girl had put her days of solitude to good use. It comes, he reflected; as surely as a woman about to give birth, her time is upon her. Ollovidius the All-Knowing has decreed it; she cannot escape her destiny.

Day by day she wandered the lonely valley, his walking stick in one hand, an old black druid's robe enshrouding her head and body. The badger she had healed always stayed nearby, scratching the soil while she sat on a rock by an ice-rimmed pool, or sleeping contentedly in her lap as the evening sun warmed them. Many a time when night approached Esus would have to fetch her before darkness fell, so lost in thought was she. He felt for her, he sensed her struggle, but there was nothing he could do. It was her battle alone, to win herself . . . or to lose.

"He liked the pouch you gave him," Esus said to the girl over their evening meal one day, as a fresh snowstorm gathered force outside the cave.

"What?" she asked, seeming startled by his voice.

133

"The deerskin pouch—the young warrior was very impressed with it," the old man repeated patiently, eyeing her in concern. She had not been eating properly; her face looked bony and pale. She nodded blankly, as if she really didn't care.

"Melangell, it will come. You cannot kill yourself seeking it," he said, grasping her small hands in his across the table. She looked up at him dumbly.

"When it comes, it comes," he repeated. "Until that time, all your starvation and neglect will not hasten it."

"But I must . . ." she whispered. He shook his head vehemently in reply.

"Yes," she insisted. "Time is short. The trees—do you know, they slumber? Deep and dreamless, like the sighing of a thousand giants . . . and I hear them. Or, I feel them . . . yet not with my ears, nor my skin. They sleep, so peacefully . . ." Her voice died away and he stared at her in open admiration.

"Melangell, child, you have a rare gift. A very rare gift indeed. It must not be abused. If you waste away to nothing, of what avail is this gift then? In a hundred years, or a thousand, whenever the All-Knowing decides it, you will be reborn, but by then it will be too late—too late for our people. You owe it to us all, to yourself, and to Loucetius, who watches over you, not to destroy yourself for what you seek."

He held her eyes with his own until she looked away sadly.

"They haunt me. The trees, the stones, all whisper, yet I cannot hear what they say. I listen, but I do not understand."

"Do not try so hard, Melangell. You must let go, let it happen, be this empty vessel we spoke of. In your very act of trying you drive it away. Does the vessel go looking for the wine, or does it wait for the wine to be brought?"

"A hundred years, or a thousand," she snorted cynically. "And what will the world hold then? Does anyone know? Has anyone seen? Will our people still live; will our gods still rule? Why not seek the peace of the gods right now, and avoid the terrors of that future?"

She looked up at him again, her gaze intense, level, insistent, and this time it was he who looked away.

"You ask a question, child, that no one can answer," he said, almost sadly, and they finished their meal in silence.

He awoke in the night, restless, haunted by the girl, and when he looked to her straw pallet, to his horror he saw she was gone. Quickly he stood, pulling a heavy blanket around his shoulders. Her black cloak, the walking stick, the badger—all gone. Gods above! he thought in panic, rushing to the cave entrance, and even before he reached it he could feel the icy blasts of wind, hear the howling snow outside. He stood at the doorway, dumbly peering into the swirling black-and-white madness before him. Her footprints had already vanished beneath the snow.

Loucetius, help her, he prayed desperately as tears of dread sprang to his eyes. If ever she needed you, it is now. Loucetius above, help her. . . .

This is all so easy, Melangell thought absently as she stood on a huge white boulder and watched the black gash of the stream rush madly past her feet.

The wind carries me on; the snow obscures all distinctions. I need do nothing, think nothing, be nothing. Flying must be like this—so free and unencumbered. Just *being;* you, alone, and nothing else in the world.

She turned her face up to the stinging white flakes and closed her eyes.

"No up or down, no high or low, no right or wrong. No nothing. Is it these which bind us to this world of death, we people of the darkness; we fools? These distinctions, these limitations?"

The young badger by her feet began to shiver violently and she tucked it inside the cloak, against her warm body.

Is this the secret known by all but mankind? she wondered, turning away from the water. All of creation accepts, except us. All are happy in their existence, except us. We must constantly strive, change, create, destroy. What peace is in it?

Probing the deep drifts with the walking stick, she crept from the boulder and, turning her back to the wind, continued to walk through the madly swirling nighttime in silence, one arm cradling the badger close. At last, tired from fighting the wind and sleepy from the cold, she paused by a huge gray shape looming out of the darkness . . . an old mossy oak tree, leaning hungrily toward the stream. She looked at it silently, pensively, but it was still. Nodding as if in agreement with herself, she stepped around to the downwind side of the broad trunk, kicked the snow aside with one foot, and sat down. Pressing her back against the comforting bark, she pulled the hood of the black robe down over her forehead, curled up on her side, and drifted to sleep.

Esus sat huddled near the fire drinking warm tea, all ideas of sleep gone from his mind. A new chill shook him with every howl of wind he heard from outside, and he desperately tried to reach Melangell, extend some of his strength to her, protect her.

But always, always, one thought lumbered heavily across his mind and back again, demolishing all his best efforts on the girl's behalf:

This one small girl has shown you up, shown you for what you really are.

Gods above! He swallowed, closing his eyes. One who needs me more than any has ever needed me, and I only think of myself, my failure.

I, who claimed for nearly a lifetime to seek wisdom, realize now how far short of it I stopped. And when one comes who not only seeks it too, but sets out to find it, no matter the cost, I try to stop her, to hold her back. I had reached a point, a comfortable point, and there I halted. And yet she . . . did she make me uncomfortable? Did I see myself, my own failure, reflected in her earnest efforts, like a false reflection of the moon in a pond? She abandons all in her search, maybe even her life . . . and I? I have always feared such abandonment, though I never realized it till now.

He lowered his face to his folded arms and began to sob dryly.

Gods above! Loucetius, help her, and . . . help me.

* * *

She arose . . . or did she? Looking back, she saw herself lying at the base of the tree, partly buried in the snow. And yet she walked . . . she could see . . .

Looking around her in awe, she felt as a spider must feel on a moonlit night when his silken web turns to bright silver. For all creation shone around her, silver-white and glimmering, all connected by gauzes and filaments and fine strands. All rustling and tinkling and seeming to laugh with a joy at living that was unknown to her. A joy, not for this reason or that, but just for the fact of existence . . . of being . . . for that, and no other, reason.

"Argadnel," she marveled. "Argadnel, the fabled Silver Land."

Here the wind did not touch her, the snow did not sting, the cold did not penetrate. Here was life, a life of which she, whoever she was, was a part. A vital, functioning part, as valued and necessary as the smallest laughing leaf, the busily humming forest mold underfoot, the water caressing the fish, the rock enfolding the stream. Like fingers on her hand, arms and legs on her body, all were separate, each with its own function, yet interconnected, all a part, all one. She could no more destroy one of them than she could destroy a part of her own self . . . for they were a part of her, and she was a part of them.

She turned in amazement as the laughing chorus seemed to bid her a joyous farewell.

There was no secret message to learn, no mystery to unfold, nothing that she did not already know, deep in her heart of hearts, if only she had been still and listened for it.

Sighing happily, she curled herself once more around the young badger and contentedly fell asleep.

Esus stumbled awkwardly through the deep drifts, pulling himself forward by roots and branches, his mittened hands cold and wet.

"Melangell!" he called again, and again his cry was quickly absorbed into the enveloping silence of the snows.

Gods above! I will never find her in all this snow, he thought as panic gripped at his heart. Not till spring; not till it melts; and by then it will be too late.

"Melangell!" he called again, defying the fate he feared for her.

How could I be so warm? the girl wondered. I am not cold at all.

Protectively she felt for the badger and found it still safe next to her body.

I should be dead . . . frozen. Dead. Am I? I think not . . . I don't feel dead . . . but what does death feel like? How can I be so warm?

At a soft sound by her ear she opened her eyes in surprise and found her startled gaze falling into a pair of eyes, golden wolf's eyes. Nechtan's eyes.

She closed her eyes in weariness. Nechtan. So he has found me . . . he has sheltered me . . . he has kept me alive.

Esus rounded a bend in the stream and his eyes fell on the partly concealed black cloak the girl had worn, a dark blob against the stark whiteness of the morning snow. And beside her, a huge furry mass which, as soon as the old man came into view, suddenly stood upright, turned, and leveled a gaze at him; an unearthly yellow-eyed stare that raised the hair on the back of Esus' neck.

Then the great wolf turned and silently loped off, up the hillside, and was gone.

Sobbing in relief, the old man rushed forward, pushed the snow aside, and felt the girl's face.

She was unconscious, but she was alive . . . warm, and alive.

He lifted her in his arms. She still clung protectively to her little pet. Before turning to stumble his way back to the cave, he paused in awed silence to gaze at the huge wolf prints vanishing up the snowy hillside.

The wolf had saved her life.

"Thank you," he whispered into the cold morning air, then headed back to their home.

He knew what to do for her. He dragged his largest oaken tub near the fire and filled it with warm water. Stripping off the girl's wet clothes, he lowered her frail body into the water.

Nechtan . . . Nechtan . . . he thought, and a chill ran through his stomach. He knew he had seen those yellow wolf's eyes before.

But when Melangell roused and weakly opened her eyes, all other thoughts fled from his mind, for he could see in the luminous green depths of her gaze that her instincts had been true, her quest a successful one.

The girl had found what she sought.

Her appetite for knowledge grew insatiable, as one recovering from illness feels a desperate need for food. She questioned him about his life, about druids, about the spirit. Their talks by the warming fire often stretched far into the night, their closeness bonding firmer as the winter day by day passed to spring. He told her of the three classes of druids; the first, the guatator, who performed the rituals and chanted the religious invocations. The souls of these were feeling the first stirrings of religion. The highest, the semnotheoi, those few who like himself abandoned the world as their need to search grew to a passion. Such a one might be living his last lifetime on this earth. And the great middle ground of wise men, the druids themselves, those whose souls were so advanced from many lessons learned in past lives that they were no longer bound by tribal laws and customs. They were beyond the allures of the world around them. Even kings held them in awe, for they could unmake rulers, pass judgments, or stop wars. Their learning was immense and covered all fields; their brotherhood was a binding one, lasting even beyond death, aiding one another from this world to the next.

"Spring comes, your health is fully restored; why don't you come with me on my journey?" Esus questioned as they sat by the hearth in the brief evening of a late winter's day. She looked up from her sewing and shrugged.

"I don't know. Is there a reason for me to go? I am happy here."

"You can gain experience, and you can be helping others who need help. Sometimes it is too much of a job for one old man like myself."

"Oh, 'not so old as all that.'" she smiled, biting off the thread. "But yes, I will go with you, and offer what help I can."

They left several days later, each with a black robe, a walking stick, and a satchel of food and medicines. Spring was coming, and the melting snows had swollen their stream to a dangerous size. The two went directly up the hills and over to the rolling grasslands beyond, rather than attempt to descend the valley and follow the stream.

They walked at an easy pace, enjoying the sun and the warmth and the newly awakening earth around them. Melangell had thrown back the hood of her cloak and let her hair blow free in the spring winds, and Esus was struck again by what a beautiful girl she was. He felt so proud of her, this odd little orphan he had saved; as proud and protective as if he was her own true father and she was the child of his own love, a child such as he had never known before.

"Let us rest here and eat," he said when they entered the edge of a dark woods. "I'll tell you about our first stop. A large, splendid farm. The son, a young man of eighteen, is deaf, a mute, and has the mind of a child; but he is an attentive boy, kind and pleasant and eager to please one and all. I always stop by on my rounds, prescribe a few potions, but the boy is really beyond help. It makes the family feel better, though, and that is a benefit to all. They still hope for some miracle to cure him."

A stocky man of middle age, his hair liberally sprinkled with gray, came to greet the two travelers when they entered the stockaded yard of his spacious hilltop farmstead. A large hound frisked around them as the man heartily clapped Esus on the shoulder.

"Welcome, friend!" he exclaimed in obvious delight. "We did not expect you so soon! And your pretty young friend? Who might she be?" he said, his gray eyes falling on the girl at the old druid's side.

"An apprentice. I am teaching her," Esus replied. The man's eyebrows rose in surprise.

"In truth!" he exclaimed. Esus nodded.

"She has rare skills which I myself do not possess," the old druid said, looking down affectionately at Melangell.

"That is unusual." The man smiled at her. "Perhaps she can be of some benefit to my son. Come! Come!"

The man's farmstead was of unusual design, a cluster of round wood huts interconnected to form a large, rambling dwelling. A serving girl waiting at the door ushered Melangell into a small room with a packed earthen floor covered with clean, sweet-smelling rushes. The servant poured several buckets of steaming water into a large tub sitting by the central hearth. She placed rough wool cloths and a large chunk of soap on a barrel nearby and waited, still without a word, while Melangell undressed and handed the girl her dirty clothes.

Melangell sank down in the delicious bath and closed her eyes. What a luxury! She sighed. What a delight! Lazily she scrubbed the dirt from her hair and body, dried herself on a clean scrap of cloth, and unfolded the clothes that had been left on the bench—a long-sleeved gown of pale blue wool with a wide band of embroidery around the neck, a lavishly patterned green-and-white short cape, and small leather slippers decorated with braid. Such fine things! she thought in astonishment; these are even better than the clothes Maia gave me. This man must be a very prosperous farmer indeed, and very kind too.

A tap on the door interrupted her thoughts, and the serving girl entered, a comb and other things in her hand.

"Your hair, lady," she said, motioning to the barrel. "Feasting will begin soon, in your honor."

Melangell allowed the girl to comb and dry her long, honey-colored hair. The girl braided portions, curled some around her face, and pinned it all atop Melangell's head with several long pins of black jet.

"Genann, a son of my master, waits to escort you to dinner," the girl said, fastening the cape around Melangell's shoulders with a large circular gold brooch.

"Is he the one who is . . . is unwell?" Melangell asked. The girl shook her head.

"No, lady, that would be Donall. You will meet him shortly. Genann is the oldest son, Donall the youngest. There is also Cai, a year younger than Genann, and two sisters."

The serving girl stood back, satisfied with her efforts as she looked Melangell up and down with a critical eye.

"You look very beautiful, lady," she remarked, a hint of envy in her voice.

"Thank you." Melangell smiled. Gods above! she thought to herself as she walked to the door. I feel like a queen. This is all so splendid—how must a real queen live?

Genann stood in the hallway, idly wondering what this young druidess his father had mentioned would look like—and living with the old hermit, at that! Doubtless some wild-eyed, wild-haired little witch, wearing leaves from the trees and living off barks and mosses. Well, he sighed, shifting his feet in impatience, he could manage to walk even a witch down the corridor and to her seat in the central hall, if that's what his father wanted. Once . . .

He looked up when the rough wooden door opened, and he straightened in shock at the lovely woods-spirit who suddenly appeared before him, looking uncertainly up at his face with eyes as green as . . . as green as . . . By the songs of Maponus, words failed him! He, the family poet, who had composed many a song for many a pretty girl, was at a loss for words.

"Genann?" she said quietly, her voice as soft and melodious as a brook. He nodded dumbly. Gods above, she is lovely, he thought, staring at her; a tiny oval face, a delightful little figure, hair like honey piled atop her head, a soft full mouth with just a hint of a smile as she waited for him to speak. But those eyes . . . those eyes . . .

"At your service, my lady," he said, collecting his wits and extending his forearm to her. She placed one tiny hand lightly on it and together they walked to the great central hall, she in bemused silence, he in awkward uncertainty.

Conn's extensive family had gathered along two low wooden tables in the central hall, set with his best silver tableware from Gaul; brothers, daughters, sons, aunts and uncles, a few good friends. A visitor was always a treat, but someone as valued and well-liked as Esus meant special feasting. And the word of his mysterious young apprentice had quickly spread; everyone wanted to see her, and to see if she could help Conn's poor, unfortunate son.

142

Genann felt the girl's hand grow tense on his forearm when they neared the noisy hall, and he knew she must be afraid. Protectively he placed his other hand atop hers.

"I will stay with you. Do not be afraid," he whispered when they reached the doorway, and she smiled a shy smile up at him that melted his heart completely.

Gods above! he thought dizzily. Now I know what the Isles of the Blessed must be like, for surely I am dead now, and gone to my reward.

A hush fell over the room when they entered, and Melangell felt too many eyes boring into her in curiosity. Oh, to run! she thought; to flee! Back to my quiet little valley, my gentle friends.

"Ah! Here they are at last!" Conn boomed jovially, rising from his low squatting-stool and walking over to them. "You all know my eldest son, Genann the Poet," he announced. "And this must be . . . Melangell, is it?" She nodded awkwardly and he wrapped one arm around her in a fond embrace. Genann saw her hand slip helplessly from his arm. Father! he thought angrily. Don't do that. Let her be . . . she is afraid . . .

Desperately Melangell's eyes searched the sea of strange faces, curious faces, a few hostile female faces, a few obviously lusty male faces, looking for Esus . . . Esus . . .

At last she saw him, seated cross-legged at the far table, almost unrecognizable in a clean blue robe. Their eyes locked for a moment, pleading desperation in her face. He understood her distress and rose to his feet.

"Conn, let your son fulfill his duty, as you asked him to," Esus said, nodding toward the sullen Genann.

"Oh . . . yes, surely," Conn said, and returned the girl to Genann's side. "We welcome you and are very pleased to have you visit with us for a few days." He nodded to his son, who proceeded to escort her around the blazing hearth, to her seat across the table and down a few places from the old druid, feeling himself swelling with pride at all the envious male eyes that followed them as they walked.

"Move!" he hissed through clenched teeth to a gangly young cousin, who would be sitting next to the girl. Not wishing to argue with the muscular young poet, the boy quickly jumped up, knocking his low stool backward in his haste, and moved elsewhere along the feasting boards as laughter welled up around them.

"Eh, Esus, you might be losing your pupil before long!" Conn roared. Melangell felt her face flush with embarrassment. Genann shook his head in good-natured amusement. Were I so lucky! he thought, casting a sideways look at the silent girl as she lowered herself daintily to a stool, sitting cross-legged as was proper for a woman, rather than squatting as men did. Were I so lucky!

Melangell, her stomach in nervous knots, picked and nibbled at the overflowing trencher a serving girl handed her. Where is this Donall? she thought curiously, taking furtive peeks around the hall when she thought no one else was looking. And then she spied him. She knew in her soul it must be he. A nice-looking young man, sitting silently at his father's side, carefully eating small chunks of meat with a little knife. She gazed at him, her eyes running over his face, his dark hair, his slim hands. Genann turned and looked at her, puzzled, and soon others nearby fell silent and watched the girl stare, trancelike, at the boy. The surrounding noises faded to a buzz, the faces melted, the room wavered and disappeared as she probed deeper and deeper into the young man's heart.

Esus folded his hands on the rough board before him and watched her curiously. Suddenly the boy looked up and his brown eyes instantly fell on Melangell. Staring at her a moment, a perplexed look pulling at his features, he abruptly stood; and Conn, who reached for the boy's arm, lowered his hand at the sight of Esus sternly shaking his head at him.

The boy quickly walked around the tables as the entire room watched in silence. Melangell turned around, her back to the table, and waited for him. He approached shyly, and she held out her arms to him without a word. He fell to his knees before her, buried his face in her lap, and, like a little child, began to sob loudly. The girl wrapped her arms around his shoulders, patted him consolingly, and laid her cheek against his freshly washed hair. Conn's mouth fell open in dumb astonishment.

Melangell stood, one arm around the crying boy, and they

walked to the door. Genann glanced uncertainly at Esus, who nodded once, and the young man rose to his feet and followed them from the room.

He found them at the far end of the dark corridor, a few slaves clustered curiously around them. Angrily he waved them away. The girl looked over her shoulder at him, and her eyes held a strange, distant look he had not seen before.

"Outside . . ." she whispered. He stepped past them and led the way to the farmyard. She walked his brother to the chopping block where firewood was cut, seated him on it, and crouched in front of him, lifting his chin. She wiped away his tears as the boy sniffled and sobbed, his eyes full of open adoration. *He looks as if he has always waited for her to come,* Genann thought in awe as he watched them. *By Arnemetia! What a miracle if he can be helped by this little woods-spirit!*

Genann sat on the rear of a nearby wagon and waited for her next move. She stroked the boy's face, his hair, gently, tenderly, like a mother would do, all the while peering intently into his eyes. Donall's sobs subsided and he seemed to be trying to return her gaze. Genann realized she was speaking quietly to his brother, and he leaned forward to listen.

"It's all right . . ." she whispered, their eyes locked and her fingers never stopping their movement. "All is forgiven . . . do not punish yourself . . . there is no need . . . it is all right." She continued to whisper to him until the sun vanished and the stars came out. Then she stood and tightly embraced him to her. Genann started to rise, thinking she was through, but she crouched and began the litany again. When his father came to see them, Genann motioned him away. The night crept on, the guests bedded down in the central hall, and still the girl continued. *It is useless,* Genann thought to himself. *He cannot be cured.*

But she persisted and Genann sat shivering in the back of a hauling wagon as the sun began creeping above the far horizon. He had just started to doze, slumped against the side of the wagon, when a sound jolted him upright and sent his father running from the house.

"Ma . . ." a voice said. "Ma . . ."

Only a sound, but a sound nevertheless. Donall spoke!

Genann stood in shocked disbelief as his brother rose, inexpressible joy lighting his face.

"Donall!" he heard his father gasp. Melangell rose and turned toward the wagon, weariness etching her features. She looked at Genann tiredly and took a few tottering steps.

"I . . ." she began, and collapsed to the ground. Genann rushed forward, lifted her in his arms, and quickly carried her back into the house.

Esus exited the small storage room near the central hall and quietly closed the door.

"She will be all right. She is just worn out from the night's efforts. All her healings seem to come at great personal cost to herself," he told the little knot of people outside the doorway.

"Praise be to Arnemetia!" Conn said with great emotion. "I must offer her a sacrifice. What a miracle she has sent to us this day!"

"Can I see her?" Genann asked. "Are you sure she is all right? When I picked her up, in the pale dawning light, she looked white and sick and . . . in pain."

Esus smiled at him kindly. "Oh, she is quite all right, but for now she sleeps. Perhaps you can come later in the day and bring her some light food, for she will be hungry when she awakens. A little wine, perhaps. Nothing too rich."

The tall young man nodded solemnly, his gray eyes grave with responsibility.

"You seem to have experience with this sort of thing, Esus," Conn said, throwing one burly arm around the druid's thin shoulders as they walked off together. "She has done this before, then?"

"A few times, but only with animals," the old man replied. "Never before with a person. I am as amazed as you, Conn; truly I am."

Genann sat on the earthen floor outside the girl's door till evening, plucking his small harp and thinking about her. When the door opened, a serving girl emerged, and seemed startled to see him sitting there.

"She is awake?" he asked, standing. The servant nodded.

"Stay with her while I fetch some food," he instructed. "The druid told me what she needs now."

He propped his harp against the wall and strode off to the cooking hearth.

A short time later he returned carrying a large wooden trencher. Entering the room, he motioned the serving girl to leave. As he turned, his eyes fell in pity on the tired face of the young apprentice, propped up on a goosedown pallet, her hair loosely falling around her shoulders, and still wearing the same light blue gown of the night before. She looks like a different person, he thought as he placed the trencher on the floor beside her. Melangell looked at him and smiled a wan little smile.

"Hello," she said softly, and he found himself wanting to sweep her into his arms in a wild, sweet embrace, until all her strength and beauty had returned. Poor little dove, he thought, squatting by the bed.

"Esus said you would be hungry when you awakened, so I have brought you a few things," he explained, helping her prop herself up a little higher.

"Your brother Donall—is he well?" she asked, and he nodded.

"More than well! He is trying to learn to speak all by himself. Eighteen years of silence to catch up with. He wanted to come to see you, but we wouldn't allow it."

She smiled and nodded in satisfaction. "Good—I'm glad that he's better," she said. "It will take time, but he will learn. I am only sorry I could do nothing for his hearing, and so little for his mind. It will improve some, I think, as he learns to speak, but it will never be normal. I am sorry."

He looked at her in astonishment.

"You've done more than anyone else ever could! He is better now than ever before. Don't apologize! It is we who should apologize for inflicting this on you. We had no idea what it would mean to you; the pain inflicted."

She shook her head and smiled slightly. "It costs a farmer to farm and a warrior to fight. We all have **our** jobs; this is mine. Now, some ale, please, for I am very thirsty."

He handed her an engraved bronze goblet, helping to steady it in her trembling hands, and she drank it eagerly.

"Here," he said, "I'll hold the food for you while you eat. You are so weak!"

She looked up gratefully into his gentle gray eyes, studying his shaggy light brown hair and clean-shaven face. She could smell the faint sweet odor of vervain-water about him; he must have freshened himself before coming to see her. He is quite a nice-looking man, she realized; and so kind, so caring, so unlike all the hotheaded warriors she was used to. When he turned his face aside to tear off a chunk of warm bread for her, she saw the cleanness of his profile in the lamplight, soft yet with an underlying strength of purpose.

"I'll be fine by tomorrow," she reassured him. "Food and rest are all I need."

His slight nod of reply didn't hide the worried look she detected in his eyes.

She awoke in the night to the achingly sweet sound of a harp being played far off in the darkness. Genann's harp, no doubt, she thought as she closed her eyes and listened to it in delight. How pure it is, how clear and sweet. It reminds me of the soft tinkling music of the trees and waters and rocks—all of creation—on that night in the Silver Land. Such a short while ago—a short while, yet now it seems like forever . . . and look what I have done! Me, an ignorant slave girl, and they all think I am a wizard. Already they come to me, asking for cures. I feel sorry for them, but I am no magician. I cannot cure every kitchen burn and stomach-ache in the land!

She rolled onto her side and pulled the blanket up to her neck. Gods above! she thought in fear. What have I done to myself? What's to become of me now?

Slowly each crystal-pure note of the harp lulled her back to sleep.

Conn slammed his fist angrily onto the table as he glared at his oldest son.

"By the gods, you will *not* go with her," he repeated. Genann stared ahead stubbornly, his jaw clenched.

"You are a moonstruck calf, that is all," Conn tried again. "Granted, she is a lovely creature, but she is an apprentice druidess, boy! What would you expect of her? Doing your washing and bearing your babies?"

Genann shook his head, a glint of triumph in his eyes.

"I have talked with Esus. Yes, she has powers, and he does teach her things he knows, but she is really no druidess. She has had none of the formal education; she has never been accepted at a druids' school. She has never even applied. She is just a girl . . . a beautiful girl I want for my own," Genann retorted.

"No!" Conn roared, rising to his feet, his face flushing red. "I, too, have spoken to Esus; he says the girl has greater powers and abilities than he has ever seen. He fears all these fools pestering her to cure their backaches only upset her. He says she needs peace, quite, solitude . . . *solitude,* boy." He glared at his son. "He will return with her to their home at dawn tomorrow, and no one but I knows where that home is, and he has asked me to keep it that way. She cannot be bothered by everyone in creation, boy, and that includes you. Now, go. I will not hear of this again. Pine for her till the end of your days if you must, but you will not go with her! That's all there is to be said on the matter."

Anger storming across his face, the young man turned and strode from the room, his fists clenched in futile rage at his sides.

"Walk with me . . . please . . . after we eat," Genann whispered to Melangell as they sat for the evening meal. She tilted her head slightly and nodded.

"Yes, for a short while. I have many things to do," she replied, and his heart fell. He knew what those things must be—preparations for leaving.

He ate his meal hurriedly, in strained silence, not responding to the jests of his brother Cai or the teasings of his younger sisters. Only Esus didn't seem puzzled by his subdued manner; he had seen that look on a young man's face many times before. Genann seemed to be waiting for the girl to finish eating, and when she was through he quickly stood beside her and walked her from the room, much to Conn's obvious annoyance. Esus shrugged mildly when Conn looked in his direction, and that small gesture seemed to cool his anger a bit . . . but he still did not like the boy openly defying him like that. He would see to it later . . . tomorrow, when his guests had gone.

Melangell walked silently at Genann's side as the sun sank behind the hills to the west, painting the sky in vivid pinks and purples, and once again he felt the same overwhelming ache of longing for her . . . *lovesick, I am truly lovesick, just as the poets sing about,* he thought sadly as they strolled out of the farmyard and down the slope of the dun, pausing at the edge of the surrounding forest.

"You wish to speak to me?" Melangell asked him, turning to watch the brilliant sunset behind the hill. The sounds of the farm settling down for the night drifted on the evening air; cows lowed comfortably, geese cackled, a serving girl called to another, a gate creaked loudly on stiff hinges. Genann looked down awkwardly at his feet, unsure of what to say, and prodded a rock with the toe of his soft leather boot.

"You could poke at the rocks by the house," she teased him. He looked at her and was startled to see her staring at him with that same intense look she'd used on his brother.

"I need no cures," he muttered, looking away.

"I think you do," she replied, and he found himself compelled to look at her lovely face once more.

"I do not even consider asking you to stay here," he said, taking her small hand in his, "but let me come with you." She shook her head firmly.

"I am not asking to wed you. Just let me be there where you are. I will be your faithful guard, your servant, your harpist . . . anything."

She shook her head again.

"I am skilled with a spear. I can play a harp, compose tunes to amuse you . . . anything you wish I will do for you. Anything!"

The pleading desperation on his face hurt her deeply, but she had to shake her head once more at his entreaties. "I must be alone, Genann. Esus and I are different. We live differently; we have different needs and requirements. You think you could live with us, but the difficulties of our lives would soon prove unbearable. Look at the home you are used to living in! Look at all the comforts and luxuries! You have never lived as we do. You could not bear it."

"No! I would! What a small price to pay—"

"You are besotted, Genann."

He looked down and closed his fingers tightly around her hand.

"My father says I am moonstruck."

"And he is right. No, Genann. Stay here in your life. Remember me fondly to the end of your days, if you must; I would be flattered, as any woman would. But I must go back to my life, and you must stay in yours."

She looked at his crestfallen face in pity. "I am sorry for this hurt that I have caused you," she said quietly, and he looked at her, his gray eyes two pools of misery.

"Yes . . . I see . . ." he said, his voice strained. "May . . . may I tell you good-bye here, now, in private?"

She smiled that dazzling smile up at him as she nodded, and he felt his heart, his life, everything, shatter into a million pieces. Slowly, tentatively, he wrapped his arms around her tiny body in a gentle embrace, closing his eyes for one ecstatic moment as he felt the warmth of her against him, smelled the soft scent of her hair beneath his cheek. Then he released her and hastily turned away, before she could see the tears in his eyes.

"Good-bye," she said, lightly touching the long sleeve of his tunic before turning and climbing the hill back to the farm.

Genann walked quickly into the edge of the forest and looked up in quiet desperation as the stars began to appear in the darkening sky.

"Gods above, I will never love another," he swore. Clenching his eyes shut, he lowered his forehead to the rough trunk of a nearby tree and began to cry softly.

Melangell could hear a loud thud-thud-thud when they walked out into the front yard to leave the next morning, and knew it was Genann, angrily practicing his spear throws behind the stables. He did not come to bid them good-bye. With parting gifts from Conn added to their satchels, she and Esus walked through the gate and down the hill, toward home.

151

Genann watched over the palisade in silence until the tall druid and the tiny girl, both in their old black robes, had disappeared into the forest. Bitterly he seized his spear and heaved it at the straw target once more.

"Well, you seem to have had a profound effect on two young men at Conn's house." Esus smiled at Melangell as they ate their first meal back at their cave. She looked up shyly and tore a chunk of bread free with her fingers—good bread, one of Conn's parting gifts.

"How did you do it?" he persisted.

"Oh, he just seems to have fallen in love with me. I did nothing to encourage him," she said, mischief in her eyes.

"Not Genann, poor boy! Everyone could see how he felt about you, and no one could condemn his taste. No, his brother Donall."

"Yes, Donall." She nodded solemnly, gazing down at the food in thought. "It was strange, very strange. As if I recognized him from somewhere. And then I knew—in another lifetime, he had strangled me. His spirit then suffered for it by his muteness, so I forgave him, totally and completely. I tried to reach his soul, to convince it, and I guess I succeeded somehow. As to his other afflictions, I cannot say. But the one that was linked to me no longer exists. That is all I can tell you."

"And he knew?" Esus asked after pondering her words. The girl nodded.

"When I have tried to reach the minds of other people, they are jumbled, clouded, full of conflicts and fears and falseness, like a churning, muddy river. But his was pure and simple and clean, like a fresh stream where you can see the bottom and watch the fish swimming among the stones. People may pity him his afflictions, but he has one thing they don't—peace of mind. In that, he is luckier than they are."

Esus gazed at her in silence as she returned to her meal. She never stops surprising me! he mused. Instinctive wisdom and knowledge such as is usually found in a very old, experienced druid. Perhaps this life of hers is only the culmination of something that began long, long ago.

"I am very tired," she said suddenly. "I think I will go to bed now."

He nodded affectionately at her. "Good night, my dear," he said. "Sleep well."

Melangell awoke in the night, screaming in terror. Esus stumbled to her side, rocking her in his arms to calm her. "Hush, little apple," he whispered, stroking her hair. "It is all over now . . . all over. It was a bad dream, and now it is gone. Hush . . ."

She clenched his shoulder and looked at him with a haunted face.

"You . . ." she choked, "you were dead, on an altar of Loucetius . . . you were dead . . . and the rest of the world was dying, dying . . ."

She moaned and clung to him desperately as new sobs shook her body.

"No . . . no," she gasped, and he patted her back consolingly.

"It is all right," he repeated, but inside he felt his blood turn to ice at her words, chilled to his very soul.

Spring crept into summer, warm and lush with wildflowers and birds, young fruits forming on the bushes and animals frolicking in the hills. Melangell spent most of her time outdoors, enjoying the beauties of the druid's valley and trying to drive the memory of the nightmare from her mind.

Esus sat by the stream, patiently braiding grasses to make a basket, while Melangell wandered the valley looking for suitable stems he could use.

"I think," she decided, "that I will go down to the mouth of the valley where the ground levels out. The soil is wetter and I should find more rushes growing there."

He nodded as he worked. "These should last me for a while. I'll have to finish this tomorrow, anyway, for the light will soon be going." He stilled the hooked bone weaving needle and glanced up at her. "Be back by supper."

She nodded, picked up a small knife, and scampered over the rocks toward the flatter hills. From a distance she could see the feathery grass heads waving in the breeze, and she smiled. The rushes were, indeed, plentiful there. Quickening her pace, she hurried to the spot and began to select and cut the best, most supple stems, putting them aside on a dry rock. She did not notice as the sun crept down the sky, nor did she see the horses trotting up from the south. They halted at a distance and a figure dismounted and cautiously approached the valley. Melangell whirled in shock at the sound of a footstep nearby, finding herself looking in fearful surprise at . . . an equally frightened-looking young Roman legionary. He glanced around nervously at the surrounding brush, obviously aware that he was in enemy territory, and one hand stayed constantly on the short sword at his side.

Melangell straightened in alarm, the knife and rushes dropping from her fingers, and backed away in fear.

"No! Lady . . . wait!" the young soldier said, his speech understandable but heavily accented.

A Roman! she gasped inwardly. A Roman! Gods above, he is . . .

"Are you . . . ah . . . Melangell?" he said slowly. She nodded, and it seemed to her he sighed with relief. With his free hand he reached inside his segmented metal chest-plate and pulled out the gold medallion of Loucetius that she had given Anarios.

"Anarios!" she whispered. The Roman nodded.

"He waits at some distance and asks that you accompany me. I will take you to him."

Anarios! A flame began to rise within her, a long-forgotten flame. But Esus—how could she just go off? He would worry.

Yet something told her not to reveal his existence to this soldier—this enemy.

"Yes . . . one moment," she said, and bent over to stack the cut rushes on the rock. When she reached for her knife, she saw the soldier stiffen, and his hand tightened around his sword hilt. She laid the knife atop the rushes, the point aimed to the south.

"There," she said, satisfied, and she could only hope that if Esus came looking for her before she returned, he would see the deliberately arranged pile, the pointing knife, and know that no calamity had befallen her. It was the best she could do.

"All right." She nodded to the Roman, who replaced the medallion, relaxed a bit, and stood aside for her to go first. Silently she walked toward the waiting horses, the soldier following warily behind her.

He helped her mount the unusual-looking saddle, a high pommel at each of the four corners of the leather seat, strapped atop an impossibly tall horse, so much larger than their own native ponies! She felt as if she was riding in the clouds when the soldier mounted his own horse, took her reins, and they trotted off toward a distant tree line to the south. When they approached, she spied another soldier rising from his resting place beneath the trees, but it took her several moments to realize that it was Anarios. He stepped out into the tall grass and peered at them expectantly, one hand shielding his eyes. He took a few eager steps forward when the soldier led the horses up and dismounted. The young man walked back to Melangell. She put her hands on his metal shoulder straps as he reached for her waist and lightly lifted her to the ground. Then, taking the reins, the legionary led the animals away, leaving Melangell and Anarios staring awkwardly at each other.

"You waited," he said, and rushed forward to hold her desperately; and she, sobbing, wound her arms around his foreign clothes in a wild embrace.

"Is it you? Anarios, is it really you?" she choked, pulling back to look at his rugged face, now cleanly shaved, running her fingers through his neatly cropped hair, and then shaking her head in astonishment.

"Yes, my dearest, my love . . . I have come for you, as I said I would. Oh, by the blessed Venus, I didn't know if you were dead or alive; what had happened to you . . ."

She felt his arms tighten around her and he kissed her wildly; her mouth, her cheeks, her eyes, her neck. She tossed her head back and laughed delightedly.

Anarios!

"Tell me," he asked her, "how did you survive? What happened?"

"Loucetius . . . he saved me," she began. He shook his head in amusement.

"Oh, no, not that again!" he laughed.

"But it's true!" she protested. "A . . . a kindly old man found me and saved my life, for the tracker had wounded me."

She pulled her sleeve up and he looked at the jagged pink scar with a professional eye.

"The spear?" he asked, and she nodded.

"Damn! I knew we should have tried to kill him at the hut. I knew it!"

"No matter." She shook her head. "All is well now. And you, Anarios—what happened to you?"

"I wanted to go back to you, so desperately, but I went on, as you'd said, and soon was picked up by a Roman patrol. What a happy day that was! Back among my own people once more! Then I was given a three-month leave to recuperate, during which time I returned to Rome. Now I am reassigned, to the Syrian archers' garrison, to the east, and I have been trying to make arrangements for us . . ."

He paused in mid-sentence and stared at her.

"You are coming back with me, aren't you? Has Nechtan found you yet? Are you a slave again?"

"No . . . I mean, I am not a slave . . . but Nechtan was tried for what he did to us, and is now banished for two years, he and Melwas and Niall. He doesn't even know I am alive."

Anarios nodded in satisfaction.

"And you?" he asked.

She looked at him again, sadly, her eyes taking in his Roman clothes, his Roman speech, his Roman manners. If it were not for the face, she would not even know it was her Anarios, so different did he look. She could not imagine a whole world so different, so odd.

"No," she said, and slowly shook her head. He straightened, his hands at her waist.

"Anarios, look at me! What do you see?" she said.

He stepped back and looked her up and down, and a shock of recognition came to his face.

"Gods above, you . . . you are a druidess. No!" he gasped.

"Yes." She nodded. "Now even more than before, I am a part of this land, these people. I cannot go with you. Do you see?" She reached for his face but he turned and strode away a few angry paces before turning back toward her.

"A druidess?" he repeated, disbelieving. "Can't you come anyway? We had plans, Melangell. Remember? The stone mountains in Egypt? The finest gowns? I can give you those things now! I can! Does all that mean nothing to you? Do I mean nothing?"

"Look at you, Anarios," she said as he stood apart, staring mutely at her.

"Look at your clothes. You are a Roman; I am a Celt. You are a physician; I am a druidess. You are a man of 'science'; I am a woman of 'superstition.' What future could we have together? Do I give up what I am, or do you give up what you are? We are two different worlds now, Anarios. For a while we met, and I shall always remember it, but now we are apart again. Don't you see?"

He nodded stiffly, his face grim and drawn, and walked up to her, placing his hands on her shoulders.

"I could abduct you, you know. My aide and I could easily carry you off, and then you'd be my slave."

She smiled at him. "But you won't." He shook his head in confirmation of her words.

"Gods above, I want to!" he said, clasping her to his chest again. "For nearly a year you are all I have thought about."

He buried his face in her blowing hair and fell silent, and then he looked at her.

"I must warn you, Melangell. Our new governor follows the precepts of the Divine Julius. He seeks to leave no single druid alive in this land. In that way he hopes to break the back of your people's resistance, as Julius Caesar did in Gaul. He is a ruthless man and will stop at nothing in his goal of subduing all the northern tribes. Please, my love, for my sake if not for your own, flee . . . get as far from this place as you can, stop wearing your black robe, or you will surely die."

She stared at him, a mixture of rage and dread rising within her.

"Why?" she muttered. "We ask only to be left alone, to live our lives as we have always done. Why must your people come here, killing and looting and destroying, Anarios? Why?"

He shook his head sadly. "If only I knew that, Melangell, then perhaps I could make them stop, for it makes no sense to me either. I could be at home, safe and warm; and I could never have met you, so my heart would not ache for you as it does now. Melangell, please, reconsider. Come with me. You, at least, will be safe."

She shook her head resolutely. "I will not leave my land or my people. No."

He sighed in resignation and nodded. "Very well . . . but leave before the winter is out. Flee to the far north, or to an island; somewhere, for that is when Agricola plans to move north and destroy your people forever."

The horror on her face was like a stab to his heart, and he looked away uncomfortably. She shook her head slowly in disbelief.

"So once again it comes," she choked. "So many deaths, so much pain and suffering . . . and for what? For what, Anarios?" She grasped his arms fiercely in her little hands and sobbed in desperation at him.

She released him and turned away, pulling her hood up over her head. Like a black specter of death she walked away, across the great windblown hillside. He stood and watched her, pain tearing at him, until she was gone from view.

"Good-bye, Melangell, my love . . ." he whispered, mounted his horse, and galloped angrily back to the Roman lines.

"So, the sacrifices begin again?"

Esus looked at the stricken girl in concern and reached out to grasp her two clenched hands.

"Sacrifices?" she whispered brokenly.

"Aye." He nodded. "To the war gods, whoever they may be. A ritual as old as mankind; send off enough of your best young men to die on the altars of the war gods, and whoever has the most pleasing offering wins the war. All wars are like that, are they not?" He gave her hands an affectionate little shake.

"So you do not go back with your Roman?" he asked. Melangell shook her head emphatically.

"He is a Roman, yes, but he is not mine anymore," she hissed darkly. Esus looked at her in alarm.

"Child . . . no . . . don't hate. It is only a canker that will eat away your soul. Don't hate."

"How can I do otherwise, Esus? All the destruction they are about to bring to this land, for no reason! What offense have we committed against them? Why do they do such a thing?"

"The gods have their reasons, I suppose, even if we do not understand them. But do not hate, Melangell. It will not change a thing that happens, and it will only destroy you."

She hung her head, defeated, and her hands fell limp at her sides. "I don't know what else to do. I truly don't," she sighed.

"Then perhaps you should look for an answer. Today, tomorrow—there is time. Come," he said, rising to his feet and putting the half-finished basket aside, "it is getting dark. Let's go and have a nice meal, to cheer you up."

"How long must I wait? How long must I sit?" she wondered as she perched on a large boulder by the stream bed. For days she had restlessly prowled the valley, like some great caged animal; thinking, arguing, waiting for some sign, any sign, to tell her what to do. Anarios had said to go. Should Esus and I flee? she wondered. But what if he does not? Should I go alone? Go where? This is the only home I have now—there is nowhere else for me. Do I take off my black robe? I am not really a druidess, after all. But that would be cowardly, and unfair to Esus. Yet if the Romans come, what then? If I am a druidess, they will kill me. If I am not, they will rape me and enslave me . . . or maybe kill me, anyway. Better to die at once, as a druidess . . . yet I do not want to die! I know what pain feels like, what a spear feels like, what rape feels like—I want none of it, none of it. But what am I to do? There is no escape for me but one—to go to Anarios. There, I will be safe, but at what price? Living with the very people who will be committing these horrors against my own kind. No! I will not do that! Better to stay here, fight them . . . and die. Yes.

She pulled the old black robe tighter around herself and

lay down on the boulder under a hazy summer sky. Watching the clouds float above her, she soon drifted to sleep.

She awoke to a far-off voice, so tiny and distant most people wouldn't have heard it. Silently raising herself from the rock, she slipped from it and slid into the afternoon shadows of the valley, as Esus had taught her; as she had learned from watching the animals.

Dear Loucetius! she thought in fear. Not more Romans! A raiding party, scouts . . . or Anarios, coming back for me? She debated again whether she should go with him as she silently flowed down the shadowed hillside to where the valley opened onto the plain beyond. Melting into a dense thicket, her hood pulled low over her face, she peered between the leafy branches toward the voices. Three men sat beside the stream, eating a little food from their traveling packs, their spears on the ground beside them, long knives tucked into their belts. Then they seemed to be quarreling and all three stood, a tall dark one arguing with a strapping youth of eighteen or nineteen. When the men turned, pointing up the valley, Melangell had to stifle a cry when she found herself looking at the dark face of Nechtan, and beside him Niall and a boy she didn't know.

What are they doing here? she thought in panic. Had they come looking for her? Did they know she was here? Only Esus knew, and he wouldn't have told them.

She frantically felt at her waist and wished she had brought her knife with her. What a fine irony that would be, she mused . . . brooding over my fate at the hands of the Romans, when my fate ends up in the hands of one of my own people instead.

She watched curiously as Nechtan and Niall, spears in hand, suddenly loped off up the far side of the valley and disappeared south, toward the Roman lines. The boy they left behind sat down dejectedly behind a bush, obviously a lookout of some sort.

And Nechtan and Niall must have gone to the Roman lines to spy!

As quietly as a breeze, she withdrew up the valley, back toward her boulder, to wait.

She awoke with the first birds of dawn and sat by the rock, listening. As the sun crept higher, she heard a wild crashing in the woods to the far side of the stream, and the pet deer came bounding down the hillside, panic in its eye. It leapt the stream in one huge bound and was gone, and Melangell stood as fear rose in her stomach. The deer was badly frightened. Nechtan and Niall, on a furtive spying mission, would not have disturbed it so. Only one thing could have happened.

Romans!

Lightly she climbed atop the huge boulder, trying to get a better view, when more noises assailed her ears, this time coming from the far end of the valley. A cold rage gripped her heart when she saw the boy warrior, knife in hand, frantically chasing a young badger.

Her badger.

She stood silent and immobile and watched the animal dart this way and that until it skittered up the rock and under her cloak to safety, and she had the satisfaction of seeing the look of surprised terror on the young man's face when he saw her.

And then she knew what she must do.

Her voice came like cold doom as she tried to control the quaking rage she felt for her pet. Sternly she warned the boy to go to Nechtan's aid. He gaped in openmouthed astonishment until she bent to pick up the trembling animal and the boy roused, sprinted across the stream, up the far hillside, and vanished over the crest of the ridge.

So now she was detected. She turned, let herself down from the boulder, and returned to the cave, to warn Esus.

She hid behind the brush at the cave's entrance, peering down the hillside in the blue evening gloaming, and listened to their return. Nechtan's face was stormy; obviously he was angry at the boy about something. He raised his hand to strike him, but Niall intervened. They talked some more, then suddenly descended the hill, crossed the stream, and approached the rock . . . her rock. The boy pointed it out and Nechtan cautiously approached it, peered around, then somewhat laboriously climbed atop it. She smiled in amusement as she watched him. His banishment didn't seem to be harming him, she thought—he looked lean and muscular and healthy. Esus' little gifts must have helped them.

He lifted out his own knife and in a loud voice thanked

her for his life, warned her of the danger of vengeful Romans, then left it on the boulder as an offering to her.

To her!

She smiled and nodded. So now the debt was paid. He had once spared her life, and now she saved his.

She almost hated to see him crawl from the rock and the three of them reverently steal away. How she missed them all; her adopted tribe, a real home, Maia, human company.

The thought came as a disturbing shock to her. She had always felt so happy, here in this isolated little valley.

After nightfall she crept from the cave. Retrieving Nechtan's knife, she clasped it in homesickness and realized the most shocking fact of all: all hatred and revenge had fled her soul. She missed Nechtan the most!

And in that instant of revelation she came to know what she must do; what the gods had revealed as their message to her: she must return to the village and try to warn them of the Roman advance. She must try to save old Maia, at least. With Nechtan in exile, the woman would have no one to help her escape to safety.

Resolved, Melangell returned to the cave, Nechtan's knife tucked safe in her belt.

It was late summer when a lone warrior stopped at the household of Conn, the prosperous farmer. He was welcomed as all travelers were, and shown to a pallet where he could sleep for as many nights as he chose to stay, but the young man declined the generous offer; he had many other places to visit before his travels were done, and one night was all he could spare. He welcomed a hearty meal, though, and squatted eagerly by the long plank table as heaping trenchers of food were put before him.

"What is your mission on this journey, young man?" Conn asked his guest, amused to see the youth hungrily downing meat, bread, beans, cakes, ale, anything within his reach.

The young man gulped awkwardly and looked at his host. "Sir, I am sent by my master, Nechtan, of the Damnonii, to warn the towns and farms to the south that next year the Romans will invade."

Conn and his sons tensed at his words.

"And where did you hear this?" Conn asked suspiciously.

"A Roman prisoner, a legionary. The Romans have a new governor, who plans to make war on us. Already troops and supplies are being gathered, new roads built—"

"What are we to do?" Genann interrupted.

The visitor rose to his feet, eagerness lighting his face. "The old men, the kings and merchants, are too lazy or disbelieving to fight. We are trying to awaken the people to the danger, for it is real. I heard the Roman with my own ears, before he was killed. We must arm and train! We must assemble an army at once! If the kings will not fight, then I am to bring any willing warriors back with me, to my master. He will train an army himself."

Conn's two elder sons began talking excitedly together, and their father could see the fire of youth hot in their eyes.

"And you—what is your name?" Conn boomed over the din.

"Cathal, sir. A Parisi archer—"

"And if this invasion comes, what do we do? The families, the children?"

"Be ready with the first melting snows of spring to flee to the north. Into the mountains, the bogs, the islands."

"What of our homes, Cathal? What of our cattle, our livestock, all our wealth?"

"What of your lives, sir, and your freedom?" the archer retorted, and the group fell silent, the eyes of Conn's daughters growing wide with fear.

"See," Conn said, "you frighten the girls. Let's have no more talk of war during the meal."

Cathal stared at him, stunned. It was just as Eber had said. None of them wanted to believe.

Cai, Conn's dark-haired son, broke the tense silence. "Where do we find your master's camp?" he said, his pale blue eyes glinting resolve. He was a tall young man, and he seemed to have nearly outgrown the yellow wool tunic that stretched over his chest.

"It is far away and I cannot return there now to show you, but there is a druid who lives hereabouts who knows of it and can take you," the visitor answered.

"Druid?" Conn said. Cathal nodded.

"We call him 'old father.' He often visits us."

"Is he semnotheoi, with bright blue eyes and wispy gray hair?" Genann asked excitedly.

Cathal nodded.

"Esus!" Cai said, a grin crossing his face as he cut his eyes around to his eager brother.

"And he knows the way to your camp?" Conn asked suspiciously.

Again Cathal nodded.

"Does he have a girl with him?" Genann pressed the boy. "A fair-haired girl named Melangell; an apprentice?"

"I know nothing of a girl." Cathal shrugged. "But my master once owned a slave girl by that name."

A slave girl! Genann thought in anger. My darling woods-spirit, a slave.

"Where does this druid live?" Genann pursued, knowing he was on the girl's trail at last.

Cathal shrugged.

"I'm not exactly sure. I know it's a valley near here, to the south, but I don't know where . . ."

Suddenly he paused when an idea hit him.

"I know of a valley where I saw a druidess shelter a young badger. Because she saved my master's life, he has given his word that we will no longer hunt her creatures there."

Genann slapped his hand to the table happily. Surely that must be his mysterious, kind-hearted Melangell.

"Where is this valley where you saw the druidess?" he asked Cathal.

"I can show you, if you want to come along. It's on my way. But I don't know if 'old father' lives there," the boy replied.

"He does," Conn spoke up, admitting his defeat.

"You speak of this druid and a girl," Cathal complained, "but what of my mission?"

Cai stood up. "I will join your master," he announced, one hand going proudly to a new sword at his side.

Conn shook his head. "I'll wait until we get more definite news. I cannot risk everything on the basis of a rumor."

"It is no rumor, sir," Cathal said, and turned to Genann.

"And you?" he asked him.

The young poet looked aside at his father before he spoke.

"I must go and find Melangell," he said. "She is too near

the Roman lines. I can bring her and Esus back here, Father, where it is safer, and then I will join this army."

Conn nodded tiredly.

"Yes, son, go and fetch them—if you can get old Esus to leave!" he chuckled.

Melangell had been gone for only two days, and already Esus missed her bright smile and happy ways. He prayed for her luck at her adopted village, but he had no real hope she would succeed. People were too stubborn, too skeptical of the truth. If she did not return shortly, he would go to this town and retrieve her, perhaps save her from an unpleasant reception. He had just put some crushed wheat on to boil when the sound of voices sent him rushing down the narrow corridor to the cave entrance. Could the girl be back already? Or perhaps it was his three young Damnonii friends.

Cold terror seized his old heart when he looked down and saw a group of Roman soldiers hacking their way through the valley underbrush as if looking for something, and instantly Melangell's words of warning dashed across his mind.

They intended to eradicate every druid in the land.

Already, he knew, they had destroyed the main druid colony on the blessed isle of Mona.

And now they searched the valley below him.

Hastily he looked around, seized the girl's slumbering badger, and shoved it out the door, to safety. Then his fox, and the deer.

With a silent prayer for their safety he tried to block the entranceway so they couldn't return to the cave.

Then he heard a soldier shouting. He knew their language. They had spied the deer, issuing forth from the cliff face, and were coming up to investigate.

He closed his eyes sickly. So here his days would end, so simply and unexpectedly. And when is death ever expected? he chided himself as he sat calmly at the table and waited. At least Melangell was gone; at least she was safe.

Soon they were upon him, bursting into the cave in a rage.

"So, we found you, eh?" one of them snapped, hauling Esus roughly to his feet.

"Filthy pagan magician. We found the head of our comrade stuck up in a tree, and saw what you did to it."

Esus had no idea what they were talking about; he made no attempt to reply.

"This one will be a pleasure, eh?" The soldier grinned to his friends, and a savage blow with the butt of his sword sent Esus crumpling to the floor.

"Burn the place," he ordered. The soldiers seized burning brands from the fire and began to set alight the table, the baskets, the straw pallets, the wicker stand.

Then they threw the torches on the barely conscious old man and, laughing loudly, left the rapidly burning cave.

Esus cried out a silent scream of agony as he tried to rise, and failed. "Dear gods above!" he gasped as the flames enveloped him, and his last thoughts were of the girl.

"You were dead, on an altar of Loucetius," her dream had said, and as his mind dropped into blackness, the realization hit him.

The altar of Loucetius . . .

Sacrifice by fire . . .

Approaching the valley, they saw five Romans jauntily marching away, and smoke billowing from the distant cliffside told them more than they wanted to know. In a rage, Cathal, Cai, and Genann attacked and, caught off guard, the Romans were easily overwhelmed. Cathal calmly slit the throats of two of the three who had not been killed outright, and bound the third for later interrogation. Grimly they marched him back into the valley and tried to enter the cave, but failed; the smoke was still too dense.

A cold fury gripped Genann and he slammed the terrified soldier into the jutting cliffside.

"What did you do with her?" he hissed, pressing his knife into the flesh on the man's throat.

"Her? No . . . her . . ." the soldier gasped brokenly. "Old man . . . no her."

"What about the old man?" Genann demanded, pressing harder with the blade as the legionary squirmed and whimpered. Blood trickled down his throat, darkening the red scarf tied around his neck.

"Dead . . . druid dead . . ." he gasped. Before they could

stop him, Genann cried out and slashed his knife into the soldier's neck. The bound man crumpled to the ground, thrashing with his legs as Genann stabbed at him again and again. Cai seized his brother's flailing arms and held him back while Cathal drew his sword and gave the Roman a merciful end to his sufferings, grabbing his short hair and slashing his head from his shoulders with one swift stroke.

Genann turned to kick the soldier's body down the cliffside. "Wait," Cathal said. "Nechtan's orders . . . his mark, for all the Romans to see. Watch."

So great was their rage that the two brothers didn't flinch when Cathal performed the ritual for them. To the contrary, it gave them a grim satisfaction and, carrying the soldier's head, bound with his own neck scarf, they returned to his four dead comrades and did the same to them.

"He took a vow," Cathal said as they washed their bloody hands in the stream, "that it would be the fate of every Roman he caught."

The two brothers grunted approval.

"We'll leave them there for their comrades to find," Cai said, looking up at the diminishing smoke coming from the cave. "Nothing more can be done for Esus, but at least we have avenged his death."

Genann nodded. "But where is the girl?"

"Perhaps she has gone back to her people. If she is the same as Nechtan's slave, she is from the chief northern village of the Damnonii, where King Annos dwells," Cathal said, rising to his feet.

Genann and Cai stood beside him, wiping their wet hands on their breeches.

"Then I will go to this town and try to find her," Genann declared.

"And I will go with Cathal on his journey, recruiting men to fight the Roman dogs and asking along the way about her," his brother added.

"We meet, then, at Nechtan's camp in the fall," Cathal said. "Anyone in his village can tell you where it is. Until that day, may the gods bless our journeys with success."

Without another word they clasped hands in farewell. Then Cathal and Cai headed on to the east; Genann turned toward the northwest, the lands of the Damnonii.

Part 4

THE ENCAMPMENT

*T*HE WIND WAS RISING AS NECHTAN STEALTHILY APPROACHED the looming black walls of the Damnonii town. Pausing in the adjoining forest, he peered through the night with narrowed eyes, trying to see any signs of a guard or patrol. There were none. Even the earthen embankments to either side of the road seemed empty. He didn't know if he should be irritated by this carelessness, or grateful for it.

Bending over in a low crouch, he held his spear parallel to the ground and placed a silencing hand on the sword at his side as he ran forward through ripening wheat fields, his cloak whipping behind him like a bat's silent wings. Reaching the fort, he loped up the steep hillside to the base of the timber wall, marveling at how easy it had been; at one time he would have been severely winded by such a climb. Slowly, his back to the upright logs, he crept to the large gate. It was locked at night to keep animals from wandering in or out of the town; a smaller doorway built into the gate was provided for the people to use.

Peering around as he reached for the iron latch, he could see no guard whatsoever, not atop the earth embankments, not on either side of the gate. He frowned in disgust at these foolish people. Annos' cattle were probably better guarded than his town.

His hand found the latch, his fingers closed around it, and slowly he lifted it out of place, then paused, waiting for some response from the far side of the wall.

None came.

Placing a hand flat against the door, he pushed it open, still waiting for a reaction and still getting none.

The door opened to a narrow crack and he slipped through it, holding his scabbard against his leg to keep it from bumping. On the other side of the door a guard sat cross-legged on the ground, slumped against the wall in deep sleep. Nechtan shook his head in disgust and crept across the dark entrance yard on silent bare feet, the wind gusting vigorously around him. He started at a sudden dry series of thumps nearby, tense until he located their source; above the doorway of the Great Hall, under the overhang of the thatch roof, the severed, preserved heads of three enemy chieftains Annos had killed in battle were knocking loudly against the log wall, buffeted by the rising wind. Shaking his head, Nechtan took a deep breath and continued on his way.

A swift rap with the butt of his sword knocked out the one guard who stood outside the door of Annos' residence. Nechtan dragged him into the shadows, tying and gagging him securely. Picking up his spear and stepping over the inert body, he walked casually across the Great Hall, threading his way through the sleeping men of the king's guard, trying to appear to be one of them. Pausing outside the walled-off sleeping area of Annos, Nechtan tried to collect his nerve, hoping the king was alone and had no warriors or women in the room with him. Pushing open the door, Nechtan stepped into the gloom.

The old king lay sleeping soundly in the darkness, sprawled across a large Gaulish bed, a coverlet of embroidered wool pulled over himself . . . and he was alone. Nechtan stood in amused silence and studied the scene for a moment. How odd, he thought, to see a wealthy and powerful king sleeping like a mere babe. I wonder if I look like that when I am asleep.

He crept across the packed earthen floor to the king's bed and reached out to touch the man's shoulder to awaken him. The king suddenly whirled to life, his knife flashing so fast that Nechtan took an instinctive leap backward to avoid the blade, nearly upsetting a large silver wine jug on the floor behind him.

Gods above! The old man has reflexes like a lightning bolt, Nechtan thought as the king in one leap sprang from the bed to face him, the knife poised in his hand.

Nechtan stood upright and spread his arms wide to show

he meant no harm, and Annos straightened, a look of surprise on his face when he recognized him.

"Nechtan? Is it Nechtan . . . the Pict?" he muttered in astonishment. Nechtan slowly nodded.

"I meant no harm, sire," he said softly. "I have only come to warn you."

"Warn me?" Annos hissed, his eyes narrowing suspiciously. "Warn me of what? You have been banished, boy; you have no business being here."

"I crept in. No one need see me but you. I must warn you, and then I will return to my exile."

"You are banished, boy," Annos repeated in irritation, lowering the knife. "It is the Law. You are as one who is dead. Just to speak with you is to pollute myself. I don't care for your warning, or your stealth, or your disobedience. Go, before I have you seized." He turned his back to the stunned young man and walked away.

"But, Annos, the Romans are massing to the south. They will attack by spring. You must get ready, train warriors, move your herds, save the women and children."

He paused in frustration, looking at the king's stony back and waiting for some reply, some response, and getting none.

"Annos! You must listen! The very fact I was so easily able to sneak in here tonight proves my point. You must believe me! I risked my life to come and tell you," Nechtan pleaded, taking a few steps toward the king's unrelenting back. It was as if the man didn't hear him, as if he wasn't even there, as if he were dead.

"Annos!" he repeated, trying to hold his voice low. "You must listen!"

The king looked up toward the low ceiling in studied disinterest.

"You are as a dead man. Get out of my house, and out of this town, and out of this territory, or I will have you killed. You violate the law one time too many, Pict."

The sneering emphasis on the last word was as a slap in Nechtan's face, and a cold rage lit his pale eyes. Angrily he clenched his spear shaft and stared at the obdurate king's unyielding back.

Curse them all, the fools, he thought, whirling fiercely and striding from the room. Let the Romans have them. I will go to my mother and spirit her out of here tonight, and then let them all go to hell.

Heavy rain was beginning to plop outside, rattling loudly on the dry thatch roofs, as Nechtan strode back through the stirring warriors in the Great Hall, stepped over the squirming, bound guard at the door, and stalked away. A brilliant flare of lightning lit the sky and he unpinned his cloak, pulling it over his head. Curses, he thought bitterly. As if the rain wasn't bad enough, now the lightning comes and someone is sure to see me and recognize me.

Hurriedly he walked down the almost deserted streets, staying in the shadows as best he could and trying to avoid the occasional huddled figures who, like him, rushed to their destinations against the whipping wind and pelting rain.

A deafening crash split the sky as he neared the edge of the settlement. He turned his face aside when another bustling figure rushed past him. Then, when he resumed his hurried walk, a light nearby caught his eye and he broke into a trot.

There! Was it . . . ? Yes. Suddenly greedy flames shot into the sky, garish against the night, defying the driving rains and threatening to catch the nearby wood palisade on fire. Curious tribesmen stumbled sleepily into the streets, and he ran faster, pushing through the knots of people, kicking aside squealing pigs and snapping dogs, his bare feet splashing carelessly in the mud.

Mother! No! He gasped, staggering when he reached the clearing and saw her house—his house—burning madly.

"Mother!" he cried out, rushing forward with one arm shielding his face from the heat. The hungry tongues of fire licked out at him and drove him back.

"Mother . . ." he sobbed, dropping to his knees in the mud and rain, the cloak falling away from his head, his black hair roped and dripping into his face.

"No . . . no," he cried, doubling over, when a scream split the air and a little cloaked figure went racing madly past him, paused briefly at the door, and then, to his horror, disappeared into the flaming house.

Stumbling to his feet, Nechtan raced after it and, pulling his wet cloak over his head, plunged into the fire behind the person.

The roof was a brilliant sea of flame over his head, dropping burning bits of thatch and wood like rain around him. The log walls danced with a rhythm of light, heat gripped at his throat, and his breathing grew labored and dry. Tables, stools, pallets, everything was ablaze, transformed from the mundane to a fierce show of glory. He looked around the room in desperate fear.

"Maia!" a voice choked to his left, and he saw a small black figure rising and falling and stumbling toward his mother's bed.

An empty bed.

"No!" he cried out. One wall began to collapse, leaning inward, and he sprinted for the figure, trying to hold his breath against the searing heat. Grabbing the person around the waist, he pulled back toward the door as the wall sagged more, but the person struggled fiercely against his grip, wriggled free, and on hands and knees began crawling toward his mother's sleeping ledge, weak arms trying desperately to pull it forward against the suffocating heat.

Nechtan collapsed to his knees, lunged toward the retreating figure, and with his last bit of strength seized it by the ankles, rose to a crouch, and dragged it bodily from the blazing room.

Emerging from the burning house, he gulped the fresh wet air like a beached fish, his eyes smarting and tearing so badly he could hardly see. At the sound of a great crash behind him he grabbed the still-struggling figure in one arm and stumbled away from the collapsing house. Village men ran around the ruins with buckets of water, trying to keep the fire from spreading.

Exhausted, Nechtan collapsed to the mud a few paces away, dropping the figure to the ground beside him and still gasping for air as he watched his house fall into a burning mass of timbers and rubble.

"Maia . . ." a voice cried, and the little figure struggled to rise to its knees.

"She wasn't there," he answered, his eyes still on the fire.

"Maia," the voice sobbed again. Glancing down, he saw two dirty little hands held up before a soot-stained face, singed and muddy hair plastered across a wet forehead.

"Melangell?" he asked, disbelieving, and pulled her hands from her face. She turned to look at him with red-rimmed eyes, tears and rain streaking down her dirty cheeks.

"She wasn't there," he repeated gently, wiping her wet hair aside.

"Nechtan?" she whispered hoarsely, squinting to see him through swollen eyes.

"Yes," he replied, holding her dirty face in his hands. He ran his fingers over her lips and lightly kissed her, and he felt her hands instinctively reach for his waist.

A firm hand suddenly fell on his shoulder. "Come," a voice said. "People are gathering around."

Nechtan looked up, startled, into the shadowed face of Brennos.

"Come," the druid repeated, helping them to their feet. Supporting each other, they made their way through the driving rain as the house subsided into blackened ash behind them.

Brennos' house was of modest size, a circular interwoven wicker wall securely anchored to a stone foundation and plastered inside and out with thick mud and chopped straw. Inside, a handmade cot stood to the right of the central stone hearth, below a small shuttered window. The low hearth fire illuminated drying racks of medicinal herbs along the far wall, above a large chest containing the druid's personal belongings. Clusters of drying mosses and fungi hung suspended from the blackened ceiling. A few partially completed wood carvings, offerings to Arnemetia from his patients, lay on a fur by the hearth where the man had been working on them when shouts outside had interrupted his concentration. The druid led them to a small back room where he usually tended seriously ill patients. Without a word he rushed away, collecting packets and jars of medicines.

"Give me your wet cloaks and I'll hang them by the fire to dry," he said, entering the room with a tray of medicines.

"Blankets are there"—he motioned to a low chest by the bed. "Wrap up and stay warm." Nechtan pulled out two heavy wool blankets, wrapped one around Melangell, and pulled the other around himself. He sat down beside the girl and took her hand in his.

"She has burns," he said to the druid, holding her hand up to view.

"Yes. I'll attend to that later. First I must see to your eyes. Tilt your heads back."

He washed their eyes with great quantities of a clear yellowish liquid. "You will be hunted," he told Nechtan. "It is almost dawn. Hide here for the day, and then leave tomorrow night. I'll tell them you left. They will not dare to search this place."

Nechtan nodded. "And my mother? What of her? Where is she?"

"If that's why you risked your life to return, I'm afraid it was a wasted trip. She died during the winter, Nechtan. I could do nothing for her. Old age . . . a broken heart—I don't know. She didn't want to live anymore, and when that happens, there is nothing a druid can do."

He placed a hand on Nechtan's slumping shoulder and looked into his stricken face.

"I'm sorry," he said simply, and Nechtan nodded.

"No! It can't be!" Melangell sobbed, raising her burned hand to her mouth.

"It's all right," Nechtan soothed, wrapping one arm around the girl's shoulders and pulling her close. "Maybe it was for the best. She at least will not have to worry about the future that looms before us."

Brennos crouched before them and pulled Melangell's burned hand out to examine it. "Yes," he agreed, unfolding her dirty fingers. "The gods always have their reasons for what they do, even if we do not understand them. She is now free of her painful, crippled body, and perhaps in her next lifetime her debts will not be so heavy to bear."

Melangell nodded, wincing as the druid cleaned her hand.

"And you, Nechtan," Brennos said as he worked, "now own all her possessions . . . including this girl."

He cut his eyes briefly up to Nechtan's face and saw it go

pale at his words. Abruptly the young warrior rose to his feet.

"I must go and wash," he muttered, walking blankly from the room. Brennos returned his attentions to the girl's injured hand.

"But . . ." Melangell began, pulling her hand away, "I cannot be his slave. You must understand! I am—"

"Hush," the druid replied firmly, retrieving her hand. "The law is the law. Now, be still."

A slave again, Melangell thought blankly, her life crumbling around her. "I was a free woman . . . and now I am a slave again."

Brennos exited the back room and found Nechtan squatting by the fire, his face and hands clean, and eating a bowl of oat gruel as he watched the flames dance on the hearth. He did not look up when the druid stood beside him.

"You have a lot to think about," Brennos said, reaching to an iron kettle suspended over the fire and scooping out a bowl of gruel for himself. Nechtan grunted absently and continued to stare at the fire.

"Why did you come here, anyway?" the druid asked, sitting on the furs and beginning to eat. The question roused the young man and he looked up angrily.

"The Romans are preparing to attack in the spring. I came to warn Annos, but he chooses not to listen," he snorted in disgust.

Brennos nodded and Nechtan suddenly looked at him. "Why don't you come and join us?" he asked.

"Join whom?" the druid replied.

"My band. We are collecting warriors, men who want to fight before it's too late. I have a camp set up at the place of our exile. Find whatever other warriors you can and join us by fall."

Brennos now gazed at the fire in thought, and silence enveloped them until the druid looked up.

"I feel sure Calum will join you," he said. "He is a restless soul and I know he is unhappy here. There may be others."

"Fine! Come, then, and join us. We need a druid. You will be welcomed!" Nechtan exclaimed with a happiness that vanished with the druid's next words.

"And what of your possessions? What of the girl, Nechtan?"

"I have been thinking about it," Nechtan answered. "Take what you need. It is of no more use to me now, except the bulk of the harvest from my fields, my horses, and my war chariot. Bring them to me when you come."

Brennos nodded. Nechtan took a deep breath.

"Brennos," he said, his words difficult to speak, "she must have loved my mother very much to risk dying for her as she did. I don't know where she has been or what she has been doing, but she now wears the robe of a druidess."

He shook his head, bewildered, and continued.

". . . And the curse, my curse—how can I fight my fate, whatever it may be? These are my reasons, why I tell you now, with you as my witness, that I give her her freedom. She is now a free woman—but don't tell her until after I'm gone. Then, if she wants to come with you and join us, tell her I would be honored."

He stood suddenly and put his bowl on the hearthstones. "I should be getting to my hiding place, before anyone comes looking for me."

Brennos nodded and rose to his feet.

"Come," he said, stepping past the tall young man and leading the way back to the sickroom.

"There"—he pointed to the far wall—"a door to a small lean-to, next to the stable. There are some things stored there, but there is enough room for you to stretch out until nightfall. Then I'll come and fetch you when it's time."

Nechtan nodded and looked at the solemn, dirty-faced girl still sitting on the edge of the cot.

"Brennos, bring my cloak," he said. The druid, seeing the look in his eyes, nodded and left the room. Nechtan stepped over to the cot and lifted the girl's chin in his hand.

"Go and wash, Melangell," he said quietly. "Get some food."

She stared down dejectedly and he tilted her head back until her green eyes were looking up at him.

"Wash, and eat," he repeated, "and then come to me."

He released her chin and turned away as Brennos reentered the room. He took his cloak from the druid, cast one final glance at the girl, and disappeared into the lean-to.

Dawn had not yet arrived when Nechtan heard the low wattle door softly scrape. A slit of light from the stone oil lamp in the sickroom fell across his legs. Quickly he sat up, fearful it might be someone other than Melangell, but he relaxed when he saw her small form, still draped in the druid's wool blanket, crouched in the doorway.

"Come," he said, rising to his feet, his head bent low against the thatch ceiling. She crept into the room and he reached behind her, pushing the door shut. Melangell stood stiffly, obviously afraid, the blanket clenched tightly in her uninjured hand. Standing in front of her, Nechtan lifted her bandaged hand to his lips and softly kissed it. Her face was freshly scrubbed and her newly washed hair hung damp and clean around her face.

I must be gentle this time, he thought, reaching out and taking the blanket from her shoulders. He spread it on the earthen floor beside them. She will be a free woman tomorrow. This might be our only time together . . . my only chance.

He did not speak as he guided her to the blanket and she, woodenly, obeyed him.

Lifting the damp hair away from her shoulders, he placed it behind her, leaned down, and kissed her neck as he pulled the shoulder of her gown aside. His lips crept down to her arm and she gasped aloud.

He straightened up and looked at her in surprise. Her face was limp, her eyes closed. Slowly he kissed her face, her eyelids, her mouth, and down her throat as she rolled her head back. He moved the other side of her simple wool shift and pulled it down. It fell to the floor at her feet and she gasped again when the cool night air hit her naked body. His hand reached for her breast as he clasped her to him, fiercely kissing her open mouth, devouring her with his lips.

Suddenly her hands were in his hair, clenching his face, his mouth, to hers, in desperation. His free hand slid down her back to her buttocks and pressed her tightly against himself.

"Melangell . . . " he whispered hoarsely into her hair as her fingers pulled feverishly at the bottom of his tunic, sliding it out from his leather belt. He felt her little hands lightly exploring up his chest, sending chills of excitement down his spine.

Then she was kissing his neck, pulling his shirt off, her soft lips exploring the muscles of his chest, and it was his turn to gasp. Gods above! he thought wildly, Seonaid always took, and took, but never gave anything back.

He glanced down at her and found her sea-green eyes looking up at him, sparkling with a strange light; and then her fingers were at his breeches, her good hand fumbling awkwardly at the heavy belt buckle. Eagerly he unfastened it, pulled his breeches off, and kicked them aside. The burning within him rose until he could stand it no longer. He entered her where they stood, clenching her to him desperately as she sobbed in brokenhearted release.

Melangell lay in the crook of Nechtan's arm, her head resting on his shoulder and her fingers stroking the dark hair on his chest as they watched the strengthening sunlight slant and sparkle through the cracks and holes in the thatch roof. A cow in the adjoining stable snorted by the wall and the girl jumped in surprise.

"Don't be afraid, my little one," Nechtan laughed as she sheepishly hid her face in his neck. "I will protect you from all the world's vicious cows."

A loud belch from the same cow sent them both into gales of muffled laughter.

"By the gods, that was right in my ear!" he complained.

"Not exactly a romantic spot, is it?" she said, settling back beside him.

"The stuff legends are made of—boy meets girl in a cow shed . . ." he whispered, running a hand down the soft curve of her waist and up to her hip. She quivered at his touch and smiled up at him.

"Do we have time? Again?" she hinted, running a finger along the heavy gold torque at his neck, and was disappointed to see him shake his head no.

"Brennos is probably looking for you. You must go," he

said, relieved to see that she did not pout as Seonaid always did; she accepted his words in good-natured disappointment and sat up.

"Yes, I suppose you're right," she said, reaching toward their feet for her shift.

"Oh, no . . . look!" she said, holding it up. "It's full of dirt! It will take Brennos exactly one breath to guess where it's been."

He laughed, sitting up beside her and retrieving his own clothes.

"Well, let him. Druids know the ways of the world too, you know," he said, shaking out his yellow tunic and pulling it on over his head. Melangell still sat, naked, futilely trying to brush the dirt from her shift.

"Let it be," he said, taking it from her lap and tossing it aside. Wrapping one arm around her, he pulled her to him and pressed his mouth to hers. Just as his lips began to creep down her neck, a light tap came at the door. They looked up in alarm and Melangell reached for her gown, pulling it on hurriedly.

"Who is it?" Nechtan hissed. Standing, he pulled on his patterned breeches and took his sword and knife from the girl.

"Brennos," came the urgently whispered reply. "Someone is here to see you both."

Embarrassed, Melangell hid her face in her hands.

"Who?" Nechtan said, going to the door and opening it a crack.

"A young man, to join your army. He has been seeking Melangell as well. His name is Genann. Come." Brennos withdrew, and was gone.

"Genann?" Nechtan questioned, turning to Melangell as he closed the door. "I know no one by that name. Do you?"

She nodded. "The son of a rich farmer. I cured his brother."

"You?" he said, his eyes full of surprise. She smiled wistfully.

"Didn't you notice? My robes? I am a druidess now, or I was."

He stared at her solemn face, then leaned down and kissed her cheek.

"Come," he said, pulling her to her feet.

Brennos stood at the doorway between the sickroom and his dwelling, waiting for them and trying to suppress the smile on his lips. He pointed to the girl's black robe, now dry and lying on the cot, and she hastily pulled it on. Nechtan stood silently beside her, unfazed by their discovery.

When Melangell was dressed, the druid motioned into the front room and a tall, cleanly shaved, fair-haired young man appeared, a large, brightly painted body shield on one arm and a spear in his hand. An ornate and little-used sword hung at his side, the tooled leather scabbard suspended from a chain belt fastened around his waist. His new tartan breeches and soft white wool tunic spoke of wealth and social standing. The young man's gaze flickered lightly over Nechtan, seeming to size him up in an instant, and then his eyes fell on Melangell, lingering on her flustered face, her disheveled hair. Quickly the young man returned his gaze to Nechtan and gave a slight nod in his direction.

"You are Nechtan of the Damnonii, who seeks men to fight?" he said.

Nechtan nodded briefly, his eyes studying the young man's expressionless face.

"I seek to join your forces," Genann began.

"You are more than welcome in our camp." Nechtan smiled. "Genann, is it?"

"Aye."

"How did you know to find me here, Genann? Did you go to my camp first?" Nechtan asked. The young man shook his head, easing his stiff stance and lowering the shield's edge to the floor.

"I came here seeking Melangell," he explained, and Brennos noted a brief look of fear cross the girl's face at his words. She seemed to relax as the explanation continued, much to the druid's curiosity. What secrets did these two share? he wondered. Lovers, perhaps?

"Your man Cathal came to my father's farm to warn us and to recruit men for your group. He, my brother Cai, and I went to the valley where she lived with the old druid Esus, to take them away to a safer place. We felt they were too close to the Roman lines."

Here he paused and exchanged a furtive glance with Brennos, which roused Nechtan's suspicions.

"Valley? Esus? Who is that? You speak in riddles, Genann."

"Melangell was an apprentice to Esus, the holy man Cathal says you called 'old father.' They lived in a rocky valley near the Roman lines."

"Is this true?" Nechtan asked, turning to Melangell. She nodded as Genann watched her.

"But she was gone," the young man continued. "Cathal said you owned a slave by that name, so I came to your village to see if she might be here. The others continued on, seeking men for your band."

Nechtan nodded. "And Esus? Where is he?"

"He is safe now," Genann lied, convincing himself that it was not altogether a lie.

"And this valley . . . near the Roman lines . . ." Nechtan mused aloud. "My life was once saved by an old druidess in such a valley."

Melangell's hands rustled in her black robe, and with a triumphant smile she held up his knife. He took it and looked at her in surprise.

"You!" he gasped. "It was you?"

She laughed and nodded.

"But how did you know I was in danger? You know, you nearly scared Cathal back to his ancestors!"

She threw her head back and laughed, a clear, sparkling laugh like a babbling brook, and once more Genann felt his heart tear within him as he watched her.

"Here . . ." Nechtan smiled, returning the knife to her. "It's yours now."

"Thank you," she said, taking it from him. "It's a long story. I—"

A loud banging on the door silenced her and the four looked at each other in alarm.

"To the lean-to," Brennos hissed. Nechtan grabbed his cloak and turned.

Genann acted just as swiftly, propping his spear and shield by the wall and unpinning the ornate gold brooch that held his cloak at his shoulder.

"Nechtan," he whispered, holding his cloak out to him. "Your cloak."

Understanding, Nechtan tossed him his cloak and took Genann's, then disappeared into the storeroom. Melangell followed Brennos into the main room, picked up a bowl of gruel Genann had been eating, and sat on a fur by the fire as Brennos crossed to the front door, where the pounding had resumed.

"I'm coming! I'm coming!" he called out, lifted the bolt, and pulled the door open.

Angus stood there, almost too tall to fit through the low doorway, his sword in hand and a grim look on his face. Abruptly he walked into the room, his eyes swiftly scanning the wicker walls, the shelves, the drying herbs, falling only briefly on the druid girl who sat by the fire, looking at him curiously. Then he spied the far doorway and studied it suspiciously.

"Where is he?" he growled, starting across the room.

"Who?" Brennos demanded, placing himself in front of the guard, his hands at the man's chest to stop him. "You cannot come breaking in here as if this were a drinking hall," he protested. "Whom do you seek?"

"Nechtan—the Pict," Angus snapped. "Annos saw him last night, and many saw him at the fire, rescuing this girl. I have orders to seize him. Now, where is he?" *He never takes his eyes from the far doorway,* Melangell noted sickly. *Where is Genann? What is he doing?*

A movement suddenly was heard in the sickroom, and Angus' grip on his sword tightened.

"Brennos," a voice muttered sleepily, "I thought you said I could get a good night's rest here." Genann stumbled wearily into view, collapsing against the door in mock exhaustion. Angus' eyes narrowed suspiciously as Genann, running a hand through his tousled hair, looked up at him in surprise.

"This is Genann," Brennos explained. "He is the girl's bodyguard. He is the only other one here. If Nechtan was in town last night, he has long since escaped."

Angus angrily stepped around the druid and strode to the doorway, shouldering Genann aside to enter the sickroom,

Brennos on his heels. Melangell exchanged a brief, frantic glance with Genann, who half-smiled at her, winked, and followed the men into the room.

Brennos entered the sickroom, fear in his heart, and stopped in surprise. The cot was messed up, the blanket carelessly tossed aside as if it had just been slept in. Genann's sword and chain belt, his knife and long dagger lay atop a barrelhead. Dust and grime of a long journey were streaked across the young man's forehead, and mud stained his green checked breeches. But when Angus spied Nechtan's cloak hanging from a peg in the wall and triumphantly seized it, Genann bolted upright and began to protest loudly.

"Here . . . careful with that!" he demanded angrily, crossing the room to face the tall guard.

"This is Nechtan's cloak!" Angus announced bluntly. "I know the pattern."

"Fool," Genann snapped, snatching it from the guard's hand. "It is mine. I am the girl's guard; she belongs to Nechtan. Is it so odd that we should wear a similar pattern? You will not mishandle my clothing like that, just because the pattern resembles Nechtan's. Do you understand me?"

"It is his," Angus persisted. "Now, where is he?"

"It is mine . . . see? Is this Nechtan's pin?" Genann said, holding out for the guard's inspection a circular gold brooch inlaid with amber, pinned to one corner of the cloth. Angus peered at it intently, then straightened up.

"Pins can be changed," he said curtly, grabbing the cloak. "Nechtan's cloak will have burns, soot from the fire last night."

He replaced his sword at his side and, with both hands, held the cloak out for closer inspection. He could see no soot, no burns, only large gray muddy stains. Flopping it into one hand, he studied Genann's face, ran one finger across his dusty forehead, then looked carefully at the dirt on his fingertip. It was gray, like the stains on the cloak. Casting one eye down, he peered at the dirt floor. The packed earth was a rich, dark brown.

"Bah!" he exclaimed, flinging the cloak to the floor and stalking from the room. "If Nechtan is in the village, we will

186

find him," he declared over his shoulder. "We have increased the guard at the gate, and men patrol the streets. He will not escape us." With a shuddering rattle the front door closed behind him, and in an instant Brennos came flying across the room, anger in his gray eyes. He flung the door open savagely.

"Annos will hear of this!" he shouted after the retreating guard. "I cannot conduct my affairs here under threat of searches at any moment. Annos will hear of this!"

He slammed the door angrily and turned, and the fire in his eyes was real. Melangell looked at him in surprise and set her bowl of gruel aside.

"Brennos?" she said quietly, rising to her feet. The rage left him; his normal placid look returned. He shook his head at her, tension still lining his mouth.

"I cannot—I will not—abide that," he said flatly, replacing the bolt.

They turned when Genann, laughing, walked into the room.

"That poor fellow will be so confused he won't know who was seen in the village last night!" He chuckled, heading for the copper washbasin to clean up.

"You were superb!" Brennos smiled, clapping him on the back. "But the dirt—where did you get it?"

"Oh, that," Genann said, splashing water over his face. "I'm afraid you'll need a new pot of whatever that grayish mud is that you druids are so fond of using."

"The mud that heals poisons?" Melangell asked, and Brennos nodded.

"I recognized the jar at once," Genann explained.

"But it was old, dried out, worthless—" the druid began.

Genann coughed awkwardly.

"Yes . . . well, that's why I thought you'd need a new jar of it. As dust to scatter over myself, it was fine, but I needed mud too, so I'm afraid I . . . um . . . urinated in it."

"Gods above!" Nechtan announced from the doorway as Melangell collapsed in gales of laughter. "My poor cloak!"

He looked at Genann, smiling, his face showing frank admiration for the young man's cleverness. Genann straightened, drying his face and hands.

"Keep my cloak if you like—" he began, but Nechtan waved his words away.

"It will wash in the first cold stream I come to. It's been through worse. But you, Genann, have proven your worth to me. You've saved my life, and I do not forget such a favor."

He glanced at Melangell, then looked at Brennos.

"Since it appears my stay here will be a bit longer than we had planned, Brennos, I will make the announcement myself. Brennos was my witness, Melangell. I have given you your freedom. You are now a free woman, to do as you please."

He paused as first a look of surprise, then a radiant joy lit her face. If he lived to be a hundred, he thought, he would never forget the open, transparent beauty that shone forth from her features at that moment. How can I meet my dreaded end at her hands? he thought sadly. How?

"But I hope what you choose to do is join us," he continued, "be our druidess if you like, and . . . be my wife."

He stared at her when he spoke, his eyes searching her face for any negative reaction. He saw only the barest moment of doubt, which flickered behind her gaze and then briefly, like a shadow, was gone.

But Brennos was watching Genann, not the happy scene unfolding by the hearth, and he nodded wisely as he suddenly understood the situation. Genann's face had gone deathly pale and he slowly lowered the tattered wool towel he held. Poor man! Brennos thought sadly. His pain is so obvious, for anyone to see . . . except those who are in love.

"Yes," Melangell whispered, unable to believe her own answer. She knew that a union with Nechtan would be different from what one with Anarios would have been; he was of her kind, and would understand her calling. Together, they would make their lives a wonderful adventure. Nechtan embraced her fiercely, a broad smile on his face. Sickly, Genann looked away.

"Genann . . ." Nechtan spoke, turning to face the shaken young man. Genann looked at his new master, his face still drawn, his eyes avoiding the girl.

"Brennos said you were Melangell's bodyguard. In these

times that are upon us, she needs such a guard, for who knows what the morrow may bring? I would be honored if you would consent to be her guard."

Genann swallowed stiffly and Brennos saw his gaze fall on the smiling girl at Nechtan's side; and when he answered, Brennos' heart turned in pity at the difficulty of the young man's decision.

"Yes," Genann croaked into the stillness of the room. "I will be her guard."

Brennos fought to hold the door against the blustering wind as he lugged several large parcels into the room. Melangell looked up from her seat by the fire, where she repaired her old black robe.

"Where are the other two?" Brennos asked, kicking the door shut.

"In back—gambling." She laughed.

He nodded. "There's not much else for them to do around here. But I have a plan. Nechtan might be able to escape sooner than we thought."

"Oh?" she asked curiously.

"I'll explain it later. But look! See what I've brought you!"

"Me?" she exclaimed, rising to her feet and putting her sewing aside.

"Yes. The women in the village believe you are under my care now, as guardian of Maia's estate, until Nechtan's exile is finished. So I went around to the wealthier women and collected some very nice things for you."

She opened one of the bundles eagerly.

"Rich women always have perfectly good things they don't want." He laughed as Melangell pulled out elegant shifts in beautiful colors, shawls brilliant with embroideries, even a packet with a few bronze and silver armbands and hair ornaments of jet and bone.

"Oh . . . they are too kind!" she exclaimed, gazing at her new treasures.

"I suspect most of that is a mark of their esteem for poor old Maia. She was a well-loved person, and everyone knows how fond she was of you."

"Please—thank them for me." She smiled, opening the

smaller parcel. It held a magnificent wool cloak, woven in soft blues and greens and yellows, complete with its own spiraling silver shoulder pin. Brennos couldn't help but smile when she stood and swirled it around herself, and the shades of color made her green eyes stand out like jewels.

"Why," she gasped, "it's new!"

"An old woman bought it for her granddaughter, who didn't like the colors." He shrugged and laughed. "So it is yours now."

"Oh, I can't believe it! I've never owned anything so splendid in my life! Thank you, Brennos, thank you!"

She ran forward, the cloak clenched around her shoulders, and gave the druid a hug.

"Now you can look special for your marriage," he laughed.

"Yes . . . I hadn't thought of that!" she replied.

"You'd better start thinking of it; it must be soon, if my plan works out as I hope it will. Now let me disturb the two gamblers in back while I hunt up a chest for you to keep your things in."

Brennos and the girl fixed as festive a meal as they could; he insisted on a celebration to announce his plan for Nechtan's escape. They set small tables and barrels in the back room, and there, in greater security, they spent a pleasant evening, eating the druid's best foods—breads, honey, spiced beans, roasted pork, finely aged cheese, and good Gaulish wine. All except the girl, Brennos noted curiously. She never so much as tasted the meat, and her wine she watered in the Greek manner. Habits learned from old Esus, he guessed.

As the meal concluded, Brennos rose to his feet and waited for their attention. Genann sat perched on a barrel of dried peas, drunkenly staring at Melangell. She seemed subdued at Nechtan's side, the two sitting together on the cot. Nechtan pulled off a chunk of warm bread, offered some to the girl, and then used it to mop the last of the meat juices from his trencher. Brennos cleared his throat loudly and the three looked up at him.

"Annos' chief for the district spoke with me when I made my rounds today."

Nechtan sat up straight, his attention keenly focused on the druid.

"He says we must clear away the rubble of Maia's house. It will harbor rats, children will be playing in it, and the fact that Loucetius, your mother's protector, chose to destroy it frightens the people. Annos wants it cleared and the land it occupied purified of its unlucky influences."

Nechtan looked across at Genann, his mouth drawn back in perplexity.

"It will take several days," Brennos went on. "We are to begin tomorrow . . . you and I, Genann. Melangell, too, if she wishes, although with her burned hand she will have to be careful. We are to gather up the rubble, take it outside the town, and dump it." He paused.

"Yes." Nechtan nodded, rising to his feet. "They will no doubt search the wagon the first day. But later, when they have grown lazy, I will be on that wagon!"

"Exactly!" Brennos exclaimed. "So I suggest that you be wed this evening, so you'll have one night together. Tomorrow you will have to spend most of the night hiding in the wagon, waiting for dawn."

"Why not?" Nechtan grinned. "We have no families to worry about dowries and such. There will be no guests to provide for. We just had a nice-enough marriage feast. Why not!"

He pulled Melangell to her feet.

"Then I must get ready," she said shyly. "I cannot get married in this old shift. And my hair!"

Brennos laughed loudly. "Well, let's clear all this out of here so the lady can use the room for her preparations."

She selected a soft yellow gown to wear, with small red embroideries and braid around the neck and long sleeves. A similarly embroidered sash she tied around her waist, and she slipped two silver armbands onto her left arm, a smaller bronze band fitting over her right wrist. Propping a small bronze mirror on one of the barrels, she combed out her long hair and pinned it loosely atop her head, trying to remember how the serving girl at Genann's house had done it. Turning her head from side to side, she nodded approval at her reflection in the mirror and patted tentatively at the hair to be sure it would stay in place.

At the sound of a soft tap on the door she turned, and Brennos' low voice floated through to her.

"We are ready," he said.

"I'm coming," she answered, and turned to fetch the short shawl she had selected to wear, of fine lamb's wool, pure white except for a narrow border of red braid. She flung it over one arm and knotted it on the other shoulder. Trying to quell the nervousness in her stomach, she stepped across the room and reached for the door.

Genann stood, his jaws clenched tightly, and waited to escort Melangell to her future husband, who stood with Brennos by the hearth. I am to spend the rest of my life doing this, he thought bitterly, and found himself hating Nechtan. I may as well get used to it. I feel nothing, he told himself fiercely. I feel nothing . . .

Nechtan watched when Melangell approached at Genann's side. He had seen her in a slave's rags, in the rich lady's things he had given her, in her white shift, her black druid's cloak, and even naked, but never had he seen her so radiantly, inexpressibly lovely. She looks like a queen, he thought; so perfect and regal. Today is surely the second-luckiest day of my life; the first was when I spared her from Niall's sword.

Reaching his side, she glanced up, nervousness in her eyes, but before Nechtan could speak to her, Brennos was draping a garland of yew and oak and mistletoe across their shoulders, and he turned and faced the druid.

"As our souls were made in the beginning of Creation, and as our souls will continue until Creation ends," Brennos began, "so may your souls, who have found each other, endure in their love and devotion. Let the garland that binds you serve as a reminder; for the yew endures in green fertility; the oak endures in its age-old strength; and the mistletoe lives by a miracle, cut off from the soil, a link between man and the gods. So may your union be ever-enduring in strength, fertility, and an awareness of your spiritual bonds."

He placed his fingertips lightly on their foreheads and

pronounced the final words of the ritual, his eyes closed in concentration.

"May the gods of your hearth and household bless your union, and may you fulfill each other and find peace and happiness until the end of your earthly days."

Opening his eyes, he looked at them and smiled. Nechtan took Melangell's face in his hands and softly kissed her, and Brennos lifted the garland from their shoulders and carried it into the sickroom, to hang above their marriage bed. He glanced at Genann as he walked by. The young man looks as festive as if a plague has just broken out, Brennos thought sadly. He stares woodenly at the far wall; he has not seen a single moment of the ritual.

Genann was perched on a barrel, gazing blankly into his wine cup when Brennos returned to the room. The druid slapped him jovially on the back, trying to cheer him up. The young man cut his eyes around to him briefly and returned them to the cup.

"A round of wine for the happy couple!" Brennos announced cheerily, seizing a silver ewer from atop the storage trunk and handing out wine cups to Nechtan and Melangell. He poured the last of his good Gaulish wine all around, and held his cup aloft.

"To Melangell and Nechtan!" he proclaimed, and waited for the other cups to rise in unison, the happy couple laughing in good spirits. Nechtan downed his wine in one great gulp, as warriors were prone to do when trying to impress one another, and then he turned to Genann.

"My little wife will not need her bodyguard tonight," he joked. "I will look after her."

Genann forced a smile and nodded, raising his cup to his lips while Nechtan swept Melangell up in his arms and carried her into the sickroom, kicking the door shut behind him.

"Brennos," Genann said, his voice like lead, "where is more wine? Or some ale? We must drink . . . be festive . . ."

The night was half gone, and still Genann sat gazing into the fire, his wine cup in hand.

"We must be getting some sleep," Brennos, sitting on the

edge of his cot, suggested gently. "Tomorrow will be a busy day for us, and we must be up early."

Genann took another swallow of ale and didn't answer, and Brennos stood and walked over to him.

"I think I know how you feel," he began, placing a hand on Genann's shoulder and looking down at him sympathetically. Genann gazed up at him, his eyes red-rimmed and bleary.

"No y'don't," he slurred, and stood. "I mus' get more ale . . ."

"No, Genann, don't do this. What has happened has happened, and you cannot change it."

Genann shook his head drunkenly and stumbled over to the clay pitcher of ale. Brennos sighed in frustration, pulled off his black robe, and stretched out on the cot.

"Well, I must get some sleep, Genann, and I think you should too," he said, looking across the hut at the young man. Genann took another long drink of ale and gave him no reply. Shaking his head, the druid rolled over to face the wall, pulling a fur up over his ears to try to muffle out the sound of Genann's drunken voice, brokenly trying to sing some old love song he knew. To Brennos' relief, he soon abandoned his efforts and fell to silence. The druid had slept for only a short while when Genann woke him again. Rolling over, Brennos looked at him in pity. Genann sat slumped forward, one hand over his eyes, and cried in dry, agonized sobs that shook his whole body, the empty wine cup fallen to the floor at his feet.

Brennos' sleep was fitful and brief, his body sweating despite the chill of the room. He woke groggily, trying to forget the dreams that had haunted him, his mind a whirling haze of memories. Again he had wandered that hot, distant land where his soul had dwelt long ago. Again he, a young priest, had gone to his beloved, the new wife of a wealthy nobleman. Cool river breezes sighed around the ruined shrine where they met, and he could still see her gown, ghostly white against the nighttime, smell the heady scent of her perfume, feel her soft body in his arms . . .

Brennos groaned, shifting uncomfortably against the

throbbing ache he felt in his groin. Yet this dream had been different; this dream left him with no wistful longing for a girl he had once known, no emptiness in his soul. This dream had left him with only certainty. The girl . . . the girl was Melangell . . .

Cursing Genann and his love songs of the previous night, he sat up and flung the fur covering aside irritably; yes, he tried to reassure himself, his moonstruck songs infected me.

The sun was already well up, the village stirring to life. Gods above! Brennos cursed himself as he jumped up and pulled on his robe, we should have been out and working long before now.

He looked at Genann, who lay on his side on the floor, deep in sleep, and shook his head slowly. Whose curse is worse, he wondered as he crossed the room—Nechtan's . . . or Genann's?

He let Genann sleep as long as possible while he brewed a potion for his hangover, then tossed some bread and cheese into a leather bag to take with them for their meal. Shaking Genann's shoulder roughly, he roused him; the young man sat up groggily, running a hand through his tangled hair.

"Here, drink this—all of it!" Brennos ordered, handing him the potion. Grimacing at the taste, Genann drank it in two gulps and rose unsteadily to his feet.

"Go and splash some cold water in your face while I yoke the horse to the wagon," Brennos said, rushing from the house.

Without replying, Genann made his way to the copper washbasin and gasped when the cold water hit his bleary eyes. It did seem to wake him, and he splashed more water on his face, up his arms, and across the back of his neck. Wiping his face with a bit of cloth, he turned away from the basin in thought.

Brennos said Melangell might want to help us, he mused, then shook his head. No . . . she would want to stay with Nechtan today. But still, he did suggest it, and she didn't object.

He crossed to the rear door and gave it a light tap, listening for a response. He heard only silence.

They are still asleep, he thought. He turned from the door,

then halted. Slowly he tried the door and found it gave easily. With one steadying hand he pressed it inward and peered into the gloom of the unlit back room.

They lay naked together, deep in sleep, Melangell on her side, curled up like a little child and facing the door. Nechtan too lay on his side, his body curved close against the girl's back, his face buried in her long hair, one arm draped across her waist and the other beneath her head. Her long pale hair was a sharp contrast to Nechtan's shaggy black hair, and as Genann's gaze slowly roamed down their bodies he thought they looked like two fine white alabaster statues from Greece, perfectly sculptured down to the last detail. Nechtan's muscles were lean and hard, and the girl . . . He closed his eyes shakily and could not help but look at her one more time—her slim white arms, her softly rounded breasts, her smooth hip curving up beneath Nechtan's arm.

He closed the door with a sigh of defeat. What wouldn't he give to have her in his arms like that, for just one night? His wealth? His life? His very soul?

Shaking his head sadly, he walked across the hut. And yet, he mused, that look on her face—so sweet, so peaceful and contented, so happy. As if she truly belonged there, sleeping in Nechtan's arms. If I really love her, then I must want her happiness, and not just my own. If this is what makes her happy, I must be happy for her.

His eyes bright with new resolve, he poured himself a cup of cold water and tore off a chunk of bread just as Brennos returned.

"All ready?" he asked the young man, who nodded eagerly, picked up the pack of food in one hand and his bread in the other, and strode across the hut past the mystified druid.

They worked only in their breeches, shirtless under a warm late-summer sun. A haze of fine gray ash and dust clouded the air and coated their bodies, streaking and smudging in their sweat. First they hauled the remains of the roofing beams onto the cart, then cleared out some of the smaller rubble. As the two men heaved the last piece of beam onto the wagon, Genann paused and wiped a grimy hand across his wet forehead.

"By the wealth of Bran, I did grow up as a rich man's son!" he exclaimed. "I have never worked so hard in my life!"

Brennos laughed and climbed aboard the wagon.

"And look at you!" Genann added. "You look hardly winded, and you must be . . . five years older than I am!"

"Probably six," the druid replied as Genann climbed up beside him and he slapped the horse into motion. "You look to be about Nechtan's age—twenty-two?"

Genann nodded.

"Well, I am twenty-eight; an old, old man." Brennos laughed, guiding the groaning cart down the narrow, twisted streets. "You will get used to the active life soon enough. It is an easy transition, and a natural one."

Genann clung to the side of the wagon as it lurched and heaved along the rutted dirt streets, watching the free-roaming pigs and geese scatter at its approach. "I think next time we'd better have a smaller load," he said, listening to the shifting beams behind them. "We'll be lucky not to lose part of this along the way."

"Aye." Brennos nodded. "I also think it will be a bigger job than we expected. I think I'll hire some help—after tomorrow."

He glanced at Genann, who looked ahead to the front gate, a grim set to his mouth.

"Now we will see," the druid muttered as a guard, spear in hand, waved them to a stop.

"The chief of the district has ordered me to—" Brennos began to explain to the man, who waved him aside impatiently.

"I know . . . I know," the guard snapped, walking to the back of the cart. He peered into the rubble with shaded eyes, bending this way and that, and then he straightened up and looked at Brennos.

"Take it out," he ordered.

"What!" the druid exclaimed in astonishment. Genann sighed wearily and rolled his eyes skyward.

"I cannot search it properly," the guard replied tersely as

Brennos climbed from the wagon, Genann at his heels. "I have my orders."

"See here," the druid retorted, anger starting to flash in his gray eyes, his low voice growing tight. "I, too, have my orders, from the chief of the district, to get that rubble cleared out of here. If we must load and unload everything twice, it will take all year! We will take off the topmost logs so that you can probe everything below it with your spear, until you are satisfied. But that's all," he concluded, folding his arms stubbornly across his bare chest as Genann looked at him in admiration.

The guard seemed to hesitate; it was not his usual practice to argue with a figure of authority such as a druid.

"If you don't trust me, send a guard over to the house site," Brennos snapped. "He can inspect everything as we load, and save us all a lot of time."

"Well . . ." the guard muttered, thinking. "All right, just the top logs, then. But I must inspect the wagon, you understand."

Brennos nodded. "Of course."

Together he and Genann lifted off the heaviest beams and piled them neatly on the ground, then stood aside. The guard poked and probed the wagon's contents with his spear, raising clouds of fine ash. Satisfied, he stepped back and motioned for them to continue on their way, while trying to wipe the dirt and grime from his face.

Genann and Brennos silently reloaded the wagon, climbed aboard, and rolled through the timber gate and down the hillside. As they neared the woods and slowed to turn onto a side track, Genann laughed aloud.

"He won't keep that up for long!" He chuckled, slapping a hand to his knee.

Brennos smiled as he guided the horse along. "We'll have to be sure to get an especially dusty load tomorrow morning," he replied, a glint of mischief in his eyes.

Genann looked around as they approached the refuse pile and noted that it was closely ringed with trees and brush encroaching along its edges. A flock of ravens rose noisily to the treetops when they neared, and a fox ran down the slope and disappeared into the surrounding forest.

"Let's toss everything here, by these scrubby trees,"

Brennos suggested. "They should afford good cover for Nechtan."

"He should have no trouble escaping," Genann said, climbing from the wagon. "We'll come early in the morning, while the light is still poor."

Brennos nodded, and together they quickly emptied the wagon.

The night had begun when the two exhausted men returned to the druid's home. Genann offered to take care of the horse, but Brennos declined; he had a few preparations to make for tomorrow's journey. Genann climbed from the wagon and tiredly walked toward the druid's dwelling.

His stomach growled hungrily when he reached for the latch and the heady smells of cooking food assailed his nose. Stepping into the hut, in the flickering firelight he saw Melangell tending several kettles of food on the hearth, and freshly-baked round bread on a stone slab nearby. Nechtan was probably safe in the back room, he mused, stumbling to the washbasin. How he would love a good hot bath, but there was no time for that now. He washed his face and arms and poured water over his dusty hair, turning when Nechtan entered the rear doorway, a questioning look on his face.

"Well?" he asked Genann.

The young man nodded and quickly dried his face. "All will be well, I think," he said. Nechtan sighed in relief, casting a glance at Melangell.

"Good," he said simply, and fell silent.

Genann walked over to a fur near the hearth and sat down heavily.

"Gods above, I am tired!" he exclaimed. He took a heaping trencher of food from Melangell.

"What happened today?" the girl asked, concern in her voice. He looked at her as he began wolfing down some hot barley, and for an instant he imagined her naked, sitting there by the fire.

"Nothing much," he said, gulping the food. "On the first trip they wanted us to unload everything, but Brennos refused, and on each trip after that they got more lax. There should be no problem tomorrow."

Nechtan nodded and Melangell gazed down absently at

the floor. She roused when Brennos came through the front door, still wearing only his breeches, his black robe over one arm, weariness etching his gray-streaked face.

"Ah . . . food!" he sighed, dropping the robe to the floor and taking a deep sniff of the air while he headed for the washbasin. The druid lowered his entire face into the water and shook it vigorously.

"I am too old for this!" he gasped, raising his face and burying it in the towel. "After tomorrow, I hire some help!"

"Genann says there'll be no problem," Nechtan remarked while the druid washed his arms and chest.

"No, I don't think so," Brennos answered. "I have made some preparations, too, in the stable. Let me eat, and I'll explain them to you."

Drying himself, he headed for the food Melangell ladled out for him.

"That's one disadvantage of being a druid," he sighed, settling back on the edge of his cot. "You don't have a wife waiting for you, with your supper cooked and ready to eat."

He smiled at the girl and Nechtan gave a short laugh. "I can think of more disadvantages than that!" He grinned.

"Yes, well, we try not to think of those things," Brennos said in mock solemnity as he ate, trying not to notice Melangell's reddening cheeks.

"We must get up before dawn," Genann said, changing the conversation. "It is best if you escape while the light is poor."

"Aye," Brennos gulped between mouthfuls, "and I think it best if you go out to hide during the middle of the night, rather than just before we leave."

Nechtan agreed.

"Come!" The druid motioned to him. "I'll explain things while I eat."

Nechtan crossed the room and sat on the cot beside him.

"Melangell can tell you," Brennos began, "that the magic and powers attributed to us druids is for the most part common sense, which most of humanity seems to be sadly lacking in, and for another part mere trickery."

He bit off a chunk of ham and looked to the girl for confirmation. She nodded, a twinkle in her eye.

"You give us away, Brennos," she jested, and he laughed.

"I said for the most part," he replied mysteriously. "The remainder is our little secret, eh?" He winked.

"So," he continued, "we have been known to smuggle things hither and yon, as the need arose. Supplies, medicines, weapons, each other . . ."

He took a few sips of ale before resuming.

"Did you notice, Genann, that the wagon is old, the boards warped and uneven?" he asked. Genann nodded, curious as to what the druid was getting to.

"Well, that was no accident. I have a similarly old and uneven board which is made to fit between two of the cracks on either side, just behind the front seat. Then the seat slides back over it, resulting in a somewhat shorter wagon, and a hiding place big enough to conceal a man."

He glanced at Nechtan, whose face brightened as he seized on the idea.

"You see, we poor old crazy druids are not quite so poor or crazy as people imagine." Brennos chuckled, looking at the astonished expressions on the faces of Nechtan and Genann. Only the girl didn't seem too taken aback by it.

"So, in a few more hours, when the night is well under way, I will go out to water the horse. Nechtan will crawl through a hole in the stable wall by the lean-to, and I will hide him in the wagon. You will not be able to get out by yourself, Nechtan, and you will not be very comfortable, but at least you'll be safe."

Nechtan stood. "Genann and I can go now and begin cutting a hole through the wall. It is only wattle, but in order to be quiet we'll have to be very slow and careful. Come," he said. Genann handed his empty trencher to Melangell, rose, and followed Nechtan from the room. Melangell watched them leave, then turned and looked at Brennos.

"I hope this works," she said quietly.

"It will," he stated, raising his cup to his mouth, and his confident manner reassured her somewhat.

The four sat around the low hearthfire, talking in hushed voices while waiting for midnight to arrive. "You will come," Nechtan said suddenly to Brennos, who nodded confidently. "Aye, and once you are safely away I will ask Calum and a few others about joining me," the druid replied.

"And you, Genann—you will bring Melangell to me, either with Brennos and the others, or perhaps sooner?"

Genann nodded, and silence again descended on the room. Time crawled by as they watched the fire sputter and flare, heard the wood softly fall to ash, watched Brennos feed more small logs to the flames. Finally the druid stood, walked over to the shuttered window, and peered through a crack up at the stars.

"It is time," he said, and his voice fell like doom on Melangell's ears.

"Genann," Nechtan said, standing and clasping the man's shoulder, "I hope to see you within the passing of the next moon. Take good care of her."

"I will," Genann replied stiffly, stepping away.

Nechtan reached for Melangell and pulled her to him. "I'll be all right," he said softly. "Don't worry. The time will pass before you know it, and you'll be back with me once more."

"Good-bye," she whispered, barely audible. He kissed her softly and peered into her solemn face.

"Good-bye," he answered, turned, and walked to the sickroom, Genann close behind. Brennos picked up a small wooden bucket, filled it with water, and carried it from the hut. Melangell bolted the door behind him, turned, and ran to the lean-to to watch Nechtan leave.

The room was so crowded she could barely squeeze in the door. The two men had moved aside some large chests, and now, on hearing Brennos' voice beyond the wall talking to the horse, Nechtan began wriggling through the hole they had cut low in the wattle siding. Genann leaned over and watched him. When Nechtan's feet disappeared through the hole, Genann passed his sword and cloak to him. Listening to be sure all was well, Melangell pushed past him, fell to her hands and knees, and peered through the opening.

The stable was dark except for one small horn lantern by the horse's stall. She could see cow's hooves, the heavy wooden wagon wheels, and the dusty bottom of Brennos' black robe as he stood beside it; nothing more.

Genann's hand fell on her shoulder and she looked up.

"Come," he said, helping her to her feet. He pushed the chests back against the wall, concealing the hole, and stood silently, one foot erasing the drag marks in the dirt floor while he listened. Soon they heard Brennos talking to the horse again, slapping its neck affectionately, and the animal snorting a reply.

Genann took Melangell's arm and led her to the main room, crossed the floor, and lifted the bolt on the door.

"It is done," the druid said simply when he entered. "Now let's all get some sleep before morning."

Melangell turned wordlessly and returned to the sick-room. She lay down woodenly on the cot, not fetching a blanket, not bothering to undress. As she stared at the cobwebs dangling under the low thatched ceiling, her mind was a leaden weight on her heart.

Just beyond this wall, secreted away in a little box, is the man I love above all else, whom I may never see alive again. And I cannot go to him, or speak with him, or touch him. Yet only last night we lay together in this very room, as happy as two people could be.

She turned her face to the wall and fought the tears that crept to the corners of her eyes.

Nechtan, I love you!

The fierce gabbling of two geese quarreling in the street outside woke them early. The last of the night hung heavy in the damp morning air, and low mists still cloaked the village streets. Melangell threw together some food for their meal, barely aware of what she was doing, while the two men yoked the horse to Brennos' cart. She heard the wagon slowly creaking to the front of the house, Genann muttering and kicking angrily at a goose who challenged him. She rushed to the door to see them off, suddenly stopping, her face frozen in fear.

Brennos was speaking, at first normally, then in rising anger, to someone else. She approached the door, listening, and wildly cursing the fates a thousand times over. It was Angus. Casually she opened the door, the food sack in one hand and a look of concern on her face.

Brennos stood by the wagon, as face-to-face as he could

203

get with the tall guard, his face red with rage. Genann sat on the wagon, reins in hand, and he caught her eyes fearfully when she appeared in the doorway.

"How am I to clean out the rubble if I am constantly having to run errands?" Brennos demanded hotly. Angus shrugged.

"The chief of the district wants to see you now; that's all I know," he said mildly, cutting his sharp blue eyes around to the girl and quickly taking in the bag of food she held.

"A meal?" he inquired, and she nodded. "Let me see it." Compliantly she held it out to him.

Angus opened the sack suspiciously, probed among the contents and, satisfied, handed it back to Melangell. Her anger, too, was now rising, vying with fear for control of her emotions. Haughtily she walked around the two men and handed the sack to Genann, who took it with a suppressed smile.

"Nice little piece, eh?" Angus muttered to Brennos when she stepped around them, and she whirled, her eyes flashing. Drawing herself up to full height, she pulled her arm back to slap the guard, when Brennos' hand shot out and seized her upraised wrist before she could strike.

"That's enough, Melangell," the druid warned sternly as Angus stepped back in surprise.

"Pretty uppity for a slave, isn't she?" the guard snapped.

"Careful what you say," Brennos cautioned, motioning his head to the wagon where Genann had now risen to his feet in alarm. "He is her guard, you know."

"Eh?" Angus smiled, looking at the strapping young man who already had one hand on his dagger hilt. "Oh—no harm done! Come, Brennos, send him on ahead of you if you like, but you must come with me to see the chief of the district . . . *now.*"

Brennos nodded, resigned, and released the girl's wrist.

"Go back in the house and bolt the door, and do not open it for anyone except me or Genann," he instructed her. "I don't suppose things have come to such a pass yet," he said bitterly to Angus as they turned to go, "that my quarters will be forcibly entered."

Genann sat down, relieved, and picked up the reins while

the druid and the guard walked away. Silently he looked at the girl, then jerked his head to the door.

"Go on," he said. Without a word Melangell turned, reentered the hut, and dropped the bolt in place.

At the sound of the bolt, Genann clucked to the horse and the wagon rolled away into the swirling mists of the dawn.

Melangell listened at the door, fear in her heart, until the sound of the wagon had vanished amidst the noises of the awakening town. Turning with a sigh, she made sure the window shutter was latched, picked up Genann's heavy sword, and sat down on Brennos' cot. Slumping back against the plastered wall, she laid the sword across her lap, closed her eyes, and prepared for the long wait.

"Damn!" Genann cursed when the burned house came in sight. "They have put a guard on it, as Brennos suggested. Oh, well . . . it will make little difference, for he cannot see anything amiss here, anyway."

He pulled the horse up beside the rubble he and Brennos had selected to be the first load to haul this morning, hopped down, and in dismay looked at the size of the beams. Easy enough for two men to handle, they would be difficult if not impossible for him to move alone. He stood by the wagon, one hand on his hip and the other running through his hair, pondering what to do. He glanced at the guard, hoping he might offer to lend a hand. The man just sat on a tree stump, a spear across his lap, watching and obviously unwilling to move from his comfortable spot.

"Damn!" Genann cursed again, shaking his head. "I'll just have to do it myself."

The guard looked on keenly when Genann began dragging the burned timbers to the wagon. The largest he would have to leave till Brennos returned; the others he could slowly heave and haul into the wagon, one end at a time, by himself.

Ignoring the guard, he hopped into the wagon and pulled in the logs he had propped against the side, jumping out of the way as each one crashed to the floor, jarring the wagon mightily.

I'm sorry for such a rough ride, Nechtan, he thought as he

pulled in the last log, leapt away, and vaulted over the side to the ground.

I'll pace myself, he decided. Now, some lighter things. Brennos might be back at any time to help me.

He tossed armfuls of burned household items, crumbled storage chests, the frame of a loom, warped and melted pots, into the back of the wagon, casting an uneasy eye at the sky. Already the morning light was fading. Where is Brennos? he wondered, trying to quell the fear rising within him. It will take me half the day on my own.

Propping more large logs along the side of the wagon, he again climbed in, wiped the sweat from his forehead, and began pulling them aboard. Something has gone wrong, he brooded. I must hurry with this load and get Nechtan out of here.

Kicking aside the rubble to find secure footing, he heaved at the last log, jumped back, and landed on a melted pot. His foot slid out from under him and before he could catch himself, the end of the log came crashing down on his thigh.

Pain shot through him and he slumped forward, clutching at the leg with both hands.

"Are you all right?" the guard asked, his face appearing beside the wagon.

"No," Genann gulped, shaking his head angrily at his carelessness, his stupidity.

"Here, I'll help you down," the guard offered, extending a hand up to him. Genann gratefully took it and climbed down, blood staining his breeches and beginning to trickle down his leg. He limped over to the guard's post and sat down, the injured leg extended stiffly in front of him. Together he and the guard bent low to examine it. Genann picked aside the shredded cloth and pulled out a few chunks of wood embedded in the wound. His whole leg was burning like fire; how could he endure it much longer?

"Water . . ." he gasped. The guard handed him a skin bag. Genann groaned when he poured it over the wound. He took off his dusty white tunic, folded it, and tied it tightly around the leg. He rose to his feet, and the guard looked at him in astonishment.

"Surely you're not going to continue?" he exclaimed.

Genann nodded, limping erratically back to the wagon, the injured leg dragging stiffly to the side and barely able to support him.

Angrily he threw a few smaller pieces of wood into the wagon, climbed to the seat, and picked up the reins. To his dismay, the guard circled to the other side and looked up at him.

"I'll come along and help you," he offered, reaching up to the wagon seat.

"N-no," Genann gulped. "I can manage. I'll just dump this load and go home."

"But you can't do it yourself!" the guard protested. "Just look at you! You ought to be seeing Brennos right now."

"No, I'll do it," Genann mumbled, snapping the reins and holding on with one hand when the wagon lurched forward. Shaking his head, the guard walked along beside the cart.

Gods above, get away! Genann thought through gritted teeth. Go and leave me alone.

To his relief, the guard nodded his consent to the other men at the gate and they waved Genann through without a halt.

The trip seemed to go on forever, each jarring lurch of the wagon sending fierce new pain tearing through his outstretched leg. He was fighting for consciousness by the time he reached the dump and pulled the horse to a halt. Half-falling, he climbed from the seat and glanced around the clearing. No one else was there.

He pushed weakly at the seat but it didn't move, and panic began to rise within him. This would surely fail; nothing was going right . . . nothing! Setting his jaw, he summoned what strength he could and gave a mighty shove to the seat. It creaked, moved, and slid forward a scant space, but it was enough for Nechtan to get his hands out and push it the rest of the way. Genann slumped heavily against the cart's side. Nechtan stood, stretched stiffly, and on cramped legs jumped to the ground, buckling his sword belt around his waist.

He eyed Genann, his pale face and crudely bandaged leg, blood already soaking through the tied shirt. Genann lifted his head and looked at him tiredly.

"Go . . . quickly," he gasped. Nechtan shook his head firmly and, walking forward, began to unyoke the horse.

"No . . ." Genann tried to protest, but Nechtan ignored him. He got the horse free and led it back to the wounded man.

"Get on," he commanded, pulling Genann on to the horse's back. "Twice now you have saved my life, Genann, and I will not forget it. I know my wife is in good hands with you. Now, get back to the druid at once."

He slapped the horse's rump and it trotted back up the narrow path, Genann slumped heavily over its shaggy neck. Shaking his head, Nechtan pinned his cloak around his shoulders, closed the secret compartment on the wagon, and trotted off into the misty woods.

The guard stopped in mid-sentence when he saw the lone pony plodding up the slope, Genann swaying precariously atop it. Seizing the bridle, the man led the horse through town, back to the druid's house, and rapped sharply on the door.

"Yes?" came a female voice from within.

"I have your guard," he answered. "He is wounded."

He heard the bolt being lifted, the door opened a crack, and a pallid face peered out, the green eyes growing large when she saw Genann, nearly falling from the horse's back. The door sprang open and she motioned to the guard.

"Bring him in," she said urgently.

Pulling Genann from the horse, the guard put an arm around him and dragged him heavily into the room.

"Over there," the girl said, pointing to a cot by the wall. "What happened?" she gasped, eyeing the bloody leg.

"A log fell on him," the man explained.

"A log?" she questioned, her fear rising. "And where is the wagon?"

"Still at the dump, I suppose. He insisted on taking it down there, but he couldn't make it back."

The man turned to go. "I'll tie up the horse for you," he said over his shoulder.

"Yes . . . thank you," she answered, unwinding the blood-soaked shirt from Genann's leg. Bless you, Genann, bless you, she thought wildly as she worked. You got Nechtan down there, and now he is safe. Bless you . . .

"It looks bad," Brennos said, pulling aside the bandage Melangell had wound around Genann's cleaned and treated leg, "but I couldn't have done a better job myself."

Replacing the cloth strips, he straightened up and looked at her; Genann slept soundly, deep in drugged sleep.

"So you're a druidess again, eh?" Brennos smiled.

"I never stopped being one," she replied.

"Aye." He nodded. "And I agree with you about Genann: better to keep him asleep the first day or two, until the pain subsides and the healing begins. You say he got Nechtan out safely?"

"Apparently so. The guard who brought him said he'd taken the wagon out, even with a wounded leg, but he couldn't bring it back. It's still at the dump."

"Well, evening approaches but there's some daylight left," Brennos said. "The horse is still harnessed; I'll fetch Calum and we'll go and get the wagon."

"Calum?" She started nervously. "Do you think that's wise?"

Brennos turned toward the door and laughed.

"Oh, he knows. He's known all along. In fact, he's led poor Angus off on several wild chases, looking for Nechtan. We'll check the secret compartment, just to be sure Nechtan got away, although I feel sure he did. He probably unyoked the horse and got Genann on it; I doubt he had the strength left to do it himself."

"Yes!" she said, brightening. "I'll wager you're right!"

"Well," the druid instructed, "keep him quiet and warm. I'll be back for the evening meal. And bolt the door behind me."

"You will be all right?" Melangell asked Genann again.

"Yes!" he exclaimed, looking at Brennos mischievously. "She acts more like my mother than my mother ever did!"

The druid laughed and held out her new cloak to the girl. "Come, Melangell. He is comfortable, he has food and drink at hand. Let's be off, if we are to return by evening."

209

She took the cloak, pinning it at her throat as she followed Brennos to the door.

"Don't try to move—" she began, a parting instruction to Genann, who sat across the cot, his back to the wall and the injured leg propped on a barrel in front of him. He raised his hands as if to ward off a blow.

"Go!" he laughed at her. "Go!" Being wounded was not so bad—he sighed, settling back after the two had departed —not with Melangell taking care of him so tenderly.

"I wear any old clothes that are given to me, but Genann is used to finer things," Brennos explained as they threaded their way through the crowded market stalls inside the main gate of the village. "I thought you could better select some nice new breeches for him. He'll be walking again soon, and one-legged breeches won't be too fashionable on the streets!"

She laughed merrily, her eyes eagerly taking in the wide array of goods presented for sale in the marketplace.

"Oh, it's splendid!" she gasped.

"I thought you'd enjoy the outing," he confided. "You sit at home too much. I have a few Roman coins I've accumulated. We may as well spend them today; they'll do us little good when we leave."

He looked down at her happy face as he steered her by the arm through the busy throng. Nechtan's a lucky man indeed, he thought with a touch of sadness. How often had he wondered what a normal life would be like—a wife, children, good times with friends. Being a druid was a lonely existence for most; one was always set apart from his fellows; one was never quite the same.

"Here," he said, pointing to a stall hung with brightly colored lengths of cloth. "Pick out a nice pattern for Genann."

She stepped forward, amazement on her face.

"Yes?" the shopkeeper asked, one eye on the druid who walked up behind the girl. This transaction, at least, would have to be an honest one.

"We're buying breeches for a tall young man of twenty-two," Brennos explained to the shopkeeper, who promptly vanished behind a stack of folded cloths, emerging with a bright pattern of red and yellow checks.

"Many of the young men prefer it," he began, but the girl shook her head.

"It is too gaudy, too bright. He is quiet . . . gentle." Her eyes roamed the stall again.

"There!" she said, pointing. "What about that one?"

"Ah, a good choice," the man agreed, pulling down a length of muted blues and yellows.

"It looks nice." Brennos nodded. "Fine. Have them made up into a good set of long breeches. The young man is of average build, and somewhat taller than I am."

The shopkeeper nodded.

"I'll pick them up in four days—" the druid began.

"Paid in advance," the man said. Brennos sighed, pulled out a leather pouch, and counted a few silver coins into the man's outstretched hand.

"They'd better be good, or I'll have you thrown out of town," Brennos threatened as he and Melangell walked away, and the shopkeeper nodded meekly.

"Anything else?" the druid asked Melangell.

"How much is a harp?" she questioned.

"A harp? Why? They are very expensive, I'm afraid . . ." he began, stopping when he saw her face fall.

"Genann is a harpist," she explained. "He plays very well. I thought it would give him something to do while he recovers."

"He is?" Brennos exclaimed in surprise.

"Yes. I know he misses his harp, but if they are too expensive . . ."

"Well, now," he said, his face a frown of concentration, "I cannot afford to buy one, but tomorrow I'll see what I can do about . . . finding one."

He winked at her, and she brightened immediately. "Our secret?" she asked. He nodded.

"All right. Our secret. Now, let's buy a little food before we finish shopping. Don't you want anything for yourself?"

"I don't know." She shrugged. "Everything's so beautiful, and I've never had much before. I just don't know."

They stepped aside when a noisy group of laughing

warriors swept by, spears resting across their shoulders, their brightly patterned cloaks fluttering in the air. Brennos looked up and down the twisting pathways while they waited for the men to pass.

"I know one thing I want to get for you," he said, walking her to the end of the market and stopping at a stall cluttered with all manner of foreign objects: large gold earrings, clay statues, Gaulish perfumes, Roman glass vases, variously colored cloths. Reaching up, the druid pulled down a small shawl that seemed to float on the air, so fine and delicate was it, and the color shimmered in the sunlight, now blue, now green. She looked at it, awestruck, and gasped when he draped it lightly over her head.

"Oh . . ." she breathed, "what is it?"

"Silk. Have you ever heard of that before? It comes from a land far, far away, and is made of very fine thread from an insect, like a spider's web."

Her mouth flew open in surprise, and he paused.

"Yes!" she exclaimed. "Anarios told me about . . ." Abruptly she stopped, looked at Brennos' startled face, and lowered her eyes.

"I . . . I'm sorry," she said, pulling the cloth from her head and handing it back to him. "I know he was your slave and—"

"Nonsense!" the druid replied, pressing the shawl into her hand. "You had nothing to do with that. You are a princeling's wife now; you deserve special things. I cannot afford an entire gown of silk, so this will have to do."

She looked at him, aghast.

"For me?" she whispered. "You would buy this for me?"

"Yes." He smiled, counting out his coins. "Now, let's buy some food and get back to the house. We must get things ready for our guests."

"Guests?" she puzzled, positioning the shawl across her shoulders.

"Yes," he replied. "A surprise. You'll see."

Melangell wore a soft green shift, with the new shawl draped across one shoulder and lightly knotted on the other. Brennos had purchased more good Roman wine from southern Gaul, and a roast of pork, and these Melangell had waiting to entertain their visitors. Brennos would not tell her who they were, only that it was important that she, as Nechtan's wife, meet them—and one of them in particular. She hovered around the hut like a brightly colored butterfly, awaiting their arrival, and whirled at the sound of a tap. Anxiously she stood, her hands clasped before her, and when the druid opened the door, she gasped aloud.

His eyes fell at once on the girl, standing by the hearth, all dressed in green and staring back in surprise. Despite her elegant appearance, the silver jewelry, the long hair pinned up from her face, he recognized her easily, and an odd feeling came to him. The last time he had seen her, rain drenched her body, fire sparked her eyes, blue flames surrounded her, and he had . . .

But yes, it was the same girl. No doubt about that. And she obviously recognized him as well.

"You . . . you are . . ." she whispered. The man's long brown hair was held down by a wide leather tie, and tooled leather armbands encircled his tightly muscled wrists and upper arms. He seemed tense, wary, like a cunning weasel, always alert to the hunt.

"Calum, ma'am," the man replied with a slight nod of his head.

"How . . . ah . . . how are your eyes?" Melangell asked slowly. Calum half-smiled.

"Pretty bad for a while, but they're fine now. I realize you could have done worse to me."

"Yes . . ." she stammered. "I . . . well, I didn't want to . . . to . . ."

"To really hurt me? Yes, I realized that, and I am grateful for it. I'm afraid I didn't repay your concern very well. My spear—did it . . . ?"

Without a word she lifted the shawl draped over her right arm and saw the surprise on his face when his eyes fell on the jagged pink scar. He walked to her, lifted the arm in one tough, scarred hand, and seemed to study it.

"It looks bad," he muttered, glancing into her face. "I am truly sorry. I was half out of my mind with rage and fear and weariness. I never should have done . . ."

She shrugged, pulled her arm free, and lowered the cloth over it.

"I won't lie and tell you it wasn't bad, because it was. But my luck was good and I was saved by a druid holy man before I bled to death."

Understanding lit Calum's eyes. "So that is how you disappeared, and why my spear was returned to me! I halfway believed you to be a goddess or a spirit, vanishing into the air!"

She laughed lightly and stepped away from him. He once had brought such terror to her heart; his proximity made her uncomfortable.

"And your name is Calum, is it?" She tried to be hospitable. "Would you like some wine?"

"Yes!" Brennos exclaimed jovially, glad that the tension had eased. "Let me introduce everyone. This is Calum, the best tracker in the territory . . ."

Calum laughed, a broad, open smile that Melangell liked at once.

"And his apprentice Mac Oag," the druid said, motioning to a tall, very thin dark-haired youth of about fifteen. The boy smiled awkwardly and nodded, clearly wishing he could be somewhere else.

"And this is Genann, one of Nechtan's men and the bodyguard of Melangell, who is now Nechtan's wife."

Calum's eyebrows lifted at this last bit of news and he eyed the girl more intently. Yes, Nechtan always did have good taste in women, he mused.

"Now let's have some food and drink, and talk," Brennos suggested, motioning to the furs and barrels by the hearth.

"So you are interested in joining our group?" Genann asked as the wine was poured around.

"Aye," Calum said. "The two of us, anyway. I don't know about any of the others, though." He took a deep gulp of wine and looked at Brennos. "What about the crops?" he asked.

"I have contracted with a few of the area boys to get them in for me, for one-fourth their total yield. Then Annos gets his fourth, and the rest we take with us when we go to join Nechtan. I have my wagon, and we will use Nechtan's war chariot. That should be enough."

Calum nodded. "I have two horses as well," he added.

"Good!" Brennos approved. "Everything else of his, and

most of mine, we will sell or trade for goods we need—cloth, weapons, other foods—such as that."

"We can herd the cattle along for eating later—" Calum began. Brennos shook his head.

"We would have no food or shelter for them," he said. "Better to sell them, and live off the wild game."

"Aye," Calum agreed, paused, then spoke again; a difficult question, it was plain to see.

"And what of the families, Brennos?" he asked. The druid frowned his understanding.

"You speak of your wife, of course," he said gently. Calum looked down at his hands.

"We have no other kin here for her to go to," he muttered. "You, the only real healer in town, will be gone, leaving only a few old women." He gazed into the fire, his face falling to worry.

"And her time is near, isn't it?" Brennos concluded. The tracker looked up in fear.

"Yes—and you said she is too narrow. The birth will be difficult. I cannot leave her here alone and with no druid. She must come with me. She could be Melangell's attendant. I will not go without her."

"Of course," Melangell announced, rising to her feet. Calum looked up at her, gratitude in his eyes.

"She can be my woman—when she is able. In the meantime, I will look after her myself. After all"—she grinned, looking at Brennos—"it is entirely possible that she and I have something in common!"

Brennos smiled and nodded. "Well, then, I suppose it's settled. The boys begin harvesting next week, and within the moon's turning we should be ready to leave."

"No!" Melangell gasped, as if the earth had just opened up and swallowed the hearth before her. "I do not believe you!"

Brennos nodded solemnly, crouched before her and holding her hands in his.

"We waited to tell you," he said, "but we leave soon, and you must know. Genann, his brother Cai, and Nechtan's archer Cathal saw it. Esus is dead, Melangell. I'm sorry."

Her face turned ashen and she felt her soul crumble within her.

Esus! Dead! No, it couldn't be! She would see him again, his old blue eyes twinkling merrily, his kind voice always knowing just the right thing to say.

In desperation she looked up at Genann, who stood behind the druid, watching her. He shook his head slightly.

"I'm sorry," he said softly, wishing he could do something, anything, to make her awful pain disappear.

"No!" she choked, her gaze returning to Brennos' worried gray eyes. She pulled her hands from his and raised them, trembling violently, to her face.

"Esus!" she screamed, and Brennos quickly pulled her close. Genann felt his eyes fill with tears as he watched her heartbreak, so transparent, so total. Turning awkwardly, he left the druid's hut and sat on a log bench outside the door, letting the poor girl shed her grief in private.

Curse this world, he thought angrily, picking absently at the scrawny rowan bush the druid had planted outside his door. Will any of us ever be happy? In all the land, why did the Romans have to find gentle, kindly Esus; and why such a terrible death? He, who had rarely harmed a creature in his entire life. And now Melangell, such a sweet, caring girl, is crushed beyond words; she, who aches so for everyone else's pain, is now overwhelmed with pain herself.

Bitterly he slammed a fist into his hand.

It isn't fair! It isn't fair . . .

He turned when the door scraped open and Brennos motioned to him. He could hear the girl still whimpering and moaning, like a frightened little animal.

"Sit with her," Brennos said. "I have a few errands to run, and I don't want to leave her alone. If she does not recover by sundown, I will give her something to calm her, but for now it is best to let her release her grief. It has been a great blow to her."

Genann nodded and walked over to the girl. His heart turned in pity at the sight of her, sitting on the edge of the cot and doubled over as if in physical pain. She looked up at him briefly when he approached, and her face was like a ravaged countryside, a study in desolation. Mutely she shook her head.

"Why?" she mumbled, closing her eyes as the tears once

more flowed. He sat beside her, pulled her to him, and wrapped his arms fiercely, protectively, around her.

"Only the gods know that, Melangell. Only the gods, and the fates that guided his life."

She began to sob again and he laid his cheek in her hair, feeling her pain in his poet's heart.

Oh, my little one, I would guard you with my life, he thought sadly. I would gladly protect you from all comers, but I can do nothing to protect you from this. Nothing.

He held her as the day progressed, and with the approaching evening Brennos returned, to find that the exhausted girl had fallen asleep in Genann's arms.

"Leave her there," the druid said. "I will sleep on the floor tonight."

They laid her on the straw mattress and pulled a blanket over her, and Brennos ran a skilled hand across her forehead, wiping the damp hair from her face.

"She will mend," he whispered, half to himself, as he studied her in the flickering firelight. "She will mend."

Genann awoke with a start at a soft rustling nearby, and raising his head from the fur where he slept, he saw that Melangell had awakened. She opened the shutter to the tiny window above the cot and stood, as motionless as a statue, gazing up at the stars beyond. He watched until she turned, picked up her cloak, and crept across the floor. As she lifted the bolt on the door, he rose to his feet, seized his sword, and followed her into the deserted nighttime streets.

Wordlessly he trailed her, around the side of the hut, past the stable in the rear, between several large grain bins, and along the length of a rack of drying, freshly dyed wool. She halted at a clearing beside a large woodpile and he stepped back into the surrounding shadows where he could watch her yet let her have her privacy.

For a long time she stood, still and silent, and gazed up at the stars as if communing with something. Her back was to him; he couldn't see what expression her face held; if she was crying, praying, what . . . Instinct told him to remain hidden, to leave her to herself. She was a druidess, he knew, and she had abilities far beyond his understanding.

In the dim light he saw her turn her head from side to side, as if looking for something. Stooping, she peered down at the ground. Seeming dissatisfied, she turned to the wood-pile. Slowly she ran her fingers over the freshly cut wood; gently, he thought in astonishment, almost tenderly, like a lover.

She seemed lost in thought again, and then she found what she sought. Reaching between two chunks of oak, she struggled a moment before standing upright, a small still-green piece of tree branch in her hand, the crushed leaves fluttering in happy release in the soft night breeze.

Turning, she walked around the clearing, peering into the shadows as if looking for intruders. Genann flattened himself against the thatch wall of the shed when she neared, paused, and passed on. When he next looked at her she was lifting several small branches from the woodpile, placing them in a circle on the ground.

She creates her own sacred grove, he thought in astonishment. Here, in this crowded, dirty, treeless village, she seeks something in her soul and creates it as best she can.

Her work completed, she stood and faced the stars again, clasping the first little branchlet in her hands, her head hung down. Then she held the branch aloft and turned her face up to the late-summer breeze.

He gazed at her until he'd lost track of the time. Shifting his feet uncomfortably, now squatting, now standing, he continued to watch her. And yet she never moved a muscle, as silent and immobile as one of the trees she so obviously loved. He was not aware of the wind rising around him, whipping at his hair and sending dust skittering across the pathway between the sheds. He only roused at the sound of a voice at his elbow.

"Gods above!" Brennos gasped when he saw the girl. Genann turned in surprise, motioning the druid to silence. Brennos stepped into the shadows beside the poet.

"Gods above!" he breathed again. "She joins herself with nature. I cannot believe what I am seeing."

Genann was turning toward the druid when the man gasped and pointed, and Genann quickly followed his gaze. A large sparkling ball of yellow fire tumbled lazily across the sky, directly across the girl's field of vision. Genann felt his knees grow weak with fear.

Just who is this girl? he marveled. What is she?

The fireball suddenly vanished and Melangell lowered her arms, her shoulders rising and falling as she took a deep breath. Slowly she bent, picked up the encircling pieces of wood, and returned them to the woodpile. Turning, she walked evenly across the clearing, past the two hidden figures; and as she passed them and stepped away down the dusty dirt track, the wind whipping at her cloak, the two men were startled to hear her voice float over her shoulder to them.

"Come . . ." she said, as if she'd known they were there all along.

In the flickering light of the hearth Melangell's face looked calm, radiant, her green eyes glowing.

"Melangell?" Brennos asked uncertainly.

"Esus is well," she said quietly, facing him, "and I know what I must do. Now I am tired and wish to sleep. Good night." Without another word she walked into the back room and closed the door, leaving the druid looking after her in confusion.

Genann smiled at the puzzled look on Brennos' face. "Sit down!" he offered, placing a friendly hand on the man's shoulder. "I think it would help if I explained a few things about her."

"Yes . . ." Brennos muttered. "To me she was a ragged slave girl, now Nechtan's wife. Caring and gentle, yes, but nothing more."

"Oh," Genann chuckled, "there is more, much more! Sit down and let me tell you."

Like a great weight Melangell's grief seemed to have lifted from her heart and vanished, burned out by the flaming star in the summer sky. Happily she busied herself around the druid's home, helping him clear out his possessions, going through old boxes and barrels, sorting through his medicines, storing away the herbs he'd been drying, packing what they would take with them and putting aside the rest to be traded or given to the poor. Genann spent the days helping Calum load the harvested grain, heaving large, full sacks into the wagon and war chariot for storage until time for their departure. Questions from curious townsfolk went unanswered as they prepared for the coming trip.

When the final evening arrived, Melangell gathered her things to pack in the carved wooden chest Brennos had given her. Her fine new clothes went in first, the silver and bronze jewelry tucked among the folds. Genann sat plucking his treasured harp, as he had done almost every evening since the druid had presented it to him, and watched the girl at work.

"Melangell?" he said idly, running his fingers along the metal strings of the harp, "you said you knew what you must do, yet you have never told us. What did you mean?"

She paused, looked at him, and smiled mysteriously.

"You'll see," she said simply, and folded her old black robe into a neat bundle.

He stilled the harp and studied her, her soft hair falling forward when she leaned over to place the robe in the trunk, and a brief flare of desperation shot through him. He could easily endure this—this not-having-her—because now, in a sense, he did have her. He was her guardian; there was no other man to be a threat. But in three days she would be back with Nechtan, and he would have to watch their looks, their smiles, their caresses.

He sighed and plucked out a tune on the harp; sad, lonely notes spilling out into the room. Melangell glanced at him. "Why so melancholy?" she asked. He did not look at her, nor answer.

"I, too, am a bit sad at leaving here," she offered. "We have so many memories of this place."

"Aye," he muttered.

"Play something nice for me, Genann, while I finish packing," she suggested.

"I will play a tune I composed myself . . . for you," he answered, and the sweet liquid notes of his harp suddenly filled the room; a sensuous song, the sounds seeming to rise and fall and swirl back again, intertwining like the sinuously curving embroideries on her gowns. She paused, entranced, and watched him as he played, lost in concentration, his eyes closed, a slight frown on his face. And then, to her surprise, he began to sing, and his voice was low and tender.

> *"You say to me*
>   *That I am wrong;*
> *That the tune I sing*
>   *Is a wayward song—*
> *But if this fine tune*
>   *Might wayward be,*
> *How lost is the mountain,*
>   *How lost the sea?*
> *How lost the stars*
>   *In heaven above*
> *When you won't acknowledge*
>   *My wayward love?"*

The harp's notes died away and he turned to look at her, and to her shock, there were tears in his eyes. They stared at each other awkwardly, until Melangell felt the color rising in her cheeks. Lowering her face, she packed the last of her clothing in the chest, closed the lid, and latched it shut.

"I . . . must go to the well," she muttered, turning to the door. Genann didn't answer; he began to pluck out the same lovely tune on his harp, this time keeping the words to himself. He didn't have the slightest regrets over what he had just done. This probably was their last time alone together. In this life you must sometimes take reckless chances, he knew. He had seen the opportunity, and he had seized it.

No, he had no regrets at all.

Calum brought five men with him, all astride their own horses; and Boann, his thin, pale young wife, walked slowly at his side. Melangell went directly to the pallid woman and put an arm around her shoulders, smiling gently at her fearful gaze.

"Come, Boann, ride with me on the wagon. It will be an easier trip for you," Melangell suggested. Boann looked questioningly at Calum. He kissed his wife's cheek, concern on his face, and Melangell appreciated at once the great sacrifice he was making in order to join Nechtan.

"I'll take good care of her," she said, and the man nodded. They walked to the front of the wagon and Calum and Genann almost bodily lifted Boann onto the seat. Then Genann stood aside to help Melangell up.

With a protective arm around Boann's shoulders, Melangell sat atop the wagon and watched the men roll out the heavily laden chariot and harness two strong mountain horses to it. Genann lifted her wooden trunk into the back of the wagon, and then he nestled his precious harp, wrapped in a blanket, between the bundles behind his seat.

A crowd was beginning to gather, curious about the preparations under way at their druid's dwelling. Genann rechecked the harnesses and yokes on the two wagon horses, climbed onto the seat beside the huddled Boann, and picked up the reins. He did not like the idea of a crowd; the sooner they were off, the better. Silently he waited, fingering the sword and dagger at his side as the last trappings on the chariot horses were secured. Mac Oag stuck his spear upright between the bundles in the chariot, handed Calum his sword, and sprang atop one of the chariot horses. Seizing the bridle of the other horse, he took his sword from Calum and replaced it at his side. Calum walked over to his waiting mount and jumped astride, winked once at his wife, and walked the horse to the front of the chariot, to lead the way through the crowds. Genann pulled the wagon up beside the laden war chariot and halted as the other horsemen fanned out around them for protection.

The crowd was growing tense, murmuring nervously when Brennos emerged from his hut, pointedly left the door open to signify that it was now vacant, and mounted his horse.

"No!" a few voices shouted.

"You are our druid! You cannot leave us!" the crowd protested, surging forward until the mounted warriors drew their swords menacingly. Brennos turned his horse to face the mob and raised his arms, and the angry crowd fell silent.

"My friends," he began, gazing at each face as he spoke. "Yes, I leave you, but—"

He motioned them to silence when their voices rose in alarm.

"Annos can get another healer for you, or he can try. You do not know it, but evil times are about to befall our lands. To those of you who claim to have seen Nechtan in the town recently, yes, it was indeed Nechtan. He risked his life to come and warn Annos to make preparations; to tell him that the Romans will be invading in the spring . . ."

He waited as gasps of shock rose and subsided, like tides on the sea.

"But Annos chose not to listen. He is your chief; handle him as you see fit. As for us, we go to join Nechtan in his exile. We will prepare ourselves to fight the Roman armies. I suggest you do likewise. But, my friends, the danger is real."

He paused, contemplating what to say next.

"For I know," he resumed, his low voice strained and tense, "I know . . . the Romans have already destroyed the druids' center of learning on the isle of Mona . . ."

Again he faltered, the words too painful to speak, his memories too vivid.

". . . and they have massacred every soul in the colony, druid and pupil alike."

A roar of anger, of disbelief, rose from the crowd, and Brennos did not try to silence them again. Turning his horse, he nodded to Calum, who led the procession through the stunned people, along the twisting streets, and out the massive gates. No one interfered, no one pursued them. As they crossed the fields and neared the heavy woods, the warriors one by one replaced their swords at their sides.

The journey that took Nechtan and his men one hard day's travel, the little group took in easy stages, a trip of three days with the slowly rolling wagons and an ill woman along.

The first afternoon, they stopped by a meadow brightly spangled with autumn flowers and sloping away to a distant rocky creek.

Calum dismounted by the wagon and lifted Melangell to the ground, then helped his wife down. She left them alone and wandered away to watch the men preparing the night's camp. Seeing the men's effortless preparations, she recalled the struggles she and Anarios had endured in order to survive. These men knew exactly what to do. Horses were unharnessed and led to the meadow to feed; wheels were secured to keep the heavy wagons from rolling on the sloping ground. Wood was gathered and soon a large fire blazed, food and drink appeared, and the travelers gathered around the warming flames as the smells of cooking food drifted through the chill evening air.

Night came swiftly over the meadow. Two of the warriors rose from the fire and walked into the darkness to guard the horses. The laughter and jests of the rest continued, everyone infused with a heady sense of new adventure. Over Boann's timid protests, Melangell stood behind her and combed out her thick, long chestnut hair as Calum watched in gratitude. His wife had never had many friends, never indulged in such feminine pastimes. Melangell seemed to know exactly what to do; not since the child began had he seen Boann's blue eyes sparkle so. Melangell leaned over, whispered something in his wife's ear, and like music to his ears she suddenly pealed out a delighted, girlish laugh, the first he had heard in months. Melangell straightened up, a mischievous look on her face, and resumed combing Boann's hair.

"There!" she announced, giving the hair a final flourish and standing aside. "How does she look, Calum?"

The tracker smiled at his wife fondly. "Like a queen," he said, and meant it. Her hair fell in shining waves around her shoulders, glinting red in the firelight, and he longed to have her in his arms once more. Boann looked at him, her face glowing happily.

"But I think you need sleep," he added. "It's late, and we have more hard travel tomorrow."

"Yes," Melangell agreed, putting the bone comb aside. "Come; we'll fix a place where we two women can be alone and talk." She helped Boann to her feet and together they walked off into the shadows, toward the parked wagons. In a few moments Melangell returned to the campfire and the group fell silent as they watched her busying herself at the log where the women had sat. She picked up the comb, some long ivory hairpins, and retrieved their two empty wine cups. Walking closer to the fire, she put the two cups on the ground, lifted the heavy bronze ewer of wine, and bent to pour some into the cups.

Six pairs of male eyes found themselves staring in fascination at the girl's softly rounded bottom when she bent, showing smoothly curved beneath the fine white wool of her gown. She shifted and moved aside to lower the jug to the ground. A few men gulped awkwardly, their eyes riveted on the girl, until she straightened up, wine cups in hand, and walked into the night.

A few nervous coughs sprang up around the fire, and the men sheepishly looked at one another.

"By the gods . . ." one man exclaimed quietly, unable to finish his sentence.

Brennos shook his head and gazed up in embarrassment at the dark treetops.

"She's turning into quite a woman," he said quietly, and Genann found himself surprised at the strain in the druid's quiet voice.

"I have known many women in many capacities in my line of work," Brennos went on, "but only one who could ever have tempted me to give up my celibacy. Melangell."

He shook his head again and gazed absently into the fire.

"Aye," Calum added, "and if you had seen her as I did, cavorting naked with her Roman lover . . ."

Brennos' head shot up in alarm but he was too late. Genann was already on his feet, his sword drawn, rage in his eyes. Brennos jumped up and intercepted him as he headed for Calum, a murderous look on his face.

"Take that back!" Genann hissed as Brennos reached for his sword arm. Calum sprang to his feet, his sword before him in a flash.

"I will not," he snapped, "for it is true. She was the Roman's lover."

Genann, a sneer on his face, lunged toward Calum. The other men around the fire quickly stood, and Brennos seized him with a surprisingly strong grip.

"Genann! Get your wits about you!" he ordered, glaring into the young man's face in exasperated anger. "You are to guard her, not be her moral defender. Now, stop this before she hears you both and you have to answer to Nechtan for it!"

Slowly Genann lowered his sword, but he continued to glare at the defiant Calum. Abruptly turning, he picked up his cloak from the ground and stalked off into the night to sleep near the girl and her companion.

He glanced at the two women as he neared. The wine cups were empty, Boann was asleep, but Melangell still lay awake, curled on her side facing the dark woods. She lifted her head and smiled slightly at him when he passed, then pulled her cloak up snugly around her ears.

Genann angrily wrapped his cloak around his shoulders and stretched out on the hard ground. He lay awake for a long time, watching the stars turn overhead, and the rage and hurt in his heart were all-consuming.

Gods above! he thought bitterly. She will have a Roman, but she will not have me.

Melangell was up early the next morning; a chill, damp day with heavy low clouds shedding mist onto the fields and treetops. Pulling her cloak tightly around her shoulders, she crept to the campfire, past a silent guard who sat on the log, and over to where Brennos slept. Crouching beside him, she gently shook his shoulder, but he was difficult to rouse.

Finally he rolled over, blinking up at her. When recognition came, he sat up abruptly.

"I must talk with you, Brennos . . . alone," she whispered urgently. Blankly he nodded, ran a hand through his tangled brown hair, and pulled his cloak aside to stand.

"One moment . . ." he muttered. He walked sleepily to the campfire, nodded briefly to the watching guard, and took a great gulp of water from the skin bag hanging near the fire. Refreshed and awakened, he returned to the girl and together they walked off a short distance into the meadow.

"Brennos," she began immediately, "remember I told you I knew what I must do?"

"Yes."

"Today I must do it. I must return to the valley and give Esus' remains a proper burial." She hesitated at Brennos' disturbed look. "His spirit cries out for it. He loved the land, the trees, the world around us. He must not be left unburied in a blackened cave. He must be returned to the earth he cherished."

226

She placed a hand tentatively on his arm. "Do you understand?"

"Yes. I understand. But I don't like it, Melangell. The area was dangerous before; it will be more so now. Nechtan waits for you; you would arrive at his camp tomorrow. If you do this, it will delay you by several days. He will be very disappointed, and he could easily be angry at us for letting you go. You know how his temper goes. No, Melangell, I can think of many reasons not to go, and none to say you should."

"Except that I must," she replied gently, and he lifted his head and looked into her defiant green eyes.

"Aye," he sighed, knowing he was defeated. "Except that you must."

She nodded, satisfied.

"When will you go?" he asked her.

"As soon as it's light. Genann knows the way. I should need no other guard. We can ride, and it will be a very quick trip. I took the precaution of packing a separate bag of food before we left, so we'll have provisions."

She paused and looked at him, breathed in the damp air, and spoke again, her voice low and hushed.

"Brennos, I am not yet sure, but I . . . I think I may be with child."

He straightened up in surprise and looked down at her, a slight smile on his gentle face. "Well, it's too soon to tell for sure," he observed. "I can examine you when you get to Nechtan's camp, if you like, but this early there is little I can do that you do not already know yourself. Of course, Nechtan doesn't know . . ."

"No. Keep it our secret for now. I may be mistaken. But if not, I will tell him when the time comes."

"Of course." He nodded.

"Now I think," she concluded, watching the distant camp stir to life, "that we had better return to camp, make preparations, and tell the others of my journey."

A steady rain was falling by the time the wagon horses were yoked to the vehicles and the others were fitted with their thick riding pads. Huddled against the rain beneath greased traveling cloaks, the men broke camp, reloaded the wagons, extinguished the remains of the campfire, and stood by, awaiting the time to mount.

"Take good care of this," Genann instructed Brennos, pulling an oiled, waterproof skin over his harp to keep it dry.

"Of course I will." The druid smiled, turning around on the wagon seat where he waited beside Boann. "I had enough trouble getting it. I will let nothing happen to it!"

Genann laughed and stepped away from the wagon, his hand raised in farewell. The warriors sprang onto their mounts and the wagons creaked and groaned to life.

"Tell Nechtan I will be there very soon!" Melangell called out as the druid snapped the reins. He nodded a silent reply, pulling the black hood of his cloak over his wet hair. Silently the two stood and watched the procession wind its way across the foggy fields until Genann turned, grimaced up at the leaden sky, and pulled his cloak over his head.

"The rain is increasing," he said. "We'd better go."

"Yes," she agreed, following him to the tethered horse they were to use; one of the larger Roman ones, sleek and well-muscled, able to carry them both easily.

"You first," he said, boosting her onto the animal's back. She clung to it uncertainly, unused to riding directly on the animal rather than in a wagon or cart. In a moment Genann was sitting behind her, reaching around her for the reins, his manner loose and easy from years of riding on his family's farm.

"You'll get used to it very quickly," he reassured her, placing one arm around her waist to steady her and manipulating the reins with the other. He clucked to the horse and she grabbed his arm fearfully when the animal suddenly moved. She could hear Genann laughing behind her.

"I won't let you fall," he joked. She wasn't very amused. She clung to his arm tightly, watching the ground slide by below her, until she found herself growing accustomed to the motion, relaxed, and enjoyed the sensation of flying above the ground like a skimming bird. Despite the cloak over her head, the heavy wet drops flew continuously into her face, dripping from her nose and running down her cheeks. The horse's large hooves sent sprays of mud flying up around their ankles, and she looked at her dirty leather boots in dismay.

"You get used to that too," he chuckled in her ear. She shrugged in resignation.

"I suppose there's little I can do about it, is there?" she said over her shoulder.

"That's the spirit!" he exclaimed, giving her waist a little shake. "Just enjoy it!"

Laughing, she tasted the rolling drops as they splattered her face and coated her lips, while the horse galloped heavily across the wet hillsides.

They stopped the first night in the shelter of a copse of trees, ate a quick cold meal, and, wrapped in their cloaks, tried to sleep atop a few dry boulders. Their rest was slight, their wakings frequent as they shifted uncomfortably, hour by hour. Wearying of the struggle, they arose stiffly well before dawn, mounted the horse, and went on their way.

The ground grew increasingly soggy and the horse slowed to a steady walk as it tried to negotiate the deep mud. The day crept by, the rain continuing unceasingly. Eventually they reached the stream, swollen and surging from the runoff that spilled from the druid's valley. Cautious, he guided the weary horse into the valley, around boulders and through sandy bogs. When the valley narrowed he pulled the animal to a halt, dismounted, and led it forward, Melangell clinging tiredly to its mane. They walked until they could go no farther, and Genann stopped and turned to the girl. Her face was upturned, her eyes fastened sadly on a spot in the cliffs ahead.

"Melangell," he called through the noise of the rain and the rushing stream. Mutely she looked at him, her wool cloak shedding water in small torrents around her face.

"We must walk," he said. Without a word she slid from the horse's back and waited while he tied it. Then, his arm around her shoulder, they set off up the rocky hillside, slipping in the wet grasses and stumbling on dripping rocks. Daylight was fast vanishing when they neared the cave entrance, now strangely black and silent, and despite herself Melangell began to cry.

Esus! No. . . .

Genann felt her sobs beneath his arm and stopped, turning her to face him.

"You wait here," he said loudly over the rain. "You shouldn't have to see this." He took off his cloak and turned, but she grabbed his arm. He saw her holding out her own new cloak to him, and he nodded, taking it and handing her his own. Wet though it was, she wrapped it around herself and stood, alone and shivering, watching him climb the last few paces and vanish as if by magic into the face of the hill.

Twilight hung heavy through the mist-shrouded valley when Genann reappeared, carrying a large weight wrapped securely in Melangell's cloak. Despite his care he found himself more than once slipping awkwardly on the steep, wet slope. Reaching the girl, he motioned her to go on, but she stood rooted to the spot, staring ashen-faced at the bundle he held in his left hand; and when she spoke, he had to lower his ear to catch her words.

"Is . . . is that . . . ?" she whispered. He nodded. She looked up at him, her green eyes wide with questions.

"Just bones, that's all," he said simply. "Come . . ." He guided her. "The light is fading. We must go."

They made a careful descent to the valley floor. She selected a spot near a large overhanging oak tree and, using his knife, Genann easily dug a large hole in the wet ground while the girl crouched nearby, hovering protectively over the brightly colored bundle.

He turned when he finished, awaiting instructions from her, some druidical ritual perhaps, a few words to speak. She only stood up solemnly. Genann lifted the bundle and gently laid it in the bottom of the hole, and he found a lump rising in his throat as he did so. Who would ever have imagined it, he reflected, looking down at the bright cloth in the bottom of the dank, muddy hole; who would ever have known, sitting at my father's feast and looking at old Esus, so dapper and jolly in his borrowed finery, that here I would be, such a short time later, burying him in the waiting earth . . . or what's left of him. . . .

He roused when Melangell suddenly knelt beside him and laid a freshly cut twig of oak atop the bundle. Silently she gazed at it and then she sobbed, loudly calling the old man's name into the pouring rain. Genann found himself near tears as he watched her lean over, extend her arm down into the hole, and lovingly caress the lumped surface of the cloth.

"Come," he said, lifting her to her feet. "It is over. We must finish what we have begun." With muddied hands he pushed the dirt back into the grave. Searching the darkening valley for suitable stones, they piled a small cairn atop the fresh earth and Melangell stepped back, wiping her hands on his wet cloak.

"I know where there is shelter for us," she said quietly. Turning, she led Genann along the stream bank. They retrieved the horse and he followed her through the gathering darkness. She walked unerringly away from the stream, back toward the hillside, and soon stopped before a dilapidated wicker shack leaning drunkenly away from the valley wall. She disappeared through the low door and, after tying the horse and pulling down the sack of food, he followed her.

Nothing has been touched, she thought sadly, entering the hut and peering around the gloomy interior . . . and especially, she was relieved to see, the small supply of firewood she and Anarios had collected.

"Genann," she said when he entered, "we can have a fire! Look!"

"Praise be to all the gods who ever were!" he laughed, dropping the wet food sack to the floor. "I am nearly frozen through!"

Hastily they pulled some wood into the hearth-pit and, using his fire-starter, he soon had a large fire blazing. Melangell took off his cloak and spread it out to dry, huddling near the fire with Genann, their hands extended to the flames for warmth.

"How did you know of this place?" he asked as he watched the dancing fire and rubbed his hands together briskly. She laughed lightly, as if it really didn't matter.

"We found it when we were trying to reach freedom. This is where Calum almost caught us."

Genann found an odd sort of anger rising within him and he turned to look at her pale face, framed by still-dripping hair.

"We?" he asked pointedly, afraid of what her answer would be.

She lifted her head and met his angry gaze, then turned away before she spoke.

"Brennos' Roman slave and I. We'd been left to die in the bogs, escaped, and sought freedom." She snorted a laugh. "It looks like we both found it, too." She gazed back into the fire, a slight smile on her face.

"So it is true then?" he asked her. She looked at him, uncomprehending.

"That you and the Roman were lovers," he said bluntly, and watched in jealous satisfaction as her mouth flew open in surprise.

"Who . . . who told you that?" she demanded.

"Calum. He watched you."

"Calum . . ." she croaked, remembering sickly how she and Anarios had played naked by the stream . . . and all the while Calum had been watching.

She rose quickly, nausea gripping her stomach.

"Yes," she gasped at Genann. "It is true. I was a foolish child, alone and afraid. He was kind, caring, so much older and wiser. It . . . it just happened, that's all. But it is over. He is a Roman, and I have learned to my sorrow what that means."

Her eyes glittered coldly as she stared at him, and he recoiled at the first sign of hatred he had ever seen on her gentle face.

"I feel sick," she gulped, and fled the hut. He closed his eyes and sighed. Some food will make us both feel better, he mused, rummaging through the food bag. She has not eaten all day.

Melangell soon returned, her tread slow and unsure, and seated herself some distance from Genann. She pulled her knees up to her chin, wrapped her arms around her folded legs, and stared in rigid silence at the fire. He studied her a moment, then carried the food to her and held out some cheese.

"Eat," he said. She looked away silently.

"By the gods," he snapped, "I am charged with protecting you. You have not eaten all day; you are cold and wet. Now, *eat,*" he repeated, placing a piece of the cheese atop her folded knees. She looked at it, picked it up, and slowly took a bite.

"Why is it anyone else's business, anyway, Genann?" she mused aloud. "Why is my life their concern?"

She turned to look at him. "Just what did he say about me?"

Genann shook his head. "You don't want to know."

"Yes I do!" she insisted, staring at his solemn face.

"He just commented about you 'cavorting naked with the Roman' and how . . . how you looked." Her hand flew to her mouth in shock and he turned away awkwardly.

"But I stood up for your honor," he added, trying to cheer her. "In an instant my sword was drawn and only Brennos' intervention saved us from a fight."

"Brennos too?" she said quietly. "He heard it too?"

Genann nodded.

"Why did he say such a thing? What concern is it of his?"

Genann shrugged. "Men are like that. Such things . . . interest them."

"Oh," she whispered. "Then I suppose I should be flattered, shouldn't I?"

"No . . . not really. Just because men are that way doesn't make it right."

"And you; are you that way?"

He laughed lightly. "I am a man too, am I not?"

She nodded absently and picked up a piece of coarse bread.

"In a way it is no different, you see," he jested. "You women dwell on your appearance, and so do we men!"

She laughed uncomfortably, looking down at the crust in her hand. "Yes, I suppose that's true," she muttered.

"You must accept the fact that you are a very attractive woman now, and men are interested in you, even if you are Nechtan's wife."

He reached out and pulled a tendril of wet hair from her face and she jerked her head up in surprise.

"A very lovely woman," he breathed, his hand still at her cheek. Slowly he leaned forward, closed his eyes, and pressed his lips to hers, caressing her face in his hand.

He pulled his mouth away and looked at her. She sat as if made of stone, her eyes closed, and then she lowered her head.

"Genann . . . don't . . ." she breathed softly.

He shook his head and ran his fingers down her cheek. "I would do nothing to offend you, my love," he said quietly.

"You . . . you try me sorely sometimes, Genann." She looked up at him. "Did you know that?"

"I? What do you mean?"

His fingers explored her chin while she spoke, and her voice came strained and heavy.

"Your songs, your ways, your gentleness, your pursuit of me. Any woman would be wild over it . . . any woman . . ." She turned her face away from his hand.

"Any woman except you. Right, Melangell?" he whispered, turning her face back to him.

She stared silently at the gold torque around his neck. "I did not say that, Genann."

He looked into her sad green eyes and again ran his fingers over her cheek. "Oh, my love," he breathed.

"But I am Nechtan's wife. I love him," she said firmly, turning her face aside when he leaned forward to kiss her. He lowered his hands and nodded. Quickly he backed away and angrily tore off a chunk of bread.

"Can you not be foolish with me, just once, as you were with the Roman?" he said, half-jesting, and she smiled at him.

"No . . . I am sorry," she answered. "I love my husband, Genann. I am sorry . . ."

He nodded glumly, chewing on the bread. "Always, always you are turning me down," he muttered.

"Genann," she said, moving closer to him. "I know how difficult it must be for you to be my guard. Would you like me to ask Nechtan to find another; to release you from your duties?"

"No!" he said emphatically. "Yes, it is hard for me, but if it's all I get of you, I will be happy for that. Please don't, Melangell . . . you don't know how I ache inside for you . . . you can't imagine . . ."

She put a hand on his arm and looked at him sympathetically.

"If only you had given me a chance before you wed Nechtan," he said, seizing her hands in his. "You had the opportunity, but you wouldn't even give me a chance. And now it is gone forever, and my hurt will be never-ending because of it."

Greedily he kissed her fingers as she stared at him in shock.

"Genann—" she began, but he suddenly pressed his mouth to hers. "I am a man," he breathed heavily into her ear. "I can love you as well as Nechtan, as well as that Roman. Melangell, let me show you what love a poet knows."

Then he was kissing her neck, enfolding her in his arms, nibbling at her ear, her throat, his breath coming in eager gasps.

"No . . . no . . . Genann, don't," she protested, pushing against his chest. "We mustn't, Genann . . . no . . ."

He kissed her mouth again to silence her. "Hush, my love. Just once . . . just this once. We may all die tomorrow; I must have you tonight."

He pulled her shift from her shoulders and frantically kissed down her bare white skin, his head whirling dizzily in his excitement.

"No . . . don't . . ." she sobbed, trying to stop him, but her strength was no match for his. He returned to her face, kissing her mouth to silence, his arms still tight about her.

"Just once, Melangell, just once . . ."

"By the gods, no!" she repeated, crying openly, one hand pushing at his shoulder while the other fumbled with the top of her gown. He seemed entranced, unhearing, uncaring, and in panic she released her shift, letting fly with a small, sharp blow that hit Genann squarely on the cheekbone. Insignificant in itself, its sting broke his frenzy and he pulled back, his eyes surprised and hurt as they stared into hers.

"Melangell . . . I . . ." he began brokenly, one hand rising slowly to the small imprint of her fist on his skin.

"Don't speak . . . don't move . . ." she hissed, slipping from his embrace and skittering crablike around the fire pit to be free of him. He stared at her in silence, a hand still at his cheek, as she withdrew her knife, held it close, and wordlessly lay down to sleep, her green eyes staring blankly into the fire.

Drawing up his knees, the poet lowered his forehead to his arms and sighed heavily.

He knew, now, that all was lost.

Melangell had slept tense and catlike all night, and when she roused with the morning light dancing through cracks in the old shed's roof, she seemed at first unsure of where she was. Genann raised his head and tried to smile at her across the dying fire. The girl sat up with a jolt with sudden remembrance. "I must go and wash," she mumbled, and hastily left the hut. Resigned, Genann stood. Stuffing the food in the sack and retrieving his sword and cloak, he kicked dirt over the fire and followed the girl from the shack.

He watched her while he loaded the horse. She knelt on a rock, splashing cold stream water over her face. Then she stood, gazing blankly into the rushing water as sunlight played and danced on her blowing hair. Untying the horse, Genann led it to her side and put a hand on her arm.

"Melangell . . ." he began. She lowered her face and turned away from him.

"We must go," she said flatly, walking to the horse and waiting for him to help her mount. He lifted her onto the animal's back and sprang up behind her. In silence he snapped the reins, turned the horse, and they walked out of the valley.

Mael looked up at the sound of a horse's tired feet thudding to the earth, and he knew at once who it was. He spied the animal with two weary figures astride it emerge from the distant woods, dropped the wood he was collecting, and raced down the narrow dirt track to their camp.

"They're here!" he called up to Nechtan, who perched atop the roof of a large new addition to their quarters, putting in place the sods Calum hoisted up to him.

Nechtan slipped down the ladder, wiped the sweat from his forehead, and strode across the clearing as the horse came into view.

Brennos looked at Genann and Melangell with a druid's critical eye when they rode into view. He couldn't help but wonder what had happened in the past few days to put such grim looks on their faces; and his instincts told him he didn't really want to know. Maybe it was just the strain of burying poor Esus, he told himself. The weary girl, snugly wrapped in Genann's cloak, brightened as soon as she saw Nechtan rushing toward them. He stopped by the horse and gazed up at her, love plain on his face. Genann lowered the girl to the ground and Nechtan swept her up in his arms, whirling her around in a circle. She clung to his neck and laughed, her head thrown back, her hair flying wildly. Then Nechtan paused and extended a hand to Genann.

"Thank you," he said simply. Genann grasped the hand and nodded once in reply. He straightened, watching sullenly as Nechtan wrapped an arm around Melangell and they strolled into the new quarters.

Without a word, Genann snapped the reins and the horse trotted off across the dusty clearing, eagerly scenting hay and water at the makeshift stables ahead.

Within a few days Eber and Osla returned to the camp, bringing with them nine warriors and the promise of many more come spring. Half the month then passed, and Nechtan welcomed Niall, Melwas, and six more men to his camp. As Niall introduced the men to their new leader, his eyes fell on a slim young girl in green emerging from the main quarters, a taller young woman at her side, and he could tell it definitely wasn't Seonaid.

Nechtan caught his gaze and laughed. "Melangell, come here!" he called. The two women turned aside and crossed the clearing.

Surely not the same Melangell, Niall thought in surprise . . . the one I drugged and left for dead, the one I raped, the one I almost killed.

The girl was lovely, but it was indeed the same Melangell, now grown into a shapely young woman. He saw his chief put an arm around the little slave girl affectionately.

"Niall, this is my wife," Nechtan announced, and the girl stared up at the tall blond warrior.

"It has been a long time," she said tightly, her smile strained.

"Aye," he said simply, and looked at Nechtan. "Congratulations! When did this happen?"

"Oh, it's a long tale. At Brennos' house, believe it or not. I'll tell you sometime. But come! You must meet the others, and we have much to discuss."

Cathal and Cai returned last, with eight men and a heavy oxcart piled high with goods. Genann rushed out to meet them, embracing his brother happily.

"You look well!" Cai exclaimed, holding him out at arm's length. Genann nodded.

"Aye," he said, but Cai wondered about the drawn look around his brother's eyes. "Your trip . . . was it a success?" Cai asked him.

"Yes. I found the girl. She is now Nechtan's wife. And we returned to the valley and buried poor Esus."

"Indeed!" Cai exclaimed, understanding the pained look in his brother's eyes. He thought it best to change the subject. "Well, my trip was a successful one too, as you can see." He waved expansively toward the wagon.

"Do I see the hand of our father in this?" Genann asked with a laugh. Cai nodded, grinning.

"That it is! We stopped by the farm on our return trip and he entertained all ten of us royally, then gave us the provisions to take along. He has sent our sisters and most of the kinfolk to the north, and he will follow them in the spring." He watched Genann peer among the load of parcels.

"Just wait," Cai laughed. "There are all kinds of treats in there. Now, come; we are all weary, and we're anxious to meet this new chief of ours." Picking up the rope lead on the sturdy ox yoked to the wagon, Cai pulled the lumbering beast along the narrow pathway to the encampment, their new home.

Nechtan called for a welcoming feast that night, to be attended by all of his group, now numbering thirty-eight fighting men, the druid, and two women.

Hasty preparations were made, foods cooked, the newly completed Great Hall swept clean, dirty bodies were washed and good clothes put on. Brennos purified the new room with aromatic smoke, to drive away any baneful influences and ensure good fortune to its occupants.

With the falling of night the men gathered around the blazing hearth, laughing and talking, getting to know one another and waiting for their chief to appear. Finally Brennos came through the side door which led to the tiny original hut, now the private quarters for Nechtan, his wife, and their personal guards. He raised his arms for silence and all eyes turned to him expectantly.

"Good men," he began, "the flower of valor, the bravest of the brave, your new chief, comes; Nechtan ap Oenghus ap Gest, king of the Cruithni."

A roar filled the hall and echoed from the low ceiling, accompanied by the loud rattle of spears on heavy oak shields. Nechtan walked into the room, resplendent in a new red-and-yellow-checked cape, gold bands on his arms glinting and flashing in the firelight. He was followed by Niall, carrying three spears, and Cathal, with his bow slung over his back. Next came Melangell, tiny amidst the tall warriors, and wearing a red shift heavily embroidered with swirling silver tendrils, a new cape of yellow and black pinned at her throat, her hair neatly piled atop her head. Boann followed at her elbow, with Genann, spear and shield in hand, bringing up the rear.

The men shouted and cheered wildly and Melangell roamed her eyes over their faces; her husband's men—her men, too, in a sense. All were strong young warriors, leaving their homes and families, all willing to risk death at the point of a Roman spear, and for what? For what?

Freedom.

Nechtan raised his arms in the air, laughing good-naturedly, his shaggy black hair tumbling from beneath a tooled-leather headband and his eyes sparkling brightly. The uproar died down, all eyes watching him intently.

"Welcome, my men . . . the bravest of the brave . . . let the Romans beware!" he shouted.

A wave of laughs and cheers swept over the hall, and Melangell laughed along as she and Boann stepped to the side of the room and sat down, apart from the men. Proudly she watched Nechtan step to his ornately carved chair and accept the choicest portions of meat from a young boar roasting over the fire. Then the feasting began. Boann, now in better health, went to fetch food and drink for her mistress and herself, and returned with two trenchers piled high with treats.

"Gracious!" Melangell gasped, taking her plate from the woman, "we'll get fat on all this!"

Boann patted her bulging stomach. "I'm afraid I already am!" she laughed, returning to her stool.

"A toast!" a voice bellowed. A stocky brown-haired man, the ends of his hair lightened with lime, stood up across the room and raised his wine cup aloft as the noise subsided around him.

"To our new chief Nechtan, to his gracious wife, and to our continuing liberty!"

Forty wine cups were lifted into the air as Nechtan and Melangell stood, smiling and nodding their gratitude to the man.

"To liberty!" Nechtan shouted, and all the cups were emptied in unison.

"Genann!" Nechtan called. The young man approached silently. "Some music for us! I've had enough of these boasting male voices!"

The crowd laughed loudly.

"Something soft and gentle . . . something sentimental."

Genann nodded and took his harp from a peg on the wall. Settling on a log stool, he tossed his cloak over one shoulder and positioned the harp in his lap. When the first sweet notes leapt out into the room, all voices fell silent, all eyes turned to the solemn young man.

He played a sad song, a tale of two ill-fated lovers, the harp plaintively rising and falling as their unlucky courtship progressed. When their pursuit began, the music rose dramatically, quickening the blood as each man envisioned their desperate flight, their stumbling and falling, their death at the vengeful husband's spear. Then Genann's hands slowed, the pure, liquid notes from the harp falling quietly, sweetly, on the ears; the lovers had found peace, the peace of the grave.

His hands stilled the strings and he looked aside at Nechtan.

"Well done!" his chief said quietly. Nechtan speared a choice bit of meat on his knife point and extended it to

Genann as a token of his admiration and approval. The poet stood, bowed slightly, and took the meat from the blade. It was a high honor.

The warriors soon shook off their pensive mood, and laughter and tall tales again filled the hall. Melangell and Boann talked quietly, nibbling their food and sipping watered wine as the evening progressed. Boann could see that her mistress grew weary, and urged her to retire.

"The men could be up till dawn, drinking and boasting," she pressed. Melangell refused and took another swallow of wine.

"I am just tired . . . a while longer and then I'll go, Boann."

"But, my lady, you do not look well!" the young woman protested.

Melangell sighed, looked into her wine cup a moment, and put it aside. "Very well, Boann. Let's tell my husband that we are leaving."

Slowly she rose, Boann at her elbow, and they walked to the side door. Boann spoke quietly to Cathal, who stepped aside to Nechtan, interrupting his animated conversation with Niall, and relayed Boann's message. The princeling looked at his wife, concern in his eyes, and was relieved to see her smile at him reassuringly. He nodded and watched Boann escort her into their quarters.

He was deep in conversation again when Cathal returned, speaking low into his ear. "Boann wishes Brennos to come at once. Your wife is ill."

Instantly Nechtan was on his feet, his wine cup clattering to the floor in an abrupt alarm that threw a silence over the room. Everyone turned to see what had happened.

"Brennos!" Nechtan bellowed. The druid put aside his cup, pressed through the crowd, and up to his chief.

"Melangell is ill . . . go at once," Nechtan said urgently, worry on his face. He moved to follow the druid, but Brennos paused, facing him, and put his hands on the young man's shoulders.

"She has probably eaten too much rich food. Why don't you wait here, and I'll send for you when I'm done?" he suggested. Nechtan mutely nodded and slumped back to his chair. Turning, Brennos strode off, his black robe swirling behind him.

Melangell lay on the bed, covered with a woolen blanket, her face gray and one hand held by a concerned Boann. She looked up when Brennos entered, and tried to smile, but she seemed to be in pain. The druid motioned Boann away and went to Melangell's side. He felt her forehead, her neck, peered into her eyes. Everything seemed normal.

"My . . . stomach," she gasped. "I have eaten too much."

He pulled the blanket away, lifted her gown, and probed her abdomen. Then he straightened up, a smile on his face.

"Henceforth you'll have to be more careful of what you eat, my dear," he announced gravely, "for before autumn you will be having a baby!"

She struggled to rise, but he pushed her back and pulled the blanket over her. "Rest," he commanded. "I'll fix something for your stomachache, but you must remember —you now have more than just yourself to think about."

She beamed up at him, the color returning to her pale face. "A baby!" she breathed, as if she could scarcely believe the news. "Are you sure?"

"Oh, quite sure. You are beginning to show. It's not a matter of guesswork now!"

Her hand slid down to her stomach and rested there gently.

"Nechtan must be told," Brennos said. "He's very worried about you."

A mischievous smile crossed the girl's face and she looked at Brennos merrily. "You tell him, Brennos. Now . . . in front of everyone."

He laughed and nodded, stepping around the wicker partition that divided the room in two and returning to the main hall.

Nechtan sprang to his feet when he saw the druid emerge from the room and walk toward him. Gods above! he thought in a panic, looking at the expression on the man's face. Something is wrong; something is seriously wrong.

Niall and Cathal stood tense at Nechtan's side. Brennos motioned Nechtan forward and placed a hand on his shoulder as all eyes watched them.

"She is fine," he began. The young man slumped in visible

relief. "She has a stomachache," the druid went on. "I'll fix her something for it."

He paused and Nechtan fixed him with his piercing wolf-stare.

"And?" the princeling questioned.

"You are to be a father, Nechtan. Congratulations."

Nechtan straightened, gazing at the far wall while an incredulous smile spread across his face. "A father?" he muttered. "I am to be a father?"

"Nechtan, are you all right?" It was Niall, concern in his eyes. Nechtan whirled happily to face them.

"A father!" he shouted. "My wife is with child! I am to be a father!"

Cheers and laughter broke out around the hall, and Nechtan turned to the druid.

"Get your medicines," he said. "I must see her." Without another word, he rushed from the hall.

Boann rose when Nechtan came around the partition, a strange look on his face.

"Leave us," he commanded, and the woman silently left the room. He paused a minute, looking at his wife's happy face, and then he slowly walked to the bedside, sat on the stool Boann had vacated, and lifted Melangell's hand in his.

"A baby," he whispered, touching her cheek lightly.

"Yes . . . next summer, Brennos says. Nechtan, I think it began that night by the cow shed."

He slapped his knee and laughed heartily. "By the gods, isn't that the way of the world? It's a lucky thing we wed then, isn't it?"

"I wouldn't care," she said quietly. "It would still be your baby . . . your son."

"A son? Do you think so?" he exclaimed.

"I feel it to be so, yes. A son for you."

"You must rest. You must take care of yourself," he said, kissing the tip of her nose.

"I'll be fine, Nechtan. It is a natural thing for a woman. All will be well." She squeezed his hand lightly, turning aside when Brennos appeared around the partition, his druid's cup in hand.

"I'll give it to her," Nechtan said, reaching out and taking the cup from him.

"She is to have nothing more to eat or drink until tomorrow, except perhaps a little water," the druid instructed. "Get a good night's sleep, and we'll see how you are in the morning, Melangell. And, Nechtan, the feast is winding down; one by one your warriors roll over in their cloaks and fall into a happy, drunken sleep."

Nechtan nodded and rose to his feet. "It has been a good night," he said. "Tell Niall, Cathal, and Genann that we are retiring now, and are not to be disturbed till morning."

He unpinned the heavy gold brooch at his shoulder and pulled his cloak off.

"And the woman too," he added. Brennos nodded and left the alcove. Nechtan hung his cloak on a peg in the wall, unbuckled his belt, and laid his sword and knives on a barrel head, and unlaced his boots. Pulling off his long tunic and breeches, he tossed them aside.

"Don't move," he said, sliding under the blanket beside Melangell. Slowly he pulled the black jet pins from her hair and let it tumble in soft waves around her face. Slipping an arm beneath her, he pulled her close.

"Oh, my little dove," he sighed, pressing his cheek against her hair, "what a lucky man I am!"

She took his hand and placed it on her stomach. "See! You can feel it!" she marveled. He ran his fingers lightly over her abdomen.

"A son . . ." he repeated softly, kissing her mouth. "A son."

He squeezed her and she laid her head on his shoulder, finding the close, warm smell of him more comforting than ale. The boars' heads at his neck grinned and glinted at her in the dim lamplight. Closing her eyes wearily, she drifted to sleep.

"Quiet!" Niall bellowed, thumping the butt of his spear on the wooden platform where Nechtan sat, his guards standing to either side of him. Quickly the dull murmur of voices died away and the men looked at Nechtan, waiting for the meeting to begin.

"I'll waste little time," Nechtan said, his wolf's eyes roaming the mass of faces before him. "My men have their reports to make, and then we must begin our planning. First, let us hear from Niall."

The tall warrior stepped forward, his long mustache failing to hide the frown on his face. "Most of the villages will join us come spring," he began, "but there is other, worse news. Romans are encamped along the western coasts, and Roman ships have been seen patrolling the seas all the way up to the northern lands of the Cruithni."

A surge of disturbed voices welled up and Nechtan raised his hands to silence them.

"That's all," Niall concluded bluntly, and Nechtan nodded. "Eber, Osla, what of your trip?" he asked. The two men stepped up grimly.

"Like Niall says, most villages will join us come spring. A few, like Annos, refuse to believe. Others believe, but feel it useless to resist. Roman garrisons dot the northeast, like droppings left behind by a fly. They seek to take the whole country," Osla stated flatly.

"Some tribes even now harry and raid them," Eber added. "Night or day, summer or winter, they attack isolated garrisons and ambush lone supply trains. They give the Romans no peace."

Grins and approving nods swept the room, and Nechtan motioned for Cathal to step forward.

"And what of you?" he said. "What of the borderlands, the routes to the south?"

"The same," the young man answered, "except that most of the people have already fled to the mountains, under constant harassment by Roman patrols. Much of the land is deserted, farms in ruin, fields overgrown. We will get little help from the southlands, I'm afraid."

"Cai, do you have anything to add?" Nechtan asked.

Cai stood and approached him, his icy blue eyes glinting. "Only to say that Cathal and I ambushed a Roman patrol of four, and their fates were as you had directed."

Nechtan narrowed his gaze and nodded grimly. "Good . . . good," he muttered, then rose to his feet.

"So that is the situation, men," he said to the group. "Cathal has brought back with him several captured Roman swords, and on inspection they have revealed one superiority to our own. Whereas our swords are for slashing and have a rounded point, these Roman swords are sharper and can stab as well as slice. Because of this, they do not have to change to a different weapon for close fighting, as we do.

"I think it wise for us to practice using these weapons as well as our own. We will have some copies made. I think the Romans will be very surprised when they find themselves facing their own weapons in battle!"

Loud laughter dotted the room, and Nechtan waited for it to subside.

"All winter we must practice with every weapon we have. When the weather is bad, we will practice in here. We will mold ourselves into an elite fighting force in these distant lands, a force to strike fear into the hearts of the Romans!

"We begin tomorrow. I will see everyone assembled here with the first light of dawn."

He sat down and watched his men fall to eager conversations among themselves. They are ready to learn, to train, to fight, he mused; they are ready.

"Who is this man?" the general bellowed, slamming his fist into the tabletop with such force that his inkwell tipped over and would have spilled its contents onto the parchment map unrolled before him were it not for the quick movement of an orderly at his side, who snatched it up before it fell, and moved it to a safer place.

The soldier in front of the wooden table gulped nervously and shifted his booted feet.

"We . . . we're not sure, sir," he stammered. "A few of the barbarians we have captured say he is a wolf, or some such nonsense. We can find out little because . . . because most of the borderlands are deserted. All we know is that two ambushed patrols have met with the same fate, plus one lone legionary who had foolishly wandered away on his own."

"And how many is it now?" the general asked, his dark eyes narrowing.

"Ten, sir."

"All the same?"

"Yes, sir."

The general paused, rocked back in his camp chair, and thought for a few minutes.

"Could it be one of their priests, their . . . what are they called?"

"Druids, sir. 'Men of the Oak.' There are a few left, here and there, but I don't think they are responsible for this. Our captives were adamant about it, even under torture; 'the wolf,' they insisted, 'the wolf.' "

The general leaned forward again.

"A wolf, eh? Sounds like more of their superstitious nonsense to me. What of our men? How are they taking it?"

The legionary shrugged, his leathery face grim. "You know how soldiers are, sir. Fearful of what they do not understand. Already there is nervous talk among them, and patrols leave as if under sentence of certain death. They are afraid, sir."

"Bah!" the general snapped, rising to his feet. "They are a bunch of women, the lot of them. There is nothing to fear from these barbarians. They are all savages, nothing more. Who is that physician who was enslaved by them?"

"Anarios, sir."

"Is he here?"

"Yes, sir."

"Send him to me at once. He might know more about what is going on."

"Leave us," the general ordered his guards when Anarios entered the sturdy log building.

"Sit down," he said as the last of the guards exited and closed the door.

"So, you were a slave of these people for three years?" the general began, looking at the physician with a critical eye. He could see nothing special about him; he did not look to be the sort who could survive an ordeal like that. An ordinary man, nothing more, his hair neatly cropped, his hands and tunic immaculate in the manner of most physicians. Only the confident cast to his dark eyes betrayed an inner strength, a certainty men of science often seemed to possess. The general pressed his fingertips together and leaned back in his chair.

"What do you know of these barbarians?" he asked.

"Only that they are not so barbaric as we suppose," the physician responded bluntly, returning the general's gaze.

"Meaning what?" the general inquired slowly.

"Meaning that they are not barbarians; they are just different from us. They have their religion, their laws, their customs . . ."

"A beehive has its way of doing things too, but that hardly makes them civilized. I understand you were severely beaten by them."

"True." Anarios nodded. "But we Romans often beat our slaves as well."

"You sound as if you like these people."

"In a way, I do. They can be a refreshing change from us jaded, corrupt Romans."

The general waved his words away angrily and came forward, his arms leaning heavily on the desk.

"Everyone fancies the primitive peoples to be somehow simpler, purer. The libraries of Rome are full of such philosophical trash. I did not call you here to discuss philosophy, physician. I have a question for you. What do these people do with wolves?"

"Wolves?" Anarios frowned. "What do you mean? They do nothing with wolves that I know of. Why?"

"Have you heard of the two murdered patrols?"

Anarios nodded. "Who hasn't heard of that!"

"We captured a few of the barbarians. A woman . . . two old men; under questioning, even under torture, all they would say was that it was done by 'the wolf, the wolf.' *What* wolf, physician? What are these people up to?"

Anarios leaned back in his chair, lost in thought. "The wolf"—not *"a* wolf," but *"the* wolf."

"There is one possibility I am acquainted with, but you realize I am familiar with only a small segment of their population. I could easily be wrong."

He looked at the general's creased face. The man nodded eagerly, his brown eyes bright.

"Yes . . . go on. Even if you are wrong, it is still more than we have to go on now."

"I knew one warrior, typically proud and arrogant, with a temper just as fierce as his pride. An odd appearance, too;

darker than most, with black hair and yellow eyes like those of a wolf. That's what many called him—'the wolf.'"

"That sounds promising," the general mused. "Where did this 'wolf' live?"

"The lands of the Damnonii, to the west . . ." Anarios began, stopping when he saw the general shake his head.

"No good," the man said. "The last patrol was found to the east."

"Well," Anarios added helpfully, "it could still be the same man. The last I heard, he had been tried and exiled for two years for trying to kill two slaves, me and another, as a matter of fact. It's a long story, but that's what led to my escape. So you see, he could be anywhere now."

"He sounds vicious enough to be the man we seek, too," the general mused aloud.

"He can be, yes. I once treated a girl of fifteen he had almost beaten to death just because she publicly embarrassed him."

The general shook his head slowly. "And you say these people are not barbarians."

Anarios shrugged. "He is only one man; one among many."

"Nevertheless," the general said, rising to his feet, "he is the man we will seek. Since you know what he looks like, I will try to have you relieved of your duties as physician. I need you to help me find this 'wolf,' and when I do, we will make an example of him that these people will not soon forget. A month's wages to the man who brings him to me alive; half a month's wages for his head."

Anarios stood abruptly and began to protest. He was a physician, a healer, a man of science, not a murderer.

"You may go," the general snapped, cutting him off. As Anarios sullenly left the room, the general sat down heavily, a final plan evolving in his mind.

Come spring, he thought, I will suggest that we move our troops first through the western lands. We will find this "wolf," and we will lay waste to the tribe that whelped him.

Another scream tore through the air, terminating in a strangled sob, and Melwas tensed, flung his spear across the doorway, and again barred the distraught Calum from entering the room to go to his wife. Cathal and Cai reached the man's side and took him back to the stool where he had waited the previous afternoon and most of the night.

"Here . . ." Cai offered, "have some more ale." Calum shook his head, burying his face in his hands.

"How long?" he sobbed. "How long must this go on?"

An unearthly moan drifted through the air and Cathal felt the hair on his neck rise. By the gods, I am glad I am not a woman, he thought as the moan rose to another pleading scream. Better to face the terrors of a battlefield than this.

Melwas stepped aside when the door flew open and Brennos emerged, his mouth set grimly, his gray eyes dark and clouded. Without a word he rushed across the packed earthen floor, seized several clay jars and packets from his store of medicines, and disappeared back into the room.

Boann squatted over a clean blanket, Melangell crouched behind to support her, wiping the hair repeatedly from the woman's damp forehead. "It's all right," the girl soothed, "Brennos has brought more medicines. It's all right."

Boann gasped and clung weakly to Melangell's hands while Brennos mixed several ingredients in a cup and held it to the woman's mouth. She tossed her head from side to side numbly and Melangell helped to steady it while the druid poured the medicine in little sips down the suffering woman's throat.

"It will relax you," he said quietly, feeling the pulse at her neck. Again she tensed, and another scream tore into Melangell's ears.

Gods above! she thought desperately. What can we do? What can we do?

Brennos crouched before the woman, peering anxiously into her face while he felt her bulging stomach.

"It has turned again," he muttered, shaking his head. "Get her on the bed. I must try to move it around." He looked up at Melangell, his eyes full of unspoken meaning, and she knew it was a final effort. Boann was failing, her strength running out.

Awkwardly they lifted the limp young woman and laid her on the straw mattress atop the bed of lashed wickerwork. Melangell supported Boann's head in her lap and took her hands firmly. Brennos removed his black robe to free his arms. The young woman writhed and twisted, and another choking scream filled the room.

"Keep her awake—slap her—anything," he instructed Melangell. "Make her bear down when I tell you. Push the baby down gently yourself if you can. But hold her tightly—this will hurt."

He leaned over, and when his fingers began to reach inside her, Boann shrieked and squirmed. The druid straightened up, shaking his head.

"Get two men in here," he said, wiping the blood from his hand. Melangell slid from the bed. "Cai and Osla . . . not Calum, and not Nechtan," he instructed.

She ran to the door and returned with the two warriors, who blanched visibly when they saw the heaving young woman, her blood seeming to be everywhere.

"Hold her down," Brennos snapped. "This is our last hope, for her or the baby."

They stood one to each side of the cot as Melangell slipped back beneath Boann's head, grasped her weak hands, and doubled over as if sheltering her with her own body.

"Hush, Boann, hush," she repeated quietly, clenching her eyes shut when another scream ripped at her ears. He must be doing it now, she thought; she sensed the two men leaning forward, holding the woman's body as Boann gasped and shrieked. Let it be easier for me, she prayed fearfully. By all the mother goddesses, let it be easier for me.

"Now!" Brennos' voice came to her, and she slapped Boann's face lightly. "Bear down, Boann, bear down . . ." she pleaded. The woman didn't respond. She slapped her harder.

"Boann!"

The young woman moaned weakly and Brennos again called out, desperation in his voice. "I have it, Melangell . . . she must . . ." But Boann would not rouse.

Wildly Melangell rose to her knees, straddling the woman's head, and leaned forward beneath the bent bodies of Cai and Osla. Her hands felt the body of the unborn baby and gently she squeezed downward, massaging the tiny shape forward, almost like milking a cow. She was nearly head to head with Brennos, and she closed her eyes sickly at the sight of all the blood around him. The mattress was soaked in it, and his arms glinted red in the flaring torch-light.

"Here it comes," he said quietly, and Boann suddenly screamed wildly as the men struggled to hold her. With her final effort the baby slid out into Brennos' waiting hands.

"I have it," he said simply, and Melangell sagged forward on her arms, hanging her head in exhaustion. She felt a hand grasp her shoulder and looked up into Cai's worried face.

"Are you all right?" he asked. She nodded dumbly, slowly crawling back to Boann's head.

"It's over, Boann," she said, wiping the sweat from the woman's pallid face. Suddenly she stopped and looked at the men in horror. "She . . . she's dead," she gasped.

"Brennos . . ." she began, stopping when she saw him frantically massaging the baby's tiny pink body in a rough wool cloth. She closed her eyes shakily. Not the child too. Poor Calum, poor Calum . . .

Sliding from the bed, she laid Boann's head on the mattress and walked to the druid's side.

"He will not breathe. I'm afraid we have failed," Brennos muttered, concentrating on his efforts to revive the baby.

Melangell looked at the little boy a moment, then held out her hands. "Give him to me," she said. Brennos shook his head sadly and handed her the infant.

Life to life, she thought, recalling a trick Esus had once shown her with a seemingly dead fox cub. Placing her lips around the tiny red mouth and nose, she gently breathed into the body once . . . twice . . .

A small fist flew up and smacked her on the cheek, and when she lifted her head a mighty wail filled the room. She held the baby close while Brennos tied and cut the cord. The three men looked at each other, astonished, as the girl walked away, cuddling the baby close, to present him to his father.

"He will be a fighter," Cai said, watching her go.

"Aye!" Osla nodded. "A fighter, all right, and one born of a miracle."

* * *

Melangell sat atop a low barrel in the great hall, the baby boy cooing and gurgling in her arms while she fed it from a skin bag filled with warm barley water and honey. Calum squatted beside her, watching his son with pride in his brown eyes.

"Boann would be so pleased with him," he said sadly as Melangell nibbled lightly on the baby's tiny fingers.

"She gave you a fine, healthy boy, Calum," Nechtan said gently. "She would want you to be proud of her son, not melancholy because of her. Ollovidius the All-Knowing has decreed that her present life be over; her spirit has now escaped to another world."

"I suppose so, but I will miss her." Calum extended a finger to the boy and the little hand closed around it fiercely. He looked up at Nechtan and smiled despite himself. "What a grip!" the tracker said. "He is sure to be a spearman!"

"We can get a goat easily enough, to feed him," Melangell offered. "I will nurse him myself when I am able."

She glanced aside at Calum. The man shook his head emphatically. "No," he replied. "A military camp is no place to raise a child, especially with a battle imminent. I have a sister far to the north, near the Western Sea. If I am able, I would rather take him to her." He looked at Nechtan, waiting for an answer.

"Of course," Nechtan agreed. "We will give you a horse, and supplies."

"Then you should leave at once," Brennos added, "for a newborn such as this needs better food than honey-water. We'll fix enough of the solution to get you back to town. Then you'd better get some milk for him. Make enough stops to get him to your sister's healthy and well-fed."

"Aye." Calum nodded. "As soon as I am able, I will return. Now," he said, standing, "I'd best prepare to leave before nightfall. If I ride hard, I can get to town by late tomorrow."

An hour later, Melangell carried the sleeping infant out to the clearing and watched Calum spring onto the bare back of a large dark Roman stallion and take the braided leather reins in his hand. They had fashioned a wool sling around the man's chest, and when he leaned down to take his son, Melangell softly kissed the baby's warm, downy forehead

253

before placing him in Calum's hands. Straightening up, he nestled the baby in the sling, against his chest. Tucking the warm honey-water bag into the sling, he pulled his heavy green cloak over himself and his son. Nechtan released the horse's bridle and stepped to Melangell's side, putting a comforting arm around her shoulders. Calum studied them for a moment before he spoke.

"Nechtan, my thanks. I will return when I can," he said gruffly.

Nechtan nodded solemnly, and Calum turned to Melangell.

"I know you did all you could for my wife, and my son owes his very life to you. I am in your debt, my lady, and one day, if Ollovidius wills it, I will pay it back to you. Good-bye."

She raised her hand in farewell as the big stallion sprang across the clearing, its tail flying in the chill wind. Calum galloped out toward the grassy hillside, then veered to the left. He slowed the great horse to a walk as he approached the lonely pile of stones atop Boann's grave and paused there for a scant moment. Then the horse sprang away again, carrying the tracker and his little son swiftly up the far hillside and out of sight.

A light snow dusted the ground and a stiff breeze caused the brittle, sun-bright winter air to seem even more chill. Melangell, her feet wrapped in warm fur boots, made her way to the nearby stream, clutching a long fur cloak around herself with one hand and carrying a small wooden bucket in the other. Genann followed a discreet distance away. She was very lonely since Boann's death; the young woman had been a good friend and a source of female companionship in the midst of so much maleness. Nechtan was usually busy with the warriors' training exercises; and the men, while showing her every courtesy as their chief's wife, could not be considered as friends. Even Genann, she thought with a sigh, taking an overhanging pine branch to support herself while she slid down the snowy embankment to the stream, even he was no longer a friend. She feared to be around him much anymore, always kept a safe distance between them, and found herself unable to tease and jest with him as she once had done. He seemed to notice it and never attempted to press himself on her.

Lifting a rock with her mittened hands, she dropped it through the thickening ice at the water's edge. As she bent to fill the bucket, she peered from the corner of her eye and saw Genann silently standing atop the bank, his spear at his side, his heavy winter cloak hanging still in the cold air. Turning away, she held the bucket down into the clear rushing water. Slowly she heaved it up and onto the icy bank, then stopped to catch her breath. Straightening up, she pressed her hands into her weary back and stretched.

"Here . . . I'll carry that for you," Genann announced, leaping lightly to the ground beside her. "You must be careful of what you do now, or you'll hurt yourself."

"Yes, thank you," she muttered, and attempted to move away from him. He picked up the bucket and looked at her.

"Melangell . . ." he said quietly, trying to stop her before she slipped away from him again, as she always seemed to be doing nowadays. She hesitated, looked down at the snowy bank, then reached out to seize the overhanging pine branch and climb the slope. Genann dropped the bucket and his hand shot out to her wrist, but she had already stopped, aghast at the sight of the wooden bucket splitting down one side when it landed on the rocks.

"Oh . . . now look what you've—" she began, but he grabbed her other wrist and jerked her around to face him. She stared at him, a mixture of fear and anger crossing her cold-nipped face.

"Curse the bucket," he snapped irritably. "I must have a chance to speak my mind to you, Melangell. Ever since we kissed that night, you have treated me as if I had some loathsome disease you want to avoid."

Horror rose to her face at his words, and she struggled to free her wrists, but he held them firmly.

"Hush!" she gasped. "Someone will hear you!"

"No one else is out here," he replied. "In itself, I do not regret what we did, but I wonder if the cost was too high. In trying to have you for one night, I seem to have lost you forever. Why, Melangell? You would have enjoyed it. I would have pleased you—"

"Such things you say!" she hissed, anger flashing in her

green eyes. "Are you so stupid, poet, that you know all about your own heart and nothing of others'? Even in the little we did, I betrayed my husband. And now I still betray him. Every day of my life henceforth will be a lie, a deception. I can never cleanse my guilt, for to do so would be to hurt him terribly, and that I could never do. I must live with this, suffer with this, every day of my life; for me, there will be no release from it. Can you understand that, Genann? Can you understand a love that is quiet, that suffers and sacrifices in silence? Not a love that possesses . . . and destroys?"

Her words stung him painfully and he released her, his gray eyes clouding with worry. "What can I say, Melangell? What can I do to remedy what I have done? My poet's dreams got the better of me, and that is a regret I, too, will have to live with for the rest of my life. In trying to have my one foolish hope realized, I have succeeded in destroying all else, betraying my chief, and hurting the woman I cherish above all else . . . and always will."

He stared at her downcast face, the shadowed trees and white snow casting stark reflections on her pale skin.

"I'll make it up to you. I swear. Melangell, for the love I bear you, I will make it up to you. I will remedy what I have done."

She looked up at him and mutely shook her head, tears forming in her eyes.

"I will," he insisted, seizing her mittened hand in his. "You say I do not understand a love that suffers in silence, yet that is what I have done with you, for so long. My will was weak; I broke. I am sorry. That's all I can say, Melangell . . . I am sorry."

He kissed her hand and released it, and she turned to reach for the pine branch.

"Only tell me, Melangell, before you go—just one time, let me hear you say it—was it all so terrible for you? Our one night together—did I stir nothing within you, nothing?"

She lifted her head and looked at him sadly.

"That is the tragedy of it, Genann," she whispered, "for you did stir me."

She paused and turned away.

"Yes," she muttered, "you did."

* * *

Genann watched Nechtan sparring with Niall, his heavy shield expertly parrying each sword stroke, his booted feet as nimble as a deer's. The two swords clanged and clashed loudly, now overhead, now down. They seemed an equal match, each man's skill a perfect foil to the other's. Nechtan laughed loudly when Niall attempted to cut in low toward his leg, and he deflected it with the iron-bound rim of his shield. Springing aside, he swung upward with a quick thrust that sent Niall's sword flying. The tall blond warrior looked up in surprise when his weapon disappeared over his head, then stood erect, his arms extended, as Nechtan's sword sliced down toward his neck.

"I am a dead man," he announced, and Nechtan, laughing, halted his weapon.

"Well done, Niall! By the gods, what a fight!" he gasped, replacing his sword at his side and wiping the sweat from his face. "Aye," Niall agreed, retrieving his sword and wiping the blade on his long breeches. "We'll give those lazy Romans a fight worth the telling, eh?"

"That we will! Now I think a little ale is in order."

Nechtan turned toward the Great Hall, Niall behind him, when Genann suddenly walked up to him, a grim look on his face.

"Nechtan, I'd like to speak with you—alone," he announced, and the heavy tone to his voice made Nechtan look at him curiously.

"All right." he nodded as the three men entered the hall. "Niall, get your drink and wait outside until I summon you."

"Now then," Nechtan said, settling himself in his chair and taking a thirsty gulp of ale. "What troubles you?"

Genann unbuckled his sword and took the dagger and short knife from his belt, stepped forward, and laid them across Nechtan's lap. "I am an unarmed man," he stated flatly. Nechtan lifted them in one hand, a startled look on his face.

"See here, Genann, what is—"

"Hear me out, my chief," Genann interrupted. "It will not take long. Hear what I have to say."

Nechtan took a deep breath and nodded, sipping another bit of ale while he studied the young man. In his months of hard camp life Genann's expensive clothes had become as frayed and stained as everyone else's, and his brown hair was now nearly as long as Cathal's.

Genann stood stiffly, staring at a spot on the newly plastered wicker wall beyond Nechtan's shoulder. "What I am about to say to you is entirely my own fault. I ask you to keep that in mind. I take full and sole responsibility. I attempted to seduce your wife . . ."

Nechtan's bronze cup froze in midair and his fingers clenched slowly around the inlaid hilt of Genann's sword.

"What did you say?" he growled, his eyes narrowing.

"I tried to seduce your wife."

A strangled cry of rage rose in Nechtan's throat and he leapt to his feet, sword and knives and cup clattering loudly to the floor.

"You bastard," he hissed, drawing his dagger and stepping slowly toward the immobile young man. Before he could reach him, Niall and Cathal were there, holding him back, wrestling his knife hand down.

Nechtan's head cleared and he glared at Genann, his eyes glittering dangerously.

"Seize him," he snapped. Niall stepped behind Genann, clamping one strong arm around his neck.

"Where is my wife?" Nechtan shouted angrily. "And Brennos? Where is he?"

"Your wife is at the stables," Cathal said, puzzled.

"Go and bring her to me at once," Nechtan snapped. "And send for the druid."

Melangell combed out the long, silky mane of a gray mare, talking sweetly to the gentle animal, when Cathal suddenly appeared at her elbow.

"Your husband wishes to see you at once," he said grimly. She held the wooden comb aloft and looked at him in alarm. He grabbed her arm roughly and, before she could put the comb down or retrieve her woolen hood, he steered her from the makeshift stable, across the clearing, and into the dim hall. Her puzzled alarm gave way to fear when she saw the group assembled before her: Nechtan, tense and fierce-looking, pacing like a mountain wildcat; Genann, resigned as he stood under guard of Niall, his long hair twisted in the blond warrior's fist; and Brennos, a perplexed expression on his face, so hastily summoned he wore only his old faded breeches and a short tunic patched at one shoulder. Cathal pushed her forward and stopped beside Niall and Genann. She looked fearfully at her husband but he would not meet her gaze, and she felt her stomach turn in dread. Gods above, what has happened here? What is going on?

Nechtan suddenly strode toward them, hatred in his face, and held his knife point menacingly at Genann's throat. Melangell gasped aloud and she felt Cathal's hand close painfully around her upper arm, chafing the rough wool of her sleeve into her skin.

"Tell them what you told me." Nechtan sneered. "Tell them!"

"I tried to seduce your wife," Genann said flatly, not seeming to care what happened to him. Then Nechtan was glaring at Melangell, and the look in his eyes made her quail in fear.

"Well?" he ordered. "Is it true? Did he seduce you?"

She felt her life crumble within her and she tried to look down, but Cathal grabbed her hair and jerked her head upright.

"No . . ." she croaked in pain. "I mean . . . he tried to, but . . ."

"So," he said coldly, and suddenly he slapped her hard across the face. "Whose bastard is it, then? Genann's, or maybe a Roman's, eh?"

"No!" Genann shouted, trying to intercept him. Brennos rushed forward in alarm and planted himself protectively in front of the dazed girl. "Stop this!" he ordered. "Didn't you hear the man? He did not succeed. In the name of the All-Knowing, Nechtan, find out the details before you throw wild accusations like that."

Brennos looked aside at Genann's gray face, sorrow in his eyes. He should have guessed something like this would happen. He should have seen it coming.

"No, Nechtan," the young man stated. "She resisted; she resisted me all the way. The fault is not hers; it is mine."

"No . . . Genann," Melangell breathed in horror. He said he would make it up to me, relieve me of my guilt, but I never dreamed . . . No . . . not this way.

Nechtan looked at her sullenly, nodded once to Cathal, and the archer released his hold on her. She remained standing by Genann until Brennos put an arm around her and gently led her to the side of the room. Her cheek was swelling painfully from Nechtan's blow, but she ignored it. Brennos pulled up a stool and made her sit, but she would not take her eyes from the devastating scene before her. The druid stood silently beside her, one hand protectively on her shoulder.

Nechtan turned back to Genann and stared at his impassive face. "I ought to kill you," he growled, pressing his knife to the guard's throat. Then his rage broke, like a torrent released by a crumbling dike, and his fist smashed into the man's face. Genann's knees crumpled and he sagged downward, but Niall hauled him upright, one arm around his chest, and Nechtan's fist flew up into his stomach. He slumped forward, gasping, as Nechtan watched in grim satisfaction.

"No!" Melangell screamed, rising to her feet. "You'll kill him! Stop!"

Nechtan looked at her coldly, then returned to Genann.

"Release him," he ordered. As Niall let go, the young man slowly collapsed to his hands and knees, blood pouring down his face and dripping to the dirt floor. Nechtan stalked away and suddenly Genann looked up, aghast, at the sound of his precious harp being smashed against the floor.

"No . . ." he gasped, trying drunkenly to rise to his feet and failing. "No!"

Melangell buried her face in her hands and turned away, crying desperately.

"Twice you saved my life, and I said I would not forget it, poet," Nechtan snarled, turning back to Genann. "For that reason only, I spare your life now."

He tossed the sword and knives to the dirt in front of Genann's bleeding face.

"Get out of here! At once! And never let me set eyes on you again."

Genann pulled himself to his feet, wiping the blood with the back of one hand as he picked up his weapons. Without a word he turned and stumbled to the door, and as he passed the horrified girl he didn't even give her a final, farewell glance.

"Melangell!" Nechtan snapped. She looked at him in fear.

"Come," he said, motioning toward their quarters. With a brief glance at Brennos, she rose to her feet and walked to the door. Nechtan stood aside, waiting, and when he said nothing, she pulled the latch herself, opened the door, and entered the side room. Fear coursed through her as she stood, her back to the door, and heard him enter.

Then she felt his hand on her shoulder and he turned her to face him. She waited for him to shout, to strike her, something. . . .

"Look at me," he whispered. Slowly she lifted her eyes to meet his. His gaze softened when he saw the swollen red bruise on her cheek, and he gently touched it with his fingertips.

"Why didn't you tell me of this before?" he said sternly.

"I . . . was afraid to. Afraid of what you would do to Genann, and afraid of hurting you." She raised her hand and clenched it atop his hand at her cheek.

"Nechtan, you must believe me. I love you with all my soul. How could I hurt you? How? And the baby . . . it's your son, Nechtan, yours."

She searched his face with pleading eyes, and he smiled slightly as his anger abated.

"I know it is mine. It was my temper again; always, it is my temper."

He pulled her to him and pressed her head to his chest. "You must tell me such things, Melangell, though let's hope it never happens again. I will select a new guard for you—one who can be trusted. Now, let's forget this day ever happened."

Winter's snows still clung heavy to the ground as the Legion IX Hispana, troops of the Emperor Vespasian, loaded their supplies aboard a train of heavy wagons and pack mules, slung their packs, their helmets and weapons and marching tools over their eager backs, and set out for the promised spring offensive with their accompanying Legions. The general at the head of the army had received the permission he'd sought from the Imperial Governor Julius Agricola. He swung his troops toward the setting sun, the lands of the Damnonii.

Dawn had not yet arrived and Nechtan slept soundly, Melangell nestled at his side. A wild pounding at the door roused him and he sat up when he heard Cathal, on the other side of the wicker partition, fling the door open.

It was Melwas, gasping heavily from a hard ride on scouting duty, and his breathless words sent Nechtan flying from the narrow cot.

"The Romans . . . they come."

Pulling on his breeches and seizing his sword, he cast a fearful look at his wife, sitting stiffly upright in bed, her face ghostly white, her eyes wide. Without a word he ran from the room and out to the Great Hall, Cathal and Niall behind him.

Cai, chosen as Melangell's new guard at his own request, in an attempt to salvage his family's honor, heard the girl softly crying on the other side of the partition.

"Lady?" he questioned, listening through the wicker wall.

"I'm all right," she sobbed. "Go . . . go and join the other men, Cai. Prepare for the coming war."

The Great Hall was strangely silent when Nechtan entered it. Smoke from the low hearthfire hung thick in the peak of the circular ceiling; no one had yet thought to tend it. Some of his men sat up sleepily; others, more alert, stood grimly and talked in hushed voices. The time had finally arrived, the culmination of all their months of arduous practice, and the men found the reality of the situation to be not at all what they had expected. Here there was no heated glory, no fame, no wild exultation. Only a grimness that settled into the soul, a heaviness in the stomach, a sudden keenness of mind. They looked to Nechtan as he strode to his chair, motioning to Melwas.

The weary scout quaffed the last of his cup of ale and walked stiffly to Nechtan's side.

"What have you seen?" Nechtan asked tensely.

"Romans, sire; several Legions. For now, they seem to have halted. They are setting up camps."

Nechtan nodded thoughtfully. "How far away are they?" he suddenly asked.

"Two days' hard ride. Much slower for men on the march."

Again Nechtan nodded, his eyes roaming the sea of curious faces pressed around him.

"You say they are setting up camps?" he repeated, and Melwas nodded. "Temporary camps? A night or two?" he pressed. Melwas shook his head.

"Not large permanent camps, but not just for an overnight stop, either. There are three camps, spaced some distance apart. The first two are much larger, and much better fortified; the third is small, protected by only a hastily dug ditch and a line of implanted tree branches, and seems to hold only one Legion. They are making themselves comfortable for a while. I think they are waiting."

"Ah!" Nechtan said, and a broad smile crossed his face. The warriors looked at one another, perplexed.

"Melwas, rest for a while, then take three men with you and return to observe our visitors. I want to know as soon as they move, do you understand? Anything they do, send a man to tell me."

Melwas nodded and left, and Nechtan looked at Niall.

"Saddle up four swift horses, and select the four best riders in camp."

He gazed coolly at his chief guard, and then his eyes began to sparkle with excitement.

"It is time to send out riders with the burning brands, to rouse the neighboring warriors."

Niall grinned wickedly, nodded, and quickly left the room as the assembled men broke into wild, reckless cheers.

Despite her fear, Melangell could not help but feel excitement stirring within her as the men assembled from all the surrounding areas—young men in their teens, warriors in their prime, older men still handy with a lance or sword. They began to trickle in within the same day the riders went out, and for three days they came—on foot, on horseback, and in war chariots. The quiet little camp turned into a noisy, dirty town.

Cai escorted the girl everywhere she went to protect her

from the hordes of unfamiliar men, and many a time he had to place a cautionary hand on his sword hilt in the face of some crude remark or suggestive leer. To his relief, the girl eventually grew tired of strolling around the camp and confined herself to her own quarters or the Great Hall.

By morning of the fourth day, with several thousand men assembled, Nechtan brought together all the chiefs, princelings, and family heads who had answered his call.

Niall banged his spear down to silence the crowd as Nechtan stood.

"I will dispense with fancy speeches," he said bluntly. "My men have seen several Roman Legions setting up camps two days' hard ride to the south. I have spies there now, to keep me informed of their every movement."

"Good!" a tall, thin middle-aged chief said, rising to his feet. "Let them come! We are ready!"

A chorus of approving murmurs rose around him, and Nechtan held up his arms to get their attention.

"No! No!" he shouted. "That is just what we don't want! We must keep them out of our lands. We must try to stop them where they stand. They visit our territories . . . it is only courtesy that we repay their visit."

He watched as a few of the men nodded slowly in understanding while others stared at him blankly, uncomprehending.

"A chance has been dropped into our laps that we must not miss! There they sit, sure of their superiority, waiting for spring to arrive, for the snows to melt and the air to warm. So sure of their superiority, in fact, that one of their camps is not adequately protected. We must strike at this camp now, when they least expect us to—a surprise attack, at night, while they sleep."

"Yes!" another chief shouted, rising to his feet. "We have harassed them at night before, and they are at a great disadvantage in the dark, for we know the land, and they do not."

"But that has always been a small raid against an outpost or convoy," another protested. "This is an entire Legion." His companions nodded agreement.

"Exactly!" the first chief said. "They would never expect us to attack an entire Legion—the surprise will be ours!"

A wave of voices rose in eager approval, and Nechtan smiled in satisfaction.

"But what of their stockade?" an older, graying family head questioned. "Years ago I came up against such a Roman defense of branches; it is no easy thing to cross."

Nechtan narrowed his eyes and gazed around the room. "Any suggestions?" he muttered. A young chieftain stood, his bare torso gleaming in the firelight.

"I fought the bastards to the south; an ambush such as we plan now," he growled. "Our trick was a simple one. Gather all the woolen cloth you can, boil it down into thick pads, and sew these together with sinew. Give one to each army. Thrown over the branches, they cover the outward-facing points until the men can get inside the camp and pull the branches away or set them afire. Others of us, meanwhile, will be forcing an entrance at the gates of their camp. They will be surrounded."

Nechtan grinned and glanced up at Niall. "Gather all the extra cloaks and blankets," he ordered his chief guard. "Boil them in the bathing tubs. The work must be unceasing, throughout the night." Turning, he glanced at the assembled chiefs. "It is agreed, then?" he challenged, rising to his feet. "We leave at dawn in two days' time. A forced march, keeping to the mountains and the forests. Grease the axles of your chariots and muffle the wheels with strips of skin to maintain silence. We must surprise them, and the longer we delay, the greater the chance they will get wind of our plan. Surprise is our greatest ally."

A tide of affirmative voices rose around him, some eagerly so, others more reluctant.

"May the Great Bran crown our enterprise with success," Nechtan said, sat heavily in his chair, and took a brimming cup of wine from Cathal.

"I will be brave," Melangell said as she sat on the bedside and watched Nechtan dress by the light of a small stone lamp. The sun was hours away, yet the huge camp already hummed with activity.

He glanced at her and smiled while he lashed his supple leather boots around his ankles. "I know you will," he replied quietly, tied off the last thong, and sat down beside her, taking her hand in his.

"I should be back in five days, and I will want to see a smile on that lovely face of yours."

He turned her face up to his and she smiled slightly.

"Now . . . no tears," he said, wiping the corners of her eyes with his fingers. "It will not do for a chieftain's wife to cry. Brennos will be here with you, to look after you. You must be brave, my little dove, and trust to fate."

"Yes," she whispered, trying to subdue the fear in her heart. "I am a warrior's wife, a princeling's wife. I must be brave."

He stood and smiled. "That's the spirit!" he exclaimed. He lashed his long breeches against his legs with thin leather ties, crossing them up his calves, his thighs, and tying them off at his waist. A heavy leather sword belt was strapped over the ties and Melangell stood to help him lace a vest of stiffened, boiled leather over his back and chest. She studied him solemnly, intently, trying to fix forever in her memory the sight of him—every hair on his head, every expression on his face, every muscle, every movement—in case it should have to last her for the rest of her life.

He placed his dagger and two swords—one Roman, one Celtic—into his belt and picked up his cloak. "Come," he said firmly. "It is time."

Turning, they walked from the room, across the deserted Great Hall, and out into the dimly lit clearing in the center of the camp.

Brennos waited by the door and fell in behind them as they walked past rank upon rank of stern, silent foot soldiers, most shirtless, bearing full body shields, lances, and long Celtic swords; rows of cavalrymen astride eager horses with forelocks braided upward in bright cords and wearing neck harnesses from which their fierce riders would dangle severed Roman heads. Precise lines of wicker chariots, some light and two-wheeled, others four-wheeled and heavier, formed a smaller chariot corps, and amidst them all were the leaders and chieftains, in chain mail and leather armor, some wearing simple leather caps while others sported plumed and crested bronze helmets. And each group had four specially detailed men, carrying suspended between them the thick rolled pads of wool that would enable them to swarm into the lightly protected Roman camp.

Nechtan, Melangell, and Brennos reached their own group near the head of the column and a quiet murmur arose in the ranks when they saw their chief approach. Stopping beside his brass-ornamented chariot, Nechtan turned to his wife.

"Why don't you wait here while I have a word with Brennos?" he suggested. Silently she seated herself on the wooden deck of the chariot while her husband and the druid walked away a few paces.

"You have the sword I gave you?" Nechtan said quietly. Brennos patted the side of his black robe reassuringly.

"And, like most druids, I know how to use it." He smiled.

"Good . . . let us hope you don't have to. I've left a swift horse for you. If anything goes amiss, get her out of here at once. Take her north, to my people, and I will join you there if I can."

The druid nodded solemnly, and Nechtan put a firm hand on his arm.

"The Romans must not get her, Brennos. Better she should die than that."

"I understand," he answered, and looked at Nechtan's worried face. "I'll take good care of her, Nechtan. Don't worry."

Silently they returned to the chariot as the first faint light of dawn began to wash above the distant treetops and a few birds chittered to life nearby. Melangell stood and Nechtan looked at her a moment, then wrapped his arms tightly around her.

"I will be back, my love," he whispered in her ear. "Never fear, I will be back."

He gazed into her green eyes a long moment, fixing them in his memory, and then he kissed her, hard and desperately, as she squeezed her arms around his back. They could hear the lead armies starting to move, and he released her, stepping into the chariot beside Niall, Melwas, and Cathal. He watched Brennos take her arm and escort her away, through the vast ranks of waiting men, until she was lost to view among the rows of faces and spears and tossing horses' heads.

Nechtan turned as a shout went out, and Niall picked up the reins, waiting for the moving line to reach them. The dull sound of shuffling feet, the muffled rattle of chariot wheels, drifted through the hushed air. Niall snapped the reins and the chariot rolled forward, mounted warriors flanking it on either side, Nechtan's foot soldiers and spearmen bringing up the rear.

So it has begun, he thought calmly, holding to the curved wicker side of the chariot, the morning breeze catching his hair.

The war has finally begun.

Anarios tossed uncomfortably on a narrow army cot, trying to stuff a wool blanket beneath himself for a little extra padding. Curse that general, he thought angrily to himself for the thousandth time; a fine pass, this, when my little backward Syrian garrison seems like a luxury compared to the rigors of an army on the march in this godforsaken land. I must get out of this army and back to Rome, where things are done properly.

He sighed, gazing into the darkness of his stuffy leather tent and waiting for sleep to come, when a thousand blood-chilling screams, like all the demons of hell turned loose, sent him flying from the cot, stumbling in his frantic haste to locate his sword, falling into trunks and folded camp chairs. Outside the tent it sounded as if the world was coming to an end.

The armies of the Caledonians had caught the sleeping Ninth Legion completely unawares, creeping up on their camp in the chill darkness and sweeping down on them from the surrounding hills. Sentries were butchered before they could sound an effective alarm, and soon Celts were swarming over the light palisades and through the earth-work gates, meeting only occasional frantic resistance from the vainly rallying guard. Long Celtic swords slashed through the darkness, slings were fired with deadly force, lances and javelins thrust and stabbed. Terrified Roman soldiers groped blindly in the night, tried to rally, to fight back, but the madly screaming demons who bore down on them and seemed to be everywhere at once broke their nerve.

Anarios ran from his tent in fear, his sword in hand, as terrified soldiers stumbled past him, throwing down weapons, helmets, and shields in their eagerness to escape.

"Stop!" he shouted, to no avail. The men's ears were deafened by their panic. The physician pushed his way forward, against the flowing tide of men, trying to reach the general's headquarters; the same general who had been so contemptuous of the native "barbarians" that he had never put up a proper fortification.

A wild yell to his right froze him in his tracks and he turned as a tall, naked barbarian sprang out of the darkness at him, his slashing sword circling high, his face twisted in a wild fury. Anarios swung desperately with his sword and managed to deflect the falling blow; and then the man was grappling with him, his well-trained young muscles easily overcoming the physician's strength. Anarios tried frantically to turn his sword, to stab the demon, but he could not. One leg was giving way as the man bore him down, and he pushed hard to right himself. Suddenly the man slumped, and Anarios, in grateful surprise, angrily pushed the body aside, an arrow sticking out of the man's back. One of his old Syrian comrades grinned at him from the darkness, saluted smartly, and vanished.

He could hear the rattle of Celtic chariots now, strangely muffled as if in a bad dream, driving their way into the heart of the camp, and savage cries of triumph sweeping toward him in an overwhelming tide. Somewhere a cornicen had located his horn and was blasting a frantic retreat to the Roman troops. The sight of their legionary standards and the Imperial Eagle moving high above the melee drew the demoralized soldiers like bees to a hive. Celtic warriors desperately tried to reach the men bearing the insignia, to strike them down and further confuse the legionaries, but a brave defense held them at bay. Anarios quickly saw the general's strategy: they were fighting their way from camp, heading for a cleared hillock nearby where a better defense could be maintained till help arrived. He tried to keep his eye on the gleaming silver eagle, shining like a beacon in the rising firelight, pressing his way toward it through the fighting throngs and deafening noise. The blaring of the horn abruptly stopped, the cornicen doubtless meeting his death, and a sudden gust of smoke from the burning tents nearly obscured the beckoning silver standard. Wild fear gripped Anarios' throat and he threw down his sword and ran.

On a hill to the far side of camp the fleeing Romans gathered, shedding their panic as the familiar voices of their commanders restored their military training and discipline. Only a remnant of their numbers remained, and they listened in horror to the cries and shrieks of their comrades who hadn't made it to safety. A cold anger began to replace their fear, making them anxious to avenge their friends' deaths.

Anarios slumped against a tree, gasping for breath and watching in awful fascination the shadowy Celts moving below them, light from the fires glinting off swords and shields and sweating bodies as they roamed about, finishing off the last of the wounded Roman soldiers and searching for loot.

The sound of a horse's wildly pounding hooves coming up on them from the rear made the Romans turn, fearful of an ambush; but it was only a messenger, from the governor Agricola himself.

"General . . ." the exhausted man gasped as he slid from his mount. "The governor comes! He had received intelligence of this attack. Even now he has sent the swiftest cavalry and infantry ahead, to sweep down on the barbarians from the northeast. You must attack at once, and trap them!"

A wild cheer went up from the vengeful soldiers, who seized what weapons they had and formed up in ranks as best they could. The rosy glow of dawn was spreading across the far horizon when they began the march back down the hillside.

It is too quiet, Nechtan thought as he roamed the ravaged camp. A blazing tent crashed crazily at his side, and he turned, tense, at the sound. Romans did not run away so

270

easily, he knew. Sooner or later their fear would pass and they would return.

Cathal loped up beside him, an arrow ready in his bow, several plundered Roman pots tied together and slung over his back.

"Where is the chariot?" Nechtan snapped. A knot of men off in the darkness laughed loudly and suddenly came galloping by on wild-eyed Roman horses, bloody Roman heads dripping from the animals' necks.

"Niall has it, I think," the young man replied. Nechtan turned abruptly and trotted off to his right, where the mounted horsemen had come from.

"There is little booty in a camp such as this," he muttered as Cathal fell in beside him. "We have done what we set out to do . . . we should be off now."

He ran up to the burning Roman stables, elbowed his way through the throngs of men pulling out the panic-stricken animals, and seized a big gray gelding from a man's startled grip.

"Hey!" the man started to protest, halting when he saw who it was.

"Get yourself another, my friend," Nechtan shouted. He jumped onto the animal's bare back, seized the reins, and waited while Cathal grabbed another horse and lightly leapt astride it, throwing the looted pans clattering to the ground.

"We are retreating *now*," Nechtan bellowed at the milling throng. "Retreat!"

The men paused dumbly for a moment at his words, then began wildly fighting for the remaining mounts.

"Retreat!" the cry went up, spreading like a blazing grass fire through the fort. Nechtan and Cathal galloped through the camp until they found his chariot, with Niall sitting in the rear, cradling a severely wounded Eber in his lap. He looked up at his chief and shook his head briefly.

"We are retreating," Nechtan said flatly, looking at Eber's pallid face, pink foam bubbling at his lips, his chest soaked in blood.

"The Wolf! The Wolf!" Cathal shouted, walking his horse around the surrounding area, calling for Nechtan's men to assemble. They swiftly materialized out of the night and gathered around expectantly, meager booty slung over their shoulders or suspended from belts. Niall stood and dragged Eber's inert body from the vehicle, placing him gently on the ground. The man's eyes were glazed; already he is half-dead, Niall thought. He hefted his spear in one hand and stood over him.

"Good-bye, old friend," he muttered, plunging the spear into Eber's heart and pulling it free. Shouts, wilder and more panic-stricken, began to well up around them.

"Romans! Romans are coming!"

Niall looked up at Nechtan openmouthed, and without pausing to remove Eber's torque, he sprang into the chariot with a few other of the men. The mounted warriors formed a protective ring around their chief and, putting their heels to their horses, sprang off toward the north, and safety.

But something was wrong. The tide of fleeing men suddenly turned and washed back toward them.

It is a trap! Nechtan suddenly knew, fear rising within him. He could hear cries arising now from behind him, to the south, as well, and he turned his horse angrily to the west, a steeper slope down the encircling ditch that they would have more difficulty negotiating.

The cries came louder, accompanied by the harsh clang of metal on metal, and through the dim morning light he could see the approaching standards of fresh legionaries, bearing down on them.

Gods above, Nechtan thought savagely as the first triumphant Roman face came into view, I will not die like a fish in a net.

With a wild cry he whirled his sword aloft and charged for a gap to the west, his eyes glittering in rage, his men galloping after him.

The terrified Celts rallied at the sight of one of their leaders plunging madly at the Romans, and with a great cry they turned and followed, hacking and stabbing and thrusting their way out of the camp by inches. They broke free and fled across the ditch around the camp, streaming up the hillsides and into the sheltering forests, the Romans in pursuit.

But the weary Romans did not follow for long, and they soon returned to the carnage at their camp, leaving the

Caledonians to make their way back to their own lands in peace.

A false peace, Nechtan knew as his men slowly marched through the dark woods. We have struck the first blow; the Romans will return for their revenge. We must pack up our supplies and head north into the mountains at once.

Stumbling away from the Roman encampment, the tribesmen split up, each group returning to its own lands to recover, regroup, and await the Romans' next move.

By afternoon of the second day the first returning warriors staggered into Nechtan's camp. Melangell rushed from the hall at the sound of their weary voices, Brennos at her side. Her face fell when she saw the men. Many were wounded, and all were grim and exhausted.

Something has gone wrong, she thought in alarm. She ran into the clearing, her eyes searching the winding trail for the chariot, her ears straining to hear the wheels creaking over the rutted earth. Still the men stumbled in, in twos and threes, supporting each other or leaning heavily on their spears and lances.

At last she heard it . . . saw it . . . rattling slowly up out of the surrounding forest, the muffling leather on the wheels hanging in tatters and the two dark horses barely keeping up a slow walk as they hung their heads tiredly. She could see Niall at the front, the reins slack in his hand, his face gray with dust. Fearfully she scanned the other figures in the chariot, looking for the familiar face, the black hair.

Running forward when the chariot pulled into the clearing, she looked up desperately at the grim, bloodied men.

Niall . . . Melwas . . . Mac Oag . . .

They jumped to the ground and stiffly walked away.

Cai . . . Osla, limping badly from a wounded leg . . .

And that was all.

She peered into the empty chariot and saw a large dark bloodstain spread across the wooden floor. Backing away in horror, she shook her head numbly. Her fingers groped emptily at her face.

"Nechtan! No!" she screamed wildly to the sky, then collapsed to the ground beside the dusty chariot wheel.

* * *

"She'll be all right," a voice said calmly—Brennos' voice. Opening her eyes, Melangell saw the familiar low ceiling of her quarters. Then a face pressed wearily against hers, a hand embraced her cheek, a familiar shock of dark hair fell across her field of vision. Weakly she struggled, her hands frantically feeling the hair, the hand, the arm; and then he raised his head and looked at her, his face streaked with sweat and dirt, his yellow wolf's eyes tired, so very tired.

"Nechtan . . ." she sobbed softly, not believing her eyes. He lifted her in his arms and held her close, as much to revive his own flagging spirits as to reassure her.

"Yes, my little dove," he sighed. "It is I, returned to you, as I said I would."

Cathal, Melwas, and Niall perched around the side room while Nechtan stripped and sank into a bath of steaming water in which healing herbs had been steeped.

"What do we do now?" Niall muttered. Nechtan relaxed in the soothing waters and closed his eyes.

"We wait for one day," he answered as Melangell poured hot water through his dirty hair. "Let Brennos finish treating the wounded. Then we pack as much food as we can carry, and burn the rest; take the horses, the chariot and wagons, and head into the mountains. The Romans will not be long in coming after us."

"Aye." Melwas nodded gruffly. "Once they bury their dead, they will look for us."

"Well," Cathal added, looking enviously at the hot bath Nechtan was so thoroughly enjoying, "at least now the others of our people will believe that the threat is real and will join us." Nechtan looked at him from the corner of his eye and laughed.

"Use my tub when I am through, you three! It'll take too long for everyone to use the two out in the hall. There's nothing like a hot bath for sore muscles."

"Aye," Niall agreed, stretching stiffly.

"How many did we lose?" Nechtan asked, sitting up in the water while Melangell scrubbed his back.

"Eighteen . . . about a third," Melwas said.

Nechtan shook his head and splashed himself clean.

"That's too many, but considering the circumstances, it

could have been much worse," Nechtan mused, before stepping from the bath and taking the clean cloak Melangell held out to him.

"By the gods, Nechtan, I *will* take your dirty bath, I am so tired." Niall laughed as he stood. "Your pardon, lady." He nodded to Melangell. Pulling off his belt and sword, he stripped quickly and sank into the steaming bath with a happy sigh.

Melangell laughed and turned to find her husband some clean clothes to wear, her mind already planning the upcoming move. A small chest, she thought, with just our barest necessities; the rest I will burn myself. No Roman will be sending my things back to his curious wife, not if I can help it.

Their items of jewelry, gold and silver, bronze and gleaming black jet, went in the bottom of the chest, wrapped in her silk shawl. These she covered with her old black druid's cloak. Then she packed one change of clothing apiece, and an extra cloak. It all fit neatly into a small, easily transported wooden box. The remaining items of clothing she gathered in her arms and carried out to the clearing, where a big fire blazed wildly in the bright spring afternoon. Occasionally a warrior approached, tossing some unneeded article of clothing, a broken weapon, an overlooked piece of crude furniture, an empty barrel, into the greedy flames. It struck her, watching the devouring fire in awful fascination, that this, and nothing else, was what war was:

Destruction.

Log benches and wicker cots vanished into the hungry maw; empty sacks and finely carved chests; cloaks and breeches and torn leather belts; all curled and flared and crumbled away to nothing. Melangell looked down at the crumpled clothes in her arms, the fine gowns Brennos had given her, the beautifully embroidered shawls, Nechtan's hunting clothes, his knee-length summer breeches.

She sighed pensively and gazed at the dancing flames. Yes, this was what war was . . . destruction, and sacrifice, and terrifying, horrifying ugliness.

Angrily she heaved the bundle into the fire. The items sat amidst the flames for several moments before they caught fire and blackened, burning dully. The Romans would find nothing . . . nothing.

Groaning under the weight, four heavily laden wagons slowly moved out to the base of the hillside, still dotted with patches of spring snow. Cathal emerged from the Great Hall carrying Melangell's small carved chest and strapped it to the back of the chariot while she hurried to the house to get her cloak, but Nechtan emerged from the doorway with it tossed over one arm. He watched silently as Niall reentered the building and returned, carrying his carved chieftain's chair from the Great Hall. The guard dragged it to the fire and tossed it in, and Nechtan stood and watched it burn, a solemn look on his face.

The last to leave the building was Brennos, his sack of medicines slung over one shoulder. He tied it over the back of a tethered horse and mounted, waiting for orders from Nechtan.

The foot soldiers and horsemen moved forward, congregating around the chariot. Cathal helped Melangell onto the rear deck, newly sanded and scrubbed to remove Eber's blood, while Nechtan waited for Niall to return from the fire. The two men stepped into the chariot and Nechtan picked up the reins, snapping them smartly. The horses sprang away, the rest of his army following as they slowly wound their way up the far hillside.

The last three men in camp waited until the group had safely gone, then gathered burning torches from the bonfire. Some they tossed into the Great Hall, against the stockade and wicker walls, while others were pitched atop the dry sod and thatch roof. Mounting their horses, they galloped up the freshening green hillside as greedy tongues of fire licked up the walls of the hall and across the timbered inner roof, enveloping the empty building in flames.

Part 5

THE ARMIES

*F*OR THREE DAYS IT RAINED AS NECHTAN'S GROUP STRUGGLED over increasingly rough terrain. For three days they didn't have a warming fire, or dry clothes to wear, or a rain-free place to sleep, save what shelter overhanging trees or a rocky hillside might afford. It was a glum, disheartened group who got the news from a passing bard: the entire Highlands were up in arms and ready to fight, united at last in their desire to drive out the Roman invader for good. Reflecting their rising spirits, the morning of the fourth day brought an end to the rain, heavy gray clouds lumbering across the sky as the weary refugees climbed higher into the great Highland massif, to join the gathering armies in the north.

"May we join you?" a voice called out of the darkness as Nechtan and his men sat around an evening campfire, a small wild boar roasting on a spit for their dinner.

Niall and Cathal took their spears and walked in the direction of the voices while Cai moved protectively to Melangell's side, one hand on his sword. In moments the two guards returned to the campfire, escorting three druids in mud-stained black robes.

"Diuran!" Brennos called out, rising to his feet as the druids approached. "I had counted you for dead these past few years!"

"No, my friend." The youngest of the three, slim and curly-haired, grinned, clasping Brennos' hand. "As luck would have it, I was not on the island when the Romans invaded."

Brennos nodded solemnly and motioned them to the

fireside. "This is our chief, Nechtan," he said. "This is an old friend of mine, Diuran. We went to the druids' school on Mona together. I'm afraid I don't know the other two."

"This is Ethal," Diuran said. A tall, pale, middle-aged man nodded in reply. "And Cathbhadh . . ." indicating a much older man, balding and with a full gray beard and mustache.

"And what brings you out here?" Nechtan asked. Niall returned to his place beside his chief while Cathal began cutting the roast for their meal.

The four druids settled themselves by the fire and gladly accepted the food that was offered to them.

"No doubt we have the same reason as you," Diuran began, hungrily cutting a chunk of meat and popping it into his mouth. "Romans. Ethal and I escaped by a hair's breadth and later met up with Cathbhadh, who was making his way north to join the armies and the few druids who are left."

"How many of us are left, do you think?" Brennos asked him. Diuran shrugged as he tore off a chunk of bread and handed the loaf to Ethal.

"Maybe twenty, I'd guess. It's hard to say. Most I've talked to are not very optimistic about a high survival rate for our kind."

"Do you have any news as to the Romans' actions?" Nechtan asked them.

"Only that they have advanced northward, with ships off the coast to support and supply them, and have set up a garrison in the northern lands of the Damnonii, who capitulated with little fight," Ethal answered.

"Gods above . . ." Niall breathed as Nechtan looked into the fire angrily. The fools! he thought bitterly. The damn lazy fools!

"Are you Damnonii, then?" Ethal asked, seeing their reaction to his words. Nechtan silently nodded.

"Well, all is not lost with your people," the druid continued. "Many fled as the Romans advanced, and now wander as you do. They seek a leader and are eager to fight."

"Well, that is some balm for the shame of it, I suppose," Nechtan said gruffly. "If only they had listened sooner . . ."

Ethal laughed lightly. "As a historian, I can tell you, my

friend, that regrets will never alter the course that time has taken."

"No, nor can words alter the minds of fools," Nechtan replied sourly.

The men turned at the soft sound of crunching leaves. Melangell approached from her comfortable resting place in the chariot. She looked aside at the three unfamiliar druids as she walked over to her husband, Cai close behind her.

"I came to tell you good night, for I am very tired," she told him. "I'll not interrupt your conversation for long."

Nechtan stood and put an arm around her affectionately, kissing the side of her forehead. "First, meet our visitors," he said. "Diuran, Ethal, and Cathbhadh. Like us, they flee the Romans and seek to join the gathering armies."

She looked in their direction and they nodded politely.

"This is my wife," Nechtan announced, and Brennos smiled at the pride in his voice.

"A baby coming soon?" Diuran noted, and the girl laughed a sunny little laugh.

"Yes. In a few more months."

"All is well, I hope?"

"Aye . . . you must be a physician yourself, to be asking such questions. I have a good doctor to see to my health, don't I, Brennos?" she joked, her green eyes sparkling. Brennos laughed and shrugged noncommittally.

"Melangell is something of a druidess herself," he told his three companions. "She has studied under Esus, the old holy man, and he thought very highly of her."

"Esus?" Cathbhadh spoke up. "I know him. A fine man."

"I'm afraid he is dead now. The Romans . . ." Brennos said simply. The other druids shook their heads sadly. "A pity," Cathbhadh said. "I suppose there will be no others like him now. And you studied under him, lady?"

"Yes," Melangell said sadly. "Perhaps I'll tell you about him as we continue on our journey. There is little that Brennos does not already know and could tell you."

"Yes, of course." Cathbhadh nodded. "Forgive me . . . you must have your rest. Perhaps we can talk tomorrow."

She smiled and nodded at the three, kissed Nechtan, and retreated into the shadows.

"A lovely girl," Diuran complimented Nechtan.

"Aye," the older druid said absently, "but a great sorrow hangs over her, a great sadness."

Nechtan paused, his drinking horn in midair, and looked at the druid suspiciously. "A sadness, old man? What sadness do you see there?"

Cathbhadh shook his head slowly. "Her life is not an easy one. She carries many burdens for others, many sacrifices, many heartaches . . . great sadness . . ." His voice died away. Nechtan's face paled visibly, and Brennos knew what he was thinking of.

His family's curse.

"Cathbhadh, I'd like to speak with you privately," Nechtan said as the camp settled down to sleep and the guards positioned themselves around the perimeter of the area.

"Certainly." The old man nodded, rising stiffly to his feet. "Let's step over into those trees yonder."

Silently they walked into the darkness, halting by a great fragrant hemlock.

"You are of the Cruithni, are you not?" the druid said suddenly, and Nechtan looked at him in astonishment.

"Half-Cruithni—" he began. The old man laughed.

"It is no mystery. Your coloring, your intensity, the tattoo on your arm. Such things are Cruithni. May I guess you are of the royal house, and concerned about the curse on your head?"

"Aye," Nechtan muttered grimly. "How can it be that such a dear, gentle girl will bring about my death? We are devoted to each other. She would never betray me. How can it happen?"

The old man shook his head slowly before he replied. "It can happen in a way you or she would least expect. Does she know of the part she plays in your life?"

"No."

"Good. Such knowledge would be an even greater burden on her. Do not give her such a burden."

"But can anything be done to end this curse? How long must it continue? When will enough vengeance be exacted by this god whose name no one even remembers?"

"And your son?"

Nechtan looked at him in surprise and nodded again. "Yes . . . she says it is a boy. Is that all I will have sired, a continuation of this curse? Can't anything be done to end it?"

"Only one thing can be done to end so great a curse."

"What? Tell me! I will do anything. If not for me, then for my son."

"Do not commit yourself so lightly, young man, without knowing what you say. A curse such as this is nothing more than an imbalance."

He peered intently at Nechtan through the shadows. The young man's face was grim, waiting, his jaws clenched tightly, his finely arched brows pushed into a frown.

"An imbalance that must be righted," he went on. "That which was taken from the god so long ago must be returned to him. In greed your ancestor took the god's sacrifice. To remedy it, some male of the line must return the sacrifice, equally great, equally valued."

Nechtan blanched at his words. "No," he whispered. "You mean . . . sacrifice her? No. Never."

The old druid placed a reassuring hand on his arm and shook his head. "You misunderstand me, son," he said quietly. "It is not the girl I speak of. Always, since the beginning, the women have only been tools, instruments . . . never the cause itself. Think of the cause and, in that, you will have your answer. I cannot tell you anything more than this. The rest is in your hands, your understanding."

He turned and walked back to the campfire, leaving Nechtan standing alone and baffled among the dark, sighing trees.

"Hello, love!"

Nechtan whirled from the cart horse he was unharnessing at the sound of the familiar voice.

"Seonaid!"

"Aye." She laughed gaily. "I never expected to see you here. Is your exile ended, then, or am I speaking to the dead?"

"I am a chieftain now, with my own warriors," he said,

turning back to the horse. She walked over to him and tried to reach up to his hair, but he seized her wrist angrily and turned on her.

"None of your tricks, girl," he snapped. "I remember well the humiliation you caused me at our last parting, and I have not forgiven it."

"I? Humiliated you?" she gasped, drawing herself upright stiffly. "And what of your humiliation of me? Attempting to rape me like some slave girl."

"Enough of this," he spat, releasing her arm angrily. "What do you want with me? Why are you here?"

"I fled from the Romans. I am Angus' woman now."

"Angus?" He laughed loudly. "A fitting pair—two unmanageable redheads. Your nights together must be remarkable."

"Not as remarkable as our nights together," she cooed, touching his ear lightly.

"Our nights together are over, Seonaid," he stated, walking up to the horse's head.

"Why?" She pouted. "Are you and Niall lovers now?"

"It is something you wouldn't understand," he said, continuing with his work.

"Ah, then you and Niall must be lovers!" She laughed. "I always knew the two of you were too close."

He grabbed her hair and jerked her head back savagely.

"It is something I doubt you've ever experienced in your entire selfish life . . . something called *love.* I am married now, and I love my wife very much. And believe me, she is twice the woman you ever were."

Seonaid glared at him, waiting for him to release her hair. With a snort of disgust he pushed her away. She put her hands on her hips defiantly.

"Well, if you ever tire of your little housewife, come and find me. Just ask—"

"And half the men in camp will know where you are." He laughed.

Enraged, she ran forward, her hand raised to strike him. He grabbed her wrists and held her fast, laughing at her impotent rage as she struggled to reach him.

"Not again, Seonaid, not again." He smiled coldly. "I am

not your horse, to be beaten whenever it suits your fancy. Be off with you, and give Angus my condolences."

He pushed her away violently and she stumbled, almost falling to the ground. Righting herself, she glared hotly at him, tossed her thick red hair over her shoulders, and indignantly walked away, her well-rounded bottom swinging in exaggeration beneath her shift. He watched her go, shook his head in amusement, and returned to his work. The entire assemblage of refugees and warriors who had answered the call of the great warlord Calgacus would be meeting that night for a final feast, while the druids held their last meeting in a copse of trees down the mountainside. Nechtan and his group, newly arrived that morning at Calgacus' camp, had much to do in preparation . . . more important things than wasting time on a spoiled child like Seonaid.

Hundreds of campfires dotted the far slopes of the mountain, eager men having gathered there from all over Caledonia, and daily more streamed in, many bringing their women with them, carts loaded with supplies, horses and baggage, chariots, oxen, all the equipage of an army on the move. An entire herd of cattle had been slaughtered for the massive feast, and wagonloads of plundered wine and good ale were distributed to the various camps.

A large and noisy group gathered around the campfires of the Damnonii and allied tribes, several thousand men strong. Many listened in silence to the repeated telling of the attack on the Roman Ninth Legion, and the loud boasting of exploits grew more exaggerated as the wine flowed.

Melangell nestled snugly beneath Nechtan's arm while they listened in amusement to yet another warrior's bragging tales of his heroics in the battle.

"It's a wonder any Romans were left to chase us out!" Nechtan chuckled, drinking some wine and handing his cup to Melangell. She sipped it lightly and returned it to him, then shifted her feet to a more comfortable position. Everyone was so packed around the fire that she hardly had room to move. Cai was nearly pressed into her side, and Niall, Cathal, and Melwas stood protectively behind them, so close she could have rested her head against their legs if she'd wanted.

"There isn't much room, is there?" Nechtan smiled, giving her shoulder an affectionate squeeze. "Are you all right? Cai can escort you away, if you'd like."

He peered around his wife to her guard, who, at the mention of his name, leaned forward to see what Nechtan wanted.

"No," she protested. "I want to stay. I am all right." At her words Cai settled back beside her, watching two warriors who suddenly darted out by the campfire in exuberant good spirits, feinting at each other in mock battle, leaping high into the air with acrobatic grace and drawing loud cheers from the watching men.

A disturbance broke out to the left and everyone turned. Nechtan's anger rose when he saw Seonaid flouncing toward them, followed by a pack of hungry male eyes. The two warriors in the circle ceased their play, pausing to watch her. She wore a deliberately provocative dress of thin gray wool, her hips and breasts swaying enticingly beneath the fabric as she walked.

Melangell felt her husband grow tense as Seonaid circled the campfire and headed straight for them. A stir passed over the men around her, Cai sitting bolt upright in surprise, the legs behind her shifting in their eagerness.

"Hello, love." Seonaid smiled, leveling her blue eyes at Nechtan, and Melangell's stare grew cold as she watched her.

"What do you want?" he muttered, taking a long, slow drink of wine.

"Just being sociable, honey," she replied. "I came to meet your loving wife, but all I see is this . . . slave girl."

Melangell felt his hand tighten on her shoulder and he lowered the drinking horn, his yellow wolf's eyes glittering dangerously.

"She is my wife," he said, his voice as cold as a winter's snowfall, but it seemed to pass right by the redhead.

"Indeed? You didn't tell me she was so . . . large." She sneered. "And you claim this . . . this little child is twice the woman I am? I find that hard to believe."

She gazed self-confidently at the sea of male faces around her and laughed dramatically, as if she could scarcely believe her eyes.

Suddenly Nechtan was on his feet, his fists clenched in rage. He seemed ready to strike her. His three guards stood by and watched, grinning, while several male voices cheered and called out from around the fire.

"You wouldn't hit me here, in front of everyone, would you, love?" She smiled coyly at him. Melangell straightened up tensely, and Cai, glancing at her out of the corner of his eye, put a restraining hand on her arm. Her face was, if anything, colder and more murderous-looking than Nechtan's.

"Can she compare to this?" Seonaid said loudly. Reaching for his hand, she placed it firmly on one ample breast, to the wild delight of the men.

"You used to like it well enough."

He jerked his hand away, and when she reached up to kiss him, Melangell was on her feet, as supple as a cat despite her swelling stomach, her knife whipped out and the point pressed to Seonaid's neck.

"That's enough," she said coldly. The men fell silent at this sudden spectacle.

"What's this!" Seonaid exclaimed as she was forced back, a step at a time, by the insistent knife point. Cai was standing now, alarmed, but pride also showing in the look on his face. Nechtan folded his arms and watched them. He knew his wife well enough; he knew she could handle herself.

"Leave him alone," Melangell hissed furiously, and jabbed with the knife, making Seonaid wince in pain. "He is mine now. If you touch him again, I will cut off that red hair of yours, and if that doesn't convince you, I'll have to cut off something you value more highly."

Wild laughter broke out around the circle, but neither of the women was very amused. Melangell continued to push the girl back a step at a time, her face a mask of cold rage. Seonaid tried to keep up her insolent facade, but real fear clouded her eyes.

"Will you go and leave us alone now?" Melangell snapped, backing the girl into the encircling crowd.

"No . . . why should I—" Seonaid began. At her words Melangell reached out and with a mighty jerk tore the flimsy gown from Seonaid's body.

"Then why keep up the pretense . . . whore!" Melangell spat at her as pandemonium broke out around them.

Nechtan was after them in a flash, Cai at his heels, and bellowing for Melwas and Niall, who were only too eager to accompany him. He seized Melangell, pulled her back, and handed her to Cai, who placed a firm hand on her shoulder as he eyed the naked but still-defiant Seonaid. Nechtan paused and made a great show of eyeing her up and down, which seemed to please her. She straightened up, thrusting her breasts out at him invitingly, and Cai had to restrain his charge when she tried to go after the redhead again.

"Niall . . . Melwas . . . can you handle Angus?" Nechtan suddenly asked over his shoulder.

"Aye, easily," Melwas replied. "He is a pompous wind-bag."

"Well," Nechtan answered, still eyeing the naked but now puzzled girl, "I know you two have always had an eye on her. Here's your chance."

He stood aside grandly.

"She's all yours. Make her happy so she'll leave us alone."

Niall and Melwas grinned wickedly and looked at each other. Niall tossed his spear to his companion and in one swift stride seized the dumbfounded girl, threw her over his shoulder, and carried her, struggling and protesting mightily, through the laughing, cheering circle of men, Melwas trotting happily behind him.

"A calamity such as this has never before happened in this land," Ethal said, rising to his feet before the small gathering of druids. "In our past, the lands of our ancestors, there have been invasions, it is true. But always there were two great differences: the invaders came for a specific reason— lands to settle, crops to eat, cattle to steal, gold to plunder; and always there was some other place we could go to, if pushed too far, if defeated."

He paused as his fellow druids nodded silent agreement to his words.

"But this, my friends, is like nothing before. The Romans rule the world. They have no need for yet more land to settle their tribes, no need for more food or cattle. They have more than enough already. And we are but a poor country, no

288

prize to be won. Our riches are few, our soil thin, our climate harsh. What, other than sheer greed and the evil in their hearts, can impel them to strike at us? And as for a place of escape, there is none. We are at the edge of the world. With us now rests the last hope of our people . . . all of them."

He sat down grimly. The druids whispered quietly among themselves for a few moments before a thin elderly man stood, leaning heavily on a knotted staff to support himself.

"Then there is nothing to do short of militarily defeating them. We have no other option. Victory, or surrender. The choice seems clear."

"Aye," said a third, "but the warriors already assemble to do battle, the largest army this northern land has ever seen. That choice is now out of our hands."

"Then what's to be done?" Brennos said angrily, standing before them. "Killing a thousand white cattle or fine stallions in sacrifice will not save us from the might of Rome. What countless sacrifices have already been offered up—to the south, in Britain, in Gaul, all the way to the gates of Rome itself? What good have those sacrifices done? Perhaps this is the will of the gods. Perhaps there is little that we, as druids, can do, other than tend the wounded and wait for our own extermination at the hands of Rome."

"Brennos, Brennos," Cathbhadh said calmly, rising to his feet and shaking his head at the man's words. "You speak as a physician now, a man of means and causes, and not as the druid you are. The purpose of this meeting is not to discuss what we can do to defeat Rome . . . it is to discuss what we can do in any capacity. If defeating Rome is out of our hands, well, you forget that there are other things we can do: one in particular—the most solemn sacrifice in our office as druids."

"The sacrifice of the prophet?" Brennos said, surprised. Cathbhadh nodded grimly as the other druids began to murmur around him.

"But who?" Diuran said, leaping to his feet in agitation. "We are a fragmented, hunted people. We have no champion anymore. Our warrior class is decimated . . ."

"There are ways," Cathbhadh replied evenly. "Most of the chiefs and kings and princelings are here. We will

289

assemble all the leaders, with their chief bodyguards. From the bodyguards I will select one who is suitable; intelligent, yet strong enough to endure the ordeal as long as possible, and of course brave."

"Aye, brave," Brennos muttered, returning to the log where he sat.

"But, Cathbhadh," he continued, suddenly looking up, "as the warriors are fragmented, so also are we. Look! Our strength is diminished; there are only eighteen of us here. Who is fit to perform it? Only you are versed in the mysteries of nature, and yet you yourself are not a holy man. Who among us is qualified?"

"There is one," Cathbhadh said slowly, fixing his old eyes on Brennos levelly. "One who is not here, yet one with powers, so I hear it said."

"Who?" Ethal demanded. "What druid with such powers is not at this meeting?"

The old man turned to look at Ethal, and his voice was as clear as a thunderclap when he answered.

"The girl."

"Melangell!" Brennos cried, jumping to his feet again. "Yes, she has powers, but she is not really a druidess . . . and she would never consent to this. She is gentle; she heals; she has never killed in her life. She does not even eat meat. Her life is conducted strictly according to what Esus taught her."

"And he was a holy man," Cathbhadh responded.

"Yes, but she will never do this, never," Brennos stated. "She cannot bear to see a bird shot from the sky. How can she kill a man?"

"She must. For her people. She must. She is all we have. She will," Cathbhadh said flatly, as if for him the discussion was closed. The old druid with a staff slowly rose to his feet and spoke, his voice soft and cracked with age.

"Esus I know," he said quietly, "but who is this girl you speak of? What powers has she? I think we would all like to know this before we entrust her with this most sacred act."

A chorus of agreement met his words, and everyone looked at Brennos expectantly.

"She is the green-eyed girl who is the wife of Nechtan, the half-Cruithni princeling," he began.

"A wife? She is not celibate? Druidesses are not supposed to lie with men," someone protested. "How could she then—"

Cathbhadh raised a hand to silence the skeptic. "My friend, do not judge by externals," he cautioned. "Anyone can put on a black robe. Hear Brennos out before you decide."

"Simply put," Brennos continued, "she was born with powers. I have heard of several miraculous happenings involving her, from those who saw them. She is protected by Loucetius. He once saved her from rape; I myself saw that. Another time she called out to him and became illumined with unearthly blue flames. A boy of eighteen, mute since birth, was restored to speech by her."

"What boy?" the skeptic asked. "Where is he now?"

"Here in this camp. He is the son of Conn the farmer, whom some of you know. They both came to fight, like everyone else, for the boy is very handy with a spear."

"I would like to see this boy."

"All right. But I have not yet told you the most remarkable thing of all, one I witnessed myself. Her power is so great that, in the midst of a dirty village, she succeeded in joining herself with nature and summoning a fireball which crossed the sky before her." The druids looked at one another, astonished. "Were you not a fellow druid, I would not believe what you have said," the skeptic replied, "but because you are, I must believe you. I would like to see this girl for myself, and the boy she cured."

"We will send for them," Cathbhadh said, and the old man with the staff sat down, satisfied. "And then I suggest we assemble the chiefs and warriors," Cathbhadh concluded. "The full moon is in two days; it will be the best time for the sacrifice."

"I will summon a messenger to fetch them," Brennos said, stepping into the night.

Brennos waited at the edge of the encampment until the messenger came into view, Melangell swathed in a cloak walking at his side. The druid went out to meet her, taking her hands in his.

"How are you, my dear?" he asked gently. She smiled and nodded sleepily at him.

"Ah . . . you were asleep!" he exclaimed. "I should have known. Come . . . this won't take long, and then I'll take you back to your camp myself."

"What am I summoned for?" she whispered fearfully as they began to walk.

"We are having a druids' meeting. We need someone with special powers to perform a ritual, and with our ranks so decimated, you are the only one we could think of who was suitable. The others wish to meet you and ask you a few questions, that is all."

"Me?" she gasped, incredulous. "I am no real druidess!"

"Nevertheless, you have powers and we do not. They have selected you."

The distant campfire came into view and Melangell's stomach fluttered fearfully at the sight of ghostly black figures seated around it.

"Don't be afraid," Brennos whispered. "They are but men, as I am. Be yourself, answer them honestly, and then we will go."

He looked down at her and she nodded solemnly. Nearing the edge of the clearing, Diuran walked out to meet them. He placed a reassuring arm around the girl's shoulders and led her into the firelight. She blinked in the glare as she tried to make out the shadowed faces.

"My brother druids," Diuran said, "this is Melangell, of whom we have just spoken." He stepped away from her side and she looked around for Brennos, fear in her heart. He sat at his place in the circle and gave her a reassuring look, and she knew that she must be alone now, with no support from Brennos or anyone else. Silently she nodded a greeting to the assembled men and waited. They seemed to sense her fear, for their questions were gentle, their voices kind. She answered them as best she could; when had her powers first manifested themselves? What other abilities had she shown? The tales of the white deer at Samhain and the wolf who saved her from the blizzard seemed to surprise them all, even Brennos.

And then she heard footsteps approaching from behind

her and saw the eldest man motion with his hand to summon someone into their circle. Melangell stood still, not even daring to turn her head until the old druid addressed her.

"My dear, turn and see if you know this person," he said, his face expressionless. She could sense all eyes on her as she turned, and a slow smile crossed her face when her eyes fell on a frightened Donall. He brightened as soon as he saw her and stood grinning until she held out her hands to him.

"Donall . . ." she said gently. With a cry of delight he rushed forward and fell to the ground at her feet. She knelt before him and lifted his tearful face, peering intently into his eyes.

"How are you, Donall?" she asked softly, wiping the dark hair from his forehead.

"I . . . I am fine," he said proudly.

"Why, that's wonderful!" She looked at him, and he gazed back at her like an adoring puppy.

"I . . . love you," he sobbed, and buried his face in her lap, crying loudly.

"Hush . . . hush . . ." she soothed, stroking his shoulder and letting him cry out his emotion.

The druids were leaning forward intently, watching. Brennos slowly straightened, triumphant, and shot a quick glance to the skeptic. The man took a deep breath, smiled, and nodded.

"She is the one," he agreed. The others murmured their unanimous assent.

"The boy certainly loves you," Brennos commented while he walked Melangell back to camp.

"Yes. It means a lot to him to be able to speak, as it would to anyone, I suppose. I must tell Cai I have seen him."

"Cai?"

"Yes. Cai, Genann, and Donall are brothers. I thought you knew."

"No." He fell silent as they climbed the steep hillside, one hand at her arm to steady her. Suddenly she stopped and turned to face him in the dim starlight.

"What must I do at this ritual?" she asked.

He sighed and looked down at the ground. "I'll tell you tomorrow. It will be a simple thing . . . nothing to memorize, no real rules to follow."

"Should I wear my old black robe?"

"No. I will provide you with another."

"When will it take place?"

"In two nights, when the moon is full."

She seemed to think about it for a moment, turned, and resumed walking.

"When we get to your camp, I must get Nechtan and his bodyguards to go back with me. We have more preparations to make for this ritual. I don't want you to be alarmed," the druid explained.

She nodded silently and looked to the crest of the hill ahead, where Nechtan's campfire came into view. She could see that most of the men were still awake and sitting around the fire, watching a naked warrior do the sword dance, his body gleaming in the light as he leapt and danced over bare sword blades.

"Melangell?" a voice came out of the night. It was Cai, waiting for her return.

"Are Nechtan, Cathal, Melwas, and Niall up there?" Brennos asked the guard when he fell in on the other side of the girl.

"Aye," Cai replied with a laugh, resting his spear over one shoulder. "Melwas and Niall are in fine spirits, too, having just returned from a tryst with Seonaid."

"That sounds an odd thing!" the druid remarked, arching his eyebrows.

"I'm sure Seonaid thought so too." Cai grinned.

"Well, I must go to see them," Brennos commented as they crested the hill. "I want you to keep watch over Melangell for the rest of the night; do you understand?"

"Yes." Cai nodded, puzzled. "But why—"

"I cannot explain now. Just guard her well until tomorrow."

Without another word he strode off toward the men around the fire, leaving a curious Cai to walk Melangell to her sleeping place by the wagons. She lay down on her pallet and pulled a cloak over herself, and soon she was deep in sleep. Cai, his spear across his lap, sat by her head, his back leaning against the wagon wheel, his keen eyes watching the darkness and wondering why little groups of men, in twos and threes or more, suddenly began to leave the encampments and creep quietly down the hillside toward the druids' meeting place.

Cathbhadh stood and raised a hand, and silence fell on the large gathering. All eyes followed the druid as he strolled around the clearing, deep in thought. Brennos left Nechtan's side and joined his fellow druids, watching Cathbhadh like the rest and dreading the outcome of this night . . . and the chore that faced him on the morrow.

Suddenly the old man spoke, and everyone jumped in surprise at the sound of his voice.

"As you know, we have had a meeting here this night, to discuss various druidical matters and the future of our land and our people."

He paused and paced to the other end of the clearing, solidly packed with chiefs and warriors.

"We have decided that there is nothing we druids can do to defeat the Romans. We are now too few; that task is in your hands."

An approving murmur rose from hundreds of confident male throats as the old druid walked and stopped, walked and stopped, always searching the faces before him. Brennos realized sickly that he had already begun the selection process, unknown to any of his potential victims. Gods above, he thought, I feel sorry for whoever is picked, but don't let it be anyone I know.

"There is, however, one thing we druids can do," Cathbhadh continued. "A very old, very unique ritual I am sure you have heard of . . . a ritual which, while not affecting the outcome of the coming battle, might enable us to see that future."

He looked at a few more faces and the men's feet began to shift nervously.

"You know, of course, that I am referring to the Sacrifice of the Prophet."

A deadly hush fell over the clearing and all eyes now seemed to try to avoid the old man's unflinching gaze. He paced slowly from one end of the gathering to the other, studying each man, looking for some quality only he could detect. Brennos turned away bitterly. By the gods, he thought, what am I, a physician dedicated to saving lives and easing suffering, doing with such a cruelty as this?

He looked up in alarm when he realized Cathbhadh had stopped pacing, shocked to see the old man standing before Nechtan and his men. Oh, dear gods, no! he thought desperately, watching in horror. The old druid raised his arm and pointed a finger straight ahead.

"You . . ." he said firmly, and Brennos saw Niall's face turn gray with shock as the finger pointed directly at him.

The men returned to their camp in stunned silence, their number diminished by one. Nechtan flopped sullenly by the fire and cast a cold glance up at Brennos.

"When will this take place?" he snapped.

"In two nights, when the moon is full."

"And in the meantime?"

"He will be kept isolated, to purify and prepare himself."

"I am not allowed to see him?"

"No." Brennos shook his head slowly, sitting down beside Nechtan.

"I don't blame you for being angry," he said, "but I had little to do with it. I am only one man. What could I do? Such rituals have always been hard enough for me to tolerate, even when they involved only slaves and war captives. But to give up one of our own, and one I know personally as well . . ."

His voice died away and he looked down into the fire.

"I'm sorry, Brennos," Nechtan said, gazing at the druid's solemn features. "Will you be there when it is done?"

"Aye. I must attend."

"And us—must we?"

"It is customary. He is your man, and therefore your gift to all the tribes. I think it would be a blow to Niall if you were not there as well."

"Yes." Nechtan nodded. "I will go."

He paused and looked at the druid again, concern in his pale eyes. "Niall is not just my guard; he is my friend. Brennos, will he suffer much?"

"I will not lie, Nechtan. Yes, he will suffer, especially near the end, as the potions take effect. But it is not as much as you would think, and when the end comes, he will be barely conscious."

Nechtan nodded grimly. "And who is to administer these drugs? Cathbhadh?" he asked. Brennos looked away awkwardly.

"Only someone with special training or special powers is entrusted with so grave a service," the druid muttered in a voice so low Nechtan had to strain to understand him. "Even Cathbhadh is not qualified to do it. They have selected another."

"Who?"

"Your wife."

Brennos tried to fall away, but before he could move, Nechtan was on him with a cry of rage, his powerful hands reaching for the druid's throat, until Melwas and Cathal pulled him off. Shaking, the druid stood and backed away from the glaring princeling, nervously straightening his black robes and trying to form the right words in his mind.

"My wife is to kill my friend! What next, druid? What else is in the future for us, eh?" Nechtan snarled savagely at him. "Does she know what she is to do? How can they ask this of her? So help me, Brennos, if anything happens to her or the baby because of this ordeal, I will hold you responsible for it. Do you hear me? If they come to any harm, you will die." His men stared, appalled that their chief would dare to threaten a druid.

"Nechtan," Brennos said grimly, "I tried to change their minds, to no avail. I like this as little as you. I told them how she is. I told them she might refuse, but they only said she must do it, for the sake of her people. Now that the victim is Niall, it is even worse. She could well refuse. She has that right. But for now it is out of my hands."

"And when do you tell her?" Nechtan asked, his rage subsiding.

"Tomorrow. I must get some sleep first, for it is already nearing dawn. Then I will tell her what is involved, and who is to die. After that, the choice is hers. Nechtan, I can understand your concern for her and the baby. I, too, am concerned. But look at it this way: regardless of her decision, Niall will die. I would rather it be at her hand than someone else's, for she with her powers might be able to alleviate his fears and sufferings, whereas another could not."

Nechtan stared at him, pondering his words, and then his shoulders sagged in defeat.

"Yes, you are right," he sighed, returning to the log. "Go and sleep, Brennos, and let us see what the morrow brings."

"Come," Brennos said. "Let us walk."

Melangell looked up at the druid and put down her empty bowl of gruel. "All right," she said quietly, looking aside at Nechtan. He too was staring at the druid, an odd expression on his face.

"Brennos," he said suddenly as the girl stood, "have a care . . ."

"Don't worry," the druid replied. "Remember, I am a physician too."

Without another word, he took Melangell's arm and together they walked out of the camp, down a gentle slope to the south, through a dense patch of hemlock woods in the sheltered lee of the mountain, until they emerged by a cascading series of rills and waterfalls, the misty air wreathed in pale rainbows.

"Oh, it's lovely," she breathed. Brennos smiled at her words.

"I thought you'd like it," he said. "It seemed a nice, quiet place for us to talk. Here . . . sit on this log. You shouldn't be on your feet so much, you know."

"Yes . . . thank you." She smiled, settling herself comfortably on the fallen trunk and gazing toward the tumbling stream. "I seem to tire so easily these days. I haven't much strength anymore."

"It's only natural," he replied, sitting down at her side. "Your body seeks to rest and conserve itself before the ordeal of birth . . . which isn't so far off now, you know!"

She laughed merrily and placed a hand on her rounded belly. "No . . . and I think he is ready, too, for he is always squirming and kicking me. He already seems to have Nechtan's intensity!"

Suddenly her face fell and Brennos looked at her, puzzled.

"What's wrong?" he said quietly, studying her solemn

features. She flickered her green eyes up to him briefly and looked away.

"I . . . I am afraid," she whispered.

"Of what!" he exclaimed. "Everything is going normally. You are fine. Many new mothers are afraid at their first birth."

"I am always thinking of Boann . . . all the pain, all the blood. What if it happens to me?"

She looked up at him, tears in her eyes, and his heart moved with pity at the ordeal all women had to undergo . . . and this one, in particular.

"That happens only rarely," he reassured her, patting her hand.

"Then you don't think . . ."

"No. I am as certain as I can be that it won't. I have examined many women over the years. Boann was far too narrow. You are not. No, my dear, I think you will be just fine."

She exhaled shakily and looked down at his hand atop hers, waiting for him to speak, to say what she knew he had brought her there to say.

"Tomorrow night . . ." he began, clasping his hand around hers, "tomorrow night, for the ritual, you must give a drug to someone, a little at a time."

"What kind of drug?"

"Berries . . . mistletoe berries . . . dipped in aconite."

She jerked upright, a look of horror on her face.

"But that . . . that is poison."

He sighed and nodded glumly.

"I am to . . . to kill someone?"

"Aye."

"No! I cannot! I will not! What manner of cruel trick is this that you play on me, Brennos?"

"You can refuse us, Melangell. That is your right. Have you never heard of the Sacrifice of the Prophet?"

She shook her head. "No. My village was small and poor. We had no druid of our own, few religious observances. I know little of your ways."

"It is one of the most sacred ceremonies we can perform, for we do not merely sacrifice a living thing, a man, but one of our own. One who, through the use of the drugs, is in communication with the gods. He speaks and tells us what he sees, what he experiences, as he is given more of the medicines and sinks deeper into a trance. The victim is a prophet, a channel between us and the gods."

"Can you not give him an antidote? Revive him?"

"No. In its deepest stages it is too late to reverse it. The heart slows. There is pain in the stomach, internal bleeding. By that time, death is the kindest release."

"And how does this person die? More poison?"

"No." The druid looked away sickly, waiting before he spoke again.

"While the heart still beats, the throat is cut so that the blood may be collected."

Melangell raised a shaking hand to her face. "And the blood?" she asked.

"It is poured around the sacred tree in the grove, to nourish it. The head is severed and mounted in a place of honor in the enclosure, and the torque, now freed from the neck, is likewise removed and hung from the sacred tree, as a reminder to all of the man's bravery and sacrifice for his people. The body is lowered into a shaft in the ground, where other sacrificial victims and offerings have been deposited over the years, and the shaft is once more sealed shut. It is really a great honor; there are worse ways for a man to die than giving his life for his people and departing his body while in divine communion with the gods."

He finished speaking and studied the girl's face as she reflected on his words. For a long time she did not move, and then she looked into his face, worry in her eyes.

"What exactly must I do?" she said quietly, and Brennos sighed in relief. The girl is wise, he reflected. She might not like it, but she realizes the awful responsibilities of one with her powers, and she sees the necessity of doing what must be done.

"All you must do is give him the berries, one at a time a few minutes apart, and dipping each third one in aconite. One of us will hold the berries for you."

"Will you?"

"Yes, if you want me to."

"I do. But the cutting—I cannot do that."

"No." The druid shook his head. "You are not expected to. One of us will do the rest. We only need you to administer the drug, try to help his strength endure as long as possible, reach him with your soul if you can, as you have done with others. With your inner strength added to his, he may be able to give us some truly useful prophecy."

She nodded her understanding as she looked out at the shimmering rainbows before them.

"And the poor man . . . who is he?" she whispered.

Brennos clasped her hand tightly. "It is Niall. I am sorry . . . it is Niall."

Melangell closed her eyes sickly and forced a swallow down her throat. How can I? she thought sadly. How can I kill a man, any man, much less my husband's best friend? How?

For many minutes she sat in silence, her eyes closed, and the druid could see war being waged within her. Her duty, her responsibility to her calling, her people . . . or her fear, her tenderness, her moralities learned from Esus?

"I will do it," she sighed in resignation, opening her eyes and looking almost fiercely at the treetops above. "I will do it, but I must see him first. Today . . . now."

Quickly rising to her feet, she tugged at Brennos' hand.

"Come!" she said urgently to him.

"Melangell . . . I don't know if they'll let you. He is not to see anyone but druids. He must prepare himself."

The girl turned on him angrily, light flaring in her eyes. "I am druid enough to perform your sacred ceremony for you, yet I am not druid enough to visit the victim? I must see him, or you will find yourself another executioner!"

She glared fiercely at him. Brennos stood wearily, shrugged, and led her away from the stream.

"You are right," he said. "Let's go and see old Cathbhadh."

Brennos pulled the leather tent flap aside and Melangell ducked inside, peering uncertainly around the gloomy interior. Niall lay stretched out on a cot to the right, and when he saw her, he sat up abruptly.

"I am to see no one," he said tightly. Slowly she made her way over to him and pulled a stool to the cot.

"It's all right," she said quietly, sitting down and searching his face with her eyes. "I have their permission." His facade was manly enough, but she could see below it real fear, real dread.

"I have come to speak with you . . . to help you, if I may."

His icy blue eyes probed her face in disbelief, and then, finding some answer he sought, he lowered his face to his hands.

"Gods above, why me?" he sobbed brokenly. "To die in battle, fierce and free, is one thing, but this . . . this . . ."

He shook his head as if his pain was beyond words.

"Why?" he gasped, looking up at her, his eyes brimming with genuine terror. Appalled at his torment, Melangell stood and caressed his sweaty forehead with her hands.

"I'm sure you have thought of all the arguments and reasons, Niall," she said gently. "I won't waste your time with them. It is only natural to fear death . . . everyone does."

He clenched her slim wrists desperately in his powerful hands and looked up at her.

"It is not the death. It is the pain . . . the suffering. Enduring such agony, for all the world to see. Why me? I have thought of killing myself here, now, and being done with it, but they have taken my weapons and they guard the tent night and day."

"I know you are strong, Niall. I know you will be able to endure it, and everyone will honor your memory because of it. And I will help you if I can, lend you what strength I can impart to you."

"You? What have you to do with this?"

She lowered her hands from his grasp and walked away a few paces, turning to look at his bewildered face.

"I am to be your executioner, Niall. I am to administer the drugs."

"But why?" he demanded, springing to his feet. "Why you for such a terrible job?"

"They chose me . . . they say I have powers." She shrugged. "But I agreed because I thought I might be able to help you. I can draw away your suffering and replace it with peace. I have done it before . . . but they do not know this, Niall. Don't tell them, or they will not let me."

She looked up at him. His face seemed to sag with relief in the dim light. Numbly he sat back on the cot, staring at her.

"It is all I can do for you," she whispered. "I am sorry it is not more."

"It is enough, and more than enough," he replied, his voice tinged with awe and genuine gratitude. "But why do such a thing for me? We two have had our clashes in the past. I have raped you, almost killed you, left you for dead . . . we have never been overly fond of one another; why take such suffering of mine upon yourself?"

"What's done is done," she muttered, returning to her seat by the cot. "I dislike suffering. I seek to alleviate it. It is the task the gods have chosen for me."

In the ensuing silence she could see the unease in Niall's pale blue eyes as he stared at her.

"Melangell . . . what will happen to me?" he asked, his voice hushed. "What will the drugs do?"

"You will gradually lose consciousness, your mind will sink to a deeper and deeper level; there will be the sensation of flying, and you will have visions. You must strive to tell us what you see in this state, for that is the purpose of the ceremony. We will try to keep you awake and coherent for as long as possible."

"And the end?"

She shook her head. "You will not feel it. You will be too drugged."

He slumped forward on his elbows and hung his head. "I suppose that is a kindness, at least," he muttered to himself.

"But now the hour grows late. I must try to establish a link with you, a bond strong enough so that I can reach you tomorrow night, to help you."

She stood and he looked at her, implicit trust in his face.

"What must I do?" he said quietly.

"Lie down."

Obediently he stretched out on the cot and she pulled the stool closer, sitting by his head. "Try to think of nothing. Have no thoughts whatsoever. Be as open and free and trusting as a babe in its mother's arms."

He nodded and closed his eyes as her fingers softly touched his temples. Lightly they explored his face and he felt himself relaxing, seeming to slip away as if in a dream, wavering back into consciousness and then drifting away again, like the ebb and flow of the sea.

The sea. . . .

Melangell could smell the tang of the salt air, see the clear blue waters lapping the shores of a rocky isle.

"Mother," a voice called out, a child's voice, her voice . . . no, not hers, Niall's, yet it was she who spoke.

"A shell! See, Mother!" the child cried, waving its treasure eagerly overhead as it ran down the shining sands toward a distant woman, slightly plump, who stood and gazed out over the water.

"Will Daddy like it?"

A warm arm engulfed her . . . him.

"Yes, my darling. Daddy will like it."

Yet in her child's heart she knew: Daddy would not return. Daddy was gone, lost at sea. Daddy . . .

A gasp from Niall brought her eyes open and she looked down at him. His face was grim, strained, his lips tightly drawn beneath his long blond mustache.

"Hush," she soothed, wiping his clammy forehead. "It's all right. The pain is gone. We will remember something happy . . . happy . . . happy."

A girlish laugh rang out in her mind and, looking up a purple-cloaked hillside she saw with Niall's eyes, felt with Niall's heart . . .

"Niall" the girl called out, waving down to him, a sprig of heather in her young hand.

She felt herself smiling, the warm sun beating down on her back, her young boy's heart full of boundless hope and enthusiasm.

And then she was running with effortless grace up the hillside, the scent of heather filling her head, her eyes on the waiting girl.

"Edainn . . ." Niall whispered aloud, and she roused again. A tranquil smile lit his face and she lifted her hands away. He is at peace now, she thought; let him remember his one true love, whom he will go to join tomorrow. A waiting heart always makes the crossing easier.

She stood quietly and turned to the door. Reaching him tomorrow would be a simple matter, she knew. Stepping away from the bed, she halted when his hand reached out and took her wrist.

"Melangell," he whispered, "thank you. I only ask that you forgive all the wrongs I have done to you."

"They are forgiven, Niall. I hope you can forgive the wrong I am about to do you, as well."

"If there is anything to forgive, then you are forgiven. But I think now that you might be doing me a kindness instead."

Smiling, she nodded her understanding, turned, and silently left the tent.

Afternoon approached and Melangell sat as she had sat all day, lost in thought while she gazed into the Damnonii campfire. She was oblivious of the bustle of activity around her, she would not eat or drink, and her mind seemed unaware when Nechtan tried to speak to her. Cai stood faithfully by—as if guarding a corpse, he thought in superstitious fear—waiting for the time to creep by, for the awful ordeal to be over with.

"Melangell." Brennos gently shook her arm. She looked at him dumbly, as if roused from a trance.

"You must come with me now," he said quietly. As one just awakened from sleep, she looked around uncertainly.

"It is all right," he soothed, helping her to her feet. "Come with me, and all will be well." He led her away, one arm around her hunched shoulders, and waved away Nechtan and Cai when they attempted to follow.

"You know the time and the place," he said over his shoulder, and Nechtan felt his stomach sink as he watched them go. The hour approached. It was becoming real, no longer a bad dream . . . his best friend was about to die.

A second leather tent had been erected in the druids' clearing and Brennos walked the silent girl into it. A small iron brazier on three legs, hot with glowing coals, occupied the center of the floor, and a low stool sat nearby. Apart from that, the tent was empty.

"You must be purified, to keep away any evil influences," he explained, handing her a folded white blanket. "I will leave; you are to undress and wrap yourself in this."

He looked at her and she nodded, and he was relieved to see that she seemed to be gathering her wits about her a bit.

Quickly he left and Melangell stripped, wrapped the stiff wool blanket around herself, and sat on the stool, waiting. Brennos soon returned, picked up her clothes, and tossed them from the tent. He set a tall bronze ewer of water beside her, with a cup fastened to the handle by a fine chain. Again he left and Melangell stared dully at the glowing coals, trying not to think of what the night would bring.

When Brennos returned, she was surprised to see him wearing a spotless white linen robe instead of his usual black one. In his hands he carried two large cedar boxes, heavily bound in gold. He set them near the brazier, crouched beside them, and lifted the lids. Melangell looked at them curiously; one held little slivers of wood, the other finely crushed dried flowers. Brennos picked up a small handful of the wood and tossed it onto the brazier, and a heady scent filled the tent.

"That is larch wood," he explained. "Its smoke drives away evil spirits."

Next he picked up the dried flowers and sprinkled a handful over the smoking wood chips, and another, lighter scent drifted around them.

"And that is vervain, one of the holiest plants we druids use. It purifies."

She took a deep breath of the scented air and closed her eyes dreamily.

"You like it, then?" he asked as he walked to the ewer, unfastened the cup, and poured some water.

"Yes." She smiled lazily. "It makes me feel . . . unusual."

"I thought it would. It is said to have powers over people with spiritual gifts." Returning to the brazier, he sprinkled the water onto the coals. A hot, hissing steam rose up and filled the tent, and he tossed more of the wood and flowers on the coals.

"Normally the tent would be heated much more, but because of the child it would not be safe for you, so I'll tend it and keep it less hot."

He nodded to the ewer.

"You may have a little water if you want, but nothing else."

"I am fine," she replied with a sigh.

Brennos crouched by the fire for hours, repeatedly wiping the sweat from his face. He walked to the ewer, drank several cups of water, and insisted Melangell drink some too. He could see beneath the tent wall that darkness was falling, and he waited, tension rising within him. Finally he heard movement outside, and Diuran's deep voice called to him. He walked to the flap and answered, and Diuran thrust a folded white robe in to him. Brennos took it, turned, and saw the alarmed look on the girl's face.

"It is time," he said, unfolding the robe. "Stand up."

Obediently she stood, and he stepped behind her, placing the robe on the stool. Seizing the white blanket, he lifted it from her shoulders and dropped it to the floor. Her skin was rosy from the heat and shone with a soft sheen of sweat. He dropped the white robe over her head and she slid her arms into the long sleeves. Picking up a white cord, he swiftly braided it into her hair, gathering it behind her neck, then turned her to face him. Her eyes were large, solemn, and beads of sweat clung to her forehead and he knew it was the sweat of fear, not from the steam. He lifted a sleeve of his robe and gently wiped her face. She jumped visibly when a loud, deep drum slowly boomed out into the night.

"I will help you all I can," he said quietly, and she nodded. Taking her arm, he led her to the tent flap, and together they stepped out into the chill night air.

The clearing was a ghostly scene, sixteen white-robed druids waiting silently in the light of flickering torches. Brennos walked Melangell to the head of the procession and they stopped directly behind two men bearing large flaring brass horns which gracefully reared high into the darkness. Silently they waited, turning at the sound of soft footsteps approaching from the tent on the far side of the clearing. It was Niall, accompanied by Cathbhadh.

Melangell ran a quick glance over his features. His face was grim, his cheeks flushed from the steam. He was naked except for the gold torque around his neck and a warrior's cloak he wore draped around his shoulders. Their eyes met for a moment and he gave her a slight nod as he walked to his place behind her. Turning, she waited for the horns to blow, high-pitched and eerie, to signal the start of the procession, and a calm resolve settled into her heart. Niall was depending on her; she must not let him down.

The horns blared a long, piercing wail and they began the slow walk down the mountainside to the small sacred grove nestled far below, around one of the few oak trees growing in the harsh northern climate.

Nechtan, Cathal, and Melwas waited nervously in the palisaded sacred enclosure, ignoring the staked bare skulls around the perimeter, the glittering torques and armbands tied in the branches of a huge sighing oak tree, and trying not to stare at the handful of high kings and their warlords and retainers who had gathered there. Even Calgacus, Chief Warlord of Caledonia, was present, standing impassively and surrounded by four imposing spearmen; but like the rest, the old gray-haired warlord turned at the sound of a horn blast beyond the high wall. Nechtan tensed when the first figures entered the grove—two men with tall horns who walked off, one to each side of the enclosure. Then came his wife, accompanied by Brennos. She stared grimly ahead as they walked to a stone slab set in the center of the circle and stepped off to one side. They were followed by Niall and Cathbhadh, and Nechtan studied his friend intently when they passed. His face could have been a mask, so well was he hiding his emotions, and he walked proudly and tall, his head high, his gaze unflinching. They stopped before the stone and waited for the rest of the procession to enter. One druid held a large gold casket, which he carried to Brennos' side. The others filed in to form a circle around the clearing, warding with their presence any evils that might try to invade the ceremony and threaten the participants while their wills were low. Last came a man with a drum, which he carried to the far side, across from Melangell and Brennos.

Even the surrounding forest seemed to pause in the ensuing hush that fell over the participants. Nechtan watched Cathbhadh lean over and speak quietly to Niall, who shook his head once in reply. Then his friend handed the old druid something and spoke to him briefly. The old man nodded and stepped aside to Melangell, handing the object to her. Nechtan saw her take it, look up at Niall, and her grim face softened. Satisfied, Niall stepped up to the flat stone, unpinned his cloak, and waited for Cathbhadh to take it from his shoulders. Turning, the warrior knelt on the stone, moving back till he was pressed against the upright stone pillar behind the rock, facing the assembled chiefs. When Cathbhadh stepped behind him to tie his hands, Niall spied Nechtan, Melwas, and Cathal. A slight smile crossed his face and he nodded to his companions, then looked away as the old druid lashed his chest upright against the post. When Cathbhadh was done, Melangell walked behind the altar, cradling in one hand the object Niall had given her. Nechtan strained to see what it was, and with a shock recognition came: it was the rock from their homeland, the land of the Damnonii, that Niall had picked up on the way to their banishment.

Niall's hand was extended to receive it and he closed his fingers tightly around the stone when he felt the girl place it in his palm. Taking a thong from Cathbhadh, she lashed his hand shut around it, then hesitantly walked to the front of the altar.

She stared at Niall's grim face and a look seemed to pass between them as he returned her gaze.

"Are you ready?" she said, her voice quaking slightly in fear. He heard her fear, smiled at her, and nodded. Brennos took the gold casket, opened it, and stepped forward. He spoke quietly to the girl, who picked up a pair of small gold tongs from the box, lifted a sticky white berry, and advanced to the waiting Niall. Lightly she touched his cheek and ran her fingertips down to his freshly shaved chin.

"Never fear, my lady, I am all right," he said quietly, and with seeming eagerness he took the berry and swallowed it. Melangell returned for a second berry, and the third she dipped into a small gold vial of liquid before giving it to the man. They watched for several minutes. Niall seemed to wince in pain, and then he waited for her to continue. The girl fed him three more berries, the third again dipped in aconite. This time he gasped aloud and his eyes took on a glazed look.

"Niall?" she said, leaning forward toward him and closing her eyes. "What is happening?"

There will be no pain, she thought grimly, trying to reach

his whirling mind. It is all right. I will take your pain. It is all right. . . .

Suddenly she gasped and Brennos caught the tongs as they fell from her limp hand.

"Stop her," Niall moaned. "She must not . . . stop her . . ."

"What is it, man?" Cathbhadh pressed him. The crowd leaned forward, tense at this unexpected development.

"The army . . ." Niall groaned. "The army . . ."

Melangell roused and reached out to Niall, but Brennos' voice stopped her short.

"Don't touch him," he ordered, and she straightened up and looked at the druid in surprise. He realized what she and Niall were doing. He knew.

Balancing the casket in one hand, he returned the gold tongs to her and held out the berries. Silently she lifted another one, and Cathbhadh steadied Niall's sagging head while she gave him the berry. The warrior roused and looked at her.

"Melangell . . . you must not . . . you . . ." he whispered, then moaned again.

"The sky is full of ravens!" he suddenly cried in anguish. "The altars run red, and the sky . . . the sky is . . ."

She fed him the next berry, and the third dipped in poison, and he threw his head back against the stone pillar, grimacing in pain. Nechtan looked away sickly as Niall strained against the bonds at his chest. Blood trickled down his back, where his writhings had cut the rough stone pillar into his bare flesh.

"You must not . . ." he moaned. "You must not . . ."

Brennos looked at Melangell in alarm. She stood still, staring at the suffering man in horror, her face a mask of white. Suddenly she threw her head back to the moonlit sky, closed her eyes, and cried aloud, as if . . . as if . . .

She felt his pain.

Nechtan started at her cry, but Cathal and Melwas held him back. Brennos had already thrust the golden chest into the hands of the young druid who had carried it in and was now savagely shaking the moaning girl.

"Melangell! Stop it! Stop it!" he commanded, but she didn't seem able to hear him.

"Brennos . . ." a voice called out, and the startled druid turned to see Niall looking at him, clearly and calmly.

"Get her out of here," the warrior said. "She takes my suffering on herself. She cannot endure it, nor can I. Let it be over with, Brennos. Get her away."

Melangell's pain subsided and she looked at the warrior glumly.

"Niall," she sobbed. "I can do nothing else for you."

"I know . . . don't try. Let me go. Do you hear? Let me go."

She nodded slowly, picked up the tongs, and again gave him the poisons. Without her aid he sank fast, his head lolled forward drunkenly, great waves of pain coursing through him at each third berry. Tears streamed down the girl's ashen face as she did her duty, but Niall had no other revelations for them. Each time the old druid lifted his head, the warrior's face looked more bluish, and Diuran stepped forward, keeping careful check on the pulse at Niall's neck.

Finally Diuran held out a hand to stop Melangell when she lifted another berry from the casket, and she replaced the tongs in the box. Diuran looked at Cathbhadh and nodded once, taking an ornate golden bowl from another druid. The old man withdrew a long knife, keened and whetted till it gleamed, stepped behind the sagging warrior and, seizing his matted blond hair, pulled his head back against the pillar.

Melangell backed away in horror as a cry shot through her like an arrow.

"No!" it screamed. Niall's voice. She turned in panic before the knife could make the first cut. He is alive . . . he is aware . . . he knows . . . he feels.

Shocked, terrified, the world suddenly a whirling torrent of cries, the girl turned blindly and pushed her way through the silent men. Sobbing wildly, she ran down the slope, through the solemn trees, as the unending cry echoed down her soul:

No . . . no . . . no . . .

A groom by the parked and waiting chariots of the kings and warlords straightened in curiosity as he watched the girl's ghostlike white figure disappear down the hillside. That wasn't part of the ritual, he knew. Something had gone wrong. Her husband must be alerted as soon as the ceremony was over.

Gasping for breath, Melangell paused by a hemlock, leaning heavily into the knotted trunk; and at the low, booming sound of the distant drum, she again hurried away.

It is over, she cried softly. Niall is now dead, his valiant head atop a bloody pole in the grove, his racked body consigned to a foul hole in the earth.

No . . . no . . . no . . .

She put her hands over her ears, trying to shut out the incessant scream. Esus, I have failed you, she cried. I have killed a man, a good man. Esus, I have failed you.

Her bare feet tripped swiftly down the moon-washed hillside and her mind churned in frantic thought.

Bloody groves, you called them, and now I have partaken of that . . . but I thought I could help him. Truly I did, Esus. I would have succeeded only in his death, and my own, and my unborn child's. The drugs were too powerful, too overwhelming. The druids have skills and knowledge I am no match for, Esus, and you knew that all along, didn't you?

She paused by a spring that bubbled from between two flat rocks. The waters were covered by a small shrine to Coventina, goddess of springs, a low thatch roof supported on four thin posts. Beneath the roof were several meager offerings to the goddess; cheap bronze rings and bracelets, crude stone carvings, a bone comb. Kneeling, Melangell splashed the cooling waters over her weary face as if washing off a pollution.

The fools! she thought bitterly. All this time reassuring themselves that there is no suffering, when I know better now. Nechtan must never know the horrifying ordeal that ended Niall's life. Never. They think they know so much, have such knowledge, but what do any of us really know? We are all, as Esus said, mortal fools in a foolish world.

She lowered her face to the spring and eagerly drank the sparkling water.

Arrogant fools, all of us.

Something sharp poked into her back and she lifted her head slowly.

"Well, what have we here?" a heavily accented voice spoke behind her, and her heart fell.

A Roman.

"Get up," the voice ordered. Awkwardly she rose to her feet, gazing off blankly across the brightly lit hillside. Romans . . . and so near . . .

They inched their way around her, as careful as if she were a strapping, fully armed warrior instead of a small druidess heavy with child.

Like a bolt, it hit her. To them she was a druidess, and Anarios had warned her of their fate.

How ironic, she thought in resignation as the spears prodded her down the hillside. Perhaps it is destined that I die this night, one way or another. There is nothing I can do now. How could I know, when I sent him on his way, that Niall was simply preceding me? Will he be waiting for me? He, and Esus, and Mother . . . Behind her she could hear one of the men kicking the shrine apart. The thatch roof and supporting poles slid easily down the hillside. Only the stone figures made noise, protesting loudly as they clattered against the rocky slope.

A man on horseback rode out from the nearby trees, the moonlight flashing silver off his helmet and heavy armor, and slid to the ground as she and her captors approached. Together they walked into the forest and paused in a large clearing. The sergeant of the patrol pulled a leather thong from his belt and roughly bound her hands behind her.

"A druidess, eh?" A soldier grinned, turning her in the moonlight the better to see her face.

"Melangell!" a voice cried out, and the girl turned in shock when Anarios, holding the four horses, rushed forward.

"You know this one?" the sergeant said, looking at him.

"Yes," the physician gasped. "You must release her. I . . . owned her once. She is no druidess."

"I'm sorry, sir." The sergeant shook his head. "You were simply to accompany us on patrol. We have strict orders that all druids are to be killed. You cannot override that order."

"But she is mine," Anarios tried again in desperation, looking at Melangell's grim face. He knew she couldn't understand what they were saying. "You have no legal right to kill her if she is mine."

The sergeant looked up into the surrounding trees, his eyes scanning the branches critically. "If we were in Rome, what you say would be true enough. But this is the army and we are on the frontier, not in Rome."

He pointed to a branch of a large old pine and one of the soldiers obediently uncoiled a rope and tossed it over the limb. The sergeant marched the silent girl to the tree, Anarios at his heels.

"I'm sorry for you, sir," the sergeant said, "for I know the value of a good slave nowadays, but out here my orders come first."

He knotted the dangling end of the rope and slipped it over the girl's head while the other soldier pulled out a heavy spike and hammered it into the tree's trunk. Sick, Anarios watched Melangell; with every pound of the mallet she flinched visibly, as if the spike was being driven into herself instead of the tree.

"Melangell . . ." he began, approaching her. She didn't respond to him.

"Watch out, sir," the third soldier said, leading a horse up to the girl and pushing the physician aside. "Hey!" he said when he boosted her onto the animal's back. "This one's been knocked up! I thought druidesses were supposed to be celibate."

"They are," Anarios said, seizing the chance. "I told you, she is not really a druidess."

The sergeant paused and scratched his stubbled chin a moment, in thought, and wild hope sprang up within Anarios' heart. He didn't care whose baby it was; he had to save her some way.

"Well," the sergeant said at last, "I don't know if she is or she isn't. All I know is the robe she wears, and my orders."

He turned toward Anarios sternly.

"Why don't you get over there by the tree and out of the way? If you try to interfere, I'll have you arrested and hauled back to camp, understand?"

He waited while the physician reluctantly walked over to the great pine trunk. "Tighten the rope," the sergeant ordered. The young legionary waiting by the spike pulled the slack out until Melangell could feel the knot pulling upward at the back of her neck. She took a deep breath, closed her eyes, and waited. *I am never to have a child in this lifetime,* she thought sadly as she savored the cool nighttime air against her face for the last time. *Nechtan, I love you . . .*

The legionary tied the rope to the spike and nodded to the sergeant. Anarios stared in horror, tears welling in his eyes. *I must watch her die . . . Melangell . . . no . . .*

Suddenly pandemonium broke out in the hushed forest. A wild whoop filled the air and, before they could turn to see the chariot bearing down on them, the sergeant in the clearing fell to the ground, an arrow through his neck, while a spear pierced the body of the legionary at his side. The third soldier ran out to the clearing in surprise and collapsed, a spear through his heart. The horse bolted in fear, and as it leapt forward, Anarios pulled out his short sword and in one savage stroke slashed the rope in two. The animal ran out from beneath Melangell, jerking her neck lightly against the rope before she fell to the ground.

Replacing his sword and heedless of his own safety, Anarios rushed to the girl's side and knelt, frantically pulling the rope from her neck and ignoring the chariot that clattered to a halt beside him. Suddenly a spear point slid up to his neck and a familiar voice spoke.

"Get up, Anarios."

He looked up at the grim faces of Nechtan, Melwas, and a young archer he didn't know.

"She is hurt," he protested, gently pulling the rope from her head. Melangell moaned weakly. Abruptly Melwas seized him, jerking him to his feet, a knife at his throat. Anarios helplessly watched Nechtan kneel by the barely conscious girl and raise her in one arm, brushing the twigs and loam from her face. *So, it is his child,* the physician realized sickly, watching them. *She is Nechtan's wife. Nechtan . . . the wolf.*

The princeling stood, the girl cradled in his arms, and looked darkly at the Roman. "Tie him," he snapped to Melwas. "Then finish your work."

Anarios felt his arms being tightly bound behind him, and then Nechtan's two men began cutting the heads from the dead soldiers, stuffing their genitals in their mouths, binding the jaws shut.

"So it is you!" Anarios muttered. Nechtan laid his wife in the chariot and turned.

"Aye," he said grimly. "I am the wolf, but you already knew that, didn't you, Roman?"

He retrieved a horse and boosted the bound man onto its back.

"For the gods' sake, get her to a physician," Anarios protested when Melwas and Cathal approached, carrying the dripping Roman heads. "Do you want her to lose the child?"

"I can take care of my own wife, Roman," Nechtan said flatly, taking the heads from his men. "Brennos is up on the hillside yonder. Do you suppose he'd be interested to know that you are here?"

One by one Nechtan tied the severed heads to the neck of Anarios' horse. "I spare you only because you saved Melangell's life," he said tersely, looking up at the man and pointedly wiping his bloody hands on the physician's bare leg. "Next time it will be you, Roman, for you are the cause of it all."

Nechtan grabbed the horse's reins and ordered Anarios to bend over. He obeyed and felt Nechtan tie the reins snug around his neck. He could barely sit erect without the leather cutting into his throat.

"Now we will let the gods decide your fate, Roman." Nechtan grinned, stepping away from the horse. "If you fall, then it is you who will hang this night. I hope the beast knows his way home," he laughed. "When you see your commander, tell him the wolf sends his greetings."

He nodded to Melwas, who slapped the horse's rump sharply. With a jolt the animal trotted away, down the silver mountainside, the bound man on its back leaning low over its neck in order to keep his balance and having to endure the sight of the gruesome heads in his face all the way back to his camp.

Cathal mounted one of the remaining horses and rounded

up the other two, then followed the chariot's swift return up the hillside to the druids' tents.

"Brennos!" Nechtan bellowed as Melwas pulled the chariot to a halt by the druids' fire. Diuran emerged from a tent, shirtless and wearing only his short breeches, a bronze razor in his hand.

"He isn't here; he should be back soon."

"Come here! Quickly!" Nechtan snapped. "She is hurt."

The druid tossed the razor into his tent, ran to the chariot, and looked at the girl's pallid face. Easing her out, he carried her into his tent, placing her on a bearskin pallet.

"Go," Diuran told Nechtan. "Send Brennos as soon as he arrives."

Grim-faced, Nechtan exited the tent as the druid began to examine Melangell. Diuran was fixing a poultice when Brennos rushed in, his face expressing his alarm. He knelt by the girl and felt her bulging stomach.

"The child seems to be all right . . . for now," Diuran said as he worked. "I think we should keep her sleeping for a few days, to let her system right itself."

"Aye." Brennos nodded. "What is that you're fixing?"

"A poultice. Nightshade and chamomile. Lift her up and look at her back."

Sitting on the side of the furs, Brennos raised the girl and flopped her over one arm, wincing when he saw a large black bruise across her shoulder blade.

"By Arnemetia!" he gasped. "Is it broken?"

"No. She is lucky. The forest floor is soft and that blow seems to have taken most of the impact. It has probably saved her child."

Brennos nodded and held her while Diuran applied the mashed herbs to her back, covered it with a clean cloth, and they gently lowered her to the pallet.

"Brennos . . ." Melangell roused, weakly reaching for his sleeve.

"Yes, dear, what is it?" he answered, leaning low over her face to hear as he pulled a blanket up to her chin.

"The baby . . . the baby . . ." she repeated.

"The baby is fine, but you must rest. Diuran will fix you something to drink while I go fetch Nechtan. Do you feel like seeing him now?"

317

"Yes . . . Nechtan . . ." she mumbled.

"Good. Now, don't move. Diuran will be here with you."
He patted her hand and left the tent.

Nechtan rushed into the small leather tent and stopped,
shocked at his wife's pale face looking up at him from the
dark fur pallet. Diuran squatted by her head, his druid's cup
in hand, but he stood and crossed over to the princeling
when he entered.

"I have just given her a tea to make her sleep. She must be
kept quiet for a few days. If anything goes amiss, she could
still lose the child. Right now rest is the best thing for her.
With your permission, we would like to keep her here where
we can better care for her. She will be asleep soon . . . so,
only a few words with her for now."

"Yes . . . of course." Nechtan nodded. He went to
Melangell's side, his nose full of the pungent smell of the
herbs the druids had used. She tried to look up at him, but
her eyelids were already growing heavy.

"My love," he said quietly, crouching to kiss her cheek.

"Nechtan," she sighed. "The baby . . . is all right."

"Yes." He smiled, taking her hand in his. "Rest now, and
I'll visit you later." She was fighting valiantly to stay awake.
"Sleep, Melangell. You and our son need the rest. Sleep."

She took a little breath, turned her face aside, and was
soon deep in sleep.

Melangell slept for three days, faintly rousing to take the
teas and watery gruels the two druids forced into her, and
then sinking back to valleys of deep sleep interspersed with
peaks of shadowed dreams, disturbing dreams that would
neither come into focus nor vanish away. On the third day
the druids allowed her drugged sleep to wear off, feeling safe
that the baby was well. As the dim dream world in which she
roamed came into clearer sight, she was horrified to see the
shadowy forms take shape:

Niall, wandering around the perimeter of her soul, was
vainly trying to tell her something, something important,
something urgent.

She tossed restlessly. The two druids slept on the far side
of the tent, unaware of her torment.

Niall . . . no . . . what are you saying? I cannot . . . No . . .

And then he was holding the gold tongs himself, advancing toward her, a berry coming purposefully to her mouth.

"No!" she screamed, struggling against the pain at her back, trying to get up, to run, to escape.

"Be still, girl, be still!" Brennos ordered, seizing her shoulders in his strong hands while Diuran hurried to light a stone lamp. "You must be still. What has happened? Was it a bad dream?"

Diuran held the small lamp high and peered anxiously over Brennos' shoulder at the girl. She fumbled nervously with the frayed edge of the wool blanket, her beautiful green eyes two wide pools of fear. She looked up at him, then back to Brennos, and tears began to slide down her trembling cheeks. Abruptly she collapsed, sobbing, against Brennos, and he put his arms around her gently.

"It was only a dream. Such a drugged sleep is often haunted by dreams," Brennos consoled her.

"No." She shook her head against him. "It was no dream. It was Niall. It was! He must tell me something . . . something important."

She clenched at Brennos' arms and looked up fearfully.

"He wants me to take the berries," she whispered in awe. "He wants me to . . ."

"No!" Nechtan thundered, rising to his feet in a rage. "This has gone on long enough. I forbid it! Do you understand? I forbid it!"

He glared at the two druids seated by the fire, their faces grim at his response.

"The last time almost killed her. What would happen this time, if she actually took some of the poisons herself? No." He shook his head firmly, pacing back and forth in frustration. "If she obeys me, then it will never happen. I forbid it."

"It would be carefully controlled this time, Nechtan." Brennos tried to calm the agitated warrior. "Diuran and I would monitor her every minute. We would have antidotes ready if anything went wrong, and in any case we would give them to her to undo the drugs after just three berries, Nechtan; just three, and no aconite."

The Pict stopped his pacing and looked at Brennos suspiciously. "And what good would that do? Three might be of no significance to her, but what of the child? And if only three are so minor a matter, what is the purpose of giving them to her at all? Let her commune with Niall in some other, safer way."

"So small an amount of the drug, traveling through her body, would probably have less of an effect on the child than the sleeping medicines we gave her after her fall," Diuran said patiently. "In any case, the antidotes would soon remedy what little drug there was."

"Then what good is any of this?" Nechtan demanded hotly. "Why risk it at all?"

"Because," Brennos calmly replied, "she insists that she must."

"And I insist that she won't!" Nechtan shouted.

"Because she feels that she will receive some message of great importance to us all," Brennos continued. "And because she is so sensitive by nature, so attuned, it will take only the slightest bit of help to nudge her over. Nechtan, you cannot deny this to her, to us all, simply because of your own fears. Something greater than all of us is at stake here—the future of our people."

Nechtan clenched his fists impotently and glared at them. He knew he was defeated; he could marshal no good argument against their words. And Melangell wanted it as well, and when she wanted something bad enough, she would defy even him to get it. His wishes counted for nothing now, and he knew it.

"Bah!" he spat angrily. "Why bother to ask me? This is all a farce. The three of you already had your minds made up. I can see that now. Go! Do it! But don't expect me to be there to watch you. I will not do that, and that is one decision I can make for myself. But guard her well, druids, for if you don't, it will be the last thing you ever do."

Bitterly he picked up his cloak from a nearby log, flung it over one shoulder, and stalked away from the fire, a darkly ominous look on his face.

In the silence that descended in his wake, the two druids sighed deeply, looked at each other uncertainly, and stood.

"We'd best go and tell her . . . and the others," Diuran muttered. Silently they returned to the druids' camp.

Nechtan stalked furiously through the encamped armies, past campfires and unfamiliar faces, by tethered horses and waiting chariots. An acquaintance jovially called his name but he ignored it. His mind whirled in dangerous, swirling currents; his face was grim and clouded. He cursed himself, the druids, the Romans, even his own dear wife. He cursed his dead friend Niall for having the gall to risk her life so. He cursed them all, muttering angrily to himself as he walked.

I, who am a chieftain, a warrior, a royal Cruithni—to them I am nothing. Just an impediment to their plans, an insignificant annoyance.

He drew up short when he saw the girl seated on a wagon yoke, her bare arms soft and white in the afternoon light, the lowering sun glinting off her thick red hair.

Seonaid, he thought darkly, and a fierce hunger flared within him. In Melangell's condition, it has been so long; not that she cares anyway. . . .

He strode up to the girl and she stared at him, a look of surprise on her face. Standing suddenly, she reached up and tickled his ear lightly, and he felt his fire burn hotter.

"Come," he said, grabbing her wrist and pulling her behind him, through the fringes of the camp, across the lengthening shadows, and into the waiting trees. Throwing his cloak to the ground, he seized her shoulders and turned her to him roughly, tangling his fingers into her hair and kissing her fiercely. He felt her quiver in delight beneath his arms. When he pulled away and looked at her, she was smiling at him.

"I knew you'd come to your senses," she whispered, wriggling out of her dress and standing naked before him. Anger fueled his passion and he reached for her, greedily devouring her with his mouth. Closing her eyes, she gasped excitedly until he pushed her to the ground, pulled down his breeches, and mounted her fiercely.

Cai returned to his camp following a brief visit with his father and brother Donall, feeling very pleased with his little brother's progress. His speech was very near normal now, his mind had improved dramatically, he could read the lips of others when they spoke, and he was an excellent spearman as well. Altogether quite a change from what he had been less than two years ago.

To save time the young man cut through the woods to avoid the crowds scattered down the mountainside. The sun was already sinking low in the sky, casting long purple shadows through the trees, and he hurried his steps in order to get back before dark. In his haste he almost stumbled over the couple lying in the forest loam, and only a moan from the girl alerted him in time to stop. The man was riding her hard, and Cai began to discreetly turn aside and leave them when recognition hit him with the force of a blow. At almost the same instant, the girl spied him and blurted out his name.

The man atop her stopped, rose up on his hands, and looked over his shoulder at Cai, and he saw that it was, indeed, Nechtan.

He stared at his chief in anger, his face cold and hard. Gods above, he thought bitterly, the hypocrite dares to banish my brother for attempting the very thing he now so lustily commits. Melangell deserves better than this . . . better than him . . . she deserves my brother, and not this . . . this . . .

Abruptly he turned and strode away, ignoring Nechtan's voice calling after him, bidding him to wait. He heard the girl's protests and then Nechtan's footsteps, pounding through the soft earth after him. The Pict grabbed his arm and whirled him around to face him as he stood gasping for breath, trying to speak.

"Cai . . . it is not what it looks like. You don't understand—"

"I know what I saw," Cai snapped, turning. He walked a few more paces before Nechtan again stopped him.

"Don't tell her . . . don't tell Melangell," he fairly begged Cai. "I was a fool. I was angry. I will get Genann back if you remain silent."

"No one knows where my brother is," Cai replied, pulling his arm free of Nechtan's grip. "You cannot buy me off like that, Nechtan. It won't work. Some of us were raised with principles we adhere to," he said pointedly, and turned once more to go. "The poor girl deserves better than you, she really does."

"No!" Nechtan protested, reaching for the young man's arm. "Let me explain! Let—"

Cai's self-control reached its limits and, with a grimace of rage, he let fly with his fist, smashing Nechtan in the face and sending him sprawling to the forest floor, blood streaming from his nose. Without another word Cai stalked off through the darkening woods. Seonaid rushed to Nechtan's side, but he sat up groggily and pushed her away, wiping his bloody nose with the back of his hand. Staggering to his feet, he retrieved his cloak and stumbled back to camp, a corner of the cloak pressed to his throbbing face.

"He does not like it, but he can give no real reasons to stop you, either," Brennos informed Melangell. He and Diuran sat beside her on a log near the druids' campfire. She wore her old black robe, and beneath it her right shoulder was swathed in the bulky poultice and bandage.

"But what exactly did he say?" she persisted, worry creasing her forehead.

"He is concerned about you and the child. We tried to reassure him, but I don't think he was listening. You know his temper."

"You mean he was angry?"

"Yes, but he will cool. He is a sensible man, once his rage goes," Brennos answered, studying the girl's drawn face. Something of her old radiance has gone, he reflected, but what caused it, he couldn't say. Harsh camp life, the child she carried, her fall, or the ordeal with Niall—maybe all of them. Briefly he wondered if this scheme of hers was such a wise idea after all. Perhaps Nechtan was right; he knew his wife better than either of them.

"We must do it soon," she blurted, looking up at their startled faces.

"But," Diuran protested, "the next full moon is long away!"

"We cannot wait," she said firmly. "I must do this at once, while Niall is still close by; otherwise there is no point to it."

"But now?" Brennos gasped. "The moon diminishes. It is

the wrong time. Wait some days, at least . . . wait till the moon is past its darkness and grows once more. You cannot do it now. It would be ill-omened and very dangerous."

"I must," she said flatly. "Niall lingers; for us he has held back his own journey. Would you so insult a guest by telling him to wait? No . . . I must do it now."

She leveled her green eyes at the two men.

"Tomorrow night."

Brennos' mouth tightened as he stared back. "You are a stubborn woman," he muttered. "Diuran and I will go and make ready the sacred grove. It must be purified, the chieftains must be alerted, and the other druids—"

"No." She shook her head. "Not the grove. It may be holy to you, but it is not to me. I will never set foot in it again. I must do this in a place of my choosing; by the little waterfalls, where the rainbows shine . . ."

She nodded in satisfaction.

"Yes, that is where I will speak with Niall."

Diuran sighed deeply and shook his head. "It is not normal, not proper, but then, none of this is a normal ritual. I suppose we must let her do what she thinks is best, eh, Brennos?"

"Aye," Brennos said. "I only hope you know what you are doing. Talking with the dead is a dangerous business. Will you still be purified; will you wear the white robe again?"

"Yes." She smiled. "That I will do, for there is peace to be found in that ceremony, and peace will help me in my task."

"Melangell!" Cai's voice cut over to them. He stepped brusquely out of the surrounding twilight. "I must speak to you a moment . . . alone." The grim set to his mouth alarmed the girl and she rose awkwardly, encumbered by her bulging stomach and bandaged shoulder.

"Yes . . . yes," she said quietly, and walked across the clearing to the front of her tent.

"Stay nearby," Cai snapped to the two druids as he followed her. Together they entered the tent, the druids watching curiously.

"Sit down, my lady," Cai said firmly to Melangell when she turned to face him.

"No, it is too difficult for me now. I—"

"Then I will help you. Sit down."

Baffled by his tone, she walked to the cot and slowly sat on it, watching him standing before her. His fine clothes had grown threadbare on their journey, his brown hair and mustache were in need of trimming, but he still held himself with an air of good breeding. His pale blue eyes seemed to cloud and he suddenly crouched and took her hand in his.

"I hereby renounce my loyalty to Nechtan and give it instead to you, to protect you and follow you for as long as my life lasts, as my brother before me had sworn to do."

She pulled her hand away in shock.

"Cai! What are you saying!"

"I am your man now. I will not serve your husband any longer, and you, if I may say so, deserve better too."

Anger flashed in her eyes at his words. "Have a care, Cai," she warned. He suddenly rose to his feet, standing stiffly before her.

"I have just found your husband in the forest, making love to Seonaid," he blurted rapidly, as if the words were a foulness in his mouth.

"No." She laughed lightly. "Surely you are mistaken, Cai. You saw how he treated her at the feast."

She looked up at his resolute face and read the truth it held, and the color drained from her cheeks.

"No . . ." she breathed, devastation in her eyes, "no."

"I am sorry," he said quietly. "I thought you should know."

"Yes . . . thank you . . . yes . . ."

She sat woodenly, staring beyond him. "Leave me. I will see no one tonight. No one."

He caught the meaning in her eyes and nodded a reply. "Yes, my lady," he said, turned, and walked from the tent, positioning himself outside the door flap, his spear in hand.

Cai glanced aside when he saw Nechtan striding angrily into the clearing, his cloak held to his face. The two druids jumped up in alarm when they saw him.

"Where is my wife?" Nechtan bellowed. Diuran pointed to the tent. He and Brennos followed Nechtan to the tent, only to be halted by Cai, who extended his spear across the door firmly.

"She will see no one," Cai said flatly, his blue eyes glinting like ice.

"You bastard . . ." Nechtan snapped, reaching to push him aside. In a flash Cai thumped his spear shaft across Nechtan's chest.

"She will see no one," he repeated.

"What is going on here?" Brennos demanded, his anger rising. "What is the meaning of this? Cai?"

"She said to admit no one . . . no one," the young man said again.

Brennos reached for the tent flap but found his way barred by the spear as well.

"She is my wife and I will see her!" Nechtan shouted, flinging his cloak to the ground and drawing his sword. He could do nothing when he found Cai's spearpoint suddenly pressed to his chest.

"She will see no one," Cai said again, and Nechtan at last heard the danger in the young man's voice. Slowly he replaced his sword and picked up the cloak.

"Very well," he said grimly. "You may be able to stop me, but not my voice . . . or will you gag me as well?" He shot a cold glance at Cai.

"Melangell," he called to her, "I love you. Please forgive me. Let me explain. Please . . ."

He waited, but no sound, no response came from the tent. Glumly he turned, his cloak dragging the ground, and walked from the druids' camp.

"Gods above!" Diuran muttered. "What has happened here? I think more and more that our little adventure tomorrow is a misguided one."

"Aye." Brennos nodded, turning from the tent. "So do I."

Cai resumed his vigil outside the tent, while within it Melangell sat stiffly on the cot, her back to the door, staring dumbly at the rear wall. Her face was blank, her heart was cold; even her eyes could not cry. Her devastation was beyond tears.

Cai admitted Brennos into the tent the next morning, and helped him carry in some food and wine for Melangell. She still sat upright on the cot, her eyes grim but heavy.

"By the gods, girl," Brennos gasped, putting the food on her wooden chest. "Have you sat there all night? You need your rest. Will you lose the child now, after all you have been through?"

She hung her head weakly and sighed.

"Eat something, and then sleep until this afternoon. Do you understand? If you do not sleep willingly, I will force something down you that will make you sleep, and if you still get no rest, we will cancel the ceremony tonight. I'll not have you ruining your health because of—"

"What does it matter?" she muttered, barely coherent from her weariness. She picked up a bowl and halfheartedly scooped some hot barley into her mouth. Brennos shook his head and handed her some cheese, which she scarcely nibbled.

"I don't know what you told her, but I hope you're happy with the results," he snapped to Cai as he tried to force some wine into the girl. She drank a little and turned her head away.

"No," she said softly. "I am tired. I must sleep." She lowered herself to her side, curled up as best she could, and in seconds was deep in sleep. The druid pulled a blanket over her, picked up the food, and the two men silently left the tent.

Cai held the tent flap aside while Brennos and Diuran carried the heavy iron brazier into Melangell's tent. She was still asleep but she quickly roused when Diuran shook her gently.

"Is it time?" she said, seemingly refreshed by her nap.

"Aye," Brennos replied, crouching before her and studying her face. "Are you sure you are ready for this? We think we should postpone it."

"No," she said firmly. "I am fine. I must do it today. I must. Have the others been told?"

"Yes." Diuran nodded. "The same chieftains and warlords as before. But the afternoon is here; we must begin. The cot and other things must be cleared from the tent."

"Yes," she said, standing. Cai picked up the cot and her small carved wooden chest and carried them away while Diuran heated coals in the brazier and Brennos swept the tent floor clean.

"Here is your blanket," Brennos said, "and as soon as you're ready, I must take the poultice from your back too."

She nodded and waited for them to leave. Quickly she removed her black robe and wrapped the blanket around herself, leaving her shoulders bare. Brennos returned and cleaned away the sticky poultice, then washed her shoulder with warm water. She sat on the stool while he tossed out her old robe and the poultice and brought in the ewer of water. He left again and she waited, listening to the familiar camp sounds outside until he returned, once more in his clean white robe and carrying the two cedar boxes of dried herbs. She sat silently, the afternoon passing and night drawing near, while the druid fed the bark and flowers to the iron pot.

I must compose myself, she thought grimly, inhaling the fragrant air. I must get Nechtan from my heart and my mind so that Niall can enter it, or else this whole night will be a waste, and Niall's message will be lost to us forever. She closed her eyes and sighed shakily, and heard Brennos walk to her side.

"Here," he said sternly, "drink some water. You look pale." She drank the cup he offered her, turning when she heard Diuran's deep voice call to Brennos. The druid crossed the tent, took the white robe that was thrust in to him, and turned to the girl.

"It is time," he said flatly. Melangell rose to her feet immediately.

"Are you absolutely sure you want to do this now?" he asked, laying the robe on the stool.

"Yes," she said emphatically. "I am prepared. I must . . ."

With a sigh he removed the white blanket, dropped the robe over her head, and tied her hair back. Then he returned to the door and came back with a small gold cup, which he held out to the girl.

"What is this?" she said, looking into the cup uncertainly. "I thought I was to have nothing but water."

"It is a drug in a little wine. It must be taken to keep your mind clear."

She looked up at his shadowed face, aghast. "You mean Niall also had this?" she whispered.

"Aye, he did," Brennos replied, puzzled by her reaction.

The drum boomed out and Melangell looked aside, her eyes staring blankly at the leather wall. So that explained it . . . his final cry . . . his knowing, his feeling.

"Drink it," the druid said firmly, "or we cannot proceed."

She took the cup from him and swallowed the wine down. Taking her arm, he walked her from the tent.

So here I am, she thought absently as the procession wound down the hillside, both the officiating druid and the victim—an odd thing indeed! Brennos and Diuran flanked her, carrying their jars and cups of antidotes. Cai walked stiffly behind her, his spear, shield, and sword left behind at the tents. The dark tree line along the stream came into view, and she could see flickering torches and shadowy figures. The horns blared once as they stepped into the rock-strewn glade, and she quickly cut her eyes around to the waiting faces. Nechtan was nowhere to be seen.

They walked forward to a large flat rock, where the two druids stopped and turned to Cai, nodding once in silence. He pulled out a length of rope and tied Melangell's hands behind her.

"What is this for?" she started to protest, but Diuran shook his head to stop her. "Lady, under the influence of the drug you will be inclined to thrash about. You must be bound to prevent that."

She nodded, swallowing hard. Only three berries, and I will thrash about? Fear began to rise within her. Perhaps I shouldn't be doing this . . . Was Nechtan right after all?

They led her to the rock and she sat cross-legged on it, facing the dancing creek, the assembled warlords, chiefs, and druids forming a warding circle around her. Cai lashed a rope across her chest twice, binding her arms to her sides and, having no post to tie her to, he took the rope ends in his hands and knelt behind her, ready to hold her tightly if need be.

Diuran stood to one side, a druid beside him holding the tray of antidotes, as Brennos handed the golden box of poisons to a fourth druid and opened the lid.

"Wait," Melangell whispered to him. "One moment . . ."

The drug in the wine was taking effect and she stared into the tossing waters before her in fascination. The sound of the torrent came louder, louder, till it grew to a thunder in her ears. As she gazed upward, the tree trunks seemed to leap out of the darkness toward her. The coldness of the stone beneath her radiated up through her body and she breathed deeply; the air seemed as sweet and liquid as wine. So this was what Niall had felt at the end—an achingly beautiful world, a feast for the senses.

"I am ready," she said quietly, closing her eyes. She felt Brennos' hand beneath her chin, the berry entered her mouth, and she swallowed it. Another hand—Diuran's—touched her neck, feeling her heartbeat. She waited expectantly, exploring the sensations of her own body as if she was her own physician, but nothing happened. A low buzzing began to rise in her ears and she opened her eyes in alarm. Brennos' face came into view, fuzzy and gray-looking. His image wavered, swam, as if she viewed him through water. I must be moving, she thought dully, for Cai is pulling me back tightly against his body.

"Another . . ." she gasped, and her voice sounded loud, impossibly loud, like thunder in the treetops . . . yet Brennos leaned closer, as if he couldn't hear her.

"Another!" she repeated, and saw him look up at Diuran. Then a berry entered her mouth and she swallowed it, watching in fascination as it slid down her throat, a tumbling silver orb, falling away into blackness.

How can I see inside myself? she wondered idly, and realized with a jolt that she was looking down at her own knees. My head must be hanging down . . . how silly I must look!

"Melangell!" Brennos was calling to her, as if from across a great void. She looked at him but her eyes would not focus.

"Melangell . . ."

"Niall?" she gasped, lifting her head and looking around. He stood between the two druids, tall and calm and proud, a cloak tossed over one shoulder, his fair hair and tanned skin glowing with health. He came forward, a grim look on his face.

"Tell them," he said intently.

"Tell them what?" she muttered.

"Beware our own kind. Tell them."

"Beware our own kind," she repeated slowly.

"Tell them to guard the right flank at all costs."

"Guard the right flank . . . at all costs."

The chiefs leaned forward, listening intently to the sagging girl as Cai held her upright with one arm, the other pulling tight on the ropes that bound her.

"Tell them to stay on the hillside," Niall continued.

"Stay on the hillside . . ." she echoed him.

"Tell them, you must give me the third berry with aconite, at once."

"You must give me . . . the third berry with . . . with aconite . . . at once."

His face was now lowered directly into hers and he looked intense, vigorous, his blue eyes boring into her. "Tell them again," he said quietly. "Scream it as loud as you can."

"I must have the third berry . . . with aconite . . . at once!" she shrieked.

"Tell them that Niall says so. It is urgent. Niall says so."

"Niall," she sobbed, "I am sorry, I know how you died . . . I am sorry."

"Tell them!" he commanded, his face wavering.

"Niall says so . . . it is urgent . . . Niall says so . . . No! Don't go! I am sorry . . . Niall . . . don't go."

She sobbed brokenly, held back against Cai's chest, her staring eyes seeing nothing. A low murmur broke out among the chiefs, and Brennos and Diuran looked at each other uncertainly. "Her pulse is still good," Diuran said quietly. Brennos felt the girl's neck himself, nodded solemnly, and motioned the druid with the box forward. Lifting out a third berry, he lightly dipped it in the aconite and wiped all but a tiny portion onto the sleeve of his white robe. Turning to the girl, he placed it in her mouth and the entire gathering watched in silence as she swallowed it.

"Behold!" Niall said in triumph, taking her hand in his. He pulled her and she rose easily, springing into the air like a bird released from its cage and winging its way heavenward. They soared upward at a dizzying pace and then he flung her free, like children playing at spinning games.

"Farewell!" he called, his form quickly vanishing below her.

"No!" she gasped as she sailed on at a frightening speed, trying vainly to halt herself. Forms began to take shape below her, at first dim and wavering, then growing clearer, sharper, brighter.

"Armies . . ." she gasped when she beheld the world below her, from horizon to horizon, covered with Roman Legions.

"Romans . . . they cover the world . . ."

Then the armies vanished and she watched the scenes unfolding below her. "Houses . . . of sand, and tall trees . . . with leaves like hair atop them."

The assembled group looked at one another, their faces creased with puzzled frowns.

"A gentle silver cloud arises from this land . . . it covers the world in the wake of the armies of Rome. No longer will our people fear the bloody sacrifices, for the silver cloud will bring peace."

Her voice suddenly fell in desolation. "The Romans are the will of the gods. Nothing can stop them but the silver cloud."

The chiefs looked at each other. A silver cloud? Some odd new weapon, perhaps? But houses of sand? Trees with hair? They shook their heads. The girl was obviously out of her mind.

"But beware," she continued. "In the wake of the silver cloud comes the lesser army of Rome. Fear not the greater army, which destroys only our Celtic bodies; fear the lesser army, which seeks to destroy our Celtic souls."

Diuran stood at the girl's side, monitoring her pulse, which began to flutter erratically. He looked at Brennos and nodded, then took a druid's cup of milky liquid from the tray.

"Beware the lesser army of Rome!" she went on. Diuran held the cup to her mouth but paused when Brennos stayed his hand.

"Behold!" she gasped, twisting in pain while Cai held her firm. "Our people shall one day rule the world, and walk among the stars, and . . . and our gift to them shall be our love of freedom."

She gasped again, turning her head desperately.

"We will rule the world! We will rule the world!" she cried, and Cai held her steady while Diuran trickled the liquid down her throat. She coughed and gagged noisily.

Brennos reached for a second cup and slowly poured it down behind the first.

Melangell thrashed wildly and Cai wrapped his arms directly around her, holding her as tightly as he dared while another warrior stepped forward to secure her legs. The antidotes gradually took effect and she collapsed. Cai looked at the druids questioningly. They felt her pulse, looked into her eyes, and nodded to each other.

"It has passed," Diuran said quietly. "Cai, carry her back to the tent for us."

The young man cut the ropes that held her, lifted her in his arms, and stepped from the rock. He walked up the dark hillside, the two druids joining him, as murmurs of excitement welled up behind them.

They had their answer. The girl had said it: the battle would be a victory—"we will rule the world!"

A delirious cheer rose from the warriors' throats. We will rule the world!

Something sweet forced its way into Melangell's mouth and the weary girl tasted it in delight. It resembled honey, and yet it wasn't. She tasted more, trying to identify the flavor. Then someone was patting her cheek lightly, and a voice spoke low and soothing by her ear.

"Wake up now, my dear. It is over."

She moaned softly and turned her face away. Again the same sweet taste came to her mouth, followed by a brief sip of watered wine.

"Come now, Melangell," Brennos persisted. "You must wake up."

Her eyes fluttered open and she squinted in the bright sunlight that streamed into the open tent flap at her feet. "What day is this? What happened?" she gasped, trying to sit.

"No!" Diuran said sharply. "You must have bed rest. The baby is moving too much. Perhaps we miscalculated and the drugs affected him. You must be still and quiet. You are not even to walk. Brennos tells me it is a month before the child is due. We must keep you well and rested until then."

The girl's hand went swiftly to her heavy stomach. "Is the baby all right?" she said fearfully.

"Aye, so far as we can tell," Brennos answered. "But you have been through too much lately. You must have strict bed rest, do you understand? We will even fetch a pot in here for you to use. You are not to be up and around under any circumstances."

She nodded solemnly and seized his sleeve. "Brennos, what happened to me? How did I do? Was it successful?"

"Don't you remember any of it?" he asked in surprise.

"Very little. Niall was there; he told me some things about armies. Then I was flying through the air. There were visions . . . Romans. How did I do? Was anything of value learned?"

A slow smile crept across his face as he looked down at her. Impulsively he leaned over and kissed her forehead. "My dearest one, you told us more than enough. They will be speaking of you and your visions for generations to come!"

"Really?" she said, brightening at his words.

"Yes; even now they hold a meeting, called by Calgacus himself, to make our plans and discuss strategies, thanks to you. Now you must finish eating this. It strengthens the heart. You are to have nothing but this and a little wine until tomorrow. We must take very good care of you from now on."

"What is it?" she asked, savouring the sweetness anew.

"Crushed red rose petals and honey. Now, stop your talking and eat."

Calgacus stood, an imposing figure with long graying hair fastened by a braided band around his head, a heavy gray Celtic mustache drooping over his mouth. Despite his advanced age, he was still a powerful man, his broad chest and arms heavily muscled. Three great war hounds reclined by his folding Roman camp chair, two a shaggy gray, the other one sleeker, colored white with red patches. Casually they lifted their regal heads when their master rose to his feet.

"The Romans have advanced steadily northward over the summer while we gathered here in these mountains waiting for their return," he boomed, his voice deep and well-trained for addressing large gatherings. "For a long time our chiefs and I have debated what action we should take to stop them. We could never come to a firm decision until now. Those of you who were not present to hear the girl's revelations last night have been told of them. Now our course is clear."

He paused and gazed dramatically at the sea of faces before him. Consummate speaker that he was, he knew just how to hold the attention of his audience, and the assembled chiefs and leaders waited tensely for him to continue.

"The sacrificed warrior Niall conveyed three messages: of the first, we know little; but the next two we can understand and act on. Guard our right flank, and stay to the mountain's slopes. And this tells us what we must do. In a few days' time the Romans will be marching past our present position, heading back to their supply ships and forts before winter. When they reach us we will be waiting for them, our ranks massed and solid on this slope they must pass by, from the crest of the hill to the plains below. When they attack us, they must attack uphill. If they try to encircle us, we will be massed as solid on our flanks as we are on our front. They will not be able to drive us away, or surround us, or divide us. And we will hold the advantage over them as long as we remain on the slope, forcing them to make the forays, forcing them to climb the hillside after us. Niall's advice was sound, and we will heed it!"

He roamed his fierce brown eyes over the crowd, and if anyone had a mind to disagree, he kept his words to himself. Satisfied, the old warlord sat down and reached to his side, his large hand scratching one of the great hounds lovingly. The dog's tail thumped loudly against the chair in response. Calgacus studied the men in silence, summoned a guard, and spoke quietly to him. The guard nodded, turned, and called out in a loud voice, "Is Nechtan of the Cruithni here?"

The sea of heads turned curiously until a tall, grim, dark-haired warrior stood to the king's left.

"I am Nechtan," he announced, his voice showing not a hint of fear or awe.

"Calgacus wishes to know if the druidess is your wife," the guard said.

"She is."

"Come forward."

Nechtan made his way through the packed men, Cathal and Melwas close behind him. He stopped when he reached the king, his two guards flanking him. The warlord leaned forward and his keen eyes seemed to appraise the younger man for a moment before he spoke.

"She is a very brave woman, to do what she did for us," he said.

"Thank you, sire." Nechtan nodded.

"I have a gift for her, to show both my gratitude and admiration. I ask that you deliver it to her."

"I would be honored," Nechtan replied.

"Lacha!" the king said quietly, and the gray hound rose to its feet, its long tail slowly sweeping back and forth in curiosity.

"This is a dog I bred myself, raised myself, and trained myself," Calgacus explained, rubbing the dog's shaggy neck affectionately. "I could give no greater gift were I to offer one of my own children."

He signaled to a guard, who handed him a leather leash.

"He is but a year old, not yet full-grown. I call him Lacha because he is as swift as the wild duck he was named after. I would trust my life to him."

He fastened the leash to the dog's wide leather collar and handed it to the dumbfounded Pict.

"He is now your wife's, with my thanks."

Nechtan looked at the lead in his hand, then up to the king in amazement. There was scarcely a gift in the land more cherished, more significant, than one of the great war hounds of a king.

"Thank you, my lord," Nechtan muttered. "I know she will be thrilled. Thank you."

He bowed low and made his way through the openly admiring crowd, the young hound trotting contentedly at his side.

Melangell rested on a cot carried into the druids' clearing, taking advantage of a cool evening breeze. She sipped watered wine and watched Cai and Brennos duel with their large swords. She hadn't realized how skilled a druid could be with a weapon. It seemed to her that Brennos was only slightly outmatched by her guard. Sweat gleamed on their bare torsos as they leapt and twisted, lunging and slashing, their eyes glaring at each other in fierce concentration. When Cai finally pinned Brennos' sword arm, the other druids around the clearing applauded and cheered loudly.

"Not bad for an old man!" Ethal jested as Brennos walked past him, wiping the sweat from his face.

"Quiet, you," Brennos laughed, "or I'll get Cai to fight you next." He poured a cup of wine, set his sword on a barrel, and flopped tiredly to the ground by the girl's cot.

"Aye," he gasped to her, "but it is true. I am not as young as I once was."

"I thought you were splendid," she consoled him, patting his sweaty shoulder.

"Thank you. I . . ." He stopped abruptly and stood when he saw Nechtan, Melwas, and Cathal walk into the clearing. Cai, wiping his sword, advanced protectively toward Melangell.

"Oh . . . look!" the girl said, startled when she saw the stately dog that walked by Nechtan's side. Nechtan came toward her and Brennos could see worry in the man's eyes when he saw her pale face.

"Cai . . . it's all right," Melangell said suddenly, waving her guard aside. He stopped in his tracks, retreated a few steps, and stood sullenly glaring at Nechtan. The girl was looking at Nechtan too, her expression withdrawn, veiled, hidden from him.

"I have brought you a gift from Calgacus," he said quietly, extending the leash to her. Her mouth flew open in astonishment and her eyes fell to the dog at his side. She clicked her tongue and the great dog leapt toward her, his tongue lolling happily.

"This is for me?" she asked. "I cannot believe it! Why does he give me such a priceless gift?"

The gray head nuzzled her neck affectionately and she laughed, scratching behind the dog's ears.

"Calgacus said it was presented with his thanks, to show his gratitude and admiration for what you did . . . for all of us. He raised and trained it himself. Its name is Lacha."

"Lacha," she repeated, and the dog lifted his ears at the sound of his name. "Oh, you are a dear one, aren't you, Lacha?" The dog wagged his tail happily and Melangell pressed her cheek to the top of his shaggy head.

"I said I would deliver it, and I have," Nechtan stated, turning to leave.

"Wait," Brennos said, resolve on his dusty face. "Come here, Nechtan. I think you have some talking to do with your wife."

"No," Nechtan replied stubbornly. "I have nothing to—"

"You *do*!" the druid snapped impatiently, jerking the princeling back toward the bedside. "Now, all of you," he commanded the guards and druids with a grand sweep of his arms, "go! Give them some privacy. Over to the far side of the clearing!"

He picked up his sword from the barrel and forced Nechtan to sit by Melangell's side. "I do believe Ethal said he would like to try a sword fight with you, Melwas," Brennos called out, crossing the clearing to join the rest of the group. He was met with a loud laugh from Melwas and strident denials from Ethal.

They sat in awkward silence, the girl stroking the dog's head, Nechtan looking down at his hands uncomfortably. Then Melangell spoke, her voice barely a hushed whisper.

"Why did you do it, Nechtan? Why?"

He looked up at her but she continued to gaze defensively at the dog, studiously avoiding her husband's eyes.

"I was angry. I didn't want you to go through with the ritual, but my wishes didn't seem to matter to anyone. So I was angry, she was sitting there, and I took advantage of the situation. It meant nothing to me, Melangell. I was just using her; venting my rage, that's all. She means less to me than one of my horses. Don't you see?"

Her green eyes swept slowly up to meet his gaze and she studied his face for a moment.

"'Passion rules all,' the bards say . . . so now we are even," she said quietly.

He looked down at his hands again and picked absently at his fingernails. "Yes," he sighed. "Cai lost no time in pointing that out to me. I will get Genann back. I was wrong. Cai says no one knows where he is now, but surely he must be around here somewhere. I will send out word. We will find him."

Nechtan moved his feet aside as the hound lowered himself to the ground by the cot and flopped lazily onto his side. Melangell reached her hand out to Nechtan and he took it firmly.

"I forgive you." She smiled. His face softened when he met her gaze.

"I will never hurt you again, Melangell. I swear it. Never." He leaned forward and softly kissed her mouth. She reached her hand desperately into his hair and held his face next to hers, her eyes closed happily.

"I will be so glad when this child is born," she whispered into his ear, "for I do so miss your arms about me at night."

He lifted his head and smiled at her, his hand touching her cheek. "Not nearly so much as I miss the feel of you beneath me—"

"Hush!" she laughed, putting a finger to his mouth. "The druids will hear you!"

"It will be soon," he said. "A month or so and you will be mine once more, and then, my little love, I will give you a night you will never forget!"

He kissed her again and stood.

"Now I must be going. We have many preparations to make. The battle comes in three days."

"As much as I dislike it, we must get you up and walking. If a battle is coming, you must be strong enough to leave with the rest of the women and camp followers."

Brennos put an arm around Melangell's back and helped her from the cot.

"I feel fine . . . really," she protested.

"Nevertheless, you are not to strain yourself in any way. One of us will walk with you everywhere. It will not do to have the child born early."

She rose to her feet unsteadily, not realizing how weak she had become. The druid supported her and, the dog protectively at her side, they strolled from the tent, across the druids' clearing and to the campfire, where Cathbhadh fetched a stool for Melangell.

"Have some of our meal with us and we can talk," the

older druid offered hospitably, scooping out a bowl of hot oat gruel for her. "I have heard that you, like Esus, eat no meat, so we fixed our foods to suit you."

"Why . . . thank you!" She smiled in surprise. Lacha sat at her side and hungrily eyed the small boar roasting over the fire. Cathbhadh looked at the hound a moment, turned, and cut off a large chunk of meat. He tossed it to the dog, who settled down happily to eat his prize.

"In my youth I had a dog like that," the old druid mused. "A magnificent animal, and a good friend. I will never forget him."

"Wine?" Brennos offered, handing a cup to Melangell. She took it, sipped the watered wine lightly, and held the cup between her knees while she ate.

"The women will be leaving tonight," Brennos said. Melangell felt the hot oats turn to lead in her stomach and she lowered the bowl.

"Leaving?" she whispered in disbelief. She had never thought much about what the coming battle would mean to her, as a woman.

"Aye," Cathbhadh said. "Your husband is providing a small wagon for you and your possessions. You can ride in comfort and safety and Cai will of course accompany you."

"No!" she stated, her voice shot through with an iron will. "I will not go. Many women stay behind to look after the wounded."

"What could you do, in your condition? You would only be in the way, and you would be endangering yourself and your child as well," Brennos said firmly. "No. Nechtan wants you taken to safety, and Diuran and I agree. You must leave tonight with—"

"No!" she shouted. The dog turned from his meal and looked at her in alarm. "I will stay with Nechtan. I will not go."

"We will not permit it, Melangell. You don't know what you are saying. You have never seen a battle like this—"

"I have been *in* a battle. My own home, my village, were destroyed in a battle. I know what battles are like."

"That was a small raid, my dear," Cathbhadh said calmly. "Nothing at all like the coming clash. You have never seen the Romans fight."

"All the more reason I will stay here," she replied angrily. "Nechtan may need me."

"No. You will go. I rarely cross your will when your mind is made up, Melangell, but on this I must. You will leave with the rest of the women tonight." Brennos' face was stern and determined.

"I will not!" she snapped, rising to her feet and throwing the wine cup and gruel to the ground. "I will stay with my husband."

Turning, she called the dog and, one hand on his back to steady herself, returned to her tent.

"I have come to walk with you," Nechtan said, entering Melangell's tent. His wife sat sullenly on her cot, watching the evening shadows gather outside and listening to the distant sounds of snorting oxen, nervous horses, and creaking wagons as the women and camp followers made ready to leave. Lacha lay at her feet but he stood and wagged his tail when Nechtan approached.

"It is not necessary that I walk," she said flatly, "for I am staying with you."

"I won't argue with you," he said, gently pulling her to her feet. "But you still need some exercise, and I want to be with you this evening. The battle is in the morning. I might not have a chance to see you tomorrow."

He put an arm around her shoulders and she leaned her head against him, fighting the tears that filled her eyes. Will there ever be a world, she wondered, where people can be safe and happy?

"Don't be sad, little one," he said, kissing her forehead. "Everything will be all right. You said yourself that we would win."

"Yes, but I am still afraid for you . . . for us."

"Fear will change nothing, and it will only poison this time we still have together. I will meet my fate tomorrow, whatever it may be, and so will you. All fighting men are fatalistic. We have to be. Worry is of no avail."

They strolled into the twilight and to the nearby trees, his warrior's cloak pulled around her shoulders like the sheltering wing of a bird. Silently they watched the stars emerge, one by one, their moment too private, too intense, for the

341

intrusion of words. Unable to bear it, Melangell lowered her head to his shoulder and began to cry softly.

Why can't we run away, my love? she thought desperately. Just the two of us. Let them fight their war, but leave us alone to find our own happiness.

"Don't cry, my dearest," he whispered, turning her face up to his and gently kissing her. "All will be well with us. I am sure of it. We will defeat the Romans and our son will have a free land to grow up in. And one day, because of us and what we do here tomorrow, his wife will never have to cry because he goes off to war, as you do now. Isn't that worth the cost? Freedom for us, and peace for our children?"

"Yes," she sniffled. "You are right."

"Good." He smiled. "Now, let's go and get some wine. All right?"

Arm in arm, they walked back to the druids' clearing, where the black-robed men sat solemnly around the fire, talking in hushed voices. Brennos rose when they approached, smiling and nodding as he offered them wine. Melangell sat tiredly on his stool and took the cup he handed her while Nechtan stood close behind her.

"To us," he said, bending low over her and tipping his wine cup to hers. Smiling at his salute, she quickly drank the wine and stared blankly at the fire, feeling Nechtan's hand firm on her shoulder.

Suddenly, to her horror, the flames began to waver and leap.

"No!" she gasped, springing to her feet in alarm, the clearing whirling dizzily around her. Through a haze she saw Brennos' face, peering at her intently, and as she collapsed she felt Nechtan lifting her in his arms.

Nechtan laid her gently in the back of a small wagon and kissed her cheek. "Guard her well," he instructed Cai, who nodded silently. "Head north, with the others, and if anything goes amiss, take her to my people. They will shelter her until I come."

He called to the dog and the great hound leapt lightly into the cart, sniffed his mistress's face, and lay down beside her.

Cai propped his spear in the wagon, jumped astride the cart horse, and without a word guided the horse and wagon into the woods, to join the other refugees who streamed away from camp.

Nechtan watched until they were lost to the shadows, then turned away grimly.

"It is for the best," Brennos consoled him as they walked back to their camp.

"Aye," Nechtan muttered. "I only wish there had been some other way."

Melangell fluttered her eyes open, her mind dazed and confused, when the cart jolted roughly over a protruding tree root. Looking up, she saw dark tree branches solemnly clasped overhead, an occasional star peeking through as they slowly creaked along. Lying quietly, she fought to clear her mind, to remember . . .

Yes . . . they had drugged her, to get her out of camp. Her wine had been drugged by Brennos.

Frowning, she gazed around, trying to decide what to do. Looking up over her head, she could not see Cai sitting on the wagon. Good, she mused. He must be on the horse.

The cart was small, of a type used for farm hauling. Three sides were enclosed by high wooden walls, but the rear was open except for a small board to keep cargo from sliding out. That is good too, she noted, squinting through the darkness to see what the cart contained.

There was Lacha, of course, looking at her happily, his breath hot on her face. Two sacks of food, and her carved wooden trunk. Reaching past the dog, she unlatched it carefully and lifted the lid. Patting her hand inside, she felt the familiar coarse weave of her black druid's robe, folded up and placed on top. Quickly she pulled it out and lowered the lid, clenching the robe happily to her breast. Not for nothing did druids wear black. It made one almost disappear into a dark forest, when the need arose.

Sitting up slowly, she slid to the rear board of the cart and tucked the robe down the front of her shift. Raising herself on all fours, her legs extended out over the board, she waited. When the cart rolled up and over another large tree root, she let herself down over the back, the cart's momentum slowed by the root, and her descent easily accomplished in secrecy. As lightly as a duck settling on the water, Lacha leapt to the ground with her, and she steadied herself against the dog's back. Stepping away into the trees, she took out the black robe and pulled it on. As silent as a shadow, she crept off through the forest, the great gray dog at her side, following the rutted trail back to the encampment, back to Nechtan.

The great Highland army, thirty thousand men strong, assembled on the slopes of Duncrub while the skies were still dark, the air shrouded in night mists. As silently as they could, the men dressed and seized their weapons and crept away from the still-burning campfires behind their chiefs; young men and old, skilled warriors and untrained craftsmen, grizzled farmers and the flower of the nobility, all assembled as one on the edge of the world, to defend their homeland and drive out the hated invader. Only the mounted horsemen and charioteers waited for the dawning light, so that not a sound would alert the encamped Romans, peacefully slumbering below in what was, to them, just another stop on the long march back to their bases. When the sun rose through the yellow mists and fogs of the mountain, the Roman sentries were astounded to see the facing slope covered with waiting warriors, and the cry went up in all the Roman camps as the sleepy soldiers sprang to life, to battle.

Melangell stumbled, exhausted, through the ghostly, deserted camps. Not a soul remained behind anywhere. Grasping the dog for support, she wandered wildly from camp to camp, looking for someone, anyone. The food had been taken, the tents packed away, personal possessions removed. Only the fires and debris and footprinted earth remained, a silent universe populated by a hundred blazing suns.

Eager horses and gleaming chariots lined the crest of the hill, waiting for the battle to begin. Thousands of eyes watched intently as the Romans formed up below them, their line stretched out long and thin to encompass the whole front of the Highland army, and the chiefs grinned and nodded to one another happily. Old Calgacus stood in his splendid chariot, surrounded by his spearmen, fluttering banners and carnyx-blowers, waiting on the highest point of the hill. Raising his arms into the air, he addressed those of his troops who could hear him:

"When I think of the reasons we fight and the dangerous position we are in, I feel that the united front we are showing today will mean the dawn of liberty for all of Britain. There are no lands behind us. Even on the sea we are menaced by Roman ships. The clash of battle, the glory of heroes, is now the safest refuge of a coward. We, the most distant dwellers on earth, the last hope of free men, have been shielded till today by our very remoteness. Now all of Britain lies open to our enemies. There are no more nations beyond us; nothing lies there but waves and rocks and the Romans, more deadly than all these, for in them is an arrogance which neither submission nor good behavior can escape. Pillagers of the world, they have exhausted the land by their indiscriminate plunder. A rich enemy excites their greed; a poor one, their lust for power. East and West alike have failed to satisfy them. To robbery, butchery, and rape they give the lying name of 'government'; they create a desolation and call it peace.

"Since you cannot hope for mercy, take courage before it is too late. We, who have never been forced to feel their yoke, shall be fighting to preserve our freedom. Let us show them, then, what manner of men Caledonia has kept in reserve."

Melangell stumbled along the rocky ridge of the mountain, following the clear sound of Calgacus' voice, and as she emerged over the crest a wild cheering broke out from the thousands of men assembled on the slopes. She stopped, gasping in awe at the vast army stretched away before her, as numberless as leaves on a tree. At the conclusion of the old warlord's speech the eager men pressed forward behind their battle standards, war horns blaring and rattling raucously, the air charged with their battle fire. The skies echoed their wild cries and the rising sun glinted like a blacksmith's sparks off the polished shields and spearpoints descending the hillside. Lifting her heavy robe, Melangell ran frantically along the crest, toward the distant chariots. Calgacus' charioteer turned his horses and, with a blood-curdling cry, the mass of vehicles thundered down the hillside, toward the waiting Romans. . . .

"No!" she cried out, sinking to her knees by the dog as the chariots disappeared in a thick cloud of dust.

"No."

Lacha pranced and galloped eagerly back and forth, sensing the excitement in the air and anxious to join the battle. Melangell slumped to the rocky soil, her stomach churning in fear and defeat.

Protect him, great Medocius, she pleaded desperately, her body racked with brokenhearted sobs.

Protect him.

"Do you see him?" the general snapped as he and Anarios stood on a little hill to the side of the Legions, watching the descending mass of enemy charioteers.

"Do you see this 'wolf'?" he demanded.

Anarios had a clear vantage point, and despite himself he felt a thrill at the wild spectacle of the charging chariots, bronze and gold glinting in the sunlight, brightly colored clothes flapping in the onrushing air. Yes, he could almost understand these people, he thought, watching the pounding charge; their fierceness, their love of freedom, their high-strung nature. They are like a fine horse, he reflected. Break that horse and make it useful, but in the process something is lost . . . something unique and wild and wonderful.

"Well? Answer me!" the general fairly shouted. "I want this 'wolf.' Where is he?"

The physician watched carefully. The chariots reached the bottom of the hill and strung out along the gap between the two armies as they turned, pounding onward in a rapidly vanishing line, raining spears and javelins on the front ranks of the Roman army to soften them up for their foot soldiers. He spied him at once, his black hair flying from beneath a leather band, the familiar cloak belted tight around his waist, a spear from his hand felling a startled soldier in the ranks. No doubt about it: it was Nechtan.

"No," Anarios answered, turning to the general. "He is not here. Perhaps he has fled to the north."

The general looked disappointed, turned, and motioned for their horses to be brought up. "We'd better get out of here before things get any worse," he said. "They'll be needing you soon, behind the lines."

Nodding grimly, Anarios mounted his horse and walked it down the far side of the hill, the battle cries rising behind him.

Go with the gods, Melangell, he thought as he rode away. May the two of you find happiness.

The little cart clattered to a halt beside the knot of druids and a few remaining women who stood on the crest and watched, awestruck, as the battle unfolded below them. Cai jumped down, breathless, and ran to the startled men.

"Is she here?" he gasped. "Melangell . . . is she here?"

"What?" Brennos demanded, stepping out from the group. "What do you mean? What happened?"

"Somewhere . . . she slipped away. I looked and she was gone."

"I knew I should have given her a stronger dose," Brennos cursed himself. "I was concerned for the child."

"Have you seen her?" Cai nearly shouted in desperation.

"No. She could be anywhere by now. Gods above! I—"

A loud bark made them turn. In the distance they saw the great gray dog, bounding in his eagerness, a huddled black figure on the ground nearby. Both men broke into a run when the figure lifted its head and gazed down the crowded mountainside.

"Melangell!" Cai gasped, falling to his knees beside her. Brennos rushed up behind him. "You should not be here!"

"Are you all right?" the druid asked tensely. "By the gods, not a baby, in the midst of a battle! Not that."

"You tricked me," she said, her voice like ice as she watched the battle. "I came to be with my husband."

"Pick her up," Brennos said, exasperated. "At least come to the wagons so we can get away quickly if we have to."

She put an arm around Cai's shoulders. He lifted her and

the three returned to the waiting group of people, the dog leaping happily beside them.

The men in the chariots sprang to the ground when the line completed its pass across the Roman ranks, running to join their own men afoot. The vehicles returned up the hillside, to wait until they should be needed for further action . . . or evacuation.

The chariots passed quickly up the far side of their army, circled around behind the lines, and formed up along the ridge, waiting. Mac Oag, at the reins of Nechtan's chariot, looked over his shoulder in surprise when he saw the girl sitting on the ground by the druids, a grim Cai at her side. Shaking his head, he turned to watch the progress of the battle as the first wounded men stumbled up the hillside to the waiting women and druids.

Nechtan seized his shield, jumped to the ground with Melwas and Cathal, and without breaking his stride, ran to join his warriors. Pulling out his long Celtic sword, he pushed through to the front line and was dismayed to find himself facing, not small disciplined Romans, but tall, fiercely grinning Germans and Gauls, advancing wildly with pointed Roman swords, shouting and screaming in their furor. With a wild cry the Caledonians returned the attack, stabbing with their lances, slashing with their swords, as the entire central rank of the Roman forces, a solid wall of Continental Celts and Germans, bore down on them.

Nechtan knew they were being pushed back under the onslaught, and in the tightly packed melee he had no room to use his slashing Celtic sword. In desperation he shouted to his men and they pulled out their Roman swords, stabbing and hacking at the startled mercenaries in front of them. Stepping backward, he almost stumbled, and glanced down in the blink of an eye. It was Osla, dead of a split skull. Then Mael fell beside him, his bow still on his back. Baring his teeth savagely, Nechtan thrust out and ripped, and a tall blond German fell to the rocks, his innards spilling over the ground. And still more men began to fall around him, silent trees toppling one by one in a forest, the roar of the battle deafening him to everything as he fought in desperate hand-to-hand combat with his own kind. His own kind.

"Beware our own kind," Niall had said, and now he understood. Mercenaries . . . traitors, pushing the center of their line back up the hill, step by desperate step.

Melangell washed wounds in clean water and applied hasty bandages, but there was little else she or any of them could do beyond that. Cai stood in the chariot beside Mac Oag to get a better view of the battle, his face grim but his eyes bright with eagerness. Nervously he fingered his spear, anxious to be on the field with his friends.

Calgacus saw the center of his army being pushed a third of the way up the slope but still fighting back valiantly, and he seized his opportunity. Sending out orders, he watched the two wings of his forces suddenly turn, advance, and press inward on the forward thrust of the Romans. A delirious cheer rose from his men when the startled enemy found themselves almost surrounded and fought back wildly in several directions at once.

"Go," Brennos said to Cai and Mac Oag, who were nearly bursting in their eagerness to be off when they saw the tide of battle turn in their favor. "Win your trophies in this battle. I will watch Melangell and the chariot."

With a loud shout Cai leapt over the side of the chariot, startling the horses. He and Mac Oag raced down the mountainside, disappearing in the rising cloud of dust.

Melangell bandaged a wounded leg and stood, smiling happily. "All is going well, then?" she said, peering below her through the haze.

"Aye." Brennos grinned. "We are strangling them in one of their own maneuvers."

The cavalry of the Romans now advanced, trying to deflect the attack along one flank or open up an escape route for their troops, but when their large horses galloped up the rock-strewn slope, they slipped, fell, slid into one another in a shrilly screaming confusion.

Brennos' gray eyes glittered with all the excitement of his Celtic blood as he watched. "Stay to the hillside is what Niall said, and by the gods, he was right!" he whooped.

Melangell stood at his side, her hands clenched together, a wild eagerness burning within her. The Roman cavalry collapsed, tangled upon itself, tried vainly to rise, and withdrew, to cheers from the excited men, who streamed down the hillside to finish the kill.

"Gods above, you were right!" the druid laughed. "We will rule the world with this one!" He looked down at the girl, but her face had suddenly gone gray.

"What are they doing?" she gasped.

"Who?" he said, following her gaze. "Our men? They are rushing forward to finish them off—"

"No!" she screamed. "They are not supposed to! Niall said to stay on the hillside . . . to guard the right flank! Look! There is no right flank! No! Stop them!"

"Melangell! Stop!" he said firmly. "They have won! See? Even now they pursue the Romans . . ."

His voice died away as wild shouts rose up from their right. The men who had streamed eagerly down the slopes a moment before now paused, turned, and in wild panic swept across the mountainside, hotly pursued by five hundred Roman cavalrymen who had circled around, found an easier access, and now raced almost unhindered across the field. The gathered Highland workmen and merchants, unused to such a sight, fled in terror, leaving only the trained warriors to try to halt the Roman hordes.

The druids ran forward, not believing their eyes, as the women screamed and fled into the woods. Wounded men, hobbling, limping, crawling, disappeared over the crest of the mountain. The leading edge of the tide of fleeing men reached them, and one by one the waiting charioteers whipped their mounts into action, trying to descend the jammed slopes to pick up their chiefs, a few turning and flying over the mountaintop to safety, panicked men scrambling to get onto the racing vehicles.

"Stop!" Melangell screamed, running out to face the mob of terrified men. "You cowards! Stop! Go back! Go back, you cowards!" The men rushed madly around her, throwing down weapons, battle standards, cloaks, and shields in their haste to escape. Lacha plastered himself to her side, growling and lunging at anyone who brushed too close.

Brennos grabbed her arm and nearly threw her into

Nechtan's chariot. "Wait here for me!" he shouted, pulling out his sword from beneath his robe, a grim look on his face. Grasping the arched wicker sides of the vehicle, she watched the other druids, all except the oldest, follow Brennos' lead, draw their swords, and run down the slope, their black robes flying like a flock of ravens descending on the carnage.

Lacha snarled savagely and lunged when a wild-eyed man attempted to board the chariot and fell away when faced with the slashing fangs of the dog. The girl looked around desperately for a weapon . . . anything. The dust was choking her, rising to the mountaintop in a thick yellow cloud, muffling the shouts and blaring horns, the screams and clanging, neighing and crashing as small groups of men tried to rally, turned, and plunged back into the dust, savagely attacking the Roman cavalry bearing down on them.

"Nechtan!" Melangell screamed wildly as panic seized her. Picking up the reins and whip, she lashed the horses and almost fell when they leapt forward, madly pounding straight downward, into the maelstrom of fighting men, fleeing men, dying men. . . .

Brennos, Ethal, and Diuran fought side by side, trying to rally the men by their example, hacking skillfully at the horses that bore down on them, and seeming to attract more than their share of action by their black druids' robes. At the sound of a shout, Brennos turned, momentarily frozen when he saw Nechtan's chariot go thundering past, Melangell clinging desperately to the sides and obviously unable to control the highly trained horses.

He did not see the spear flying toward him and turned just as Ethal lunged forward, intercepted it, and fell to the ground, dead. Grabbing Diuran's sleeve, he pulled him sideways, hacking and pushing through the surging armies, trying to reach Melangell.

"Look!" Cathal shouted, and Nechtan turned briefly. They had fought their way backward up the slope, trying to reach safety but always pursued by the raging Germans. Blood ran down his leg, his arms felt like lead, but still he forced his weary body to fight on, to retreat, to escape. There was no hope here . . . all was lost.

A fire of rage rose within him when he saw his own chariot rapidly approaching, wild and uncontrolled, driven not by Mac Oag but by a panic-stricken Melangell, pulling desperately but futilely on the reins. With an anguished cry he stabbed and sliced with his sword, Cathal at his side, trying frantically to extricate himself, to save his wife.

"A druid!" the cry went up, and the enemy soldiers pulled away to his left, after the rampaging chariot and the black-clad girl. And then, to his astonishment, he saw a large dark stallion bearing down on it, two bearded men on its back racing at breakneck speed to catch it, the one to the rear leaning out desperately when they reached the flying vehicle; and in that instant, as if a door had suddenly opened to reveal an entire stunning view, Nechtan knew what he must do to end the curse on his son. He could try to get away today, survive to face his future death at the hands of his own sweet Melangell; or he could meet his end now, voluntarily, and spare his son the awful curse that had haunted his own life. It was not a woman who had begun the curse, he realized; it was a man. To end it, a man must die, a sacrifice himself. Either way, he was doomed. The choice was his to make. . . .

His mother's Celtic blood had bequeathed to him his height and his eyes. Now he drew on yet another gift she had given him. Flinging aside his Roman weapon, he drew his own sword as a hot battle furor welled within him. Snarling savagely, he charged forward, his sword whirling overhead, leading his men down into the pressing mass of Germans and Romans and Gauls, trying to divert them from the flying chariot. A free man! he cried out as he went. My son shall live as I die . . . a free man.

He saw from the corner of his eye the chariot slow, turn, and race back up the slope. She is yours now, Genann, he thought grimly, fighting on. You have saved her . . . she is yours.

Melangell screamed in terror when a Roman tried to leap onto the chariot and fell back, Lacha ripping at his throat. The dog tumbled from the back of the vehicle as the horses fled down the mountainside, and the girl heard a few savage snarls amid the chaos, then silence. Suddenly she became aware of a large dark horse bearing down on her from her left, and she turned in panic when a bearded man leaned out toward her, reaching for the side of the chariot as the horse drew near. Raising the whip, she lashed out at the man. He jumped into the chariot beside her, reaching for the reins in her hand and shouting hoarsely to her as he did so.

"No! Melangell! It is Genann . . . no!"

Then Calum vaulted atop one of the wild-eyed chariot horses, pulling frantically at their bridles to slow them, turn them, head them back up the crowded slope.

"No! Stop!" the girl screamed, savagely fighting Genann to get the reins away from him. "I must save Nechtan! No!"

She pulled at his arm, dug her nails into his hands until they bled, pounded him with her fists.

"Don't," she pleaded desperately when he clamped her firmly against himself with one arm. "I must save Nechtan."

Kicking and biting, she tried to get free of his grasp. Calum turned the horses and, leaning low over them for protection, raced them up the mountainside. When the chariot turned, Genann saw Nechtan glance quickly in his direction, still fighting bravely against the encroaching Germans. Then Cathal went down, rose briefly, and fell again. As the chariot clattered away, Genann looked one last time over his shoulder. Nechtan was nowhere to be seen.

Brennos and Diuran ran frantically, hotly pursued by several eager Romans. Brennos' left arm hung limp and useless at his side, his shoulder nearly severed by a sword blow. Despite the pain, the blood soaking his robe, he tried to fight on, supported by Diuran when his feet slipped on the gory hillside.

Calum saw the two druids and pulled the horses to a trot. They ran forward, the Romans on their heels, and Diuran thrust his stumbling friend toward the vehicle. Turning, he ran headlong back toward the Roman swords.

Melangell and Genann grabbed the slumping Brennos and pulled him into the chariot. Calum whipped the horses away; the girl cradled the druid's head in her lap and Genann stood astride his body, slashing his sword at the Romans who raced after them. He could see the other druid lying on the hillside, his body a trampled, bloody heap.

"Faster!" he shouted to Calum. The horses, more sure-footed than their Roman counterparts, gradually pulled away, flew to the crest of the mountain, shot over the top, and vanished into the encircling woods.

"Halt!" a voice shouted, and Cai slowly dropped his sword. He, Mac Oag, and Melwas had joined up together and had nearly reached their chief when pandemonium broke out and, turning, they had fled.

Now several Romans surrounded them, their faces stern. Melwas tossed his sword to the ground and it clattered jarringly on the rocks.

"Move," one soldier ordered, and the three obediently walked down the mountainside. Reaching the bottom, they were forced forward, toward the Roman encampment and a large group of chained captives.

"See what a little taste of Roman slavery will do to these barbarians, eh?" one legionary joked to another as they pushed them to the camp.

Melwas spied the chains being readied for him and in a final desperate burst of energy bolted from the group, racing madly for the cover of the nearby brush. Feet pounded after him, he felt a violent blow to his back, and he sprawled headlong to the ground, his mouth full of dirt. He tried once to rise, knew it was useless, and lay still, waiting for death to overtake him and feeling for the last time the cool, sweet soil beneath his cheek.

Cai stood tight-lipped while iron manacles clamped his wrists behind his back. By the time the Romans led him away with the other captives, Melwas' body had already been stripped and dragged from the camp.

The chariot raced crazily through the woods, weaving in and out of the trees, swerving to avoid fleeing people, animals, vehicles. They could hear Roman patrols crashing through the forests behind them, coarse shouts, frenzied screams. . . .

Midday approached before they slowed to a walk. Calum hung wearily over the horse's neck and Melangell still cradled Brennos' pale face in her arms. He winced and gasped with each jolt of the chariot, and she looked up at Genann in desperation.

"We must stop so I can help him."

"Soon. Down the next slope, and we will stop."

The sounds of pursuit were rapidly fading and the Roman cavalry seemed to have given up their hunt. An occasional shadowed figure crept silently through the trees around them, another refugee fleeing to the north. Feeling safer, Calum pulled the exhausted horses to a halt in a little glade and jumped stiffly to the ground. He and Genann lifted the druid from the floor of the chariot and laid him under a tree before unharnessing the two horses. Melangell knelt at Brennos' side and began to pull off his bloody robe, but his hand reached for her wrist and he stopped her.

"No," he said weakly. "I will die as a druid. It has been my life."

"Let me help you!" she protested. "I must see it!"

"No," he sighed. "There is nothing you or I can do for it now. My life is over."

"No! Don't say that! I can help you!"

He smiled wanly and shook his head. "No, my dear. Not this time, I'm afraid."

He gasped aloud as pain flared through him, and the girl ran her hand gently over his clammy forehead, fighting back the tears in her eyes.

"Brennos?" she whispered. He looked up at her.

"One favor, before I go?" he asked quietly.

"Anything."

"Kiss me."

Melangell looked into his gentle gray eyes, now so filled with suffering, and read things there she had not seen before. Smiling, she nodded and softly pressed her lips to his. When she lifted her head and looked at him, he ran his hand lightly down her cheek, and it was the touch, not of a druid or a physician, but of a man.

"Another time, perhaps . . ." he whispered, and she clenched his hand in hers.

"Yes . . . another time."

He smiled at her answer and looked aside. Genann approached, leading one of the chariot horses. Melangell released the druid's hand and Genann helped her to her feet.

"You must give Calum your black robe," Genann said tersely.

"No! I am a druidess! I will not—"

"Time grows short," Calum snapped. "I must have it if I am to attempt to save your life."

She ceased her protests and looked at the tracker, dumbfounded, as understanding came to her. Without a word she pulled the robe off and handed it to him, pinning his dusty cloak around her shoulders instead.

"For my son's life," he said simply, pulling the exhausted horse closer to them and waiting for them to depart.

"But what of Brennos?" she objected. "I cannot go and leave him here like—"

"Go with Genann, Melangell," the druid said weakly. "Calum and I will manage. Have a fine, healthy son for Nechtan. Go."

She looked down at him uncertainly, and a brief, reassuring smile crossed between them. Turning, she allowed Genann to boost her onto the waiting horse. He sprang lightly behind her, wrapped one arm around her, and took the reins from Calum. Brennos watched them walk into the shadows, Melangell turning once to gaze over her shoulder at him.

As soon as the two were gone from sight, Calum stepped to the druid's side. "It is a brave thing you do for her," Brennos said. Calum shrugged.

"I am a tracker. This is my country. I expect I can outwit the Romans easily enough."

Briefly they stared at each other. Abruptly Calum dropped the girl's black robe to the ground, knelt astride the waiting druid, and pulled out his dagger.

"When I nod," Brennos whispered. "And be quick. Like most men, I fear pain."

"Aye," Calum said, positioning the blade above the druid's heart.

Brennos glanced around at the treetops and closed his eyes wearily, his fingers probing the soft forest floor and lifting a crumbling bit of rocky soil.

Let your final thoughts be lofty ones, he told himself, for

that helps determine your entrance into the next lifetime. His fingertips explored the bits of dirt with the intensity of approaching death. Each a tiny jagged orb, complete and perfect; a myriad of grains, each a world unto itself.

A world unto itself. . . .

Once more he was on Mona, a mere boy of ten, sitting on a wide beach as his old teacher put a mound of sand into his plump, childish hand. He stared at the glittering grains in fascination, the sun warm on his back, the sea breeze blowing his hair.

"Such as this is what you are; such as this is the world," the old man said as the tiny bits sparkled and shone in the sunlight. "For you are made up of a myriad of worlds, and our world is but one among many. Where does the one end and the other begin? Where do you stop and start? Infinity upon infinity, boy; infinity upon infinity."

Brennos sighed and his fingers released the soil.

Infinity upon infinity. . . .

Above me, below me, around me, within me . . .

He nodded.

All is one. . . .

Calum stood and wiped his blade before replacing it in his belt. Putting on the girl's black robe, he mounted the remaining horse and quickly trotted off, back toward the searching Romans, to detour them away from Melangell and Genann as they chased what they would think to be another druid.

Night came swiftly to the barren mountains as the horse wearily stumbled and slid down the slopes of wet grass and rock. Reaching a small meadow on the mountainside, Genann pulled the exhausted animal to a halt and dismounted. Reaching up for Melangell, he lifted her to the ground.

"It's too steep now, and I'm afraid the horse might fall," he said. "We must walk."

With his steadying arm around her back, they descended the steep hillside. Melangell soon slumped wearily against him.

"I cannot . . . go on," she sobbed dryly.

Wordlessly he picked her up and carried her down the incline. A waning moon rose over the indigo valley, illuminating his way with a faint, ghostly light. Melangell clung to him weakly, her face buried in his shoulder. Suddenly she gasped and her fingers clenched at the back of his neck.

"What is it?" he whispered, alarmed. She gasped again, her body tensing in a fierce spasm.

"The baby . . . it's coming!" she moaned.

Gods above! he thought wildly, looking around for a place to stop. He spied a rock overhang a few paces away and crept toward it as another spasm wracked the girl.

"Put me down," she panted. He lowered her to the ground and she knelt on all fours, like an animal, her head hanging down until another pain shot through her.

"It is coming." She grimaced. "Help me."

"What do I do?"

"Kneel . . . help me up . . . I must squat."

He pulled her upright and she squatted between his knees, leaning forward in pain.

"Hold me . . . wait till the waters come, and then put a cloak beneath me to catch the baby. And, Genann . . ."

"Yes?"

"I must not scream. Put a gag in my mouth . . . at once."

She heard him pull out his knife and cut a strip of cloth from the old brown cloak he wore. He folded it lengthwise, put it in her mouth, and tied it firmly. Moving close behind her, he wrapped his arms around her and held her as another pain came . . . and another . . .

The moon slipped up into the heavens while they crouched on the ledge, the girl straining against his grasp. The child was ready and it soon slipped out, pink and squirming.

"It's a boy," he said, removing her gag. "Just as you'd said. Nechtan has a son."

She picked up the infant and tied and cut the cord with Genann's knife. "Yes," she sighed, wiping the tiny face with one finger, "Nechtan has a son."

The baby gave out a strangled gurgle. A lusty cry followed, and she pressed him close to silence him. "Hush, little one," she cooed, "don't cry . . . don't cry."

Genann watched her stroke the tiny head, already haloed with Nechtan's dark hair. He did not hear the stealthy footsteps approaching from behind; not until a spear descended between them did he know they had been watched. Seizing his knife, he crouched to defend the startled girl. His gaze rose up along the spear's shaft and he suddenly broke into relieved laughter.

Two men stood beside them, with silver bands on their arms and heavy silver chains around their necks. They both bore blue spiral tattoos on their arms and faces and one wore a splendid cloak of dense otter fur. Genann could see where Nechtan got his looks. These men were dark, intense, hungry-looking. He would not want to tangle with them on a battlefield.

"Gods above!" Genann gasped. "Am I glad to see you! This is the wife of Nechtan, son of Oenghus, son of your King Gest, and she has just borne him a son. We are fleeing the Romans."

"Many are fleeing the Romans," the taller of the two said, putting his spear aside and crouching to look at the baby. The young warrior spoke true, the man noted to himself, studying the ruddy-faced infant; the child's dark hair was Cruithni and came from no Celtic father.

"Come," the man in the otterskin cloak said, "we have a cart."

Genann lifted Melangell and the baby and carried them down to the valley floor. The taller man folded Genann's cloak around the afterbirth and followed them. It must be preserved for ritual disposal by their wise men. The otterskin cloak was spread in the back of a small wooden cart and Genann laid the girl on it. He sat beside her, one arm around her shoulders, and watched her holding the tiny infant in her arms.

"Thank you," she whispered, caressing the small dark head with one hand, "for my life, and my son's life."

She looked up at him and tried to smile, but the tears filling her eyes spoke more eloquently than words: she knew the awful reality of this day, and she accepted it.

Wearily she laid her head on his shoulder. The men took the pony's halter and the cart creaked into motion, the bright half-moon lighting their way to the distant Cruithni village, home of Nechtan's people.

Genann and Melangell were married the following spring, for Nechtan did not return. He died as he had predicted, on the blood-soaked slopes of Mons Graupius, with a Roman spear through his body, and the fire of the Celt in his eyes.

The warriors arose together, together they met, together they attacked, with single purpose; short were their lives, long the mourning left to their kinsmen . . . may their souls get welcome in the land of heaven, the dwelling place of plenty.

—Welsh

BOOK *II*
The Heavens Turn

She is my treasure, she whose eye is green as grass, she who would not put her arm under my head, she who would not lie with me for gold. . . .

Sad is my plight, strange how long I take to die; she who would not come near me, on my oath, she is my love.

—Irish

Ah blackbird, it is well for you where your nest is in the bushes; a hermit that clangs no bell, sweet, soft and peaceful is your call.

—Irish

Part 1

ACHIVIR THE KING

*T*HIN ORANGE FLAMES LAPPED AGAINST THE SKY LIKE SEAWEED along the shore; orange on blue, yellow to gray, snapping and crackling in a rising swell until Melangell turned away, sick at the sight, and groped for the steadying arm of her son.

"Resad . . ." she gasped, feeling her knees grow weak beneath her as the finality of the day descended.

"It's all right, Mother," he consoled her, his arms strong and supporting. She leaned heavily against him, fighting back the tears as he held her close.

What's to become of me now? she thought desperately as the fire grew to a roar behind her. She could not watch . . . must not see. Genann is dead, and I am alone. Alone. . . .

"No!" she cried out, throwing her cry heavenward with the ascending smoke of his funeral pyre.

Genann . . . no . . .

They laid him to rest beside his two dead children, his ashes in a clay urn, the urn placed within a rough box of stone slabs set into the ground. Only a handful of people attended the burial: Genann's widow and their two surviving children, frail Anor, an ethereal-looking girl of sixteen, and Cadvan, only twelve but already as sturdy and stocky as his grandfather Conn had been. The son of Nechtan whom Genann had raised as his own, proud Resad, stood behind his mother, his dark hair whipped by the gale coming in off the northern sea, his intense blue eyes gentle with concern as he watched her shoulders heave with desperate sobs. Beside him stood his best friend, Drosten, clad in a dark sealskin cape, a brown wool tunic, and the native leather breeches. He was tall for a Cruithni but still not matching Resad in height. Drosten's brown eyes were on Anor, that delicate flower who lit his life as no other could do, and at every movement that looked like a faint, he started toward her, ready to catch her should she collapse under the weight of her emotions. Despite her frail appearance, her delicate coloring, Anor was as tough as her Celtic blood would allow, and she clenched her mother's hand tightly, one arm around the woman's quaking shoulders, seeming to forget her own grief while she consoled her. To Resad's left stood stout old Severa, serving woman from King Achivir's household, fighting valiantly for control as the man she had loved like a son was consigned to the earth before her. Apart from the druid Broichan, quietly chanting the appropriate rituals for the dead, that was all. And it did not escape the notice of either Resad or Drosten that the king for whom Genann had played and sung so faithfully for eighteen years was not present, nor had he sent a single envoy on his behalf.

Out of the entire Cruithni village, only seven people came to Genann's funeral.

Perhaps such a callous betrayal, Resad thought grimly, only adds to the intensity of my mother's heartbreak.

Every morning Melangell left her tiny stone home in the Pictish town shortly after sunrise, a heavy wool cloak clenched against the ocean breezes as she wandered the lonely moors along the clifftop; and every morning her children watched her go, unable to dissuade her, unable to lighten her grief, and increasingly concerned about their mother's unrelenting pain. The world no longer seemed to interest her; she had lost all will to live.

"She cannot forget the accident," Anor said quietly, kneeling by the stone hearth kneading bread. "She cries out in the night; it haunts her during the day . . ."

Lifting her pale blue eyes, she glanced across the hut to her half-brother. Resad seemed to be working a small piece of deerhide, rubbing it to a buttery softness, but she could tell his restless mind, like hers, churned with worry.

"And Cadvan?" he said suddenly, meeting her gaze.

She paused her kneading and sat back on her heels. "I

think he still mourns our father too much to notice much else. But I feel he is aware of Mother's pain, in his own immature way. You know how boys his age are, Resad—so puffed with pride and self-importance at their learning to be warriors."

"It has been five years now?" he asked, putting aside the deerhide.

"Yes." She resumed her work. "Five years since his warrior's training began. He is away much of the time, and I hear he practices unceasingly. They say he is very good for his age."

"Then it is just as well that he is not preoccupied with our mother's grief. Let him stay concerned with his training. It's best for him, I suppose."

"But what can we do for Mother, Resad?" the girl went on, slamming the dough to a flat stone with a satisfying thud. "So many she has cared about, and all met with tragic ends. Her mother, her uncle, the druids Esus and Brennos, your own father, and now my father. I think she is afraid to care anymore."

"And what is hardest," the young man mused, "is that she has never liked horses that much. It must have been horrifying for her, riding behind her husband when suddenly his horse slips and he vanishes over the edge of a cliff. I know she was screaming and babbling when they brought her home, half out of her mind from shock, and it was all I could do to calm her. She watched him fall, Anor . . . all the way down, the horse thrashing and tumbling atop him . . . and there was not a thing she could do."

Anor blinked back tears, her eyes gazing absently at the lump of coarse dough. "I know, Resad," she whispered, "I know."

A light tap outside interrupted them and they looked up to see Drosten enter the low wooden doorway, his dark eyes catching at once the grief on the face of the girl.

"I might have some good news for you," he said, seating himself on a stool beside Resad. Anor resumed her work, cutting the dough into smaller pieces and rolling them into neat round loaves. She stood, wiping her messy hands, and crossed to the far wall, pulling down several dry bunches of herbs. Drosten had watched her grow from a skinny child to a graceful woman, and he'd been ready to ask Genann for her to be his wife when the accident happened. Now, he knew, it was out of the question—for a while, at least. She must stay with her mother, help to care for her, until he could accumulate enough wealth and position to provide for them both, or until Melangell could chance upon another life of her own . . . which was why he'd come to call.

"I have talked with my uncle," he began, turning to look at Resad, whose amused smile at his friend's moonstruck gaze turned to abrupt interest at his words.

"Yes?" Resad prodded.

"I have asked him to try to find out the king's intentions toward your mother and you, her family, in light of Genann's faithful service for so many years."

"It is no doubt as I suspected," Resad muttered darkly. "He only provided for them out of kindness, because my father was a kinsman."

"Resad!" Anor spoke in shock, the knife she was using to chop the herbs poised in midair.

"Well, it's true," he retorted. "Achivir has no love for music, no matter how talented your father was. He was wasted here."

"Regardless," Drosten continued, "my uncle dines with the king tomorrow, to report to him on the status of the crops and herds. He will bring up the subject then. I'll tell you as soon as I hear something."

Silence descended on the room and the two young men watched Anor flatten the bottom of each round loaf in the chopped herbs, then put them on an iron slab mounted by the hearth. Soon the warm fragrance of baking bread and browning herbs filled the room.

"Will you stay and dine with us?" Anor asked, stirring a great iron kettle of stew suspended over the fire and glancing at Drosten shyly.

"It would be my greatest pleasure," he replied solemnly, gazing back at her.

"Come then," Resad said, rising to his feet. "We must go and fetch Mother. Once again she has spent the day wandering the moors."

* * *

Anor insisted on dressing her mother's hair and getting out one of her best gowns to wear. Despite her daughter's reassurances, Melangell still felt a bit foolish at the splendid-looking reflection that met her in the small silver mirror. For days, since Genann's death, her appearance had mattered little and she had contented herself with looking as drab as a sparrow. But this was an important presentation, Anor had explained; her future and the future of her family could rest on its outcome. She was still a young and attractive woman, and a little feminine charm never hurt any man. So their precious oak tub was dragged out and Melangell was made to bathe and scent herself with fragrant herbs. Bathing was not customary among the Cruithni, but she and Genann had insisted on it for themselves and their children, and now her daughter insisted on it for her.

"You look beautiful, Mother!" Anor smiled, adjusting the bronze brooch on her cloak and looking her up and down with a critical eye.

"I feel a fool," Melangell answered, patting tentatively at her braided and curled hair. In her youth she would have welcomed such finery, for the feast at Conn's farm, her marriage to Nechtan . . . "I must go," she muttered, turning abruptly and walking to the door. "Is Drosten waiting?"

"Yes, Mother. He is outside."

"Good," she replied, flinging the wooden door open with no little irritation. *They treat me as if I am a child . . . or an old dottard. I am neither; I can choose my own life. I need no keepers and nursemaids.*

Her anger eased when she stepped out under the leaden gray sky and Drosten stood to greet her. She had always liked him.

"If I were an older man, lady, you would not need to see the king today, for I would claim you as my own." He grinned, sweeping a grand bow before her.

"You jest, Drosten!" Melangell laughed, placing her hand on his arm. He chatted amiably while they strolled the narrow, twisting streets, and she studied his face intently. He had always reminded her a bit of Nechtan, so much so that at times it hurt to see him. The same dark hair, the same mouth, the same lopsided grin. *Perhaps they are*

371

distant kin, she mused, turning away from him. She knew he had eyes for her daughter, and she had long suspected a proposal was in the offing. If Genann had consented or not would be a different matter; Anor had always been his pet, spoiled and indulged and doted on no end. Melangell didn't know if she would have agreed to the match, either. Drosten was of a good family, highly placed, wealthy, but he was Cruithni and Anor was not. Melangell wasn't at all sure she wanted her grandchildren to be half-breeds like Nechtan had been, a product of two worlds yet belonging to neither. . . .

"Here we are," Drosten said, interrupting her thoughts. She gazed up at a massive gateway, the stones rough and dark under the cloudy sky, while Drosten spoke briefly in their tongue to the two stern guards who flanked it. Satisfied with his explanations, the men rapped on an iron-bound wooden door and stood aside for Drosten to guide his charge into the palace.

She had been there a few times with Genann when he went to play a banquet or a reception, but her stomach still fluttered nervously when they crossed the inner passageway and stepped into the cool gloom of the building opposite. It was Achivir's own residence, almost splendid in its spareness and austerity. It was the home of a man, lived in by men, guarded and cared for and tidied by men. No woman's touch brightened it anywhere, save a few servants, cooks, and laundrywomen. And they did the bidding of men. Its very masculinity frightened her, and she suddenly wished she did not look so fine and feminine. Dark laughing warriors fell silent when they passed; lounging princes and royal kinsmen watched her walk by, their brown eyes quick and intense. Drosten too seemed to have noticed them, and his free hand went casually to the sword at his side.

To her great relief, they were finally admitted to the private room of the king, and her tensions eased when she heard the door shut solidly behind them. Achivir sat near the central hearth, deep in conversation with two of his counselors, but he stood as soon as he saw her waiting.

"Leave us," he said, waving his hand toward the men. Silently they gathered their wooden tallies and tablets and left, and at a nod from the king, Drosten followed them from the room.

Melangell could not forget his neglect of Genann's burial, and when he put an arm around her shoulders in a brotherly gesture, she was not for an instant deceived.

"I am so sorry about your loss," the king said gently, his voice carrying the peculiar lilting accent of the Cruithni when speaking her tongue. "A king could have asked for no finer musician or more loyal servant. We miss your husband already; he brought a touch of culture to this barren pile of rocks."

He guided her to the wide central hearth and she was relieved when he insisted she sit on the stone bench his counselors had vacated. His nearness made her uncomfortable.

"And now what's to be done for you?" he said, seating himself opposite her and studying her face. "You are still a lovely woman. Why don't you remarry?"

She gazed back at him, refusing to be awed. "I do not wish to," she replied.

"But surely you must have prospects! Most widows have many suitors who suddenly appear on their doorsteps, especially widows as attractive as you."

"No." She shook her head. "I have no suitors, no prospects. You forget, perhaps, that I am an outsider here. What man would want a foreigner for a wife?"

"Then what do you intend to do to support yourself and your family? I hear from my men that your young daughter is as lovely as a flower. What of her future, her suitors, her dowry, if you have no income or means of support?"

Melangell stiffened uncomfortably at the very mention of Anor and "his men," and her fingers clenched in her lap. She well knew how soldiers could be with women; she did not like the idea at all.

"She has a suitor," she replied tightly. "She is already spoken for."

"Indeed? Then that is fortunate for you, isn't it, my dear? And what of your two sons? The elder is a warrior now, as his father was, and no longer lives in your house. What of the younger boy?"

"He is in training. He is seldom home; he lives with his teachers and the other boys."

"So then, when your daughter weds, you will be alone. And then what will you do?"

She didn't like the persistence of his questions, or the uncomfortable direction they seemed to be taking. Abruptly she looked down, turning her fingers nervously. "I suppose I would live with Anor and her husband," she muttered almost apologetically. "I hadn't thought about it. Everything has been so sudden. I . . ." She found herself wishing she could leave; the harsh reality of the situation suddenly thrust before her was too unsettling.

"I know, my dear," Achivir said calmly, reaching out and placing one strong hand atop hers. "That is why I have been giving it some thought."

Something in his voice frightened Melangell, and she refused to look up and meet his gaze.

"As you know, my wife died many years ago. Childbearing did not suit her. I never took another." He paused, waiting for some response from her and getting none. "You are lovely enough and cultured enough that I would take you for my wife . . ."

Melangell gasped and looked up at him in shock.

". . . but of course," he went on, "I cannot do that. It is our custom that the inheritance comes through the mother. For that reason, my wife must be of royal Cruithni blood. But still, there might be a way . . ."

His hand closed firmly around hers as his dark eyes studied her face. He had that same probing, intense gaze Nechtan had had, and she turned away awkwardly. She didn't want to hear any more of what the king had to say; she'd heard too much already.

"It would benefit you, and me, and your family, if you were to become my mistress," he concluded, leaning toward her as his voice dropped away.

"Mistress?" she croaked, looking down at the rough stone slabs of the floor. "I cannot—"

"Before you answer," he interrupted, "think it over well. Your family, your children, would be under my protection. I would see that they are well provided for, that your daughter has a suitable dowry and a fine wedding. You would live here in my palace, in your own quarters, with a serving woman and every comfort you could want. . . ."

She lifted her head and looked at him levelly. "Until I grew too old or you tired of me. And then what?"

He shrugged, releasing her hand and sitting back. "Live with one of your children then, unless you had given me a few children of my own. Then your position would be assured to the end of your days, for a Cruithni does not neglect his children, nor the women who bear them."

The king stood abruptly, smoothed the creases in his heavy brown wool tunic, and walked to the door. Melangell took it as a sign her meeting with him was finished. Rising, she silently followed him, studying his back, his broad, stocky shoulders, the powerful muscles beneath the long leather breeches he wore. He must be fifty or older, yet he was still fit and nice-looking for a man his age. A little gray in his hair, a few lines around his eyes, a waist that had thickened from his youth, yet he was vigorous and active enough. But could she ever consent to such a thing?

Achivir rested his hand on the massive iron door latch, turning and looking down at Melangell's bewildered face. "Take your time," he said quietly, "think it over. I am in no hurry. When your bed has grown too cold at night, I think you will see the wisdom of my words."

She expected him to grab her, to kiss her, something . . . but he did nothing, merely opened the door and let her out. Drosten, squatting in the shadows while chatting with the other guards, rose to meet her. The king summoned one of his stewards into the room.

"Well?" the man said, glancing over his shoulder at Melangell's retreating figure.

"See that the three small rooms by the wall are cleaned and furnished," Achivir said, his voice low and certain.

"Then she has agreed?" the steward asked.

"Not yet," the king replied, a slow smile spreading across his face as he caught the man's eye, "but she will . . . she will."

They stopped at a food stand perched beneath a tattered leather roof in the tradesmen's quarters and Drosten insisted on getting a cup of warm, fresh ale for Melangell. The paleness of her cheeks, the grim set to her mouth, alarmed him. They perched atop a low stone wall and he watched her absently sip the drink, her mind obviously dwelling elsewhere. She seemed unwilling to speak of what had happened at the palace, but his curiosity would not be stilled.

"Has the king any plans for you?" he probed. Melangell lowered the wooden cup to her lap, cradling it in both hands, and took a deep breath.

"Drosten," she began, her discomfort evident, "what do you know of Achivir? What kind of man is he?"

He shrugged. "A man, that's all. A fair enough king. With him the people have been content, prosperous, and secure, which is the main function of any king, I suppose."

"But as a man, Drosten. A person. What of him then?" she urged, looking up, and he could see a puzzling worry in her green eyes.

"A man?" he began. "I don't know. Kings don't usually let such things be known. Their mystery is part of their power. To know that one suffers from wind and has a sweet tooth is a bit demeaning. I know he loved his wife dearly and was crushed by her death. I assume any man capable of such love could not be too bad a person. Why do you ask?"

"Because," she said, returning her gaze to the dark ale, "he wants me to live in the palace and . . . and be his mistress."

Drosten's face darkened at her words and his hands clenched into angry fists. "And surely you said no . . ." he began, and was horrified at the placid look that greeted him when she lifted her head. "Forgive me, lady, but you must be mad to even consider such a thing. What life would you have? The palace is full of men, nothing but men, and Achivir himself . . ."

He stopped abruptly when he saw tears filling her eyes.

"I know, Drosten," she whispered, "but what choice do I have? How can I provide for my family? How can I arrange a dowry for Anor?"

He looked away angrily. "I care little for a dowry. You know that. My family is wealthy enough."

"Nevertheless, I would not humiliate Anor and shame my family by having none."

376

"And so you would prostitute yourself for your honor?" he snapped. "It makes no sense at all."

Tears spilled down her cheeks at the harshness of his words and she wiped them awkwardly with one hand. "I have not yet decided," she whispered. "Perhaps I can try to live on my own. Resume my healings. Sell embroideries . . . I don't know . . . there must be something I can do."

"Yes." He tried to sound encouraging. "Resad and I will help. We can finance Cadvan's training for you. And as for Anor, I will wed her as soon as it can be arranged. Then she will be my concern, and not yours."

She looked at him, gratitude lighting her eyes, and nodded. How could I ever have doubted the wisdom in letting him marry my daughter? she wondered. I could ask for no finer kinsman.

"You have my permission, Drosten, and my prayers for your future happiness. Please . . . say nothing to the others about this. Let's hope things work out so that I can tell Achivir no, as I should. We will have to let the fates decide."

They roused at the sound of a brief tap on the door, and Anor, curious, rose from her grass pallet, pulling a cloak around her shift and glancing at the faint gray light that trickled in around the small shuttered window. It must be early dawn, she mused; who can have come at this hour?

Her mother, too, was awake and puzzled, her hand going fearfully to the long dagger she always slept with since Genann's death. Anor cautiously opened the door a crack, peering out into the misty morning gloom. She could see no one outside. Pulling the door open, she stuck her head out, glancing up and down the silent street. No one was to be seen. As she turned to close the door, her eyes fell on a large wicker box sitting by the step.

"Mother! Look!" Anor gasped. Melangell rose and crossed the packed dirt floor. Together the two women dragged the heavy chest into the room and over to the dim light from the central hearth.

377

"Open it, Mother!" Anor squealed, as excited as when she was a child and her father brought her little surprises from his banquets at the palace. Smiling, Melangell untied the leather thong that held the lid in place. Who on earth can have sent this? she wondered. If it was a gift from Resad or Drosten, they would not have been so secretive. Then who else?

Anor gasped aloud when the lid came off, and Melangell suddenly knew the source of the mysterious gift.

Achivir.

Folded in the top of the chest was a splendid wool cloak, dyed with woad the favorite Cruithni blue, and delicately embroidered in silver and gold threads. Melangell lifted it out, almost afraid to touch it, it looked so exquisite. A small scrap of Roman paper fell from its folds, and Anor snatched it up. "What does it say, Mother?" the girl puzzled, studying the black markings it bore. "Perhaps it is the name of the person who sent this."

Just as Melangell knew a few words of the Cruithni language, so also she knew a few words of the Roman writing the Picts sometimes used in their official records. "No, Anor," she answered, glancing at the marks on the paper. "It is not our benefactor. It is my name."

Anor grinned wickedly, her pale blue eyes shining. "Mother! You have a suitor . . . and a very rich one, at that. How splendid! Now all your worries will be over."

"Yes," Melangell sighed, folding the blue cloak and putting it aside. "See what else is in here."

She let Anor have the fun of unpacking the chest, and derived more pleasure from the girl's feverish excitement than she did from the gift itself. A matching blue wool gown with long sleeves came out next, and then an ornate silver neck chain such as the Picts were fond of wearing; a pair of soft leather boots; and food boxes of aged cheese, spiced beans, rich hazelnut cakes. Even a small Roman glass flagon of wine. He seemed to have sent an entire meal.

"Wait till Resad and Drosten see this!" Anor gasped, opening a wooden box and lifting out a rich dark cake heavy with fruit. "I have not eaten so well in months, Mother! I am so sick of herbed bread and stew and gruel. We must have a feast tonight!"

"Yes," Melangell sighed, tearing off a chunk of the cake and savoring it, "we will have a feast tonight."

By the time the fourth box arrived a week later, Melangell knew she could not deceive her family much longer as to their source. With every new delivery, Anor's curiosity increased tenfold, Resad's keen suspicions rose higher, and Drosten's mood darkened. He was not deceived by Melangell's feigned ignorance; he knew full well the identity of her benefactor. And soon, she feared, the others must be told as well.

But suddenly, as abruptly as the boxes had come, they stopped. Anor's heart fell when each dawn greeted her with another empty doorstep and a dwindling supply of food. Melangell missed the luxuries, but she was also relieved; perhaps Achivir had changed his mind. Despite the contributions of flour, barley, ale, and beans brought by Resad and Drosten, she knew their supplies would not last much longer; she must soon give in to Achivir, or find some way to support herself, no easy task for a woman alone.

It soon became plain that the Cruithni knew nothing of her healing abilities and medical knowledge, and showed scant interest once they found out. They were not a mystic race as the Celts were. They cared little for trances and miracles, unseen presences and unknown quantities. To them life was what surrounded them. Their needs were met by the druid Broichan and a few midwives in the village. What did they care for some flaxen-haired alien woman who was said to possess strange gifts? Such a thing was of no concern to them. In desperation, Melangell turned to her embroideries for a livelihood.

The bronze needle stabbed Melangell's finger for the third time that evening. She winced and sucked it in frustration, stretching her cramped back and trying to shift to a more comfortable position.

"Mother," Anor said, rolling over on her pallet and eyeing her in concern, "why don't you come to bed? It is late, and you can barely see by the firelight. Finish that in the morning."

"I can't," Melangell answered tiredly. "The old woman

379

needed this shawl finished in three days, and if it is not ready in time, I might not get paid. A small wheel of cheese and some bread will last us several days."

Anor shook her head and stared at the firelight dancing against the low sod ceiling. "So much work, for so little pay, Mother!" she gently chided her. "You exhaust yourself. Your sewing is the finest in the town, yet you let people take advantage of you. Cheese and bread for three days' work!"

Melangell shrugged and leaned toward the hearth, trying to get more light on the running spirals she was sewing along one edge of the fine wool shawl. "It is enough to live on," she muttered absently as she worked. "If I ask too much, I might find myself with no job. Go to sleep. I'll be finished with this soon, and then I, too, will retire. Now I must concentrate."

Anor rolled over, facing the cold stone wall, and pulled a thick wool blanket over her ears. Her worry over her mother was mercifully brief, for the girl was exhausted from her own day's labors at housekeeping, and she soon fell into a deep, restful sleep.

Melangell worked until near high moon, and by the time she stopped, her eyes burned and her body ached. But she did not retire. Folding the shawl and putting it with her other work, she opened a wicker chest and lifted out a beautiful gown of pale green wool. Anor didn't know it, but the wool she'd used to make it was part of her payment from one client; a special arrangement with the village dyer produced the soft green color in exchange for an embroidered belt for his wife; various threads set aside from her many jobs provided the startlingly vivid embroidery of a Celtic Vine of Life, twining around the neckline and cascading down the front of the gown in riotous abandon. It was breathtaking, she had to admit, holding it out at arm's length and examining it. And it would be Anor's wedding dress.

"Genann," she whispered to herself as she sat by the fire and began to work on the gown, "I can afford no dowry for our daughter, but I will see to it that she is the loveliest bride ever to grace this barren stone village."

She suddenly found her concentration wavering as her eyes filled with tears. She wiped them slowly with one hand, trying to avoid spotting the precious dress. It seemed like only yesterday . . . her own wedding to Genann. A small feast provided by Achivir's uncle. A gown given her by one of the village women. The newly awakening earth of spring a stark contrast to the horrors that still plagued her soul. All the loss, all the death. She had thought she could never forget Nechtan, and Genann had patiently waited with her for the return they both knew would never come. He had worked hard to purchase a harp, with which he supported her and her infant son for many months, as kindly and loyally as the most solicitous brother. And when their wedding night finally came, he held her tenderly, letting her cry out all her desolation into his willing arms. He had waited so long for her; what was one more night? He realized the last man to love her had been Nechtan, and he knew the memory would never leave her soul.

Melangell sighed deeply, folded the gown, and returned it to the wicker chest. I am too tired to continue, she told herself. And besides, my heart is not in it tonight.

Silently she lay on her pallet, staring stiffly at the fire, and let the tears flow freely. Genann, how I miss you! she sobbed quietly. My life closed on the day yours ended, and now all that is left to me is to see my children safely on their way. Beyond that, I am nothing.

Resad's handsome face clouded and he turned away from his friend angrily. "Why didn't you tell me this before?" he snapped, clenching his fists at his sides.

"She asked me not to. I gave her my word," Drosten answered, studying Resad's grim expression. He looked ready to strike him; he couldn't really blame him if he did.

"Then why tell me now? Why not continue the deception?" Resad said, cutting his piercing blue eyes around to bore into Drosten's.

"Because I think Achivir has something planned . . . some trick or two at hand, to force your mother to his will. I have seen signs, heard things . . ."

"What things?"

"Gossip, mostly. The mothers, aunts, and sisters of our fellow warriors who would do business with your mother are suddenly discouraged from doing so. Her work is very fine; she could easily earn enough to live comfortably, were it not for the . . . discreet pressures."

"What kind of pressures?" Resad said suspiciously, turning to gaze out across the dark evening sea below the cliff where they stood. Drosten paused, pulling his fur cloak to against the chill wind and trying to compose his thoughts. His friend's temper was too short to risk saying the wrong thing to him.

"There are," he went on, "a few who would even go to your mother for cures, but they are dissuaded by Broichan. At first a simple word was sufficient, but now he resorts to other tricks."

"Such as?"

"Rumors. Resad, you will not like this, but you must keep your head and think clearly what to do. He says she is a witch, in league with demons, and children have died at her hand."

Resad whirled, his dark green cloak whipping against him in the breeze, his eyes flashing unbridled rage. "And you think Achivir put him up to it?" he growled.

"Yes. I think he is behind it all. He seeks to drive her into his bed through poverty and hunger. And he will, too."

"Then we must leave here. Take my mother and Anor and travel to the west, where my stepfather's surviving sister lives. Among her own people Mother will be better treated, happier. They will know her talents, and appreciate them."

He paused when Drosten gazed down at the rocky clifftop and slowly shook his head. "We cannot," the Pict muttered, the wind catching his words and blowing them to the air. "I have not told you the worst news, Resad. We—you and I—are being sent on an errand. For Achivir. Delivering something to a relative; I'm not sure. But he wants us out of the way. He knows we help support her. With us gone, his task will be that much easier."

He glanced up uneasily at his tall friend. Resad's face had gone blank, as if he wore a mask, and his eyes were fixed darkly on the horizon. "I will not go," he stated flatly, his expression unbroken.

"What choice do we have?" Drosten protested. "He is

powerful. What can you do? Try to flee? You would be hunted down and killed, and your mother seized after all . . . and no doubt Anor too. If you act rashly, Resad, you condemn us all."

Resad sighed, his heart drained of emotion, and studied a faint star that glimmered above the sea. He knew he was beaten. All his anger, all his strength, all his skill and cunning would avail him nothing now.

"When do we leave?" he muttered, turning his back to the sea and pulling the cloak tighter around his shoulders.

"In six days. It should take a few months, all told."

Resad nodded, lost in thought. "Don't tell Mother of your suspicions, Drosten," he said as they slowly walked from the cliff. "She is a clever woman, and stubborn too. Perhaps if she is unaware of the forces arrayed against her, she can hold out until we return. Then we will think of some other way to help her."

He looked aside at his friend. "And Anor?" Resad asked gently. Drosten's face grew strained.

"She will have to be patient and wait until I return," he answered. "I had hoped to wed her sooner, but there is no way it can be arranged in six days."

Resad heard the bitterness plain in Drosten's voice and he put a brotherly arm around the young man's shoulders. "The months will pass swiftly, Drosten," he reassured him, "and then you will have my sister, and Mother will have a different future."

The wind howled dismally through the empty streets of the Pictish village, whistling down the narrow stone corridors between the low buildings like air through a flute. Melangell and Anor sat huddled by the small central fire in their home, deliberately kept low to conserve their dwindling supply of dried peat. Anor looked dull and passive, shivering beneath a wool blanket and fur cloak, and Melangell hugged a clay cup of hot ale between her hands as if it was her very life's blood. She too had a luxurious cloak of dense otter fur, like Anor's, a parting gift from Drosten, and she pulled it up against her cheeks to try to warm them.

"It shouldn't be too much longer, Mother," Anor said

quietly, her delicate face pinched by the cold. "Half a month, and Drosten and Resad will be back. We can manage till then."

Melangell looked up at her daughter and gave a silent prayer of thanks that the girl was still unaware of the dilemma caused by Achivir and his proposal. "Yes," she replied simply. "If only our food and fuel hold out, then we can—"

A sharp rap on the door interrupted her, and she rose stiffly, clenching the fur to her neck as she crossed the hut. A young soldier stood outside, swathed head to toe in fur leggings and boots, long jacket and cap, his face heavily bearded, a spear in one hand and a small round shield on his arm.

"Melangell, wife of Genann the harpist?" he said briskly. She nodded, knowing before he resumed what his mission was.

"I am to escort you to see the king," he said. "At once. Please come, lady."

He stood aside as if expecting an immediate exit, and Melangell looked uncertainly over her shoulder at Anor. The girl had risen to her feet, her eyes wide, at mention of the king.

"Now!" the soldier pressed her, and she feared to refuse him. "Bolt the door," she instructed her daughter as the guard took her arm and led her away.

"Good lady, your hardships are taking their toll on you," Achivir said, leaning back in a massive carved chair draped in tapestry as Melangell stood stiffly before him.

"You look worn and ill and half-starved," he went on solicitously. "Give my steward your fur and I'll have some food brought."

"No . . . I—" she began to protest, but he waved her words aside.

"I insist. Some food, and then we will talk."

The silent steward took her wrap, left the room, and in a moment a procession of foods obviously prepared in advance was brought in. Melangell's empty stomach knotted painfully at the aromas.

"Eat!" Achivir smiled, leaning forward. "A little wine?"

He poured it himself, holding the silver goblet to her. She could smell the heady tang, see the dark redness shining in the depths of the cup; she could not resist it. Taking the goblet in trembling hands, she sipped it once . . . and again . . . and then drank it greedily, as if she was dying of thirst. Her appetite whetted, she put the empty cup down, suppressing a sudden belch that slid its way up her throat, and picked up a bowl of steaming oats and vegetables. Hungrily she scooped them into her mouth, then reached for fresh hot bread thick with butter. And spiced fruits, and cheese, and dark, heavy cakes, and honeyed beans, and . . .

Sated, she closed her eyes contentedly, leaning back in the chair and savoring the unaccustomed feeling of a full belly.

"Better?" the king asked, pouring them each a cup of wine and motioning the steward to remove the food tables.

"Yes," she said quietly, opening her eyes and looking at him when he handed her the wine. They waited in silence until the steward and servants left the room.

"I said I was a patient man, but you try my patience, dear lady. It has been several months, and still I receive no word from you. Do I assume your silence is your answer?"

Melangell straightened herself awkwardly in the chair, gazing into the depths of her wine cup, and felt suddenly uncomfortable in her old gown, her hair hanging loose, simple fur boots on her feet. She didn't know how to answer him . . . what to say.

"Come," he said, rising to his feet and taking her hand in his. "I have something to show you."

He led her through a side door of his private quarters, past several small cells where stewards were busy with their tallies and accounts, by a guard's cubbyhole set into the wall, to the end of a long narrow corridor. Opening a carved wooden door, he ushered her into a tiny suite of rooms, immaculately clean and lavishly furnished.

Melangell gazed around, awed, and slowly turned, taking it all in. Embroidered tapestries warmed the cold stone walls; fragrant rushes covered the floor. A bed, a real bed, such as she had not seen in twenty years, stood to the right, its goosedown pad covered by a brightly patterned wool blanket. A few carved wooden chests lined the far wall, and two low chairs were placed near the central hearth.

"It's . . . it's lovely," she breathed. Achivir smiled broadly, his brown eyes gleaming.

"I'm glad you like it, good lady," he said, stepping to her side. "It has been waiting for you these past few months."

"For me?" she gasped, weary amazement overcoming her caution.

"Yes. And see . . . there are two smaller rooms. One for your maidservant, perhaps, and one for your daughter. Or a private dressing room for you. Whatever you like."

He ran a hand slowly down her cheek as he spoke, and she looked away awkwardly.

"Why do you want me?" she muttered. "Surely you could have any woman you want."

"I have always been struck by your beauty, since the first day you came to my village. But you soon were married again, and I was already married, so what could I do? I loved my wife, and you loved your husband. But the gods had a fate planned for us, and now we both are free . . . free, and alone . . ."

"No," she said quietly, moving to step away from him. He took her arm and held it firm.

"It is true I could have many other women, but what are they to me? A diversion in the night. But you . . . you are different. Your fair hair and green eyes and gentle manner. I have never had a Celtic woman before, and the thought of you in my arms drives me near to madness."

"No!" she repeated, freeing her arm and backing away from him. He made no attempt to pursue her.

"You are free to go, Melangell. I will not force you, nor hold you against your will. But the day will come when you will come to me, and by your own choosing. Go, if you must, but remember all this"—he waved his arm around the room—"when next you are cold and hungry and alone. It will be waiting for you."

He turned and left her. Stunned and angered, Melangell gave one last longing look at the comfort and luxury around her. When she exited the palace, the silent steward gave her a neatly wrapped parcel of food. It was for Anor, he said, compliments of the king.

* * *

Snow blustered around Melangell as she turned from the door that had just closed in her face. Another "no." She sighed, hanging her head in undisguised despair. An occasional bundled figure hurried past, giving her only a cursory glance as she stood on the old woman's doorstep, her fur cloak pulled close, as immobile as if she had frozen in the bitter winter gale.

Another good customer had suddenly, inexplicably, turned her down. A total of six since winter began; she was running out of resources. And try as she might, she could not imagine why everyone was suddenly so dissatisfied with her work. The old woman who'd just refused her had been thrilled with the shawl she'd embroidered, and had even talked of an entire coverlet she wanted sewn for a nephew's marriage gift. Melangell had counted on enough food from that to last until Resad and Drosten returned. As it was, they were almost out of food now. A mere cupful of beans and a chunk of bread the size of her fist was all she had to eat on most days. Anor wheedled pieces of old dry ham or salted fish from families she knew, but despite her increasing hunger, Melangell steadfastly refused to eat the meat. That, at least, is one dignity I will maintain, despite all else, she thought glumly. I will be true to Esus and all he taught me, if not to myself.

Turning, she stumbled wearily down the gusty street, her thin shoulders shivering violently in the cold. If I could, I would take Anor and flee Achivir's kingdom, she mused, but I know what folly that would be. Here all is at his whim; we would be hunted down and returned to him, or if we were lucky we would merely starve or freeze on these cold, treeless moors. No, this is not my land and these are not my people. With no kinsmen here to protect me, I am totally at the king's mercy, and his mercy lately seems a slim thing indeed. I must survive somehow until the boys return. For Anor's sake. She must not be left alone. And then, if I die, I die. I am weary of this life anyway.

She tripped over a protruding stone in the street and fell to her knees in the snow, her mittened hands splayed outward in the drifts. Gods above, I did not realize I was so weak, she gasped, finding herself barely able to rise. Slowly, awkwardly, she pulled herself up, clinging to the jutting rocks of the nearby wall for support. Trembling from the exertion, she closed her eyes to the stinging flakes and tried to find the strength to continue.

Die! she urged herself. It is so easy . . . you know that. Remember the blizzard of your youth, when you quietly slipped away to the Silver Land? How simple it was? Just lie down here in the snow and slip away again, only this time there will be no one to save you. No wolf, no Esus, no one.

She sobbed aloud as the refrain echoed down her desolate soul. No one . . . no one . . . no one . . .

No! She roused herself. Anor cannot survive alone. I must go on, for her sake. And then I will go to join my friends. I have none here. I must go on . . . I must.

Grasping the wall for support, her bony fingers clenching each protruding stone, she slowly progressed down the street, only her mother's love and stubborn determination fueling her efforts.

Anor scraped black mold from a hard piece of cheese she'd snatched from a garbage heap before the village dogs could get it, and eyed her sleeping mother in concern. Drosten is already overdue, she thought desperately; she did not know how much longer they could stay alive. For some reason, her mother's work had stopped; no more gifts came from the king either. She realized now that's where they'd come from, but she couldn't imagine why. She was reduced to scavenging the streets and begging at wealthier households, for her mother could scarcely rise from her pallet now. Even Drosten's family, she thought bitterly, had given her a mere pittance, some beans and curdled milk; and their distaste for their future daughter-in-law was plain to see. She dropped the hard cheese into a pot of simmering, watery gruel and wondered at the wisdom of marrying him. He was so gentle, so caring, and she loved him dearly, but when one weds, one weds the entire family as well, and his had never been shy about showing their disapproval of her. Aside from the fact that she was a foreigner, she was of lowly birth, no better than a servant or tradesman's daughter would be.

She stirred the gruel and watched the cheese melting through it. What good fortune that I chanced upon this cheese, she thought, brightening a little. It will provide a filling, nourishing meal for Mother. Scooping out a large bowlful, she carried it to Melangell's pallet and sat it on the floor. Kneeling, the girl shook her mother's shoulder. The woman roused slowly, her sunken eyes staring blankly at Anor for a few moments before recognition came.

"Here, Mother, I have some food for you," Anor said gently, helping her to sit.

"Food?" Melangell muttered blankly, and fear rose in Anor's heart. First her mother's strength had gone, and now her mind seemed to be going. At this rate she would not live much longer.

"Eat, Mother," the girl prodded, scooping a bit of the mix onto the edge of a large wooden ladle and holding it to her mother's mouth. She ate it listlessly, but Anor fed her until the bowl was emptied.

"Mother, let me go to see the king. He was kind enough to send us food before; he probably doesn't know what hard luck we have been having. Please, Mother, let me go to him."

Her mother roused at the suggestion, a spark of light showing in her eyes. "No . . . you must not . . . never," she snapped. "He is the cause of this . . . all this."

"Cause?" Anor puzzled. "I do not understand, Mother."

"It is he who has put an end to my work, I feel sure of that. And he who sent Resad and Drosten away."

"But why?" the girl gasped.

"He seeks to force me to his bed, child . . . as his mistress."

Anor's face went pale, all the recent puzzles suddenly solved. "No . . ." she breathed, at once fearful and panicked by the awful forces arrayed against them; two women, cold, starving, and alone. "Then we will never yield to him, Mother," she said stoutly, hugging her mother. Melangell smiled at her words.

"How like your father you are," she whispered to the girl. "The king will not have me. I will outwit him, in the end, if it takes my death to do it."

"And I, Mother." Anor stared grimly at the far wall as she held her mother close. "If we must, then I will lie here with you and we will die together, and let Resad and Drosten handle him when they return. We will never give in to his treachery . . . or to his cruel betrayal of my father's memory. Never!"

Melangell patted Anor's arm reassuringly and closed her eyes. Yes, she mused, perhaps death is the kindest solution after all.

"Melangell!"

She opened her eyes slowly when she heard her name called, for it was not Anor's voice that spoke. The room was dark, the fire was nearly out, and she narrowed her eyes, trying to peer through the heavy shadows.

"Resad?" she muttered. "Is that you?"

"No, my dear," the voice responded.

"Then who?" she demanded, rising easily on one elbow. "Who has entered my house in the nighttime?"

She sat abruptly, surprised by her recovered strength, until she looked around the room and saw the objects of her everyday life—the stew kettle, her loom, barrels and low stools—all lit by a strange white glow, and then she knew. She had risen from her body and once more roamed the Silver Land.

"Who are you?" she thought aloud, and the words became living things that fled into the ether.

"Don't you remember me?" the voice replied. She turned and was overcome with a wild rush of joy. It was Brennos.

"Brennos!" she gasped, advancing toward him. "Have you come to take me now? Am I to die?"

"No." He smiled. "It is not yet your time. I only came to help you; now, when your will is lowest. Do not despair, my dear. Always remember what I tell you. The finest gold must first be purified. The wheat must be flayed from the stalk, threshed and ground in violence, before it can be made use of. Remember that, Melangell. Your time is fast approaching, but it is a time of life, not death."

He came toward her and she felt like crying out when she saw his gentle gray eyes, now shining with an intense, fiery light.

"Help me, Brennos," she gasped, reaching for him.

"I will, my dear one, but you must live, you must survive.

You must never give up. And then, when your life is at its lowest ebb, I will come once more . . ."

His form began to waver and fade.

"Brennos! No!" she cried.

"I will come; never fear. When you need me most, I will come."

She woke up, a wild cry strangling in her throat, as the door burst open with a crash. "Brennos!" she cried, sitting up and sobbing into her hands. "Don't go . . . don't leave me . . . don't . . ."

"It's all right, Mother," a strong voice said, and she felt Resad clasping her to his chest, the smell of winter's cold and travel weariness heavy around him. "We are here, we have food; all is well now."

She looked up at him, disbelieving, and glanced over his shoulder to Anor's pallet. Drosten had gathered the frail girl in his arms, hugging her in a frantic embrace as she cried brokenly into his shoulder.

As Drosten listened to his father's words, his face grew grim.

"There are legal matters to be considered, son," the old man said calmly, turning from the hearthside, his wispy gray hair floating out from his bony head. "It will take time—"

"Time!" Drosten exploded. "What more time do you need? It has been months, and still you delay. Do you think I am such a fool, Father, that I cannot see what you are doing? You have never approved of her. None of you have. She told me how you treated her when she came in desperate search of help."

"I was not at home then, son. I am not responsible for—"

"What difference would it have made if you were home? Would you have treated her fairly and decently? Or would you, too, just as soon have seen her starve to death and be out of your way? You shame me, Father; that my own family could be so callous to such a sweet girl . . ."

"Sweet in more than one way, I'd say, from the way she has taken your fancy." The old man sneered, and Drosten seized his thin shoulder menacingly.

"You are my father, it is true," he growled, "but by the gods, for the little respect I feel for you I would break you in two for that remark. You judge her so blithely, yet you have never taken the time to meet her properly or get to know her."

"It is not necessary. Everyone knows the nature of Celtic women. It is why the Romans prefer them, the Germans, we Cruithni—"

"Hold your tongue, you foolish old man!" Drosten snapped, clenching his father's shoulder painfully in one powerful hand.

"And besides," the man went on maliciously, "her mother is a witch. It is common knowledge. I think the two of them have cast a spell on you."

Drosten raised his arm to strike his father, thought better of it, and slowly clenched his upraised hand into a fist. "I renounce you, Father," he shouted. "I renounce the whole damn lot of you. I have my own resources from my grandfather's estates, and I will take nothing more from you."

Turning, he stormed from the room, brusquely pushing his startled mother aside when she walked toward him. Without a parting word, he slammed the heavy wooden door in his wake.

"Another month," he repeated, looking into Anor's stricken face. She gazed up at him, pain in her eyes, the ocean breeze pulling wildly at the patterned Celtic cloak she held around her tiny shoulders.

"A month! But why?" she asked quietly.

"I have broken with my family, Anor. There is no forgiving them for the way they treated you. But because I have, I must now lay claim to all that is coming to me of my inheritance. And that will take more time. A month, at most."

He took her hand in his and together they strolled a few more paces along the gusty clifftop.

"Then," he continued, stopping and turning her to face him, "I will have ample funds to provide a nice wedding for us, and to take care of your mother, as well."

"Oh, Drosten, it almost seems worth the long wait!" She smiled, twining her fingers between his.

"It will be, my love," he murmured. "We have waited so long, but like most Cruithni, I am not an impulsive man. I must be ready to care for you properly. A little extra delay will be worthwhile."

"Yes, I suppose so," she sighed, looking into his dark eyes. He leaned down, his breath warm on her cheek, and pressed his mouth to hers. She flung her arms around his neck.

"Drosten, I do love you so!" she whispered into his ear. He kissed her again, his mouth hungry on hers, and one hand tentatively reached for her breast. She pulled her mouth away and backed off a step.

"No," she laughed. "You know we must wait."

"Wait! Always wait!" he sighed in dramatic exasperation, throwing his arms wide and looking heavenward. "You don't know what self-control you ask of me!"

"It will be worth it, I promise." She took his hand and pulled him behind her as she set off for the low stone walls of their village. "We must return now. Mother is fixing the evening meal, and Resad will be coming, with news of Cadvan. They say he is the favorite of his teacher, a born warrior."

"Like most Celts." Drosten nodded, wrapping one arm around the girl's waist and pulling her close. They approached the town walls, nodding politely when they passed the creaking tinker's cart heavily laden with various old bits of junk. Two tattered men futilely switched the rump of a skinny pony, which desperately tried to avoid their blows. Drosten laughed in high spirits at the ludicrous sight. He spoke briefly to the guard outside the town gate, who admitted them and quickly closed the gate, waiting to inspect the rickety cart approaching at a snail's pace.

The days flew by, and the wedding plans proceeded swiftly. Broichan plotted the heavens and chose an auspicious day for the ceremony. Melangell spent every afternoon finishing the embroidery on the precious wedding dress while Anor was gone on her usual walks with Drosten before he had to report for guard duty at the Treasury. The girl still had no inkling of her mother's surprise, and Melangell thrilled with anticipation at the expression of joy that would light Anor's face when she saw the dress. It was truly a work of art, the most exquisite thing she had sewn in her long years of practice. And every thread was stitched with all the love her soul possessed, both for her fair daughter and for the man who had sired her.

She started at a sound outside, slid the bronze needle into a fold of cloth, and lowered the dress into the chest where she kept it hidden. Were Drosten and Anor back so soon? she wondered, crossing to the door and unbolting it. Pulling it open, she found herself face-to-face with a grubby peddler, his hand raised to rap on the door.

"Pardon, lady," he wheezed, bowing slightly when he saw her. He clenched his hands nervously before himself like a groveling sycophant, and Melangell felt an instinctive dislike for the man.

"What do you want?" she snapped.

"Repairs, ma'am?" he muttered, avoiding her gaze as he motioned to his waiting wagon. "Any broken pots, belts that need sewing, a new wooden ladle for the soup pot, perhaps? We have some fine items for sale, and can repair your damaged things as good as new."

"No . . . I have nothing to be repaired, and I can't afford to buy anything of . . ." She stopped when something on the jumbled cart caught her eye, and she stepped past the tattered man, taking care to close her front door as she did so. The man would no doubt love a chance to slip into her house and add to his stores, if he could.

"Where did you get this?" she demanded, pulling an ornate gold torque from the clutter.

"Ah!" He nodded knowingly. His partner, a chunky man with an ugly scar across his forehead, hovered nearby. "The lady has excellent taste. A gold necklace such as that is a rare find in these parts."

"I said, where did you get it?" she repeated, fingering the twisted gold wire.

"The necklace? It was found beneath the mold of a forest, bent and trampled underfoot, no doubt by the Romans, for it was very near their territory. It was come by honestly, lady. Would you like it? It would look lovely on you."

"Fool," she snapped, "it is a warrior's torque. I am not a warrior."

He shrugged mildly. "I know nothing of such things. It is yours, if you meet my price. Solid gold, you see . . . very valuable."

"I can see that," she said, irritation rising within her. She handed it back to him and turned to her house. "Wait here," she ordered. In a moment she was back, the ornate blue cloak Achivir had sent her tossed over one arm. The peddler's shrewd eyes lit up when he saw it.

"A fair trade, I think," she said, holding it out for his inspection. "A very fine cloak any woman would pay handsomely for, in exchange for that bent and dirty torque, and one promise."

"A promise?" the man said, his eyes narrowing suspiciously. He had not believed he could be the recipient of such a wildly favorable deal; this, no doubt, was the catch.

"Yes," Melangell answered simply. "Do not attempt to sell this in the village. That is all. Keep it hidden until you reach the next town."

"That's all?" he asked, disbelieving. The robe was easily worth three old battered pieces of Celtic jewelry. No one was interested in those . . . except, obviously, this Celtic woman.

"Lady," he said slyly, "you have just acquired a gold necklace." He handed it to her and seized the cloak as if he expected it to disappear.

Melangell turned, carrying the torque as carefully as if it were a holy relic. When was the last time I saw this? she mused, reentering her house. She poured a small bowlful of hot water and with a brush slowly cleaned the dirt from the tiny twisted wires and the savage eagles' heads that formed the ends.

"Never fear, my lady," he had said. And then she had killed him.

"Niall . . ." she whispered into the silent room. Brennos said your torque would be hung in the sacred grove as a reminder to all of your sacrifice. But it fell, was trampled underfoot, and fate sent it into my hands once more. You will be remembered, Niall. Your torque will adorn the neck of your best friend's son, where now only a Pictish silver neck chain rests. We will respect your memory, Niall, and my son will, for the first time in his life, honor the Celtic blood that beats so strongly in his veins. He will reclaim his heritage.

The wedding was only days away, and Drosten and Anor spent every spare minute in each other's company, strolling arm in arm along the shore or sitting quietly atop the town walls, gazing up at the stars, to the vast amusement of his fellow warriors, who passed by on their rounds with many a snicker and an elbow to each other's ribs. Drosten ignored them. His spirits were too high to be annoyed by their crude jokes and lewd suggestions when he reported for duty at the Treasury. A few more days and Anor would be his, and he knew their first night together would be a sweet and sleepless one. He could scarcely wait.

"Come!" Drosten said, pulling Anor atop the boulder where he stood. "See how the sun has bloodied the sea."

"What a choice of words you use, Drosten!" Anor shuddered, sliding her arm around his heavily belted waist and watching the setting sun color the sea to the west of the jutting peninsula of land where they stood. It was cluttered with huge rocks and he'd had to help her more than once as she stumbled on the slippery stones. Neither of them minded too much, though. It gave him a chance to be gallant, and her an excuse to feel his strong arms about her. I know he can't wait for our wedding night, she reflected, gazing up at his strong, clean profile against the darkening sky. All men are like that. But I, too, feel such a fire within me at the very thought. Is that normal for a woman, I wonder? What will it be like? His body; the feel of him, his strength, his gentleness? For despite the fact that he is a warrior, he has always been only gentle with me. Will it also be gentle, his loving me? I wonder . . ..

She stilled her wandering mind when she suddenly became aware of him staring at her, a slight smile pulling at his mouth.

"So serious?" he chided her, and even in the fading light he could see her blush deeply.

"Oh ho!" he laughed aloud, wrapping his arms around her

and whirling her in a circle. "I know what you were thinking about!"

"Drosten! Put me down! We'll fall!"

"No we won't. I've been out here a hundred times and haven't fallen yet. A few more days and then your thoughts will become reality!" He kissed her, hard and fierce, and she felt the fire within her blazing again.

"Oh, Drosten," she sighed, and he could tell by the look on her face that she was ready for him. The thought briefly crossed his mind that he could take her now, if he wanted, and it was probable that she wouldn't refuse him this time. Shall I? he argued with himself. It would be so easy . . . but no . . . we have waited this long. A few more days, and then it will all be new and special. No . . . we will wait . . . for our wedding night.

He kissed down her slender neck and felt her shudder violently in his arms. Slowly his mouth crept lower; pulling her gown aside, he felt the soft downy curve of one breast beneath his lips. Replacing the gown, he picked her up in his arms.

"We'd best get back before it's completely dark," he said, and she sighed dreamily, resting her head on his shoulder.

"Drosten," she whispered softly.

"Yes?"

"I love you."

He carried her over the rocky peninsula, settling her to the ground where the rock-strewn slope gave way to level sod. Hand in hand, they began the long walk back to their village, its massive walls now an indistinct line of black in the heavy dusk and dotted with occasional torchlights from the sentry posts. They followed a narrow footpath through flower-spangled meadows and up to the windy clifftop, where they paused briefly for another quick kiss before they hurried on. The night was fast descending, and the call of the watch atop the town walls drifted out to them. Drosten did not like to be outside the safety of the village once darkness fell.

"Come!" he urged her, striding so hurriedly that Anor nearly had to run to keep up with him.

"Drosten . . . wait!" she panted. "I am not so swift as you! You must go slower!"

"I'm sorry, love," he said, easing his strides. "We have tarried too long. You must try to hurry."

"How unsafe can it be?" she protested, pointing a short distance ahead. "See? The two old peddlers are out and traveling to the next town. Do you think they would risk losing one bit of silver if the nighttime was so unsafe? They travel all the time, Drosten. Who better than they should know if it is risky?"

"I suppose you're right," he sighed, slowing and giving her hand a little squeeze. "I doubt those two would part willingly with a single hair of their filthy heads."

"Yes!" She smiled. "We'll be home in plenty of time."

They walked on in silence, nodding to the two peddlers when they passed. They seemed to have acquired a decent horse, Drosten noted, eyeing the well-muscled gelding that trotted briskly along the path, scarcely winded by the old cart it pulled. A fine-looking animal, he mused with a warrior's keen suspicions. I wonder what of such value they could have possessed, to trade for such a splendid beast?

They continued on a few more paces before some instinctive wariness began to prod Drosten's mind. The cart! he noted with rising alarm. The wheels no longer squeaked and groaned behind them. The cart had stopped for some reason. Now, why . . . ?

A silent rush came through the night and Anor was jerked to the side, her hand pulled helplessly from his grasp.

"Anor!" he began to shout, when with the swiftness of a hawk the taller of the two peddlers was on him, a long pole in his hands flying full force into Drosten's stomach. The young man doubled over, gasping, one hand groping for the sword at his side as he stumbled forward. The next blow crashed down across the back of his head and he sprawled to the ground, light flashing and spangling through his numbed brain. But he was tough as well as powerful, and he refused to let the blackness descend.

"Anor . . . no . . ." he croaked as he heard her being dragged away. She was fighting and the men seemed to be having trouble controlling her.

"Anor!" he bellowed, dragging himself to his hands and knees. Through the gloom he could see her face, as pallid as the moon, her eyes staring wildly at him from above the hand clamped roughly across her mouth. He staggered to his feet, and his fingers had just clenched the hilt of his sword when the wicked pole again sailed out of the night, striking him full across the face. He sprawled backward, blood erupting in a hot torrent, and this time the blackness was too powerful to resist. It enveloped him slowly, closing over his head like the sea.

Melangell removed the kettle of gruel from the hearth and stirred it slowly, anger and fear vying for control of her heart. *It will be ruined*, she fretted. *The gruel is thickening, and I cannot add much more water. Where can they be?*

She stuck the wooden ladle in the congealing mass and crossed to the small window. Opening the shutter, she peered up at the sparkling stars. *Gods above*, she thought in rising alarm, *it is nearly time for Drosten's duty at the Treasury. I will skin him with my own two hands for keeping Anor out so late. It is so unlike him . . . he is usually so responsible . . .*

She turned, gazing around the empty room. *So odd*, she mused, *for me to be here all alone now. Always there has been someone here—Genann, the children, Drosten . . .*

Drosten, she thought again, anger pulling at her mouth as she closed the shutter. *He will get a piece of my mind about this, make no mistake. And to leave me worrying so, without sending word or . . .*

Something scraped at the door, an odd sound she couldn't place. Crossing the floor, she cocked her head and listened as the sound repeated, followed by a loud clumsy knock. Then came a voice, a strangled voice, Drosten's voice, and she threw the door open in alarm.

"Lady . . ." he gasped, stumbling into the room, dried blood caked across his face like a mask, "help me . . . Anor . . . is gone . . ."

Melangell seized his arm and guided him to her pallet. He seemed near collapse, barely able to stand. His thick dark hair hung with sweat, and blood stained the front of his gray wool tunic.

"Lie down, Drosten," she ordered. "Where is Anor? What happened to her? Tell me!"

His face was raw, his lip split open, his nose grotesquely

bruised and swollen. She examined him quickly and, without waiting for a reply to her questions, ran to fetch water and cloths to clean his wounds. When she knelt beside him, he brushed her away, sitting up awkwardly and grabbing her shoulders.

"No! There is no time!" he shouted, staring into her eyes in near-panic. She had never seen such wild emotion in his steady brown gaze before; his self-control was obviously near to breaking. "Get Resad!" he choked, clenching her tighter. "We must go after them!"

"Who?" she answered, trying to free herself from his grip. He seemed unaware of the pain his strength was causing her.

"Anor! Those two peddlers . . . have taken her . . ."

At the words, Drosten's will broke and he began to sob, his tears etching lines in the dried blood on his face. Melangell stared at him in horror, the color drained from her face, all life gone from her soul. "No . . ." she breathed, unable to comprehend his words. He leaned forward, collapsing against her like a child as he cried, and she wrapped her arms around him gently.

"I couldn't save her," he sobbed, "I couldn't help her."

"Hush, Drosten," Melangell soothed, pulling him away from her and brushing the sweaty hair from his face. "I must get Resad. I want you to lie down and rest till I return. Do you understand? Rest . . ."

She forced him back to the pallet, dipped a cloth in fresh cool water and held it to his swollen face. "Now, stay here, Drosten. Hold this to your lip and nose. I will be back soon."

He nodded dumbly, gazing up at the low ceiling while tears trickled from his eyes. Grabbing her cloak from its peg on the wall, she pulled it around her shoulders, trying to conceal the bloodied front of her dress. Running lightly across the floor, she flung the door open and flew out into the silent night.

Her feet fairly skimmed the uneven stones of the village streets, and by the time she rounded the last corner and saw the torches before the warriors' quarters, she was gasping for breath and her heart pounded wildly. Running up to the guard at the door, she pressed one hand to her burning lungs as he looked at her quizzically.

"Resad!" she gasped, searching desperately for the right Cruithni word. "Quickly!"

The man nodded, turned, and spoke through a small window set into the center of the wooden door. Melangell waited for what seemed an eternity, hungrily gulping the thick night air, until the door opened and a sleepy Resad stumbled into view. The flush of her face, the wildness of her eyes, roused him instantly.

"Mother!" he said, grabbing her arms as she looked up at him. "What is it?"

She could see other curious faces appearing in the gloom behind him, and she swallowed hard before she spoke.

"Come at once!" she breathed raggedly. "Drosten has been beaten and the two peddlers . . . have taken Anor."

The rage that had been his father's now crossed Resad's face like a brushfire. "Wait . . ." he said curtly, turned, and vanished into the dark barracks. With a silent nod of thanks Melangell took a cup of ale that was offered to her, drinking it quickly to ease the dryness of her throat. Resad soon returned, still shirtless, fastening a sword belt diagonally across his chest and carrying his cloak draped over one arm.

"Come," he said, steering her into the courtyard with one hand. She broke into a frenzied run and his long legs easily kept pace with her as they raced back to their home.

Drosten still lay on her pallet, one arm flung across his throbbing forehead and the other hand pressing the compress to his face. When Melangell and Resad burst into the hut, he struggled to sit, pulling himself shakily to his feet and nearly stumbling, until Resad grabbed him and forced him to a stool by the fire. Drosten held his head in his hands, as if the pain he felt was nearly unbearable.

"They waylaid us . . ." he muttered thickly through his swollen lip. "I tried to get my sword, but he had a pole . . ."

Drosten looked up at his friend, fighting valiantly for control. "They dragged her away, Resad. I saw her . . . the terror in her eyes, and I could do nothing . . . nothing. I was hit in the face, and that's the last I remember. I'm sorry, Resad. I could do nothing. I'm sorry . . ."

Tears collected in his eyes and Melangell pushed her son aside, seating herself in front of the battered young man.

"We must get this cleaned, Drosten, or it will become poisoned," she calmed him. "You must sit still. Resad will know what to do now."

She glanced over her shoulder at her son while she wet another cloth in clean water, and for a moment her heart nearly stopped. Standing in the dim firelight, shirtless and with the gold torque gleaming at his neck, he looked so like his father. She swallowed hard against the lump in her throat and turned away.

"I will be back," Resad said tightly. Before Melangell could respond, he was gone.

"I must get some medicine into these wounds," she told Drosten, trying to control her quaking voice and the suffocating panic she was beginning to feel. "Don't move. I'll get something for the pain as well."

"What is going on?" Achivir bellowed, flinging open his door to the noisy confusion in the narrow hall outside his quarters. He was shirtless and barefoot, wearing only a pair of embroidered crimson trousers.

"Sire," a guard said, turning to him, "Resad insists he must see you . . . that it cannot wait until morning. Every time I try to have him removed, he fights and shouts, no doubt trying to awaken you."

"And he has succeeded," the king said dryly, cutting his dark eyes over to the sullen young man who stood between two of his spearmen.

"Why did you do it, Achivir?" Resad shouted at him. "Is this another of your tricks to break my mother's will? Tell me, Achivir! Why did you do it?"

"What is he talking about?" the king said, raking his tangled hair down with his fingers. The guard shrugged and shook his head.

"You know what I am talking about!" Resad snarled, trying to advance to the king but finding his way barred by several sharp spearpoints. "My sister! How much did you pay them to take her? Would you really stoop so low, Achivir? Would you?" he sneered.

"I don't know what you're talking about, boy," the king said, his curiosity sharpened. He motioned to two of his guards. "Take his weapons, then let him in my room. I wish to speak alone with him."

The guards nodded and Achivir retreated into his quarters.

"Now, then, boy, what on earth are you ranting about?" Achivir said, pulling on a white wool tunic while Resad, his sword belt removed, stood glaring at him.

"Those two peddlers who had been in town these past few days beat Drosten and abducted my sister Anor," Resad began. The king looked up, anger in his eyes.

"When did this happen?" he snapped.

"At dusk, out by the clifftops. Drosten has just now made his way to my mother's house with the news. He is there now, being treated by her."

Achivir passed to the blazing hearth and turned to study Resad's stormy face. "And you think I had a hand in it?" he said quietly. Resad nodded sharply at the question.

"We had not been deceived by your tricks, Achivir," he said. "How you have tried to force my mother into your bed."

"Yes," the king said, recrossing the room. "It's true I tried to force my will on your mother. But she is a noble woman, despite her lowly birth, and I can see why she was so esteemed by your father. Not once did her refusals waver. But I swear to you, son, I had no hand in this."

He stopped before Resad, gazing thoughtfully at the young man's face. "And to prove my innocence of the matter," Achivir went on, "I give you and Drosten leave of your duties here to track the rascals down and retrieve your sister. I will detail two of my own men to accompany you, and have food and supplies packed. We must bring these ruffians to a swift justice, boy; leave as soon as you wish. Capture them and I will pay for your sister's wedding out of my own purse."

He paused, eyeing Resad. The young man's face sagged in surprise.

"Sire . . . I . . ." he stammered awkwardly. Achivir waved his words aside.

"Go," he said tiredly. "The sooner you leave, the sooner you will rescue her."

Resad turned and strode to the door. When his hand reached for the massive latch, the king's voice halted him.

"Tell your mother I am truly sorry," Achivir said quietly. "If she needs anything of me, she only need ask."

"Thank you, sire," Resad replied. "I will tell her."

"Don't try to speak," Melangell chided the young man. "I do not approve of your going off with the other three in the shape you're in, but I know there could be no stopping you. At least stay quiet, to let your lip heal."

"I must speak, lady," he mumbled, and Melangell had to strain to understand him. His swollen lip and nose were thickly coated with an ointment she'd made, and he had trouble forming his words properly through the encumbrances.

"I leave you the profits from my inheritance until I return, so you will have some means to sustain yourself."

He looked down at her face, her normal sweet expression now etched with strain and worry.

"Do you understand me?" he asked, taking his spear from Simal, one of the two men detailed by the king to accompany them.

"Yes, Drosten," she whispered, "I understand you. Thank you."

"We'd best be going," Resad said, walking to Melangell's side and placing an arm around her shoulders. "Is everyone ready?"

He glanced at the assembled men: Drosten, stooping slightly but determination firing his eyes; Simal and Aniel, eager to be off, their bows and javelins and heavy swords ready for action. He had no doubt, with such a company, that they would soon catch up with the two peddlers and rescue Anor. The trail would still be fresh, and Aniel was said to be an excellent tracker.

"We must go," he said abruptly, hugging his mother to him. "We will find her, never fear. We will not come back until we have, however long it takes."

Melangell fought back her tears and reached up, fingering the torque at her son's neck. "Find her, Resad," she whispered. "Bring honor to this torque, and to the blood in your veins. Find her . . ."

He nodded, holding her out at arm's length. "Be careful, Mother. Take care of yourself. Go to Achivir if you need help; remember that. Cadvan will come when he is able. Now we must be going."

He stepped away from her, adjusted his leather traveling pack, and with a slight wave of his hand led the others to the door. Simal and Aniel nodded when they passed her, but Drosten paused, eyeing her solemnly.

"I would kiss you farewell, lady"—he shrugged—"but my face . . ."

She laughed at his jest and seized his hand affectionately. "I have something for you, Drosten," she said quietly. Turning aside to the wicker chest, she removed the folded and wrapped marriage gown she'd made. "If you are late in catching them, if they have gone too far south, go west to Genann's sister. Do not return here, Drosten. Wed her there, and give her this. It is my gift for her. Will you promise?"

He took the bundle, a puzzled look on his face. "Yes, lady, but what of you? The ceremony . . ."

Melangell smiled and touched his cheek. "You deserve her, Drosten. After so long a wait, you deserve her. Send word and I will join you, in time to see my first grandchild born. It is time I left this land and returned to my own people anyway. Now, go . . . the sun is already rising. May the gods be with you."

He placed the parcel in his pack and hoisted it over his shoulder, wincing at the pain it caused his bruised stomach. With a deep bow and resolve in his eyes, he marched out to join his companions.

May the gods be with you all, Melangell prayed silently, standing in the empty street and watching the four figures disappear in the morning haze. May you meet with success, she thought forlornly, for surely I will die of a broken heart if you do not.

The days dragged by, a weight Melangell labored under like a slave in the gold mines. Hour by hour she watched the sun cross the sky; sleepless nights without end awaited her at the close of each evening. Every footstep in the street, every voice passing by, sent her heart leaping to her throat. Was it

Anor? Were they back? But they did not return, and the repeated disappointments slowly bored their way into her soul; it would be harder than they had hoped. The peddlers must have made a swift and clever escape of some sort. Wearily she accepted the facts and tried to settle herself for a long wait.

After half a month she was startled when a messenger came to fetch her to see the king. He had something important to tell her. Fear gripping her throat, she grabbed her cloak and hurriedly followed the man to the palace.

Achivir had prepared some sweets and wine for her, and he insisted that she sit and refresh herself. But her dread would not permit relaxation.

"What news have you, Achivir?" she fairly begged him. He could see the fear in her eyes and understood her agitation.

"No, Melangell, I have no word on your daughter," he reassured her. "Would to god I had, for your sake. No, this is about your son."

"Resad!" She jumped to her feet in horror. "What has—"

"No, no," the king said, reaching for her hand and pulling her back to the chair. "You are too tense, dear! Have some wine to relax you. It is about your other son."

"Cadvan?" she questioned, sipping the wine he offered her.

"Yes. I have just received word through the usual channels. It seems his military prowess has gone to his head. He has left his training, and the word is that he has gone to join his half-brother in his search."

Melangell set the wine cup jarringly on the table and anger flashed in her green eyes. "The little fool," she muttered darkly. "I will thrash him good when I find him!"

Achivir laughed heartily at her threats. "I'm afraid it is too late for that! He is already taller than his mother, I hear, and as muscular as a young bull. Seriously, Melangell"—he patted her hand lightly—"I will send word to neighboring towns and to my fellow kings. We will keep an eye out for your errant son, as well as your daughter, and I will let you know as soon as I hear anything about them."

He stared at her and saw her anger abate at his words. "Yes . . . thank you," she sighed, picking up the wine cup.

"You have been very kind to us all, throughout this . . . this ordeal." She glanced at him briefly and found his open stare unsettling. "Thank you," she repeated, looking away and sipping the wine evenly.

"I am only trying to help, dear," he said kindly, closing his hand tightly around hers. She shut her eyes nervously. It was plain . . .

Oh, gods, she thought sickly, he still wants me, and I am once more alone. What am I to do now?

"I'm sorry, lady," the steward said, turning away from Melangell's stricken face in obvious discomfort. "There is nothing I can do for you."

"Nothing . . ." she muttered, the word dying in the still air of the Treasury. She felt as if everything in existence had suddenly turned to stone; hard, unyielding, unfriendly. The tiny room where she stood, the brown-robed man who sat before her . . . her very soul . . . all cold stone . . .

"But . . ." she tried to protest, but the fire was gone from within her. "Can't you speak with them? Tell them what their son said?"

The steward glanced up at her, and he could not help but be moved by the pallid fear on the young woman's face. "I explained to them your situation, and the words of Drosten," the man said gently. "They had but one reply: there was only your word on the matter. How could they believe that, with no other proof? No witnesses . . ."

"They are all gone," Melangell whispered. "Three others heard his words, and they are gone with him."

"I'm sorry, lady," the steward said, watching her turn numbly and walk to the door. She was fighting tears when she left him.

"They said if you had a witness, or some written expression of Drosten's wishes, they would consider that to be proof," he said, trying to instill some small hope in her. "Until then he has, so far as they know, done nothing official about changing the status of his holdings. In his absence, they remain with the family."

The woman didn't give any sign that she heard, or cared. Her shoulders sagging, she silently opened the low wooden door and let herself into the damp stone hallway. Shaking

407

his head, the steward returned to his tallies. Kindness had kept him from finishing his parting sentence to the poor lady:

". . . and you will receive not a single grain of wheat from them," he concluded, trying to concentrate again on his work.

Melangell walked blindly down the long dark corridors of the Treasury, desperate to escape the place. Her eyes seemed sightless things as sheer instinct guided her feet on their way; a turn to the left, and another, past small, dimly lit rooms containing busy men, by silent, watchful guards; clutching her cloak around her shoulders, she emerged into a mockingly bright day, the sun washing over her jarringly as she broke into a trot across the bustling courtyard in front of the building. She would brush the sunlight angrily away if she could; like a scurrying lizard, she only wanted escape, the soothing comfort of darkness, coolness, peace.

Avoiding the people who passed her by, she studied the familiar paths that swept beneath her hurried feet. She must reach home soon! She must! She felt her will crumbling within her, like an empty house toppling from the neglect of sitting too long without a happy hand to maintain it. Desperate for solitude, she felt her heart spring up with relief when her own rude doorway came into view. Eagerly she unlatched the door, flung it open, disappeared into the welcoming embrace of her home. Slamming the door behind her, she stood still, breathing shakily, her gaze roaming the empty room.

All these years I have been an adult, she thought dully. Mature, responsible, in control . . .

Like an errant child, she dropped her cloak from her shoulders and let it fall to the floor, little caring if it got dirty or torn.

Who is there to be responsible for now? She sighed, walking to a stool by the fire. She settled on it slowly, gazing blankly at the low flames upon the hearth. The room's very silence seemed to mock her; ghostly sounds rising up like puffs of ash. Genann's cheery voice as he returned from a late evening's playing at the palace; the childish squabbles of

Anor and Cadvan; the horrifying croupy cough as her second-born girl slowly died before her eyes . . .

She let the tears spill down her cheeks unchecked. Who was there to see, or care? What was left of her life, all she had devoted herself to, loved, cared about . . . and now only a future of slow starvation faced her.

Why? She looked up at the smoke-blackened ceiling. All the promise I once had, all the hopes, all the dreams . . . gone. Why? She shook her head mutely. Won't anyone answer? Doesn't anyone care? Anyone . . .

Hugging both arms forlornly around her stomach, she slumped forward and cried loudly, openly, without shame or fear or hope.

Evening was settling over the village when Melangell finished packing the last of her few belongings in a wicker chest. She had washed her tearstained face, dressed her hair, put on a clean gown. Sighing, she latched the chest and straightened up, letting her eyes study the dear familiarity of her home for the last time.

A grim resolve lighting her eyes, she picked up her cloak from the floor where she had dropped it, shook out the dirt, and spread it over her shoulders, fastening it with a long thorn from the fields. Its brooch had long since been traded for food. Seizing one handle of the chest, she dragged it to the door and out into the evening-stilled streets. She did not pause to look back.

Brennos said to survive, she told herself as she walked away, and to do that I have but one recourse.

She dragged the chest around a narrow corner and looked ahead, through the gathering gloom of dusk. May the gods grant that my decision is a wise one, she thought, approaching the massive front gate of Achivir's residence. She was relieved when one of the guards recognized her and stepped forward. Hoisting her wicker chest over one burly shoulder, he escorted her into the palace.

The servant pushed open the door she recognized as leading to "her" quarters. Inside, all was as she remembered it from her first visit. The guard followed her into the suite, put her chest on a small stand by the far wall, and left.

"I will notify the king of your arrival," the steward said, bowing low. The door creaked shut behind him, and Melangell was alone.

She walked around the room, fingering the heavy wool tapestries on the walls, sliding her weary feet through the sweet rushes on the stone floor, pausing at the massive bed. The bed, she thought, and a heavy feeling settled into her stomach. She sat on it stiffly. The goosedown pad sank beneath her as if she rested on a cloud. Will you be a tranquil cloud of summer, she mused, or a threatening storm? I do not love this man, but is that odd? I feel as if I can never . . . will never . . . love another man. I seek only peace, and comfort, and these he can provide. Is that so bad? I will survive, as Brennos directed. I will await the return of my children, for they are my life now. Like any mother, human or animal, I will do what I must for my children. Little matter that they would not approve of what I do. Little matter that I am scarcely more than a whore now. I am alive, and I will survive.

She stood abruptly when the door opened and Achivir entered. His hair was tangled and he wore a long saffron tunic hastily pulled on over gray-and-brown breeches; it was plain he had retired early, a fact which surprised her. She had imagined kings to be ever busy, ever pressed for time.

"You look tired," he said, standing by the door and studying her. "Would you like food?"

"Yes," she whispered, looking awkwardly at him. "It has been . . . a hard day for me . . ."

"I heard." He nodded, turning aside and muttering a few quick directions to the servant behind him. "Gossip spreads among the guards as quickly as it does among a group of bored old grandmothers. I am sorry for your misfortunes, Melangell; truly I am."

She looked at him, touched by the concern in his voice.

"You must rest, my dear," he said, advancing to her and lifting her hand in his. "Restore your spirits. I would have our first night together as pleasurable for you as it will be for me, and so I will not press you now. You must have a servant, a guard, a good night's sleep, a bath if you like. Things must be done properly . . ."

Despite her gloom, a slight smile played at the corners of

Melangell's mouth while she listened to him. Would she ever get used to these methodical Picts? she wondered. How unlike an impetuous man of her own people! By now she'd have been tossed to the bed and half-stripped, instead of standing and listening to a fine speech about propriety. Still, at her age, his deliberations were a welcome change. She felt old tonight . . . incredibly old, and frail, and inept. She couldn't take too much wild passion; not here, not now.

"Thank you." She smiled at him as he softly squeezed her hand.

"I have the perfect guard for you. He speaks your language very well, having grown up on lands near your people's. Do you have a choice for a serving woman?"

Her answer was immediate and certain. "Severa," she replied.

"The old woman who does the washing?" he said, surprise on his weathered face. Melangell nodded.

"I have known her a long time," she said. "Genann was like a son to her. I would feel comfortable with her."

"Very well. I'll have her sent in the morning, along with your guard. For tonight I will detail one of my own men outside your door. If you need anything, ask him."

He studied her face intently, waiting for some reply, but the only one she could force was a slight nod. When the servant came in carrying a small tray of food and drink, Achivir leaned down and brushed his lips to her cheek. Turning, he left the room without a parting word, and as he returned to his own bed he found his steps were somehow lighter, his heart more alive than it had felt in years, and the fierce burning in his loins was almost impossible to control. One more day, he told himself eagerly; tomorrow night, and the little Celtic prize will be mine.

"My name is Talorc, ma'am," the powerful young guard said, with a slight nod toward Melangell. His young face was broad and open; his long brown tunic and breeches were spotlessly clean. He wore two heavy silver neck chains, and a wide tooled leather armband divided a blue tattoo that twined down his right arm. The woman looks frail, he thought cynically, eyeing her sitting in a chair while the old woman dressed her long wheaten hair. But then, most Celtic women looked frail to him. Probably the fair coloring, he reflected, studying her. She, however, was especially delicate-looking, shorter than even most Cruithni women, and her figure still tiny despite the children she'd borne. Her skin looked like fresh cream, and only her bright green eyes punctuated all the paleness and fragility of her appearance. Still, he could see why Achivir had wanted her for so long; she was not a bad-looking woman at all.

"Talorc, is it?" she said quietly, and he ceased his musing when he realized she was studying him as intently as he had been studying her.

"Yes, lady." He bowed again, feeling slightly foolish.

"The same Talorc my future kinsman Drosten has often spoken of?" she asked, still eyeing him. He nodded, fingering the handgrip of his round shield awkwardly.

"I can assume so, lady, since he and I have been friends since we began our warriors' training together, although if he spoke too highly of Talorc I am sure he meant someone else."

Melangell laughed and the young man was surprised at how that one small action lit her face and eased the lines of worry and strain around her eyes. She was, indeed, a lovely woman, and he enjoyed making her laugh.

"Only when he was drunk would Drosten think highly of me, I'm afraid," he said solemnly.

"Oh, I don't believe you!" She smiled. "You look like a good man to me, and my instincts are seldom wrong. I am pleased to have you as my guard."

"Thank you, lady. I'll do my best to live up to your good opinion of me."

"I'm sure you will, Talorc." She nodded at him, and he took it as a sign of dismissal. Turning, he exited the suite and stationed himself outside the door, checking his sword and dagger, positioning his shield on his left arm, and placing the butt of his spear on the floor at his side. His first real duty, guarding the woman of the king, and by the gods, he would see that it was carried out to perfection! As evening approached, he admitted three servants carrying steaming trays of food, silver ewers of wine, a beautiful cloak for his mistress, embroidered drapery for Achivir's chair. Finally the king himself appeared, escorted by two advisers, eagerness lighting his eyes like a youth with his first love. He had attired himself royally in embroidered shirt and breeches, a leather belt inlaid with jewels around his waist, gold and silver jewelry glinting from his arms and neck. Talorc stood aside respectfully while they passed. When the door opened to admit them, he glimpsed the lady standing shyly by the hearth, and he found himself envying the king. She looked like a doll a princess might own, tiny and perfect from her glinting golden hair to the shimmering embroidery of the cloak she wore over one shoulder, Celtic-style.

The two advisers hovered over Achivir's shoulders like annoying flies as he dined with his mistress—pouring his wine, cutting his meat, dishing out more stew, offering him sweets on a chased-silver tray—until at last, with no little annoyance, he waved them away. Obediently they stood by the door, finding their enforced silence and inactivity difficult to maintain. Achivir poured his own wine, and the young woman's. He offered her the finest cakes his cooks could create, and the choicest portions of meat, which she politely declined. She ate little, in fact, and he attributed it to a tense stomach. Of course she is frightened, he thought, studying her; bedding with a king is a new thing for her.

Comfortably full, the king leaned back in his chair and motioned for the food to be removed. The advisers jumped at the hint, like two overeager horses waiting for a race.

"Leave us," Achivir ordered when they exited the room, to save them the trouble of returning. Melangell's serving woman, seated behind her lady, rose uncertainly to her feet, unsure if the command applied to her as well. Melangell turned her head at the sound, glanced back at Achivir, and spoke quietly to the old woman.

"You may go, Severa," she said. "I'll call if you are needed." The old woman quickly went to her room off the side of the suite and closed the door, leaving Achivir and his lady alone.

The king sipped his wine, put the cup aside, and looked at Melangell for a long moment. She seemed to be waiting for him, and her forthright manner pleased him. "Come here," he said, pulling his sealskin cloak aside and patting one knee. Obediently the young woman stood, came to him, and seated herself on his knee. He put one arm around her waist and pulled her close. The sweet warmth of her sent the blood rushing in his head, and he lightly ran a hand down her cheek as she gazed at her lap.

"Gods above, you are lovely," he whispered, sliding his hand across her chin, down her neck, to the heavy silver brooch at her right shoulder. He pulled the pin loose and let her cloak fall free over the arm of his chair. She was too tense, too afraid. He stroked her slim white arm, pulling her close and running his tongue along the delicate curve of one ear. She gasped and he felt her shiver in his lap, and he was pleased by it. No frigid widow, this. Perhaps she contained all the fire attributed to Celtic women, if only he could stoke it properly.

She seemed to be going limp in his arm, and his tongue explored down her neck, lingered at the base of her throat, and continued on as he slid the gown from her shoulders. Her excitement seemed to be springing forth in full bloom, for when he pulled the gown to her waist and his eager hand took her breast, she moaned weakly. By the gods, he thought wildly, she is hotter than a mare in season! What have I stumbled on here in this little Celtic witch?

Sliding her from his lap, he stood and removed his cloak, his heavy belt, his shirt, boots, breeches. It seemed to take forever, and he dropped them hastily to the floor like a heap of discarded refuse. She, too, was naked, the gown around her ankles, and he sat back in the chair, pulling her to him, kissing her mouth fiercely as he put her astride his lap. She brought out things in him he had not thought he still possessed! Again and again she roused him as the night wore on, until the king thought it was he who was being kept, she who was doing the keeping. When dawn approached, he found himself too exhausted to return to his own room, as was customary. With morning a worried Severa poked her head from her room, to find Achivir and Melangell sprawled deep in sleep beneath the patterned wool blanket, looks of contented weariness on both their faces.

"She treats him more like a king than he's ever been treated before," a guard in the hallway outside Achivir's private quarters whispered to another when Melangell passed by, a tray of foods in her hands. It had become her custom to oversee his evening meal herself, instructing the cooks, choosing nutritious foods and interesting new dishes, even preparing an occasional specialty herself. Today her surprise was a wine sauce for his beef.

A guard opened the door and she passed into Achivir's room. In the few short weeks she'd been there, the appearance of the palace had changed dramatically. Achivir's stark rooms were now hung with bright tapestries, and large bearskin rugs covered the neatly swept floors. The servants grumbled at the unaccustomed chores they were expected to perform, but she insisted nonetheless. Hearths were cleaned, ashes carried out, cobwebs removed from ceilings, shuttered windows opened to admit light and fresh air. The stored household items of the king's dead wife were brought out, all the tapestries, hangings, coverlets, and cushions that made Achivir's spare barracks once more a home.

No, I do not love him, Melangell reflected, putting the tray down and setting out his meal, but he is not a bad man, and I am content. I am well fed, well cared for, and able to wait for my children's return. I keep busy so I do not go mad with worry over them. Achivir has sent out messages to all the surrounding lands; as soon as something is heard, I will know it.

She arranged a few wildflowers in a small green Roman glass vase and put it on her table. The Cruithni are too industrious a race, she reflected; they seldom have the need for art or culture or beauty for its own sake. A few flowers will brighten the room.

She turned when the door opened and Achivir entered, several stewards and advisers clustered around trying to discuss some important matter of state. He seemed only half-interested, and when he spied Melangell standing there, wearing the pale yellow Cruithni gown he'd given her, the long full sleeves and hem lavishly trimmed with gold embroidery, her green eyes shining like jewels, he waved the chattering throng away angrily.

"Leave us," he barked, walking to his tapestried chair and sitting down heavily. The men looked at one another in dumb surprise, bowed low, and left the room. Melangell caught the looks on their faces and turned to the king in concern.

"You shouldn't have turned them away so abruptly," she gently chided, pouring some honeyed wine for him. "They must have had something important to discuss with you, and you know the pride of these men who—"

"They are at me all day," he said, taking a great gulp of the wine. "I can enjoy my evening meal in peace. Come here . . ."

He motioned her closer, reaching into a leather pouch suspended at his hip. "I had this made for you," he said, pulling out an exquisite silver necklace ornamented with plaques of various woodland animals. Melangell's mouth fell open in surprise and he smiled at her reaction. "I know how you like animals, and so I hoped it would please you," he said, rising to his feet and fastening it around her neck.

"I . . . I don't know what to say," she breathed, holding the chain out and studying the meticulous craftsmanship. "It is too lovely, Achivir. You shouldn't have . . ."

"Nonsense!" he replied, seating himself and spearing a chunk of beef with his knife. "Sit down and dine with me. Tell me what surprises you've prepared for me today."

She laughed, fingering the treasure as she sat at her own table and explained the foods to him. He nodded and looked at her while he began to eat.

"I have managed to keep myself fit for all these years," he said, "but you threaten to make me into a fat old man, eating all day and lying abed all night."

"It is not the bed that will make you fat, sire," she retorted, and he roared with laughter.

"By the gods, woman, not when you are in it! I suppose the increase in activity makes up for the increase in food, eh?"

She smiled at him and he wiped his fingers on his shirt and gazed at her hotly. "Everything you do arouses me, lady," he said, his voice husky with feeling. "You sit there and eat a meal and I find you more enticing than a dancing girl from Greece. Come . . ." he said, pushing the table aside and rising to his feet. "To the bed. I want you . . . now."

"But, Achivir . . . the food . . ." she started to protest. He pulled her to her feet.

"We will eat later. I want you now. In bed, on the floor, I care not."

His clothes were coming off and she could see the hunger burning in his eyes. Quietly she slipped from her gown and laid it on the chair. Naked, he came toward her, gliding his hands eagerly up her body. Stopping at her face, he kissed her fiercely, his tongue exploring her mouth as he lifted her in his arms and carried her to the bed.

"Let him take her all he will," one of the dismissed advisers snapped as they walked down the hall.

"Let him?" asked another. "Already he neglects his work. Would you have other hands, more wicked hands perhaps, taking more and more of his power? The man is bewitched, I say, and it must be stopped."

"And soon," agreed a third.

"Exactly," said the first. "He has been alone so long, his desire is natural. Let him take her all he will, and soon she must be got with child. She is not too old. Then he will have to leave her alone, and can return to his duties, as is proper."

"And if she does not?"

The first man shrugged noncommittally. "Then some other means must be found to remove her."

Severa held Melangell's head low as she leaned over the side of her bed, retching violently into a large wooden bucket.

"By the gods . . ." the young woman gasped, clenching the coverlet tightly in one shaky hand when another spasm hit her.

"Easy, dear," Severa soothed, stroking her charge's damp hair. "Broichan will be here soon. He will help you."

Melangell flopped back on the bed, grimacing at the foul taste in her mouth, and pushed the old woman's hand away in irritation. "I told you not to send for him, Severa," she muttered, gazing blankly at the dark peat smoke rising from the hearth. "I dislike him, and besides, I know what ails me. I can care for myself."

"But, lady," Severa protested, "he can give you something

for the nausea. You may know what ails you, and even what to do for it, but you have no medicines here to treat yourself."

She turned her head when the door opened a crack and Talorc looked in, his keen dark eyes scanning the pallid face of his mistress. "Broichan is here," he said. Before Melangell could protest, Severa nodded to the guard. He opened the door and a tall bony-looking middle-aged man came in, a long graying beard adorning his chin, his hands clasped professionally in front of the fur cloak he wore. He strode to the bedside and without a word picked up the bucket, examining its contents briefly before he turned his attentions to Melangell. Severa stood to one side, watching the man examine his reluctant patient.

"You know, of course, that you are with child," he observed casually as he worked.

"Aye," the young woman muttered dully.

"You don't wish it?" he asked, glancing at her pale features.

"I am a woman. Of course I do. But after carrying five in my lifetime, I cannot be too excited about it, can I?"

"You'd best be excited about it," he said dryly, feeling her abdomen, "for when the king finds out, you will be treated as the queen you are not."

Melangell narrowed her eyes and looked at the man. She did not like the implication of his words. "Meaning what, Broichan?" she said angrily.

"Only this, lady," he said, straightening up and replacing the bedcovers. "You are not queen. Achivir is desperate for a child, even by a concubine. Give him one, and your future here will be assured."

Their eyes locked for an instant, defiance to defiance, before he turned to the door.

"I will have some medicines sent for you. Eat lightly, sparingly. No heavy drink. A little dry bread will help settle your stomach. And for the gods' sake, woman, take care of yourself and your child. It will be worth your while to do so. I will inform Achivir. Clean up this mess, for he will no doubt be here at once to see you."

He brushed past Severa, opened the door, and like a swooping falcon was gone. Melangell looked at Severa, took a deep breath, and closed her eyes wearily. "Fetch a washbasin," she muttered, "and throw out the bucket. I must get myself in a more presentable state for the king."

Achivir treated her like a delicate bird, she mused as she sat in a large wooden chair comfortably padded with down-stuffed cushions, and listened to a flute player entertain them at their evening meal. Severa had tucked his latest gift around her swelling lap—a lovely white lamb's-wool coverlet, lightly embroidered with silver thread. Broichan is right, she reflected, picking at her spare dinner: a queen could not be more lavishly honored than he now honors me. She turned aside and looked at him. The king seemed lost in thought at the sweet sounds of the flute he'd gone to the trouble of bringing up from the Celtic lands to the south. He caught her glance, turned, and smiled at her.

"More wine?" he asked. She shook her head and smiled back, returning her attentions to the flute player.

What will my children think of me when they return? she mused, closing her eyes and listening to the music. If they return. So long, and still no word from them. No sightings. Nothing . . ..

She opened her eyes and found tears clouding her vision. No, she chided herself resolutely, I must not cry. Tears do no good; I have learned that long ago. I am surviving, and that is not so bad a thing. Though when I will need Brennos again, as he predicted, I cannot see. Every fate now seems to be working in my favor.

She sighed and looked down into her wine cup. The wine was watered, on Broichan's recommendation, and the glimmering pink depths scarcely cast a reflection back at her. The fates, she pondered; as weak and insubstantial as this wine, yet as all-consuming, all-directing. Achivir and I, we don't love each other. There is passion, yes; and we fulfill needs we each feel, but there is no love. That is what the fates have decreed for me, in the end. Not security, or love, but need. Two tottering trees, limbs entwined, leaning against each other for mutual support.

She looked up at the flute player and found her tired eyes refreshed by his Celtic good looks. He was fairly tall and his long hair hung down his back in the coveted Three Colors—

brown on top, then reddish, and ending nearly blond. He had tied it into a thick plait to show off the colors to best advantage, and she saw that his sparkling blue eyes were framed in long, dark lashes. Melangell looked away bitterly as a wave of homesickness engulfed her.

Maybe Brennos was right, she thought, suddenly somber, sipping the watered wine. Even the mightiest tree will eventually fall. None are immune to the winds of fate.

Talorc stood before the king, fingering his spear while he waited for the man to look up from his work.

"Yes?" Achivir said, impatience clear in his voice as he pushed a pile of ivory tallies aside. His mood lifted when he recognized the dark young man who stood before him. "You're Melangell's guard, aren't you?" he said, his voice calming.

"Yes . . ." Talorc stammered, swallowing the nervousness in his throat. The king had never addressed him directly before.

"Well?" Achivir said mildly, leaning back in his chair and seeming, at heart, grateful for the interruption. "Is something wrong?"

"No, sire," the young man said, shifting his feet. "I . . . I thought you should be told."

"Told what?"

"Your Lady Melangell wishes to go for walks. I . . . ah . . . I told her she could not, without your permission."

Achivir studied the young man's flushed face. A sensible fellow, he reflected; obviously he'd made a good choice for Melangell's guard.

"Why does she wish to go for walks?" the king said, trying to put the young man at ease. "Isn't she happy here? I have provided every comfort for her. A musician, games to play, embroideries . . . what more does she want?"

"To walk, my lord. She says all the inactivity is unhealthful. She must see the sun, feel the wind—those are her words." He shrugged. "She is Celtic, sire. You know how they are."

"I do," Achivir said, gazing down thoughtfully at his folded hands. "They seem to need nature more than we do.

Their mystical communion, the sacred groves, all that nonsense."

"Yes, sire; exactly. She says it will be healthier for her and her child to go for walks, to be once more surrounded by nature, as she puts it. She is unused to a town such as ours."

"Yes." The king nodded to himself. "Their towns usually consist of a small collection of crude wooden huts thrown up atop a hill, soon to rot away into the soil they sprang from." He fell silent a moment, then looked up at Talorc. "You did well to consult me first, my man." He smiled. "Yes, she may go for brief walks. Brief, do you hear? And you must always accompany her. Take the old woman too, if she can manage it. But guard her well, Talorc. Keep her away from any rocks, or the cliffs by the shore. Nothing must happen to my child, do you understand?"

Talorc straightened up, clenching his spear firmly. "Yes, sire."

"Good," Achivir said, waving a hand at him absently as he returned to his work. "You may go."

His mistress had been right, Talorc noted as they strolled across a wide flat meadow beyond the town walls. In just these few short weeks he could see color returning to her pale cheeks, her eyes sparkling with renewed happiness, her strength and vigor growing. Celts must be like wild birds, he reflected, able to live in captivity, but truly happy only when set free.

The brisk salty wind from the sea whipped his long hair across his eyes and he paused to tie a leather band around his head. He could not have a little thing like blowing hair interfere with his guard duties. Melangell strolled on ahead of him, deep in animated conversation with the Celtic musician. They chatted so rapidly in their own language that at times he had trouble keeping up with their words. She seems to find great pleasure in the company of one of her own, he mused, tying off the thong behind his head as he watched her throw back her head and laugh like a little girl at something the man had said. The wind was tossing their words aside; he couldn't tell what they were discussing. Seizing his spear, he trotted to catch up to them.

"Talorc . . ." Melangell laughed when he reached her side. "Eldol was just telling me about a grossly fat old man he once played for. Totally bald, and as pink and round as a mother sow. He said . . ."—she gulped, pressing one hand lightly to her chest as if gasping for air—"that the man even grunted and wheezed like a pig, and when he began to play the flute, the old man got to his feet and . . ."

She stopped abruptly at the sound of a shout behind them. They turned and Talorc placed a cautious hand on his sword hilt when he saw a palace guard coming toward them, panting heavily from his long run.

"What is it?" Talorc demanded, stepping in front of Melangell protectively.

"The king sends for his lady," the man said. "At once. He has word . . . on her children . . ."

The color drained from Melangell's face. Alarmed, Eldol placed an arm around her back to catch her if she should faint. "We must go," she muttered, her voice as thin as an insect's wing. "My children . . . we must . . ."

Despite her swelling stomach, she began to run, but both Eldol and Talorc seized her arms and restrained her. "No," her guard said firmly, "we walk."

She was too numb to argue. Puppetlike, she set off between her two escorts, hurrying to the distant town as fast as they dared.

Achivir made her sit, when she didn't want to sit. He sent for wine, and she wasn't thirsty. He waited, he delayed, till she thought she would scream from the silence.

"Tell me!" she begged, seizing his hand when he walked past her. "My children! By the names of all the gods, tell me! What do you know?"

Achivir paused and looked down at her stricken face. He took a deep breath, glancing quickly to the musician and her guard. They looked nearly as grim as she was. "Simal has returned," he said, taking her hands in his.

"Simal?" she squeaked, her voice tiny and afraid.

"Yes. Resad sent him to tell you—"

"Tell me what? What of Resad?" She jumped to her feet. Achivir forced her back into the chair with a stern warning. "For the sake of the child, woman, if not for yourself, stay calm or I'll have Broichan give you something to make you calm."

Melangell slumped back in her chair, defeated. The news must be bad . . . terribly bad. She must prepare herself for the worst.

"Simal was sent to tell you that they are well," the king continued. "Your two sons, and Drosten. They are in Celtic lands now, and on the trail of your daughter, though they have not yet caught her."

He paused, nodding to the guard by the door. The man opened the door to the hallway and Simal entered, tired and dirty from his hard journey, a beard growing on his unshaven face. He carried a large cloth sack over one shoulder.

"Simal . . ." Melangell said, rising slowly to her feet when he approached her.

"Lady." He bowed, lowering the heavy sack to the floor.

"What else did Resad say? What of Cadvan? And Anor? Where is she?" she pressed him.

"Your son sends a gift, lady," he said, motioning to the bag at his feet. "Drosten says they are now so far south that, as you wished, when Anor is recovered they will head to the west and be married there. They will send word."

Melangell sat back in her chair, her heart racing wildly in fear. "The gift?" she questioned. Simal opened the sack, lifting out the washed and bound heads of the two traders who'd kidnapped Anor.

"Resad said to tell you that justice has been done to these two, and honor brought to the torque he wears."

Despite the gruesomeness of the gift, Melangell felt relief at Resad's message and found herself smiling at the words. "Then surely, if you caught these two," she went on, looking away while Simal returned the heads to the sack, "you must have found Anor."

"No, lady," the weary man said, straightening and casting a nervous glance at the king. Achivir moved cautiously to Melangell's side, and alarm gripped her throat at their odd behavior.

"Anor . . . what of Anor?" she demanded, rising to her feet and confronting the startled warrior. She could feel Achivir's hands clenched insistently on her shoulders, and Simal's dark gray eyes suddenly turned pitying.

"Tell me!" she screamed, reaching for his arms.

"She has been sold, lady," the warrior said as gently as he could.

"Sold?" she breathed in horror. Sold? A slave?

"To the Romans . . ." he began, but before he could finish, she collapsed with a moan into the king's arms.

"Get Broichan!" Achivir bellowed, lifting Melangell and carrying her to the bed. "Leave! All of you! Go! And get Broichan at once!"

Talorc stood aside when Broichan left Melangell's room. The young man could tell by the grim set to the druid's mouth that the lady's condition was unchanged. Closing the door, he glanced around the corner and caught Severa's eye. The old woman still sat by the bed, where she had waited and watched for three days, and she shook her head slowly when she spied Talorc's worried expression. Glumly the guard closed the door, reflecting on the sudden turn events had taken. The shadow of death hung heavy in her room, though he couldn't be sure the victim it would claim—the lady, her child, or even poor Anor, in some distant Roman town. He shook his head and looked up at the sound of approaching footsteps. It was Eldol, carrying his polished wooden flute in one hand.

"She will see no one," Talorc muttered, looking up at the tall young musician. Eldol glanced at the flute, sighed, and returned Talorc's gaze.

"I wish there was something we could do for her," he said.

"I know." Talorc nodded. "I have thought the same myself."

"Perhaps if I played anyway, it might ease her mind. We Celts love our music."

"No," Talorc said resolutely. "She has ordered me. I am sorry."

Eldol nodded his understanding. "She has given up, hasn't she?" he asked.

"Yes. So they say. Rumor is that soon the child will go, and she will quickly follow."

"Then you must help me, Talorc," Eldol said eagerly as an idea seized him. "The moon is full. We must take her for a walk . . . tonight. I understand her, perhaps as no one else here does. She says she was once a druidess, that she had powers she has now lost. My people do not lose their abilities. They just go dormant at times, like a sleeping bear in the winter. Perhaps this has been the winter of her life, and it is now time for her to emerge. Help me, Talorc, and we can restore her to her old self. Will you?"

Talorc looked at him with a cautious eye. Such mysticism was beyond him. Yet the man seemed so certain, so sure.

"What must I do?" he sighed, and Eldol smiled broadly at his words.

The indigo night soothed Melangell like a balm as she walked slowly, woodenly, to the rocky clifftops by the beach. Despite her gloom, the mystical lyricism of the night danced her spirits higher. Bless Eldol, she thought while she walked; Celt that he is, he knew just what I needed and he insisted, despite my stubbornness, that I get it.

She stopped at the cliff's edge and heard her two escorts, Eldol and Talorc, halt a short distance behind her. Taking a deep breath of the tangy air, she pulled her cloak from her head and let her hair stream free in the breeze. Moonlight washed her like molten silver and bathed the choppy sea in gaudy sparkles.

The moon . . . She sighed, seating herself on a rock and gazing up at the heavens. Like a human soul, you enter this dark world, grow, age, die, and grow again. Over and over, like our earthly cycle of lives. And we do not fear when you go, for we know you will be back. Just as we come back, again and again. The sun may be the gods, steady and eternal and never-changing. But you, moon, you are us. Frail humans. Changeable humans. Humans . . .

She placed a hand on her stomach and sighed again. Who are you, child? What are you? Why can't I love you? You are a product of need, of lust, not of love. You are not mine . . . you are someone else's. Achivir's, not mine.

She stood as an idea gripped her. Extending her arms to the moon, she closed her eyes and her mind and opened her heart. She could hear Eldol whisper harshly to Talorc when her guard started forward in alarm. The Celt knew what she was doing. He knew she must be alone.

Alone . . . she mused, her mind sinking beneath her. My

feet are rooted to the soil, my hands reach to the skies; like a tree I bridge the gap between heaven and earth. Solid and eternal, I let the power of creation course through me, like sap in a tree. Like a tree I am alone, on this barren, windswept moor; the only tree, the only mystic, the only . . .

"Melangell . . ."

She looked around uncertainly in the radiant night. Who spoke? she wondered. The world had a strangely still quality, like a painting or a dream.

"Little apple, what do you do to yourself?"

"Esus?" she gasped, and tears began to silver her cheeks.

"You have a rare gift, my child. You must not abuse it."

He stood on a nearby rock, as white and insubstantial as the silent moonlight.

"What do you do to yourself?" he repeated, his blue eyes twinkling brightly like two stars in the night. She looked down at her swelling belly in sudden shame. How must I look to others? she thought. To Simal? To Eldol? To my children, when they return? I am a whore, nothing more . . .

"Help me, Esus. I am lost . . . help me," she gasped, trying to reach for him. "My life is gone, lost. Help me . . ."

He smiled at her, but his message was the same. "You have a rare gift, Melangell . . . a rare gift . . ."

She could almost smell the warmed summer grasses in a little valley nineteen years ago; nearly feel the kindly touch of his hand on hers.

"Esus . . ." she sobbed, and then she knew. For too long her life had been others, and she had suffered for it. Her husbands, her children, her duties, and in all the press, her own destiny had been abandoned. Such was the lot of women, she knew, but that did not make it right, nor desirable. Like the moon, all die and come again. Her friends, her husbands, her children, too, dear as they were to her, were souls, lives, of their own. Their destinies were not hers. And she? What was she?

Nodding her understanding, she watched Esus slowly fade from view.

A rare gift.

"I'm sorry, little child," she whispered, and flung herself from the cliff.

Part 2

ANOR'S STORY

*C*OLD METAL PRESSED JAGGEDLY INTO ANOR'S CHEEK, AND SHE turned her head to avoid it.

Gods above! She gasped, choking against the tight gag in her mouth. Her body felt leaden, heavy, as it had when she'd had a fever three winters ago. She could feel the cart lurching hurriedly over the rough ground, hear the clang and jangle of the peddlers' pots and pans shifting overhead. She tried to move but found her arms were securely tied behind her. Her legs, too, seemed to be bound, for when she attempted to kick them free of the encumbering junk, the best she could manage was a small twist. Panic rose at the overwhelming tide of helplessness that engulfed her and she squirmed mightily, trying to somehow free herself, to escape into the surrounding night.

The cart pulled to a halt and the clamor around her fell silent. Above her the clutter was tossed aside and a man's scarred face appeared in the gloom.

"Here! What's this?" he growled down at her. "Best be still, my darling, or we'll have to quiet you ourselves. Uncomfortable, are you, eh?" He grinned. "Just wait there like a good girl and we'll soon have you out of your hideaway. Right?"

A callused, foul-smelling hand reached down and roughly patted her cheek, and Anor clenched her eyes shut in sick fear. Helplessly she waited while she was again concealed beneath their tattered goods and the cart swayed into motion once more.

What do they want of me? she wondered desperately. What will happen . . . ? Mother! she cried silently. Drosten,

429

my love! The horror of his gaze when she had last seen him, sprawling to the ground, the pallid moonlight turning the blood on his face a sickly purple, crushed her heart like dry leaves.

Will I ever see you again? She sobbed, lowering her cheek to the scant comfort of a bent bronze ewer.

"Now we walk."

Anor roused from a restless night by a low campfire at the sound of a voice nearby. She had scarcely slept for three days, so maddening was her fear and heartbreak, until the distinctions between waking and sleeping vanished and she spent the unending days in the same trancelike weariness that marked her nights.

"Get up, little vixen!" the man snapped, grabbing her bound arms and jerking her roughly to her feet. "I said it is time to walk!"

Anor gazed at him dully, her mind full of hatred. It was plain they intended to skip the morning meal, as the taller of the two kicked the campfire out, picked up their food rations, and followed her and his companion into the forest. Ever since they'd traded their pony for food at a farmstead, they seemed to be in a hurry, and the girl wondered at the reason for it. Perhaps they were being followed. Surely someone would have found Drosten, even if the blow had killed him. Achivir could not allow such things in his land. A party of warriors would have been sent out to track them down, to save her. Yes, that must be it! And now they hurry away, to whatever safety they think they can find. If they are fast enough, they will succeed, and with it all hopes for rescue will die.

As if sent by Nemetona, a looped and protruding tree root crossed the path ahead and Anor slid her foot beneath it. She fell heavily to her face, unable to catch herself, her bound arms slipping from the startled peddler's grasp. Her forehead struck the ground and for a moment light splashed across her mind. Weakly she tried to lift her head from the forest loam.

"What the . . ." her captor hissed. She felt his hands on her arms, lifting her to her feet.

"I told you to bind her arms in front!" the other man protested. "You have her trussed up like a goose; it's no wonder she fell."

"Shut up!" the shorter of the two retorted. "She fell because she is weak. She will not eat; she will not sleep."

Jerking her upright, he roughly brushed the dirt from her, his scarred face twisted in disgust. When Anor's weight fell on her twisted ankle, a sharp pain shot up her leg and she moaned weakly through her gag, slumping toward the man.

The taller man grimaced. "Now see what you've—"

"Will you be quiet!" the other snapped. "It is twisted, that's all. Sit her down and we'll pack it in mud."

"This will never work, never," the first muttered, wandering off in search of mud. "Peddlers we were and peddlers we should have stayed, but no, you had grand ideas. Sell her to the Romans, you said. They will pay a pretty price for so fair a flower. But look at her, eh? Look at her!" he suddenly called out through the trees, turning toward his companion. "The fair flower has withered. Skinny and dirty, her face scratched, her eyes sunken, and now a twisted ankle. We will be lucky if some raw legionary wants her, never mind a centurion or general. What of your fine plans now, eh? What now?"

The man turned angrily and strode off through the woods, and Anor looked at her captor in horror. So now she knew her fate. It was not to be the loving wife of Drosten, but the slave and mistress of some foul Roman.

She stared at the man, tears welling in her eyes. Oh, gods, not that! Please! Not that! He slouched back against a tree, his face a frown as he tried to shut out his companion's words, and did not return her gaze.

Simal and Drosten tensed at the soft sound of footsteps in the forest, expecting it to be Aniel returning to camp but unwilling to allow any laxity in their watch. Both men studied the scout's face intently when he crept into the dim circle of firelight, trying to read his mission and finding only a carefully practiced blankness of expression. Scouts and trackers were not emotional men.

"Well?" Drosten said testily, his fingers nervously playing

along his spear. Aniel squatted by the fire, his eyes on the fierce gaze of Resad opposite, the golden torque glinting like flames around the Celt's neck.

"I have found their trail," Aniel said quietly. "They must be flying like the wind in their haste to escape."

"And my sister?" Resad said grimly. Aniel shrugged.

"I see only the tracks of the two men and the pony cart. They take turns riding and walking. The girl must be in the cart, for I see no trace of her so far. Soon she must be allowed out, to relieve herself if nothing else, and then I will know. By their haste, though, we can judge rightly that she is with them."

"And their path?" Drosten snapped, lowering his spear across his lap.

Aniel nodded confirmation of everyone's suspicions. "To the south . . . the Roman camps," he said simply.

"Then we must go!" Drosten declared, standing. "Follow them before they escape! Catch them! We must . . ."

Resad rose to his feet as silently as a great stag of the forest, trying to avoid waking his sleeping younger brother, whose valiant attempt to stay awake with the warriors had ended in failure.

"Drosten," Resad said levelly, circling the fire and placing a hand on the young warrior's knotted shoulder, "we have traveled three days without rest. It will do little good to grow so weary we miss clues or are unable to outwit them. She is my sister; I want her back as much as you. But we lack the stamina of gods; we must eat and rest. Tomorrow we will continue."

He fixed his piercing blue eyes on Drosten's battered face in pity. The Pict's bruises and cuts still showed blue and purple, and Melangell's ointment flaked from his swollen lip like a gruesome plague. Drosten stared back, then turned away with a small shake of his head. "We must find her," he muttered woodenly, walking back to his guard post. "We must."

The old couple hovered nervously at the doorway of their thatch hut while the group of warriors examined their newly acquired pony.

"When did you purchase it?" the tallest of the five

demanded, stepping away from his companions and striding toward the pair.

"Yesterday morning," the old man croaked. "I . . . we did not know anything was amiss. Please . . . if it is yours, take it and go. Only do us no harm. We didn't mean to cause trouble. Please . . ."

Resad smiled grimly at their agitation but felt too angry to try to reassure them. "It is not ours," he snapped. "It belonged to one we seek. Tell us who traded it."

"Two peddlers," the old woman mumbled. "They had no cart, but a runaway slave—"

Resad's hand shot out and intercepted Drosten when he started toward the couple. "A slave?" Drosten growled. The man and woman shrank away in fear.

"Please . . . we know nothing. Do not harm us," the man begged.

"Peace, old man," Resad said tersely. "We do you no harm. We are sent by the king. Tell us of this slave."

"A girl, fair and frail. She was not of the Cruithni; they said she had escaped from the Romans and they were returning her for the reward."

Drosten turned away bitterly, his spear clenched overhead between his two fists as if he meant to snap it in two. The rage within him seemed near to exploding, and without a word he stalked into the forest, following the clear trail of the peddlers. Puzzled, the old couple watched him go.

"We gave them food," the man explained to Resad. "We believed their word."

"What of the girl?" Resad pressed. "Was she well? Had she been injured?"

The old man shrugged and looked at his wife. "They kept her apart," the woman whispered slowly. "I saw her but once, and then she was bound and gagged. She seemed thin and weary, but otherwise well. I could not see that she was injured."

They stared at the tall warrior fearfully until, to their immense relief, he turned and led the other men into the forest after their companion.

"They know they are being followed," Aniel observed as they ate a quick evening meal. "Anor has done what she can

433

to slow them, but still they press on." He looked aside at Drosten, who lay on his back by the fire, his head on his traveling pack, gazing up at the stars.

"So now they have split up, to trick us," Drosten muttered into the night air.

"Then we will do likewise," Simal said, tearing off a chunk of bread.

"Yes!" Cadvan interjected. "Split up, trail them both, and find Anor, whichever one she is with. I can catch one. I know I can!" he boasted, tossing his dagger with a sharp thud into the trunk of a nearby tree.

"Not with your weapon needlessly dulled, boy," Aniel chided him. He reached out, removed the knife, and tossed it back to the boy. It landed point down in the narrow gap of sod between the startled boy's feet.

"I think Cadvan had better go with me and Drosten," Resad laughed, "so that we can keep an eye on him."

"But I—" the boy began to protest.

"I was just about to suggest that." Aniel nodded. "Simal and I will track the taller one, and you three follow the shorter. We are bound to catch them, especially since whichever of them has your sister over his shoulder will be traveling much slower."

Resad nodded. "An hour's sleep apiece, then," he said, tossing a cleaned squirrel bone into the fire, "and then we set out again, while it is still dark."

He kept to the high ground, carefully avoiding mud and leaves and anything else that would leave too clear a trail. His trip was considerably slowed by his precautions, and by the excess weight of the girl he carried over his shoulder, and he wondered in rising fear if he would be swift enough to reach the Roman campsite before his pursuers caught him. Perhaps he should dump the girl and flee? A quick slash with his knife, or drop her into a stream and seek his own safety. But no . . . the thought of a bag full of fine Roman coins spurred him on. All had been arranged. The centurion would be waiting for him come morning, with the payment at hand. His pursuers would never expect Romans so near; their plans would be thrown off considerably. If he could just avoid them half the night, his ends would be achieved;

secure in Roman protection, with a reward of Roman silver. He'd worry about his damned companion later, wherever he'd gone to.

Salvation! He sighed when a wide, shallow river came in sight. Wearily he splashed down the grassy bank and out across the pebbled stream bed. Now, he knew, his trail would be all but lost, and all he had to do was wade through the knee-deep water until he reached the Roman camp downstream. Then his troubles would be over.

Anor, too, saw the thought behind her captor's actions, and she began to struggle with the last strength she possessed. To no avail. The short, stocky man clamped her firmly with one strong arm and continued on his way.

Drosten paced down one side of the stream, Resad and Cadvan down the other. Sooner or later the man must come out, and when he did, they would have him. He glanced across the meandering river and had to scan the dancing leaves and shadows before he caught a glimpse of Resad and Cadvan, loping low along the far bank like two great silent cats, their patterned Celtic cloaks making them nearly invisible in the dappled light. They were so near to catching the man now, he thought eagerly, his rage settling within him like a cold, blanketing snowfall. With Anor or without, when we find that bastard I will give him the longest, slowest taste of death I can devise. I will show him all the mercy he has shown us. Death will be a blessing . . .

He stopped abruptly at the scent of wood smoke, and with a warrior's instinct he dropped to the ground behind some streamside grasses. Glancing across the river, he saw that Resad and Cadvan had vanished; they, too, must be wary of something. At the sudden sound of two sparrows chittering furiously from the far bank, he froze, recognizing it as a warning from his companions: danger ahead. He whistled a soft song in reply, and hearing no answer, relaxed: the warning was real, but the danger was not imminent. He crept through the blue shadows of early dawn, the smoke smell growing in his nostrils until the freshness of the ash itself could be detected. And then he heard it—voices, laughing, talking Roman voices—and his hopes crumbled.

They had just struck camp, sixteen of them, and their

goods were already piled atop two large pack mules. The mules snorted in the chill morning air, protesting their burdens. Legionaries, obviously; foot soldiers, for the two pack mules were the only mounts visible. The soldiers stood sleepily around the dying campfire, long red cloaks pulled close against the cold, awaiting orders to leave.

He could not attack them, alone as he was, and they stayed too close together for him to pick off one or two. Try as he might, he could see no evidence of the peddler, or Anor. Perhaps their presence was just an odd twist of fate. Perhaps the man had emerged on the opposite bank and Resad had caught him. The thought excited him with a savage need for revenge, and after giving the Romans a last examination, he quietly withdrew.

The man had been easy enough to catch, his trail clumsy and amateurishly concealed. Aniel and Simal followed him at an easy pace, certain from the man's freedom of movement that he did not have the girl. Sure enough, when they spied him through the forest, hungrily downing blackberries from a thicket of brambles, they saw that he was alone. Well enough, Aniel mused as the two circled around to capture their unsuspecting victim, let Drosten rescue his lady himself. The man was either very confident or very stupid, because he seemed to be totally off his guard as he ate his fill. At a quick trilling whistle from Simal across the clearing, Aniel pulled out his sword, crouched, and in one wild rush the warriors burst upon the startled man, who dropped his pack, turned, and fled a few brief steps before a dagger to his thigh dropped him. Killing would have been simpler, but Resad's orders had been clear: bring him back alive for interrogation. And then let Drosten decide his fate.

Drosten knew something was wrong when he retreated upstream and saw no sign of Resad or Cadvan. Had they been captured? Or were they still waiting near the Roman camp? But surely the Romans had gone by now. Then where were they? What had happened?

Feeling himself safely distanced from enemy eyes, he found a shaded bend in the river and decided to cross to the other side. The sun was already descending down the sky, and he knew he must hurry if he hoped to find them before nightfall. Lifting his weapons and traveling pack above the water, Drosten slid into the rushing current and waded to the far bank. Emerging into the dusky woods, he squeezed what water he could from his dripping breeches and loped off downstream.

Twilight was falling when the vacated Roman camp came into view across the river, the hastily erected earthen dike around it looking forlorn and ghostly in the shadows. Crouched behind a bush, Drosten peered around, wondering where his companions were. A hand suddenly fell on his shoulder and he found himself staring into Resad's grim face.

"We have the man," the Celt said, and Drosten slowly rose to his feet.

"And Anor?" he asked numbly.

Resad shook his head and watched tears of anguish brim Drosten's eyes when he read the answer.

"She is gone," he said quietly. "The Romans have her."

Blood ran from the peddler's nose and broken lip when Drosten hauled him to his feet. Cadvan looked uncertainly at his older brother as Drosten let fly with another blow to the man's face. Resad stood impassively, seemingly unconcerned with the beating going on before him, but Cadvan knew him well enough to recognize the keenly searching cast of his eye, and it reassured him. So far Drosten's "interrogation" had produced nothing more than cries and moans and pleas for mercy. Surely, the boy thought, the peddler would have more information of use to them; information that would be lost if the man were beaten to death.

"Drosten!" Resad's voice cut through the silent forest as the young warrior pummeled the bound man's stomach, all the while sobbing in rage. When his word went unheeded, Resad strode across the glade and seized his friend's arm.

"That is enough," he said firmly. Suddenly aware of his presence, Drosten looked at him dumbly, grief and anger etching his scabbed face.

"I said it is enough," Resad repeated, pulling Drosten away from the gasping man and thrusting him toward his brother. Cadvan took his arm and led him to a tree, and he found the Cruithni to be as insensate as if he had been gripped by the battle fire of the Celts.

Resad crouched before the battered peddler and hauled him into a sitting position against a tree trunk. The man sagged sideways and Resad seized him in sudden irritation, slapping him across the face. "Speak, worm, if you value your life," he snarled. The man's head lolled drunkenly and he squinted at Resad through swollen eyes.

"Where is my sister?" Resad demanded.

"The Romans . . . gone . . ." the man mumbled, barely audible.

"I know she's gone!" Resad shouted, shaking the man. "Gone where? Tell me now, or die!"

"No!" the peddler gasped. "Centurion . . . bought her . . . I don't know . . . he said . . . said he would sell her to . . . to a tribune . . ."

"Where? What tribune?"

"The west . . . the borders . . . a small fort . . . he said the tribune wants a . . . a beautiful Celtic woman . . . will pay well."

"Who is he? What is his name?"

The peddler gasped again, trying to lick the dripping blood from his mouth.

"Tell me!" Resad repeated, grabbing the peddler's coarse woolen tunic and shaking him till his head rolled from side to side.

"Marcus . . . Marcus . . ." the man sobbed. "That's all I know. Please . . . I didn't know she was your sister. Spare me. I will give you my silver—"

"Silver? What silver?" Drosten growled, advancing toward the man, who cringed in terror at the sight of him.

"In my tunic . . . silver . . . payment . . ."

Resad ripped the man's tattered tunic and his eyes fell on a bulging leather purse tied to his side beneath one arm. Angrily he tore it free and tossed it to Drosten.

"This . . . for Anor?" the Pict gasped, disbelieving, as he looked into the bag. "Her life, our future, our happiness . . . for this?" Slowly he dumped the small silver coins to the ground, one by one, as the peddler watched sickly, and in the livid rage on the Pict's face the man read his fate. Resad stood and walked to his brother's side as Drosten pulled his dagger from his belt.

"Today you become a man, little brother," he said grimly while they watched. "Today you see your first killing."

Cadvan felt sick, but pride would not let him turn away. For five years he'd been in training for this moment. He would not lose face now, shame himself in front of his older brother. He'd been warned by his instructors that the first time was the worst. He would endure it.

The man screamed weakly when Drosten slit open his belly. Stuffing the empty leather purse into his mouth to silence him, the Pict scooped up a handful of the coins and forced them into the man's steaming innards as he thrashed on the ground.

"For Anor . . ." Drosten snarled, slashing the man's chest with tiny cuts and pushing pieces of Roman silver into each wound. "Die from your precious treasure, worm. Feel it with your last breath . . . Roman coin, tormenting you to the end."

He seemed to take malicious delight in the man's sufferings, and Cadvan fought to control his rising nausea. Even an animal is given a kinder death than this, the boy thought, swallowing hard as he stared at the glinting coins sliding around in the man's open abdomen, dark blood covering Drosten's arms, the inhuman moans of the man filling his head.

"For Anor . . . for Anor . . ." Drosten kept saying; and then, the peddler's body ludicrously reflecting the bits and pieces of his payment while he squirmed and thrashed, the Pict stood up, his knife poised in front of him, and glared down at his victim.

"Think of her," he said, slowly pressing the knife point into the side of the man's neck. Blood spurted out and the peddler stared at Drosten in horror.

"Think of her," Drosten repeated. "Let her be your final thought on this earth. The innocence your greed has destroyed. Is it worth it? Is it?"

He kicked savagely at the man and he flopped to one side, his life draining away, his abdomen spilling onto the ground, the coins rolling and bouncing crazily across the rocky soil.

Cadvan retched violently, and as he collapsed to the ground he heard Drosten's voice brokenly calling Anor's name into the silent trees.

Cadvan awoke to darkness, hushed voices, and the soothing smells of a campfire nearby. He struggled to sit, his stocky young body quaking, and grimaced at the foulness in his mouth.

"Some wine?" a voice offered, and Cadvan looked aside at Aniel's dark, grinning face, his even white teeth shining in the night.

"Wine?" he croaked, taking the Roman flask from the scout.

"Yes, puppy. You have had wine before, haven't you?" Aniel laughed. Cadvan stiffened at his jest.

"Aniel . . . enough," Drosten cautioned from beyond the fire.

"Yes . . . you are right." Aniel nodded, lounging back on one elbow. "It was a rough killing, to be your first one, Cadvan. But you are a man now. Drink, and then we must make plans."

Cadvan took a tentative swallow and found the unwatered wine strangely rich and pleasing. "Where did this come from?" he asked, taking another long swallow before Aniel retrieved the flask. "And why are you here? We had split up . . ."

"Easy, little brother!" Resad smiled, leaning toward him. "Let the wine settle your stomach a bit. They caught the other peddler and brought him here. He had little to tell us, however, and he now rests yonder with his companion. The wine and some food were his parting gift to us." Resad tossed a hunk of cheese to his brother and the boy caught it, sniffing it curiously before taking a bite.

"Roman cheese, Roman wine, Roman silver," Simal grunted. "Those two must have been a small spy network in themselves. We are well to be rid of them."

"But what do we do now?" Cadvan asked, eating the odd cheese hungrily.

"The only thing we can do," Resad said grimly, poking at the fire with a stick. "Try to find this fortress, and retrieve

our sister"—he cut his eyes across the fire to Drosten—
"whatever condition she might be in."

The Pict lifted his head and looked at Rèsad stonily. "If
she carries a Roman bastard, I will kill it when it is born.
Beyond that, I care little what condition she is in, so long as
I get her back. Her life matters more to me than her
virginity. I know the Romans will not long leave her pure. I
am no fool . . ." Angrily he snapped a pebble into the fire,
sending a shower of sparks into the night air.

"But," Cadvan interjected, "shouldn't someone let Mother know how we fare? She must be half-mad with worry by
now."

"I will go back," Simal offered. "It will not be so long a
journey at my own speed. What message should I give her?"

"Tell her we will find Anor . . ." Drosten began, stopping
when Resad suddenly stood, one hand absently fingering the
torque at his neck.

"Hand me the food sack the man carried," he directed
Aniel, who tossed the bag to him across the fire. The men
watched curiously as Resad walked to the bodies of the two
peddlers, drew his sword, and swiftly sliced their heads off.
One by one he put them in the sack and tied the top.

"Give her this," he said, extending the bag to a grinning
Simal. "It is the custom among her people. Tell her that we
will soon have Anor, and that the torque I wear has not been
dishonored."

Simal nodded, rose to his feet, and took a final swallow of
wine before hoisting the sack over one shoulder and disappearing into the forest.

"Tomorrow we head west," Drosten muttered, rolling
into his sealskin cloak by the fire. "We will leave the thieves'
bodies to rot into the loam. Let anyone have the coins who
dares to take them from a putrid corpse; otherwise may the
hooded crows and ravens claim them as they clean their
flesh. And when I find this Marcus, his fate will be no
kinder."

"Do you really think anyone will want such a skinny
wench?" the young legionary muttered to his centurion as
they ate a quick evening meal of beans and hard biscuits

washed down with sour wine. The men both looked across the campfire to where the Celtic girl lay sleeping, a rough army blanket pulled close around her neck. Her face was gray with travel dust and a few scratches marred her forehead, but they could see that beneath the filth and bony features lay a real beauty, a delicate quality such as northern women often manifested but which was almost unknown among their own females. A quality many men craved, lusted after, and a few, who were able to, paid handsomely for.

"You speak her tongue?" the centurion said gruffly, ladling more beans from the rough iron stew pot into his mess tin.

"Yes." The legionary nodded.

"Then wake her and tell her the situation she is in. Explain that it is in her interest to eat, restore her health and her looks, and be found pleasing to this Marcus fellow. Her life will go easier for her if she does. Otherwise I will be forced to sell her for what I can get, and only the kindness of her fates will decide whose bed that will bring her to. Tell her that, Rufus. Explain it simply, so she will understand. These barbarians are filled with rages and passions, but their mental capacity is not so great as ours."

The young soldier laid his tin patera on the ground and stood.

"She must be made to do as you say, boy." The centurion looked up at him, his eyes narrowing meaningfully. "I paid handsomely for her; I intend to make a nice profit from the purse of young Marcus. Understood?"

"Yes, sir." Rufus nodded and crossed the clearing, past his fellow soldiers, talking and jesting as they ate their meal, till he reached the slumbering girl. Pity moved him when he crouched beside her, his eyes falling on the stiff ropes around her little wrists, the makeshift leather hobble that fastened her ankles to a tree. She is scarcely more than a child, he thought, grasping one thin shoulder and shaking her gently.

Despite her weary sleep, the girl awakened instantly, her eyes springing wide in fear. The young soldier tried to smile at her, leaving his hand on her shoulder in what he hoped would be a comforting gesture. The girl just stared at him, her pale blue eyes like two icy northern lakes.

"I wish to talk to you," Rufus began, carefully choosing his words and trying to remember the right pronunciations. "Do you understand me?"

The girl nodded slowly, and he sensed her tensions easing beneath his hand. Relieved, he lowered himself to the ground and extended his legs stiffly. He saw her gaze flicker curiously over his strange clothes—the scarlet wool tunic and scarf he wore over warm leather knee breeches, his chest covered by segmented body armor, heavy studded boots on his feet, the foreign sword and dagger at his waist, a bronze helmet strapped over his right shoulder.

"What is your name?" he asked quietly. Her eyes roamed up to his face suspiciously and she made no reply.

"I want to help you," he persisted. "Tell me your name."

"I have no name," she whispered, "and the only help I seek is freedom. Will you give me that?" Sliding her arms up to her head, she rested one cheek on her hands and stared blankly ahead.

"Well, then, child-without-a-name," Rufus went on mildly, "I will tell you what is necessary to say, and then I will leave you. Your only freedom is to decide your future, for it is in your hands to determine it. There is a tribune to the west, Marcus by name, who is wealthy and handsome and of noble lineage. He is here for a few years of military duty before going on to a political career in Rome. He has long sought a lovely Celtic woman to . . . ah . . . warm his nights. It is hoped you will be to his liking, and will bring a good price to the centurion yonder. But your chances will increase, girl, if you eat properly, get cleaned up, and look a little more attractive . . ." He shrugged and looked down at her grimy face.

"It is for you to decide. Otherwise, the centurion will sell you for whatever price he can get and then your future, I can promise you, will not be so pleasant a one."

He shifted his legs to stand, but the girl's bound hands reached out and seized his wrist. "Wait," she whispered. "What is your name?"

"Rufus."

"I . . . I am Anor. Might I have some food, please, Rufus?"

The young legionary sighed in relief, nodded, and rose to his feet.

They camped two days later by a small trading post along the frontier, and Rufus was sent to take the girl into town to buy her some clean clothes, rent a room, and see that she was bathed, dressed, whatever was necessary to put her at her best. Then, it was planned, she would ride one of the mules for the remainder of their journey, to preserve her delicate beauty, restore her health, and bring the best possible price from the tribune.

Rufus had seen the looks many times before: the furtive glances or stares of open hatred from the hostile natives; or, more unnerving yet, the groveling and sniveling from the numerous hangers-on who survived by living off the Roman army and were always ready to curry favor from their masters, by whatever means it took. He found them as disgusting as maggots and nearly as trustworthy, but it was to one of these that he turned his steps, leading the bound girl as he entered the low wooden door of a small log-built hostel.

The girl instinctively drew back in fear when curious male eyes suddenly fell on her and the clamor of the tavern rooms died away. "Come," Rufus snapped, jerking her toward the advancing innkeeper and fingering his short sword with his free hand, "the sooner we are out of here, the better."

The innkeeper's hands were clasped lightly before him and he bowed low when he reached the soldier, his black eyes taking in the frightened slave girl at the Roman's side.

"Yes?" He smiled smoothly.

"A room," Rufus growled, his right hand pointedly on his sword. The movement was not lost on the man and he straightened stiffly, his hands falling to his sides.

"A bath for the girl," Rufus went on. "Send your wife for some women's things, a gown, combs, ointments, and such. You will be paid, of course."

"Of course." The innkeeper nodded with a slight tilt of his head. "And food and wine?" he questioned.

"Yes, food and wine," the legionary replied.

"This way," the man said, leading them through the hushed room as hungry male eyes followed the girl's gracefully swaying hips.

"Eat." Rufus motioned to Anor, settling back on a rickety bench and pulling a chunk of roast pork from a large wooden platter. "It will take a while for the man's wife to gather the necessary things."

Anor sat slowly on the edge of a narrow Roman-style cot and extended her bound hands to the food.

"Here . . ." Rufus wiped his mouth with one hand and pulled out a short knife. In one swift stroke he cut the ropes at her wrists and she looked at him, surprise and gratitude lighting her face.

"Can I trust you?" He smiled and she half-nodded, picking the stiff knots loose and dropping the ropes to the floor.

"This is the closest to freedom I will ever know," she muttered, rubbing her chafed wrists gently.

"Oh, no!" the soldier laughed. "Be good and trustworthy and you will be surprised at the freedoms you'll have. It won't be as bad as you imagine. We have laws against mistreatment of slaves, you know, and you no doubt will be cleaner and more comfortable than you ever were in the past."

"But I will not be free," she sighed, tearing off a chunk of stale dry bread.

"Who is free, anyway?" He shrugged, looking at her downcast face. "Am I free, made to do the bidding of the army for twenty-five long years? Was my father free, working every day of his miserable life as a potter? Or my mother, chained to her household and ten squalling children? Are you so much worse off, then?"

"I had no choice in the matter, though," she replied, lifting her gaze to meet his. "It was thrust on me against my will. I suppose a slavery we choose ourselves is infinitely more bearable."

"Whom has fate not intruded on in such a way, girl? The course of a whole life can turn on the smallest event. Life happens, and your only freedom is in how you handle it. You can be luckier than most; it is up to you. A slave has only two choices: he can die rather than submit, or he can submit. It is simple."

Anor looked away from him bitterly. "You speak my tongue and you seem a pleasant sort," she said, "but at heart you are just a Roman. It is simple for you; what do you know of slavery?"

He leaned back against the log wall and gazed at the raw beams of the low ceiling. "I know this of slavery; that my sister was taken by the Gauls, sold to the Germans, and none of us ever saw her again. I pray that she is alive and well, but that is all I can do."

"I'm sorry," Anor replied, "but knowing that, how can you help enslave the sister of another?"

He shrugged and leaned toward the table again. "What can I do? Were I executed for insubordination, would it make you any less a slave? No, Anor, we are both trapped, and little can either of us do to change things . . ."

He sprang to his feet when the door opened and the innkeeper's bony wife entered, several fine women's garments folded over one arm. Behind her came a procession of street boys, three dragging a large wooden tub, two with steaming kettles of water, and two more bearing a motley collection of boxes and clay jars. Under the woman's brusque direction the bath was made ready, the clothes and ointments were laid out, and the boys were shooed from the room. The woman silently approached Rufus, one gnarled hand extended toward him. He made a show of examining her preparations, taking his time as he fingered the new gown and cloak, sniffed the ointments and perfumes, checked the bone combs and hairpins. Seeming satisfied, he counted out a few bronze coins for the woman. She looked at them, pulled her mouth into a frown, and still without a word left the room.

"By Jove, she took less than I was prepared to pay!" Rufus chortled, turning to the solemn girl. "The fool should have held out for more." He untied his red cloak and draped it over the bench before he sat again.

"And now I am to prepare myself for my new master," Anor said, standing. "Will you leave?"

"You think I am so simple as that?" He smiled, loosening the scarf at his neck. "As soon as my back is turned, you will be out the window and gone. No, little one, I must stay and guard you, as I was ordered."

She looked at his dark eyes in shock and turned away stiffly. "I . . . cannot have you watch me," she mumbled.

"You have no choice. Do it willingly or I will force you."

"I will scream."

"Scream, then." He dipped the hard bread into some meat juices and took a casual bite. "In this place they will only think it is one more girl being raped by a nasty Roman. Isn't that what we Romans are best at? Now, get started, while the water is still hot, the way you people like it."

He stretched back against the wall, extended his booted feet, and watched her smugly. Anor's stomach sank and she turned away from him, keeping her back to him as she removed her torn, dusty cloak and slid the fringed brown Cruithni gown from her shoulders. She could hear him moving behind her, and suddenly, to her horror, she felt his calloused hand on her shoulder.

"Turn around," he said, and his voice had a strange, heavy sound to it.

"No . . . I . . ."

Abruptly he turned her to face him and she instinctively raised her arms, trying to cover herself.

"Don't," he said, gazing down at her. "You are too lovely to hide. Marcus is a fool if he doesn't buy you . . ."

Roughly he jerked her arms aside and his hands slid down her cringing body. No man had ever touched her so . . . only Drosten, and he had been gentle, tender.

"No!" She tried to pull away when his hand seized her breast. "Will Marcus want me if I am violated?"

"I will not harm you, little wench," Rufus muttered, staring transfixed at her soft white body, "only have a little sport before we go."

Before she could react, he had grabbed her wrists, lowered himself, and begun hungrily biting at her. She recoiled in horror at the sheer animal feel of it, as if a ravenous dog was trying to tear her apart.

"No . . . stop . . ." she sobbed, trying to free herself, but he held her tight, his mouth so noisy on her flesh she felt like vomiting. Gods above, was this making love? Was this what Drosten wanted of her?

Rufus sank to his knees, his hands still clamped around her wrists. Her momentary relief vanished when she felt his mouth nearing her legs.

"By the gods, don't!" she screamed, twisting away from him. He seized her hips so tightly it hurt and pressed his face against her. Frantic, she grabbed two great handfuls of his dark hair, swung sideways with one foot, and caught him hard in the side with a piercing blow from her heel. He released her, gasping, and slouched to the floor. Anor ran to the far side of the room, trying to plant the steaming tub between them.

"Don't touch me again," she hissed, clenching her old cloak protectively. "Don't touch me again . . ."

He nodded and waved her aside as he stumbled back to his seat. "Bathe," he gasped. "Go on . . . bathe . . ." He slumped back weakly, holding his aching side in one hand.

In two days they reached the fort where Marcus served as tribune, and shabby quarters were rented for Anor's comfort in the outlying vicus, while the necessary preparations were made with the tribune and his underlings. A drawn-looking middle-aged woman was hired to watch over her, and for one unending night Anor had lain on the hard, unfamiliar bed, sleep eluding her as she listened to the nighttime sounds of the bustling village and nearby fort. Hobnailed boots hurried over streets paved with logs or smooth stone; carts, wagons, and chariots creaked and rattled, the horses' metal-clad feet unnaturally loud on the paved byways. Drunken knots of soldiers and merrymakers occasionally passed by, laughing or loudly singing in a tongue she couldn't understand. And regularly throughout the night, from the nearby fort came cries and trumpet blasts when the watch was changed atop the heavy stone-and-timber walls. She felt the last vestiges of hope sink in a swirling mist of fear as the night wore on. They will not save me. They cannot. Drosten, Resad; has something happened to them? Tomorrow my life ends. My freedom, my hopes, everything. If Marcus is too unbearable, if I am sold instead to some demon, I will show them what stuff Celtic women are made of. I will end my life in dignity rather than endure it in shame and humiliation. Wearily she dozed off, dawn washing the surrounding tiled rooftops, when the centurion sent word to awaken her.

"Stand erect, girl," the stocky man ordered, removing his high crested helmet when he entered the low room. "Is her hair fixed properly?" he snapped to her guardian, who was meticulously smoothing the pleats in Anor's fine new woolen gown.

"The best I could manage," the woman retorted, her gray eyes flashing. "Her hair has a fine texture. It is difficult to fix in a Roman woman's hairstyle."

The man walked around Anor, eyeing her critically, the crest of his helmet brushing her arm as he circled. A long knotted wood staff in his hand seemed never still, always tapping tensely against his leg. "Eh! I know nothing of such matters, woman!" he growled. "Is this the best you can do with her? She looks pale."

"All Celtic women are pale, fool! She slept little during the night . . ." Abruptly the woman stood, seizing sharp wads of flesh from Anor's wan cheeks and pinching them firmly. Anor winced and tried to evade the woman's insistent hands.

"Be still, girl!" the woman barked, continuing with her rough ministrations. "There!" She nodded, patting the girl's reddened cheeks approvingly.

"Better . . ." The centurion nodded. "Fix her cloak. He should be here soon."

The woman shook out the girl's new brightly checked cloak and placed it around Anor's slumping shoulders. "Stand, girl!" she snapped, gathering several folds of fabric in her hands and pinning them at the base of Anor's throat with a large bronze brooch. Wearily Anor straightened herself, her ears focused keenly on the door at the end of the long hallway outside her room. Soon he would be here. Soon she would see her future, her surrogate husband . . . her master.

Her stomach jumped and she clenched her fists tensely into the cloak at the sound of a heavy iron latch lifting in the distance. Then several deep male voices floated down the hall, speaking that language she couldn't understand. He comes . . . oh, gods, he comes.

She quelled the urge to study the faces of the three men

who entered the room, instead keeping her gaze resolutely focused on the log wall ahead, her hands still grasping the cloak. They talked rapidly with the centurion a few moments, and then to her surprise she heard her own tongue spoken; heavily accented, obviously of a different tribal dialect, but understandable nonetheless.

"What is your name, girl?" the man said, advancing toward her. She kept her eyes averted, afraid to look at him.

"Anor," she replied shakily.

"And how old are you?"

"Sixteen."

He moved to intercept her gaze, and she shifted her eyes to the side. Again he moved, and again she looked away. She could hear low chuckles coming from his companions.

"Why do you avoid me, Anor?" he said calmly, moving in front of her once more. "Look at me!" His voice, though kind, carried the authority of an officer. Slowly she turned her gaze toward him, first staring at the gleaming engraved cuirass he wore over his chest, to the white scarf knotted at his throat, her eyes roaming up his dark Roman skin, briefly flickering over his mouth, his lips full and pulled back into a slight smile.

"My eyes, Anor," he said, and she tilted her head until she found herself looking into two typically dark Roman eyes, like two black coals in his face, his lids heavy and rimmed with long, beautiful lashes she found fascinating.

"There!" He smiled. "That's better! Mother Hera, you are a lovely little thing." He lifted one hand to her cheek and she closed her eyes abruptly, tensing at his touch, memories of Rufus flooding her mind.

"Ah! You are shy," he said quietly. "Good. I like that. I am tired of brazen women. A sweet flower will be a welcome change."

He turned to the centurion, and his next words brought a mixture of relief and despair to her heart.

"Very good, my friend," Marcus said. "I will take her."

"You will be well provided for, child," Marcus' old Gaulish cook said kindly, her plump hands working to unfasten the heavy brooch at Anor's throat. "He is a generous master, and kind as long as you cause him no trouble. You are fortunate he has selected you." She studied the girl's drawn face critically. She had seen her sort before; numbed from the sudden reality of slavery, attempting escape as soon as the initial shock wore off.

"Understand me, child," the old woman repeated, anxious for the girl's safety. "Accept your fate. It will not be so unkind, especially for one as lovely as you. Marcus is a good man; you will be showered with luxuries. Out here the slave-master relationship is not so strictly kept as it is to the south. Listen, girl! You will be trusted here, given the freedom of his modest house, but the first time you try to escape, all that will end. He does not take kindly to betrayals of his trust. Your escape will fail, and your good treatment will end. Do you understand me?"

She was relieved to see light come to the girl's pale eyes. The old woman folded the cloak as Anor gazed around the comfortably furnished living quarters of the small private house Marcus had bought in the vicus outside the fort. "Yes." Anor nodded. "I understand."

The sandals were too large and the leather straps tied around her ankles cut into her flesh. "Must I wear these?" Anor complained as the cook piled her hair atop her head, attempting to crimp it into curls with stale beer and heated metal tongs.

"Yes. Now, be still! Your hair will not dress properly. What am I to do? The food must be prepared, and that fool of a kitchen boy cannot do it himself. I cannot get your hair fixed . . . what am I to do?"

"Leave it, Cordelia," Anor said, pushing the woman's hand away kindly. "My hair was not meant for Roman fashions. I will fix it my own way."

The cook sighed and laid the curling tongs on a small charcoal brazier. "All right, but it must look nice. Marcus only occasionally gets a chance to come here. You must always look your best for him. Remember that, child; that's the way to keep a man."

"Yes . . . I know. Now, go to your kitchens," Anor answered, pulling the silver hairpins and fine nets from her hair. It tumbled in luxuriant golden waves around her shoulders and she picked up a large silver mirror and examined it critically. A light combing, she thought, and it will be fine as it is.

Turning her head from side to side, she suddenly paused, her gaze fixed solemnly on her reflection. So tonight it comes, she thought dully, fighting the tears that rose in her eyes. The end of my journey, the reason I was bought. Tonight I will go to his bed. I will know what it is like, I will endure it, and it will be over. Mother had explained it to me. Cordelia tried, in her own fumbling way. Tonight I will know. The love I imagined in Drosten's arms will instead be an ordeal inflicted by a Roman. But I will survive. I must. Mother was once a slave, and look where it led her. She did not fight it. That is the trick. I must be strong, and I must survive. I must be like mother was, and accept the guidance of the fates. My past is over, and I have no future. Only the present, and I will live it as it comes, one day at a time.

She closed her eyes weakly when she heard the kitchen boy open the front door. Tilting her head back to the painted ceiling, she cut her ties with the past.

"Drosten, I love you, and always will . . ." she whispered, put the mirror down, and rose as Marcus entered the room.

They sat upright at a small table in Anor's room while they ate, the kitchen boy bringing out an unending stream of food from Cordelia's ample kitchen. Anor found little of it to her liking; it seemed too fancy, too highly seasoned and overcooked, and everything that wasn't covered with some foul-tasting oil, Marcus doused with a smelly fish sauce. Yet she forced herself to eat polite portions as Marcus watched her approvingly.

"You like my house?" he asked, lifting a small fruit-filled pastry from a silver plate.

"Yes . . . but it seems rather odd," she said softly.

"Odd? Explain that to me, though I can well imagine how different it must be from the sort of hovels you are used to."

She ignored his insult and picked absently at a small roasted bird she'd been served. Everything was so dainty, so feminine. Didn't the Romans eat any great chunks of cheese, whole roast boar, haunches of beef, kettles of gruel? Do all Romans eat like picky children? she wondered. How do their great warriors feed themselves?

"I am used to things the gods made," she answered, glancing up at him.

"I don't understand."

"Look up. What do you see?" she asked. He tilted his head and looked at the bright red and yellow geometrics marching across the plastered, painted ceiling.

"A painted ceiling," he said, his curiosity roused.

"And who made it?"

He shrugged. "Some local artisan of mediocre talent, I suppose. Why?"

"A man made it. I am used to seeing wood and thatch, made by the gods, over my head. Beneath my feet the packed soil of the earth, not this . . ." She slid one sandaled foot across the smooth clay tiles of the floor. "How can one feel the spirits of the gods, be strengthened and refreshed by them, in such a house as this? This house is pretty, and comfortable, but it is not natural. I am not used to it," she muttered, looking down at her food awkwardly.

"And the food is not natural either?" he observed. Silently she nodded. "And a Roman hairstyle is not natural," he continued, studying her, "so you fixed your hair after your own fashion."

Anor absently toyed with the loose golden waves at her shoulders and looked at him in fear. Perhaps she had said too much. "I tried to fix it . . . the cook helped . . . but it wouldn't stay properly," she explained hurriedly. "I tried. Truly I did . . ."

He laughed and the girl eased her tensions. I like him, she thought uncomfortably. He is handsome, and nice, and I like him. Yet I am afraid of him too . . . so afraid.

"Your hair looks fine. It is lovely," he reassured her, seeing the worried haze in her large pale eyes. "Dear Venus, you are beautiful," he suddenly blurted, and she looked aside awkwardly. "It is no wonder you love 'natural things,' as you so quaintly put it. You are a natural woman, with the glint of the sun in your hair and the mountain mists in your exquisite blue eyes."

His words died away and in the ensuing silence she began to tremble. She knew the fine words. She knew the path and where it led. So now it comes . . .

"Boy!" he called. "Take the food away. Leave the wine, and do not disturb us further."

Obediently the sullen youth piled the trays and dishes and tiny spoons atop the table and carried them from the room. As the latch fell on the door, Marcus reached across the vacated space between them and took Anor's quaking hands in his. "Do not be afraid, little flower," he said gently. "We will progress slowly, so as not to frighten you. All right?"

He lifted one of her hands to his lips and kissed the back of it as he studied her face. She nodded stiffly, her eyes averted from his. Turning the hand over, he softly kissed her palm, then her limply extended fingers.

"Like a little pink seashell," he muttered, studying her tiny hand. Her fear was galloping unbridled, yet she found him different from Rufus . . . not so savage and animalistic. Nearly as tender as a mother would be.

Her heart pounded wildly when he kissed up her bare arm, his lips lingering lightly inside her elbow, and her breath came quickly, labored, as if she was preparing to run from him. She watched in horrified fascination as his dark, curly hair drew closer to her face. No! she gasped, trying to withdraw her arm, but he held it firm.

"Hush. It will be all right," he soothed, taking her face in his hands and brushing the hair from her cheeks.

"No . . . please . . ." she sobbed weakly.

"You must. You know you must. Just relax and trust me, eh?" His thumbs were tracing the finely chiseled lines of her cheekbones as he studied her frightened face. "Has a man abused you before, that you should be so terrified?" he asked quietly.

"Once . . . in a way . . . but he stopped. I did not like it. Like an animal . . ."

"But he did not violate you?" he asked, his voice taking on a harder edge as his fingers ran lightly across her lips.

"No . . . no, he didn't . . ." She tried to turn her head away, but he held it and gently pressed his mouth to hers.

"Well, I am not an animal, Anor. I am a man. It will be different, I promise you." Again he moved his mouth to hers, but this time she felt the tip of his tongue brushing along her lips. She knew his patience would not last forever. She knew the way men were when the fire struck them; she'd seen many a lusty warrior and his woman together at a drunken banquet, when her parents hadn't known she was watching. She knew she must submit.

His lips crept over her chin, down her neck, and despite herself she felt a chill of excitement run along her spine. *What will it be like?* she wondered blankly as he ran one hand up her leg. *Soon I will know. It is like animals. Like the warriors, like Rufus, like dogs and cattle and horses. I must submit, I must. . . .*

Tensing, she waited for his hand to reach its goal, but to her surprise, it only slid over her hip and up to her waist.

"Come . . ." he said suddenly, standing and pulling her to her feet. They walked to her sleeping couch and he turned her to face him. "Is it so bad?" he asked, moving one side of her gown from her shoulder. "Is it so bad, or is it only your fears and imaginings that are bad?"

"No . . ." she croaked, bracing herself.

"You know it is time, don't you?" he said, sliding the other shoulder free.

"Yes," she replied, waiting. He pulled the gown and it fell to the floor at her ankles. He stared at her in silence a moment, his hands resting lightly on her shoulders, and then he began to stroke her body, carefully, soothingly, and she found herself relaxing at his touch. Gently he kissed her mouth again, and she was surprised to find her own mouth responding. She scarcely noticed his hands as she explored the sensation of his lips on hers, until she suddenly became aware that he was lightly stroking her breasts. She turned her face away and gasped aloud. His lips lingered by her cheek, his breath warm, and she felt her knees weakening.

"No . . ." she whispered. Strange fires were rising within her and she didn't know if she should scream, collapse, or flee. Looking down, she saw him kissing her, his eyes closed contentedly, and she ran a hand through his thick hair.

"Marcus . . ." she sobbed. He pushed her backward onto the couch, his mouth crossing to the other breast while he fumbled at the hem of his tunic. Standing, he pulled it off, throwing it to the floor while he stared at her. Sprawled on the couch, she looked back in fear, her hands awkwardly trying to cover herself. Naked and with deliberate speed, before she could see him and be frightened, he was atop her, moving her arms away to lay his chest on hers. Sliding between her legs, he cradled her head in one arm, pressing her face into his neck to smother her cries while reassuring her with his words. She was difficult, as much so as any virgin he'd ever taken, and he pitied her weak struggles and protests. But he forced himself, ignoring the sticky blood he could feel between her legs. He finished sooner than he'd have liked, but for her sake he supposed it was best. Rolling onto his side, he pulled her into his arms and let her cry her hurt and fear into his chest. The night was half over before she calmed, and he rose and fetched some wine for them both. She was solemn but recovered, and her soft warmth proved irresistible to him. He made love to her three times more before dawn, and each time he succeeded in having her enjoy it a little more.

Aniel raised a hand to silence his companions. Drosten, Resad, and Cadvan immediately dropped behind the brush and brambles along a small rise of land near a stream. They could hear loud splashing coming from the waters below, and a man's smooth voice singing a ribald warrior's tune with as much ease and grace as if it were a lullaby. Resad and Drosten looked at each other, mystified. Whoever it was, he was not Roman or Cruithni. The man's speech was too natural, his knowledge of the song too perfect, to be anything but a Celt. But who?

Silently the four crept through the dappled morning light. Parting the leaves before his face, Resad peered down the shadowed stream bank. A giant of a man knelt by the water, shirtless, his powerful back muscles rippling in the soft light as he bent over, washing a luxuriant mane of long chestnut hair as carefully as a woman would do. Resad looked at Drosten and a slight smile crept across his face. Motioning quietly, the two circled down to the riverbank, to where the stranger had placed his tunic, cloak, and leather boots atop a dry rock.

His song had reached its climax, the bedding of the village harlot by the crafty one-eyed, one-legged shepherd. Resad fought to control his laughter at the lyrics as he drew his sword, extended it from the bushes, and lifted the man's neatly folded tunic with the sword point. Retrieving it, he reached for the cloak while Drosten's sword fetched the two deerskin boots. Having secured their trophies, they crept back up the hillside, rejoining a chuckling Aniel and Cadvan.

"Wait," Drosten hissed, tucking the boots beneath his arm. "He will surely notice their loss soon."

They waited while the giant finished washing his hair. Launching into a few verses of a song he'd obviously made up himself, he shook his hair like a wet dog, carefully spreading and untangling it with long, slim fingers.

"Vain, isn't he?" Aniel winked.

"Perhaps we should return his things," Cadvan worried, his ears burning from the rawness of the man's tune. "He looks awfully strong."

"We three can handle him," Aniel whispered, his dark eyes glinting, "and if not, we'll send you down to fix things, eh?"

"Shh . . . see!" Drosten gasped, one hand trying to suppress a laugh. The warrior had finished with his hair and stood, his hands on his hips, staring in perplexity at the bare rock where he'd left his clothes. Peeking under a few nearby bushes, he paced a slow circle around the rock, his heavy brows knitted into a frown.

"By Ialonus, I know I left them there . . ." they could hear him muttering, his hair dripping wet tracks down his broad back as he walked.

"Stay here and wait," Resad hissed, rising to his feet. The stranger whirled in alarm, one hand quickly on his sword.

"You look puzzled, friend." Resad grinned, descending the slope. The giant's blue eyes narrowed suspiciously. "Can I be of help?"

The man quickly took in Resad's height, his well-muscled shoulders and alert eyes, and his glance crossed over the man's obviously skilled right hand, firmly grasped around his sword hilt, the flesh nicked and scarred from many a practice session.

"I seem to have misplaced my clothes," the giant began, when a movement up the slope caught his eye. Like a deer he was up the hill, his long legs racing around Resad, who just as quickly intercepted him, his sword out and ready to fight. Drosten, Cadvan, and Aniel stood from the bushes, the man's clothes in hand, and watched Resad face the giant without flinching. The man's sword, too, was out, and the two warriors circled each other like two hostile rams, their eyes locked menacingly. The giant suddenly lunged, quickly and powerfully, and the blow as Resad intercepted the sword stroke jarred deep into his bones. No mistaking it, he thought grimly; the man is a giant. More here than skill to take him.

Their swords clanged loudly again and again, Resad gripping his fiercely in two hands to keep it from flying loose under the giant's powerful strokes. He watched for his opening, and when the giant swung his weapon down and to his left, Resad cut his own directly across between them, a sharp slicing motion that in one move deflected the giant's blow with the butt of his sword and then cut directly up and horizontally across the man's chest. The giant froze, surprise on his face, and looked down at Resad's blade, poised and ready to slice him open. Then he laughed loudly.

"You win, friend!" he bellowed. "A neat move, that one! Where did you learn it?"

Resad slowly lowered his sword and studied the man, and a smile pulled at his mouth. "First, your name, vain giant." He grinned.

"Fortrenn. I am Fortrenn," the man replied, sheathing his sword as Resad's companions descended the slope, "and I see where my clothes have gone."

"You won them back fairly." Resad nodded, replacing his own sword. The warriors tossed the man's things to him. "My trick is a Cruithni one," he explained, watching the young giant pull on his boots and tie them around his ankles. Despite his size and power, he had something of the grace of a woman in his movements.

"Cruithni, eh?" the giant said, pulling a gray tunic over his head. "Are you Picts, then?"

"Two of us are. I am part Cruithni, and my brother is a Celt."

"A motley band, then," the giant laughed, tossing his cloak over one shoulder and pulling his drying hair from beneath it. "What tribe of Celts do you come from, boy?" he asked, leveling his bright blue eyes at an awed Cadvan.

"My parents were of . . . of the Damnonii," the boy said.

"Is that so? Damnonii? My parents, too, were of the Damnonii, though of course no one lives there now but Romans and traitors. Perhaps we are kin, boy. Is that possible?"

Cadvan shrugged weakly as a powerful clap on the back from the giant sent him stumbling forward a few paces.

"You say your name is Fortrenn?" Drosten interjected. "It means 'powerful.' Is that really your name?"

The giant tilted his head quizzically. "It is the only name I know. My mother died at my birth. Besides"—he grinned, spreading his muscular arms wide—"don't you think it fits me?"

"That it does!" Aniel agreed, nodding. "But why is so powerful a warrior out here alone, with no war band to accompany him?"

"I am newly come down from the north. I got wind of the unrest and came to join the rebels."

"Rebels?" Resad perked up, his blue eyes shining eagerly. "What rebels?"

"Ah." Fortrenn shook his head. "You have not heard? Under a series of weak governors, the Roman hold along our borders is not what it once was."

They waited, uncomprehending, for him to continue.

"Don't you see? The southern tribes are planning an uprising. We will sweep over the Roman forts and outposts and kill them without mercy. We will drive them from our lands forever!"

Resad and Drosten looked at each other in mute astonishment, and the glint of cold hatred that settled into their eyes was not lost on Fortrenn. "Come, then, and join me," he suggested jovially.

"Which way do you head, powerful warrior?" Drosten asked.

"To the west . . ."

Drosten nodded, satisfied. "Then we will join you."

"We should reach Allectus' camp by moonrise tomorrow," Fortrenn announced, standing atop an open bluff and gazing across the silvered hilltops that stretched away before them.

"And which way is that?" Resad asked, peering through

the clear summer night for some sign of the camp the giant had mentioned.

"To the northwest," Fortrenn answered, pointing to an oddly shaped hilltop in the distance. "Safely nestled in a wild gorge yonder, away from prying Roman eyes. The only spies who see it are soon enough dead spies, so I hear it said."

"It sounds risky to me. Who's to say we won't end up dead ourselves?" Aniel muttered darkly. Fortrenn turned to the Pict in amusement.

"Look at us, my friend!" he laughed. "What nationality would be stupid enough to have the lot of us for spies? Not even the Romans, I'll wager!"

Aniel glanced at the dirty faces and odd assortment of clothes on his companions, some Cruithni, some Celtic, some items military and others civilian, and laughed as well. "Surely you are right, Fortrenn," he replied. "We look more like beggars than spies!"

"A moment there!" Drosten protested. "I have tried to keep myself looking like a proud warrior, difficult as that might be!"

"Easy, friend." Fortrenn smiled, placing a broad hand on the Pict's squared shoulder. "You look as fine as can be expected of one on so long a journey. Allectus runs a generous hostel, so I hear. A good bath and cleaned clothes will fix you up nicely."

"Well, then, let's finish our journey," Resad suggested, hefting his spear eagerly. "I am anxious to get back into training, and to hear the plans for this invasion you speak of."

"And I," Drosten added, and the plain hatred on his face made Fortrenn shake his head sadly. Such a warrior does not last long, he knew; in battle his heart rules, instead of his head.

Nervously the five warriors crept between looming black masses of mountains on either side of them. The night air was warm and buoyant, and a gentle breeze ruffled their hair and set the surrounding vegetation to dancing. Cadvan started fearfully when a bush rustled nearby, and Resad pulled him protectively between himself and Aniel. He could see Fortrenn's broad back in the moonlight ahead, picking out a path through the dense undergrowth as unerringly as a fox would do; he seemed to have a special sense for seeing in the night—a gift, he'd said simply, inherited from his father.

"Hold!" the giant suddenly hissed, and the group froze. Before their weapons could be drawn, a circle of grim warriors had descended on them from the surrounding slopes, spears and swords at the ready, seeming to spring from the forest like woodland spirits.

"Who are you?" one of them demanded.

"Warriors, Cruithni and Celt, seeking lodging," Fortrenn answered carefully, eyeing the tall, bearded leader who advanced toward them, his clothing a camouflage of muted grays and browns.

"Lodging of whom?" the man replied evenly, as if it were the questions and not the answers that mattered most.

"Of the noble and generous lord Allectus," Fortrenn responded, staring at the man's face. "We heard he has a hostel hereabouts for weary travelers."

"And what is your destination?" the man continued, his eyes narrowing.

"The south," Fortrenn answered, and the man stood aside.

"Pass," he said, and motioned them into the gorge with a silent wave of his hand. Obediently the five crept between the steep rock walls that sliced down from the mountainside, picking their way around a bend in the valley. When they rounded the corner and gazed ahead, an astounding sight met their eyes; sheltered in the heavy darkness of the rising mountain walls were hundreds of small campfires, and the low murmur of voices rising from them was like the hum of a thriving beehive.

"Allectus . . ." Resad bowed low before the seated warrior, who stared at him critically with grim brown eyes. The man waited silently for greetings from each of the new men: a chestnut-haired giant; a stern, powerfully muscled Pict with fresh scars on his face; a young Celtic boy; and another Pict, slimmer, as quick and sleek as a cat.

"Are you the leader?" he asked Resad once the greetings

461

were completed to his satisfaction. The young warrior's piercing blue eyes gazed back confidently, a gesture Allectus found both admirable and annoying.

"We have none, sire," Resad replied levelly.

"Then you wander alone, unattached to any lord?" the man inquired suspiciously.

"No, sire," Resad explained. "Excepting Fortrenn, we are the men of the Cruithni King Achivir, sent by him to bring two ruffians to justice and retrieve my stolen sister."

"Your sister?"

Resad explained their mission as Allectus listened carefully. "And you?" He nodded to Fortrenn.

"I came from the north, where I was raised by an aunt. I belong to no lord; I only seek to fight the Romans, and if I can help my friends recover their kinswoman, all the better," the giant responded.

"And this is why you seek to join me? To recover this girl?" the lord asked slowly. "I hope you realize there is more at stake here than the life of one mere girl."

Drosten stiffened at the man's words and stepped forward hotly. Resad moved to intercept him, but too late. He knew if they were not accepted into Allectus' army, they would not be allowed to leave the valley alive, and Drosten's current mood would not help the situation any.

"I aim to recover her, sire," the Pict snapped, and Allectus raised his eyebrows in surprise at the young man's tone. "With others, or alone, I care little. But if you plan on attacking, and we do so on our own before you can act, it will put the Romans on their guard and no doubt foil your plans. It is in our mutual interest to aid each other. We fight for you, and heed your plans; your spies tell us where Anor is, so that we can rescue her when the time comes."

He paused, staring at the lord, who leaned back on his piled bearskins, the slight smile on his face hidden beneath a heavy beard and mustache. Insolent Pict, he mused, to threaten him so, when all he had to do was lift a hand to have the lot of them cut down where they stood. Still, he liked his spirit. Obviously their journey had tested and tempered them, made them real warriors and not just school-trained pups. He needed men like that.

"Tell me what you know of your sister's whereabouts, and

when next my spies report to me I will alert them. We will see if we can restore her to her rightful place, in exchange for your services. Welcome, warriors, to the army of Allectus."

"I think you have an admirer." Aniel laughed at Resad. The men took turns bathing in several large oaken tubs near the laundry, and Aniel had just emerged from the steaming water, rubbing himself briskly with his clean cloak. Resad stripped, handing his dirty clothes to one of the old washerwomen attached to the camp. He followed Aniel's gaze and saw the girl again, hovering shyly in the shadows, her large dark eyes as solemn as a deer's.

"She is not the first . . ." Resad grinned, stepping into the tub and sinking back lazily.

"How many broken hearts did you leave behind in your village, eh, Resad?" Fortrenn boomed, glancing at the girl lingering nearby. "She's not a bad-looking kitten. Why don't you give her a go?"

Resad snorted and began washing himself. "She is a child, Fortrenn. You take her if you want. We all heard your song; we know what you do with women."

"Oh ho!" Aniel chortled, propping a bronze mirror in a tree fork and attempting to shave by the low firelight. "Don't let him have her, Resad. Better I should take her."

"Stop it, you three," Drosten snapped, turning around in his tub to look at the girl. "It is one thing to talk so among yourselves, but not where she can hear you."

"Yes, you're right," Resad said with a sly wink. He sat up in the tub and motioned to the girl. A startled look crossed her young face and she took an eager step forward, thought the better of it, and paused, peering at him from beneath a thick, dark mop of hair.

"You . . ." he prodded. "Come here!"

She advanced a few more hesitant steps, then stopped again.

"Come . . ." Resad repeated, holding out a bit of cloth. "Wash my back."

The girl's face brightened as if a ray of sunshine had suddenly illuminated her life, and she came forward, taking the scrap of cloth with trembling hands. His companions tried to put on straight faces as Resad leaned forward. The girl soaped the cloth and gently rubbed it down his back, as if she were bathing a tiny infant.

"Harder, if you please," he prodded. "I am very dirty, you see."

Obediently she put her elbow to it, scrubbing hard. He closed his eyes happily. "Very good. That felt very good," he complimented her. She rinsed off the soap and as shyly as before she handed him the cloth, moving to skitter away again, back to the safety of the shadows, but he quickly seized her wrist.

"What is your name, girl?" he said kindly. She pulled back from him in fear.

"I won't hurt you, child." He smiled. "What is your name?"

The girl shook her head, a pleading look in her brown eyes, and slid her wrist free of his wet grasp. Turning, she ran away. Aniel broke into muffled laughter.

"You render her speechless with your charms," he snickered. Resad turned and glared at him.

"No, good men," the old washerwoman interjected, returning Drosten's cleaned clothes to him. "She cannot speak. She is mute, you see. And a sweeter child you will never hope to find, despite the fact that her mother was a Roman."

"A Roman?" Resad asked curiously.

"Aye." The woman nodded. "But she is dead now. The child lives with her father, who is a warrior from the west. Marcia is her name, sir, and she is but fourteen years old." With a polite nod, the old woman left them. Resad sank back in his tub, a thoughtful look on his face, and his friends deemed it best to stop their jesting for the remainder of the night.

A strong hand shook Resad's shoulder and he roused slowly, the ale of the night before still clouding his brain.

"Allectus sends for you. He has word on your sister," the spearman said, and Resad sprang to his feet. "Drosten . . ." he began, but the Pict was already awake and strapping on his sword belt.

"Hurry!" Resad snapped, seizing his sword and stepping over his slumbering companions. He followed the guard to the lord's quarters; it was the only structure on the site, a hastily constructed building of saplings and wattle, but the walls inside, he noted in surprise, were lavishly hung with wool tapestries.

He could feel the tension radiating like heat from Drosten when he joined him. Allectus was still fully dressed, having just completed lengthy meetings with his spies and advisers, and when he looked up from his bearskins, his face was gray with weariness.

"We have located this Marcus fellow," he began, and Resad and Drosten tensed, waiting.

"He is, indeed, a tribune, with a small house of his own he goes to whenever his duties permit. It is staffed with an old Gaulish cook, a kitchen boy who does odd chores, and a young Celtic girl."

"Anor . . ." Drosten breathed.

"Aye." Allectus nodded. "She would seem to fit your description. Fair and delicate, and it is reported to me that she seems well and healthy."

"Who has seen her?" Drosten demanded eagerly.

"A chain, boy," the lord replied tiredly, "and you must not know who the links are in it. Sufficient to say it is one she deals with at the marketplace."

"Has he seen her? Spoken with her?"

"Aye, he has. So now we know where she is. When the time comes, she will be safe from the slaughter."

"I must see her," Drosten fairly sobbed.

"What?" Allectus bolted upright.

"Surely you can smuggle me in somehow. I must see her, have a word with her. Give her some hope. I am dark; I can pass as a Roman. A beggar, a peddler. You must."

Allectus studied the Pict's face in silence for a moment. He had been young once, and in love; he knew how it felt.

"It will have to be discussed," the lord muttered, his weariness suddenly returning. "If it is not approved, then this knowledge alone will have to satisfy you, boy. Now, leave me."

Resad and Drosten exited the hut, their minds grim, their thoughts whirling. Anor was alive, and well, and the possession of a Roman.

* * *

Marcus was gone nearly all summer, on expeditions along the borders, on forays into the north, or at training camp with his men, and for months the only companionship Anor had was that of Cordelia, the old cook, or the inanities of the kitchen boy, which was worse than no companionship at all. She'd felt herself growing fond of Marcus, and on his infrequent visits home they'd bedded together in mutual delight. He was kind and generous and cared for her, but despite that they were not really close. She knew that in his eyes she would never be more than what she was: his slave. And she also knew that he was betrothed to a senator's daughter in Rome. As soon as his few obligatory years of military duty were over, he would be off to Rome, to a marriage, to a career in politics. And she? She would be handed on to someone else, like a used garment, and on and on until she ended up like Cordelia, old before her time, a cook or washerwoman, waiting for her life to be over with, marking time one endless day after another.

He did not know, though Cordelia suspected, that she had aborted his child, deliberately so; and the stomachache that had laid her low for a few days earlier in the summer had been in reality the aftermath of that abortion. She knew it was risky, that it endangered her life, but so be it; she would never bear the child of a Roman.

Still, considering her circumstances, she could not complain. For a slave she was lucky, and fairly free to do as she pleased. She especially looked forward to market day in the outlying vicus, to the bustle of the marketplace, the change of scenery it afforded her, and, most important, the chance to speak with her own kind, the area farmers and craftsmen who were permitted to set up stalls and hawk their wares. Only with them did homesickness engulf her; only then did wild ideas of escape cross her mind.

Today she needed a few things and so she went alone to the busy market, with a little wicker basket to carry her purchases. Marcus always left her with a small purse of coins, and these she carried tied to her waist and safely hidden beneath her cloak. Roman towns were generally safe, but one could never be too sure, especially with so many unsavory types in town to take advantage of the crowds.

Threading her way down the busy street, she nodded

several times to various men she knew through Marcus:
other rich young noblemen like himself, in Britain to
complete their military duty, perhaps win a few commenda-
tions and medals, and return to Rome; a grizzled old
centurion who'd been to the house—Pannonian, she
thought Marcus had said; two young legionaries, standing
watch as the long market stalls came into view. They smiled
and nodded pleasantly, and the sly wink the taller of the two
gave her did not pass unnoticed. She laughed merrily, her
spirits high, and continued on her way. No, this life was not
so bad after all.

She suspected that Marcus would soon return for a visit,
and the few gowns he'd had Cordelia purchase for her
originally were beginning to look ratty; her first stop was to
purchase an inexpensive gown, Roman in style and nicely
made, from an old woman she'd bought from before.
Carefully folding the fine blue woolen fabric, she laid it in
the bottom of her basket and roamed down the row of stalls,
her eyes studying the wares critically. She had thought of a
new bracelet, but the dress had been a bit more than she'd
expected and so, after pausing to eye some fine Greek
jewelry, she walked on. Best to be frugal, she cautioned
herself. Some fresh fruit for his meal would be more
appreciated. He got none while on campaign, and he said
his Mediterranean blood craved it. To her fruit had always
been a luxury, a rare treat, except for a few wild apples and
forest berries; to him apparently it was a necessity. A nice
melon, perhaps, or a few imported figs if they were not too
dear.

She rounded a corner in the street of stalls and walked to
the produce sellers, set up in the coolness next to a long
stone wall. If he was here, for one could never be sure from
one week to the next who would come, she would go to an
elderly man she'd often dealt with. Not only was his
selection of fruits fresh, varied, and fairly priced, but he was
a Celt like herself, and she welcomed the chance to speak her
own tongue instead of the little strained Latin she knew.

She spied him at once, tucked into a far corner, busily
arranging some yellow melons into an artful pile. "Good
morning," she said, smiling, and the old man straightened
and faced her with a polite nod.

THE SILVER LAND

"Lady. What can I do for you this fine morning?" he replied.

"I was looking for a nice melon, and some figs, if you have any."

"Figs?" He shook his head. "It is the season, but I hear the crop was very bad this year. A blight, I believe. Any figs you find here will be very poor in quality and not worth the price. Some dates, perhaps, or late cherries?" he suggested.

"No . . . just the melon, I suppose," Anor answered, her eyes roaming the flat wicker baskets of fruit he had on display. "Do you have anything else from the south? Mediterranean? My master wants fruit he misses from his home."

The old man nodded. "Come with me, lady, if you please. I have a few things in back which might interest you."

"Can't you bring them here?" she suggested, feeling vaguely uneasy at his words. He shrugged in reply.

"They are too few to put on display," he said. "I cannot spend my time bringing out such little bits to show you, when I could be waiting on other customers more profitably. You will have to trust me, lady, or look elsewhere for your master's treats."

She studied his leathery old face a few moments and decided to take the gamble. "All right."

"My boy will show them to you. Tell him what you want." He tapped his head knowingly. "He is slow, so I keep him in the back."

"Your boy? I didn't know you had a son!" She smiled.

"He is nothing to bring pride to a father's heart," the man snorted. "Still, he is strong and a willing worker. Boy!" he called out, clapping his hands. Anor saw the leather tent flap spread across the back of the stall part and a heavily bearded hunchbacked young man peered out.

"Show this good lady the things in the small box," he explained slowly. The young man nodded. Hesitantly Anor stepped between the piles of fruit and entered the gloomy back room, narrow and cramped and abutting the high stone wall of the fort.

"Here . . ." the young man croaked hoarsely, motioning to a few things in a flat wooden box. Anor poked through them critically—a nice selection of plump olives, small blush-red foreign apples, several clusters of sweet dessert grapes, and a few other indistinguishable fruits she didn't recognize.

"I'll take a few of these olives," she said, speaking slowly, as his father had done, "and some grapes. Have you anything to put them in so I don't stain my new gown?"

The young man nodded gruffly and reached to take the fruit from her, and when he did so, she noticed scars and nicks on his right hand, such as a warrior bears.

"Were you a warrior once?" she asked gently, pitying him for whatever affliction had left him in his present state. He withdrew his hand quickly and turned from her, searching the cluttered room for some scrap of cloth or leather to wrap her purchases in.

"Did you understand me?" she repeated, her suspicions rising. "Were you a warrior once?" Still he didn't respond, and she stepped in front of his hunched body, her curiosity insistent. He stopped abruptly, almost colliding with her in his awkwardness, and then he paused, his head hanging low.

"My life is in your hands, Anor," he said, and she was startled to hear that the words were Cruithni. Suddenly he stood, his afflictions gone, and stared at her with intense brown eyes. She gasped, studying the bearded face, and took an involuntary step backward.

"Drosten!" she choked, her eyes searching his in disbelief.

"Yes." He nodded, afraid to touch her in her Roman finery; afraid of what his reception would be.

"How . . . how did you find me?" she whispered, her voice trembling. "Is Resad here? How is Mother?"

"I cannot tell you," he answered, studying her dear face in desperation. "I am sworn to silence, Anor. Resad is nearby, and Cadvan. Word has been sent to your mother."

"Why have you come so far?" She began to sob. "You cannot save me now. You know that, don't you, Drosten? I am the woman of an officer. Were I to vanish, a search would be made until I was found."

She reached and ran a quaking hand down his bearded cheek, fighting the tears that filled her eyes. "Forget me, my love," she murmured. "I am lost to you now. Forget me."

469

He put his hands on her shoulders and she lowered her head, wiping her eyes roughly. "Send Mother my love," she cried, "and Resad, and Cadvan—"

"No!" he stopped her. "There will be a way, Anor. I will rescue you. You do still love me, don't you?" He was shocked to see her shake her head no.

"You cannot mean that!" he protested. She turned away blankly, trying to regain her composure. "Leave me, Drosten," she whispered. "Please. Don't you understand? I am not yours anymore. I can never be yours. Look at me! I am Roman now! I lie abed with a Roman. I am a whore, Drosten—the whore of a Roman. Find another . . . please . . . leave me."

She reached past him, seizing her basket and the wrapped fruit. Clumsily she counted out a few bronze coins and pressed them into his hand.

"This should be enough for the fruit." She glanced up at his solemn eyes and he raised a hand and caressed her soft cheek.

"You are still mine, Anor," he said quietly, and she closed her eyes, relishing the gentleness of his touch.

"Oh, gods, Drosten, don't," she gasped. "Have pity on me . . ."

"I will never give you up," he replied. Wrapping her in his arms, he pressed his lips to hers and she dropped her parcels, flinging her arms around his neck. Hers was no longer the kiss of a shy girl, but a woman, and he knew the Roman had been teaching her well. Hungrily she responded to him, and then pulled away, resting her head against his shoulder.

"Oh, my love," she sobbed, "forget me. You must. There is no way for us . . . no way . . ."

He shook his head resolutely, smelling the sweetness of her neatly dressed hair. "There will be a way," he retorted. "I will never give you up . . . never."

At a sudden cough from the old man outside, Drosten pushed the girl away and stooped into his crippled position. Anor patted her hair and picked up her parcels just as the two legionaries poked their heads through the flap.

"Lady . . . are you all right?" one of them questioned.

"Yes." She laughed lightly, nodding knowingly toward

Drosten. "I was unwise enough to pay this poor fellow instead of his father, and he seems to have trouble deciding if it is enough."

Drosten clenched the coins to his chest and peered foolishly over his shoulder at the soldiers. "Here!" the old man interjected, pushing his way past the men. "Let me see what you have, boy!"

Drosten held out the coins obediently and the old man counted them. "And what did you purchase?" he asked Anor.

"Ten olives and a bunch of dessert grapes."

"Eh? Then you have paid too much! Here . . ." He handed back four of the coins and cuffed Drosten's ear roughly. "I am sorry for the inconvenience, lady," he apologized. Anor stepped past them and exited the tent.

"Oh, it is all right. I am sure the fruit will be well worth the trouble." She smiled. When she walked away, the hunchbacked son peered from the flap and watched her go, vanishing into the market bustle while chatting brightly with a Roman soldier on either side. He clenched the bronze coins tightly in his fist and pressed them to his chest in desperate rage.

Marcus returned late in the night, weary from a long ride, and Anor didn't have a chance to put on her new gown before he stumbled into her room, rousing her from a restless sleep. Pulling a cloak around her nightshift, she ran to the kitchen to wake Cordelia. Something light, she instructed the old woman; a little cold meat, the fresh fruit, some good wine.

Marcus was nearly undressed when she returned, his dirty clothes and dusty armor in a heap by his chair. He slumped back tiredly, but his face brightened when he saw her enter.

"Let me wash off the dust and dirt," she suggested, fetching her bronze washbasin and a large ewer of water. He stretched out comfortably in the chair and closed his eyes while she washed his tired face, his arms, his grimy neck.

"Mmmm . . ." He smiled lazily. "I should take you back to Rome with me when I return next year."

She laughed and continued to wash him, but her heart had frozen in her breast. To Rome . . . What if he did take her to

Rome? All would be lost then, all lost. How could she endure it, with her one faint glimmer of hope gone?

"You needn't have come so far, as tired as you are," she said solicitously, turning when Cordelia brought in a tray laid out with hastily prepared foods, the sleepy kitchen boy behind her bearing a silver ewer of wine.

"Leave them," Anor directed, returning to Marcus. He ran an appreciative hand over her bottom and smiled up at her.

"I wanted to see you, my little one," he said, "and I had business here, anyway."

"Business?" she questioned, pulling a chair to the table and pouring the wine.

"Yes." He emptied the cup and held it out for more. "With the general who is, for the time being, staying at the fort. Some plans for a spring offensive next year." He shrugged. "I'll know more once I have talked to him."

Anor felt her emotions being torn two ways. An offensive against her own people—Resad, Drosten, Cadvan—and the chance that Marcus might be wounded, even killed.

"Why so glum, Anor?" he asked, reaching for her hand. She looked up at him and found the thought of him dead to be profoundly disturbing.

"I . . . I was hoping you would not be injured in this . . . this offensive you speak of." Tears filled her eyes and she awkwardly shielded them with her free hand, shaking her head at the hopelessness of her life.

"Or killed," she choked, and her composure broke. Pulling her fingers from his grasp, she buried her face in her hands, sobbing openly.

"Here, now!" he exclaimed, rising from the chair and circling to her side. He lifted her to her feet and she collapsed against him, crying wildly, her hands feeling the reassuring warmth of his chest next to her cheek.

"It's all right," he soothed. "I can promise you I will be careful. Hush, now. We have months to worry about that. It is even possible I won't be sent out into the field. They may stick me behind a desk at headquarters, filling out the general's reports to Rome."

She sniffed and looked up at him dubiously. "Will you tell

me . . . when you know?" she whispered, and he kissed her forehead.

"Of course! Now, dry your tears and let's eat Cordelia's food, drink the wine, and be off to bed."

She returned to her chair and watched him settle to his meal. If I get any useful news, she wondered, studying him, will I relay it to Drosten and risk Marcus' life, or do I remain silent, and endanger Drosten and Resad? What should I do? What?

She ate little, and when they went to bed, despite his best efforts to arouse her, Anor's mind was elsewhere—in a gloomy tent behind the fruit seller's stall, with the longing eyes and gentle hand of a man she wished she could forget.

"She is well, as the spies said," Drosten told Resad, his mouth set tightly, and Resad could see the strain around his friend's eyes.

"Did she recognize you?" Resad asked.

Drosten nodded glumly and looked up, hurt plain on his face. He had changed back to his long brown Cruithni tunic and leather breeches, his massive silver warrior's neck chain again gleaming around his neck. "She tried to make me leave her, Resad," he muttered. "She said it is hopeless, that there is no escape for her . . . that I should forget her. I could not tell her of our plans, that she would soon be rescued. She is happy, yet she despairs . . . and I could say nothing to alleviate her fears . . . nothing."

Resad clasped his hand on Drosten's slumping shoulder. "You did what you had to do, my friend. Some things require time, and this is one of them."

"But I wish I could have done more! Her quick thinking saved me when the two soldiers came, too. She still cares . . . I know she does. And then to have to watch her walk away with Roman soldiers . . . in the name of the gods, Roman soldiers! Chatting and laughing as brightly as a bird, and I could do nothing, Resad, nothing."

He stood up, rage clouding his dark features, and clenched one hand fiercely around the leather-wrapped hilt of his sword. Without a word he strode away into the gathering shadows of evening, and Resad left him to himself. He rose from the boulder where they'd sat and headed back to their assigned campsite. Perhaps Aniel or Fortrenn had thrown together some gruel or a roast for their supper. He hoped so, for he was hungry, and he hoped it was Fortrenn who'd done the cooking. Aniel was hopeless as a cook, his food barely palatable even to the camp dogs that roamed about. How someone could manage to ruin something as simple as a spitted chunk of meat, he couldn't see, but Aniel had done it. The man needed a wife, and fast, before he poisoned himself with his own meals.

A loud laugh in the trees to his left brought Resad to an abrupt halt. The laugh came again, followed by a hard slap. A man grunted angrily and the scuffling sounds of a fight broke out. Resad narrowed his eyes and stepped into the forest, his suspicions confirmed when he saw the couple rolling on the leafy ground—a drunken warrior clad only in torque, long breeches, and chain sword belt, and a valiantly struggling Marcia, her clothes nearly ripped from her body, her eyes wide with fear.

Resad kicked the man aside and he sprawled to the dirt, surprise on his bleary face. The girl was gasping heavily and she crawled into a huddle, watching as the man suddenly sprang to his feet, his sword drawn. Resad too had drawn his weapon, and he waved it slowly in front of the man, taunting him, a sneer on his face.

"Come on," he muttered fiercely. "You drunken fool, I'll take you on. Come and try me."

The man made a clumsy move to strike, thought better of it, and unsteadily replaced his sword. "Is she your woman, then?" he snapped, turning to leave. "A mute Roman bastard . . . is she yours, eh?" The man laughed cynically and walked away. Resad straightened up, sheathed his sword, and turned to the huddled girl. The attack had not unnerved her, but the man's parting words were obviously ones she had heard too many times before, and they had cut her like a knife. She hung her head, her dark hair tumbling about her face, and Resad could see her bare shoulders shaking as she cried.

"Here, now." He tried to calm her, having had little experience in such matters. "He was drunk. Pay him no mind."

He placed a hand on her thin shoulders and she flinched away from him, shaking her head violently. She rose to her knees, preparing to leave, and trying awkwardly to pull her torn gown over herself. The man had ripped it savagely and her efforts would have been almost comical were she not so pathetic a figure. Resad quickly unpinned his cloak and draped it around her.

"Come," he said kindly, "I will walk you back to your father's camp."

She looked up at him, and the open adoration in her large dark eyes hit him with the force of a blow. By the gods, he thought in irritation as they stood, I feel sorry for the little thing, but I wish she'd get me out of her blood. She is just a child.

His irritation increased during their long walk to her father's fireside, their stroll being met with snickers, loud laughs, and crude comments. It was plain many men had tried to take advantage of her youth and muteness, and it was also plain the sight of her walking at his side, wrapped in his cloak, gave the wrong impression to everyone they passed. He was glad to turn her over to her father, a fierce-looking man in his thirties who obviously loved his only child very much. Sighing in relief, Resad tossed his cloak over one shoulder and returned to his camp and the latest disappointing meal prepared by Aniel.

Anor tried to quell the fear in her heart as she applied a careful bit of Roman makeup to redden her cheeks and lips. Marcus had specifically requested it, to go with the splendid white linen gown, long and bloused over at her waist, a delicately embroidered wool overmantle, and a new pair of plaited leather sandals he had bought her. They were the most fashionable things to be had in this remote location, for he wanted her to look impressive for this special occasion: the newly appointed general was coming to dine.

Marcus' mother had packed a few pieces of family silver for his use when he was assigned to far-off Caledonia, and he'd borrowed enough tableware from his fellow tribunes to complete a respectable dining service. Anor and Cordelia spent the day preparing lavish foods with the help of another cook on loan from a friend's kitchens. The sitting room was cleaned and decorated with tall vases of wildflowers. Small dining tables were moved together to handle the coming banquet, and three carved chairs with embroidered cushions were placed at the proper locations—the honored guest's at the center, Marcus at his side, and Anor a discreet distance away. Marcus was as nervous as a new mother as he made sure everything was ready and as perfect as possible. Then he retired to don his best armor and ceremonial swords, and when he and Anor emerged from their quarters and looked at each other's finery for the first time, they broke into delighted laughter.

"Don't we look splendid!" He grinned, straightening his engraved bronze cuirass in an exaggerated show of vanity.

"Two strutting gamecocks!" Anor replied merrily, appreciatively eyeing the splendid figure he made. He was in full formal uniform, with decorated bronze greaves on his legs, a long white cloak thrown back over his shoulders, and a narrow purple sash, badge of his rank, tied around his chest.

"Well, the general had better be impressed," Marcus agreed, putting his elaborate bronze helmet on a wooden stand and straightening the feather crest as he spoke. "It's been a year since I've had to polish up this parade armor. He can't help but be struck by you, Anor . . . you look like a goddess."

She blushed and looked at him, her eyes shining with open longing. He caught her gaze, smiled slyly, and winked at her. "Tonight, little flower," he whispered as he heard the front door opening. "We'll have a night at the races, eh?"

Anor laughed brightly and tried to regain her composure before the general entered the room. He was a much older man, graying, his face wrinkled from so many seasons campaigning in the hot summer sun and cold winds of winter. His uniform was even more ornate and lavish than Marcus', and Anor half-wondered when such displays of male vanity among the Roman officers reached their limits. What must a governor wear, or an emperor? The general's grim soldier's bearing eased as he was shown to his seat, and Anor was relieved to find him a very nice man at heart. Witty to talk to and obviously quite a charmer with the ladies, he eyed her openly whenever Marcus was diverted, teasing and flattering her and seeming to take great pleasure in the blushes he brought to her cheeks. She looked fearfully at Marcus more than once, expecting to see anger on his face but relieved and puzzled to find him seemingly unconcerned. The meal lasted for hours, eaten slowly and punctuated by much idle chatter she could barely understand. When the feasting drew to a close, Marcus stood and his gaze fell on Anor's curious face.

"You must go to your room now, Anor," he said quietly. "The time has come for our private discussion."

Obediently the girl rose and made her farewells to the general, who turned, unconcerned with Marcus' presence, and watched her swaying hips as she left the room. "By the gods, Marcus, where did you get her?" the man said, turning to the young officer.

"A long search, but well worth it." Marcus shrugged. "I paid handsomely for her, too, believe me."

"Well, my man, when you return to Rome next year, I'll be glad to take her off your hands for you. At a fair price, of course."

"Of course." Marcus grinned, pouring fresh wine and settling back for their talk.

Anor went to her room and quickly removed her sandals. On silent bare feet she crept to the closed door, pressed her ear to the roughly planned wood, and nearly stilled her breathing as she strained to catch the men's hushed words. Marcus' seeming unconcern about selling her to the general stung her for only a moment; she was, after all, a slave. What more could she expect? But their next words caught in her throat and sent her heart crashing wildly in her chest. A camp of rebels had been found, and as soon as the men were assembled, a surprise raid would be carried out.

Drosten . . . She gasped, and her course of action suddenly became clear.

Marcus left early the next morning, his step jaunty from the success of the night before. He could nearly taste a promotion to prefect under the general, and what it would mean to his political career in Rome. Anor watched him go, rushed to her room, and with trembling hands quickly dressed herself.

"Cordelia!" she called, forcing normality into her voice as she pinned her cloak around her shoulders and crossed the main room, still cluttered from the night before. The old cook came scurrying, clad in her nightshift.

"I believe we ate the last of the melon last night," Anor said, tying the purse around her waist. "I am off to the market to select a few more, before they get picked over. Do we need anything else?"

"A little fresh cream. But, lady," the old woman protested, "the master will be gone for a long while. We don't need any fruit now, do we?"

Anor stared at Cordelia and tried to look coy. "I can't explain it, Cordelia," she stammered, "but I seem to have developed a . . . a craving for fresh fruit."

The old woman's face brightened and she nodded wisely. "Yes, lady . . . by all means, buy some fruit. It is good for you!"

Satisfied with Cordelia's reaction, Anor walked from the house and hurried her steps to the marketplace.

The old fruit seller was in his usual place, just setting up his displays as Anor approached. Her eyes scanned his booth eagerly, but she saw no sign of his "son." He seemed surprised to see her out at so early an hour.

"I need more melons," she began, "and I came to apologize for any trouble I caused your poor son on my last visit. The cuff you gave his ears was a bit rough. Is he here?"

"No, lady." The man shook his head, putting a few of his best melons on the rickety wooden counter for her inspection. "He is at home. It is so difficult to bring him with me."

"I understand." Anor nodded, examining the fruit. "Do you think, with his simple mind, that he would be able to understand a message from me?" she inquired, leveling her pale eyes at him.

He nodded briefly. "I am sure I can make him understand it," he replied.

"Tell him I am sorry, and . . . Oh, gracious—look!" she shrieked, pointing over his shoulder. "A rat! My master, the tribune, was just saying last night that they had discovered a nest of the vermin and within days they expect to wipe them out."

Startled, the old man glanced over his shoulder and looked back at her suspiciously. He had seen no rat.

"I suppose I'll take these," she said, tapping two of the yellow melons with one finger.

"And the message for my son?"

"No matter." She shrugged. "The rat has so unnerved me I can scarcely think straight. Romans hate such vermin, you know."

Without another word she put the fruit in her basket, turned, and walked away. She had done what she could, risked as much as she dared. The rest was up to them.

Marcus was back a week later, tired and dejected. He threw his muddy cloak to the floor with unusual anger.

"What is wrong?" Anor asked fearfully. He had been on campaign. She knew the signs—the mud and dust, the scratches, the stubble of a beard he'd had no chance to shave.

"Fetch the wine," he snapped, sinking to the chair with a heavy sigh.

She scurried from the room and soon returned. Marcus was bent forward, unlacing his heavy leather army boots. Placing the ewer on the table, Anor poured a cup of wine and held it out to him. He grabbed it, gulped it down, and looked at her, his dark eyes sparking anger. "So close . . ." he muttered. "It would have been such a boost to my career, too, for I was leading the forward assault." He thumped the cup to the table and bent back to his boots. "Damn!" he muttered under his breath.

"Marcus! What has happened?" she pressed him.

He did not sit up to look at her, only continued with his work, but his next words made her heart sing.

"A secret rebel camp. We invaded it, but somehow they knew. When we got there they were gone, every last damn one of them, and all they left behind were their burning campfires."

"I am to stay here for several days." Marcus grinned, kissing her cheek while his orderly put his heavy traveling pack on the floor by the door.

"But why?" Anor puzzled. "You usually are not home till the weather turns. Is something wrong?"

"No." He shook his head, removing his cloak and tossing

479

it to a nearby chair. "It seems we have new plans afoot, and I believe the general wishes to return our hospitality. We are to dine with him tomorrow."

"We?" she gasped. "You mean I am to go too?"

"Yes," he laughed. "I think it is obvious he was quite taken with you. No doubt the old man wants to gaze at your fair face and lovely figure again, and dream his foolish dreams."

"Marcus! Don't be so unkind!" she chided him.

"It is not unkind. Do you know, he even offered to buy you when I leave here? As if I would sell you."

"You mean . . . you will take me to Rome with you?" she gasped, fear and astonishment flooding her heart.

"I've been thinking of it." He smiled. "My betrothed is a skinny young thing, high-bred and no doubt as flighty as a mare. I will need you there for relief from her."

She didn't know what to say, how to respond.

"But mind you," he cautioned, "I have only been thinking of it. I haven't decided yet. Would you object to the general if I chose to leave you?"

"Me? What choice do I have in the matter?" she muttered.

"Ah . . . I'd want you to be happy. He is rich, but old. You might prefer a younger master in your bed."

Her hopes again crumbled, and she suddenly realized the utter futility of her life. Like a series of blind alleys, every course she could take led her nowhere. Did he care for her, or didn't he? She could stay here near Drosten, hope for a rescue that might never come, but in the bargain belong to another stranger. Or she could go with Marcus and have no chance of ever seeing Drosten and her family again. Over and over, every road came to nothing. . . .

The general's attentions proved almost unbearable, but for Marcus' sake she forced herself to endure them. His hand repeatedly fondled her knee, he stared at her as she ate, he even dared to kiss her ear when Marcus wasn't looking. Her anger was rising and she was relieved when the lengthy meal finally came to a close and she was told to leave the room. Marcus went to greet several other young tribunes and prefects who'd been summoned to the meeting, and as she exited past the general, the old man went so far as to caress her bottom when she walked by. She tried to ignore him, but she determined that Marcus would be told of his insulting behavior later; though what he could do about it, she didn't know. She felt she was merely a pawn in Marcus' game for power and prestige, and for that, she knew, her Celtic sense of decency would have to be sacrificed.

Marcus snored drunkenly, his breath sour on Anor's cheek as she lay awake staring at the painted ceiling above. It was past midnight when they'd returned from the general's borrowed house in the vicus. She had toyed with Marcus a few brief moments, trying to find out the subject of the meeting he'd attended. But he'd had too much of the general's good wine and he soon fell into an exhausted slumber, leaving her with only one disturbing bit of news:

The general had somehow learned the names of the rebel leaders, and come morning, he was going to send out word to have them eliminated. The Roman network of spies and assassins was nothing to be taken lightly. Oh, gods, she thought sickly, what must I do? What can I do? There is no time to send word through the fruit seller. Must I sit by while my people are murdered, and do nothing? But what can I do?

She turned and looked at Marcus. He was sleeping soundly. Softly she kissed his cheek, slid from the bed, and located her discarded gown where she'd tossed it over a chair. Slipping it on, she picked up her sandals, cloak, and Marcus' dagger, and silently let herself out of the room.

The general was still awake, sipping a heavy local beer while he studied a map unrolled on the table before him. He looked up and wiped his tired eyes when an orderly poked his head in the door. "Yes?" he snapped.

"Someone wishes to see you, sir," the soldier began. "She says it is urgent and cannot wait till morning."

"She?" the general asked, his interest suddenly roused.

"Yes, sir. The Celtic woman of the tribune Marcus, who was here earlier this evening."

Anor? He gasped. Mother Hera, what would she be doing out at this time of night? Quickly he stood, straightening his rumpled white tunic and smoothing his hair. "Send her in," he ordered. "Take this ale away, and bring wine."

The orderly nodded and left, and in a moment the girl entered the room, a cloak draped over her head, her hair hanging in loose waves around her shadowed face.

"My dear!" The man smiled, advancing and taking her hand in his. "What brings you here at this hour? Is something wrong with Marcus?"

She gazed at him, her eyes wide and almost innocent. Almost.

"No." She shook her head, letting the cloak fall away from her hair. "Marcus is asleep . . . drunk. I came to see you."

A sudden fire sprang up within him at her words, and he jerked his head in irritation when the orderly returned, bearing a tray with two small silver cups and a glass flagon of wine. "Leave us," the general fairly shouted, trying to control the annoyance he felt. "Do not disturb me until morning, do you understand? Not till the morning watch is changed."

The young man nodded once, casting a quick glance at the silent girl who gazed shyly at the floor. The old fool, he thought, leaving the room; such a jewel as that does not willingly lie with an old man like him unless she wants something in return.

"Wine?" the general asked. "Here . . . let me take your cloak."

Anor crossed the painted floor hurriedly, concealing the knife in the folds of her cloak as she casually laid it on a chair, and continued walking until she was gazing from the window by his study table.

"What a lovely view this must be by daylight," she mused, tossing her hair over one shoulder with studied ease. She could hear him walk up behind her, feel his breath suddenly warm on her neck, and she graciously took the wine he offered her.

"Not nearly so lovely as the view in here," he whispered. She smiled at him, moving aside to push open the wooden shutter and gaze out over the tiled rooftops.

"No traffic noise or stench from the marketplace," she observed, carefully noting the easy descent to the roofs below. "Just a nice, quiet residential area." She turned to him. "How I envy you."

"Perhaps one day you will share it with me," he said, setting his wine atop the unrolled map and leaning forward to kiss her.

"No . . ." She giggled like a silly young girl. "Not here by the window! What if someone sees me?"

He smiled eagerly and traced a finger down her slim white neck. "What a fool young Marcus is, to choose wine and drunkenness over you."

She blushed enchantingly and walked to his couch, setting her wine on a table nearby and slowly untying the sash at her waist. The old man quivered in excitement when she slid her gown from her body and stood naked before him.

"Gods above . . ." he gasped hoarsely, eyeing her up and down. He crossed the room in three swift strides, seized her, and began kissing her body, biting and nibbling in his eagerness. Anor fought to control the revulsion she felt. He is just like Rufus, she thought sickly; like an animal, trying to devour me.

"Here, now," she crooned, unfastening his army belt while he frantically fondled her breasts. "Now you." The belt fell to the floor and her fingers went to the neck of his tunic. Quickly he pulled it off and threw it to the couch.

"And now, my little dove," he laughed low, pressing himself against her, "now begins the best part!"

He was still well-muscled for a man his age, and thin rather than paunchy, but he was no Marcus . . . or Drosten. His hands groped over her soft skin, squeezing one breast painfully before he reached down between her legs and forced his fingers into her, a slight leer on his face. The strength of his movements hurt her, but she made herself endure it. She must, for her people. She must.

"I want you," she whispered, licking his ear lightly, trying to dissuade him from his sport. Hungrily he clamped his mouth to hers, and the foulness of his breath sickened her. Wrenching her face aside, she tried to pull away from him while still appearing eager.

"Come . . ." She backed to the couch. Pulling him onto the wool blanket, she clasped his face to one breast and moaned as if in utmost delight.

"Take me . . . please . . . take me," she gasped, and he seemed only too willing to comply. He crawled between her legs, forcing his way into her violently, and just as violently thrusting. He pulled her hips up to him as he knelt, his excitement growing at the sight of her stretched out before him. He finished quickly, and she thanked the gods for that, but still his hunger was not sated. Pulling roughly at her breasts, he managed to rouse himself again, and again he raped her . . . or made love to her . . . she wasn't sure which term fit the circumstances. But this time his age caught up with him and he stretched out on the couch beside her, one arm thrown across her bare stomach, and fell into a deep, satisfied sleep.

Anor lay still, scarcely daring to breathe, and watched the darkness outside the open shutter. The night will soon be over, she thought, and if there is any hope at all of my escaping, it must be while it is still dark. I must act soon, or not at all.

Fear coursed through her body as she slid from beneath the general's arm and paused, watching him. He didn't rouse. Tiptoeing from the couch, she pulled on her gown, picked up the cloak, and extricated Marcus' long army knife from the folds. Stopping to steady her quaking legs, she took a deep breath and looked across the room at the sleeping man. How can I kill him? she thought wildly. I have never killed before . . . how can I kill him? And yet if I do not, how many more will die? Maybe even Drosten and Resad and Cadvan . . . and all because of the knowledge this man carries in his head. I must. I must. . . .

She slipped back across the floor on silent bare feet, clasping the knife in both hands. I pray you have told no one else what you know, she thought grimly, listening to the wild beating of her heart in her ears. She held the knife high and then, with all the force her arms possessed, she plunged the dagger downward.

The general's eyes flew open when the blade sank into his chest, and Anor gasped and jumped backward. Gods above, she thought, he is not dead yet. It is harder than it looks . . . all the bone, all the muscle . . . I have failed.

Eyes wide with horror, she watched the man slowly roll onto his side, groaning and reaching for her. Blindly she turned, bolting for the open window as a wild scream erupted from the dying man's throat. She reached the windowsill, flinging one leg out into the open air beyond as the door crashed inward behind her. The general fell to the floor with a thud, and in nearly the same instant rough hands seized her, dragging her back into the room. She did not struggle, she did not resist; she knew her fate was sealed, and she accepted it.

Drosten and Fortrenn sparred with swords and spears, choosing to leave their shields aside and attempt the much more difficult two-handed fighting. For this Fortrenn seemed to have the advantage, his sheer size and bulk making the wielding of two weapons an easier task. Yet Drosten was a muscular warrior as well, and he turned his smaller size to good advantage, feinting with his spear while he nimbly sprang aside, as quick as a deer, to avoid Fortrenn's answering blow. Drosten slashed with his sword, trying to throw the giant's concentration, but Fortrenn anticipated it and a swift blow jarred the sword from Drosten's right hand. Unfazed, the Pict took the spear shaft between his two hands and glared at the grinning warrior. This was fighting such as his people excelled at, and he welcomed it; the lethal poles, tipped with spear points, hooks, or barbs. Or nothing, in a pinch; it mattered little. Lightning-fast, Drosten advanced on the giant, whose smile faded under the sudden onslaught of blows delivered by the Pict. A crowd was gathering, silently appreciative of the skill being shown before them. A sudden jab with the butt of Drosten's spear sent the air from Fortrenn's stomach and he dropped his spear in surprise. The giant's face flushed red in anger; he did not like to be bested in a fight, and, by Medocius, he would not be! The match began in earnest, Cruithni against Celt, when a spearman from Allectus stepped between them, bringing the fight to a halt. The crowd, muttering its anger at the interruption, dispersed as the two combatants wiped the sweat from their faces and turned to the man.

"Well?" Fortrenn asked in ill-disguised irritation. He knew he could have beaten the little Pict, if only he hadn't been stopped.

"Allectus sends for you," the guard replied icily. "He has news of the girl you seek."

He hadn't finished his sentence before Drosten retrieved his sword from the ground, sprinting away through the forest toward the hastily erected new shelter of the lord.

Resad and Cadvan stood in the dim interior, waiting for him. Allectus paced the packed earthen floor in unusual agitation, and Drosten caught Resad's eye quizzically when he joined them. Allectus abruptly turned to them, and the look on his bearded face was grim. "The girl has been arrested," he blurted unceremoniously. Shock stilled the young men's voices, and they waited for the lord to continue.

"Last night," he said. "She killed a general."

"Killed?" Resad choked, disbelieving. Not fair Anor, his delicate little sister?

"Why?" Drosten demanded, fear rising in his blood.

Allectus shrugged. "In light of the valuable information she passed to us earlier, I can only assume it was for some dire reason, a reason she could not wait to inform us of by the usual channels. The question is, what information could have been so important that she had to kill a general and throw away her own life?"

"What do you mean, throw away her life?" Drosten growled. Allectus' spearmen stepped closer to their lord protectively.

"It seems she was caught at the scene, son. The Romans have their laws, but for her there will be no defense. She will be executed."

"No!" Drosten shouted, and the spearmen lowered their weapons at him in warning. "We must save her! We must!"

"We cannot, Drosten." Allectus tried to calm him. "To do so would be to risk all of our plans. No. No matter how much she means to you all, she cannot be saved."

"Then I will save her!" he sobbed, his composure breaking. "I will not let them harm one hair on her head!"

Allectus brushed his guards aside and seized the Pict's shoulders in his powerful hands. "Listen to me!" he snapped. "In the name of Medocius, we will not endanger hundreds of people and the future of our lands for the life of one girl. Do you understand me? She must have known the dangers of what she did, but she did it anyway. She is a brave woman; one we will long remember. Are you any less brave than she is, boy—throwing it all away for the life of one person? In war there are always casualties; this is war, and you must consider her just one more death among the many to come."

Drosten looked at the man, agony in his eyes like a raw wound. "No," he gasped. "Not Anor dead . . . no."

Allectus motioned to Resad and Cadvan. "Take him away and talk with him. She is your sister, I know, and I am sorry for her fate, but you see the position I am in."

Resad nodded, his mouth set grimly against the leaden weight in his heart.

"Good." Allectus smiled consolingly. "Make him see reason, will you? Your mother can take comfort in the fact that her daughter died for the freedom of her people. I am sorry . . ."

Cadvan stoutly fought the tears in his eyes as he took one of Drosten's limp arms, his brother took the other, and they steered the sobbing Pict from Allectus' lodge.

"When will it be?" one of the guards asked the warlord as they watched the three forlorn figures walk away.

"What?"

"The execution of the girl."

"Oh . . . not many days. They must observe their formalities. A military trial, a swift execution. Four days at most."

"And the method?"

Allectus shook his head. "Crucifixion is usual for common criminals, but this was no common crime. Who knows what torment they will devise for her, to teach us a lesson? I would not want to take her place, not for all the gold in Rome."

Marcia emerged ghostlike from the dark woods, her solemn eyes gleaming with sympathy for the glum group that confronted her. Each man seemed to have just lost his nearest and dearest, all sprawled by their campfire, their food pots and spits empty. Her own noble warrior gazed blankly at the ground, and one of the Cruithni cried like a little boy, his heart obviously broken by some tragic news. Unobtrusively the girl passed through them, attracting barely a glance, and began to prepare a nourishing stew in their kettle. Tending it until it was done, she scooped out a bowlful and carried it first to the crying warrior. She shook his shoulder lightly and he lifted his head and looked at her, his eyes red and swollen from his tears. Thrusting the bowl at him, she motioned for him to eat. He turned away blankly. She repeated her efforts, lifting one of his hands and placing the bowl in it. Carefully she brushed his tears away, pointed to his weapons, and made a gesture of strength with her arms. He was a warrior, he was strong; he should not cry. She nodded encouragement, her eyes searching his face in pity. Lightly she touched his lips and motioned to the food. To her relief, a slight smile pulled at the man's mouth and he looked down at the bowl sheepishly.

"Thank you," he whispered, patting her cheek gently. She nodded, smiling, and rose to serve the other men.

They ate in strained silence, and Resad watched as the girl seemed to instinctively sense Cadvan's fears. Despite his weapons and his swagger, he was still very much a boy, and the reality of what was to happen to his beloved sister was driving him near to breaking, a thing no warrior could endure. Marcia knew this and sat at his side, admiring his weapons, fetching more food when his bowl was emptied, diverting him whenever she saw his will failing. Alone, she helped him through his crisis, saving his honor and his pride from collapse until, the worst over, Cadvan rolled over in his cloak and drifted to sleep. Resad sighed in relief when he saw him; come morning, he knew, his little brother's spirits would be strengthened, his willpower restored. The girl had saved him.

The other men were also falling asleep around the fire, and the girl rose from Cadvan's side, cast a shy farewell glance at Resad, and walked into the forest. He watched her go, roamed his eyes over his sleeping companions, and stood to follow her.

She walked as silently as a deer, the leaves scarcely disturbed under her bare feet, and he followed her until the campfires were far behind them. Suddenly she stopped and turned, obviously aware that she'd been followed.

"Thank you for helping Drosten and Cadvan," he said quietly, studying her solemn face. "Do you understand what I am saying?"

She nodded brightly, her eyes searching his face with undisguised longing. Gods above, why did I follow her here? he thought uncomfortably. Has she put a spell on me? I could have thanked her back at the camp.

Suddenly the girl pointed to him and ran her fingers lightly like tears down his cheeks, a puzzled look on her face.

"Aye." He nodded. "We are sad. Our sister, the beloved of the Pict, is to be killed by the Romans."

Marcia's hands flew to her cheeks and a look of horror crossed her face. She shook her head, disbelieving his words.

"Yes, it is true," he said, his composure breaking. "My sister is to die a lingering death, and I cannot save her." His lips were trembling and he fought to control the tears in his eyes. Slowly he sank to the forest floor, his shoulders quaking in silent sobs. The girl knelt beside him and wrapped her arms around him tenderly. Pressing him to her chest, she soothed him like a mother as he brokenly cried out his heartbreak.

"What do the spies say?" Allectus demanded of his druid, Eliseg. The old man rose stiffly from his stool by the fire.

"News of the girl is that she murdered a general in his bed, was caught trying to escape, and is now in their military prison, awaiting trial and execution."

"And what of their troops? On summer maneuvers as usual?"

"Oddly enough, my lord, no. For several days they have been returning to their forts along the southwest border, as if summoned for a purpose."

"Ah!" Allectus nodded. "That could explain a lot. Perhaps the general planned an attack on us, and the girl killed him to try to save us, or at least to serve as a warning."

The old druid nodded solemnly. "A brave one, that. I will offer sacrifices to her soul."

"That may not be necessary," the lord mused, motioning the old man to return to his seat. He looked grimly around the circle at his assembled chiefs and advisers. "Well, my war council, there you have the news. The Romans obviously have wind of something, and are making preparations to move. The death of a general will only set them back a few days in their plans. What shall we do about it?"

A tall, fierce-looking chief stood up, his long red hair braided down his back. "It is likely they know of our plans, Allectus," he said. "They knew of our previous camp. They must know of our revolt. I say we advance our schedule and attack at once, before they can get their forces massed and well-organized."

"Aye," a chorus of voices rose around them, "attack now . . . surprise them . . . kill them all."

"And the girl?" Allectus asked the chieftain. The man narrowed his steely blue eyes menacingly.

"If she lives, when we attack we will save her. If she is dead, we will avenge her death. Ten heads of traitor women for every year of her life."

He gazed around the circle and the chiefs nodded their approval. Who among them didn't have a daughter, a sister, the same age as the brave girl in the Roman prison? Who among them couldn't help but shudder in fear and rage at the fate that awaited her?

"And who will be detailed to save her?" Allectus asked.

"Who else?" The chieftain shrugged, returning to his seat. "The Cruithni and her brothers. She is their kinswoman. Let them have the honor . . . or the revenge."

"It is agreed, then?" Allectus concluded the meeting, his eyes roaming the determined faces before him. "We send out runners to alert the other rebels and camps along the border. It should take two days at most to warn them. On the night of the second day, we attack. May their gods have mercy on their souls, for we will show them none."

Drosten practiced unceasingly, throwing his spear at a makeshift sod target until it fell apart, hacking at a crude human figure of bound grasses and reeds until it was cut fine enough to stuff a mattress. Rage fueled his efforts, rage and revenge. His chance was coming, at long last; his months of impotent waiting would soon find vent. Word had been received in all the camps that afternoon. The attack had been advanced; they were to leave at dusk tomorrow.

The sleepy camps suddenly became hives of activity. This was what the men had assembled for, waited for, hoped for. Weapons practice became an obsession with them. Equipment was made ready, torn belts and leather body armor were mended, iron blades and points were honed and polished with fine wood ash and pumice stone. Eagerly they awaited the passing of the final day, the arrival of the hours of glory, the destruction of the hated Romans.

Marcia had become something of a permanent fixture around Resad's camp, fixing their meals, mending their clothes, helping them bathe. None of the men minded handing over the women's chores to her, but they were amused when her fierce father suddenly appeared one morning, solemnly informing them that Marcia had chosen to be Resad's woman and asking if, should anything happen to him in the coming battle, Resad or one of his companions would look out for her. They all had sworn it, to a man, realizing the difficulties of the man's circumstances, but their jests and laughter at Resad's expense continued long after the man had gone, much to Resad's annoyance. Confound the girl, he thought sourly as he watched her cook their evening meal, I have only tried to be her friend, and she has taken it all wrong. She is sweet, and attractive, but I am a man. I need a woman, not a girl.

And women there were aplenty, roaming about the camps, openly eyeing the warriors who'd gathered there, bestowing their favors on a select few. Fortrenn had attracted more than his share of attention, much to his delight, and Aniel's dark good looks appealed to the women with a taste for the foreign. A few girls had even approached Cadvan, but he'd just blushed and turned away awkwardly. Drosten rebuffed every advance, his heart on Anor and Anor alone.

By the gods, Resad thought angrily, time grows short. I, too, will find myself a willing woman and put this moonstruck girl in her place. Abruptly he rose, wiping the wood ash from the knife blade he'd been polishing, and tucked it into his belt. He stalked off silently, a puzzled Marcia staring after him, and he did not return till near dawn, sated and satisfied. He'd slept only a short time when a light touch on his arm roused him. Lifting his head, he saw that it was the girl.

"Go away," he muttered, rolling over. Undaunted, Marcia crawled around to face him again.

"What do you want?" he sighed in exasperation. Gently she lifted his hand in hers, touched it over her heart, then pressed it to his chest.

"I don't understand . . ." he began. Pointedly she clenched his hand once more to her chest and slowly bent, laying her head on his shoulder.

"Marcia . . ." He pushed her aside, sitting up. "You cannot love me. You are a young girl with an infatuation."

She shook her head vehemently and stared at him. Slowly she slid his hand down until it was resting atop her breast, and she held it there firmly.

"No, Marcia. You are a child. Now, leave me."

She tightened her grip on his hand, shaking her head, and slid his fingers over her slim waist and up to one full hip. He felt the curves of a woman beneath his hand, and despite himself the first stirrings of passion rose in his loins.

"You want me so much, then?" he whispered, and she nodded happily, his hand still clenched in hers. She kissed it and pressed it to her cheek, closing her eyes contentedly, and he ran his free hand through her thick, dark hair, touched by her simple sincerity. She looked at him, released his hand, and shyly slid her old brown shift from her shoulders. Awkwardly she sat, naked to the waist and unsure of what to do next, but assuming he would show her. He eyed her small breasts hungrily, bent down, and gently began to kiss them. The girl sat stiffly but the quivers he felt beneath his hands told him she was enjoying it. He slid one hand along her leg and lifted the hem of her dress. She felt enticingly warm between her legs and he released her long enough to lower his breeches, lay her back on his cloak, and slide between her legs. Her face suddenly looked fearful, her hands grasping tentatively along his arms, and when he began to enter her she flinched violently at the pain. A virgin, he mused, and found the fact somewhat surprising in light of all the attempts that had been made on her. Twining his fingers in hers, he held her hands down overhead to keep her from scratching him—a fate he'd never live down. Reassuringly he kissed her neck, her strained face, as he slowly forced his way into her. She stared overhead, fighting the pain, but when he began to move against her she relaxed and closed her eyes, exhaling a soft sigh against his cheek that moved his heart. Brave little one, he thought admiringly, wrapping his arms tightly around her. He prolonged it as long as he could, deriving pleasure from her pleasure; and when he was finished and she rose and walked away, he found himself wondering eagerly when next he could bed her again.

Marcia's father gave her his shaggy mountain pony and the small two-wheeled cart they used for their meager possessions. In it Resad and his companions piled their few belongings, for safekeeping with the girl until their return.

Drosten lifted the gift from Melangell and held it up, still folded and tied as it was when it was given to him so many months ago. "I want you to keep this for me," he said solemnly. Marcia studied his face. "It is a marriage gown for my beloved. I hope the gods will be kind and she will wear it when we return. Do you understand?" Marcia nodded and took the parcel from him with reverent hands. A dress for his bride, and she was charged with its care. She felt deeply honored by the trust he showed her, and impulsively she stretched upward and kissed Drosten's cheek, wishing him in her silent heart all the luck he could possess in recovering his woman. Turning, she put the bundle in her own traveling pack to protect it, and then she cast a sidelong glance at Resad. He stood stiffly at his brother's side, watching her with his intense blue eyes. She was unsure what to do next—go to him, content herself with a brief wave of farewell, or simply climb atop the pony and be gone. She knew her attentions annoyed him, and she did not want this parting to be a strained one.

Placing a hand on the pony's yoke, she raised the other in a small salute to him, lightly sprang to the animal's back, and urged it away with her knees, sitting astride it as expertly as a boy.

"Marcia!" he called, and she halted the cart. He was

striding toward her, an odd, happy look on his face, and she felt she would never forget the beauty of him as he approached—his dark hair, longer now, as black and glinting as a raven's feather, his fine skin like ivory from the Northern Seas, his eyes as blue as the summer sky. Reaching her side, he lifted her from the pony and stood her on the ground before him. The closeness of him twisted her heart unbearably and she turned her face aside, closing her eyes against the awful pain she felt within. Suddenly, to her unending delight, he wrapped his strong arms around her, lifted her into the air, and when she looked at him in astonishment, she found his mouth on hers, kissing her long and passionately.

"I will be back for you, Marcia," he whispered, returning her to the ground. "Wait for me."

She nodded, choking on the tears in her throat. They embraced one last time, her heart raging in desperation at her affliction. So much to say to him, so many words she could never utter, so many things he might never know. . . . He lifted her back atop the pony and watched the cart roll away, and when he turned to face his startled companions, the fierce look on his face stopped the jests from even the most foolhardy of them.

Night rapidly approached, the camp strangely silent with the women and animals gone, the men now grimly preoccupied with the coming attack and their preparations for it. The second hour of moonrise was the appointed time, all along the border, for the raid to be launched, and the men cast tense eyes at the settling night above the treetops, awaiting the hour of their departure.

"It is nearly ready," Aniel said, turning from a small black kettle simmering over their campfire. Drosten sat stonily, trancelike, and accompanied by three other Cruithni who'd joined them. Like most of the other warriors, the newcomers drank ales to fortify their courage and give them energy; a welcome offering to Braciaca, god of drunkenness, to strengthen anyone's faltering courage. Drosten had declined. His concentration was growing, focusing to such an extent that his companions wondered in awe what would be the results when he was finally unleashed on the Romans, and all his months of frustration and heartache came to an end.

At the word from Aniel, Drosten stood and removed his Cruithni clothes, methodically laying them atop a rock with those of his companions. Naked, the men advanced to the fire, taking small shallow bowls of steaming liquid handed to them by Aniel. A bad cook he might be, but there was one thing he knew how to fix properly: the blue dye made from boiling the woad plant, the dye all Picts used to color themselves before going into battle.

Drosten set the bowl on the ground and knelt before it as if in silent ritual. Swiftly he tied his shaggy dark hair behind his neck, removed his silver armbands and neck chain, and dipped a wad of clean wool into the dye. He rubbed it briskly over his face, wiping with his hands to be sure it was well distributed to a fine, even sheen of blue. Next he colored his neck, chest, and shoulders, rubbing the dye along his powerful arms and watching it cover and darken the ornate spiraling tattoo that ran from his left shoulder and across his left breast. Standing, he covered his abdomen, his hips, his genitals and legs and feet with the dye, and waited patiently for one of his companions to come and color his back. Tonight he saved Anor or he avenged her; tonight his warrior's preparations must be perfect.

It was Aniel who helped him, also naked and partly dyed, and when Drosten's back and buttocks were colored, he turned and finished Aniel's preparations for him. Satisfied that he was done, the Pict cast a grim eye to the sky and knew the hour was at hand. Quickly he donned his massive silver neck chain and armbands. Fastening a narrow leather belt around his bare waist, he tucked his knife and dagger into it. Strapping a sword belt diagonally across his chest, he slid his round shield over his left arm and took a lethal five-barbed spear from Aniel. Let the hour arrive, he thought fiercely. Let this night commence. For good or ill, I am ready. . . .

The sound of footsteps woke Anor from an uncomfortable slumber, and she tried to raise herself on her manacled hands. Her wrists were raw and bleeding, and the pain when the iron bands cut into the open wounds made her gasp aloud. Weakly she pushed herself upright, sagging against the damp stone prison wall and trying to cradle her burning wrists in her lap. She could hear a rat scurrying in the darkness of her cell, rustling noisily in the old straw tossed across the floor; and where normally she would have shuddered in revulsion, she could do little else now but ignore the creature. Her tiny room was dark, its only light filtering in through a small square window in the heavy wooden door—torchlight from the dimly lit hallway outside.

What now? she thought dully when a brighter light suddenly gleamed beyond the door, making her squint in the unaccustomed glare. At the sound of a key turning, her heart sank. Another beating . . . or had her final hour arrived? She was so weary, so wracked with pain, she almost didn't care anymore.

"Anor . . ." a voice roused her, and she opened her swollen eyes in surprise. The guards had gone, locking the door behind them, and she was astounded to see Marcus standing before her.

"They have beaten you!" he said, crouching and pushing the blood-matted hair from her face.

"After the trial," she mumbled through scabbed lips. "They wanted more information from me, but I had none to give."

"Why did you do it, Anor?" he choked, his voice heavy with emotion. She rolled her head against the stones behind her and looked past him, watching a torch on the wall flicker and flare in the drafty air.

"I had a hard time convincing them I had no part in it," he continued, rising and pacing the cell, his immaculate white cloak a sharp contrast to her fetid surroundings. "Now they see plots everywhere, and every slave and barbarian lives under a cloud of suspicion. Didn't you know what you were doing? In the name of all the gods, why did you do it?"

She cut her eyes around to him and shifted her chained feet uncomfortably. "Were you sent to find out for them?" she muttered. "Or do you seek to salvage your career by helping them?"

"Don't speak nonsense, Anor!" he snapped. "It is true my

career is in shambles; all I have so carefully built up now lies in ruins. But I cared for you . . . I tried to be good to you. Didn't that **matter** to you? Why did you throw it all away?"

Pulling his cloak from the dirty floor, he crouched before her again and she could see that the pain on his face was real.

"I am sorry for the hurt I have caused you, Marcus," she whispered, "for you were kind and you treated me well. It was merely something I had to do, and beyond that I can say nothing more."

Gently he placed his hands over her bloodied fingers. "And is there anything more to say?"

She shook her head slowly. "No. What I did, I did on my own. There was no plot, no spies. By the names of my ancestors, I give you my word on that, Marcus. I acted alone."

He studied her battered face in pity. "I believe you, Anor," he said, wrapping his hands around hers. "I will miss you."

She closed her eyes and turned her head away stiffly. "When will I die, Marcus?" she muttered.

"At dawn tomorrow."

"And what time is it now? I cannot see the sun in here; I do not know if it is day or night."

"It is early afternoon. Anor . . . that is why I came to see you. Your death will not be easy; they have planned it that way. But I hope I can help ease it for you, in the end."

"How . . . how will I die, Marcus?" she said, her voice suddenly quaking in fear.

"You are to be stripped and whipped through the vicus, as a warning to your people. And then, at the edge of town, where all can see . . ."

He paused and looked down, finding his next words difficult.

". . . you are to be impaled and left till you die."

"Oh, gods," she sobbed, rolling her head back and looking up at the dark ceiling. "I suppose mercy is more than I could expect of them."

"No." He shook his head. "Not after what you did. It is an old method we learned from the Persians. Were you a man, it would be quicker, for the weight would soon force the point into your heart, but you are not heavy . . ."

His voice caught and he looked away awkwardly.

"All I can tell you is to struggle mightily, Anor, for the sooner the stake cuts through you, the sooner your sufferings will be over. And if you are still alive tomorrow night, I will try to have poison sent, in a little water, to end your torments. We often allow the dying a drink of vinegar and water. They say it is out of mercy, but its real purpose is to refresh the condemned and prolong their sufferings. Do you understand, Anor? If someone brings water to you, drink it and hope your stomach is still whole enough for it to take effect. Beyond that, there is nothing I can do for you."

He stood, and even in the dim light he could see the shocked whiteness of her face as she pondered his words. "I must go now, Anor." He reached down and touched her cheek lightly. "Good-bye."

She looked up at him, tears washing her battered features. "Good-bye, Marcus," she whispered, and put her hands over her face so she would not have to see him leave.

It was a night like any other, the respectable citizens and shopkeepers safe in their beds while little knots of merrymakers unsteadily threaded their way through the dark streets, from alehouse to oyster bar, veering to avoid the occasional horse or chariot clattering over the uneven stone pavements. Secure in the protection of the nearby Roman fort, the vicus serving it had grown up without protective walls, and in the fort itself the watch scarcely gazed out over the gently rolling moonlit hillsides, so intent were they on gambling their monthly wages atop the wooden parapets. They did not notice the shadowy figures who filtered into the town on bare feet, stealthy as cats, swiftly butchering any citizens who were unlucky enough to stumble upon them. Nor did they see the loyal servants of their officers who slipped across the courtyard below, cut the throats of the guard at the gate, and drew back the huge bolt that locked the fortress in for the night. Not till the gates burst open with a wild, unholy shriek from a thousand vengeful throats did citizens and soldiers alike realize that something was wrong, and by then it was too late.

* * *

Anor roused, unsure if she'd heard voices or if it was only another of her half-delirious dreams. She'd had little food or water for three days, and at times her misery was such that she didn't think she would survive to face her execution. The flickering torch in the hallway cast a comforting square of light across her feet, and she stared at it while she strained her ears to hear beyond the confines of her cell. Her heart pounded wildly when footsteps approached, and she found her forced calm rapidly crumbling. No! she choked, hearing two guards stop outside her door, the rattle and clang of their weapons and armor an unmistakable sound. It must be time to take me! I don't want to die!

The men seemed to fumble with the keys until one succeeded in unlocking the door, and the manner in which they rushed into her cell puzzled her. Are they so anxious, then, to be rid of me? she thought, struggling to sit. The men stopped, eyeing her, and then, to her horror, one threw his cloak back and pulled out his long army dagger.

"We have orders to kill you at the first sign of a rescue attempt," he began, and her fear came near to choking her when he advanced.

"No . . . please . . ." she begged, cowering into the corner, her arms raised protectively over her heart. The guard came closer, grabbing her shoulder and raising the knife.

"Don't kill me . . . please . . . please . . ." she sobbed, kicking her legs against the chains that held her to the wall, feebly trying to twist from his grasp.

Suddenly the man grunted, his face sagged, and he sprawled forward, the dagger in his dead hand driving deep into her hip.

Oh, gods! She gasped and slumped back into the wall, the weight of the man crushing her, his blade cutting into the joint every time she tried to move. Dimly she heard the second guard fall . . . the sound of footsteps. The heavy body was pulled aside and she looked up, her startled gaze falling on a powerful warrior, naked, his skin gleaming blue in the torchlight.

"Drosten . . ." she cried, reaching weakly for him. "Help me."

Cadvan pulled his spear from the second Roman's body,

hastily wiping the blade before he trotted to his sister's side. Drosten had already pulled the dagger from her hip and was trying to stanch the blood with a corner of her filthy dress. Quickly the boy tore his cloak into strips and handed them to the Pict, and with the practiced skill of a warrior he bound the wound, easing her onto her side as gently as he could.

"Look what they have done to her!" Cadvan muttered darkly, studying her battered face and raw wrists.

"We must get her out of here," Drosten snapped, moving to lift her but stopping when he saw the chain that bound her ankles to the wall. "Damn!" he cursed, tugging futilely at the securely fastened shackles. "Check the guards. See if there are keys to this."

Cadvan kicked the bodies over and checked the Romans' belts and purses, but the only keys he could find were the heavy door keys. Frantic, Drosten pulled mightily at the chain, but it refused to yield.

"Fortrenn . . . where is Fortrenn?" he shouted, rising from Anor's side and rushing to the door, looking down the shadowed hallway for the giant. He could hear the sounds of fighting in the distance, and his panic flared like a bonfire.

"Fortrenn!" he bellowed, and was relieved to see him emerge from a distant cell, accompanied by Resad and Aniel, a glinting Roman sword in his hand.

"Hurry! I need you!" Drosten shouted, and the three men broke into a run. The sharp clangs and grunts of fighting were growing nearer, and Aniel stood guard at the cell door while his companions rushed inside.

"Gods above!" Resad gasped when he saw his sister. Cadvan sat beside her, her head cradled in his lap, and the fleeting look of awareness that crossed her face told him that she was only dimly conscious.

"So you have found your lady, eh?" Fortrenn boomed, looking down at the bloodied girl. He unslung a drinking horn from his belt and tossed it to Cadvan. "Here," he ordered, "give the poor thing some water."

"The chains, Fortrenn." Drosten pointed. "Can you pull them free?"

The giant looked down solemnly, examining the iron ring

that held the shackles to the wall, and nodded. Tucking the Roman sword into his belt, he bent over the girl's bandaged hip, positioned his feet, and gripped the chain. The men watched as the muscles in his powerful back knotted and tensed, and then, with a mighty jerk, the ring broke loose from the wall.

"Get her out of here," Resad snapped, watching the Pict lift Anor in his arms. They ran for the door, Resad leading the way, as the first of a fleeing band of Roman auxiliaries rounded the distant corner, weapons flailing mightily at anything that stood to halt their underground escape.

Fortrenn seized Cadvan and thrust him from the cell behind the retreating form of Drosten. The boy already had his sword out, ready to fight. Fortrenn fled next, with Aniel bringing up the rear. They raced madly along the dark corridor, the pursuing soldiers shouting and steadily gaining on them as they matched their pace to Drosten's slowed strides.

"Hurry!" Aniel shouted, throwing his spear at their pursuers. A man screamed in the darkness and the auxiliaries slowed for a scant moment. They rounded a corner, and Aniel hesitated, dodging one spear that flew at him from the flickering shadows but failing to see the second. It ran through his abdomen at an angle and he stumbled, dropping his sword as he fell backward. The protruding iron point of the spear lodged between two stones of the floor, trapping him, flailing and helpless in the face of the approaching soldiers. Frantically he reached for his sword, his fingers groping blindly for the hilt, the spear shaft twisting painfully in his body.

"No!" Cadvan shouted, flinging his spear at the men in an attempt to save his friend. One pursuer fell, but it was a hopeless try. Grabbing the boy, Fortrenn raced down the hallway, leaving Aniel still desperately searching for his weapon until the soldiers reached him and a swift stroke from a sword ended his struggles.

"You let him die!" Cadvan choked as they ran. "You let him die!"

"Shut up, boy, and run," the giant snapped. Turning the next corner, they saw light coming in an open doorway, and

Resad and Drosten waiting for them, panting heavily. Aniel's death had bought them a few precious moments of time.

"Aniel?" Resad gasped. Fortrenn wordlessly shook his head.

"Cadvan, Drosten, get Anor to the central compound," Resad barked. "Allectus will be there, and the druids to care for her. Hurry!"

"And you?" Drosten demanded.

"I will follow. Now, go!"

Without a word the Pict and the boy trotted off toward the beckoning light of the doorway. "I will hold them off for a while," Fortrenn said, fastening his shield over his back and taking his sword and spear in hand. "You go on."

"No," Resad said firmly. "I will help you."

"You will not," the giant snapped. "There is no time to argue. What I do is no more than what my father did to save the green-eyed druidess at Duncrub. Now, go."

"Druidess?" Resad gasped. "But . . . that was my mother!"

"Aye? Was it now?" Fortrenn grinned. "All the more reason you must go. Return to your mother and thank her for me. I had nineteen good years of life because of her; nineteen more than I'd have had without her. The world has turned full circle. The son of another, whom she once saved, now saves her daughter in return. It is the plan of the All-Knowing. Now, go!"

Resad took a few hesitant steps down the hall and turned back to the grim giant. Fortrenn suddenly broke into a broad smile.

"Resad, my friend," he called out as the sounds of pursuit drew nearer, "if any little bastards are born in camp nine months hence who look like me, foster them, will you, and raise them as your own?"

"I will." Resad nodded. "You have my oath on it." Turning, he fled the tunnel.

Cordelia woke to the sound of a strangled sob from the kitchen boy, and shouts and screams from the streets outside. The old woman sat up abruptly, to find herself confronted by a tall Celt, his teeth and eyes shining white in the dark room. Before she could think a coherent thought, his sword flashed and her head silently fell from its shoulders, her heavy body tumbling to one side and taking the cot with it, blood pooling on the gleaming tiles of the floor. Screaming in terror, the kitchen boy bolted across the room, his hands frantically clawing at one corner of the wall in his desperation to escape. A swift slice of the sword ended his panic, and his spirit joined that of Cordelia in the great Void.

They knew they could not hold out for long. Already the bolted door of the storeroom was beginning to splinter under the onslaught of the eager natives. The Roman officers milled nervously in the dank room, the single torch on the wall dimly illuminating the spreading cracks in the oaken door. Marcus knew the bolt would not hold much longer, and he looked around desperately for some other defense, some way of escape. There was none. The handful of officers had fled into a trap, with no other exits, no hiding places, no additional weapons stores, and little room to fight. Another blow struck the door and he could see the end of a log protruding partway through it. The officers instinctively drew to the rear of the small room like nervous sheep as the log withdrew and the shouts of the natives, scenting victory, came to them. Several of the men fell to their knees, praying loudly to Mithras or Mars or whoever gave them solace, while others drew their swords for a final fight. They heard loud grunts from the hallway as the log was swung back and with a final heave came crashing through the door.

All the Roman officers and their women—wives and daughters, mistresses and slaves—were bound and herded into the clearing before the principia, the main headquarters building, while the slaughter of the soldiers and townsfolk went on around them. Allectus and his druids and war council waited patiently, studying each new group of captives brought to join the others. The raid had been a success, he knew. Caught off their guard, the Romans had been overwhelmed. Victory was theirs.

His spearmen suddenly stirred when two figures appeared in the gloom, trotting from the rear of the fort toward the warlord. With a silent nod Allectus sent two druids to see to the bloodied girl the Pict carried tenderly in his arms. They crossed to a small side building and Allectus settled back in a plundered chair to wait, eyeing the frightened, sobbing Roman women coldly. Their fate depended on the druids' verdict: would the girl live, or would she die?

"Drosten . . ." Anor moaned. The Pict moved to her head, stroking her cheek softly while one of the druids cut the bandage from her hip.

"It's all right, my love," he soothed, kissing her dirty forehead. "You are safe. All is well now." He glanced at the druid's grim face, and the man's words brought relief to Drosten's heart.

"I must get my medicines," the druid said, rising, "and a smith to remove these irons."

She will live! Drosten sighed. She will live!

Abruptly he stood, hatred etching his weary face, and left the building.

"You must send help!" Resad gasped to Allectus. "He is in the tunnel, holding off the pursuing Romans. Hurry!"

The lord acted swiftly. With a wave of his hand he sent twenty of his personal spearmen with Resad, to try to save the giant Fortrenn.

Drosten strode to the principia, his face dark and dangerous. "Who speaks their tongue?" he demanded of a warrior nearby. The man shrugged and pointed to a druid. Drosten crossed to the old man.

"Ask for the tribune Marcus, owner of the slave girl Anor," he snapped. The druid called out an unintelligible sentence and an aristocratic-looking soldier, his armor and weapons removed, his arms tied behind his back, wormed forward through the packed mass of officers.

"I am Marcus," he said, staring at the naked blue man curiously. He had often heard of the blue Picts of the north, but this was the first he had seen.

"Tell him I was the man Anor was to marry," Drosten growled, his eyes unflinching as he stared at the Roman. By the time the druid finished speaking, the curiosity had fled Marcus' face, replaced by a rising fear. Abruptly the Pict seized his hair in one powerful hand and pushed him aside to a small supply building.

"Look at her! See what you have done!" the Pict barked in broken Celtic, and Marcus could make out enough of the man's angry words to know what he meant. Anor lay on a pallet of empty grain sacks. Her leg shackles had been removed by a smith, who now worked as gently as he could to free her torn wrists. One black-robed druid was feeding her some liquid from a metal cup while another skillfully cleaned a raw wound to her hip. Marcus started at the sight of her, so pale and fragile in the clutter of the ransacked storeroom.

"Anor . . ." he gasped, flinching when the Pict jerked his head roughly. The girl turned her face from the druid's cup and looked at him with her battered eyes.

"Marcus?" she puzzled, and her gaze turned to Drosten's livid face in sudden understanding.

"See her, bastard!" Drosten snarled, twisting a handful of hair savagely.

"No . . . Drosten . . . please," the girl cried, attempting to rise from the startled grip of the druid and smith. "He was good to me. Please, Drosten, spare him. He tried to help me, Drosten!"

Abruptly the Pict turned, shoving his bound captive from the room as Anor's desperate pleas followed in his ears. Outside, the first gusts of smoke from the burning vicus tainted the cool night air. Marcus saw the man pull out his knife and waited stoically for the end, but to his surprise the Pict cut the ropes tying his arms. Crossing to a stocky fair-haired boy warrior who stood guard outside the storeroom, the Pict pulled the boy's sword from its sheath and tossed it to him. Marcus seized it, hefting its unfamiliar weight and balance in his hands. When the Pict picked up a barbed spear from the ground and clasped it between his two hands, Marcus understood: he was to fight to the death.

"Die like a man," the Pict snarled, feinting with the spear. "Because Anor pleads for you, I allow you this one mercy."

The Pict lunged, the butt of the spear catching Marcus in

the side. It was a hopeless fight, he knew, and just a matter of time before he fell. The Pict knew it too, his brown eyes burning in hot revenge as he toyed with him, sparring and lunging and easily dodging Marcus' awkward strikes. Still, he tried to put up a good fight, slashing the best he could with the unfamiliar weapon he'd been given. It was almost a relief when the spear ran into his abdomen, the five barbs tearing at his innards like a wolf's claws. Groaning, Marcus dropped the sword and sank to his knees, his hands feebly grasping the shaft that protruded from his stomach. Through a haze of pain he watched the Pict draw his sword, raise it high, and with a wild cry of rage send it slicing toward his neck. . . .

Fire coursed through Resad when he entered the torchlit courtyard and saw a handful of Roman auxiliaries wandering about, their odd uniforms a strange sight in the gloom. He and Allectus' men watched them in silence for a few moments; they seemed to be searching for another safe passageway, peering cautiously into doorways and down corridors. Cowards! Resad thought savagely, pulling out his sword. For Fortrenn, he swore, and with a wild cry he led the men in a charge on the startled soldiers.

He sliced the first legionary nearly in half, and the body fell to the ground, thrashed a moment, and was still. Satisfied with his handiwork, Resad ran to the next soldier, a more experienced swordsman, who met him bravely, cutting and thrusting as skillfully as Resad himself. They fought fiercely, across the open floor and into a dark doorway where Resad could scarcely see his opponent. Baring his teeth, he struck savagely at the man's upraised arm. "Die!" he snarled, and was startled when his sword met only air. A shadow, he realized sickly. But it was enough. His balance thrown off, his concentration broken, he missed seeing the man's counterattack until it was nearly too late. Whirling, he tried to dodge the downward slice. It cut into his calf muscle and, helpless, Resad fell to the ground, waiting for the end. The soldier pointed his sword to thrust, but before he could move, a silent shadow leapt on him from the darkness, breaking his neck with a loud crack.

"How will you foster my sons when you cannot even look after your own hide?" a familiar voice laughed.

"Fortrenn . . ." Resad gasped, rising on one shaky elbow.

"Aye," the giant boomed, pulling off his tunic and tying it around Resad's bleeding leg.

"But . . . how did you survive?" Resad began. Fortrenn waved his words aside with a grin.

"Outnumbered twelve to one, I decided hiding was the bravest course. Lucky for me, the Romans put many hiding places in their buildings. Now, come." He took Resad's arms and lifted him over his broad back. "We must get you away from here and to the druids."

"Fortrenn, you scoundrel," Resad groaned, fighting the pain searing his leg, "if I had another sister, I'd give her to you, sure enough."

"And break the hearts of all my other women?" The giant laughed loudly. "No, my friend, I will furrow a few more fields before I settle down to one crop." Chuckling, he carried Resad along the building's low wooden wall, avoiding the fighting going on in the center of the yard, until he reached the gateway and slipped safely out.

Allectus heard the news he'd been waiting for; one of the druids attending the girl informed him that she would live, perhaps with a slight limp, but she would live. Summoning the Pict, Allectus gave him his final instructions: get a cart and pony for Anor and Resad, and take the girl safely back to her family. A woman should not have to witness what was about to happen here. Removing an inlaid gold band from his arm, he pressed it into the startled young man's hand and smiled. For your firstborn son, with my gratitude to the woman who is to be your wife. Without her, our plans would surely have failed. With the skill of his father and the courage of his mother in his veins, your son will surely be deserving of so fine a token.

With a nod of thanks, Drosten crossed to the supply building to reclaim his bride. As he passed the huddled captives, he picked up the severed head of Marcus and pointedly tossed it between Allectus and the Roman officers. The lord caught his eye and nodded, laughing loudly. A last

favor for the Pict; his victim the start of a pile of severed
Roman heads. The lord ordered the terrified women removed, herded away to a life of slavery, and waited until the
cart bearing the girl had rolled from the ravaged fort. Then,
with a silent wave of his hand, his men moved forward,
swords drawn, to begin the final slaughter.

Part 3

REUNIONS

M ELANGELL COULD SEE THEM, SILHOUETTED AGAINST THE
luminous nighttime sky, and turned her head away with a
groan.

I am still alive! she cursed silently, gasping at the fiery
aches that racked her body.

Oh, gods!

She could see Talorc leaping down the rocky cliff face, as
agile as a mountain pony, and Eldol not far behind him.
Closing her eyes, she dropped her head to the cushioning
sand and listened to the reassuring splash of the waves
nearby. Leave me, she pleaded silently when she heard the
two men approaching. Let me die! Leave me!

She was awkwardly sprawled. Talorc reached her side,
unsure of what to do. "Lady . . ." he choked, and Melangell
opened her eyes at the fear in his voice.

"I cannot move," she gasped weakly. "My leg . . ."

Talorc looked aside, bewildered, when Eldol joined him.
They could see, even in the shadows of the cliff, that her leg
was twisted grotesquely, possibly broken.

"We must move her and check that leg before we carry her
back," Talorc decided. Eldol crouched beside Melangell,
sliding his folded cloak beneath her head. "Lady, we must
lift you from these rocks. It will hurt."

"No," she mumbled, turning her face toward him, "no
. . . the pain . . . don't . . ."

"We must," Talorc stated. He slipped his hands beneath
her shoulders while Eldol supported her legs. Gently they
lifted her from her skewed position, and Melangell gritted
her teeth against the pain that engulfed her.

511

Gods above, I hurt all over, she gasped, feeling them probe her injured leg. Is every bone in my body broken? And the child . . . what of the child?

Like a rising tide, the pain surged upward, and before she could cry out, it overwhelmed her, drawing her away into a peaceful, painless oblivion.

Severa opened the door cautiously, unsure of where her charge had gone and afraid to find out. Her weary old eyes flew open in horror when one of the king's guards pushed his way in, followed by Talorc and the musician Eldol, carrying between them a battered and unconscious Melangell.

"What happened?" the woman choked, her gray eyes flashing in sudden motherly concern. "What have you done—?"

"Quiet, woman," Talorc snapped, laying Melangell on the bed. "She fell from the cliff. Don't just stand there gawking. Get Broichan! Quickly!"

"Gods above! The baby!" Severa sobbed aloud. "If the child dies, it will be all our heads for it."

"Go!" Talorc shouted, sliding his arm from beneath his mistress and turning angrily to the old woman. "Fetch him now or I'll kick your lazy ass to get you moving!"

The king's guard eyed the scene silently. When Severa ran crying from the room, he turned on his heel and followed her down the hall, turning left at the end and demanding immediate entry into Achivir's quarters. In minutes the palace was in an uproar, Achivir storming from his room clad only in his breeches and followed by a chain of sleepy retainers and grim guards. He nearly collided with Broichan in the corridor outside Melangell's rooms. The druid carried a large sack of medicines and his hastily donned clothes looked rumpled and ill-fitting.

"The child!" Achivir bellowed. "The child!"

"Yes, sire." The druid nodded. "I will do what I can, though the old woman says she is severly battered . . ."

Rage crossed the king's face at the unfinished sentence the druid dangled before him. "Who is responsible for this?" he growled, his voice like an icy winter's storm. Broichan shrugged.

"I know as little as you, sire," he said calmly. "Now, I must go." He rushed into the young woman's room, an agitated Severa close behind him. The king followed more slowly, his mind churning dangerously, his eyes narrowed like an angry dog's. I will find who is responsible, he swore to himself, and he will pay dearly, whoever he is.

Melangell woke to pain, unending pain, like a fine garment clinging to her body.

"Don't move," a soothing voice commanded, and through the fogs in her brain she recognized it as Severa's. A cool cloth bathed her forehead and cheeks; the clashing smells of medicinal herbs filled the air.

"Severa . . ." she mumbled, trying to turn her head to see the old woman.

"Keep her still!" Broichan snapped from somewhere near her feet. He sounded remote, distant, shouting across a wide valley.

"I fell, Severa, I . . ." she explained, and felt Severa grasp her hand reassuringly.

"We know, dear, we know."

"Hold her," Broichan said. Melangell found the old woman suddenly flung in an odd embrace across her shoulders. In the swift gasp of pain that followed, she knew the reason. The child—Achivir's child—was gone.

"What were you doing out on the cliffs, against my orders, at that hour of the night?" the king demanded, his hands on his hips as he stood by her bed, as threatening a presence as a building thunderhead.

Melangell gazed at him through the awful pounding in her head, not wanting to reply, not even wanting to see him. "A walk . . ." she muttered brokenly, for even the act of breathing caused her pain. "I needed to walk . . . it helps."

"Then why at night? And why was that musician there?" he snapped, pacing to the hearth and stopping, his back to her, waiting for an answer.

"He thought to help."

"He?" Achivir shouted. "By the gods, woman, what place was it of his to help you?"

"He was kind, Achivir. He—"

"Was he your lover?" he growled, turning on her with a sudden fury that startled her. "That Celt . . . was he?"

"No! He never even suggested . . . No!" she tried to protest, as vehemently as her frailty would allow. Her head was fairly sailing from the pain and she desperately wished he would go, would stop shouting so.

"No . . ." she gasped, lolling her head back to the bed. "No . . . never."

"We will see," he retorted, turned, and stormed from the room.

"Severa, some tea," Melangell moaned as welcome silence engulfed her. "My head . . . Severa, get tea for it."

When the old woman lifted her charge's head to feed her the painkilling willow tea, she noted the flushed look to her face, the dullness of her eyes. A casual hand to the young woman's forehead confirmed her suspicions. Severa put the empty bronze cup aside, pulled a patterned coverlet to Melangell's chin, and slipped across the room. Opening the door, she motioned to Talorc, standing guard in the hallway outside.

"Fetch Broichan at once," she whispered urgently.

"Why? What is wrong?" Talorc asked, alarmed.

"The fever . . . she has childbirth fever."

Talorc watched suspiciously while the druid examined his mistress. Old Severa hovered nearby like a nervous dragonfly, her plump hands twining monotonously. "Well?" the old woman whispered fearfully. "Has she?"

Broichan took her aside, nodded once, and began picking up his jars and packets of medicines.

"What are you doing?" Severa hissed. "Aren't you going to treat her for it?"

The druid shook his head and glanced at the woman. "A cure for this is long, difficult, and uncertain. If she survives, which is unlikely, she will never be able to bear children again, which is the main thing that interests Achivir now. It is a kindness to us all if she dies."

"No!" Severa gasped in horror. "Surely you don't—"

"Let Achivir find a proper wife. Let him return to his

duties, as he should, and stop wasting his time on this little witch. Besides, woman, what future will she have if she lives? Unable to bear children, she will be of no more use to Achivir. What then, eh? No, let her die, I say, and thank the gods for it."

"Broichan! You must help her!" Severa pleaded, tears rising in her eyes. "Don't let her die!" She seized his arm but he jerked it away angrily, lifted his bag of potions, and turned to the door.

"Make her as comfortable as you can in her last days, woman," he snapped, glancing over his shoulder as he spoke, "for soon she—"

Strong hands suddenly grabbed him by the shoulders, whirled him about, and flung him hard into the rough stone wall by the door, driving the wind from his lungs. Before he could utter a sound, he found a dagger slicing threateningly across his throat, and Talorc's angry face directly in his.

"My sister had the fever," the guard snarled at him, his dark eyes like two burning coals. "She was treated and lived. Save her, druid, or you die."

"Are you threatening me, boy?" Broichan said, his voice strained but cold. Talorc nodded slowly and pressed the blade against the druid's flesh.

"And what will you do, boy, if I do not save her? One word to Achivir and it will be your head for it. Your threats are hollow. Now, release me."

"It will be a simple matter, druid." Talorc sneered. "A sudden rush in the night, when you least expect it. First your pretty mistress, whom the king knows nothing of, and then you. A slit throat is very quick and quiet. You won't even be sure if it was me or another who did you in as your life's blood drains away."

Broichan's face sagged at the guard's words, and as if to add emphasis to his threat, the young man slammed the druid into the wall again. The honesty of his anger and the power of his muscles were not lost on Broichan, and he nodded. "Yes," he croaked. "Release me. I will do my best to save her."

Talorc stepped away from the man, replacing his knife in his belt. "You'd better do more than your best, druid," he snapped, "for if she dies, you die." Glancing at a relieved Severa, the young man left the room.

For five days Melangell hovered at the edge of her life, rousing to the aches and fires and poundings of her battered body and throbbing head, then sinking back mercifully into oblivion. For five days Broichan came as regularly as the passage of the sun; giving her potent teas, applying poultices, heating the room with medicinal steam, flushing her out with healing washes. Talorc eyed him threateningly each time he arrived, and checked the lady's progress with Severa before he would allow the druid to depart. When, on the morning of the sixth day, he heard Melangell's soft voice greet Broichan when he entered her room, Talorc was satisfied; he knew her crisis had passed. She would live.

But at what cost? Broichan thought bitterly, passing a smiling Talorc on his way from Melangell's room. The young fool has got his wish: the lady will live. Yet in all these days of my unceasing care, Achivir has never known the truth about her. He doesn't know that my seeming devotion to her cure will be for nothing. Had he known, he doubtless would have agreed with my assessment: better she should die. And when he does find out, what then? Will he blame me? Do I dare plead ignorance of a simple fact even the youngest apprentice healer knows? He will have no more use for the woman then. The young fool has had his way . . . but at what cost?

Achivir came to see Melangell frequently, and while his concern seemed genuine, she could see behind his studied smile and light conversation that some care he'd once had for her had died. It was the child, she knew; not her. He frequently mentioned it, as if to constantly remind her of her failure; and her lack of tears, of heartbreak, puzzled him. She'd just lost a child; why wasn't she devastated by it?

"We will have another," he said in feigned reassurance, studying her pale face for a reaction. She sat propped up in the bed, a trencher on her lap, and picked at the light meal Severa had prepared. She must not have heard him, for she gave no reaction whatsoever.

"I said, we will have another," he repeated, rising from his chair, pushing his meal table aside, and crossing to her bed. She looked up at him blankly but still made no reply.

"Why don't you answer me, lady?" he persisted, his anger rising at her listlessness. "Your carelessness killed my first child; we will have another."

"Weren't you told?" she said quietly, looking down at the trencher. "I can have no others."

"What?" he said coldly, a hardness settling into his voice.

"The fever . . . I am scarred too badly inside. I can have no more chil—"

Her word was cut off by a violent blow to her cheek. She sprawled sideways across the bed, spilling the food and wrenching her bruised leg.

"Bitch!" he snarled. She did not reply, only lay numbly, her stinging face resting atop one outstretched arm. "You will pay," he growled, and the tone of his voice sent ice into her soul. Turning, he stormed from the room.

I am beyond tears, beyond fear, she told herself resolutely, pulling her weary body upright and trying to clean the bed. No matter what he does to me, I am free once more. Esus has said it, and I did it. I have no regrets . . . none.

Severa's eyes were round with fear when she woke Melangell in the night. "What is it, Severa?" the young woman asked, alarmed at the look on the old lady's face.

"I am to leave," she sobbed, tears spilling down her plump cheeks. "The king has sent a message. You are to have no more of my services."

"What!" Melangell gasped, pulling herself upright in the bed. "But my injuries . . . how can I manage?"

"I don't know, lady," Severa cried. "I am to go at once. Lady . . . I am afraid . . ."

"It's all right, Severa," Melangell said, patting the woman's arm reassuringly. "It will all be for the best, in the end."

She seemed lost in thought, and Severa studied her a moment, then rose to collect her things. As she stepped to the door, Melangell quietly called to her. Severa paused, not daring to turn and look at her.

"My children, Severa . . ." The lady choked, and Severa could tell from the sound that she was fighting tears.

"Yes, lady?"

"If they return, tell them . . . tell them I did not fail them."

Severa nodded. "Yes, lady, I will."

Melangell hobbled about as best she could, fighting the aches and bruises that racked her body. Talorc helped her as much as possible, but the silent thought occupied both their minds as the first long day without Severa dragged by: Talorc, too, would no doubt soon be gone, so she must learn to manage on her own. Always Talorc stood at his post outside the door, ready to come at her call.

Loud laughter woke him when the night was half over, and Talorc looked up from the blanket where he slept across Melangell's doorway when a brightly blazing torch rounded the corner and came toward him. Springing to his feet, he saw that it was Achivir, weaving unsteadily on his feet and accompanied by two stern guards.

"Where is she?" the king bellowed. Talorc could see that he was drunk. "The little bitch . . . where is she?"

Fear rose in the young man at the tone of the king's voice, and he stood at the door, gently trying to dissuade him. "Sire . . . she is asleep."

"With whom?" Achivir shouted, swaying from side to side as he laughed.

"She has been ill and needs her rest."

"Ill . . . bah! She is a witch. Have you had her yet, boy? Eh? Stand aside. I will see my little lady now."

"But, sire, you shouldn't—" Talorc protested. On a signal from the king, one of the guards shoved him back to the wall.

"Out of the way, boy, and let me pass," Achivir muttered, opening the door and entering the gloom of the girl's room. The guards followed, the torch flaring eerily on the stone walls as the door closed behind them.

Talorc straightened and listened sickly to the sounds coming from the room. The lady awoke, protesting mightily as Achivir made his intentions known in the crudest of terms. Evidently she resisted him, for the noises of a halfhearted struggle followed, ending with the king heaving up his dinner, the sound of a violent slap, and the door flew open. Achivir emerged, a look of sickness all over his bleary face, and followed by the two guards. One caught Talorc's eye and quickly motioned with his head toward the lady's room. Then, in silence, they passed into the night.

Talorc turned and hurried into the room, taking a torch from the wall and lighting it on the hearth.

"Lady . . ." he questioned, peering around the room. He finally detected her, sitting upright on the bed, the coverlet in a foul-smelling heap on the floor.

"He . . . he tried to rape me," she gasped, her face pale and ghostly in the dim light. "In front of his men, he tried to rape me."

He wasn't sure what to say. "I know," he muttered, picking up the soiled coverlet. "I will throw this out and fetch you another." Glancing at her when he passed, he saw tears sliding down her ashen cheeks.

"Perhaps Achivir is sorry for what happened last night," Talorc suggested brightly when he entered Melangell's room the next morning.

"Why?" she said dully. She'd managed to seat herself in a chair and was now combing out her long wheaten hair.

"He sent word to tell you to prepare yourself. Eldol will be coming to dine with you."

"Eldol?" She brightened. "I have heard nothing of him since . . . since I fell. Is he well? Where has he been?"

Talorc shrugged and opened the window shutter on the far wall to let some fresh air clear out the stench from the night before. "Word was he was thrown into the dungeon. It seems Achivir blamed him for what happened."

Melangell's face fell and she lowered the bone comb to her lap.

"Then they said the king would send him back from whence he came. That was the last I heard. But he must still be here, if he comes to eat with you this morning."

"I hope he is well," she muttered. "I never meant to get him in trouble for his kindness."

"Well, you'll soon find out." Talorc smiled, putting a few blocks of dried peat on the fire. "Perhaps if the king's anger has cooled, he'll let Severa come back too."

"Yes." She nodded, returning her attentions to her hair.

"Gods above, Talorc, I will be so glad when my strength returns and I can get around again."

He laughed and crossed to the door when a curt knock interrupted her words. A small parade of servants entered, bearing trays heavy with elaborately prepared dishes and a large ewer of wine. Melangell looked at Talorc, mystified by this sudden change in Achivir's heart. One by one the trays were placed on tables before her and she looked at the sumptuous layout in sudden hunger.

"Won't you stay and have some, Talorc?" she asked when the servants left the room. He pulled a chair close for Eldol, then stood and grinned at her.

"No, lady, I will wait at my post for your guest to arrive. If I may say, it looks like your fortunes have changed."

"Perhaps." She smiled, tasting a small cake heavy with cream and honey.

He left the room and had barely positioned his spear in hand when a wild scream came from the lady's room, followed by a strangled sob and a loud crash. Panicked and puzzled, he rushed into the room as Melangell struggled to crawl from beneath her toppled chair.

"Lady . . ." he gasped, running to her side and lifting her up in his arms. She clung to him desperately, choking and gasping in terror, and when his gaze followed her wildly waving arm, his stomach turned in nausea.

Centered on a covered silver platter was the severed head of Eldol.

Talorc could do nothing, and his impotence enraged him. Once again Achivir came in the night, like some dread demon swooping down on the innocent at rest. Again the king stalked into Melangell's room, but this time he was sober. Sober, angry, and vicious. And this time Talorc was ordered in as well. He was made to stand and watch as the lady tried to fight the king; as his two guards held her down; as Achivir brutally raped her, caring little for her weakened condition or injuries. And he knew, as he watched, that this was his punishment for having allowed her to go out for that nighttime walk. His fate was no less horrid than Eldol's, if less swift. Degraded himself, he would be made to endure her degradation, again and again, until the king tired of his sport and put a merciful end to the both of them.

He stood woodenly, seeming to see but refusing his eyes their vision, until the king finished with the lady and left, taking the guards and torches with him. Numbly Talorc stumbled to her side, pulling the coverlet over her naked body as she sobbed into the soft down mattress; and a cold resolve settled into his heart.

For the friendship I bear Drosten, for my admiration of Resad, I will get you out of here, lady. I will not let Achivir win.

On the third nightly visit of the king, Melangell was still as unyielding as before. She knew it was futile, that Achivir only need beat her or have his guards hold her to have his way, but still she resisted, as if determined to stop him or die trying. The fourth night was the same, and the fifth, till Talorc could stand her weakening protests and feeble struggles no longer. When, on the sixth night, Achivir ordered him into the room with the others, he balked.

"Sire," he said calmly, aware of the king's dangerous mood of late, "such behavior does not become you."

"Do you defy me, boy?" Achivir threatened.

"No, sire. I only seek to warn you. You have long held the respect of your people for your fairness and wisdom. This will not add to your reputation—nightly raping an ill woman who came here only through your schemes in the first place."

A hardness passed across Achivir's face, then eased. "I see." He nodded. "So you do not think it is fit for me to do this?"

"No, my lord," Talorc said, relieved that the king was being so reasonable.

"Very well; I agree. Come into the room, my good man. All of you, come."

The three guards followed the king into Melangell's room and waited expectantly. *Maybe he will release her,* Talorc thought hopefully. *An apology, perhaps.*

Achivir seated himself in a chair and motioned for the guards to put their torches on the walls. They did as he commanded and turned to face him, puzzled by his attitude. Melangell had awakened from a restless sleep and now peered from the edge of her coverlet, her face drawn and fearful.

"Talorc feels it is not fitting for me to have you nightly," the king addressed her. "And, on reflection, I agree with him. You are of common birth; surely I deserve better. So, in light of your continuing need for punishment for the death of my son, which you caused, and for the torment you have brought me, I direct my guards to take you instead."

The two guards looked at each other, dumbfounded, but made no move to comply. "Sire—" one began to protest. Achivir cut him off.

"Do you disobey me, man?" he thundered. "I will not have a disobedient guard. Do you strip and take her, or do I relieve you of your duties?"

The guards looked at each other again, laid down their weapons, and slowly began to undress.

"No . . ." Melangell gasped, horrified when they started toward her. Wildly she flung herself to the far side of the bed, crashing to the floor with a groan.

"Well? Go on!" Achivir snapped when the two men hesitated. He seemed amused by the spectacle. "Take her, or leave. You will enjoy it. Go on."

Reluctantly they rounded the bed and lifted the struggling young woman from the floor. "No!" she screamed, flailing with her arms.

"Lady," one of the men hissed at her, "it will go easier on us all if you stop fighting. What choice do we have? We must obey him."

"Please . . ." she sobbed. "Don't . . . please . . ."

"We must, lady. Be still, we will finish with you, and be gone."

The other guard was caressing her body, his fingers frantic against her pale skin, and she could see that both of them were becoming aroused by her. "No! Help me . . . Talorc!" she cried when one of the men climbed atop her.

Talorc started toward her at the cry, his nerves so taut at the spectacle he thought he would choke on his rage. The bastard, he thought savagely, glancing at the king's smirking face. The filthy, no-good bastard . . .

"Hold your place, boy," Achivir snapped when he saw Talorc move. "Stand where I directed or you lose your head."

The young man froze, his fists clenched in fury. The second guard was now atop Melangell, but she seemed to have stopped her fighting. Perhaps she sees the uselessness of it, Talorc mused; or perhaps she has given up.

"Now you," the king ordered, turning to Talorc when the second man climbed from the bed.

"Me . . ." Talorc said, the word dying on his lips. The other two guards, still naked, looked at the king in shock.

"No . . . I am her guard. I cannot." Talorc protested.

"You will, boy. I have commanded it!" Achivir said, and the calmness of his voice was a warning. "Strip off your clothes and take her. Surely it is not the first time, is it?"

Talorc stared at the king, dumbfounded. "I cannot. It is a violation of my duty . . . my oath. I am to protect her, not . . . not rape her."

"Take off your clothes, boy," the king repeated, rising menacingly to his feet. Silently Talorc removed his wide sword belt, his long wool tunic and leather breeches, and the hate spilling from his eyes was almost tangible. He dropped the clothes in a heap on the floor and stood grimly before the king.

"Seize him," Achivir directed the two guards. They took the young man's arms as the king pulled out his long knife. Casually he slid the point through the hair on Talorc's chest, over his stomach, and the young guard tried to cringe when the point reached his genitals.

"If your manhood is worth anything"—Achivir sneered, toying with him with the knife point—"you will do as I say. If not, I will make a eunuch out of you, and you can be her companion for the rest of your miserable life."

Talorc swallowed hard, his gaze focused stonily on the far wall, a nervous sweat breaking out across his forehead.

"No!" Melangell gasped, sitting up in the bed. "Achivir, don't. Not because of me. Please . . . I am begging you. Don't."

The king grinned and replaced his knife. "Just as I suspected. The lady cares. Then she must also care enough to help you achieve what you so obviously lack right now, for if you do not take her as I have ordered, you will leave this room less a man than when you entered it. Is that clear?"

"Yes," Talorc croaked, trying to still the wildness of his heart. At a nod from the king, the guards released him, and Achivir returned to his chair. Slowly the young man turned, and the short walk across the floor was the longest he had ever taken in his life. Reaching the bed, he looked down glumly at the lady, still sitting up, the coverlet clutched awkwardly to her breast.

"It is all right," she whispered. "Do what you must, Talorc. It is your future at stake. I have none. It is all right."

She reached up and slid one small hand delicately along his hip, and despite his fear, he felt himself stirring.

"I cannot . . ." he gulped, looking away.

"You must. Come . . ." She flung the coverlet aside and took his hand gently. "Quickly, Talorc. Give him little pleasure from us. Come."

He looked down at her bare white shoulders, the graceful curve of her breasts, and he could see them rising and falling as she breathed.

"By the gods!" he whispered, his excitement growing. Girls, he had had. Young girls, silly girls, girls aplenty. But never a woman. Never . . .

He sat on the bed, tentatively gliding his hand down her body.

"Lady . . . forgive me," he whispered, jerking his hand away.

"It's all right. Forget who I am. Just take me, and be done with it."

"No. I cannot . . . my oath . . ."

She slid her hand between his legs and was pleased to see that Achivir's threats seemed to be having little effect on his hot young blood. Gently she helped him, and he closed his eyes and swallowed hard.

"Gods above!" he whispered hoarsely, and his hand returned instinctively to her breast. She lay back on the bed, pulling him down with her, and he began to eagerly kiss her neck.

"Now, Talorc, now," she urged. He finished in a few brief

minutes, but before he could rise from the bed, the king stood, laughing heartily.

"Well done, Talorc, well done!" he boomed. "You have just saved your skin, in more ways than one. Come!" He motioned to his guards, who stood transfixed, eyeing the scene on the bed. "Let's leave the two lovers alone."

The guards roused, gathered their clothes, and followed Achivir from the room, leaving the torches guttering low on the walls.

"I will kill him," Talorc muttered, rising from the bed and turning away from Melangell in shame. He pulled on his clothes, retrieved his weapons, and hurried to his post outside the door.

"Esus," she whispered into the night, "I am trying, but in the name of the All-Knowing, it is so hard! Shamed and humiliated, used like a slave, abused like a cart horse. Why, Esus? What is the reason for it? Am I to endure this until a merciful death releases me? Until my children return? But what can they do? I hope they never return to this place. Here, all are subject to Achivir's whim, and he is now a madman. I have thrown my life away, Esus; shattered on the rocks that night like a fragile vessel. All that I had is now gone. Why, Esus? You directed me down this path—for what reason? Why?"

She turned her gaze to the flickering hearth, thinking on her life. Her husbands, her children. How joyous and simple things had been then! But now there was nothing. Nothing but cold hatred, a need for revenge like a ravening wolf, and emptiness. . . . Like a black, gaping maw, the blackness in her soul devoured every hope, every light, every dream she could muster. She had not thought such emptiness to be possible; or that a human soul could long endure it if it came. This very absence of anything was the only something life had left her. . . .

She felt a movement against her forehead, a light gust from the drafty air . . . or was it? If she closed her eyes, she could almost feel it to be Brennos' gentle hand, as light as a butterfly's wings across her skin. But no . . . And yet . . . Did something move in the shadows across the room, over by the far doorway? One could think it to be a ghostly druid, robed in black, gliding away from her bedside. Druidry formed a bond that existed even beyond death. "I will come . . ." she heard Brennos speak again in her mind, and with that her soul felt peace. She was not alone.

She turned in sudden fear at the sound of voices in the hall. It has been days, she thought sickly when she heard Talorc speaking to Achivir. Not since he forced Talorc to break his oath, destroy his honor . . . I had hoped that had been too much, even for the king's twisted mind. That he would now leave us alone. But no, it is night, and once again he comes. Once again the nightmare begins. Brennos, help me to endure. . . .

Talorc stood aside helplessly when Achivir opened the door, ushering in a resplendently dressed envoy from a neighboring tribe. This night his guards did not enter Melangell's room, nor did Talorc. The young man's hatred flared higher when the door closed behind the two men, and he glanced hotly at the guards who stood across the hall from him.

So it begins again, he thought sickly, gazing up at the low ceiling. Only now he has thought of a new sport; she is to entertain his distinguished guests. He has turned her into a harlot.

He waited for the inevitable protests from the lady. The blows, the curses from Achivir. Instead, an astounding sound drifted out to the three waiting men; Melangell's soft voice, singing a gentle lullaby every mother in the village had sung to her child at one time.

"What in the name of . . ." Talorc puzzled, glancing at the other guards. They were trying to suppress the smiles that broke out on their faces. Leaning closer to the door, the men listened to what was going on. Achivir and the envoy seemed to be arguing. Melangell's voice showed occasional stress, but she never wavered from her song, and Talorc realized what she was doing. The men's voices within became more agitated, and still she sang, as sweet and gentle as she could manage.

"By the gods, you have quite a mistress there!" One of the guards grinned at Talorc. The men straightened at the sound of approaching footsteps. The door flew open and Achivir and the envoy stormed into the hallway, still arguing loudly.

"Gods above, man!" fumed the envoy. "It would be like lying with my own damn mother."

"She will stop if I order it," Achivir protested. "She is willful. You know how—"

"Forget it, Achivir," the man retorted, retreating down the hall. "How you expect me to find excitement in a skinny woman with an injured leg, who sings lullabies the whole while, I don't see. Why didn't you instead find . . ."

They rounded a corner, the two grinning guards following behind, and were gone. Heaving a sigh of relief, Talorc peeked into Melangell's room. She sat in a chair near the hearth, calmly sipping some ale. She gave him a brief nod, a sly wink, and continued her silent musings.

Talorc roused before dawn, confronted by a small army of servants led by a grim steward. "Stand aside," the man snapped, kicking Talorc's heavy blanket away from the door before he could retrieve it.

"By the gods, what now?" Talorc sighed, watching the men enter the lady's rooms. "We all grow tired of this game the king plays. When will he, too, weary of it and put us all to a kindly end?"

It did not surprise him when the servants soon emerged from the room, bearing in their arms and over their backs everything she had been given. Tapestries were pulled from the walls, chairs and chests were removed, the bed was dismantled, the soft down pad rolled up and clumsily hauled off down the hallway. They took everything—cups and dishes, coverlets and gaming boards, even the dried peat by the hearth. As the last man vanished down the hallway, bearing on his shoulders Melangell's own wicker chest, Talorc entered the suite, and the sight that greeted him would have softened a man of stone.

"It won't be long now, will it?" she whispered calmly from where she sat, crudely dumped to the dirty rushes on the floor, her bandaged leg extended stiffly in front of her. "See?" She smiled. "They were kind enough to leave me this . . ." and she held up a wooden waste bucket.

"I can stumble about, and I can relieve myself"—she

laughed lightly—"but as for sleep and food and heat in the coming winter, well . . ." She shrugged and looked up at him, and then her resolve broke. "They even took my own trunk, Talorc. My jewelry, my children's things . . ." Tears brimmed her eyes. "They took it all . . . everything."

He crossed the floor and helped her from the rushes, his own eyes tearing at her simple desolation. "No, lady," he said quietly, sitting on the stone hearthside and holding her close, "it will not be long now, for either of us. You have shamed him in front of another, and for that we will surely die."

He shared his warrior's rations with her that day, but she seemed to have little appetite. When dusk approached she pulled her cloak around her thin shoulders, curled up near what warmth remained on the hearth, and drifted to sleep. Talorc sat inside the doorway and watched her until the night was well under way, and then he rose, spread his own blanket over her, and went to his post in the hallway. When he stepped from the room, a welcome sight met his eyes: several small bundles had been left in the shadows, and he could tell by the manner in which they were tied that they'd been left by a sympathetic guard. A small parcel of dried peat, a bag of bread and cheese, and an old, worn, but still warm soldier's blanket from the barracks. But the silent message the gifts conveyed was nearly as valued as their utility: all he and Melangell had endured had won admirers. They had allies, and in that simple fact Talorc found unending hope.

For another week they existed on the charity of shadowy figures who approached in the night, left food and fuel, and as quietly vanished. Talorc sometimes saw them, sometimes not, but he never spoke or inquired when they came. A brief nod in greeting, a firm handclasp of solidarity, and then their benefactors left, asking nothing in return. But the young man had heard gossip in the palace. It had begun with Achivir's two guards, who seethed with resentment at being ordered to lie with the king's woman, as if they were mere slaves to be ordered about and not proud, freeborn warriors. The forced violation of Talorc's vow was an even greater scandal, and like a brushfire the word spread—guard to guard, and then to appalled families in the village. Surely the king is mad, the people said, and sympathy for Talorc and his Celtic charge ran rampant. Soon better foods appeared in their nightly parcels—a drinking horn of ale, homemade treats brought in by the guards from sympathetic womenfolk, even a clean gown for Melangell, and it brightened her spirits to see it, as if it were the most sumptuous robe in Achivir's storerooms. Perhaps there is hope, she and Talorc told themselves as their burden eased, borne now on other willing shoulders. Perhaps all is not lost.

Their peaceful period of neglect came to an end nearly a month after Achivir's visit with the envoy. Talorc awoke in the night, not to another benefactor, but to the king stalking down the hallway, two silent guards at his heels. His eyes glittered hotly and Talorc could see the need etching his face like a starkly chiseled carving. Jumping to his feet, Talorc pulled his blanket away and hesitated. He must obey his king, yet he chided himself for his cowardice, allowing such abuse of the woman he had sworn to protect. Staring at the king, he drew his sword and stepped in front of the door.

"Move!" Achivir barked, his vicious mood rising at the young guard's act. Talorc merely shook his head, his jaw set resolutely.

"No, sire. This has gone on long enough. For the lady's sake as well as your own, it must stop."

The king's mouth fell open in astonishment at this defiance, and his eyes narrowed. "Did you hear me, boy? Move, or I'll have you taken—"

"I am no boy," he retorted, "and I will not move. Leave her now, and give her her freedom. She has done you no harm; she does not deserve such abuse."

"By the gods, boy," Achivir thundered, "my child is dead thanks to her. Now, stand aside. She is my woman, and I will take her as I see fit."

He motioned his two guards forward, but before they could act, the door to Melangell's room opened and she appeared, sliding Talorc's long dagger from his belt and holding it before her menacingly.

"Talorc is right," she said tightly. "This has gone on long enough. I am not your woman, Achivir, and never was. I am a freeborn Celt, and if you lay a hand on me again you will die."

Outraged, Achivir signaled his men and they pressed forward around him in the narrow corridor, but they were too late. Melangell and her guard slipped into her room, bolting the door behind them. "Batter it down!" the king bellowed. "Send men around to the outside! They must not get out of here alive!"

Melangell and Talorc looked at each other, dumbfounded by the step they had just taken. "We only have a few moments," the young man said, glancing around the empty room. "Get your cloak . . . come . . ."

He was striding toward the small high window on the far wall, barely big enough for them to squeeze through. Melangell joined him, her cloak belted around her waist, warrior fashion. She reached for the stone ledge and Talorc boosted her up. Wriggling through it, she pulled herself to the flat sod roof of the palace. Talorc followed, his sword drawn. "Come," he urged, taking her hand and running low across the roofs. Shouts were rising from the courtyards below. Soon, he knew, someone would be on the roof and after them. He must find a more defensible place to make their last stand . . . however brief it might be.

Circling the high round tower that marked the center of the palace, Melangell and Talorc ran toward the front gate. If they could avoid their pursuers, it was possible they could reach the stone walls surrounding the palace, jump down, and escape into the labyrinth of the twisting village streets. He didn't really believe they could, for if they eluded the guards in the village, then what? Another escape across the vast, empty moors? He pushed the thought of impending death from his mind as he'd been trained to do, squeezed Melangell's hand tighter, and raced for the distant wall.

But too late. Men were streaming up the narrow stone staircase and running toward them. Desperate, Talorc pushed Melangell to the side, toward a scaffolding used by stonemasons repairing the tower. He thrust her under it, into the scant safety of the lashed saplings and hanging ropes, and turned to face their attackers.

He slashed at the first man to reach them, trying to keep the wall to his back and one arm against Melangell, forcing her beneath the scaffolding where the advancing swords couldn't reach her. The guards, tasting victory, seemed in no hurry, their dark faces grinning eagerly at the sport.

"Alive!" Broichan suddenly bellowed, appearing over the far wall, his long tunic whipping against his body. "I want the woman alive, do you hear me?" His voice, rising with the wind, had an odd screeching quality to it that made Melangell's blood run cold. *I must turn the knife on myself,* she thought, fighting to free herself from Talorc's well-meant protection. *Broichan must not take me alive.*

She looked at the heavens. The moon was sinking down the western sky, silvering the vast moorlands stretched away beyond the village. A nearly full moon. The moon of Samhain, time for sacrifices. . . .

A swift slice from a sword cut into Talorc's leg and he stumbled, dropping his weapon. Melangell grabbed at his arm, righting him on the slippery sods, her eyes growing hot with fury. *Wicked men!* She tried to support the sagging Talorc with one hand while holding his dagger with the other.

"Leave me . . ." her guard gasped, stumbling toward a flimsy ladder and grasping his bleeding leg. "Go . . ."

"Alive!" Broichan screamed again, advancing toward them, a smiling Achivir at his side. Whatever fate they had planned for her, she didn't want to live to see it.

Releasing Talorc, Melangell suddenly stood erect, raising her arms heavenward, her eyes sparking fire.

"Achivir . . ." she screamed over the eager warriors and rising winds. The king halted, fearing some trick.

"You say I am a witch. Very well, then I am a witch. And I curse you . . . your death will not be an easy one . . . betrayed by a woman, a revenge from the woman you betrayed."

Achivir quailed, her barbed words striking some long-buried fear in his heart. Such is the way of a curse, she knew, for it was not the thing itself that destroyed, but fear of the thing.

The king's face paled and he reached for Broichan's arm when the druid advanced to rally the men. Scornful, the druid pulled free and stepped in front of the hushed crowd, his eyes narrowed menacingly.

"I have no fear of you, woman," he hissed. "You are an

531

impostor, no witch at all. You merely feed on the ignorance of others."

"A trick you know well, eh, Broichan? I too know a bit about druids, and how they work their magic."

The warriors murmured uneasily, not liking such blasphemous talk in their midst. Broichan saw his chance, and took it.

"See what wickedness she speaks?" he shouted, turning to face the guards. "First she curses your king, and now she maligns druidry. She must be taken, and she must be burned at Samhain."

The men advanced, fearful of her, yet angry, goaded on by Broichan's solemn warnings. Talorc pulled himself to his feet, vainly trying to protect Melangell from the first advancing guard.

"Remember me, Achivir!" Melangell tried again, playing on the man's fear. "With my dying breath I will curse you from the flames. Remember that."

"No!" the king bellowed, trying to override the druid. His fear was genuine and visceral, a fear she could not know; a fear of the ancient curse on Cruithni male royalty. "No!"

Ignoring Achivir, the guards rushed them, taking first Talorc and then Melangell in an overwhelming tide. Talorc was dragged away, nearly helpless in his pain, but Melangell fought back, unwilling to be taken alive, trying to retreat up the scaffolding and fling herself from the tower. Her dagger slashed one man's arm and he grunted, stumbling back into his startled companions. His move was brief, but it gave her a few precious moments of time. Scurrying like a squirrel, she reached the top and prepared herself to die. Flinging her arms skyward, she called out the name of her protector, long forgotten in the busy life she had lived.

"Loucetius!" she screamed, closing her eyes when she heard the guards climbing the ladder. Her foot slid backward, reached the edge of the rough stone wall, and stopped. So this is death, she thought briefly. It must be now, if I am to avoid Broichan's fires. Now.

A fierce roar suddenly filled the sky and Melangell opened her eyes in disbelief. How could such a thing be, here in this northern land, where storms were a rarity? How?

She looked up, tears flooding her eyes. A large black cloud

mass had obscured the setting moon and half the stars, flashing orange and yellow and gold. A storm, thunder . . . Loucetius.

The guards were backing down from the tower, suddenly terrified at the magic this Celt had summoned, and even Broichan ceased his rantings. Melangell closed her eyes when the first heavy drops began to fall, washing away her tears like a benediction. She was not abandoned, she was saved.

I will cry, she sobbed into the driving storm; let me cry, for my exile is at an end. My protector has not abandoned me, Esus and Brennos have not abandoned me, my Celtic blood has not abandoned me. It is time for me to go home.

She knew they would not harm her. Secure in the protection of Loucetius, she lowered the dagger, stepped down the ladder, and walked through the frightened men. They released Talorc and he fell in behind her, limping past a dumbfounded Broichan, toward the stairs that descended the wall; and when she passed, Achivir the King was glad to see her go.

"Gods above, we did it!" Melangell whispered to Talorc, limping hurriedly at her side, urging her across the square before the palace.

"We are not free yet, lady," he replied in her ear, "for we are being followed." Melangell's heart pounded and her elation gave way to wild fear. Two men, cloaked and dripping from the storm, were approaching. They stopped and she could make out only scattered bits of their hurried conversation with Talorc.

"Come," Talorc muttered in her ear, turning to follow the men, "they are on our side and will help you on your way."

"Talorc," she hissed when they turned into one of the narrow, twisting streets of the village.

"Yes?"

"If this is a trap, kill me at once. A knife to my back. Don't let me reenter that foul palace alive."

He squeezed her arm gently. "As you wish, lady," he said, guiding her down another rain-washed turn in the street. "But I do not think it will be necessary now."

A dark figure stepped from the shadows, motioned silently, and led them into a narrow crevice between two low stone buildings. He tapped twice on a rough wooden door and it opened a crack, then wider. Directing with his hand, the figure motioned them into a room, turned, and disappeared into the storm. Bending low, Melangell and Talorc crept through the doorway.

Two warriors waited in the tiny storeroom, cramped among an assortment of wood barrels, reed matting, and iron smithy tools. "This is the one?" one of the warriors muttered, stepping toward them. Talorc nodded suspiciously.

The second man tossed a bundle of old clothes at her. "Remove her cloak. She must change into these . . ." he began. "Tell her."

"But why?" Melangell protested, understanding their words and fearful of their intent.

Talorc conversed hastily with the men, then turned to her with a grin. "It's all right. They had been planning an escape for you. Tonight you just hurried things along for them. These are the clothes of a Cruithni boy, to enable you to escape the town should Achivir change his mind. There is a wagon waiting for you, beyond the walls."

Nodding, she untied the bundle and pulled out the clothes—a tattered pair of wool breeches, a short tunic, and an old brown hunting cloak. Turning from them, she changed quickly, draping the cloak around her shoulders as men did, pinning her wet hair up before pulling the water-proof hood low over her forehead. They handed her a worn pair of boots and she tied them around her ankles. A short sword, belt, and traveling pouches of food and water completed her disguise. When Talorc stood back and looked at her, he would hardly have guessed her true identity.

"Perfect!" he said, nodding. "Now we must go."

She followed Talorc and one of the warriors from the hut. They walked side by side, for all the world like three hunters going out to the moors for some night hunting, huddled against the easing rain. Sauntering to the gates of the town, they were given barely a notice by the guards on duty. Walking on to the windswept bluffs, they halted.

Melangell turned at a touch from Talorc. He pointed to the distant tree line, barely visible through the storm, where an old cart creaked into view and stopped, safely hidden in the shadows.

"Who is that?" she whispered, afraid of a trick. He shook his head mutely, cutting his eyes to the warrior at his side. The man seemed unperturbed, and Talorc's fears eased.

"Is this part of your plan?" he questioned the guard. The man grunted. "Yes, it's time," he said flatly, drawing his sword. Melangell flinched, seeing a sudden deception. "No . . ." she gasped, pressing to Talorc's side and reaching for her knife.

"It's all right, lady," Talorc said. "I know what his plan is, and I will go along with it. It is an old warrior's trick." He straightened himself on his injured leg, pulling his round shield from his back and taking the retrieved sword from his belt. "To go with you would only confirm Achivir's sick suspicions, and he might change his mind and have us hunted down."

She began to understand his meaning and tried to protest, but he shook his head, putting a hand on her wet shoulder and looking into her face. "I will be all right, lady." He smiled. "I must remain behind, to make it look real. They will think you were kidnapped when we fled the village, as your daughter was. Then Achivir will not care what happens to you, and you will be free. And besides"—he grinned, the easing rain dripping from his hair—"they all saw the storm you summoned. I need only tell them that you had bewitched me, as well. Achivir is such a fool, he will believe it."

"But what is this plan, Talorc? What will you do?"

"You will see, lady, if you promise not to interfere or cry out. Do you promise?"

"Yes, but . . . " She felt a lump rising in her throat at their parting. He saw the pain on her face and gently kissed her damp forehead.

"Go to your people; find your children. I deem it an honor to have been your guard."

"A woman could ask for no better one, Talorc," she whispered, looking into his dark eyes. "When I find Drosten, I will tell him his fine words about his friend Talorc were not misplaced."

He laughed and released her. "Farewell, lady," he said,

stepping away and taking his shield in his left hand. Pulling her woman's cloak from his belt where he'd hidden it, he tossed it aside and stood, facing the other warrior. The man nodded once, raised his sword, and in two swift blows struck at Talorc's shield. Talorc deflected them easily, but their aim had been accomplished; his shield was freshly cut and battered. The guard picked up her cloak and ripped it in several places while Talorc drew his knife. He knelt awkwardly on his injured leg. the knife poised in his left hand, and stared at the sky, steadying himself. Then, in a movement so swift she could barely see it, he slashed with the blade, cutting his right forearm twice and finishing with a broad slice across his chest. He sagged forward in pain and Melangell moved to run to him, but the warrior held out a warning hand.

"Leave him," he warned her. "He knows what he does. He has prepared himself."

She watched in horror. The warrior spoke to him quietly and Talorc roused, looked up at the man, and nodded. He took her torn cloak and dabbed it in his blood, then handed it back to the shrouded guard. The man tossed it aside, kicked it in the mud a few times, and left it.

Talorc managed to stumble to his feet and stood erect, gazing resolutely past Melangell as the blood dripped down his right arm and darkened the front of his tunic. The guard stepped in front of him, an old piece of wood in his hand.

"Ready?" she heard him ask, and Talorc nodded. Abruptly the man hit her guard across the stomach, and when he doubled over, another blow to the back of his skull sent him sprawling to the ground, unconscious. Melangell's hands flew to her mouth, trying to suppress a cry when she saw him fall. By the gods, such suffering, so bravely endured, and all to save her! "Talorc!" she gasped, staring at his inert body.

The warrior rushed to her and thrust her toward the distant wagon. "Go!" he hissed. "Walk calmly—those at the wagon will help you." Sick and frightened, she stumbled away, alone on the wide, windswept moor, a young boy out for a night's hunt.

A withered old man waited at the cart. He jumped to the ground when Melangell approached, taking her arm and pulling her forward. His wagon contained a load of animal skins such as the Picts often traded with southern tribes. Pulling the stiff hides up, he shoved her into the wagon and lowered the bulky cargo in place over her.

"Stay quiet," the old man hissed. He climbed aboard the wagon and slapped the ponies into motion. "I will get you out with the dawn."

The wagon lurched away and Melangell didn't know which made her feel sicker, the stifling smell of the furs or the painful ordeal Talorc had just been through. Closing her eyes wearily, she lowered her head to her arm and listened as the cart creaked from Achivir's lands.

The shrouded warrior watched the wagon go, turned, and as silent as a shadow loped back to the village, leaving Talorc lying on the clifftop, battered and alone in the dying storm.

Sleep would not come to her, no matter how desperately she wished it. She'd managed to locate a crack in the weathered floorboards through which she could see the muddy soil and tufts of weeds pass by below her, and she greedily sucked in the cool air that wafted upward through it. The whole cargo weighting down on her seemed to reek of death and suffering and uncleanliness, and she felt she would go mad if she was not soon released from her tomb.

Forcing herself to study the rocks passing by below, she tried to deflect her mind from her present predicament. She could feel sweat dripping between her breasts and collecting on her back. To her great relief, she realized the soil beneath the wagon was gradually lightening as the darkness of the night's storm gave way to gray, and then pale colors became discernable—the varied greens of the weeds, here a red stone, there a small yellow flower. She strained her ears for some sound from the old man, a word to the ponies, any sign that he was calling a halt. All she could detect was the unending creak of the wooden wheels, the groan of the wagon poles, the slapping and rubbing of the pony yoke, and the thudding hooves and gentle snorts of the animals. Like one about to drown, she gasped another draft of fresh air, her attention rousing when she felt the cart roll to a stop. The ponies shuffled tiredly, whickering and shaking their weary necks while the old man climbed stiffly to the ground. She waited, her keen ears following the man's slow footsteps, but to her disappointment she heard him walking away from the wagon. She began to shift, but her movement froze at the sound of another voice nearby.

"'Morning . . ." it said amiably, a man's voice, and Melangell's heart sank. Was it a friend of the old man? she wondered wildly. Or an ally, someone to take her on the next leg of her journey? Or a guard, searching for her? Surely by now they would have found poor Talorc. Signal fires would quickly alert adjoining villages, if Achivir was determined to have her burned under his own roof rather than die a slave in Roman hands.

The furs overhead rustled and shifted and she tried to slide her hand to the knife at her side. They will never take me back alive, she vowed. Never.

The rush of fresh air that blasted her face was almost overpowering in its sweetness, and she gasped aloud, reflexively closing her eyes when it hit her. The bright morning light pierced her closed eyelids and she squinted when a hand seized her upper arm, trying to see who it was. The strength was far too great for the old man's gnarled hands. Reaching for her knife, she futilely began to struggle. Her other arm was taken and she was lifted from the cart as easily as if she were an infant dandled in its father's hands.

"Hold . . ." a deep voice commanded, and in the flooding sunlight she could just make out the lines of a giant of a man before her, a long blond mustache glinting like ice when his head turned, shoulder-length hair so pale it was almost white delicately flying from beneath a wide leather band around his forehead.

"This little one?" the man spoke aside, and Melangell could hear a strange, heavy accent in his voice. The old man was beside the giant, nodding.

The man lifted her into the air and gave her a good-natured shake before lowering her to the ground. "I have children bigger than she is!" He laughed loudly. Melangell stepped back in fear, one hand shading her eyes, when the giant released her.

"This is Cherdic," the old man explained, seeing the look of alarm on her face. "He will take you on the next part of your journey . . . back to your own people."

"Cherdic?" she muttered, studying the stranger. He was a

foreigner, no doubt about it, and probably from across the northern sea, from the looks of him. He would have dwarfed even tall Niall, and his chest was as broad as a barrel. He wore a fur tunic, his brawny arms bare except for several gold armbands. Below it were short fur breeches, bare feet, a wide leather belt, and a huge sword hanging at his hip. A necklace of a few pierced Roman silver coins glittered at his neck.

"Like what you see, little one, eh?" He grinned. "By Woden, you are a sight! You must wash before we get into the boat, for I don't think I can take the sight of you as you are for the few days our voyage will take."

"Voyage?" she croaked.

"Yes," the old man said. "He has a small boat. Normally he smuggles things up and down the coast, but he has a grievance with Achivir and has agreed to take you down to the Celtic lands."

"The weasel," Cherdic spat, a sudden fire in his eye, "took a cargo of Roman cloth and never paid me for it. 'Lost,' he said. Bah! If getting you away injures the bastard's pride, I'll gladly do it. I hear he gave you a rough time, eh?"

Melangell lowered her head, finding the subject too painful to discuss with a stranger. Cherdic stared at her, puzzled, until the old man gave him a meaningful glance and shook his head. Taking the young woman's arm, the old man steered her toward a nearby stream. "Come, little one, and wash," he said kindly, and when she turned away from him Cherdic's keen sailor's eye caught the blue bruises on her arms, a slight limp to her walk, and he understood her silence. The king had obviously abused her as no decent man abuses his woman.

The bastard, Cherdic thought again, following the two to the stream.

They walked throughout the day, Cherdic matching his long strides to Melangell's weakened, limping gait. "You must get your strength back, little one," he observed, watching her struggle over the uneven ground. "You have a long journey ahead of you, once I put you ashore."

"Yes." She nodded. The man seemed kind enough, but could a smuggler really be trusted? His very size unnerved her; she felt he could crush her with one massive arm if he wanted to. And they would be together, alone, on a small boat for several days. After what she had been through with Achivir, it was no surprise that she no longer trusted men.

"I will not harm you, lady." Cherdic smiled, as if reading her thoughts. She looked up at him, mildly embarrassed at his keen insight.

"It's all right!" He laughed, throwing his great blond head back happily. "Most women are afraid of me. It is my size. And you are such a tiny thing, like a little wren, it would be only natural for you. I am not offended and I can understand your fears. I have seen many such bastards as Achivir in my years on the sea. It has always been a mystery, too, why something as beautiful as the ocean attracts so many rogues and scoundrels."

He grinned broadly and winked at her.

"Like me," he boomed, slowing his jaunty strides again to match hers. "I smell the sea already," he said quietly, closing his eyes and inhaling deeply. "Soon we will be at the boat, and when dusk comes we will be on our way."

Melangell lay back in Cherdic's boat, a small, low wooden skiff of odd hybrid Roman design, and reclined against the rolled leather of the sail, her cloak and hood removed and the warming sun soaking into her weary body. The man had rowed all night and into the morning, stopping for brief rests, a little food, or some fortifying wine, which he seemed to have in great quantities. Now he rowed again, always heading south, keeping in sight of the mountainous coastline, and she watched, homesick, the green hills and ridges creeping past. Home! She sighed, her eager eyes taking in the scenery, the streaks of white clouds above, the curious gulls that flew overhead and then vanished.

"The sea is a lovely thing," she said over the rhythmic splash of the oars.

"It is," Cherdic grunted, looking down at the young woman's peaceful face. *Already it is working its magic on her*, he observed. *The lines of pain and fear have eased, her pallor goes.*

"Why don't you use your sail?" she asked, watching him ply the heavy oars.

"Too dangerous," he said, and saw the lady suddenly sit up in alarm.

"Danger? From whom?" she said, her sea-green eyes wide. Cherdic studied her a moment, shipped the oars, and slumped forward wearily on his elbows, flexing his stiff hands.

"The Romans, little one," he answered, glancing at her. "If we get through here safely tonight and early tomorrow, all will be well, for it will be the riskiest part of our trip. The Romans do not control the northern lands, but by Woden, they patrol the seas all around."

"Do you think we will see any?" she whispered fearfully. His blue eyes crinkled in merriment.

"By your words, I'd say you've had dealings with the bastards before, eh?" he observed, reaching for an old cracked leather food sack and rummaging through it.

"Yes," she said dryly, "many dealings, all unpleasant."

"Is there any other kind?" he replied, offering her some coarse barley bread.

"They have taken from me everything I hold dear," she retorted bitterly, looking up at him with hatred in her eyes. "My father, my grandfather, dear friends, my husband at Duncrub . . ."

Her voice died away and she looked down sadly at her thin hands.

"And now they have my only daughter. A slave. And my sons have gone to find her. So you see, Cherdic, I have nothing now, thanks to the Romans."

He looked at her downturned face in sympathy, reached out, and clasped one huge hand over hers. She glanced up at him resolutely and he nodded his head, a knowing look on his face.

"I wish you luck," was all he said, and resumed eating his meal.

At dusk he pulled into shallow water, afraid to go closer to shore to sleep but finding himself in great need of rest.

"I will watch," Melangell offered. He lowered a heavy stone anchor into the depths and nodded his thanks.

"There will be lights landward," he told her. "Ignore them. They will be your people, watching the coast for the

Romans. They are no danger, and they cannot see us anyway. That is why my boat is so low to the water, and painted gray . . . it makes us very hard to spot.

He stretched his powerful back tiredly and pointed to the sea. "That is where the danger comes from. Roman patrol ships, sleek and fast. They are on you before you know it, but at least at night you can see their lights. Keep watch that way, little one, and let me know if you see anything odd."

Melangell nodded, turning and making herself comfortable against the sail. Cherdic lowered himself to his side, curled his long legs over the mast and oars lying amidship, and was soon deep in sleep.

Her day's rest had done her well, for despite the gentleness of the night, the rhythmic rise and fall of the boat, she did not doze. Cherdic slept soundly, his breathing deep and regular, his weary body seeming too exhausted to move. With the first dusky yellow glow of morning lighting the far horizon and reflecting eerily off the low mists around them, the muffled sound of an oar's splash nearby whirled her into alertness. Crouching, she stumbled to Cherdic and frantically shook his broad shoulder, as if trying to rouse a massive tree. Despite his deep sleep he was awake instantly, springing to a tense crouch so quickly that he threw her off balance and she nearly toppled into the sea before he grabbed her waist and pulled her back to safety.

She trembled in fear at the near-disaster, but when she made a move to speak he hissed her to silence. He, too, heard it and he knew the sound well enough.

Roman warships. Patrols. Swiftly slicing their way through the morning mists around them.

Grimly he narrowed his eyes, trying to see through the surrounding fog. He needed some hint of their location, their number. The mist was too thick. The rapidly approaching sounds muffled and echoed in the air in a crazy distortion and he found himself unable to get his bearings. All he knew was one sick fact: they were bearing down on them fast.

"Get down!" be breathed, reaching over her to unlash the ties that bound the sail. Melangell flung herself into the bottom of the boat. Cherdic loomed over her, pulling the sail loose and dragging it over them both. He lay down atop her, trying to keep his weight from crushing her, his arms splayed to either side of the hull. A stifling humid darkness enveloped them.

"Not a sound, no matter what happens," he warned. "Can you swim?"

"Yes."

"If we are discovered, slip over the side and into the water. It is our only hope. Quiet, now."

She lowered her forehead to the damp, smelly wood and listened. The ships were near now . . . very near. She could feel Cherdic's massive muscles tensing atop her. Slice, slice, slice came the oars, as steady as a heartbeat, and the sound seemed to be coming from several directions at once. The ships must be passing all around them.

The little boat began to rise and fall, heaving and rocking in the wash from the ships, and Melangell closed her eyes in sick fear. Don't let them catch me, she prayed desperately. Not now, within sight of my home. Please . . .

The boat continued to toss and bob, pulling at the anchor as it danced. Then, abruptly, the movement eased, slowed, died, and Cherdic slumped in relief over her.

"By Woden . . ." he gasped, lifting one corner of the stiff leather and peering out over the side of the boat. "See?" he whispered. Melangell raised her head beneath his, fearfully gazing out into the mist. To the left and the right three low, massive ships disappeared into the dawn, the lanterns fastened to their sterns swinging slowly as they went. She could just see the long, thin lines of the oars as they rose and fell, like the delicate legs of an insect skimming across the water.

Cherdic listened for a moment, to be sure no other ships approached, and then he sat up, flinging the heavy sail aside. "That was close!" he sighed, watching the last of the Roman patrol vanish. "And see," he said, pointing to shore, "we are not the only ones observing them."

Melangell turned, and felt as if she would cry out at the sights of signal fires and torches flickering along the coast. Her people. The Celts. Home.

Cherdic rowed to shore that afternoon, pulling the boat

onto a sandy, shelving beach and lifting Melangell to dry land. She stretched happily, looking at the clouded sky, blue twilight already descending the steep hillside above her.

"It should take you two days' walk to reach Duncrub," Cherdic said, handing her the brown hunting cloak she'd worn. "It is visible from the sea. From there you can find your way to the pass through the mountains and reach your family in the west."

"Yes." She nodded, looking at him. "I crossed once at the pass many years ago, on the way to the battle. I can find it again."

He nodded slightly at her words and studied her, his full lips pursed beneath his long blond mustache. "Take care of yourself," he said quietly. "You are such a little thing, to be wandering the land alone."

She smiled and touched one massive arm lightly. "And you, Cherdic," she replied. "Thank you for your help. My life may be cursed as far as my family goes, but no one could ask for better friends than I've had." .

He grinned and stepped away a few paces in the sand. Turning, he looked up the beach at her. "May luck be with you, little one," he called out. "If ever I meet Achivir alone on the shore, the first blow I strike will be for you."

She laughed and waved, watching the blond giant lope down to the boat and push it out, the water splashing high around his bare legs. He climbed aboard, returned her wave, picked up the oars, and the craft quickly slid into the gathering gloom of evening. She followed with her eyes until he turned, heading north, and was lost to the mists and rocks offshore.

Sad at his leaving and weighted with the looming aloneness she suddenly felt, Melangell pulled the cloak around her shoulders, tied the hood over her head, and trudged up the grassy hillside sloping away from the beach. There were many villages hereabouts, she knew. Perhaps one could be found before darkness fell.

She awoke to a drizzly dawn, her muscles stiff and sore from sleeping in a small thatch storage shed hastily erected at the edge of a plot of ripened barley. Rude though her shelter might be, at least it was Celtic, and she was glad to be once more in a dwelling buoyant with fresh air, built of something other than Cruithni stone. Harvesting was well under way, for several iron scythes hung on the walls. Well, she thought, rising and stretching, there will be no harvest today, not in this rain.

Best conserve my food, she planned, fingering the small sack at her belt. The ale I will drink, for refilling it from a stream will be simple enough. She pulled the cap from the polished drinking horn and eagerly gulped the warm, pungent brew. It satisfied almost as well as a meal would, and she decided to save half in case she needed it later. Pulling the cloak around her shoulders and taking care to cover her head, she crept out into the rain.

Perhaps I can beg a meal, she mused, following a narrow, rutted footpath through the dark forest. Do a little work, although I haven't the strength a boy my size would. My only alternative is to steal, and that might be simple enough, now, at harvesttime. Fields will be full of ripe grain, beans drying on the vine, plump berries and apples waiting. I dare not raid a storehouse for a hunk of curing cheese or more ale; the risk is too great. Do the best I can until I reach a village, where my reception might be kinder than on an isolated farm.

She trudged on, emerging from the woods at dusk and pausing to eat some currants from a bush by a meadow, leaving some on a flat stone as a thank offering to Ialonus, god of the meadow. The mere act of offering to her own gods again soothed her soul. Taking another quick gulp of ale, she looked around for a dry, safe place to sleep, but saw none. What shall I do now? she brooded as the sky darkened above her and the rain increased with the approaching night. Nowhere to go, no fire to warm me, and this old cloak is too thin to afford much protection.

She halted abruptly at a brief glint of light across the gray meadow. A house, perhaps? Or a campfire? Swallowing her fear, she set off for it, hoping to find a friendly face or at least a kind offer of shelter.

"Cruithni, eh?" a young man said when she approached his campfire uncertainly. He was not a warrior, she noted. Probably a hunter, judging by the bow she saw propped beneath a dry pine tree. "Welcome," he went on amiably, motioning her to the fire. Melangell grunted, saying a thank you in Pictish, and advanced to the warmth of the flames. She did not dare extend her hands to the fire, for fear he would see them as a woman's. Huddled miserably in her wet cloak, she leaned forward, trying to find what comfort she could.

The young man eyed her suspiciously. "Some food?" he asked, holding a haunch of roasted pork toward her. She shook her head abruptly, unease rising, and decided it was best to leave.

"A village?" she asked gruffly, trying to imitate the odd Cruithni accent. "I seek a village."

"A village?" he answered, tearing into the meat with greasy fingers. "The only one hereabouts is to the southwest. At the base of the mountains, near the sea. Two days' walk. Do you understand?"

He glanced at her and she looked down at the campfire, trying to hide her face in the shadows. He shrugged and resumed eating. Whatever this stranger's reason for secrecy, it was none of his affair.

"Past Duncrub," he went on. "You know of it?"

"Yes," she mumbled.

"A path to the south . . . half a day from there. But stay the night. Warm yourself. I have more ale." He held up a leather bag and grinned at her.

"Yes . . . thanks . . ." she muttered, and curled on her side, keeping one wary eye on the young hunter squatting across the clearing as he finished his meal. Despite her best efforts she soon drifted to sleep, her weariness overcoming her caution, and when she awoke midway into the next day the sun was shining, a warm breeze rustled the trees, and the man was gone. Before going, however, he'd left her two small round loaves of bread, sitting on a rock by her head.

Melangell emerged from the scrubby woods and paused, her eyes wandering slowly over the rocky slope before her.

Duncrub.

She did not want to move from the spot; didn't want to traverse the bloody ground. Her gaze swept upward, to the top of the small mountain, to the rocky crest where she'd watched the horror unfolding. It seemed only yesterday, so vivid were her memories, like a bad dream that would never leave her soul.

She could not help but wonder the inevitable, the question that had haunted her for eighteen long years, as she slowly turned her head, down the slope, to the position of the Roman lines.

Where had Nechtan been? Where did he die? Was it swift and painless, or slow and lingering? Did he think of me at the end? Or was there, for him, no end? Only an abrupt tomorrow, bringing to a conclusion the today in which he dwelt?

"Nechtan!" she sobbed, turning numbly away from the tranquil slope. How cruel, to see such peace here! The birds chitter merrily, the sun glints from the rocks, tiny flowers nod silently in the breeze.

What mad fate has brought me here? she thought bitterly, wiping her tears away in frustration. Of all the spots of ground in this fair land, this is the one I never wanted to see again. So many memories, so many tears . . .

And yet I must. Sad irony; I cannot avoid it. In order to rejoin my children, I must set foot on Duncrub once more; an older, wiser, but no less sad woman than when I last was here. I must cross it, find the steep mountain pass, and locate my children. Genann's children. And Nechtan's son.

She inhaled the warm air slowly, deeply, and squared her shoulders. I cannot go on to my future unless I am able to confront my past, she chided herself. It is a hill, like any other. I can cross it. I must.

Stepping lightly onto the bright slope, she walked fearfully, tentatively, as if she expected the very earth to quake underfoot from the memories it held. But it did not. It was soil, like any other. Soil, and stones, and grasses. Her steps veered unerringly downward, to the base of the hill, and when she reached it she looked upward in mild surprise. Her wild chariot ride during the battle had seemed so short, so swift, yet the slope was immense, stretching up to the blue sky above her. How must it have looked to the Romans, she wondered, waking from their camps to see the entire vast mountainside covered with eager warriors?

And for what? She laughed cynically. So many dead, so many become fugitives in the forest, the homesteads burned, the farms ravaged. For what? We are free once more. Poorer, proud still, and free. Was it worth the cost?

She could see no trace of the pyre where the Romans had burned the bodies. Their own dead in one, attended by the proper ceremonies and rituals. The enemy in another, stripped and piled indiscriminately with the dead horses and war hounds, their ashes mingling in the soil as their spirits mingled in the air. Nechtan and Cathal, Melwas, Lacha the war hound. Perhaps Cai and Donall and their father, Conn. The druids Ethal and Diuran. All the brave and good and valiant men, all except Brennos. He left the world in greater peace, as he would have wished.

She turned away dully, and the wind off the distant sea seemed to carry the voices of a thousand dead to her ears. The cries and groans of the dying, the shrieks and shouts of those yet alive. She could almost smell the choking dust, the nauseating stench of blood. Walking slowly up the mountainside, she paused near the summit when a glint caught her eye. Bending, she picked at the crumbly soil with her fingers, working free a bronze lance point, flattened and folded back on itself where it had struck the ground and been trampled. She studied it, recognizing it as one of her people's. Pensively turning it in the sunlight, she wondered what tales it could tell. Then she stooped, replacing it in its grave and pressing the soil once more over it. It seemed only fitting that it stay were it fell.

She resumed her walk to the crest of the hill, and in the darkening shadows of the flanking forests she could almost detect the knot of black-robed druids, ghostly forms still watching the battle, hovering calmly on the edge of the world.

But no . . . She sighed wearily as she reached the top. It is only the shadows, only my imagination. The druids are not here anymore. They are gone, and with them our way of life. Only a few old ones remain, and the wise men of the Cruithni, or the half-mad hermits, hiding in the Highlands. The Romans have succeeded in their goal. The druids are gone.

Melangell roamed the stony ground until she found the sloping rock where she'd sat beside Brennos and the rest. Where Cai stood, his blue eyes bright with battle-fire. She sat on the stone and pulled the hood from her head. She could see the distant sparkle of the sea, and the vast mountainside stretched away below her, empty and still but for the occasional foraging bird.

Strange, she thought, closing her eyes, it is a peaceful place now. Quiet. Serene. No hint of the horrors that once happened here. It is like a sacred grove, a nemeton. Is that what the druids knew? That the spilled blood of humans sanctifies a gound? The shedding of violence and terror leaves peace in its wake?

The warm midday sun lulled her into sleepiness and she removed the old brown cloak, folded it, and slid it beneath her head as she stretched out on her back. Gazing at the clouds sailing overhead, her eyes grew heavy and she drifted to sleep.

She woke abruptly to the sharp slap of a lance blade against her cheek.

"Get up!" a voice commanded. She opened her eyes to the descending twilight and two tall warriors who loomed over her, their patterned cloaks hanging still in the quiet evening air. Slowly she sat, clutching the folded cloak awkwardly to her breast.

"And who are you?" one demanded gruffly, eyeing her Pictish clothes in suspicion. "A spy, perhaps?"

"No . . ." she croaked, suddenly aware that her disguise was gone. They could plainly see that she was a woman, no Cruithni lad at all.

"Who, then?" growled the other, jerking the cloak from her arms and examining it thoroughly.

"I . . . I was the wife of a princeling who was killed here, at the battle," she stammered, beginning to fear for her safety. "I came here seeking the pass through the mountains. My daughter was . . . was taken by the Romans . . ."

"Aye?" the first said, thrusting the cloak back at her. "And when was this?"

"Months ago. I am trying to find her."

The two warriors studied her and one took her arm, pulled her to her feet, and marched her briskly over the ridge and into the forest. "We will let our chief decide," he snapped. Melangell stumbled painfully over the uneven ground, trying desperately to keep up with them.

The forced march was mercifully brief, and by moonrise a squalid settlement appeared, perched as securely as possible atop a rise of cleared ground. Melangell cut her eyes around in surprise when she walked through a crude gate of saplings. This was no fine village or mighty fortress. It was little more than a cattle enclosure, a collection of rickety wattle huts surrounded by a crude brush palisade, the streets foul with refuse and roaming animals. She was forced through a low doorway beneath an overhanging thatch roof and into a dark, smoky room.

"What's this?" a voice said to her left. Her captors turned her to face a low sleeping ledge jutting out from the wall, on which an overweight man of about fifty had been resting atop piled bearskins.

Or had he? When he sat up, his white chest bare in the dim firelight, Melangell saw a slim young woman rise behind him, her breasts plainly naked in the gloom.

"A young woman, sire," one of the guards replied stiffly. The chief made no move to rise from the bed as he studied Melangell.

"She says she is seeking her daughter, who was taken by Romans," added the second guard, "and that her husband was killed at Duncrub."

"Then why your Cruithni clothes, woman?" the chief barked at her. "Perhaps you are a spy. A woman in the clothes of a Pictish man."

"No, sire," she answered, her voice quaking with fear. "I have lived in a Cruithni village since my escape from Duncrub. My husband was half-Pictish, a princeling. I swear to you by the god who watches over me, I am no spy."

"Escape?" he said, his interest rising. "You were there?" She nodded slowly.

"I was there too! Was lucky to escape with only a spear wound to my leg. Who was your husband?"

"Nechtan."

The chief's round face suddenly froze, his gaze hardening. "I know of him. His wife was the druidess who prophesied a victory for us. Is that you?" he demanded hotly. Melangell nodded again, puzzled by his sudden change of mood.

"Get out of my village!" he shouted, waving one heavy arm for emphasis. Her two young captors straightened in surprise. The chief picked up a small bronze cup and aimed it at her head, throwing it with remarkable accuracy. She ducked and it sailed past her ear so close she could feel the rush of air in its wake.

"Witch!" he bellowed, his agitation growing. "Get out of here! Go! Witch!"

The guards grabbed her arms and bodily dragged her, stunned and bewildered, from the hut. A few people had come from their hovels at the noise, and at the sight of the guards dragging the young woman to the compound gate, several picked up stones and flung them after her. The guard to her right yelped in pain when one hit his shoulder, and he turned menacingly, putting her tormentors temporarily at bay.

"Witch!" they shouted, following her to the gate. The guards tossed her from the compound and she stumbled, barely keeping her balance on the rutted path. A stone flew from the gate and stung her arm, and she grabbed the rising welt with one hand, running as fast as she could to the safety of the woods.

Her name preceded her, the word spreading like a brushfire to all the adjoining duns and farmsteads. Time after time her reception was the same; the word she came to fear, the cold, angry faces, the shut door if she was lucky, the stinging stone if she was not. The force of their hatred stunned her; the fame and immortality Brennos had assured her of had come to pass, but for all the wrong reasons. She almost didn't care anymore as she wandered dully from place to place, knowing beforehand what she would meet there, like a dog returning to its master, knowing full well a kick would be the only greeting it received. Her food was gone, so she resorted to thievery, stealing from fields and storage sheds and fleeing like an outlaw into the forests with her meager booty. Still she inched her way westward, desperately hoping to make the mountain pass before winter fell. If not, she would freeze to death in the crossing. And gladly so, she told herself time and again as yet another taunt stung her ears, another pebble stung her huddled back. But the fame that preceded her reached other ears too. Ears that were only too eager to hear of the green-eyed witch of

Duncrub. Ears that had taken over for sightless eyes, searching for five long years for the wife of Nechtan, the Pict.

Melangell could scarcely believe her luck. The old woman actually seemed kind, and either hadn't heard the gossip or didn't care. When she'd been caught before dawn, stealing a few hasty handfuls of barley from a barrel near a doorway, Melangell had feared for her life. But the old lady, up early to do her washing, looked at the thin face and tattered clothing of the girl thief and invited her in! She had set out warm milk and oat gruel for her visitor, and the exhausted young woman had downed it in minutes. Not really surprised by her visitor's gnawing hunger, the old woman next gave her some stale brown bread, which Melangell gnawed and tore at like a starving dog, speaking not a word as she ate, only eyeing the woman suspiciously. And when the kindly woman next gave her a fatty chunk of pork from her stewpot, Melangell's hunger was so great that she paused only briefly before tearing at it with her teeth and downing it in two bites. She had begun a piece of moldy cheese when the door opened and a young couple entered the hut. Like a cornered wild thing, Melangell started at their hostile glares, her hands clenching the plank table, her body tensed to flee.

"Mother!" the young woman gasped in horror. "What's she doing here? Don't you know who she is?"

The old woman began to protest, but her words died when the man advanced menacingly toward Melangell. She crouched, wary, and circled the room, heading to the doorway and escape.

"Get out, witch!" he hissed, seizing an iron pot-hook and wielding it threateningly.

"No!" the old woman cried. Melangell bolted for the door and flung it open, the man at her heels.

"Witch!" he bellowed, and soon sleepy people began to spill into the compound.

"My father died because of you!" the young man shouted. Again Melangell felt the sting of a pebble on her back. She ran as desperately as she could in her weakened state, the gathering crowd following leisurely, taunting her at their whim.

"And my brothers . . ." a woman shrieked. The voices behind her were growing uglier, louder, and Melangell looked around desperately for an escape. The only woods she saw were many paces ahead, dark and thick along the slopes of a rising mountain peak. She veered toward them, flinching and stumbling under the onslaught of rocks and pebbles.

"Yes!" the crowd roared. "Go on, witch!" They were laughing, and Melangell wondered why. "Let the wild man catch you. He'll have your blood for his dinner!"

She looked ahead at the black forest shadows, sickened when she saw two bleached skulls posted atop stakes at the woods' edge. Oh, gods, she thought, I am trapped! Trapped between a wild mob and a madman in the woods. A large stone thudded into her back and she stumbled to all fours. The crowd saw its chance and advanced, raining rocks on her. Gasping from the pain, Melangell rose to her feet, staggering toward the forest and trying to ward off the blows with her arms. A small boy ran out to her side, laughing wildly at the sport, and let fly with a sharp pebble that grazed her forehead, snapping her head to the side when it struck.

"No . . ." she gasped, feeling blood run into her eyes. Several other boys joined her tormentor, pelting stones at her face, and she crouched, pulling her cloak over her head in a desperate attempt to protect herself.

"Witch!" the crowd laughed, watching her lurch like a staggering drunkard. Another large stone hit her in the side and she sank to her knees with a groan. "Kill me!" she sobbed, falling to the ground in a huddle, the cloak dropping uselessly from her face. "Kill me!"

The individual pains and stings and welts merged into one vast torment and she groveled helplessly, her arms around her head, blood running into her eyes as blackness slowly descended. The last thing she heard was a sudden yowl of pain from one of her attackers, and the sharp whistle of a sling being whirled.

The mob backed away, their faces angry at the interruption of their sport. A tall beggar on the hillside, oddly clad in a sleeveless Roman tunic and tattered Celtic breeches, advanced another step, let fly with his sling, and another pebble found its mark. A young man howled in pain, grasped his arm, and fled the scene.

"Go on . . ." the stranger growled, and the people milled nervously. The man seemed blind, his eyes horribly scarred, yet his aim was unerring. Again he whirled the sling and the crowd retreated a few more respectful paces. The stranger seemed satisfied, lowered the sling, and crouched by the witch.

"Lady . . ." he said quietly, his hands patting her shoulder, her arm. Lifting the old cloak, he pulled it away and gently felt her face. He knew the hot, sticky feel of blood, and he ran his hand down the woman's throat until he located the reassuring feel of a pulse at her neck. She was alive.

"Lady?" he repeated, but she did not rouse. Tucking the sling in his rope belt, he slid his arms beneath Melangell, lifting her as he stood. He could just make out the dark shadows of the woods ahead, smell the heavy richness of the forest mold. He advanced to the trees, past the grinning skulls posted in warning.

"Let them go!" the crowd murmured. "The wild man will have them both! Let them go!"

A stone flew from the crowd, and another. They hit the beggar's back squarely, but he ignored them. His long search was over, his oath of loyalty fulfilled.

Cai, son of Conn, had found his mistress.

A rough cloth cool with water wiped across Melangell's forehead, and she moaned weakly at the pain.

"You are safe now," a deep voice said, and she felt a hand lift her head.

"Water?" the voice asked, and she found the leather rim of a water bag hovering awkwardly near her mouth.

"No . . ." she muttered, turning her head aside and fighting the pain that seared her body. Her head was slowly lowered to the thick hemlock needles of the forest floor and the wet cloth was again pressed to her injured forehead.

Curious at her benefactor's odd manner, she peered through the dark shadows, trying to identify him, to confirm her rising suspicions. All she could see was his outline above her, his hair long and matted, his motley clothing thread-bare, a full beard on his face.

"Who . . . who are you?" she muttered.

"Lady? Don't you recognize me?" the man said, sitting back on his heels. "Granted, I must not look the same as I once did, but surely I am not that different."

Melangell narrowed her eyes in the gloom, studying the man. He did, indeed, seem familiar, but the skin around his eyes was badly scarred and, as she suspected, he was blind. She still could not identify him.

"I leapt over the side of Nechtan's chariot and ran to win my trophies." He grinned, and in the smile she knew him.

"Cai!" she gasped, struggling to sit.

"No!" he ordered, his hands locating her shoulders and pushing her to the ground. "You are injured. You must lie still until I can find help."

"Who will help me, Cai?" she sobbed, her pent-up tensions breaking. "You heard them. They all blame me for Duncrub. Who will help me?"

She began to cry helplessly and he patted his hands to her face. "Lady . . . don't . . . have I failed you before? I will find help. Perhaps this wild man they spoke of. He must know medicine, as most hermits do."

"No, Cai," she gasped, seizing his dirty hand in hers. "I have no life left. Don't try to save me. Please."

He ran his free hand gently down her cheek, feeling the tears flowing. "There is always hope, lady," he said quietly. "Look at me! Even when my eyes were put out, I did not give up. Always the one thought spurred me on—that I must honor my vow. I must find you. And now I have."

"But, Cai, all those years . . . I thought you were dead. You, and all the others."

He sat wearily beside her, leaning back against a tree, and she held tightly to his hand, as if it alone kept her alive, preserved her sanity.

"We have a lot of catching up to do, no doubt." He sighed, turning his face upward to the canopy of trees. "I was captured by the Romans—me, Mac Oag, and Melwas. They killed Melwas, and Mac Oag and I were soon separated. I knew resistance was useless, so I waited, biding my time. I was sold south, to the town they call Manucium. First I worked their fields, then I fed the furnaces at one of their great baths. And three times I tried to escape. Three times they caught me. And on the third, my owner had my eyes put out. But see," he said, turning his scarred face to hers and pointing to his left eye, "in my struggles and the slavemaster's haste, he only sealed this lid shut. The eye is still intact, and I have a small opening through which I can see . . . after a fashion."

Her heart turned in pity at his tale, but it seemed to bother him little, for his expression never changed.

"And your escape?" she asked gently.

He smiled slightly and lowered his face. "For four years I pretended to be blind. They never knew how poorly the slavemaster had done his job. But a woman at the baths, an officer's daughter, took pity on me . . ."

He lifted his head and grinned.

"We'd been lovers. Bored Roman women love a strong Celtic man in their beds—"

"Oh, Cai!" Melangell laughed, squeezing his hand. "You'll never change!"

He chuckled. "She arranged my escape. I made the most of it, pretending to be a blind beggar as I crossed the Roman borders to the south. They paid me little mind."

A solemn look crossed his face and his voice fell to a whisper. "I searched for you, lady, for five long years. My only will was in the vow I'd given you in your tent. To serve you till I died. I could not live with the knowledge that I had abandoned you in the midst of a battle. I had to find you, lady . . ."

His voice broke and he turned his scarred face toward her. "You kept me alive, lady. Only you . . ."

He gasped aloud and fell to dry, anguished sobs, and Melangell was overcome with pity for his plight and raw emotion at his loyalty.

"Cai . . ." she choked, dragging herself upright and reaching for his arms. He pulled her to him and they clenched each other desperately, crying as the night descended around them.

From the darkness of the nearby brush a grim pair of eyes

watched the scene in the glade, then silently withdrew into the depths of the forest.

Cai managed to light a small fire, and their food the next day consisted of a mass of boiled weeds collected from the forest, slowly cooked in Cai's skin water bag. Melangell ate it listlessly, finding little in her situation or the pain that racked her body to brighten her.

"So I have a niece and a nephew?" Cai remarked, finishing the last of his meager meal.

"Yes," she muttered, "though where they are now, I cannot say, nor if you'll ever see them alive."

"Not so glum, lady!" he chided her, licking his fingers. "Remember me when next you feel so low."

She looked at him and was amazed to see him grinning at her. How he managed to keep his spirits so high was a mystery to her. "Here," she sighed, handing him the rest of her food. "I am not hungry."

He felt the small pile of wet greens on the piece of bark and shook his head disapprovingly. "You must eat better than this if you expect to heal!" he said. "You will never find your children if you die."

"I know," she answered listlessly. He tilted his head in attention.

"You are in pain, aren't you, lady?" he observed.

"Yes. Great pain," she muttered. "I feel like sleeping a month until I am well."

"I can tell. Your voice is strained. Where is it worst? Perhaps I can help."

He set the plate aside and crawled toward her, his hand patting the ground until he felt her leg. Slowly he moved upward till his fingers touched her forehead. "I know little of such things," he said, "but perhaps if you told me what to look for . . ."

"No, Cai . . ."

"You don't feel feverish to me."

"I'll be all right," she insisted.

He ran a hand over her swollen face and a frown pulled at his mouth. "You will not give up, lady," he stated. "Your spirit is gone, and I will not allow you to die. You must find your children, and I must see my sister again, and my niece and nephew. Come . . ." he ordered, lifting her in his arms, "You direct my steps. We will find this wild man and restore you to your health."

She leaned wearily on his shoulder, her arms around his neck, and tried as best she could to be the eyes he so tragically had lost.

They slept the night beneath a great rotting log, Cai protectively at her side, but as weary as she was, Melangell found little rest. The strangeness of the deepening evergreen woods unnerved her. Mysterious shadows flickered past them as Cai carried her along what she took to be a path into the heart of the forest. An owl hooted nearby, always nearby, even in the daytime, and she'd felt her skin crawl at the unnaturalness of it. Once Cai nearly stumbled over a series of half-rotted wood carvings erected in a dim clearing, their vaguely human faces mossy and demonic-looking. She wanted then to turn back, to take their chances with the villagers, but he would have none of it. He carried her on despite her protests, and she had to look away in fear when they passed the vacant, hollow-eyed stares of the moldering figures.

By the gods, she thought wildly when the cursed owl hooted in the darkness nearby, I am so weary, so pained, and so afraid. I would die, but Cai needs me. I am now his eyes; how can I abandon him here, in this forest, with a wild man lurking nearby?

She listened to his soft, rhythmic breathing and felt tears gathering in her eyes. Is there no justice in this mad world? Why must all the good souls suffer so, like Cai has suffered, while rascals like Achivir remain untouched? Why?

She turned, sensing the comforting warmth of his body. Dear Arnemetia, my head is splitting, my forehead is burning, and my whole body aches. If we do not find help soon, I may well die, despite my best efforts to remain alive.

"Lady . . ."

Cai was shaking her shoulder vigorously, fear in his voice, and Melangell felt his hand at her neck, as if to reassure himself that she still lived. Groggily she turned her head, gasping when a searing pain cut behind her eyes.

"What is it?" he asked, alarmed at the sound. "What's wrong?"

"My head . . . Cai . . ." She tried to look at him and was terrified to find that her eyes would not focus. "No!" she choked, reaching for him. "Find help, Cai! My eyes . . . my head . . ."

He lifted her quickly, trying to make his way through the enshrouding forest. More than once he stumbled into the brush or felt a low-hanging tree branch lash his face.

"Cai," she moaned repeatedly, but it was not till her moans stopped that his fears rose. He crouched to the ground, lowering her in one arm, his free hand frantically feeling her burning, swollen forehead.

"No . . ." he sobbed, hugging her limp body to his chest. "Melangell . . . don't die . . . don't . . ."

Desperately he lifted her again, staggering his way through the woods, going he knew not where, nor what he hoped to find. He only knew that he must keep going.

"Help me!" he called out, his voice choking. "She is dying . . . help us!"

His words sank into the dripping heaviness of the forest, as if no sound would be allowed in this forbidding domain. "Help!" he gasped again, quieter, holding the woman protectively as if to stave off her fate.

"Help . . ."

The woods suddenly rustled to his right, and before he could turn, a stern hand fell on his arm.

"Come," a voice commanded, and Cai followed a darkly cloaked figure that pushed its way through the dense underbrush.

"Put her here," the figure said, leading Cai to a low bed on one side of the small round wicker hut they had entered. When he laid her down, the fragrant odor of heather wafted to his nose.

"Here," their benefactor said, guiding Cai to a squatting-stool and lowering him to it. "I must have room to treat her." He thumped a wooden mug of water to a large chest beside Cai and rushed away. The guard located the cup and sipped it as he tried to watch the man. For it was a man.

He'd thrown his old cloak carelessly to the dirt floor and now seemed busy at his work. Cai could see that he wore brown knee breeches and a long gray tunic, as drab and dank-looking as the lichen-covered trees around them.

"Are you the wild man?" he asked abruptly.

"Perhaps," the man said, carrying several objects to the bedside.

"Do you know healing?" Cai asked suspiciously. The villagers' taunts about the wild man having their blood came back to him vividly. Curse the gods, he thought angrily, for now we are at his mercy, and I cannot even see what he is doing to her!

"I do," the man replied, and Cai could smell the mingled odors of herbs and teas and ointments drifting through the hut.

"What happened to her?" the man suddenly demanded. Cai was surprised at the anger in his low voice.

"She was stoned."

"But why?" he asked, rising and crossing to the shallow hearth-pit in the center of the floor. Cai heard water being poured, and the man walked back to the heather bed.

"They say she is a witch," Cai replied. "They blame her for Duncrub."

"The fools," the man muttered bitterly, and again Cai was struck by his manner. Melangell suddenly moaned and he sprang to his feet.

"Easy, my friend," the wild man said. "The wound on her forehead is poisoned and must be cleaned. It will hurt her, without a doubt, but she will die if I do not."

The man seemed to be turning his head toward him, and Cai slumped to the stool in resignation. "Yes, I understand," he sighed, not feeling too well himself. He heard the lady moan several more times while the man treated her. Then, his voice deep and kind, he gave her tea and she soon fell silent, to Cai's immense relief.

"Is she . . . is she going to live?" Cai muttered to the man as he gathered up his potions.

"Yes," he answered simply, and crossed the floor to Cai's side. Cai felt a hand on his face and he tensed instinctively, wishing he had a knife for protection. The man tilted Cai's head back and seemed to be examining his battered eyes. Abruptly he withdrew, and Cai heard him thump loudly on the chest by his side.

"Food is here," he announced. "My home is yours."

"But . . . where are you going!" Cai protested.

"I will sleep in the forest."

"But I cannot see! What do I do for Melangell?"

Cai could detect a smile in the man's voice. "I will be back. Tonight. When it is dark."

Cai heard the rickety wicker door scrape, and the wild man was gone.

Melangell awoke two days later to a darkened hut, the only light coming from a low fire in the center of the packed earthen floor. Familiar smells of drying herbs came to her nose and she tried to sit.

"Cai?" she whispered uncertainly. Where was he? And where was she? How did she come to be in this tiny hut, on a fragrantly soft bed of heather tops?

"He is asleep," a voice said. She turned her head uneasily and saw someone sitting cross-legged on the floor across the room. The figure rose and as silently as a cat crossed over to her.

"How are you feeling?" it asked kindly. She narrowed her eyes in the gloom, studying it.

"Who are you?" she whispered. He gave no reply, but began to remove the bandage at her forehead. He worked oddly, awkwardly, and she noted that his left arm seemed to be almost useless.

"Are you the wild man?" she persisted. He had a thick beard and long, wavy brown hair that reached past his shoulders, and she found nothing threatening in his manner whatsoever.

"Yes," he said simply, dabbing medicine on her cut forehead. He seemed reluctant to speak, so she honored his wish and lay silent, allowing him to minister to her. When he pulled aside the coarse blanket that covered her, she suddenly realized, to her discomfort, that she was undressed. Calmly he changed a poultice on her side, where the large stone had struck her.

"You have been mistreated," he observed. She tensed uncomfortably and he seemed to sense it, glancing at her face as he worked.

"You have had several children," he went on, "and an injured leg. A man has abused you, as well."

She turned her head away in embarrassment and felt color rising in her cheeks. He certainly was observant! He must have examined her thoroughly while she lay feverish and ill.

"Who are you?" she demanded again, suddenly annoyed. He didn't answer and she watched, bewildered, while he put away his potions and wordlessly left the hut.

Cai handed Melangell a trencher of gruel and coarse bread. "Why does he come only at night?" she puzzled.

"Perhaps he does not wish to be seen." He shrugged.

"But why?"

"If his appearance is anything like mine, I can understand it," Cai answered, a hint of bitterness in his voice. "The screams and shrieks or laughs I've received would weigh down a Roman mule."

"Yes," she muttered, "perhaps you're right. His arm seems to be afflicted in some way. Have you seen?"

She looked at Cai and he shrugged and snorted a laugh. "I see his clothes, his size, and little else," he said.

"Yes . . . I'm sorry," Melangell answered. "I thought perhaps you—"

"No matter," Cai interrupted her. "I only say that, whatever his reasons, we must respect them. He has saved your life."

"Yes," she muttered, looking down pensively at her food. "Yes, he has."

Melangell slept soundly when the wild man slipped into the hut that night, her recovering health allowing her the luxury of a restful sleep. But Cai had kept himself awake, and when the man bent over the slumbering woman, Cai peered as carefully as he could at the shapes illuminated by the flickering fire. He saw the wild man check her forehead, her side, and then he straightened up, gazing at her peaceful face. Suddenly, to Cai's shock, he leaned down and gently kissed her bandaged forehead.

The next day was blustery and cold, full of the threat of coming winter. Melangell huddled all day in several blankets while Cai kept the fire in the hearth-pit blazing. They ate hot gruel for supper and tried to find enough warmth to allow sleep. But Melangell was still awake when the wild man came to check her, and as he approached the bed the cold radiating from his body brought shame to her heart. She lay quietly while he checked her, feigning sleep. When she knew he was through, she reached out and seized his wrist. "Wait," she whispered. With a jerk he pulled his arm free and she struggled to sit. "No! Stay!" she called after him as he quickly crossed the floor. "This is your home . . . stay!"

"No," he muttered almost angrily, and rushed out.

Melangell lay back on the bed, feeling the dry heather tops crunch beneath her body. Cai turned over by the fire, awakened by her outburst.

"Melangell?" he asked tentatively.

"Why won't he stay?" she puzzled. "He could get sick out in this weather."

"I'm sure he is used to it. His home is the forest now."

"Now?" She turned her head toward him. He lay on his side, the firelight glimmering off his scarred face. "What do you mean, 'now,' Cai?"

"Don't you recognize him, Melangell? Are you more blind than I am?"

"What do you mean? How could I recognize him?"

"You really don't know, then?" He sighed, turning his face toward her.

"No. Who is he? Who?"

"One whom you long thought was dead. Melangell, it is Brennos."

She waited for him the next night, and the next, and the next. The wild man did not return. She didn't want to believe it was Brennos. He had died . . . or she had always thought he had. The brutality of his wound, his pain, the loss of blood. Even he himself had believed it. "Another time," he had said after their tender farewell kiss. Another time. . . .

No, it couldn't be.

Yet the wild man's crippled arm was the same one Brennos had wounded. The gentle hand, the medical skill, were the same. But she couldn't be sure until she saw his face, his eyes, his smile.

No, she decided, it couldn't be Brennos. This man was no druid, and Brennos had said it was his life. Cai must be mistaken, despite the superficial resemblance. It could not be Brennos. He would never give up his calling.

Still, night after night she waited for him, doubts engulfing her, her hurt growing, her heart aching gently for a man she knew was gone forever.

Brennos. . . .

Her strength returned, her battered body healed, and despite Cai's concern, she insisted on walking around the hut and out into the falling autumn leaves. Hours passed as she sat in the dirt by the door, desperately listening for a footfall in the dry leaves. And time after time she returned to the hut, her heart fallen, her hopes dashed. The man would not reveal himself.

"Melangell . . . don't," Cai pleaded, grabbing her arm with unaccustomed roughness. The skies had opened up and cold rain drove into the cracks in the wild man's hut, but despite the harsh weather the woman donned her old cloak and prepared for her customary vigil.

"I must, Cai," she retorted. "Release me."

"Then I will come too," he protested. "I am your guard. Something might happen."

"No," she said as gently as she could. "Cai, it is odd, but when I am out there, I always feel he is nearby, watching me. I know that if anything happened, he would come. Just yesterday I saw that owl again, sitting in a tall tree. Suddenly it turned and flew silently away, as if following someone. I know he is out there, Cai."

"You cannot know that, Melangell. If something happened and he didn't come, I could never find you in the forest. You would be lost. You mustn't go out today."

She removed his hand from her arm and guided him back to the stool. "Wait here for me, Cai," she said, patting his shoulder. "I will be back at my usual hour."

He began to protest, rising to his feet, but he was too late.

His unease flared when he heard the door scrape shut behind her, and an ominous silence descended on the room.

She had seen something suspicious on her previous day's wanderings, and she felt she must investigate it. Oddly spaced holly trees, snaking away through the woods, as if marking a trail. Sure enough, she noted when she followed them, they seemed to be leading somewhere. Up a tangled slope to the left, circling around down a gully, until she saw a surging stream below her, the water gray and roiling from the heavy rains. And beside it, silent and pensive, the seated figure of a man.

She approached him slowly, fearfully. He seemed as lifeless as one of the wooden statues he'd placed in the glade to frighten away intruders. Perhaps it is someone else, she thought in sudden uncertainty. A hunter, a warrior, and not the wild man at all. But when she saw the great gray owl rise from nearby and glide away through the forest, she knew.

"So you have found me," the man said suddenly, rising to his feet and turning to face her.

"Brennos?" she whispered, still unsure it was him. "Is it you, Brennos?"

She stepped closer, but he turned and walked brusquely away from her. "I am not the same Brennos you knew, Melangell," he said tightly, lifting his head and gazing at her, and she recognized the gray eyes at once.

"Not? What do you mean? I thought you were dead, Brennos. All these years I have mourned you, prayed for your soul, and hoped for your future. Why didn't you tell me it was you, Brennos? Why have you avoided me, been so deceptive?"

"I am not the Brennos you once knew," he repeated.

"I don't understand," she protested, fingering the neck of her cloak. "You are Brennos. My physician, my druid, my friend."

"No." He shook his head, turning his face up to the pelting rain. It silvered his beard and dripped heavily down the front of his dark checked cloak. "Is your training so far behind you that you cannot see what has happened?" he asked her. "I am a hermit now . . . semnotheoi . . . no longer a druid. I have abandoned the world."

"But why, Brennos!" she choked.

"Why?" he asked, closing his eyes. "The world has gone mad, Melangell. It is inhabited by fools. The wounds and scars I saw on your body are a testament to that. I could not endure it. I have left it."

"But, Brennos, the world has always been a mad place. What druid does not learn that in his first year? No . . . what has happened to change you so?"

"I cannot tell you," he replied, turning his head and looking at her. His gray eyes, soft in the darkness of his tanned face and heavy beard, seemed to be seeing through her, beyond her, to worlds past this one. "Use my hovel as long as you like. I have no real need of it. It is only a luxury I indulge myself in every so often."

She came toward him, her heart twisting within her. He retreated a few more steps and looked up at the clouded sky once more. "Don't Melangell," he sighed. "Leave me. It is the only request I make of you, in the name of our friendship. Stay in my hut, but do not seek me out. Please . . ."

She lowered her hands, the rain dripping around her hooded face and running into her eyes. "Brennos, I have nothing now. Nothing . . ." she croaked into the gathering storm. "I married Genann, and he is dead. Two of my babies died. My daughter was stolen on the eve of her marriage and sold to the Romans. My two sons are gone, searching for her. I was mistress to a king, who used me and raped me and beat me. I was stoned repeatedly by people who blamed me for something I had no part of. And now I find this. My guard is blind, and my druid does not care."

"I am sorry for your misfortunes, Melangell. Truly I am, for you are a fine woman and deserve more than what life has handed you. But there is nothing I can do for you, save one thing."

"What?" she asked, eagerness lighting her face.

"I can open Cai's scarred eyelid. I can restore some small measure of sight to him."

Cai cocked his head curiously when he heard footfalls returning to the hut . . . not one pair, but two, both sounding as similar, as gentle, as the four feet of a deer.

"Brennos?" he questioned when he saw the figure of a man behind Melangell.

"Aye," the man sighed. "It is Brennos. I must talk with you, Cai."

"Yes . . . what of?" he blurted, starting to rise to his feet. The firm hand of the man forced him back to the stool.

"Melangell has told me what happened to your eyes. I have examined them briefly and I think it will be a small matter to open the lid over your good eye, if you wish it."

"If?" Cai gulped, disbelieving. "You mean . . . I could see again?"

"Somewhat. No doubt in the intervening years the eye has become damaged from the unnaturalness of its predicament, but Melangell tells me that even now you can see shapes and colors."

"Yes." Cai nodded. "I can."

"Well, I can't say for certain that it will be much better than that, but at least you will be able to see more of the shapes and colors. Do you wish it?"

Cai sat, too stunned for words, his face a blank mask of disbelief. "Yes . . ." he whispered. "Brennos, do what you can."

Brennos turned and gazed around his hut. "Here, by the light of the fire, will be best," he remarked. "I must be able to see clearly." He looked aside at Melangell. "You will help me?"

She nodded. "Gladly. Just tell me what I must do."

He moved to his shelf of medicines and began selecting jars and packets and bandages. "Here," he said, handing her a slim, sharp knife. "Hold this in the fire. It must be cleansed."

She crossed to the hearth while Brennos prepared his various medicines.

"Come to the light, Cai," he instructed, carrying a tray to the hearth. The guard rose to his feet and made his way toward the glow of the fire. Brennos helped him to the floor, propping his head on a folded fur.

"Come, Melangell, and put the knife here," he said, motioning to a clean wool bandage. "First, Cai, some drugs to make you sleep."

He lifted Cai's head and held an old battered druid's cup to his mouth. The guard drank the contents quickly and rested his head back on the fur.

Brennos replaced the druid's cup on the tray. "Wash his face and eye with the tea in that bowl while we wait for the medicine to work," he instructed Melangell. Washing Cai's face, she noted his features growing slack.

"Cai?" she whispered, shaking his shoulder. He did not respond. Brennos laid clean linens around the eye and picked up the knife from the tray.

"It is such a simple thing, I am surprised it has not been done before," he said, holding the knife over the eye.

"I doubt he had the time or fees. He has spent the last five years, since his escape, looking for me," she replied.

Brennos paused, glanced at Melangell's solemn green eyes, and shook his head. "By the gods . . ." he muttered, turning back to the eye. Swiftly he cut along the juncture of the scarred lids and took the wad of wool Melangell handed him. He wiped the blood away and gently pulled the lids. They gave easily, sliding apart over Cai's pale blue eye.

"You did it!" she gasped when she saw it. "Brennos, you did it!"

She glanced up at him but his face was grim, studied. "The ointment," he directed. "The trick now is to keep it from growing back as it heals."

He wiped the thick ointment, made of herbal infusions and beeswax, expertly across the bleeding scars and placed a clean pad atop the eye. "I will lift him and you bandage this in place. Then I must go, but I'll return every day to check on him, until he is healed."

Her happiness over Cai's well-deserved good fortune vied with her own heavy heart as she wound linen strips around Cai's sagging head. What a joy it had been, working at Brennos' side once more! But it obviously meant nothing to him. Still he insisted on leaving. If only he would stay!

"Keep him calm," he instructed, rising and crossing to the door. Melangell pushed the cluttered tray aside and ran to follow him when he stepped into the rain.

"Brennos, wait," she begged.

He paused briefly beyond the door, his face toward the dripping sky. "No, Melangell, I cannot," he murmured, and walked into the forest gloom, thankful for the kind assistance of the raindrops. They hid from her pleading eyes the tears that had trickled down his cheeks.

Cai stirred impatiently, listening to Brennos pour hot water from the iron kettle by the fire. Melangell moved, off to his left, and he tilted his head expectantly.

"Will you sit still!" She laughed. "You remind me of your nephew when he was four years old!"

Cai slumped, grinning sheepishly. "You cannot know how eager I am to have this bandage off," he explained. "I never realized how I valued the one bit of sight left to me, until it was removed from me entirely these past few days."

"I can only imagine, Cai," Melangell said kindly, placing a hand on his shoulder. At a nod from Brennos she unwound the bandage around Cai's head. He sat tensely, his hands clenched on his knees.

"Be still and do not open the eye until it is rinsed with this medicine," Brennos directed, stepping up beside the young woman and watching her deft hands at work. Cai sat woodenly while the last of the bandages came off and Melangell tilted his head back, slowly lifting the linen pad over the eye. She was relieved to see that it was clean; no seeping blood, no yellowed poisons stained it.

Cai pulled his mouth back when he felt her little fingers at his eye, carefully pulling at the lid. A warm, soothing liquid flooded it, pouring down his cheek and into his ear. She wiped it away and moved his head upright.

"See what you can do with it," Brennos instructed, stepping away and watching him critically. Cai moved the lid tentatively; it felt stiff, unnatural, the scars limiting its flexibility. He turned his head, blinking, until the eye began to focus.

"By the gods!" he cried, leaping to his feet. "I can see!"

Brennos smiled slowly and nodded, satisfaction evident on his face.

"Everything is hazy, like a fog, but I can see!" Cai gasped, turning around. "In the name of Arnemetia, I can see!"

He faced Melangell, grinning broadly, and seized her hands in his. "Gods above, you look beautiful!" he laughed. "You are the first woman I've seen in nine years . . . and the last one I saw was a Roman." He wrapped his arms around her abruptly and lifted her from the floor, planting a big kiss on her cheek. "Sister-in-law, I love you!" he whooped, whirling her around. His joy was infectious, for when she looked over his shoulder she saw that Brennos, too, was laughing, a light in his level gray eyes. Cai suddenly remembered him and lowered Melangell to the ground. Turning, he took the druid's hand fiercely.

"Thank you, Brennos," he said, his voice choked with emotion. "I owe you a greater debt than if you had saved my life. Thank you . . ." Impulsively he threw an arm around Brennos' shoulder, hugging him in an awkward embrace.

"Thank you," he repeated, turning away and wiping the eye.

"I am glad it turned out so well, Cai," Brennos said quietly, walking to the door. "Wash his eye several times with that liquid until you're certain that the tears have resumed their natural function," he instructed Melangell, slipped through the door, and was gone.

"Well," Cai said, looking around the room like a delighted child, "I think the time has come for the two of us to discuss our future plans."

He turned to look at the young woman. By the stiff way she held herself he could tell that Brennos' abrupt departure had disturbed her.

"Come," he said, extending a hand to her. "We must plan to leave here, while there is still time to cross the pass before winter. I can see now; I am fit and strong. We will go west, and find what remains of our family."

She stitched Cai a large sack for food, and managed to find a leather drinking bag in the chest that held Brennos' supplies. She made a soft leather patch to cover his bad eye and make his appearance less frightening to others. After cleaning his clothes in the chilly stream, Melangell cut his long hair and helped him shave his beard with Brennos' surgical knife. He insisted on leaving his warrior's mustache. Except for his old tattered clothes, he made a fairly respectable appearance, and Melangell thought he should have little difficulty on his journey.

"Here," she said, rolling up a heavy wool blanket and

tying it over one of his shoulders. "This should keep you warm enough. If it turns too cold, wet it in a stream. It will freeze like a snug cocoon and protect you from the winds."

"A good idea." Cai nodded. "Where did you hear that?"

"From the Cruithni. They are an inventive race and used to surviving in the coldest weather." She paused, looking at him as he stood before her. "You need a knife. Some weapon besides your sling."

"There is a box of weapons and such behind the door," he suggested. "I suppose Brennos would let me have one."

Dragging the heavy chest to the hearth, he opened it, and Melangell gasped when she saw the contents. "Where ever did he get these?" she wondered, lifting a beautifully made short sword in her hands. Cai shrugged and picked out a sleek long dagger with a handle of carved ash wood.

"I hadn't realized the quality of all this before," he marveled. "It looks as if he made them himself."

"Brennos . . . made these?" Melangell shook her head. "I cannot believe it. They are so exquisite. And the handles! Look—elaborately carved of bone or wood or wrapped in leather strips. This must be his life's work."

Cai returned the knife to the chest and looked at Melangell. "I will delay my departure a day or two," he said, removing his gear. "I have an idea. A small way I can repay him his kindness."

Melangell walked with Cai a short way into the forest, one hand on his arm.

"Tell them where I am," she said, and he nodded. "Send word, and I will come."

"Aye, I will," he said.

"Your sister lives in a village at the foot of the Bristling Mountains. Its chief is Firtan; he has the blood of the Gael in him."

"I'm sure I can find him," Cai replied.

"And Anor and Cadvan," Melangell sighed. "You will know them at once. She has your eyes, pale and cool, and is as delicate as a spring flower. Cadvan is already as stocky as your father was . . . and as bullheaded."

He laughed and turned to her. "And Nechtan's son?"

"He is dark, with skin like mellow ivory and eyes as blue

as the heavens. At times he looked so like his father that it would break my heart. There is no mistaking him."

Cai looked awkwardly at the stony ground, one hand checking the short sword at his side. "And you? Will you be all right here? I don't feel right, leaving you again, after seeking you for so long."

"Cai," she said, seizing his hand, "the wars are over. I am safe here. You have been a loyal guard such as the bards sing about, but now you are my kinsman. I need no more guard. Cai, I release you from your vow."

He looked at her, his scarred eye scanning her face slowly. Suddenly he fell to one knee and raised her hand to his lips. "Lady . . ." he said gruffly, his emotion choking him as he kissed her hand. Then he stood, embracing her fiercely. "Good-bye, Melangell," he muttered. "I will send word."

"Good-bye, Cai," she replied as he stepped away from her. "Have a safe journey. Good-bye."

He waved silently and walked into the dark forest, and when she could see no more of him, nor hear the careful tread of his feet, she returned to the hut. Closing the door behind her, she roamed her eyes around the room, and a lump rose in her throat when she saw the parting gift he'd made for Brennos: an exquisitely carved rack of wood, hung on the wall and fitted with six of Brennos' most beautiful blades.

She awoke many nights later to the sound of movement in the room. Sitting abruptly and reaching for the knife she kept nearby, she was relieved to see that it was Brennos, bustling quietly on some errand or other. He seemed startled to see her, but after first moving toward the door he changed his mind and lowered himself to the floor by the fire.

"You stayed," he muttered.

"Yes," she answered, studying his shadowed face. "I hope you don't mind; Cai took one of your swords. He needed a weapon."

Brennos shook his head silently.

"They are beautiful. Did you make them yourself?" she continued.

"Yes." He sighed, looking up at her. "With my bad arm I

cannot manage the larger items, though. It keeps me busy, and I occasionally trade one for supplies."

"Cai left you a gift," she pointed out. "A small thank-you, he said."

Brennos half-smiled and looked at the rack on the wall. "I know. I saw it . . . very nice. Thank him for me, when next you see him."

They fell silent, listening to the popping of the fire. "Brennos . . ." Melangell spoke up, "how did you survive? What happened to you?"

He sat grimly, his eyes reflecting the fire before him. "I had determined that I was to die," he began, "but Calum determined otherwise. When I had made my preparations, he merely knocked me unconscious with the butt of his knife, cut away my bloodied robe, and bound the wound tightly. Then he left me while he lured the Romans away. But he returned by dawn, took me to an old woman's hut, and left. I never saw him again."

He paused and took a slow, deep breath.

"I hovered near death for days, but the woman was a skilled healer and pulled me through. She hid me from the Romans several times, and sewed my wound together with gut strings—"

"Sewed?" Melangell gasped.

"Aye." He nodded. "Some trick she learned from who knows where. It probably saved my life, but of course the inner fibers of my arm were never repaired, and the result is as you see now. I can move the arm, use my hand to grasp, and the muscles are fairly strong, but I cannot use the fingers properly. It flops awkwardly, like a dog's broken leg." He snorted a cynical laugh and fell silent.

"But why did you leave? Abandon all?" she questioned. He looked up, a vague expression suddenly clouding his face.

"I cannot say. You should not have stayed here, Melangell. I can offer you nothing."

"There is peace here, Brennos. The one thing my life has lacked."

"But you are young still. Attractive. You should have gone with Cai, found your children, married again, and had another family."

573

"No, Brennos," she said resolutely. "I want no more husbands. It is too painful. And as for children, I can have no others."

"But you are not so old—"

"No, but I had the fever. I carried the bastard of a Cruithni king, and in shame over my state I flung myself from a cliff. I did not die, but the child did, and the result was the fever, which has ended my childbearing forever."

"I am sorry," he muttered, rising to his feet. "You are welcome to stay and enjoy whatever it is you seek. I will leave you food from time to time. Now I must go."

She did not try to call him back, did not protest. She knew it was useless. She watched him leave, and listened to his footsteps fade into the night.

Autumn was well under way, the trees nearly bare, harsh wind rattling dryly at the wild man's hut. One evening Melangell returned early from a walk and was startled to find Brennos there. Like a cornered animal he turned quickly at her approach, and she smiled in an effort to calm him.

"I . . . I brought you something," he mumbled, pointing to the bed. Looking, she saw two expensive women's gowns and an embroidered wool overblouse laid out on the rough wool blanket.

"Why . . . where did you get these?" she gasped, lifting one and studying the fineness of the material.

"I stole them." He shrugged nonchalantly.

"Stole? Brennos, you shouldn't have done that!"

"I do it all the time," he said, squatting by the fire and extending his hands to the flames. "I thought you needed more than . . . than those Pictish boy's things you wear."

"Well, I do, but I'm not sure you should have stolen them. What if you are pursued?"

"Oh, I won't be." He smiled, looking at her. "I creep in by night, and no one knows I am there. Some wealthy woman had her laundry draped on a bush, so I took what I fancied. But I left something in return."

"A knife?"

"No," he laughed. "I collected a few bits and pieces from the forest before I went—a dead bird, half a turtle shell, a squirrel's leg bone. I tied them into a suitably gruesome-looking charm and left it where she would find it. She will know it was the wild man who came in the night and took her things, and she will summon their wise man to lift the curse she thinks I have put on her. So, you see, you will get your gowns, the wise man will get a good meal for his belly, and the woman will be glad she got off so lightly from me, with only the loss of a few clothes. Everyone is happy!"

"Brennos . . ." She smiled, shaking her head in exasperation.

"People are such fools," he muttered, gazing back to the fire. "No one stops to think anymore. I find a few moldering skulls in the forest and peg them near the village, and everyone thinks the woods are cursed. They let themselves be used."

"Don't be so hard on them, Brennos," Melangell said quietly, lowering the gown to the bed. "In your seclusion you cannot know what hardships they now labor under. The old carefree days are gone. In my journey here, I saw such things as I never dreamed possible in this fair land. The border the Romans have set up is strangling us, like a bound limb withering away. Where once we traded freely with our kinsmen to the south for luxuries as well as necessities, now the people are hard-pressed to find enough food even to survive. The towns and fine hostels and palaces are gone, dismantled by desperate people, the wood and iron used and reused in the meager hovels they now call their homes. Life is hard, Brennos, and the people are sullen and embittered. You must not fault them for their weaknesses."

A wry smile pulled at his mouth. "You have always been too gentle for your own good," he said. "Gentle people do not survive long in this world."

"Is it any better to harden my heart, as you have done?"

He stood, brushing the dirt from his old worn breeches. "Perhaps you are right," he said, walking to the door. "I hope you like the gowns. It does not suit you to dress as a boy."

"I do, Brennos. Thank you."

She watched him pull the door open. "Brennos . . . when the weather turns, please come here for shelter. It is your home, not mine. I feel bad enough, keeping you turned out

575

just by my presence. I give you my word: I will not annoy you or question you. I will leave you alone. Please, Brennos . . ."

"I'll see," he replied brusquely. Before she could speak again, he left.

"You seem pensive," Brennos noted over their supper, a hot, filling gruel Melangell had prepared. Outside, the wind howled dismally, and the two sat on the floor by the fire, huddled under furs and woolen blankets.

She looked up at him and half-smiled. He had come at first only during the nights, but as winter progressed, his stays grew longer until eventually he remained around the hut almost the entire day. And his silence, too, had eased; indeed, he seemed almost glad to have someone to talk with.

"I am thinking of what I always think of," she replied. "My children. My life. Why it must be the way it is."

"And how is that?" he asked mildly.

She looked at him blankly. "You know how it is," she began to protest. "Luck has never been with me."

"Do you know why that is?" he responded. "Because all your happiness rests with others. Yet nothing in this life is permanent, and so you mourn when the happiness is taken from you."

"That is unfair, Brennos!" she objected.

"Unfair, perhaps, but true. Let me show you something." He rose, crossed the floor, and left the hut. She watched him go, puzzled, until his voice floated in to her.

"I am gone, am I not?" he called over the whistle of the wind.

"No, you are on the other side of the wall."

"But you cannot see me, touch me. I must be gone."

"You are not, Brennos! Stop this!"

"And where is Nechtan? Genann? They are gone too."

"Yes . . ."

"How do you know that, Melangell?"

"Because I cannot see them . . . or touch them," she muttered, realizing his message. Abruptly he reentered the room and returned to the fire.

"Then what is the difference, eh?" he asked, rubbing his

cold hands briskly. "All are gone, because by your measure you can no longer see them or touch them. Is it them you miss, or the comfort of their physical presence? Yet that physical presence changes from lifetime to lifetime. The body you love today is not the body you love tomorrow. The body is the only thing gone, Melangell. You know," he said quietly, studying his hands, "I often think that if I could develop the ability to leave my body at will, the world would hail me as a wonder. Yet when the gods take us from our bodies at their directing, not our own, we deem it a tragedy and call it 'death.' Perhaps it is only our own helplessness that so enrages us about dying."

He looked across the fire and saw tears in her eyes.

"You are right, Brennos," she whispered. "All these years, all the pain I have carried inside me, and all because I refused to see the truth."

"This life is like water," he replied. "Everything seen through it is distorted."

He smiled softly and studied her face, and she could feel peace and contentment radiating from him like heat from a bake-oven. How different he seemed now, his kindness and gentleness strengthened and magnified, calm and tranquil like the sea at rest, or a moon-washed pool in the forest.

"Please," she said shyly, "tell me what happened to change you so. Please, Brennos."

"All right." He gazed into the fire. "After Duncrub, when I made myself ready to die, my thoughts were on the intricacies of life, the oneness of the world. It was my final thought—'all is one.' Perhaps believing I was dead, even though I was not, my soul had a vision."

She leaned forward eagerly, her solemn green eyes on his pensive face.

"I stood on a path," he continued, "and I knew it was the path of my soul's journey. But obscuring it as it stretched off to the horizon were clouds and mists. They suddenly parted, showing me the way in clarity and brilliance . . . and then I knew, Melangell."

He glanced at her, and his eyes held a strange look. Intense, fired.

"I knew the clouds were the creeds and philosophies of

577

man; his beliefs and religions. And I knew that, contrary to what I had thought all my life, they do not illuminate the path, but obscure it. My druidical teachings were a waste; all was a waste. The very efforts I devoted myself to, in an attempt to progress, in truth only held me back."

"So what did you do?" she breathed.

"I abandoned my druidism. I abandoned the world, I abandoned everything, as nearly as I could. I came to see that religions and philosophies are not the truth; they are the creations of men, as imperfect as their creators, and like men, they too change and evolve, grow and die. They are not the answer. I determined that I would seek the truth, as other semnotheoi have done, but with the difference that I would discard my druidism, whereas they had not. I would leave the imperfect systems of men behind me. One day druidism will be gone, and the doctrines of the Romans. Who knows what creeds will arise to light the dark corners of the world? But that is not what I want, Melangell. I want the true peace of the gods, not the falsehoods of men's minds."

"I understand," she whispered. "Esus sought the same thing, and he often said that druids are as foolish as anyone else. He taught me to be no respecter of person or position, but to try to see what lives within. I once adhered to that teaching, and tried to follow his lead, but my will has left me now, Brennos. In my busy life, so often lived for others, I have lost sight of myself."

She looked down at her lap awkwardly, discomfited by the emotion of her words. He was so much more than she was; he had seen visions, dedicated himself to his goal, and she had not. He was a "clear vessel for the gods"; she was a shattered remnant. A widow, a whore . . .

"I must get some sleep," she choked, rising to her feet and walking from the fire. He watched her go in silence, saw her curl on her side atop his heather bed beneath a mass of furs and blankets, and heard a soft sob as she gently cried.

"Melangell," he said quietly, "show yourself a little of the kindness and understanding you so lavish on others."

Her sobs subsided, and he sat by the fire till near dawn, watching her sleeping while his mind wandered in thought.

* * *

Winter gave way to spring, the warming sun softening the frozen soil and bringing a fine greenness to the awakening forest. Melangell was eager for the icy stream to warm so she could bathe off the winter's grime; Brennos had no proper tub she could use. Ice was melting in the swollen stream and she took her gowns to wash, donning again the Pictish clothes Brennos found so unattractive.

Brennos . . . She sighed, slipping in the mud as she walked to the stream. They had grown a bit closer during their winter in the hut, but now with the warmth of spring he again stayed away from her, wandering the forests or sleeping beneath the overhanging rock he called his cave. He seemed to draw strength from the forest, and wisdom, and she envied him for it. She still knew no peace, nor did she think she ever would.

Sighing, she dunked one gown in the rushing water and watched it flow outward from her hand. Like through water, she thought dully, studying its tossing, everything seen in this life is distorted.

"See what I have found," Brennos spoke behind her. She straightened abruptly, the heavy wet gown dripping in her hands. He knelt to the rocks, his good hand cupped around a tiny green frog. "It has awakened early, seeking the warmth of the sun," he said, studying it. He had been gone for five days, and she had missed their talks desperately.

"Do you know what some say about frogs?" he asked, glancing at her while she ran one finger down the frog's soft wet back. She shook her head at his question.

"They say the frog is the highest animal created, the one closest to the gods, for it has no teeth, no claws or scales, no weapons of violence. It alone is a truly peaceful creature."

He lowered the animal to a warmed spot of rock and it squatted comfortably, soaking up the sun.

"Man has that ability, if only he were wise enough to use it," he muttered, rising to his feet.

Yes, she thought dully, watching the frog a moment before returning to her washing, run away from me again. Leave me, Brennos, as if I had some disease you might catch. You preach a philosophy of love and caring, yet when it is offered to you, you turn away. Go quickly, Brennos . . . run. . . .

She held the wet gown in her hands, listening, but he said nothing more. Her heart fell when she heard him walk away.

Oh, gods, she cried, her composure breaking in the silent forest, what can I do? The thought of his deep voice made her heart ache; the memory of his gentle touch, his solemn gray eyes, crumbled her soul. She wanted to run after him, to fling herself at his feet, beg for mercy, plead for his love; a crumb of attention, a morsel of indulgence, anything. The lovers of her youth had been heated, impetuous, but this was different. This was gentle, slow, deep, like a mighty river, tearing her to pieces by its very power.

What am I to do? she sobbed into the humid air, for she suddenly saw the truth, and admitted it:

She loved him.

He knelt by a still, quiet pool and gazed at his ragged reflection. Gods above, what a sight I am! he mused. No wonder the people are afraid of me.

Running his good hand through his thick beard, he turned his face from side to side, examining it. It is difficult, I know, he told himself, but I have done it before and can do it again. He lifted the sharp surgical knife he'd made and began scraping the beard from his face. The hair must go next. Wash it out, and while it is still wet, perhaps my poor hand can grip it while my good hand cuts it shorter. It will be slow, it may take a few days of trying, but it must be done. It is too long . . .. too ugly.

Melangell was trying to transplant a few wildflowers to the doorstep when Brennos approached, and at first her heart jumped in fear at the strangeness of his appearance. His clothes were washed, his face cleanly shaved, his hair clumsily cut and combed back with his fingers.

"Brennos!" she gasped, standing and wiping her dirty hands on her skirt. "I . . . I didn't recognize you at first."

"I thought, with warm weather coming, I would get rid of some of my excess hair." He smiled, and in that small gesture her old Brennos had returned, his gray eyes twinkling merrily.

"It looks nice," she complimented him. "I . . . I have stew cooking, if you'd like to stay. Some young greens and herbs added to the usual gruel. I thought it would be nice to have something different."

"Yes . . . many thanks," he muttered, looking down curiously at her work on the ground.

"Oh," she laughed lightly, "I thought a few flowers would be nice, but I don't know how well they will do. Wild things do not like being transplanted."

"No," he said abruptly, and stepped into the hut.

Dusk was gathering by the time they finished their meal, a slow, leisurely dinner of stew and fresh herbed bread. The silence between them was thick, their spoken words brief and awkward.

Why did he do that? she wondered, watching him wipe his trencher with the last of the bread. His face beneath the beard is somewhat older—after all, it has been nearly twenty years—but it is still the same Brennos. Has he done this to taunt me? To raise my hopes foolishly and then foolishly dash them again? Hopes? By the gods, hopes for what? For him? For marriage? Just what is it I hope for, anyway?

"Melangell?" he asked, seeing the worried frown on her face. "Is something wrong?"

"No," she lied, putting her trencher aside. "You say your beard and hair are hot in the summer?"

"Aye." He nodded. "And when I do my smithy work, they get filthy with sweat."

"I'm surprised you did not cut them off before now," she prodded, hoping for some encouraging answer, a brightening hint.

"So am I," he said, and her heart fell. "Would you like to watch when I make the next blade?" he asked. "Perhaps I could make you a small knife, for protection when you leave here."

"Yes." She nodded, hope crumbling within her. "I would like that."

"I have learned a secret, you know," he went on, reclining on one elbow by the fire and stretching his legs comfortably. "While the blade is still hot, I temper it in blood."

"Blood!" she gasped, looking up. "But why? Surely you don't kill things for it."

"No," he laughed. "The villagers bring it, in spring and fall after slaughtering. I leave them a few knives in exchange. They think I drink it, never dreaming that it contains some special force which keens and hardens the very blades they covet so. They think I use magic to produce them."

"Really?" she asked curiously. "Blood does that?"

"Aye. I can't say why, though. But the blades are far superior to ordinary ones."

"Yes, I'd like to see it." She nodded. "When Nechtan had the Roman swords copied, he was not entirely happy with their quality."

Brennos studied her intently as her face fell in sorrow.

"Perhaps if the blades had been better, he would not have died," she whispered.

He sat up slowly, never taking his eyes from her solemn face. "You have never stopped missing him, have you, Melangell?" he asked gently. She looked at him, her eyes brimming tears, and mutely shook her head.

"With Genann, I had eighteen years. There are happy memories, comforts. But with Nechtan it all happened so fast. Suddenly he was gone, and I will never know how, or why, or anything." Her voice dropped away. "It rests like a stone in my heart, Brennos, that will never go away." Tears slipped down her cheeks when her gaze met his, and his heart moved in pity.

"Melangell . . ." he began, his voice low and soothing, "Cathbhadh and I once talked about something secret, something you never knew; something about Nechtan. I think now that you should be told."

"Told what?" she sniffed brokenly.

"Nechtan labored under a curse. It haunted his life."

"A curse?" she gasped.

"Aye. On a remote Cruithni ancestor, exacted on all the males of his line. They all met horrid deaths at the hands of the women they loved most. And then the curse passed on to their firstborn son."

Her face paled visibly in the dancing firelight. "Resad . . ." she choked.

"It is why he had you left to die in the bog. He was afraid. Then he abandoned himself to his fate, but always he hid it from you. He did not want you burdened with the knowledge."

"But Resad!" she cried. "He is out there somewhere, at great risk, and if he is under a curse as well . . ."

"No, Melangell," Brennos tried to calm her. "Listen to me! Have you never thought it strange that Nechtan was not able to escape the battle at Duncrub? Many did so. But think of it. Of him and his band, not a one survived. To a man, they died with their chief."

Her face was puzzled, her eyes searching his quizzically.

"Melangell, I believe he died deliberately, both to spare you your part in his fate and to end the curse on his son."

Her face sagged in horror, as if a demon had come and snatched her soul away.

"No . . ." she croaked woodenly, shaking her head in disbelief. "Nechtan would not have left me like that. I cannot believe you, Brennos. I will not."

Clumsily she stumbled to her feet, ran to the door, and disappeared into the indigo twilight.

He waited till well beyond midnight, and when she still had not returned, he fed the fire, rose, and determined to find her. If she had not met with some misfortune, at least she would need comforting.

He found her as the nearly full moon crept down the sky. In a broken glade not far from the stream, she had selected a small upright white stone and made it into an altar for Nechtan's departed soul. Unwilling to make a blood sacrifice, she had placed a few pretty things on it that she had gathered from the forest—a small bunch of wildflowers, a few colored pebbles, a broken piece of smoky crystal, some bird feathers. Not much, but it came from her heart, and Brennos was touched by the simplicity of her gesture. Now she lay on her side at the foot of the stone, deep in exhausted sleep, and he crouched and studied her thoughtfully. Her cheek rested gently on the mossy ground, her small hands curled before her like a child's, the flooding moonlight washing the delicate skin of her face, her tear-swollen eyes, and turning her hair to silver.

Melangell, he sighed, how else could I tell you? Yet the peaceful look on her face reassured him. Here, in this glade, she had finally been able to do what she could not for nearly twenty years. Truth enlightening her heart, she had erected an altar for Nechtan, communed with his spirit, made her offerings, sought peace for his soul . . . and hers. She had laid the dead to rest.

Dawn etched the far horizon when he rose, leaving her sleeping at the foot of Nechtan's altar, and crept away into the forest depths.

Melangell left the offerings intact and walked to the stream. Kneeling, she splashed the bracing waters over her hot, swollen eyes, pausing when her gaze fell on her wavering, dancing reflection.

You fool, she thought savagely, dashing the solemn face peering up at her with one brush of her hand. All this time you have lived in pity and grief, your silly mind dwelling on your heartaches, your losses, and never finding peace. Never knowing, never daring to imagine the sacrifices others have made for you. Nechtan, Genann, Calum, Talorc, even poor Eldol. All sacrificing for you, while all you do is cry over your misfortunes.

The green eyes stared back at her from the depths, suddenly grim, resolved.

But sacrifice is the answer, isn't it, fool? she mused. In sacrifice there is peace, nobility. Yet what sacrifice have you ever made? What deep longing have you denied yourself? What pain have you suffered, to unselfishly benefit another? None.

She splashed her eyes one last time and stood, an idea taking shape in her mind. There is one sacrifice I can still make, she realized, brightening. One left to me whom I love enough to sacrifice for. Brennos. He has turned away from the world in a sincere effort to find the truth he seeks. Yet here I am, hovering around him like an annoying insect, and already he wavers from his path. I, of all the world, should be able to understand his motivations, his desires. Just because life has led me from my path does not mean I should do the same to him. No . . .

She walked back to the hut, resolve firm in her heart. Yes, Brennos, she told herself, for the love I bear you I will make this one great sacrifice of my life; and in this sacrifice, I hope you will come to see that I did understand your search. Let it be my love's testament. I will go and leave you to yourself, as you have wished all along.

Brennos awoke, bathed in sweat despite the evening chill. Oh, gods, he groaned, sitting up and wiping his face with one unsteady hand, how long has it been since I've had those dreams? Why must they come again? He could still see the flames leaping before the girl's stricken face, hear the simple cry, like a startled child's, when the fire reached her gown. No, he shuddered, burying his face in his hands at the horror of it. Again and again in the dreams, the girl he had loved with all his soul, the nobleman's young wife, dying for their adultery, while he was forced to watch. The young woman . . . Melangell . . . and her last scream was a heart-rending one: help me . . . help me. . . .

This child of Loucetius, coming back as one with such a tender heart, one whose protective deity ironically prefers burnings as sacrifice. How odd, the world, he sighed, trying to push the dream from his mind. I, a priest, caused her death in another lifetime. In this one I tried to control my feelings, and I had succeeded, until she came into my life once more. For what reason?

Slowly she had been creeping into his life the past few months, until he found his need for her beginning to consume him. Why?

He sat under the overhanging rock, a gentle rain dripping around him. He poked at the muddy soil with a twig, his mind roaming to idle corners. Yes, he had found peace here, an outlet for his strivings. But was he content? Had he achieved much? Could he honestly say his very loneliness hadn't been a hindrance in itself? Celibacy had always been a labor for him, but he had willingly endured it. But loneliness? The times when he had wanted to share a sudden thought with someone and had been reduced to talking to his owl. The solitary walks he had taken, following a deer's trail and trying to feel he was one of them, just for the sake of belonging. The nights he had hovered at the edge of the forest, watching with silent longing the lights glimmering in the warm huts of the village. No, he sighed, man is a gregarious creature, no denying it, and sometimes my loneliness comes near to driving me mad. Then how could such madness serve to enlighten me? Or do I only make excuses, excuses for the thing I want now above all else . . . her sea-green eyes across from me at mealtime, her soft hand on my arm when I need a friend, her merry laugh when I am sad, her companionship, and even, the gods be kind, her love. . . .

He threw the stick aside in sudden irritation. My choice is plain, he thought. I must have her, or I must go away. I cannot continue as I have.

Grimly he rose to his feet and walked off through the dripping springtime forest.

Melangell was relieved that Brennos was not at the hut when she returned. A gentle rain had begun to fall outside, and she picked up her brown cloak and pulled it over her shoulders. I need nothing more, she told herself, surveying the empty room. I will go, walk out of his life, and not worry about the morrow. Cai has never sent word—did he make it across the pass? No matter, she sighed. The passes will still be snowed in. I cannot go that way. That leaves me this part of the land, where they stone me and call me "witch."

Absently she turned, straightening the room, smoothing the blanket on the heather bed, putting away a few carved wooden bowls from the hearthside, tidying Brennos' medicine shelf.

Dear Brennos. She smiled, running a hand over the neatly stored herbs and ointments. Abandoning all, living alone, but still he has the heart of a physician, a healer. That, alone, he could not abandon, even though out here in his solitude there is no one for him to heal. None save an occasional wanderer, unafraid of the fearsome wild man with a gentle soul. Like me . . . and Cai . . . yes, he saved me when I most needed him, as his spirit had promised me, so long ago.

She picked up a cup, filled it at the water bucket, and left it on the large supply chest. From the edges of the forest she gathered a small bunch of early wildflowers and arranged them in the cup.

For you, Brennos, she thought sadly, moving it to the

center of the trunk. Pulling the hood of her cloak over her head, she walked out into the rain.

It was nearing dusk when Brennos returned to the hut. He knew what he must do, and he tried to quell the uncertainty in his heart when he pulled the door open.

"Melangell?" he called, glancing around the room. Only silence met him. Alarmed, he stepped into the hut; it was not like her to go out in the rain, with darkness falling.

The peg on the wall was empty, her cloak gone. Frantically he looked around, his apprehensions rising. Had something happened to her? The hearthfire was nearly out, and her Pictish knife still lay on the trunk.

He groaned aloud. The trunk. He saw the flowers she'd left him, and suddenly he understood. His persistence had paid off. Melangell was gone.

She decided to head for the mountain pass. It was her kindest fate, she knew, for then she would either cross over to the west and find her family, or die in the attempt, frozen atop the great snow fields hugging the peaks and meadows. Either way, her release was assured. She spent the first night huddled miserably beneath her old cloak, shivering in the cold dampness. Her meal the next day was a few handfuls of tender spring weeds she gathered, eaten raw and washed down with icy stream water. Toward the mountain passes the number of farmsteads she could steal from grew fewer, and she could not bring herself to kill and eat the creatures of the forest. On the second day she raided a squirrel's nest, filling her skirt with fresh hazel nuts and plump seeds. The nuts she cracked between two rocks and ate immediately. The seeds she saved, wrapped in several large oak leaves. When the third day dawned, she woke stiffly from an uncomfortable night beneath a great hemlock tree, looking forward to the gruel she would make with the seeds. Brushing the forest litter from her cloak, she planned her meal: pound the seeds between two rocks, grind them fine, and mix them with a little water and perhaps a few herbs. It would make a passable gruel, even if it was cold and raw. Pulling the cloak around her shoulders to ward off the early chill, she turned to retrieve her food. To her horror, she saw the oak leaves torn, scattered, and a large raven picking at the seeds.

"Shoo!" she shouted, angry at the thief and panicked at the thought of her only meal disappearing. The bird looked at her, unconcerned, and wiped its heavy black beak against the rock where it stood.

"Get away! Go on!" she repeated, running toward the raven, her arms waving wildly. With a loud cry of protest the bird rose and settled himself on a nearby branch, watching Melangell grovel among the weeds and pebbles on the ground, picking out what seeds she could find and putting them into her cupped hand.

No . . . she sobbed, wiping her tears against one shoulder while she searched. Can nothing go right for me . . . nothing? Once more I am alone, destitute, starving.

The dim morning gloom grew more indistinct through her tears and she looked at the small pile of seeds she held in dismay. This isn't even a mouthful, she thought. What's the use?

"Take them!" she screamed, stumbling to her feet and flinging the seeds at the bird. The creature seemed to mock her, cocking its head and ruffling its glistening feathers indignantly. Staring at it, hatred flaring in her eyes, she noticed an oddity: sprinkled among the raven's black wing feathers were a few snowy white ones, standing out like snowflakes in the night.

No! Melangell gasped, stumbling back a few involuntary steps. An omen. Esus had always deemed it one of the most potent, a sign of good fortune such as few were privileged to see.

"You mock me," she muttered to the silent bird, turned, and hurried away, following the steep incline to the rising mountain peak. Unconcerned, the raven flew back to the ground to finish its meal.

She had made no effort to conceal her trail, and Brennos followed it easily, along the swollen, surging stream, circling around in seeming uncertainty, and then striking off with unerring accuracy toward the high mountain pass. The direction she had chosen and the fact that she hadn't even taken her knife disturbed him; without knowing her reasons, he couldn't help but draw the conclusion that she had given up on her life, no longer cared. He must find her, before it was too late. He must.

Midday approached and Melangell knelt by a trickling stream, drinking her fill of the cold water in an attempt to ease the hunger pains tearing at her stomach. Low clouds were gathering on the surrounding mountain peaks and she could feel the threat of rain in the air. A sudden raucous cry in the distance roused her and she stood, listening to the raven's alarmed call. Someone was coming. Panic gripped her throat at the thought of a villager approaching, or a hunter or warrior, and she a lone woman, wandering the mountainside without even a knife for protection.

A gentle misty rain began, and through the dripping trees she could see a man approaching. Pulling her cloak tight, she turned and rushed into the safety of the forest.

The man's footfalls followed her. Ducking into a tangled hazel thicket, she peered out at her pursuer. The man saw where she went, and now stood, not twenty paces away, unfastening a heavy gray cloak as he prepared to follow her. He was young and muscular, and she could tell by the weapons he carried that he was a hunter, not a warrior. He placed his bow and arrows atop his cloak on the ground, eager sport lighting his eyes, and she realized sickly how his other victims must have felt in their final moments—the deer, boar, or squirrels that had been the recipients of that same cold grin. She bolted from the thicket, hoping his temporary inattention would give her an edge. Racing through the trees, she weaved and dodged like a terrified animal. But the man was a hunter; the forest was his element. In a flash he was after her, and the pounding of his feet told her that flight was useless. She looped around a tree, trying to evade him. Her cloak seemed to catch and snag on every twig and thorn she passed, and she frantically fumbled to untie it. Gasping, she reached an open glade, drove her feet harder into the soft earth, ran from the man as she had not done since Calum had pursued her and Anarios so long ago.

Was it his feet pounding in her ears . . . or her heart? Her lungs were burning and she fought to clear the numbing buzz from her head. Thud . . . thud . . . thud . . . until she heard a rush, a grunt, and she crashed headlong into a spiked fernbrake.

She lifted her face from the jabbing fern stems, spitting leaves and dirt from her mouth. He had her pinned; she had no way to fight him.

"Come here, you," he muttered, pulling himself up her body, and by his voice he seemed hardly winded by their run. Rolling her over, he fumbled at her gown, his face flushed with excitement. But he could not strip her and hold her down at the same time; freeing her arms, she tried to push him away. Her feeble efforts only amused him, and the laugh that was his response drove her fear into sickness. *Raped again; gods above, raped again! Why was I ever born a woman?*

When she felt his mouth at her neck, his body clenching against hers in anticipation, she knew she would not submit. Not this time; not if it was the last thing she did on this earth.

"No!" she screamed, and sent her fist flying directly into his ear. Struggling was all right for a woman, she knew, but not a direct violence that could hurt a man. The man was always stronger, and to injure his body as well as his pride was a sure invitation to battering, even death. This she knew. But she didn't care.

The blow stunned the man for a moment and she tried to twist away from his heavy body. "Bitch!" he snarled, slapping her hard across the face. She allowed herself to be stunned only a moment. *You will not rape me,* she thought fiercely. *You will not.* When he moved to lower his face, she reached up, her fingers spread, and aimed her nails directly at his eyes.

He howled and jerked his head away and managed to limit her attack to several deep gouges beneath one eye. But her actions had their desired effect, for all thoughts of rape fled as he sprang to his feet, blood trickling down his cheek. Before she could escape, he grabbed her wrists, jerking her to her feet and tossing her around angrily as if she were a helpless child.

"No!" she screamed again, fighting to free herself. His

face looked murderous and she knew he must exact some revenge from her. When he jerked her toward him she raised one knee, but before she could make contact with his groin she heard a thud, felt him drag her a few startled steps to the side, and then he released her. She stumbled backward, almost falling. The hunter turned, stunned to see Brennos standing there, a broken tree limb in his hands. Before the hunter's head could clear from the first blow, Brennos struck again, a quick, glancing thrust to the stomach, throwing the man off balance. He sprawled to the forest floor with a moan. Brennos swooped down on him, snatching the hunter's sword from his side and waving it menacingly in his face.

"Get up," he snapped. Obediently the man pulled himself upright, one hand furtively reaching for his hunting knife. Brennos saw it and sliced the sword to the left, cutting the man's arm as a warning, and the hunter froze. His eyes grew wide with astonishment when his attacker suddenly began to whirl the sword tip before him, looping and circling like a swift and annoying wasp, threatening to sting he knew not where. It was a druid's swordplay, designed to awe and dazzle, wound if need be, but not necessarily to kill. The only escape route open to him was to retreat, for any movement to either side was quickly halted by the dancing sword tip.

The man's mouth fell open in disbelief. "You . . . you're a druid!" he gasped, recognizing the famed wild man of the woods and realizing that only a druid could know the deft sword strokes being displayed before him.

"Aye, I am a druid." The hermit grinned coldly, circling and looping the weapon before the hunter's pounding heart. "How does it feel, eh, to be the victim for a change?"

The hunter's hands were trembling violently and he backed away, desperately seeking to escape the hermit's games. The man's face before him was not that of a rational druid or skilled warrior; it was the murderous look of an enraged man defending his woman.

"I . . . I didn't know she was yours," he whined, still retreating. "Truthfully . . . how could I know? I would never have—"

"She is a human being!" Brennos bellowed, and before the hunter could dodge the blade, the druid sent it slicing across his chest, not once, but twice. The hunter looked down at the blood staining his gray tunic and groaned. To the end of his days he would be a marked man, always wearing on his flesh the double-winged scar fanning outward from his breastbone left and right; the mark that would tell the world he had dared to fight with a druid, and had lost.

"No!" the man moaned, sinking to his knees, his hands clutched feebly to his bleeding chest. The pain was beginning to tear at him, and as he collapsed to the ground he saw the enraged druid raise the sword high to strike off his head. The double-winged mark had been instinctive; the druid did not intend to let him live.

"Don't!" Melangell screamed in horror, rushing forward, her arms raised to the druid's sword. "By the gods, Brennos, don't kill him!"

She planted herself protectively between the druid and his victim, her green eyes flashing fear and concern. Brennos seemed in a trance, nearly a warrior's rage, but when he realized who it was who stood before him, her small hands reaching for his arm, her bruised face pleading with him, the distorted hatred drained from his expression and he blinked, lowering the weapon.

"You must not kill him," she said gently. Brennos looked past her, his cold eyes surveying the huddled, whimpering man.

"All you have striven for and believed in . . . Brennos, you must not take his life," Melangell pleaded. To her relief, calm returned to his face and his shoulders sagged. The druid took a slow, deep breath, looked at the sword in his hand, and flung it angrily into the woods.

"Come," he said, seizing her wrist.

"No." She stood firm. "I must see to him first."

"Him?" Brennos snorted, scorn in his voice. "He should be glad enough you saved his life. Let him see to himself."

"No," she repeated, turning to the man and kneeling beside him. Brennos watched her a moment, reached down, and pulled the hunting knife from the man's belt. He flung it into the underbrush, stepped across the glade, and sat down next to a tree, watching the young woman tend the wounded man. The hunter sobbed and whimpered like a frightened child and Brennos could hear her voice, speaking low and soothingly to the man. Gently she rolled him onto his back, ripping his tunic to see his wounds.

"Hush now," she muttered, tearing strips from her skirt to bandage him. "I know it hurts, but it is not so bad a wound." She looked down at his face and brushed some dirt from his cheek. "We'll have you fixed up and on your way soon." She smiled. The hunter seemed only dimly aware of her, through his pain, but her very manner seemed to touch some corner of his soul and calm him. As Brennos watched her treating her attacker, his anger slowly gave way to awe, and then to understanding.

This was her calling, he realized. This was her path to wisdom. Not the abstract seeking he had so long pursued, but an active striving. Not the thinking mind, but the overflowing heart. He would have killed the man, so great was his rage, his sense of possessiveness of her, his feeling of personal violation. In the end, all his fine words and thoughts and musings had vanished like mists before a hot summer sun. She, orphan, widow, mother, and druidess, knew the way. She forgave her attacker and returned only love and caring to him. And now, as he watched her, the marvel of it all slowly dawned on the druid. She leaned over the man, talking as reassuringly to him as if she were his mother. Through his fear, through his pain, the hunter gazed up at her in gratitude. She would have no bonds with this man to work out in a future lifetime, no bonds to hold back her soul's progress, to condemn her to yet another earthly existence. She was free, and only gentleness had severed the chains.

"Here," Brennos said, rising to his feet, "let me help you," and in the brimming gaze she turned on him, Brennos felt that his soul, like the hunter's, had found peace.

She did not rest until the hunter's pain subsided, until they had helped him to his feet and, dusk falling, retrieved his cloak and led him downhill toward the nearest settlement. Faint light from distant huts winked and glimmered through the gathering night as the three paused. Melangell instinctively withdrew from the proximity of the people she had come to fear, hovering nervously at the forest's edge.

"You can make it on your own now," Brennos said tightly, trying to feel some small measure of charity in his heart but finding chiefly bitterness at the violation he had almost witnessed.

"Aye," the man said weakly, turning his bandaged body to face the young woman. "I am truly sorry for what I did, and for striking you so hard. Please believe that I will spread the word to all about the true nature of the wild man and his lady."

"No," Melangell interrupted him. "On your honor, say nothing to anyone about us. Only by remaining the wild man and the witch of Duncrub will we have the peace we seek."

He looked at her quizzically and gave a silent nod. "As you wish," he muttered, "but you have my word that you will always have my loyalty and admiration. Thank you . . . thank you both."

He cast a quick glance to Brennos' cold face, turned, and made his way into the darkness, toward the welcoming hearths of the village ahead.

Wearily Melangell turned, pulling her worn cloak close against the evening breeze. "Our task is done here," she sighed. "I must be on my way."

"To where?" Brennos blurted, concern etching his face. Walking away from him, she shrugged and gave no reply.

"Wait!" he called quietly, trotting after her. "Melangell, we must talk."

"I have nothing to say, Brennos," she answered firmly, never slowing her pace. "I thank you for saving me, but now I must go."

He hesitated, unsure if he should follow her. Her mind seemed made up. Who was he to try to change it? Confused, he watched her form vanish into the shadows. Then panic seized his heart and he ran after her.

"No!" he persisted, grabbing her arm and turning her to him. He put his hands on her shoulders and looked into her startled green eyes. "Why did you leave?" he whispered. She studied him for a moment, and then she looked down.

"I came to realize that I was in the way. I knew your calling, and I respected it. I would not stand in the way of that, Brennos, or even presume to. All I could do to help you was to leave."

"No! That is not true!"

"The way you distanced yourself from me made it plain enough. You did not wish me to stay. I know I was a hindrance. It is your calling, Brennos . . . your life."

He could see tears gathering along her lowered lashes, and his heart moved in fear and pity. He raised his good hand and ran his fingers over her cheek. "It has taken me lifetimes to see it, Melangell, but you are my calling. You. We can continue our search together, for in all the world you are the only woman who understands it. Our aims are the same. Like two arrows, we shoot for the same mark. Why should we not share what remains of our lives together? Melangell," he said, lifting her chin, "stay with me."

She looked at him, aghast. "No. Brennos, what of your calling, your life?"

"Without you, my life would be nothing. I have loved you far longer than you can imagine. Now that you are here, I cannot lose you again. Please . . . come back and stay with me. But before you answer, I must warn you. I am as a starving man. You would be my banquet. I cannot do otherwise, Melangell . . . I am only human."

She looked into his gray eyes in silence, and then a slow smile crossed her face. "Yes," she said, "I will return with you."

He lowered his hand and his eyes suddenly held a pain, an intensity of emotion beyond all bearing. "Come," he said simply, taking her arm, "let's go home."

Melangell awoke the second morning of their return journey when Brennos shook her shoulder. Opening her eyes, she was surprised to see him smiling mischievously.

"What is it, Brennos?" she muttered sleepily, brushing the hair from her eyes and sitting up. Grinning, he thrust a triangle of bread and a chunk of soft white cheese at her.

"Food!" she gasped, disbelieving, her stomach turning painfully at the sweet fragrance of the cheese. "Where did you get it?"

She saw a familiar glint in his eye and shook her head in mock dismay. "Brennos—" she began.

"It came from a nearby farmstead," he explained, sitting back on his heels and tearing the bread in two. "I awoke before dawn, the faint odor of wood smoke in my nose. I followed it until I came to the farm. The good housewife was baking bread, and her husband sat in the yard sharpening a scythe. I knew I was hungry, and I guessed you were too, so I walked up to the man and called on my right as a druid to partake of his hospitality."

"And?"

"Well," he went on, tearing a hungry mouthful of the bread, "as young as he was, I doubt he'd seen many druids in his lifetime . . . and I had no robe. He didn't seem to believe that I was a druid. So I drew myself up full height, my eyes flashing in indignation, and raised my arms to pronounce 'geiss' on him."

Melangell was laughing merrily at his tale, fearing the worst was yet to come. Brennos enjoyed the sound and continued his story with gusto.

"It seemed to convince the poor fellow that I was the genuine article, for his eyes grew wide, he dropped the scythe and whetstone, and rushed into his dwelling. Soon he, his plump wife, and a brood of young children emerged, all staring like owls. He pushed the bread and cheese into my hands and was no doubt glad to see the back of me . . . so there you have your morning meal!"

"Brennos," she laughed, biting into the crusty bread, "I thank you for the food, but I'm afraid you have turned into quite a rascal!"

"Aye"—he winked at her—"that I have!"

They walked through the day, a light, misty rain falling that put a sheen to their faces and hung the fresh green treetops earthward. Awkward and seemingly afraid to touch each other, they nevertheless felt young and happy, like two giddy children. Melangell laughed when Brennos slipped and nearly fell on a leaf-covered rock, and he shook an overhanging branch to shower her with wet drops in response. With dusk the humid warmth of the day vanished and a crisp northerly breeze sprang up. They found a dry evergreen to sit beneath and Melangell huddled, cold and shivering, under her threadbare cloak while Brennos scouted the area for some dry wood for a fire.

"It's no use," he sighed, settling himself against the tree trunk and pulling his cloak close. "I did not carry my fire-starter with me, and there are no dry wood and tinder to be found anywhere. It would be impossible to start a fire without them."

He glanced aside at Melangell. "I know," she muttered. "I have had to start a fire from nothing, and it is not an easy task, even under the best conditions." She slouched her chin to her knees as if seeming to gaze into a roaring campfire might somehow make her warmer. He could see her shivering, even under her cloak, and he flung one side of his cloak open and extended an arm to her.

"Come here . . ." he said gently. "I cannot bear to see you so cold."

She looked up, hesitation in her eyes, and then she rose to a crouch and hurried to him. Wrapping his arm around her, he pulled the cloak up to enfold them both and held her close.

"Better?" he said, and felt her nodding beneath his chin. She sat stiff and erect, and he found himself feeling unnaturally tense as well. Always before they had been free and open with each other because the shield of his professionalism had safely come between them, but now that shield was gone, and they both seemed uncomfortably aware of it.

"Well," he muttered, "here we are, as cozy as two logs propped together."

She laughed lightly; she seemed to be having trouble deciding where to put her hands. One minute they were clenched absently before her; then they rested awkwardly on her upturned hip. Putting them near his lap seemed too intimate.

"Gods above," he joked, "we are going to have some interesting times ahead of us."

"Brennos, hush!" she giggled, settling for resting her hands in the cleft between their huddled bodies. Lightly he kissed her forehead and rested his cheek in her hair, and when the next morning dawned and they resumed their trek, the two walked quietly together, holding hands like children.

The door of the hut still stood ajar, where he had flung it in his haste to catch her. Inside, the hearth was cold, but the room was as neat and tidy as she had left it. "It isn't much," he began to apologize, seeing her solemn gaze as she took in the tiny room.

"It is all I need," she replied, removing her wet cloak and hanging it from a peg. Brennos crossed to the hearth, poked at the cold ashes, and began making a fire. How long have I known this man? she pondered, watching him work. Most of my life . . . and all the things we have been through! Happiness and heartache, pain and sacrifice, and how often has it seemed that when I needed help most, he was there? Brennos . . . my druid, my physician, my protector, and my friend. And now? Who can say? Three is a number sacred to the gods; perhaps this third love will be the luckiest of all. But for now, I am content, and that is the most important thing. For he, alone, of all the men I have known, can boast of one proud claim. I have never once felt a moment's discomfort with him, and that is the greatest happiness there is.

He stood and turned to face her, removing his wet cloak and tossing it to the trunk. "You are sure?" he said, his voice low and tightly controlled. She smiled and nodded. He grasped the neck of his tunic and quickly pulled it off. Then the tie at the waist of his old breeches was loosed and they fell to the floor. Advancing toward her, he stepped out of them and she could not help but stare. In all their time together she had never seen him naked, and his lean living and smithy work had kept him as trim and muscular as a man decades younger. She slid her gown from her shoulders, laying it neatly atop the bed.

"Don't move," he said when he reached her. He moved closer and she could smell the masculine warmth of his body. Her head began to whirl in excitement when he ran his good hand across her lips, down one cheek, caressing her throat, gliding across one shoulder as delicately as if she were a fragile statue. There was scarcely a bit of her anatomy he had not seen at one time or another, yet this was different, incredibly different. His skilled physician's hands had become sensual; his gentle gray eyes were almost pained in the intensity of their longing.

"Melangell . . ." he sighed. Bending his head, he softly kissed her neck, moving from one side to the other, nuzzling under her chin like a kitten at its mother's belly.

"Oh, gods!" she gasped, flinging her head back and clenching her eyes shut. She felt his mouth move lower, seeming in no hurry, his lips tenderly crossing from shoulder to shoulder, and he clenched her arms firmly, afraid she might flee from him.

Her eagerness was maddening, but still his lips were slow and deliberate, as if for him time meant nothing and urgency was to be avoided. Was it intentional or merely a quirk? Some druid's trick or physician's knowledge? By the time his relentless search from shoulder to shoulder stopped and she felt his mouth creep down the languid curve of one breast, tears crept from her eyes and she fought for control. Oh, gods! she thought wildly, this cannot be happening! It has been so long . . . so long . . . it cannot be.

Suddenly he buried his face between her breasts, his hands clenching her hips desperately, and she felt his shoulders heave.

"Brennos?" she said, looking down at his shaggy brown hair. He glanced up at her and she was shocked to see tears in his eyes.

"What is wrong, my love?" she soothed, leaning her face close to his. Abruptly he stood, smoothing her hair and gazing into her eyes.

"You cannot know how long I have waited for this moment," he whispered, "the longings I have felt, the dreams I have dreamed, the foolish notions I have denied myself. And now you are here, it is real, and I want this moment to go on forever. You are every good thing my life has ever lacked."

She looked at him, moved by his simple declaration. "Come," she said, taking his hand. She led him to the heather bed and they reclined on it, his good arm cradling her close to his body. She could feel his breath warm on her cheek and she gently pressed her lips to his. He responded, slowly at first, then hungrily, his arms tightening about her, his tongue eagerly probing her mouth. He seemed ready to devour her, and the fire rising within her ran unchecked. Her hands slid across his back, caressing the muscles in his shoulders, lingering in the dark hair on his chest, and she felt him quiver at her touch. "By the gods . . ." he gasped as her slim fingers searched his body. How many lonely nights had he awakened, his seed unwittingly spilled onto his pallet, no willing receptacle there to receive it? But now the vessel was here, the vessel was eager and willing, and . . .

Pushing her legs apart, he slid between them, rolling her onto her back. He'd wanted to go slowly, to prolong their pleasure, but he could not control his eagerness. All the years of frustration, all the decades of denial, spilled out in a wild rush and he rode her harder than he had ever ridden a woman in his youth. No abstinence was ever so exquisite, no denial so profound. He finished too soon, his arms about her so tight he was afraid he would crush her. And then he lay still atop her, studying her long lashes, the delicate curve of her mouth, the graceful sweep of her nose. Once Nechtan lay where I now lie, he mused, and then Genann, but now, my dear one, you are mine. His exhaustion was complete, his happiness was total. Lowering his head to her hair, he took a deep breath, and when she turned her face and softly kissed his cheek, he could not help himself.

He cried like a little child.

How long have I waited for thee?
How many lifetimes have turned through the
heavens?
How long would I wait for thee?
Till the heavens no longer turned.

EPILOGUE

(Twelve Years Later)

AFTER HAVING LIVED SO EVENTFUL A LIFE, HER DEATH WAS quiet and simple. Returning from her yearly visit with her children and grandchildren in the west, she caught another of the fevers to which her small body seemed increasingly prone as the years wore on, as if she grew unable to fight off the ills of the world; only this time, all my skills and medicines could not save her. She died in my arms, and the last word on her lips was my name.

"I built her funeral pyre as best I could with my failing strength, dismantling the hut where we'd lived in order to have enough dry wood to use. I have no need of it anymore. After having lived most of my life without her, I cannot do so again. I will light the fire, hold her in my arms, and take this poison I have made, and soon there will be no trace of our passing—our home gone, our ashes melting into the soil, as if we had never been. Then we shall be once more together.

"I do not know if my Search would have been more successful without her. I cannot tell if her presence held me back. Only the gods can judge that. But I would not exchange our twelve years together for all the wisdom in Creation, and there is one thing I am sure of:

"Having known her, and having loved her, my life was not a waste."

Journeying to the western mountains of Caledonia following the native uprising, Anor and Drosten were married at her aunt's farmstead. They had three children—twin daughters and a son she named for her father. Drosten later visited his native village and reclaimed what he could of his inheritance, returning to the Bristling Mountains of the west with a fine herd of cattle, a small quantity of gold, and eight disgruntled warriors and four women who had chosen to leave Achivir's village.

Resad and Marcia were also married, and had three sons and a daughter. The firstborn son Resad named after his father, Nechtan, and the lastborn and youngest child he bestowed with the name of his friend Brennos, whose many talks with the young man had left him feeling as if he had known his father himself. When the boy reached seven years of age Resad made a point of finding a willing hermit who would take him under his wing and teach him to become a druid like his namesake, who had died the year before his birth.

Cadvan never married, choosing instead to make soldiering his life. He died at the age of twenty-six, of pneumonia incurred on a winter raid against the Romans.

Fortrenn finally settled down with one of the Pictish women who had returned with Drosten. They had one daughter, the light of the genial giant's life, and he named her after the mother he never knew, Boann of the chestnut hair.

Cai also eventually married, a plump widow with a kind heart. She brought two children to the marriage, and bore Cai six more—two sons and four daughters. The sons he named for his father and dead brother Donall; the lastborn daughter, a shy and solemn child with oddly green eyes, he named for the woman who had had such an influence on his life, Melangell of Duncrub, who had died four years earlier.

And Achivir the King finally met the fate he had so long been courting. His delectable young wife poisoned him after sharing his bed for eight years, installing on his throne her lover and co-conspirator, the chief of the palace guards, Talorc. He soon proved to be a wise and able ruler, and the people, realizing their good fortune, chose not to quarrel with the unorthodox means of his ascendancy.

Afterword

IN A.D. 78 JULIUS AGRICOLA WAS MADE ROMAN GOVERNOR OF Britain, and in his six years in office he conducted one campaign in Wales and six in northern England and Scotland. His troops finished the destruction of the druids' stronghold on the island of Mona (Anglesey, Wales) begun twenty-four years earlier by a predecessor. He then turned his attentions to Scotland, where many hitherto independent tribes submitted to him. In the spring of A.D. 84, advancing his troops into southern Scotland, his Ninth Legion narrowly escaped annihilation in a surprise native raid. That autumn Agricola reentered the Highlands and somewhere in northeastern Scotland his troops met the assembled native armies under the leadership of a warlord named Calgacus, in an engagement known as the Battle of Mons Graupius. According to the only surviving account of this battle, written by the Roman historian Tacitus, the native armies were defeated and one-third of their men were killed. A legionary fort was built at Inchtuthil, north of Perth, the northernmost garrison of the Roman Empire. Because the climate was too harsh, the supply routes too difficult, and the natives too intractable, the fort was dismantled and abandoned three years later and the Romans withdrew to southern Scotland.

There is no written history of Britain for over thirty years after the governorship of Agricola. About A.D. 100 all Roman garrisons north of the Cheviot Hills in southern Scotland were withdrawn. Within a generation of the Battle of Mons Graupius (Duncrub) the natives of Scotland had begun to once more attack and harass the Roman armies stationed along the borders, at first sporadically, then with increasing strength, culminating in "The British War" of A.D. 117–119. This was a full-scale war the details of which are not known, but it was so serious that Roman casualties in it were compared to those of the Jewish Revolt in Palestine a few years later. Perhaps because of a great defeat suffered in this war, the Roman Ninth Legion was disbanded. In 120 the Emperor Hadrian ordered construction of a great wall of stone and turf, earthworks and ditches, built along the entire Roman border with Scotland in an attempt to contain the Celtic hostilities. The effort was only partly successful, for native raids continued until the Romans abandoned Britain in A.D. 410. They had controlled the island for over four hundred years, but from the year A.D. 87 northern Scotland remained forever beyond the Roman grasp.

Glossary and List of Characters

Achivir—Pictish king, Melangell's antagonist

Agricola, Julius—Roman governor of Britain, A.D. 78–85, leader of Roman forces at the Battle of Mons Graupius

Allectus—Celtic rebel leader, benefactor of Drosten and Resad

Anarios—Roman military physician, slave of Brennos, lover of Melangell

Angus—guard in service of Damnonii king Annos

Aniel—Pictish warrior who aids in the search for Anor

Annos—king of a tribe of the Damnonii people

Anor—daughter of Melangell and Genann, slave of the Roman tribune Marcus

Aramo—"the gentle," north British god

Arnemetia—north British goddess of healing

Artogenos—elder druid and chief Lawgiver of the Damnonii people

blood—perhaps used by druid smiths to temper sword blades due to its high phosphorus content; possible origin of the favorite Celtic theme of superior and mystically created swords

Boann—wife of Calum, mother of Fortrenn

Braciaca—north British god of intoxication

Brennos—physician and druid to Nechtan and his men, ally of Melangell

Brigantes—great north British tribe, Northumberland area

Broichan—Pictish druid of King Achivir

Cadvan—son of Melangell and Genann

Cai—son of Conn, one of Nechtan's men, and Melangell's personal guard

Caledonia—ancient name for what is today Scotland

Calgacus—chief warlord of the native tribes at the Battle of Mons Graupius

Calum—skilled tracker of the Damnonii, father of Fortrenn

carnyx—tall animal-headed battle horn of the Celts

Cathal—Parisi archer (modern Yorkshire area), one of Nechtan's men and personal guard

Cathbhadh—elderly druid mystic

centurion—professional military man in the Roman army, in charge of a "century" of eighty men

Cherdic—Germanic smuggler

Conn—prosperous farmer, father of Genann, Cai, and Donall

Cordelia—Gaulish cook and housekeeper in the private home of the tribune Marcus

Cornicen—Roman military hornblower

Coventina—Brittannic goddess of springs and wells

Cruithni—native name for the north Scottish non-Celtic people called "Picts" (painted men) by the Romans

curiass—one-piece "muscle armor" of chest and back plates worn by higher Roman officers

Damnonii—Celtic tribe in southwest Scotland, present Glasgow area

Diuran—druid physician, friend and classmate of Brennos

Donall—retarded son of Conn, partly healed by Melangell

Drosten—Pictish warrior, Anor's fiancée

druid—a class of wise men, physicians and "moral philosophers" who held sway over most aspects of Celtic learning and society

dun—Celtic hill or small mountain; usually refers to the native fortress or settlement atop it

Duncrub—native name for Mons Graupius

Eber—one of Nechtan's spearmen

Eldol—Celtic flute player at King Achivir's court

Eliseg—druid of Allectus

Esus—wandering druid "holy man," teacher of Melangell

Ethal—druid specializing in history and genealogy, friend of Diuran

Fortrenn—"powerful," Celtic warrior, friend of Resad, son of Calum and Boann

geiss—a combination curse and taboo pronounced by a druid; to violate it brought death or disaster

Genann—Conn's eldest son, a harpist, poet, and one of Nechtan's men; later Melangell's guard, her husband, and father of Anor and Cadvan

greaves—leg armor worn on the front of the lower legs by centurions and Roman officers

guatator—"the Invoker," one of three druidical classes, they performed the rituals and ceremonies

Ialonus—north Britannic god of meadows and glades

Lacha—war hound of Calgacus, gift to Melangell, of Irish wolfhound type

legionary—the common foot soldier of the Roman army

Loucetius—Britannic god of lightning; his consort was Nemetona, goddess of sacred groves

Mac Oag—"young boy," apprentice to Calum and Nechtan's charioteer

Mael—an archer, one of Nechtan's men

Maia—crippled foster mother and aunt of Nechtan, briefly the owner of Melangell; named for the Caledonian goddess of spring

Manucium—Roman town, modern Manchester, England

Maponus—north Britannic god of youth and music

Marcus—Roman military tribune, owner of Anor

Medocius—Caledonian war god

Melangell—young girl enslaved by Nechtan, later his wife and a druidess; wife of Genann; mistress of Pictish King Achivir; mother of Resad, Anor, and Cadvan

Melwas—one of Nechtan's spearmen and personal guard

Mona—modern Anglesey, Wales; stronghold of the druids, conquered by Agricola

Mons Graupius—site of a battle in A.D. 84 between 30,000 natives and 29,000 Romans; exact location unknown

Nechtan—half-Pictish princeling, captor and husband of Melangell, father of Resad

nemeton—a sacred place, usually a grove, in the woods

Niall—one of Nechtan's spearmen and personal guards, sacrificed before the Battle of Mons Graupius

Ollovidius—"the All-Knowing," Britannic god, possibly connected with the Celtic doctrine of reincarnation and karma

Osla—one of Nechtan's spearmen

Ordovices—Celtic tribe of northern Wales

patera—"mess tin" of the Roman foot soldier, similar to a porringer of today

Pict—*see* Cruithni

prefect—aide to a Roman general, often appointed from the ranks of tribunes

principia—main headquarters building in a Roman camp or fort

raven—bird sacred to Bran, the war god; a raven with white feathers was considered good luck

Resad—warrior son of Melangell and Nechtan

Rufus—Roman legionary who briefly guarded Anor during her initial enslavement

Selgovae—Celtic tribe of lowland Scotland

semnotheoi—druidical class of hermits, "holy men"; name means "reverence to the gods"

Seonaid—Nechtan's girlfriend

Severa—Melangell's serving woman while living in the palace of King Achivir

Silures—Celtic tribe of southern Wales; ethnic background of Melangell

Simal—Pictish warrior who aided in tracking down Anor

Talorc—Melangell's Pictish guard while living with King Achivir

tribune—usually a Roman nobleman's son in his early twenties who served three years in the army as an officer with no specific duties, to gain military experience before

going on to a political career in Rome; six were attached
to each Legion

Tuatha de Danann—people of the goddess Danu, the Celts;
"people of art"

vicus—military town which grew up around a Roman fort
Vintios—Britannic god of winds
Vitucadrus—"brilliant in energy," Britannic god

wolf—thought by the Celts to be helpful to humans and
associated by the Britons with healing

Author's Note

IN WRITING THIS STORY I HAVE ATTEMPTED TO RECONSTRUCT THE institution of the druid as close to reality as it is possible to determine today. So much that is fanciful or erroneous has been put forth as "the truth" about this key element of Celtic culture, ranging from the exalted mystic privy to a higher wisdom to animal-skin-wearing shamans or bloodthirsty satanists. Some ancient Greek writers saw their philosophy as originating with "the wise men of the Celts," and so in my research I read the works of such early Greek philosophers as Plato, Pythagoras, and Socrates. A few modern authorities see striking similarities between the culture of old Ireland (Iron Age Celtic) and the Hindu of India; to that end, I delved into Hindu religion and philosophy. In truth, the druid was probably similar to the Hindu pundit, a wise man versed in Sanskrit and the religion, philosophy, and culture of India, or the Latin "doctor" in its original sense retained today in "Doctor of Letters," "Doctor of Philosophy," etc. It is probably no coincidence that all three of these cultures—Indian, Latin, and Celtic—derive from the same original Indo-European root stock. I feel my portrayal of the druids is the most accurate in popular circulation, and the reader is asked to keep in mind the words of the druid Brennos in summing up what I have tried to portray: "They are but men, as I am."